THE
PUSHCART PRIZE, XXXII

2008
PUSHCART PRIZE XXXII
BEST OF THE
SMALL PRESSES

EDITED BY BILL HENDERSON
WITH THE PUSHCART PRIZE EDITORS

Note: nominations for this series are invited from any small, independent, literary book press or magazine in the world, print or online. Up to six nominations—tear sheets or copies, selected from work published, or about to be published, in the calendar year—are accepted by our December 1 deadline each year. Write to Pushcart Press, P.O. Box 380, Wainscott, N.Y. 11975 for more information or consult our websites www.pushcartprize.com. or pushcartpress.org.

Acknowledgments

Selections for The Pushcart Prize are reprinted with the permission of authors and presses cited. Copyright reverts to authors and presses immediately after publication.

Distributed by W. W. Norton & Co.
500 Fifth Ave., New York, N.Y. 10110

Library of Congress Card Number: 76–58675
ISBN (hardcover): 978-1-888889-48-2
ISBN (paperback): 978-1-888889-46-8
ISSN: 0149–7863

For Hannah

INTRODUCTION

Hᴏᴡ ʜᴀs ᴛʜɪs sᴇʀɪᴇs, published from an 8'x8' backyard shack and staffed by hundreds of unpaid volunteers across the country, survived and thrived for over three decades?

The commercial world informs us that this is an impossible dream. Money is the yellow brick road. Oligarchs pick our entertainments, our celebrities, our presidents and our wars. We children of the spirit are yesterday's news, if we ever were news.

Yet for three decades the Pushcart Prize—and the small presses and authors we honor—have flourished. The reason? (Simple, stupid). Spirit will never be quelled, certainly not by mere bucks and bluster. Each edition of the Pushcart Prize is evidence of this. Many new presses—such as the wondrous *A Public Space*, with two selections herein—and dozens of new authors emerge annually. And so the Pushcart Prize has been renewed since our first edition in 1976. We celebrate this renewal in PPXXXII and every year. This is our joy.

I have always thought of the Pushcart Prize as a "small good thing"—which also happens to be the title of one of my favorite Ray Carver short stories, featured in PPVIII (1983). To me it's the small good things that really count—a helping hand, the smile to a stranger, the anonymous gift—not the big buzz, the shock and awe.

Such a small good thing blessed another Ray Carver story recently. Way back in 1976, in the very first Pushcart Prize, we reprinted a story by the then little known Carver titled "So Much Water So Close to Home" from an obscure and since vanished journal, *Spectrum*. It's the profoundly moving story of a husband's fishing trip, his discovery of a woman's body, and the consequences for his marriage.

After three decades the story might have been considered lost like its original publisher. Yet just recently it was released as a feature film, "Jindabyne" starring Laura Linney and Gabriel Byrne, based in, of all places Australia—far from Carver's and *Spectrum*'s California home, and Pushcart's original office in Yonkers, New York. The reviews have been terrific.

Carver's story has been reborn for a new generation, thanks to *Spectrum*'s small good publishing.

A jolt of rebirth was in the air towards the end of winter when a packed house at New York's Baruch College assembled to salute editor Joan Murray's *The Pushcart Book of Poetry: The Best Poems from 30 Years of the Pushcart Prize*. This whopping 640 page collection, just published by Pushcart Press, was gathered by Joan and 49 past poetry editors of this series and includes 180 poems from 154 poets.

On stage for the event were a former Poet Laureate of the US and winners of several Pulitzer Prizes, National Book Awards, and National Book Critics Circle recognitions: Lucille Clifton, Billy Collins, Maxine Kumin, Grace Schulman, Gerald Stern and C.K. Williams. That night poetry, so long the heart of this anthology, really sang out.

Publishers Weekly stated in an article about the book and the event: "The Pushcart spirit it seems is stronger than ever." Indeed.

In March of 2008, National Public Radio will broadcast nationally a PP fiction reading by some of our best actors from New York's Symphony Space. The stories will scan the entire thirty-two year history of this series. Try not to miss it.

Sadly, Pushcart has lost a big chunk of its heart and energy—Hannah Turner, managing editor of this series, died in February 2007. She was 88 years old. Hannah alone was responsible for informing thousands of writers that they had been nominated for a Pushcart Prize. She did this by meticulously filling out announcements in calligraphy.

When she died she had just finished mailing over 1,000 nomination letters to authors for this edition, as she had done for a quarter century. In all those years she lovingly inscribed over 20,000 announcements from her small apartment in Maryland. She did it for a pittance, tirelessly, and she was adamant that we not change the nomination format to make it easier for her.

"Why not a pre-printed, general form?" I suggested to Hannah early in 2007.

"Never" was her reply.

We probably will not see another person like Hannah at Pushcart. I know from many letters and conversations with nominated authors how important those handwritten forms were to them. In a computer age somebody out there cared to tell them personally that their work was valued. This was a tremendous boost to writers, so often writing for love and receiving little appreciation in return.

This edition was honored by the labors of two distinguished poets who served as poetry co-editors: Ray Gonzalez and Philip Schultz. As usual, they worked many months for a tiny honorarium at a totally impossible task of selecting a few dozen poems out of thousands.

Ray Gonzalez is the author of nine books of poetry including *Consideration of the Guitar: New and Selected Poems* (BOA Editions, 2005). His other titles from BOA include *The Hawk Temple at Tierra Grande* (2002), a winner of a 2003 Minnesota Book Award in Poetry, *Cabato Sentora* (1999); and *The Heat of Arrivals* (1996), a winner of a 1997 PEN/Josephine Miles Book Award.

He is the author of two books of nonfiction: *Memory Fever* (1999), a memoir about growing up in the Southwest, and *The Underground Heart* (2002), which received the 2003 Carr P. Collins/Texas Institute of Letters Award for Best Book of Nonfiction. He is also the author of two books of short stories: *The Ghost of John Wayne* (2001) and *Circling the Tortilla Dragon* (2002). His poetry has appeared in *The Best American Poetry* and *The Pushcart Prize*.

He has served as Poetry Editor of *The Bloomsbury Review* for twenty-five years and founded *LUNA*, a poetry journal, in 1998. He is a Full Professor in the MFA Creative Writing Program at the University of Minnesota in Minneapolis.

Philip Schultz is the founder and director of The Writers Studio in New York, now in its 20th year. His fifth book of poems, *Failure*, will soon be published by Harcourt.

His first poetry collection, *Like Wings* (Viking, 1978), was nominated for a National Book Award. In 1984 he won a Lamont Prize from the Academy of American Poets. He has also won a Pushcart Prize, a Guggenheim grant, and a Levinson Prize from *Poetry* magazine for his collection, *The Holy Worm of Praise* (Harcourt,

2002). He is the author of a chapbook from State Street Press, *My Guardian Angel Stein* (1986), and most recently *Living In the Past* (Harcourt, 2004)

My thanks to all of you who wrote to me about the death of my beloved mutt Lulu and my own health concerns as mentioned in last year's introduction. Your comments were most appreciated.

Lulu is still never far away from me in many ways. Her ashes are scattered nearby on a beach named by me "Lulu's Leap". It was her favorite spot. Lulu leapt there many times, after gulls (which she never caught and never intended to) and after old tennis balls and sticks. More successful there. She was and is a source of joy to me. She voted with her heart.

My thanks also to the more than 350 members of the Pushcart Prize Fellowships, the donors to our endowment. Recently Cedering Fox in Los Angeles and Phil Schultz and Cynthia Weiner in New York have organized sold out readings to benefit the Fellowships. We are very grateful for their mighty efforts. If you want to help us please write to the Fellowships at PO Box 380, Wainscott, NY 11975. All donors are listed in each edition of the Prize. Our endowment insures that our non-profit project will endure despite the oligarchs.

Our only overhead is that 8'x8' backyard shack, and it's real sturdy.

And finally, thanks to you, the reader. Without you none of us would exist.

BILL HENDERSON

THE PEOPLE WHO HELPED

FOUNDING EDITORS—Anaïs Nin (1903–1977), Buckminster Fuller (1895–1983), Charles Newman (1938–2006), Daniel Halpern, Gordon Lish, Hary Smith, Hugh Fox, Ishmael Reed, Joyce Carol Oates, Len Fulton, Leonard Randolph, Leslie Fiedler (1917–2003), Nona Balakian (1918–1991), Paul Bowles (1910–1999), Paul Engle (1908–1991), Ralph Ellison (1914–1994), Reynolds Price, Rhoda Schwartz, Richard Morris, Ted Wilentz (1915–2001), Tom Montag, William Phillips (1907–2002). Poetry editor: H. L. Van Brunt:

CONTRIBUTING EDITORS FOR THIS EDITION—*Stacey Richter, Nami Mun, Richard Garcia, John Fulton, Tracy Mayor, Dick Allen, Judith Kitchen, Philip White, John Kistner, Ron Tanner, Jody Stewart, Beth Ann Fennelly, Kenneth Gangemi, Richard Kostelanetz, Wally Lamb, Jeffrey Hammond, W. S. Merwin, Benjamin Percy, Daniel Henry, Jeffrey Harrison, Maura Stanton, Ed Falco, Michael Waters, Jane Hirshfield, Edward Hirsch, David Jauss, Joyce Carol Oates, Kate Braverman, Roger Weingarten, David Wojahn, Dorianne Laux, Mark Irwin, Ellen Bass, Laura Kasischke, Roger Shepherd, Sherod Santos, Joan Murray, Suzanne Cleary, Steve Kowit, Arthur Smith, David St. John, Andrea Hollander Budy, Joe Hurka, Atsuro Riley, Alice Mattison, Brenda Miller, Robert McBrearty, Lucia Perillo, Paul Maliszewski, Lee Upton, Daniel Hoffman, Thomas E. Kennedy, Rebecca McClanahan, Katherine Taylor, Dana Levin, Susan Terris, Jim Moore, Reneé Ashley, Karl Elder, John Allman, Lysley Tenorio, Terese Svoboda, Karen Bender, Gerald Shapiro, David Schuman, Mark Wisniewski, Jack Pendarvis, Philip*

Levine, Rosellen Brown, Robert Boyers, Pauls Toutonghi, Daniel Orozco, H. E. Francis, Caroline Langston, George Keithley, Jean Nordhaus, Michael Bowden, Mike Newirth, Elizabeth McKenzie, Jessica Roeder, Kristin King, Nancy Richard, C. E. Poverman, Jack Marshall, Carolyn Alessio, Averill Curdy, Eliot Khalil Wilson, Michael Czyzniejewski, Gary Gildner, Dzvinia Orlowsky, Alice Schell, Bonnie Jo Campbell, Joe Ashby Porter, George Gessert, DeWitt Henry, Dennis Vannatta, Maureen P. Stanton, Kathleen Hill, Eamon Grennan, Mark Halliday, Matt Yurdana, Sharon Dilworth, Scott Geiger, Kathy Callaway, Maxine Kumin, Molly Bendall, Natasha Trethewey, Kirk Nesset, Gary Fincke, Daniel S. Libman, Kevin Moffett, Deb Olin Unferth, Tony Ardizzone, Nancy McCabe, Tom Filer, Diann Blakely, Claire Davis, Thomas Lux, Kim Addonizio, Meredith Hall, Salvatore Scibona, Mary Ann Samyn, Nicola Mason, Joan Swift, Charles Harper Webb, Laura Krughoff, John Drury, Rita Dove, Donald Platt, Nance Van Winckel, Michael Heffernan, Colette Inez, William Olsen, Philip Appleman, Carl Phillips, Billy Collins, Grace Schulman, David Rivard, Debra Spark, Bruce Beasley, Angie Estes, James Harms, Antler, Kevin Prufer, Gibbons Ruark, Rachel Hadas, Elizabeth Spires, Lloyd Schwartz, Christopher Buckley, Lance Olsen, Gerry Locklin, Joan Connor, R.T Smith, Susan Hahn, Kent Nelson, Dara Wier, Daniel Anderson, Robert Wrigley, Christopher Howell, Timothy Geiger, Martha Collins, Pinckney Benedict, Jacqueline Osherow, Stuart Dischell, Marianne Boruch, Claire Bateman, Henry Carlile, Rosanna Warren, Ted Deppe, Kim Barnes, Paul Zimmer, Ralph Angel, Jane Brox, Jean Thompson, Reginald Gibbons, Robert Thomas, Richard Burgin, Linda Gregerson, Linda Bierds, Vern Rutsala, Alan Michael Parker, Bob Hicok, Floyd Skloot, Michael Martone, Tony Barnstone, Michael Dennis Browne, Marilyn Hacker, Maureen Seaton, Erin McGraw, Michael Collier, Jim Barnes, Ed Ochester, David Baker, Fred Leebron, Len Roberts, Kathy Fagan, Eleanor Wilner, Kim Chinquee, Christina Zawadiwsky, Katrina Roberts, Rachel Loden, Sydney Lea, Wesley McNair, BJ Ward, Stephen Corey, Chard deNiord, Robert Pinsky, Lia Purpura, Andrew Hudgins, Robin Hemley, S.L. Wisenberg, Melanie Rae Thon, Robert Cording, Jana Harris, Brigit Kelly, Dan Masterson, William Wenthe, Tony Quagliano, Daisy Fried, James Reiss, Dina Ben-Lev, Catherine Barnett, Reginald Shepherd, Marianna Cherry, Kay Ryan, Helen H. Houghton, Edward Hirsch, Ethan Bumas

CONTENTS

THE
PUSHCART PRIZE, XXXII

CARTAGENA

fiction by NAM LE

from A PUBLIC SPACE

In CARTAGENA, Luis says, the beach is gray at dawn. He points to the barrel of his G3 when he says this, *steel gray*, he says. He smiles. The sand is white, he says, this color, tapping his teeth. And when the sun comes up on your right, man, it is a slow-motion explosion like in the movies, a big kerosene flash and then the water is sparkling gray and orange and red. Luis is full of shit, of course, but he can talk and it is true that he is the only one of our *gallada* who has seen the Caribbean. Who has been to Cartagena.

And the girls? Edwardo asks.

Luis tosses back his greasy, black hair. He knows we will wait for his answer. He is the oldest of us (except for Claudia who doesn't count because she is a girl), and he has recounted this story many times with pleasure.

The girls, he says. He looks at me and it is proper, he is showing respect. Together we smirk at the immaturity of Edwardo.

No, says Claudia. The fishermen. Tell us the part—

The girls, Luis says, speaking over Claudia, they are the best in all of Colombia. They wear skirts up to here, like on MTV, and boots up to here, and it is not like the country, where the *autodefensas* will shoot them for it. They are taller and whiter and have beautiful teeth and can talk about real things. Nothing like here.

He pauses. Luis has grown a mustache that looks like it has been drawn on with wet charcoal, and now he strokes it with his thumb and finger. I remember a line from a movie.

With that mustache, I say, you look like a shit-eating faggot. Ed-

21

wardo laughs happily. And it is you who would be shot for your long hair.

Luis ignores me. He says, speaking slowly—In Cartagena, everything is nothing like here.

We are five, including Claudia, and we are going downtown to do some business on behalf of Luis. Apart from me and Luis and Claudia and Edwardo, there is little Pedro, who walks behind the group with his hands in his torn pant pockets in order to fondle his testicles. It is not even funny any more.

I have not seen any of them, except for Claudia, in the last four months. Claudia—the only one who knows where I have been staying—told me yesterday about this business. I did not want to come, but she told me how strongly Luis insisted.

All of them look younger than I remember. Pedro is the only one who has grown—he looks like he has been seized by a fistful of hair and stretched two inches. I wait for him to catch up, and say to him, *Ay*, you are almost a man now!

Ask him if he has any hair on his *pipi*, says Edwardo.

Pedro keeps his hands in his pockets and does not react.

See, even now he is molesting it!

Come on, says Luis. He sounds distracted. Claudia is smiling to herself. I look away from her.

To do this business, there would usually be more of us, but our old *gallada*, the core of it anyway, is three short. Carlos was shot in the throat outside the Parque del Poblado: it was night and he was selling *basuco* to the crackheads when the rich kids came in their yellow Jeep and cleansed him. Salésio joined his elder brother in the local militia, where he sent back a photo of himself in a balaclava, holding an Uzi sub and a Berreta .45. You could see the shape of his stupid smile through the black cotton.

And then there is Hernando. I do not want to think about Hernando now.

We stop at the border of our barrio, in a dump at the bottom of a ridge. A thin ditch of water runs through the debris. Without a word, Pedro and Claudia take lookout positions. Luis and Edwardo straddle the sludge, one foot on either bank, and clear away the molding cardboard and plastic junk. Soon they uncover the nylon three-seater that we stole, months ago, from a public bus. They tip it forward to reveal the large concrete tunnel into which the water runs. I stand sentinel as they crawl, one by one, into the hole.

This is one of our old *mocós*. Only the five of us know its location. It is a runoff from the main storm sewer, but smells like a sewage pipe. I am glad it is dark.

Over there, I say.

Edwardo and Pedro go where I point, navigating by the blue light of their cell phones. At a waist-high ledge they peel back a thick, water-resistant cover, and Pedro lets out a whoop, then muffles his mouth. The sound echoes against the wet concrete.

Luis grins. You come back after four months, he says, and already you think you are the dog's balls. He is grinning widely. These are yours?

On trust, I say.

Handheld grenades, he says, picking them up, weighing them in his hand like they are pieces of fruit. A new AR-15. And these?

Glock nine millimeters. You can throw away your thirty-eights now.

I heard the forty-fives are better.

They look like toy guns, Claudia murmurs from the darkness.

Well, Luis says to me, still grinning. Well, well. El Padre is a generous man.

Aside from Luis's G3, we take one of the Colts and the two pistols. As this is Luis's mission, I do not ask whether this is too much or too little firepower. Pedro is a child and will carry the bullet bag. He insists on bringing a couple of grenades. Just in case, he says.

In case what? jeers Edwardo. In case the target is hiding in a FARC tank?

It is getting dark when we finally arrive in the correct neighborhood. We are on foreign turf and I am uneasy because it is the worst time of day to identify a target. I am also pissed off at Luis because he made a detour to check his emails. Luis is pissed off at me because I told him we could take a bus, and he replied, No, *puto*, they don't go that way, and just now a green one came by and almost ran us over on the narrow street. And we are all pissed off at Edwardo, who failed to dodge a pile of warm dog turd.

You sure you have done the recon? I ask Luis.

Fuck you, he says. Maybe I have no office job but I am no child.

And the target is not protected?

Listen to you and your fancy language, says Edwardo. Is the *target* not *protected*?

It is nearly dark now and everything melts into shapes of brown

23

and gray. We pass buildings made of brick, of cement blocks, of wood and plastic. Faces of people merge back into the material of their houses. Street kids scavenge for food by the roadside; some of them inhaling the pale yellow *sacol* from supermarket bags—their eyes half-open and animal and unblinking. We pass unattended stalls, half-filled wheelbarrows, hot pillow joints, then there are no more houses and we reach an abandoned railway line running parallel along the edge of a cliff. We cross the tracks and look down. The road dips steeply into a gorge that is jumbled full of bamboo sticks and torn tarpaulin sheets and hundreds upon hundreds of boxes. It is our destination: the *tigurio*: the city of cardboard.

The few inhabitants we see do not interfere. We walk through dimly lit trenches, toward the northeast corner. Shadows of faces move behind candles and gas lamps. Luis lifts his fingers to his lips and points to a shack at the end of an alley. He creeps forward. Yellow gaslight glows from behind the gaps in the cardboard. Coming closer, I see a black man on his back chewing a sugared red donut. Luis grabs him by the hair and flips him onto his stomach. If it is the right person, Luis has done his recon excellently. The target looks older than all of us—even Claudia, who has sixteen years. His skin is a darker black than mine, and burnished with sweat in the gaslight. His mouth is still crusted with little sugar bits. Luis rests his boot on the side of the target's face as he reaches inside his pants to pull out the rifle. He frowns as the magazine gets stuck in his waistband—this is a common hazard with the G3—a beginner's mistake. Edwardo has dropped to his knees, pinning the target's legs down.

Who is the son of a bitch now? Luis says. His voice is light and breathy as it is when he is excited.

You are, *puto*, squeaks the target. His lips strain to spit, and fail.

Claudia comes in and crouches down; there is not enough room to stand. We all sweat from the heat of the gas lamp. Luis succeeds at last in removing his rifle from his trousers and jams the barrel into the target's eye socket.

Do I kill him fast? he says. He is looking at me. Claudia and Edwardo are looking at me too. Pedro stands watch at the edge of the *tigurio*.

For a moment I am taken aback. Killing has never been the business of the *gallada*, unless things have changed with that, too, in the four months I have been away. Maybe they are seeking to impress me, now that I have my office job. Or maybe that is why they asked me to come with them.

Do I kill him fast? Luis says again. His voice is tight—it sounds as though he is really asking for my answer.

What is his crime?

Luis falls silent. He lifts his gun and paces two steps this way, two steps the other way, stooped underneath the cardboard roof. The target twists his head from the dirt and looks up for the first time. He sees Edwardo, who is holding his legs, and Claudia and then Luis. He sees Luis's hand, trembling on the trigger-guard.

He has many crimes, says Luis. But he called my mother the offspring of a dog.

I don't even know you, the target says instantly. He swings around in my direction. And I am protected. Ask anyone.

I glance quickly at Luis, who opens his mouth.

The target twists around to face Luis and looks at his hand again. When he speaks, his voice is low and sly. What are you doing? he murmurs. His face is shiny in the gaslight. We both know you are no *sicario*.

Breathing hard, Luis grabs the G3 with both hands and jams the barrel into the target's mouth. I can hear the metal muzzle clatter against his teeth.

Ask him who is the offspring of a dog now, I say. I find myself thinking of four days ago, the calm face in front of my Glock. Ask if he will tell you that.

I will tell you, the target cries out, whatever you want me to! He is not a tough any more; no *soldado*, that is for certain. His words are slurred because his mouth is forced half-open—it moves like the mouth of Claudia's demented mother. Please, he says.

Don't you get it? Luis shouts. His black hair gleams with sweat.

From the ground, mouth ajar, the target shakes his head. I'm sorry, he croaks.

Why are you sorry? I don't want you to say what I want you to say! We all watch Luis.

I want you to want to say it.

Okay, man.

Okay?

Okay, man.

What are you going to do? He removes the gun from the target's mouth and presses it against his cheek.

I'm going to say what you want—

Luis's frown deepens.

I mean, I'm going to want to say it, I'm going to—

What are you? Luis breaks in.

It takes a second for the target to comprehend. I am the son of a dog, he says.

What kind of dog?

A dog. A bitch. A dirty, flea-bitten, whore of a bitch.

What else?

I am a dog that is ugly, that is an imbecile, that looks like a disease-ridden rat, that smells like shit . . .

You eat your own shit, too, don't you?

For a moment Luis sounds like a gangster in an American movie I recently saw in the city. His face even carries the same sneer.

Yes, yes. The target reaches for a piece of red donut next to his face, rubs it into the dirt before pressing it in his mouth. Claudia turns away. It is strange the things a girl will tolerate and will not.

From a distance comes the sound of ringing bells. I move to a gap in the cardboard to check with Pedro. After a moment he shakes his head and calls out in his high voice, Gasoline trucks.

Luis says, What else?

His mouth full of dirt, the target says, I am a dog that eats its own shit, and drinks its own piss, and—

But he cannot fully untangle his mess of words because at that moment Luis lifts his G3, twirls it around and smashes the aluminum butt into the target's head. I think I hear a soft crack. For a brief moment Luis looks surprised, then he waves one finger from side to side in the manner of a parent scolding a child.

You are lucky, *puto*, he says, that my friends here are full of compassion. He spits on the ground next to the bleeding head. But they will not be so full next time.

You broke his head, says Claudia. He cannot hear you. She half-stands and shuffles over to the target—I think at first she is bending over to examine his wound—then she does something startling: she leans back and kicks him, hard, in the chest. Edwardo gets up from his knees and copies her. We know the target is still alive because his feet shake in response.

Luis gestures at the target with his G3, and says to me, Are you sure?

They all look at me. Their faces are flushed and full in the warm

26

yellow light. It is strange, I think—their readiness to kill—for as far as I know, none of them has ever committed the act. This business is personal.

As we leave, Luis picks up a plastic bag that contains two donuts. The icing on them is green and yellow. For Pedro, he explains gruffly. He likes this sort of shit.

Outside it has turned into night. At the bus stop I ask Luis again what was the man's crime.

A shipment of *basuco*, he says. Or marijuana. I forget.

I thought you said a game of poker, says Edwardo.

Shut up, says Luis. Shut up, you fat punk.

*   *   *

My name is Juan Pablo Merendez, and I have been hiding at my mother's place for four days. People call me Ron from the time when I was a child and, on a dare, finished a *medio* of Ron de Medellín and then another, and did not vomit.

I am a *sicario*, a hit man, an assassin. I have been a *sicario* for four months, although my agent, El Padre, says that in truth I am *soldado*, fighting for a cause. It is no cause, however, but my own hands that have brought death to fourteen people for certain, and perhaps another two. For this El Padre offers me a safe house in the barrio, where I live alone, and pays me 800,000 pesos a month and another 300,000 for each hit. Of this at least 400,000 pesos a month goes to my mother, who prays to her God about my *delincuencia*, but takes the money for her medicines and her clothes and her cable TV and asks no questions.

They call it an office job, as the *sicario* is waiting always by the phone. In Medellín, it is a prized thing to have an office job.

My agent is named Xavier—I do not know his last name, for everywhere he is known as El Padre. I have never met him. They say he is a large, light-skinned man with perhaps twenty-five years. They say he is the only agent in Medellín who is permitted a personal army. I am not sure who he works for, but it is evident from the pattern of hits he has ordered that he is connected with drugs.

El Padre has a powerful reputation. They say, when he had only six years, he was under the bed where the guerrillas came at night and killed his father, then raped his mother and stabbed her to death. The story goes that he memorized the killers' feet and their voices and their smell and tracked them down and made his revenge, one by one. The story goes that he allowed them each one final prayer and then, when they were only halfway finished, took his knife and opened their throats from behind. For this element of prayer they named him El Padre.

But the better story is that he was present, ten years ago, when his friend assassinated defenseman Escobar for the horrible sin of scoring a goal against his own country in the World Cup. The story goes that some time later he killed this friend over a spilled drink. It is something to murder a *sicario* of such reputation, but to do it over such a small failure of respect—an eyebrow revenge—this is a formidable thing. They say he now has hundreds of deaths to his name.

I have worked for El Padre for four months and have been a good *sicario*, a loyal *soldado*, never failing him until four days ago. Four days ago I was assigned a hit and did not make this hit. Of course, he is not interested in my reasons.

According to our usual practice, he called me three days ago on my cell phone to confirm the hit.

Bueno, I said, getting up and walking outside so that my mother, who was watching TV, could not listen in. Of course I had not told her I was in hiding. On the street I said to him, I could not find the target.

The phone line went quiet. You could not find the target, he said. His voice was soft, like he was recovering from a cold: Maybe the information was incorrect. Sometimes it is that way . . . the information is incorrect.

It had been a whole day and still I could not think of a better excuse.

I said, Maybe it is best to wait until Sunday. We both knew that Sunday is the best day to do the business as the target is usually at home.

You were ordered to do it yesterday.

I could not find the target, I lied again. Maybe he will be there on Sunday.

We have never met, have we, Ron?

No, sir.

You have been a good *soldado*, he said. I think it is time we met. In three days, I think.

Yes, sir.

I will call you with the details.

28

Yes, sir.

I am no child, wet behind the ears. I have now fourteen years and two months. I know how things work. That there is not supposed to be contact between a *sicario* and his agent. I know that I have been summoned.

*　*　*

When I return from the business with Luis and the others, my mother is sitting in a dark room watching an American soap show. I quickly scan the street as I close the front door.

I switch a lamp on for her. In the yellow flood of light I see she is still wearing her makeup and her going-out clothes. For a moment I watch her as she watches the screen. She does not blink. The concentration of her face is calming.

Your friend called, she says, not turning her head from the TV. It is a large forty-inch Sony model and was in almost new condition when Carlos sold it to us.

Claudia?

I wrote it all down, she says and gestures vaguely. On the screen a white woman with large lips is hugging her elbows and crying. I catch my mother's hand and make a show of kissing it gallantly, like I see in the old movies. It smells of fish and nail polish.

Oh darling! I say in high-voiced English, Come back to me for I am . . . *embarazada* . . . with your secret love child! I say this last part in Spanish so she will understand.

She shushes me and waves me away, then, as the commercials come on, she half-turns and says, Do you think I should dye my hair more blonde?

Why do you want to, dear Mother?

I don't know, she says. Maybe it will make me look younger.

Younger? You already look young. In the streets, people do not think you are my mother. They think you are my sister. My mother has heard this before but still her face beams. I continue: They say, Is she your sister? And I say, Are you joking?

Tonto! she cries. I go into the kitchen to get some *panela* from the large urn. You should learn from your friend, Xavier, she calls out.

Xavier?

I feel a tightening in my stomach, like the tightening when you walk into a room with your weapon ready and the target is not there. It is stupid to feel surprised, I think.

29

He has nice manners on the phone. Who is this friend? He said you are lucky to have a mother such as me.

He said that.

I add milk to the *panela* and bring it out to her with some Saltina biscuits.

We need more candles, she says absently. They say there will be another blackout tonight.

What did Xavier say? I ask, putting the tray down, but the commercials have ended and my mother is once again lost to the soap show.

I pick up the note paper next to the phone. She has written down an address in her large, girlish writing. It means nothing to me. I put the paper in my jacket, my heart beating *pá pá pá* from what I have just heard, and bend over the chair to kiss my mother's forehead.

Outside, I catch a bus to Aures. Claudia's house is the old cement one painted blue, halfway up the hill.

She turns from the large window when I arrive and says, *Buenas noches, guapo*. I am calmer now. The night air has cooled me. Claudia comes and lifts her hand to almost touch my face, then lets it drop. She knows I do not like to be touched around the head.

Let's go to the park, she says, like a question.

I nod. I am watching her. The window gap behind her is bigger than her whole body, and the dark openness is somehow beautiful; it is rare that any window in this city is not nailed up with grilles or latticework. Behind the window is a sheer drop of twenty meters into a marsh of mud and rocks and rubbish.

We walk up the hill together. The night air is cold and clean. All this time I am thinking about Claudia's window, and how it used to be filled with glass until one day her mother came home from the market, pulled the glass pane so far back the wrong way the hinges broke, climbed up onto the ledge and stood upright before throwing herself out. Even then, she only managed to ruin the right half of her body.

We arrive at the spot. It is dark. Ever since I showed it to Claudia she thinks of it as our spot, but in fact I prefer to go there without her. It is high, above the barrio, past the reach of the electricity cables, at the top of the hill where there are fields of yellow ichu grass and you can feel the wind from all four directions. Recently I have come here every day to sit in the long grass and sometimes drink or do the *basuco*. From this place I see the deep, narrow, long valley where the city of Medellín lies, cradled by mountains. I see the nameless streets, *carreras* running one way and *callés* the other. And in the evening I see the streetlights come on, running in gridded patterns until they reach the mountainsides where they race up and spread out until all the barrios that surround the city shimmer like constellations.

It is like that tonight, everything upside down. The stars are under us and above, a sky like dirt.

So you are really going to Cartagena? Claudia says.

Yes.

Why?

Why? I think, To see the ocean. But I say, What did you want to talk to me about? I have important business tonight.

What business?

There is no reason not to tell her. I say, I am meeting with my agent.

So it is real, she says. You have been summoned.

I am silent. Everywhere around us is the whine of grasshoppers, and further away the noise of people and machines sounds to me like the wash of the ocean. From far enough away everything sounds like the ocean.

There is a night bus to Tolù from the Terminal del Norte, says Claudia.

I shake my head.

I know about Hernando, she says. Everybody does.

What do you know?

She opens her mouth as though to say something, then stops. Then she says, The contract placed on him. By your agent.

You do not know everything, I say.

I watch Claudia's face carefully and it is hard, the face of a *soldado* with its thin cigarette mouth.

I must ask my agent for leave, I explain. Or he will find my mother.

How is she?

My mother, I think, who I had assumed was safely hidden. She is glad I am home, I say. Four whole days. I continue to watch Claudia. Excepting the business today, in the *tigurio*.

But she ignores me. Instead, she says, And you—how do you feel?

It is a question only a girl would ask.

Feel? I say.

She is right, though. Tonight, of all nights, I should feel something.

31

If you ask me, then I am scared, yes, and sad, but it is like that person who feels is someone other than me. In truth I sit here and I do not know what to feel. I have become dead of surprise. In truth, I come up here to feel nothing.

The last time she asked me that had been at Carlos's funeral, six months ago, at the *Cemeterio Universal*. It was the first death in our *gallada*. Everyone agreed he had died well. Then, too, I did not know what I felt standing before his grave. The hole was so small—he was never big, even though of us all he had the most hair on his legs and chest. My head was full of voices. One voice said, You should be crying, the other said, I want to, and behind both I could see myself, the fresh dirt on the mound, the bouquet of fake flowers, the statuettes of Marias and angels bobbing above the streets of headstones; I could hear the singing of birds and smell the *plumeria* and then feel the tears come, fake tears, watching my body and my hands so clearly as they moved, as through polished glass.

It is like that now; I am watching myself and it is a different person.

You want to do some *basuco?* Claudia asks, reaching into her bag.

I have to go, I say to her.

Then I will come with you, she says.

*   *   *

Chicas, they are a distraction from the important things, and as Luis says, sometimes to go between the legs of a chica is more dangerous than walking under a bridge in a strange barrio. As for Claudia, we used to go together, as far as that goes. I am fond of her but in truth I would not call her a friend. There has only been one who I would call my friend, and that one is Hernando.

Hernando used to be the head of our *gallada*, if such could be said, although nobody would have admitted it. (Especially not Luis, who had the same age.) There were more of us then, perhaps fifteen, and Hernando organized the *mocós* and arranged with restaurants and market-sellers for food in return for protection. The children he sent cleaning windshields, shining shoes, minding cars, juggling machetes, making sales. The older ones he organized to steal cigarettes, flowers, and gum for the children to sell. Only a few of us did the serious robbery. We worked only for ourselves. I learned much from Hernando—how to run the tag-team, when to wear the private-school uniform, how to spot targets, such as the gringos who go to an ATM and put the bills into dirty socks in their laundry bag. As one of the oldest, I did most of these things with him.

He talked differently to me when the others were not around. Sometimes he liked to watch people going about their business, particularly in crowded places, at times when we were supposed to be looking for marks. Once, in a plaza at noontime, he pointed to a farmer at a market stall, then a man at a construction site, and asked if I thought they were happy.

I don't know.

What about them?

I looked where he pointed.

They are probably happier, I said, half-jokingly.

Pah! he spat on the parched grass. The suits, they are richer, yes. He turned back to the construction worker, lean and black-skinned and slow-moving in the heat. He thought for a moment, frowning all the while, then said, But to work with your hands, and to work with others—that is real work. He spat on the ground again. I had heard from others that his father had been a farmer in the west country, but the past had never been discussed between us.

It may not make a man happy, he said, but at least there is honor in it.

In that way, too, he was different. While most of the *gallada* was concerned with buying the new things, Hernando talked to me about happiness and honor, even politics; about a future unconnected to money.

Then the day came when we became friends. Everyone was playing football in a park on the edge of the city. Hernando was one of the better players and looked like a bronze statue in motion. Someone kicked the ball off the field. It went a long way, then stopped at the leg of a man sitting on a stationary motorcycle. The man got off his bike, removed his sunglasses, and kicked the ball—in the opposite direction—into the traffic away from the park.

Hernando had been chasing the ball. I had followed him because I wanted to speak in secret about a new strategy for the game.

What are you doing? Hernando called out to the man.

Hey, *puto!* the man said. Why aren't you working? Life isn't a bowl of cherries.

You should not have kicked our ball away, said Hernando.

I am doing you a favor. The man paused briefly, then looked over his shoulder. At that moment I realized he was there with another man, a uniformed policeman, also sitting on a motorbike.

Come here, the policeman said to Hernando. He was smiling. The first man began to smile too.

Hernando walked over without hesitating. He was wearing only pants and his sweating body looked large and powerful next to the shape of the sitting policeman. I watched and said nothing.

You would argue with a business leader in our community? the policeman said cheerfully. He unclipped his holster. Hernando did not move. Turn around, the policeman said. You will argue at the station.

I watched as the policeman handcuffed Hernando. Then I felt my arms being jerked behind my back—the other man had approached silently—and I felt the cold click of metal around my wrists. This man led me to his motorbike and sat me down behind him, facing backwards. He smelled of alcohol.

As the motorbike started moving, I slouched into the man's back to keep my balance. I saw the park diminishing—everyone had vanished from the football game—but could not see where we were going.

Hernando's bike was in front of ours so I could not see him either. The handcuffs cut into my wrists. Soon I realized we were going away from downtown Medellín. We were not going to the police station. Then we began to climb a hill leading us west. It became hotter the higher we climbed.

The man said something but I could not hear it in the wind.

We turned onto a road where there were no houses. The motorbike slowed.

Jump! someone yelled. It was Hernando. Automatically I leaned to the side of the bike. I tried to jump but my pants got caught in the chain. Then the bike skidded onto its right side and I began to roll down the hill, my hands cuffed behind me. I heard a couple of gunshots. I kept rolling until the ground leveled off. My head hurt badly. Moments later I felt someone's boots roll me onto my stomach. I waited for the shot. All I could smell was earth, and grass, and it smelled richer than anything I had ever smelled before. I waited. But the gunshot did not come, and then I felt someone unlock and remove my handcuffs. Hernando helped me to my feet. Blood leaked from his right armpit. He led me up the grassy hill to where my captor, the businessman, lay under the bike, one leg bent so far the wrong way it almost touched his hip. Hernando handed me a gun.

It is his, he said.

And the policeman? I asked.

Your corrupted friend is dead, Hernando barked at the man, as though it were he who had asked the question.

The man groaned. The flesh around his mouth had gone loose. I did not know then—as I do now—that this was a sign of fear.

You must do this, said Hernando. He looked at me like a brother. He said, Ron, you must do this so we are in it together.

I took the gun, which felt unexpectedly warm and heavy in my hand, and which gave off a smell like a match being lit in a dark room. I pointed it at the man's head. His sunglasses were broken and bent around his ear and the fragments shone in the afternoon light. I aimed at the blackness in the middle of his ear and shot.

After a while, I turned my back to the man's face and tried to lift the motorbike from his broken lower body. I felt filled with a tremendous lightness, as if every breath I took expanded inside me. Then I remembered something.

The policeman. How did you—

Hernando let out a short, burp-sounding laugh. He bent his knees as though about to sit down on an invisible chair, then tipped on to his ass. He seemed suddenly drunk.

The stupid *puto* stopped, he said, because the handcuffs were uncomfortable against his back. But he would not turn me around to face the same way as him—he said he did not want a faggot rubbing up behind him. Hernando burped again. So he handcuffed my hands in front. At the top of the hill, I stopped him like this.

Hernando tilted his head backwards and lifted his arms up, high up, over his head. I saw the gashes in his right armpit that the policeman's fingernails must have made when the cuffs looped over his face and under his throat.

I watched his pale face and he laughed again. Inside, the light air filled me like *sacol*. Help me lift this, I said. But he did not look at the bike. He remained sitting on the grass, half-naked, embracing his legs tightly.

For me too, he said. That was my first time too. He frowned, looking straight ahead. His face was as white as a plastic bag. Then a change came over it as though he was going to be sick. Then his face changed again and he smiled, but now the smile only affected his mouth.

35

Finally, I lifted the bike and rested it on its side stand. We have to go, I said. You ride behind me.

He nodded. I helped him to his feet and onto the motorbike. All the way down the hill he gripped me tightly, like a *chica* on her first ride.

❖　❖　❖

After that, of course, things changed more than just the fact that Hernando and I became friends. You do not kill a policeman and business leader and expect the streets to owe you protection.

El Padre approached me—through a *nero* whom I knew but did not know to be employed by El Padre—and told me he would protect me. He would take me off the streets, like he took other kids off the onion farms, but he would raise me above these farm kids: I would be given an office job. There was strength in me, he said on the telephone. I could go back to my own barrio where, with my new status, I would be safe. We are similar, he said. We are both *soldados*, we do what needs to be done, and we have both lost our fathers to the conflict of Colombia. He said, I will be your benefactor.

Hernando, meanwhile, had disappeared from the *gallada*. His reputation had increased as a consequence of killing the policeman, and we all assumed he was hiding. Then several weeks later someone reported seeing him at one of the gringo-led programs in the city that are known to combat violence and drugs and poverty by staging plays in public parks.

I tracked him down and told him about my new job and said that I could ask my agent to give him an office job as well, or at least employ him as a *soldado*. What is this shit? I said. I gestured at his windowless, white-plastered room, clogged with stacks of cardboard and paper. The room smelled strongly of bleach. Hernando sat behind a scratched steel desk and behind him was a poster depicting a gun with a melted barrel, and underneath, the words: *This makes you a man?*

Forget all this, I said. You can start again. My agent will get you a stainless police record.

Hernando looked at me for a long time. He had cropped his hair and it changed his face, making his features seem somehow tired, muted. Finally he said, So now you have an office job. What is it like?

I told him about everything: the salary, the bonuses, the weapons. The respect from the barrio. He listened carefully. Then he leaned

36

back in his chair and closed his eyes for a long time. I sat down, watching him, wondering what he did in this room all day. He looked older.

But what is it like? he asked at last.

I realized he was asking about the killing. At that point, I had not yet been given my first assignment and the question irritated me. It is easy, I said.

Who is your agent?

I told him.

He paused again.

What?

You must listen to me, Ron. The man you know as El Padre is a dangerous man.

I laughed, thinking he was joking.

Listen to me.

Of course he is dangerous. He is a legend.

Yes, said Hernando, speaking slowly. And even so, in the game, he is a small player. He leaned suddenly forward, the steel desk wobbling under his weight. Listen, Ron, you must stop. You must quit your office job.

You are joking, no?

I was embarrassed for him. What had the *nero* said who had found him? That Hernando, looking like a peasant, instructed him to return to school or he would surely end up the victim of the never-ending culture of violence—at which the *nero* applauded and told Hernando to return to his new faggot friends. I had hidden my uneasiness. No one in the *gallada* would have dared to talk to Hernando in that manner before.

This is what your gringo friends tell you?

I do not need a gringo to see with my eyes. He looked away from me. But they are right about some things. About El Padre, for instance, who is a dog of the drug lords. He is a man who kills the innocent to protect the rich.

They are not innocent, I said quickly. He is cleaning the streets of the very people you denounce. I caught myself at the last moment from saying "I." His words affected me. I calmed my breathing. You say this when you do not even know him.

He came to me too, Hernando said.

Neither of us spoke for a while. His clothes were faded and worn, his left shoe ripped at the toe. I became conscious of my Nike Mercurial Vapor shoes and my Adidas Squadra jersey with its ClimaCool fabric and mesh panels.

It is dangerous for you to say this shit in public.

Hernando said softly, as though to himself, No one should have to do what you do. He stood up and walked around the desk.

They pay you? Where you work, this program?

Hernando smiled. His smile was heavy at the corners of his mouth. I am happy here, he said.

I can help you. I have made almost one million pesos already.

You are my family, he said simply, and I want to see you safe. He frowned briefly, trying to follow a thought with words. We cannot help each other, Ron. Maybe it is too late. But maybe you can help your own family.

Maybe you should leave the city, I said.

He smiled again, then leaned over to embrace me. Maybe, he said.

The next week I used a proxy to buy a house in the barrio next to El Poblado, and moved my mother there in secret. I did not speak to Hernando again until four days ago, when I was given the order by El Padre to assassinate him.

❊   ❊   ❊

When we were still living at the old place, and I had nine years and my mother twenty-four, it rained for a week and another two days. School was canceled—the rain so heavy the roads were waist-high with mud, people trapped in their houses. On the tenth day the rain stopped and it felt like a holiday. People wandered outdoors, as though for the first time, and the sun was warm against their skin and the grass and the trees deeper in their color and the faces of strangers flushed like ripe fruit. During this time a militia set up roadblocks along the Avenida Oriental and hijacked a public bus at the exit to our barrio. They raped two of the women and killed my father, then dumped his body and his guitar outside the back alley of my school. The papers said some of the hijackers were police agents.

They broke his guitar? my mother asked when the uniformed men came, their shirts wet at the armpits and their leather shoes splashed with mud. Of course we already knew by that time.

Why? one of them asked. Would you like it? He looked surprised. Maybe—

He stopped talking at his partner's look.

That evening it rained again, heavily, the air a mix of gray and green before the night came down. A couple of neighbors visited—my mother exchanged soft words with them at the front door—then afterward no one else came. All night she did not speak and I did not know what to think. She sat on the brown carpet in the main room, in the dark, with my father's notepapers and sheet music. The gaslight from the kitchen made her face seem misshapen. For hours, I sat on my parents' bed with the door open, watching her arranging the papers in careful piles, calmed by how her fingers moved individual pieces from pile to pile, without pause, as though following some special sequence. I watched her fingers and her strange face, and I watched the rain leaking from the thatched kitchen ceiling behind her, and I waited for her to tell me what would happen to us.

The rain did not stop for two days. My mother stayed cross-legged on the carpet, which, in the rain-dimmed light, changed color to dull orange. She wore the same gray dress and did not eat. On the third morning, a car with mounted speakers drove past and announced that Andrés Pastrana Arango had won the presidential election. I remembered that my father liked to call him the hippie candidate. I took some money from my mother's purse and went out into the street to buy some food. I played football with some kids.

That night, when I put two mangoes and a bag of boiled water in front of her, my mother saw me again. She told me to sit by her. We sat in silence. Then, in the dark, she leaned toward me and kissed whatever part of my body was closest to her, the outside of my knee, she kissed it twice, then two more times. And then she spoke my name, Juan Pablo, she said, and I looked at her and she said, You must say nothing of it, and think nothing, for you are a man now. I said, Mother? But her only answer was my name, spoken again like a chant, *Juan Pablo, Juan Pablo, Juan Pablo*.

❁　❁　❁

There are blackouts every month in the barrios, sometimes for days in a row. As Claudia and I enter the barrio where El Padre's headquarters is based, the entire mountainside stops humming and everything turns black. In the sudden dark, ghosts of light dance at the edge of my vision like memories, trapped at the back of my eyes. There are no stars. Gradually the glow of city rises over the black line of mountains, and beneath the clouds the effect is one of torchlight smothered by gray blankets.

We continue up the hill in the half-darkness. Dim lights begin to shine onto the street from candles placed in windows. At last I see at a high lookout on the hill what must be my destination: two youths stand outside the gate holding mini Uzi submachine guns. Even from this distance I can see that they are nine millimeter with twenty-five-round clips. The house is two-storied, with a balcony on the second floor overlooking the hill. Another guard patrols the balcony. The shadow of yet another glides and starts behind dimly lit windows. On the perimeter, the outer wall is topped by shards of glass of different shapes and colors, and shimmers in the candlelight.

From the midst of the slum, the house rises like a palace.

Stay here, I say to Claudia.

To my surprise, she does not argue. I will wait here, she says, and then pulls back into the shadows of an alley.

At the gate, I say my name and am searched roughly, profession-ally, and then escorted to the house by one of the guards. He opens the front door, gestures for me to enter, and returns to the gate. In-side it is dark, and the air is heavy, as in one of those houses where the windows have been left closed through the heat of the day. It smells as though someone has been smoking a spliff laced with co-caine.

You are Ron, a female voice sounds out from the corner, where a triangle of light slants down at an angle. I see someone coming down some stairs, her pointy boots first, her tight jeans, and then her bare stomach and then her tank-top breasts and then her face and her tied-up hair, all white and amber in the light. She is extremely beau-tiful.

Yes.

Xavier is waiting for you, she says. She comes directly to me and takes my hand. Her touch is warm and smooth, and the tips of her fingers lightly trace a circle on my palm. Here is a *chica*, I think, who would fuck me as soon as slit my throat.

Upstairs, El Padre is sitting behind a large wooden desk that looks out over a set of balcony bay windows. The room is filled with can-dles—candles placed on every flat surface, in every window, like in a basilica. I glance around, almost expecting to see a statue of a cruci-fixion. It is ten o'clock at night and El Padre is wearing a suit with an open-necked shirt. Even sitting, he is tall and broad at the shoulders and, consistent with the rumors, his complexion is light, but mainly I notice his hair, which is braided into cornrows. I find this surprising.

There is oil in his hair—it holds each individual braid as tight as a cable—and the oil glistens in the candlelight.

Sit down, he says.

The wooden planks creak under my weight as I walk to the chair in front of the desk. He is thumbing through some papers. Aside from his hair, he looks like he could be any businessman leaving the office at the end of the day. His features seem somehow strange to me—then I realize that even though his skin is fair, he has the wide nose and thick lips of a black man. His eyes, also, are black. I watch the play of candlelight on El Padre's braids, on his fair skin, on his slow-moving hands. He gathers up a pile of papers and taps them on the table to align them, then pulls a pen from his breast pocket and signs the top sheet with a gesture that makes plain his disgust. He puts the pen away. Then he looks up at me with cold, snake eyes.

So we meet, he says.

Yes.

His eyes flick to something behind me. I remember from when I first walked in that there are two others behind me: the *chica* and another guard who carries a rifle and has a joint in his mouth. El Padre looks at me again.

You know, Ron, you will never become an agent. His voice is soft.

Because I'm too dark?

Because you think you are smarter than your superiors.

I do not say anything.

You were given an assignment and you refused to carry it out.

I did not find the target, I say quietly.

He pauses. A good *soldado* does not choose which orders to obey from his general, does he?

No.

He swivels around on his chair, leans back and speaks out through the bay windows as though addressing the night. I am your general, he says. I must look after an entire army. If two women fight, I shave their heads. If somebody cheats me, I shoot them in the hand. If a *soldado* fails me, or betrays me . . . what choice do I have?

I watch as a gecko runs along the top frame of the bay window. It stops, testing the night air with its tongue. El Padre turns back around to me and frowns.

You have been getting high on the *sacol*, he says.

I recognize the insult. I do not do that stuff any more, I say. It is for children.

The heat from the candles on the desk, the scent of wax, the smells of marijuana and cocaine from the guard's spliff combine and my head feels very heavy.

You disobeyed me, he says, I—who have been your benefactor—and decided instead to spare your friend.

I do not say anything.

Do you know what your friend has been saying? For the first time he raises his voice. Do you know what ears listen to those kinds of words? Do you know what it costs to quiet those words? He takes a long, slow breath. You mock the hand that feeds you.

I remain silent.

And worse, you make me lose face. Respect.

You can send other *sicarios* for him, I hear myself say.

When you have already told him to run?

I told you I could not find him.

I have already sent Zeno, he says.

I do not know Zeno. But I hear he is good.

Yes, Zeno is good. His thick lips purse together, then part. Already he has achieved his mission. Two days ago.

I feel my mouth pool with cold spit. I remember I am sitting before a snake. I remember that Hernando is skilled in the ways of leaving the city unseen. And that he has had four days.

Yes?

I do not lie, he says, as though reading my thoughts. In fact, Zeno told me this himself when I visited him earlier today. In the *Hospital San Vicente de Paul*. He looks at me intently with his dark empty eyes. Then he says, Where he was admitted for a severe fracture of the skull.

I feel my body becoming heavier. I am once again going away from myself, watching myself as though watching a stranger.

This is peculiar, El Padre goes on, because Zeno said Hernando did not resist. An easy hit. So his injuries must have been caused afterward. But of course you do not know anything of this?

It is not easy for me to contain my surprise. I am looking at El Padre but all I see is the black body underneath the cardboard roof, the red donut crumbs and the sugar on his lips. My mind races like a fast-rewinding movie. So they all knew, I think, Luis and Claudia and Edwardo. I should not have gone into hiding. But I had to go into hiding—to give him time to escape. Above all this I think of Claudia, who knew, who knew where I was hiding, and who had made a choice not to tell me. Then I realize El Padre is still waiting for me to speak.

If you do not trust in my ability, I say, I can go away. My voice sounds like a series of echoes inside my head. You can take my salary for this month as compensation.

That is generous of you, Juan. Perhaps I will return the favor and give it to your mother.

He has not taken his eyes from me. I say to him, I am a *soldado*. You said this. There is no reason to involve my mother.

We look at each other. On the desk between us a thick candle sputters in a sudden draft, but neither of us blinks. His eyes are black puddles.

A bell rings in the outside darkness. I cannot hold my eyes to his—I look away. Everywhere I look are the flames of candles. It is truly like the inside of a church, I think, although I cannot remember having been inside one for years. I feel hot and slightly faint. I look at El Padre again and realize that I cannot remember the words to any prayers. Hail Mary, full of grace, I think, but after that my mind is as dark as an empty barrel. I wonder if the stories are true. I wonder where he conceals the knife. I wonder if he will ask me to turn my back to him, or if he will come to stand behind me.

*   *   *

Hernando was reading the newspaper over an evening meal as I watched from my concealed position, behind a thick shrub, in his back yard. Four days ago. My Glock loaded and ready. I watched him for a long time before coming in. When he saw me his face was grave with surprise, his eyes blinking down and up from the gun. Then he stood to embrace me.

They sent you? he asked quietly.

I nodded.

And?

He looked at me, calmly, as though I were a brother he had grown up with every day of his life. He looked at me as though he already knew what I would say. I wondered whether he knew better than me what I had been thinking as I stood outside in his yard, underneath the warm, polished leaves, testing the trigger in the half-dark.

I told you, I said. I told you.

He smiled. My fingers tightened around the Glock. I looked at his forehead. Then, as though following its own will, my hand lowered the gun to the table, let go of it.

Run.

I was not sure if I said it aloud or merely thought it.

His smile froze. Run?

He will send others. You must go. Now.

What of you?

I did not know. I had never thought it would happen this way. My mind was still clear—as it was whenever I did the business—but before the broad calm of Hernando's look I could feel the clarity slipping away.

He asked, Are you sure? After a while he frowned, then said abruptly: Come with me.

He nodded, as if it had been I who had made the suggestion, then nodded again, more vigorously, saying to himself, Yes, yes. But where? Far away. The coast. North is better. Cartagena. Come with me to Cartagena. We will be fishermen. He laughed aloud. After all this! he said.

Cartagena?

Yes, he said. Why not? He spoke playfully now, as if we were kids again, as if we were in one of our *mocós* and bragging to each other about our day's score.

I cannot go, I said.

I will not go without you, he said. When I looked at him I knew he was serious.

Even then, I understood the consequences. He was my brother but I owed him nothing—he knew that. I had not seen him for three months. He knew I had come in from the streets and—like them—had promised nothing, was incapable of betrayal. He laughed, and as I watched him laughing, his face made childlike in the act, I suddenly saw a glimpse of the old Hernando and in that moment I realized how completely he had left that person behind. I remembered him tall and bronze-skinned, then handing me the gun on the hill, then weak-kneed and pale, and now as I watched him his face was again new. It was unlike any of the faces I had seen in their last moments—always too tight or too loose—his was settled somehow, clear of weakness, the face of a *soldado* ready to die—for what, I did not understand—but whatever it was, I knew then it was not mine to impede. I would let him go. I thought of El Padre. I thought of my mother, and of Claudia. I thought of Cartagena and wondered how many times a person could start over. After a while I started laughing as well.

Yes, he said again. Yes, yes. He paused, his face sly: Claudia likes Cartagena.

Fishermen, I said.

Yes, he nodded, grinning widely. Do you remember how Luis described it?

I brought my hand to my mouth, tapped my teeth with my fingernail. This sent Hernando into a renewed fit of laughter. We were like two drunken schoolgirls. Do I remember? I said. Only after the fortieth time.

❊　❊　❊

After a long time in silence, El Padre sighs, his breath fluttering the candle flames on his desk, then smiles with his mouth and says:

You are right. You have been a good *soldado*.

I do not say anything. My head feels humid and heavy. He leans back in his large chair and clasps his hands behind his neck. Even the darkness of his armpits somehow suggests violence. Hail Mary, full of grace . . .

When I was your age, he says—even younger—I, too, had to kill my friends. He pauses. His voice has changed; it is damper now, softer. I did not mark your friend as a hit, he says. But I chose you to make the hit.

I bow my head, not knowing what to say. I remind myself that, of course, I already knew this. I think of the World Cup story, and wonder distantly if El Padre's face looked then as it does now: like a gangster in an American music video.

He continues speaking. As he speaks, it seems that his voice sinks lower and lower. His words harden into deep noises in my head. Afterward, he says—he is saying—afterward, I learned to not care so much about death, only the details. Death is just a transaction. A string of consequences.

I nod. I am becoming heavier. His words are weighing me down. My body is a rock in this chair.

Take me, for example, El Padre says, looking at me carefully. If I die, do you know how many deaths will follow? He tells me the number. I do not know whether he is saying it with pride or sorrow or disbelief.

But part of me is capable of thinking that this is an extraordinary thing. That one life can hold so many others up. And that the other lives can be ignorant of this. It reminds me of a game of wooden blocks I used to play with my parents, where the push of a single piece could bring the whole tower crashing down.

El Padre watches me and I watch him back, and when the realization comes through the hot swamp of my mind it comes with no satisfaction. You are no Hernando, a voice says in my head, and at that moment I know it to be true. Then another voice says, You are no El Padre. And as it speaks I watch him—this man sitting in front of me with a head of gleaming cornrows, in this warm room of candles—I watch him, alive, and absolutely alone in a power he cannot share.

I understand, I say.

You have been a good *soldado*, he says again. He takes a deep breath. You understand that you cannot continue in your job, however?

Yes.

And I will require the weapons back.

Of course.

I will send Damita to tell your friend who waits in the alley. She knows where they are?

I pause. Hail Mary. Then I say, I must tell my friend myself or she will not go.

He watches me impassively.

The weapons are at our *mocó*, I add.

He thinks, and then nods. Then go with Damita, he says. And come back afterward for a drink.

In the front yard outside, before we reach the gate, Damita says, He likes you.

I laugh shortly, the first time tonight. There is something about the coolness of the air that brings me back closer to myself. It is almost over, I tell myself.

No, he does, she says. I can tell. He always acts that way, the first time. She gives me a sidelong look. Her face is the kind they put on the cover of shiny magazines. The first time I met him, *ay*! I heard the same speech! If two women fight, I shave their heads, she mimics, then laughs, a quick darting laugh that makes me imagine sparks from a fire racing into a night sky.

She stops at the gate to have a cigarette with one of the guards.

Stand where I can see you, she says, waving to me like a schoolgirl stepping down from a bus.

At first I cannot find Claudia, then I hear her harsh whisper from the opposite alley.

Just come out, I say. They know you're here.

She comes as far as the corner, her forehead and knees glowing white under the streetlights, and I walk to meet her there. She frowns, and it makes her face look angry.

He is letting you go?

I don't know, I say.

She begins to cry—and I realize it is the first time I have ever seen her cry. Not even after her mother tried to kill herself did I see Claudia's face like this. It is all soft.

Hernando is dead, I say. I have to force myself to say it rather than ask it.

I know.

I think for a moment. Then, I say, tell Luis I thank him. For organizing the business today.

She nods.

He knew you would want revenge. But he did not want to tell you about Hernando's death, she says, if you were in hiding and did not already know, and there was no need—

She trails off, seeing where that leads. Everyone knew, I think again. But I do not feel bitter at all.

El Padre knows you are here, I say. He wants you to go to our *mocó* and bring back the guns.

She nods again.

I do not want to look at her crying face. I look into the half-dark behind her, make out the contours of a ditch, the banks of rubbish packed hard as rock. I think I see the face of a child appear behind a candle, and then disappear. The sky feels like it is sinking closer and closer to earth.

My mother, I say.

Don't worry about that, she says. I will take her away.

I turn back toward her. The revenge killings will not finish for a few weeks.

She nods again. Then a strange look crosses her face, and her narrow shoulders lurch toward me. Her teeth scrape across my lips. I feel embarrassed. I try to kiss her back but I have difficulty controlling my mouth. Her lips are on my ear. She is saying something. She is saying something but I cannot hear her, and when I try to listen I cannot remember what her voice sounds like. I am pulled back into myself.

She is saying, Take it. She presses it into my hand, guides it into my pocket. It is hard and cold and shaped like an apple. It is one of Pedro's grenades. I do not dare to look down.

How do you feel? she asks me for the second time tonight. She asks it with a small laugh.

I do not know what to say. Can I say, My body feels like it is all water? Can I say, Perhaps, perhaps I am glad?

You must be scared, she says.

Her left hand is still wrapped around mine and it is trembling. This, I think, from Claudia, who has the steadiest hands I know. I look at her and then, in her eyes, I see a window, framed by her mother's body, and I find myself thinking about how easy it seemed for her mother to jump to a death she did not want that badly.

Yes, I lie to her. Yes, I am scared.

I look back toward the house and it is clear from Damita's posture that she has finished her cigarette, is bored with the guards, is cold and is waiting for me. The house, with its candlelights, looks somehow sacred under the gray clouds, and the moon, which has come out beneath them, looks like a huge yellow magnet.

My fingers rub against the cold metal in my pocket. I must go, I say.

Claudia embraces me again, her fingers tight against my ribs. She is breathing shallowly now. Tell him you will never come back. Tell him he can trust you. She says it quietly but there is a pressure behind her words.

Yes, I say. But first you must go get the guns.

She will not let go of me.

I hate this place, she says, wiping her eyes on my shoulder. We will leave together. Your mother too.

My mother, I say.

I look up at the house, shimmering high on the black rise before me. Claudia clings to my chest. Her body is warmer than I can remember it ever being. From the gate, Damita looks in our direction and I step back, away from Claudia, and see her now as though from a growing distance. She is soft, and small, and alone, and I force myself to look away from her.

You must get the guns, I say.

He will let you go.

She has gathered her voice with effort. I smile at her. He will let me go, I tell her.

This time, the guards do not search me. At the front door Damita loops her arm around my elbow and leads me inside. As we walk up the stairs, her hips bump against mine and her bare stomach shifts and lengthens in the angled light. El Padre is behind the bay windows, standing on the balcony, looking out. He gestures for me to join him.

From the balcony, the brightness of the house makes the hillside seem even blacker. We stand there in silence—El Padre and I and a guard motionless against the far railing. As my eyes adjust, I can make out hazy lagoons of light in the distance.

El Padre makes a quick gesture with one hand. I spin around: another guard holding an Uzi submachine gun is jogging toward me. I fumble against the leathery skin of the grenade in my pocket; find the pin.

Better than *basuco*, says El Padre. He continues to look out over the hill. It is only when the guard is next to me that I realize he is holding out a spliff. El Padre takes it from him, takes a long drag, then holds it out to me.

I nod—I am unable to speak—and unclench my fingers from the pin of the grenade. When I pull in the smoke it sinks deeper and deeper, without seeming to stop, into the space of my body.

Much cleaner, no?

He smiles now: a charming host. In the deflected light, I notice for the first time a flabbiness in his cheeks. His braided hair looks wet. We stand on the balcony and look out over the blacked-out barrio. It is beautiful how, in the candlelight, the glass on top of the walls shimmers with hints of every color. For a moment I imagine the house is a ship floating on the silent ocean, high in the wind. This thought calms me and it is strange, for I have never in my life seen the ocean, and I am reminded of evenings when I have stood on the cobbled yard outside my mother's back window, watching her asleep with her makeup on, or taking her medicine with *aguardiente* when she thinks no one sees, or coming out of the glowing bathroom with her hands in her hair, a towel and a quick unthinking motion. It calms me, watching her like this.

El Padre says something. His words are sounds, splintering endlessly down the black well of my thoughts. *Vámonos*, he is saying. *Vámonos*, I need something to warm my stomach.

I look at his smiling face, the black moons of his eyes.

Come on, he says. I have a special room for drinking. We will wait for your friend there.

The two guards on the balcony do not move.

We will toast your farewell, says El Padre. I hear you like to drink. He begins to walk indoors. Where will you go? Have you decided?

I don't know, I say. Maybe Cartagena.

Cartagena, he repeats. Then he beckons, and the two guards fall into line behind me. Cartagena, I think, where Hernando waits for me. Even now, at the last, we are connected. I can feel Claudia's teeth, her dry lips against my mouth. I rotate the grenade in my pocket—Hail Mary, I think—my palms damp with sweat—and finally, when my thumb finds purchase on the safety lever, I thread my middle finger through the pin and pull it out, hard. It falls free. El Padre looks back at me and smiles.

So, he asks, have you ever been there?

Gripping the lever tightly, I follow my benefactor into the house. A third guard opens a door from the main office and goes in ahead. No candlelight shines from inside. El Padre goes next and I follow him, as though deep into a cave, the two guards unfailingly behind me. The smell of Damita's perfume is strong in the darkness. Somewhere in front of me, El Padre's voice asks again about Cartagena, and this time I say, No, and as I say it, my thumb wet and unsteady on the lever, the memory returns to me, the picture as I have imagined it so many times in the past. Luis is sitting on the old colonial wall and looking out toward the ocean. As the sun rises, he says, you can see ten black lines leading into the steel gray water, each line maybe twenty meters apart, and as the water turns orange, then red, you can see that each line is made up of small black shapes and that they are moving away from the water, together, all in harmony, and then as the sun rises higher on your right you can see that each black shape is a man, there are hundreds of them, and they are hauling one enormous fishing net in from the ocean, slowly, step by step.

Nominated by Salvatore Scibona, A Public Space

THOSE WHO CLEAN AFTER

by CHARLES SIMIC

from FIVE POINTS

Evil things are being done in our name.
Someone scrubs the blood,
As we look away,
Getting the cell ready for another day.

I can't make out the faces,
Only buckets and mops
Being carried down stone steps
Into the dark basement.

How quietly they hose the floor,
Unfurl the musty old rags
To wipe the hooks on the wall.
I hear only the sounds of summer night,

The leaves worried as always
By that nameless something
That may be lurking out there
Beyond the barn and the chicken coop.

Nominated by Philip Levine, Five Points

HYACINTHE AND THE BEAR

by PAUL ZIMMER

from THE GEORGIA REVIEW

HYACINTHE IS DANCING with the Bear outside my window again. I can hear them shuffling and rounding on the pavement. Hyacinthe is very old, and I can hear him breathing hard. The Bear groans a little. How many nights have they been out there, turning their circles? Time inches along. How do you measure its passage? Calendars yellow and crumble away. Clocks grow still and stop forever.

How do you measure seven centuries? Count out loud slowly to seven hundred, and imagine one year each time you say a number. Spring, summer, autumn, winter; the good and the bad, the hot and the cold—think of all of this as you say each number. Yes, doing such a thing is impossibly tedious; yet if you were able to bring yourself to do it, you might gain a very small sense of the passage of seven centuries. Seventy decades. Six million, one hundred and thirty-six thousand, two hundred hours. How can conditions and events that occurred all those years and hours ago be recounted? Memories blanched by time, distorted, lost, gone into the cracks and crumbles of whatever rock and residue remain. Documents translated, lost, found, retranslated, obscured, destroyed, lost again, faked, and reinvented until they are utterly distorted or disappear altogether.

Arthur Schlesinger Jr. writes, "The past is a chaos of events and personalities into which we cannot penetrate. It is beyond retrieval and it is beyond reconstruction." What we have then is a barely reliable motley, a patching together of partial stories, hopes, lies, memories, records, imaginings, and opinions—not a complete record of the "truth," just some things that suggest narrative, giving a small hint of a time and a place.

The Cathars in the Languedoc of France were obliterated, murdered, completely wiped out, "ethnically cleansed" from the earth seven centuries ago. There are no small, historically pertinent bits and pieces of them left—only some spectacular ruins of wind-battered stone ramparts and rubble on jagged peaks in the foothills of the Pyrenees. As far as I can tell, there are no pictures, tools, scriptures, treaties, songs, texts, funeral objects, weapons, boats, jewelry, or utensils left from the lives of these people—only remote ruins on Pyrenean mountaintops. Almost every small trace of the Cathars was burned to cinders, even the bones of these heretics, by the righteous crusaders of the Catholic Church.

What little I have been able to learn of them comes from scattered scholarly references, guide leaflets about the ruins, and local legends. Though the Cathars were Christians, they practiced an aberrant, dualistic faith *in petto*, and apparently their beliefs appealed broadly enough to make them seem a significant threat to the pope. Cathars believed that human beings are embodiments of the tainted souls who were inspired by Satan to revolt in heaven and who were thus driven out and banished to the earth, doomed to live and die here, eternally imprisoned in the form of human or animal bodies.

The Cathars maintained that the only way to escape this predicament was through strict dedication to their belief in a spiritual and physical discipline that would lead at death to a Beatific Vision and immortal life. Baptism was the Cathars' central rite and the only panacea for the disaster of the Fall. But baptism was not a beginning; it was a conclusion, earned only through a life of extreme constraint and effort. Those ultimately earning this blessing became "Perfects," who would be accepted into heaven at their deaths, and these constituted the ordained Cathar priesthood on earth. The temporal life of the Perfect was so demanding and perilous (because of persecution by the Inquisition) that many Cathars postponed baptism until they were on their deathbeds. Perfects lived lives of extreme denial—no sex, and no eating meat, cheese, eggs, or milk because these were the products of intercourse. Eating fish was permitted because Cathars believed that marine creatures procreated without coition.

Who can imagine such hearts beating all those centuries ago—the strange yearnings and beliefs of thousands of large and small lives, their forgotten struggles, the rock-bottom desolation of an oppressed population under constant siege? Because they were so relentlessly persecuted they were driven to construct amazing fortifications, where they could practice their faith and protect themselves, on the most inaccessible peaks of the foothills in the Languedoc.

If I lean out from the balcony of our little house in Puivert in southern France, I can see the remains of a smaller Cathar fortress on a rise just on the other side of the village—crumbled, partially restored walls and turrets, and a square tower built from the rubble by troubadours a century and a half after the massacre of the heretics. There are even more imposing Cathar ruins in the area—Montségur, Peyrepertuse, Quéribus—like dream castles on the endpapers of fairy tale books, rising high into the clouds and mist. One wonders how these ancient people, so restricted by diet and physical regimen, were able to build such formidable structures on the most unapproachable crags. At their finish, when the Cathars were under total siege from the knights of the Inquisition, they were able to hold out in these strongholds for months, even years in some cases, before perishing on the pyres of their doom.

Only a few barely creditable details of their lives have passed down to us. For certain, it is known that they excelled at weaving and farming. Those novitiates who had not yet attained the Beatific Vision and immortal life always bowed down to the ground three times when they encountered a Perfect. Their main food was a vegetable and grain gruel seasoned only with onions and shallots, and they ate fish and fruit in season.

There are, in addition, many bizarre legends and unsupported rumors about Cathars: They wore black robes exclusively and never cut their hair; they consumed in some quantity a hallucinatory soup made of secret mushrooms; they moved about only at night; and if pressed, they could live for weeks on a diet of pulverized stones. It is surmised that the basic symbol of their belief was a circle and that their dances and rituals were essentially circular. Some of the more profane rumors claim that Cathars committed buggery with goats, accounting for their astonishing ability to build on such impossible precipices; that they eliminated waste through their mouths and ears; that they kept pet bears and danced with them in the moonlight. Most of this is balderdash, of course, but the legends endure. The

Cathars were buried by the centuries, obscured by time, space, and the church. Their secrets reside in the winds.

We know the Cathars believed that hell is on earth, and that human beings are the embodiment of the evil angels who rebelled against God and were cast out of heaven by His good angels.

The *Fall*. That's what we are talking about, friends, but Cathars took it one step further than the Bible. They believed that Satan and his minions populate this world and that hell is on this earth. *We* are the evil minions, friends. Here we are. Stop counting the years now, and think about this. Do you doubt it?

The year is 2006. Several weeks' editions of the *Herald Tribune* are stacked on a small table near where I am sitting in my little house in Puivert. Let me read some of the headlines from just a few weeks: *Hindus Killed by Muslims in Kashmir, Taliban Threat Grows in Afghan South, Laser Weapon Planned, Bombings and Attacks in Chechen, Three Years of Darfur Carnage, Crippled Gaza under Siege Faces a Plague of Health Woes, Indonesian Anguish, Iraq Car Bombs Kill 34, New Orleans Citizens Suffer as New Hurricane Season Approaches, Bush Vows to Stay the Course, AIDs Continues Rampant in Nigeria, C.E.O. Sentenced, Bin Laden Calls for New Attacks in Audiotape, 30 Killed in Sinai as Bombs Rock Resort, North Korea Brandishes Atomic Weapons, Mugabe Orders Further Displacement of Zimbabweans, Iran Defiant on Nuclear Issue, Ideals Clash as Vatican Rethinks Ban on Condoms, Prison Abuse Charges Set for U.S. Guards, Chernobyl Recalled, New Attacks Aimed at Peacekeepers in Egypt, U.N. Cuts Rations to Sudan Victims, Rumsfeld Claims War Progress Despite Mounting Casualties, Latest Suicide Bombs Stir Fear of Terrorists.*

One evening, as I was coming in from a late dinner with friends in Puivert, I parked my rented Peugeot at the end of our narrow street and walked up the lane of row houses. Only a few lights were flickering in the distant countryside.

Rural France is a dark place at night. The French pull their shutters tight, keeping the light inside; road lamps are rare and widely scattered. Two or three dogs were barking across the fields as I made my way slowly in the glimmer. Nightingales in the woods just up the hill were lilting *pieu-pieu-pieu* and then abruptly their coda, *chuck-chuck-chuck*—always in threes, always a surprising sound in the night to my American ears. Other movements also aroused my curiosity—unseen rustlings in this quiet neighborhood on the edge of town. But I figure, when I am in the French countryside almost everything is none of my business. At night especially, I am a stranger in a strange land, and I keep my nose out of things.

I unlocked, hung coat and cap in the entryway, and trudged upstairs to close the shutters. But as I leaned out my front window to pull the panels, I noticed shadows moving on the moonlit street. They were turning in some sort of pattern, two men circling each other as if they might be boxing. Had they been there when I came in?

The scene was obscure, but in the dim light I recognized one of the figures—a heavy, always silent man whom I often glimpse during my evening rambles, who makes me uneasy by slipping off into narrow passageways when he sees me. He appears not to have cut his hair in decades—or ever. He is all brown hair, only his eyes and nose visible in the tangle down to the small of his back. I see this guy occasionally in town. The shopkeepers and locals seem to be used to him, but his lurking, hirsute appearance always gives me the willies.

The other guy in the dark street was equally startling—a sticklike phantom of a man with a tremendous shock of glowing white hair, wearing a black coat over his shoulders, or perhaps it is a cape.

I am not readily spooked, but I must admit that these specters moving under my window in the moonshine sent chills up my shoulders into my ears. They appeared to be doing a sort of dance—not holding each other, but standing apart, their arms held high, hooking fingers and turning, their movement dead slow as they rotated around each other. They made no sounds, but seemed to be circling to some secret, inner music. Their muted movements went on for minutes, until I accidentally bumped one of my shutters and made it creak.

They stopped and looked up, these two strange wraiths brushed by moonlight. I had interrupted them—the snooper, the foreigner obviously spying on their dance. It was up to me to say something. My voice was high and strained as I uttered a weak *"Bonsoir"* from my window. They did not respond, but stood staring at me. Hastily I pulled my shutters and hooked them, hurried back downstairs, and secured my door. Surely they heard the lock tumbling.

Later that night, as I read in bed, I thought I heard footsteps in the street in front of my house. I listened carefully, but heard no further sounds except the clicking of an electric heater at the other end of my bedroom. I was a long time getting to sleep and read my book far into the night.

After this, occasionally in the evenings I thought I heard some movement outside my locked door. A strange rhythm, a kind of shuffling, and a hint of—or at least the sense of—outré musical sounds, more felt than heard. Perhaps a strumming, coiling softly through my hearing aids into my head, but only for a few moments at a time. One night when I felt certain I heard something outside, I sucked up my courage and threw open the shutters suddenly, but there was only a startled cat in the street.

Chateau de Puivert was able to hold out for only a day or two when the Inquisition's soldiers finally came to dispatch the heretics. It is set on a rise lower than the more spectacular Cathar fortresses, but it is still imposing. One cool spring day I climbed to the stones and towers. Chill wind came up from the valley to flap my scarf and numb my nose as I panted up the hill.

I entered the gate in the walls, walked through the courtyard, and entered the main oblong tower to climb the pitch-dark stairs. My fingertips grew numb from scrabbling on the old stone walls as I groped my way up. By the time I reached the open parapet on top, the day had grown even more blustery. I felt so weary and uncertain that I had to stand back from the notched walls for fear of being blown off.

I tried to imagine day-to-day existence in such a chill, wind-blasted place. Like most castles, Puivert's seems a mad, desperate edifice, built out of fear and aggression. But it remains magical, even after seven hundred years, strangely looming, perhaps haunted by presences in its howling shafts and frigid crannies.

Cathars were strict, but they seemed to have been devoted nevertheless to amity. They defended themselves stiffly against impossible odds, yet legend has it that they were gentle folks. Their self-denial and fasting must have led them to remarkable spiritual discoveries as they faced oppression. They were such pious people, so confident in their faith, that when they were overrun they willingly hurled themselves into the huge fires prepared for their execution, as if they were almost grateful to be taken from this hell on earth.

His name is Hyacinthe Duchin—the white-haired guy. I found this out from one of the local matrons who speaks a bit of English, the old woman who manages the *marché de fruits et legumes* in the village. Hyacinthe's family has always lived in the Languedoc, she said, "from way back," and he was a language teacher in the local *lycée* until he retired a decade ago.

"He is a *personne étrange*," she admitted, "but he is very *érudit*. He is okay. He is my best customer. He belongs here." I took it that the last remark was intended to remind me I am really a stranger here. I did not inquire further about Hyacinthe, who is none of my business, but I was relieved to hear that he is "okay." I feel a bit more comfortable during the evenings when I hear him dancing with the hairy guy outside my door.

As I grow older, I take little dozes. Lately in my driftings—in my imagination—I sometimes dream that the last Cathars are dancing out there. This is an uneasy, almost crazy feeling, and yet in some ways I feel honored even to imagine it: Hyacinthe, *le Cathar finale*, the last descendent of the Perfects, orbiting with his Bear in my street.

Then I become appalled with myself. Come on, Zimmer, old man! Get a doctor. You are beginning to dither. Seven centuries! Count to seven hundred slowly again. Think. Don't slide. These are a couple of French hippies boogying in the dark. Maybe they're escapees from the *maison de fous*.

Now, sometimes, when I open my shutters the men allow me to watch them dance: so slowly, the two of them, barely moving as they round. In the dark they almost seem to elevate. Are they stepping off the Cathar circles? Why do they hang around in my street? If they decide to knock some night, I swear I won't answer. I've read my Yeats. I know what to do if shades come knocking.

When I see Hyacinthe around town, he looks at me knowingly. He thinks he is getting to me. Is he trying to cast some spell? He looks at me as if I might be some sort of "possibility." Maybe I am. I am old and getting a little ditzy as I head toward the finish. I am chill and stiff all the time. Perhaps if I danced with Hyacinthe and the Bear I would not feel so cold. He gazes at me as if I am a candidate for an epiphany—a revelation, a burning bush.

Late one night there actually does come a rapping on my door.

My shutters are still open. Why have I left them open? Am I subconsciously giving off some sort of signal? I regret not closing them. As I listen through my window I hear the timbre of a thousand night peepers rolling like the voices of the stars. Solemn doves are lined up and moaning in silhouette along the ridges of the rooftops across the way. The moon is bright, and coquelicot is vibrating bright orange in the shine along the field roads. Nightingales are going *pieu-pieu-pieu* in the trees. Is this the music I have been secretly trying to hear?

I have been reading a book and am close to dropping off for a doze when the knocking comes. I put down my book and stand up. There is another knock. What do I do? Do I go downstairs and open the door? Do I go dancing with the shades?

Friends, I am sorry. It is unfair that I have taken you this far only to leave you hanging. But this is as far as I can go. I am not going to tell you what happened when the knock came. You will think that I have not been telling the truth, that I have been leading you on. But think as you will—I am not going to tell you what happened. Please do not press me.

Now you are thinking, this old guy has gone over the top, some of his lights are unplugged—he has made me read all these words, and now he is trying to trick me. Friends, if you must think this way, then so be it, but do not ask me for more than I can tell. Think yourself fortunate that I have given you at least this much of the story.

I like to think I am a generous man, a peaceful man. I won't frustrate you completely. If you are serious about life and death, I can suggest certain things: Eat no meat, drink no milk, control your desires. Trust in the Lord and avoid the Devil. Consume only water and the juice of fruits. You may eat fish because they do not profane the water. Take vegetables and mushrooms.

If you imagine hearing music when the moon is full, you might consider turning a few circles in its light. There are chances worth taking. Some people will think you have given over, but what do they matter? The world is harsh, and we must do what we can do. At the very least, if someone comes to your door one night, consider answering the knock.

Nominated by Gary Gildner, Philip Appleman, Marvin Bell

WAR LULLABY

by MEGHAN O'ROURKE

from THE KENYON REVIEW

Wet daggers of grass
cast shadows over one another
beneath the porch light—

the boy stretched on the lawn,
fighting sleep,
fingers the tournament ring:

inside the house
his mother shouts, blinds
slap in the breeze,

and upstairs the smallest stir
as they sleep, eyelashes like
tiny whips against their cheeks.

The dogs bark, a door slams,
the boys breathe deep,
then shudder—

I have seen them
sleepwalk
out of the arms of mothers.

Nominated by David Baker, Billy Collins, David St. John

GOATS

fiction by RICK BASS

from THE IDAHO REVIEW

Ⓘт WOULD BE EASY TO SAY that he lured me into the fields of disrepair like Pan, calling out with his flute to come join in on the secret chaos of the world: but I already had my own disrepair within, and my own hungers, and I needed no flute call, no urging. I've read recently that scientists have measured the brains of adolescent boys and have determined that there is a period of transformation in which the ridges of the brain swell and then flatten out, becoming smoother, like mere rolling hills, rather than the deep ravines and canyons of the highly intelligent: and that during this physiological metamorphosis, it is for the boys as if they have received some debilitating injury, some blow to the head, so that, neurologically speaking, they glide, or perhaps stumble, through the world as if in a borderline coma during that time.

Simple commands, much less reason and rules of consequence, are beyond their ken, and if heard at all, sound perhaps like the clinking of oars or paddles against the side of a boat heard by one underwater, or like hard rain drumming on a tin roof: as if the boys are wearing a helmet of iron, against which the world, for a while, cannot, and will not, intrude.

In this regard, Moxley and I were no different. We heard no flute calls. Indeed, we heard nothing. But we could sense the world's seams of weaknesses—or believed we could—and we moved toward them.

Moxley wanted to be a cattle baron. It wasn't about the money—we both knew we'd go on to college, Moxley to Texas A&M, and me to the University of Texas—and that we'd float along in something or another. He wanted to become a veterinarian, too, in addition to a cattle baron—back then, excess did not seem incompatible with the future—and I thought I might like to study geography. But that was all eons away, and in the meantime, the simple math of cattle ranching—one mother cow yielding a baby, which yielded a baby, which yielded a baby—appealed to us. All we had to do was let them eat grass. We had no expenses, we were living at home, we just needed to find some cheap calves. The money would begin pouring from the cattle, like coins and bills from their mouths. With each sale, we planned to buy more calves—four more from the sale of the fatted first one, then sixteen from the sale of those four, and so on.

I lived in the suburbs of Houston, with both my parents (my father was a geologist, my mother a schoolteacher), neither of whom had a clue about my secret life with cattle (nor was there any trace of ranching in our family's history), while Moxley lived with his grandfather, Old Ben, on forty acres of grassland about ten miles north of what were then the Houston city limits.

Old Ben's pasture was rolling hill country, gently swelling, punctuated by brush and thorns—land which possessed only a single stock tank, one aging tractor, and a sagging, rusting barbed-wire fence that was good for retaining nothing, with rotting fence posts.

Weeds grew chest-high in the abandoned fields. Old Ben had fought in the first World War as a horse soldier and had been injured repeatedly, and was often in and out of the V.A. clinic, having various pieces of shrapnel removed, which he kept in a bloodstained gruesome collection, first on the windowsills of their little house, but then, as the collection grew, on the back porch, scattered in clutter, like the collections of interesting rocks that sometimes accrue in people's yards over the course of a lifetime.

Old Ben had lost most of his hearing in the war, and some of his nerves as well, so that even on the days when he was home, he was not always fully present, and Moxley was free to navigate the rapids of adolescence largely unregulated.

We began to haunt the auction barns on Wednesdays and Thursdays, even before we had our driver's licenses—skipping school and walking there, or riding our bikes—and we began to scrimp and save, to buy at those auctions the cheapest cattle available: young calves, newly weaned, little multicolored lightweights of uncertain pedigree, costing seventy or eighty dollars each.

We watched the sleek velvety gray Brahma calves, so clearly superior, pass on to other bidders for $125, or $150, and longed for such an animal; but why spend that money on one animal, when for the same amount we could get two?

After parting with our money, we would go claim our prize. Sometimes another rancher offered to put our calf in the back of his truck or trailer and ferry it home for us, though other times we hobbled the calf with ropes and chains and led it, wild and bucking, down the side of the highway, with the deadweight of a log or creosote-soaked railroad tie attached behind it like an anchor, to keep the animal—far stronger, already, than the two of us combined—from breaking loose and galloping away unowned and now unclaimed, disappearing into the countryside, our investment now no more than a kite snatched by the wind.

We gripped the calf's leash tightly and dug in our heels, and were half-hauled home by the calf itself. In the creature's terror it would be spraying and jetting algae-green plumes of excrement in all directions, which we would have to dodge, and were anyone to seek to follow us—to counsel us, perhaps, to turn away from our chosen path, still experimental at this point—the follower would have been able to track us easily, by the scuffed-up heel marks and divots of where we had resisted the animal's pull, and by the violent fans of green-drying-to-brown diarrhea: the latter an inauspicious sign for an animal whose existence was predicated on how much weight it would be able to gain, and quite often the reason these marginal calves had been sent to the auction in the first place.

Arriving finally at Moxley's grandfather's farm, bruised and scratched, and with the calf in worse condition, we would turn it loose into the wilderness of weeds and brambles circumscribed by the sagging fence.

We had attempted, in typical adolescent half-assed fashion, to shore up the fence with loose coils of scrap wire, lacking expertise with the fence stretcher, and in some places where we had run out of wire we had used the orange nylon twine gathered from bales of hay, and lengths of odd-sorted rope, to weave a kind of cat's cradle, a spiderweb of thin restraint, should the calf decide to try and leave our wooly, brushy, brittle pasture.

We had woven the fence with vertical stays also, limbs and branches sawed or snapped to a height of about four feet, in the hopes that these might help to provide a visual deterrent, so that the curving, staggering, collapsing fence looked more like the boundaries of some cunning trap or funnel hastily constructed by Paleolithics in an attempt to veer some driven game toward slaughter.

We had money only for cattle or fence, but not both. Impulsive, eager, and impatient, we chose cattle, and the cattle slipped through our ramshackle fence like the wind itself—sometimes belly-wriggling beneath it, other times vaulting it like kangaroos.

Other times the calves simply went straight through the weakened fence, popping loose the rusted fence staples and shattering the rotted, leaning fence posts and crude branches stacked and piled as barricades. Sometimes the calves, fresh from the terror and trauma of their drive from auction, never slowed when first released through the gate at Old Ben's farm, but kept running, galloping with their heads lowered all the way down the hill, building more and more speed, and they would hit the fence square on.

Sometimes they would sail right on through it, like a football player charging through the paper wrapped between goalposts before a football game, though other times they would bounce back in an awkward cartwheel before scrambling to their feet and running laterally some distance until they found a weaker seam and slipped through it not like anything of this world of flesh and bone, but like magicians, vanishing.

When that happened, we would have to leap on the old red tractor, starting it with a belch and clatter that inevitably frightened the calf into even wilder flight; and with Moxley driving the old tractor flat out in high gear, and me standing upright with a boot planted wobbly on each of the sweeping wide rear fenders, riding the tractor like a surfer and swinging a lariat (about which I knew nothing), we would go racing down the hill after the calf, out onto the highway, the tractor roaring and the calf running as if from some demon of hell that had been designed solely to pursue that one calf, and which would never relent.

We never caught the calves, and only on the rarest of occasions were we ever even able to draw near enough to one—wearing it down with our relentlessness—to even attempt a throw of the lariat, which was never successful.

Usually the animal would feint and weave at the last instant, as the tractor and whizzing gold lariat bore down on it, and the calf would shoot or crash through another fence, or cross a ditch and vault a fence strung so tightly that as the calf's rear hoofs clipped the fence going over, the vibration would emit a high taut hum, which we could hear even over the sound of the tractor.

It was like the sound of a fishing line snapping, and by the time we found an unlocked gate to that pasture, the calf would have escaped to yet another field or pasture, or might be down in some wooded creek bottom, reverting to instincts more feral and cunning than those of even the deer and turkeys that frequented those creeks; and we would scour the surrounding hills for all the rest of that day— sometimes mistakenly pursuing, for a short distance, a calf which might look like ours, until that calf's owner would come charging out on his own tractor, shouting and cursing, angling to intercept us like a jouster.

Old Ben fell too ill to drive, and then began to become a problem while Moxley was in school; he had begun to wander out into the same fields in which the rogue calves had been released, and was similarly trying to escape his lifelong home, though he was too feeble to bash or batter his way through the patchwork fence, and instead endeavored to climb over it.

Even on the instances when he made good his escape, he snagged his shirt or pants on a barb and left behind flag-size scraps of bright fabric fluttering in the breeze, and we were able to track him that way, driving the roads in his old station wagon, searching for him.

Sometimes Old Ben lay down in a ditch, trembling and exhausted from his travels, and pulled a piece of cardboard over him like a tent to shield him from the heat, and we would pass on by him, so that it might be a day or two before we or a neighbor could find him.

Other times however Old Ben would become so entangled in his own fence that he would be unable to pull free, and when we came home from school we would see him down there, sometimes waving and struggling though other times motionless, quickly spent, with his arms and legs akimbo, and his torn jacket and jeans looking like the husk from some chrysalis or other emerging insect: and we'd go pluck him from those wires, and Moxley mended his torn jacket with the crude loops of his own self-taught sewing; but again and again Old Ben sought to flow through those fences.

There were other times though when Old Ben was fine, fit as a fid- dle; times when the disintegrating fabric of his old wartorn mind, frayed by mustard gas and by the general juices of war's horror, shifted, like tiny tectonic movements, reassembling into the puzzle- piece grace his mind had possessed earlier in life—the grandfather

Moxley had known and loved, and who loved him, and who had raised him. On those occasions, it felt as if we had taken a step back in time. It was confusing to feel this, for it was pleasant; and yet, being young, we were eager to press on. We knew we should be enjoying the time with Old Ben—that he was not long for the world, and that our time with him, particularly Moxley's, was precious and rare, more valuable than any gold, or certainly any rogue cattle.

On the nights when the past reassembled itself in Old Ben and he was healthy again, even if only for a while, the three of us ate dinner together. We sat on the back porch feeling the Gulf breezes, coming from over a hundred miles to the southeast, watching the tall ungrazed grass before us bend in oceanic waves, with strange little gusts and accelerations stirring the grass in streaks and ribbons, looking briefly like the braids of a rushing river; or as if animals-in-hiding were running along those paths, just beneath the surface and unseen.

We would grill steaks on the barbecue, roast golden ears of corn, and drink fresh-squeezed lemonade, to which Ben was addicted. "Are these steaks from your cattle?" he would ask us, cutting into his steak and examining each bite as if there might be some indication of ownership within; and when we lied and told him yes, he seemed pleased—as if we had amounted to something in the world, and as if we were no longer children. He would savor each bite, then, as if he could taste some intangible yet exceptional quality.

We kept patching and then repatching the ragged-ass fence, lacing it back together with twine and scraps of rope, with ancient twists of baling wire, and with coat hangers; propping splintered shipping pallets against the gaps, stacking them and leaning them here and there in an attempt to plug the many gaps. (The calves ended up merely using these pallets as ladders and springboards.)

In his own bedraggled state, however, Ben saw none of the failures. "That's what being a cattleman's about," he said—he, who had never owned a cow in his life. "Ninety-five percent of it is the grunt work, and five percent is buying low and selling high. I like how you boys work at it," he said, and he never dreamed or knew that in our own half-assedness, we were making so much more work for ourselves than if we'd done the job right the first time.

After we got our driver's licenses we used Ben's old station wagon—he was no longer able to drive—and after getting him to bed, and hasping the doors to his house shut, as if stabling some wild horse, and latching the windows from the outside, we left the darkened farmhouse and headed for the lights of the city, which cast a golden half-dome high into the fog and scudding clouds.

It was a vast glowing ball of light, seeming close enough that we could have walked or ridden our bikes to reach it: and driving Ben's big station wagon, with its power steering and gas-sucking engine, was like piloting a rocket ship. There were no shades of gray, out in the country like that: there was only the quiet stillness of night, with crickets chirping, and fireflies, too, back then—and the instrument panels on the dashboard were the only light of fixed reference as we powered through that darkness, hungry for that nearing dome of city light. The gauges and dials before us were as nearly mysterious to us as the instrument panel of a jet airplane, and neither Moxley nor I paid much attention to them. For the most part, he knew only the basics: to aim the car, steering it crudely like the iron gunboat it was, and how to use the accelerator and the brakes.

And after but a few miles of such darkness, there would suddenly be light, blazes of it hurled at us from all directions—grids and window squares and spears of light, sundials and radials of inflorescence and neon; and we were swallowed by it, were born into it, and suddenly we could see before us the hood of the old Detroit ironhorse that had carried us into the city and swallowed us, as the city, and Westheimer Avenue, seemed to be swallowing the car, and we were no longer driving so much as being driven.

All-night gas stations, all-night grocery stores, movie theaters, restaurants, massage parlors, oil-change garages, floral shops, apartment complexes, dentists' offices, car dealerships—it was all jammed shoulder-to-shoulder, there was no zoning, and though we had seen it all before in the daytime, and were accustomed to it, it looked entirely different at night—alluring, even beautiful, rather than squalid and chaotic.

The neon strip fascinated us, as might a carnival, but what ultimately caught our imagination on these night sojourns was not the glamorous, exotic urban core, but the strange seams of disintegrating roughness on the perimeters: pockets toward and around which the expanding city spilled and flowed like lava: little passed-by islands of the past, not unlike our own on the western edge. We passed through the blaze of light and strip malls, the loneliness of illuminated commerce, and came out the other side, on the poorer, eastern edge, where all the high-voltage power grids were clustered, and the multinational refineries.

Here the air was dense with the odor of burning plastic, vaporous benzenes and toluenes adhering to the palate with every breath, and the night-fog sky glowed with blue, pink, orange flickers from the flares of waste gas jetting from a thousand smokestacks. The blaze of commerce faded over our shoulders and behind us, and often we found ourselves driving through neighborhoods that seemed to be sinking into the black soil, the muck of peat, as if pressed down by the immense weight of the industrial demands placed upon that spongy soil—gigantic tanks and water towers and chemical vats, strange intestinal folds and coils of tarnished aluminum towering above us, creeping through the remnant forests like nighttime serpents.

Snowy egrets and night herons passed through the flames, or so it seemed, and floated amidst the puffs of pollution as serenely as if in a dream of grace; and on those back roads, totally lost, splashing through puddles axle-deep and deeper, and thudding over potholes big enough to lose a bowling ball in, Moxley would sometimes turn the lights off and navigate the darkened streets in that manner, passing through pools of rainbow-colored poisonous light and wisps and tatters of toxic fog, as if gliding with the same grace and purpose as the egrets above us. Many of the rotting old homes had ancient live oaks out in front, their yards bare due to the trees' complete shading of the soil. In the rainy season, the water stood a foot deep in the streets, so that driving up and down them was more like poling the canals of Venice than driving: and the heat from our car's undercarriage hissed steam as we plowed slowly up and down these streets.

We were drawn to these rougher, ranker places at night, and yet we wanted to see them in the full light of day also; and when we traveled to these eastern edges during school, while taking a long lunch break or cutting classes entirely, we discovered little hanging-on businesses run out of those disintegrating houses, places where old men and women still made tortillas by hand, or repaired leather boots and work shoes, or did drywall masonry, or made horseshoes by hand even though there were increasingly few horses and ever more cars and trucks, especially trucks, as urban Texas began the calcification of its myths in full earnest.

Places where a patch of corn might exist next to a ten-story office building, places where people still hung their clothes on the line to dry, and little five- and ten-acre groves in which there might still exist a ghost-herd of deer. Ponds in which there might still lurk giant, sullen, doomed catfish, even with the city's advancing hulk blocking now partially the rising and setting of the sun.

Through such explorations, we found the Goat Man as surely and directly as if he had been standing on the roof of his shed calling to us with some foxhunter's horn, leading us straight to the hand-painted rotting-plywood sign tilted in the mire outside his hovel.

BABY CLAVES, $15 read the sign, each letter painted a different color, as if by a child. We parked in his muddy driveway, the low-slung station wagon dragging its belly over the corrugated troughs of countless such turnings-around, wallowing and slithering and splashing up to the front porch of a collapsing clapboard shed-house that seemed to be held up by nothing more than the thick braids and ghost vines of dead ivy.

Attached to the outside of the hovel was a gerrymandered assemblage of corrals and stables, ramshackle slats of mixed-dimension scrap lumber, from behind which came an anguished cacophony of bleats and bawls and whinnies and outright bloodcurdling screams, as we got out of the car and sought to make our way dry-footed from one mud hummock to the next, up toward the sagging porch, to inquire about the baby claves, hoping very much that they were indeed calves, and not some odd bivalve oyster we'd never heard of.

We peered through dusty windows (some of the panes were cracked, held together with fraying duct tape) and saw that the rooms were filled with tilted mounds of newspapers so ancient and yellowing that they had begun to form mulch.

An old man answered the door when we knocked, the man blinking, not so much as having been just awakened but as if instead rousing himself from some other communion or reverie, some lost-world voyage. He appeared to be in his sixties, with a long wild silver beard and equally wild silver hair, in the filaments of which fluttered a few moths, as if he were an old bear that had just been roused from his work of snuffling through a rotting log in search of grubs.

His teeth were no better than the slats that framed the walls of his jury-rigged corrals, and, barefooted, he was dressed in only a pair of hole-sprung, oil-stained, forest-green workpants, on which we recognized the dried-brown flecks of manure-splatter, and an equally stained sleeveless ribbed-underwear T-shirt that had once been white, but which was now the color of his skin, and appeared to have been on his body so long as to have become like a second kind of skin—one which, if it were ever removed, might peel off with it large patches of his original birthskin.

The odor coming from the house was quite different from the general barnyard stench of uncleansed feces, and somehow even more offensive.

Despite the general air of filth and torpor radiating from the house and its host, however, his carriage and bearing was erect, almost military—as if our presence had electrified him with hungry possibility; as if we were the first customers, or potential customers, he might have encountered in so long a time that he had forgotten his old patterns of defeat.

When he first spoke, however, to announce his name, the crispness of his posture was undercut somewhat by the shining trickle of tobacco drool that escaped through some gaps in his lower teeth, like a slow release of gleaming venom.

"Sloat," he said, and at first I thought it was some language of his own making: that he was attempting to fix us, tentatively, with a curse. "Heironymous Sloat," he said, reaching out a gnarly spittle- and mucous-stained hand. We exchanged looks of daring and double daring, and finally, Moxley offered his own pale and unscarred hand.

"Come on in," Sloat said, making a sweeping gesture that was both grand and yet familial—as if, horrifically, he recognized in us some kindred spirit—and despite our horror, after another pause we followed him in.

Since all the other rooms were filled with newspapers and tin cans. Sloat's bed had been dragged into the center room. The kitchen was nearly filled with unwashed pots and dishes, in which phalanxes of roaches stirred themselves into sudden scuttling escape as we entered. The rug in the center room was wet underfoot—the water-stained, sagging ceiling was still dripping from the previous night's rain, and on the headboard of the bed there was a small fish bowl, filled with cloudy water, in which a goldfish hung suspended, slowly finning in place, with nothing else in the bowl but a single short decaying sprig of seaweed.

The fish's water was so cloudy with its own befoulment as to seem almost viscous, and for some reason the fish so caught my attention that I felt hypnotized, suspended in the strange house—as if I had become the fish. I had no desire to move, nor could I look anywhere

70

else. All of my focus was on that one little scrap of color, once bright but now muted, though still living.

I glanced over at Moxley and was disturbed to see that he seemed somehow invigorated, even stimulated, by the rampant disorder.

So severe was my hypnosis, and so disoriented were both of us, that neither of us had noticed there was someone sleeping in the rumpled, unmade bed beside which we stood: and when the person stirred, we stepped back, alarmed.

The sleeper was a young woman, not much older than we were, sleeping in a nightgown only slightly less dingy than the shirt of the older man—and though it was midafternoon, and bright outside, the girl's face was puffy with sleep, and she stirred with such languor that I felt certain she had been sleeping all day.

She sat up and stared at us as if trying to make sense of us, and brushed her hair from her shoulders. Her hair was orange, very nearly the same color as the fish's dull scales, and Sloat stared at her in a way that was both dismissive and yet slightly curious—as if wondering why, on this particular day, she had awakened so early.

She swung her feet off the bed and stood unsteadily, and watched us with unblinking raptness.

"Let's go look at the stock," Sloat said, and we could tell that it gave him pleasure to say the word stock.

The three of us went through the cluttered kitchen and out to the backyard—it surprised me that there were no dogs or cats in the house—and the girl followed us to the door but no farther, and stood there on the other side of the screen. Her bare feet, I had noticed, were dirty, as if she had made the journey out to the stables before, but on this occasion lingered behind, as if perhaps made shy.

Sloat was wearing old sharp-toed cowboy boots, his thin shanks shoved into them in such a way that I knew he wasn't wearing socks, and he walked in a brisk, almost fierce line straight through the puddles and troughs toward the stables, as if he enjoyed splashing through the muck and grime, while Moxley and I pussyfooted from little hummock to hummock, sometimes slipping and dipping a foot in one water-filled rut or another. Foam floated on the top of many of the puddles, as if someone, or something, had been urinating in them.

Sloat pushed through a rickety one-hinge gate, and goats, chickens, and other fleeting, unidentified animals scattered before his explosive entrance. Sloat began cursing and shouting at them, picked up a stick and rat-tat-tatted it along the pickets to excite them further, like a small boy, and as if to demonstrate their vigor to their potential buyers.

A pig, a pony, a rooster. A calf, or something that looked like a calf, except for its huge head, which was so out of proportion for the tiny body that it seemed more like the head of an elephant.

"I buy them from the Feist Brothers," he said. "The ones that don't get sold at auction. They give me a special deal," he said.

The animals continued to bleat and caterwaul, flowing away, flinging themselves against the fences. Some of them ran in demented circles, and others tried to burrow in the mud, while the goats, the most nimble of them, leapt to the tops of the little crude-hammered, straw-lined doghouses and peered down with their wildly disconcerting vertical-slit lantern-green eyes as if welcoming Moxley and me into some new and alien fraternity of half-man, half-animal: and as if, now that Moxley and I were inside the corral, the goats had us exactly where they wanted us.

Moxley had eyes only for the calves, thin ribbed though they were, dehydrated and listless, almost sleepwalkerish compared to the frenzy and exodus of the other animals. Six of them were huddled over in one corner of the makeshift corral, quivering collectively, their stringy tails and flanks crusted green.

"Which are the fifteen-dollar ones?" he asked, and, sensing weakness, Sloat replied, "Those are all gone now. The only ones I have left are thirty-five."

Moxley paused. "What about that little Brahma?" he asked, pointing to the one animal that was clearly superior, perhaps even still healthy.

"Oh, that's my little prize bull," Sloat said. "I couldn't let you have him for less than seventy-five."

Between us, we had only sixty-five, which in the end turned out to be precisely enough. We had no trailer attached to the back of Old Ben's station wagon, but Sloat showed us how we could pull out the backseat, lash it to the roof for the drive home, and line the floor and walls of the station wagon with squares of cardboard, in case the calf soiled it, and drive home with him in that manner. "I've done it many a time myself," Sloat said.

The girl had come out to watch us, had waded barefooted through the same puddles in which her father, or whatever his relation was to her, had waded. She now stood on the other side of the gate, still wearing her nightgown, and watched us as Sloat and Moxley and me, our financial transaction completed, chased the bull calf around the corral, slipping in the muck, Sloat swatting the calf hard with a splintered baseball bat, whacking it whenever he could, and Moxley and me trying to tackle the calf and wrestle it to the ground.

The calf was three times as strong as any one of us, however, and time and again no sooner had one of us gotten a headlock on it than it would run into the side of the corral, smashing the would-be tackler hard against the wall; and soon both Moxley and I were bleeding from our shins, noses and foreheads, and I had a split lip: and still Sloat kept circling the corral, following the terrified calf, smacking him hard with the baseball bat.

Somehow, all the other creatures had disappeared—had vanished into other, adjacent corrals, or perhaps through a maze of secret passageways—and leaning against one of the wobbly slat walls, blood dripping from my nose, I saw now what Sloat had been doing with his wild tirade: that each time, as the calf rounded a corner, Sloat had pushed open another gap or gate and ushered two or three more non-target animals into one of the outlying pens, until finally, the calf was isolated.

Sloat was winded, and he stood there gasping and sucking air, the bat held loosely in his hands. The calf stood facing the three of us, panting likewise, and suddenly Sloat rushed him, seemingly having waited to gauge when the animal would be midbreath, too startled or tired to bolt, and he struck the calf as hard as he could with the baseball bat, hitting it on the bony plate of its forehead.

The calf neither buckled nor wobbled, but seemed only to sag a little: as if for a long time he had been tense or worried about something, but could now finally relax.

Sloat hit the calf again quickly and then a third and fourth time, striking it now like a man trying to hammer a wooden stake into the ground; and that was how the calf sank, shutting its eyes and folding, sinking lower: and still Sloat kept striking it, as if he intended to punish it or kill it, or both.

He did not stop until the calf was unconscious, or perhaps dead, and lying on its side. Then he laid his bat down tenderly, as if it were some valuable instrument, and to be accorded great respect.

The Goat Girl watched as if she had seen it all before. Sloat paused to catch his breath and then called to us to help him heft the calf quickly, before it came back to consciousness, though we could not imagine such a thing, and I was thinking at first that he had just stolen our money: had taken our sixty-five dollars, killed our calf, and was now demanding our assistance in burying it.

The Goat Girl roused herself finally, and splashed through the puddles of foam and slime, out toward the car in advance of us, as if intending to lay palm fronds before our approach. She opened our car door and placed the scraps of cardboard in the car's interior, for when the calf resurrected.

"How long will he be out?" Moxley asked.

"Where are you taking him?" Sloat asked, and I told him, west Houston—about an hour and a half away.

"An hour and a half," said Sloat, whom I had now begun to think of as the Goat Man. He shook our proffered hands—cattlemen!— and told us, as we were driving off, to come back soon, that he had a lot of volume come through, and that he would keep an eye out for good stock, for buyers as discerning as we were, and that he would probably be able to give us a better break next time.

Moxley slithered the station wagon out to the end of the drive— the Goat Man and Goat Girl followed—and Moxley stopped and rolled his window down and thanked them both again and asked the girl what her name was.

But she had fallen into a reverie and was staring at us in much the same manner as the calf had after receiving his first blow; and as we drove away she did not raise her hand to return our waves, nor did she give any other sign of having seen or heard us, or that she was aware of our existence in the world.

Driving away, I was troubled deeply by the ragtag, slovenly, almost calculated half-assedness of the operation; and on the drive home, though Moxley and I for the most part were pleased and excited about having gotten another calf, and so cheaply, I was discomforted, could feel a rumbling confusion, the protest that sometimes precedes revolution, though other times leads to nothing, only acquiescence, then senescence. I could see that Moxley did not feel it, however; and sensing this, I felt weaker, and slightly alone.

The calf woke up when we were still an hour from Ben's ranch. The calf did not awaken gradually, as a human might, stirring and blinking and looking around to ascertain his new surroundings, but awoke instead explosively, denting a crumple in the roof immediately with his bony head. He squealed and then began crashing against the sides of the car's interior so violently, and with such a clacking of hoofs, that we were afraid he would break the glass and escape; and his frenzied thrashings (unable to stand to his full height in the back of the car, and instead crawling), reminded me of how, hours earlier, the calf had been rounding the makeshift corral.

We attempted to shoo the calf to the back, swatting at him with our hands, but these gestures held no more meaning for the bull than if we had been waving flyswatters at him, and his squeals transformed to full roars, amplified to terrifying proportions within the confines of the car. At one point he was in the front seat with us, having lunged over it, and in his flailings managed to head butt me, and he cut Moxley's shins so deeply with swift kicks of his sharp little hoofs that they were bruised and bleeding, and he nearly ran off the road—but then the calf decided it preferred the space and relative freedom of the backseat, and vaulted back over the seat again and into its cardboard lair, where it continued to hurl itself against the walls.

As the Goat Man had foreseen, and as a symptom of the ailment that had caused it to not be bid upon in the first place at the regular auction—the auction that had preceded the mysterious Feist Brothers obtaining him—the calf in its fright began emitting fountains of greenish, watery diarrhea, spraying it midwhirl as if from a hose, so that we were yelling and ducking, and soon the interior of the car was nearly coated with dripping green slime: and though panicked, we were fierce in our determination to see this thing through, and we knew that if we stopped and turned the calf out into the open, we would never capture it again.

Somehow we made it home, and in the darkness of the new evening, with fireflies blinking in the fields, we drove straight out into Old Ben's pasture, ghostly-gray weeds scraping and scratching against the sides of the wagon with an eerie, clawing keen that further terrified the calf: and when we rolled down the tailgate's window, he leapt out through the window into that clean sweet fresh night air; and this calf, too, we never saw again, though the residue of his journey, his passage, remained with us for weeks afterward, in cracks and crevices of the old station wagon, despite our best scrubbing.

Old Ben fell further into the rot. Moxley and I could both see it, in his increasing lapses of memory, and his increasingly erratic behavior—and though I had perceived Moxley to be somehow more mature than I—more confident in the world—I was surprised by how vulnerable Moxley seemed to be made by Ben's fading.

Ben was ancient, a papery husk of a man—dusty, tottering history, having already far exceeded the odds by having lived as long as he had, and was going downhill fast. Such descent could not be pleasant for Old Ben, who, after all, had once been a young man much like ourselves. His quality of life was plummeting, even as ours, fueled by the strength of our youth, was ascending; did Moxley really expect, or even want, for the old man to hang on forever, an eternal hostage to his failed and failing body, just so Moxley would have the luxury of having an older surviving family member?

We couldn't keep him locked up all the time. Moxley had taken over control of the car completely, took it to school each day, and hid the keys whenever he was home, but Old Ben's will was every bit as fierce as Moxley's, and Ben continued to escape. We often found him floating in the stock tank, using an inner tube for a life vest, fishing, with no hook tied to his line, flailing at the water determinedly.

He disappeared for a week once, after rummaging through the drawers and finding the key to the tractor, which he drove away, blowing a hole through the back wall of the barn. We didn't notice the hole, nor the fact that the tractor was missing, and it was not until a sheriff called from Raton County, New Mexico, asking if Moxley knew an elderly gentleman named Ben, before we had any clue of where he was. We skipped school and drove out there to get him, pulling a rented flatbed on which to strap the tractor, and he was as glad to see us as a child would have been; and Moxley, in his relief, was like a child himself, his eyes tearing with joy.

All through that winter, we continued to buy more stock from the Goat Man: knowing better, but unable to help ourselves, and lured, too, by the low prices. Even if one in ten of his scour-ridden wastrels survived to market, we would come out ahead, we told ourselves; but none of them did, they all escaped through our failed fence, usually in the very first afternoon of their freedom, and we never saw any of them again.

We imagined their various fates. We envisioned certain of them being carried away by the panthers that were rumored to still slink through the Brazos riverbottoms, and the black jaguars that were reported to have come up from Mexico, following those same creeks and rivers as if summoned, to snack on our cheap and ill-begotten calves, or claves, as we called them. We imagined immense gargoyles and winged harpies that swooped down to snatch up our renegade runaway crops. We envisioned modern-day cattle rustlers congregating around the perimeter of our ranch like fishermen. It was easy to imagine that even the Goat Man himself followed us home and scooped up each runaway calf in a net, and returned with it then to his lair, where he would sell it a second time to another customer.

Or perhaps there was some hole in the earth, some cavern, into which all the calves disappeared, as if sucked there by a monstrous and irresistible force. Any or all of these paranoias might as well have been true, given the completeness of the calves' vanishings.

With each purchase we made, I felt more certain that we were traveling down a wrong path, and yet we found ourselves returning to the Goat Man's hovel again and again, and giving him more and more money.

We ferried our stock in U-Haul trailers—and across the months, as we purchased more cowflesh from the Goat Man—meat vanishing into the ether again and again, as if into some quarkish void—we became familiar enough with Sloat and his daughter to learn that her name was Flozelle, and to visit with them about matters other than stock.

We would linger in that center room—bedroom, dining room, living room, all—and talk briefly, first about the weather and then about the Houston Oilers, before venturing out into what Moxley and I had taken to calling the Pissyard. We learned that Flozelle's mother had died when she was born, that Flozelle had no brothers or sisters, and that Sloat loathed schools.

"I homeschool her," he said. "Go ahead, ask her anything."

We could have been wiseasses. We could have flaunted our ridiculous little knowledge—the names of signatories to various historical documents, the critical dates of various armistices—but in the presence of such abject filth, and before her shell-shocked quietude, we were uncharacteristically humbled. Instead, Moxley asked, almost gently, "How long have you had that fish?" and before Flozelle could answer, Sloat bullshitted us by telling us that the fish had been given to his grandmother on her wedding day, almost a hundred years ago.

"What's its name?" I asked, and this time, before Sloat could reply, Flozelle answered.

"Goldy," she said proudly, and a shiver ran down my back. If I had known what sadness or loneliness really felt like, I think I might have recognized it as such; but as it was, I felt only a shiver, and then felt it again as she climbed up onto the unmade bed (the bottoms of her bare feet unwashed and bearing little crumb-fragments) and unscrewed the lid to a jar of uncooked oatmeal she kept beside the bowl, and sprinkled a few flakes into the viscous water.

Moxley was watching her with what seemed to me to be a troubled look—and after she had finished feeding the bloated fish, she turned and climbed back down off the lumpen bed, and then we filed out through the kitchen and on out into the Pissyard to go look at, and purchase, more stock.

Back before Ben had begun falling to pieces, Moxley and I had sometimes gone by my house after school to do homework and hang out. My mother would make cookies, and if Moxley was still there when my father got home from work, Moxley would occasionally have supper with us. But those days had gone by long ago, Ben now requiring almost all of his waking care. I helped as I could, doing little things like helping clean up the house. Whenever Ben discovered that he was trapped, he would ransack the house, pulling books down off of shelves and hurling his clothes out of his drawer; once, he rolled up the carpet and tried to set the end of it on fire, as if lighting a giant cigar: when we arrived at the farmhouse, we could see the toxic gray smoke seeping from out of the windows; and rushing inside, we found Ben passed out next to the rug, which had smoldered and burned a big hole in the plywood flooring, revealing the gaping darkened maw of basement below, with the perimeter of that burned-out crater circular, like a caldera, having burned so close to Ben that his arm hung down into the pit; and all the next day we hammered and sawed new sheets of plywood to patch that abyss. For a few days afterward, Ben seemed contrite, and neither misbehaved nor otherwise suffered any departures from sentience: as if such lapses were, after all, at least partially willful.

I helped cook dinners, and some nights I stayed over at their farmhouse and helped make breakfast, and helped Moxley batten down the doors and windows before leaving for school. Knives, scissors, matches, guns, fishhooks, lighter fluid, gasoline, household cleaners—it all had to be put away. Moxley had tied a hundred-and-fifty-foot length of rope around Ben's waist each night, so that if Ben awoke and went sleepwalking, wandering the dewy hills, he could be tracked and reeled in like a marlin or other sportfish.

The farmhouse was a pleasant place to awaken in the morning—the coppery sun rising just above the tops of the trees, and the un-grazed fields lush and tall and green, with mourning doves cooing and pecking red grit and gravel from the driveway—and the interior of the house would be spangled with the prisms of light from all the little pieces of glass arrayed on the windowsill, Ben's shrapnel collection. The spectral casts of rainbow would be splashed all over the walls, like the light that passes through stained glass windows, and there would be no sound but the ticking of the grandfather clock in the front hallway, and the cooing of those doves, and the lowing of distant cows not ours. Moxley and I would fix breakfast, gather our homework, then lock up the house and leave, hurrying toward school.

I had some money from mowing lawns, and Moxley was pretty flush, or so it seemed to us, from Ben's pension checks. As much from habit now as from desire, we made further pilgrimages to Sloat's corrals, that winter and spring.

And following each purchase, upon our return to Ben's ranch, sometimes our new crop of sickly calves would remain in the pasture for a few days, though never longer than a week, after which, always, they disappeared, carrying with them their daunting and damnable genes, the strange double-crossed combination of recessive alleles that had caused the strangeness to blossom in them in the first place—the abnormality, the weakness, that had led to the unfortu-nate chain of circumstances that resulted in their passing from a real auction to the Feist Brothers, who would sell them for dog meat if they could, and then to Sloat and a short life of squalor, and then to us, and to whatever freedom or destiny awaited them.

Ben caught pneumonia after one of his escapes. (He had broken out a window and crawled through, leaving a trail of blood as well as new glass scattered amidst his windowsill-sparkling shards of glass from fifty years earlier; we trailed him down to the pond, his favorite resting spot, where he stood shivering waist deep, as if awaiting a baptism.) Moxley had to check him into the hospital, and after he was gone, the silence in the farmhouse was profound.

Moxley was edgy, waiting for the day when Old Ben would be

coming home, but that day never came; and although it had been clear that Ben's days at home were numbered, the abyss of his absence still came as a surprise, as did Moxley's new anger.

We continued with our old rituals, as if Ben was still with us—cooking the steaks on the back porch grill, and buying cattle—but the ground beneath our feet seemed less firm.

With Old Ben's last pension check, Moxley and I went to a real auction, and bought a real calf—not one of Sloat's misfits, but a registered Brahma—a stout little bull calf. And rather than risking losing this one, we kept it tethered, like a dog on a leash, in the barn. It was not as wild as Sloat's terrified refugees, and soon we were able to feed and water it by hand: and it grew fatter week by week. We fed it a diet rich in protein, purchasing sweet alfalfa and pellet cubes. We brushed it and curried it and estimated its weight daily as we fatted it for market. And it seemed to me that with some success having finally been achieved, Moxley's anger and loneliness had stabilized, and I was glad that this calf, at least, had not escaped. It was a strange thought to both of us, to consider that we were raising the animal so someone else could eat him, but that was what cattlemen did.

As this calf finally grew fatter, Moxley seemed to grow angry at the Goat Man, and barely spoke to him now when we traveled out there: and though we still went out there with the same, if not greater, frequency, we had stopped purchasing stock from the Goat Man, and instead merely went out into the Pissyards to look. After having purchased the calf from the regular auction, Sloat's offerings were revealed to us in their full haplessness, and we could not bring ourselves to take them at any price; though still, we went to look, almost morbidly curious about what misfits might have passed through his gates that week.

Moxley asked Flozelle out on what I suppose could be labeled a date, even though I was with them. I wanted to believe the best of him, but it seemed to me that it was a meanness, a bedevilment. Moxley still had the same aspirations—he was intent upon going to school and becoming a vet—but the moments of harshness seemed to emerge from him at odd and unpredictable times, like fragments of bone or glass emerging from beneath the thinnest of skin.

The three of us began to ride places together once or twice a week, and for a while, Flozelle fascinated us. She knew how to fix things—how to rebuild a carburetor, how to peel a tire from its rim and plug it with gum and canvas and seat it back onto its rim—and sometimes, out in the country, we stopped beside the fields of strangers and got out and climbed over the barbed-wire fence and went out to where other people's horses were grazing. We would slip up onto those horses bareback and ride them around strangers' fields for hours at a time. Flozelle knew how to gentle even the most unruly or skittish horse by biting its ears with her teeth and hanging on like a pit bull until Moxley or I had climbed up, and then she'd release her bitehold, and we'd rocket across the pasture, the barrel ribs of the horse beneath us heaving: the expensive thoroughbreds of oilmen, the sleek and fatted horses farting wildly from their too-rich diets of grain.

She had never been to a movie before, and when we took her, she stared rapt, ate three buckets of popcorn, chewing ceaselessly through *Star Wars*. She began spending some afternoons with Moxley out at his farm, and helping him with chores—mowing with the tractor the unkempt grass, bush-hogging brush and cutting bales of hay for our young bull. She showed us how to castrate him, to make him put on even more weight even faster, and she set about repairing the shabby, sorry fence we had never gotten around to fixing properly.

The calf, the steer, was getting immense, or so it seemed to us, and though he still was friendly and manageable, his strength concerned us. We worried that he might strangle himself on his harness, his leash, should he ever attempt to break out of the barn, and so not long after Flozelle had completed her repairs on the fence, we turned him out into the field, unfastening his rope and opening the barn doors, whereupon he emerged slowly, blinking, and then descended to the fresh green fields below and began grazing confidently, as if he had known all his life those fields were waiting for him, and that he would reach them in due time.

I had the strange thought that if only Old Ben could have still been alive to see it, the sight might somehow have helped heal him, even though I knew that to be an impossibility. He had been an old man, war torn, and at the end of his line; no amount of care, nor even miracles, could have kept him from going downhill.

To the best of my knowledge, Flozelle did not shower, as if such a practice might be alien to her or her father's religious beliefs. In my parents' car, I drove up to the farm one warm day in the spring, unannounced, and surprised Moxley and Flozelle, who were out in the backyard. Moxley was dressed, but Flozelle was not, and Moxley was spraying her down with the hose—not in fun, as I might have suspected, but in a manner strangely more workmanlike, as one might wash a car, or even a horse; and when they saw me, Moxley was embarrassed and shut the hose off, though Flozelle was not discomfited at all, and merely took an old towel, little larger than a washcloth, and began drying off.

And later, after he had taken her home—after we had both driven out to Sloat's and dropped her off, without going inside, and without going back into the Pissyards to look around, I asked him, "Are you sleeping with her?"—and he looked at me with true surprise and then said, "I am," and when I asked him if she ever spent the night over at the farmhouse, he looked less surprised, less proud, and said yes.

What did it matter to me? It was nothing but an act, almost lavatory-like in nature, I supposed—workmanlike and without emotion, if not insensate. I imagined it to be for Moxley like the filling of a hole, the shoveling in of something, and the tamping down. It was not anything. He was doing what he had to do, almost as if taking care of her; and she, with all the things the Goat Man had taught her, had fixed his fences, had repaired the old tractor, the barn.

She had not led him down any errant path, nor was his life, nor mine, going to change or deviate from our destinies as a result of any choices made, or not made. She was like fodder, was all. We were just filling the days. We were still fattening up. We were still strong in the world, and moving forward. I had no call to feel lonely or worried. We still had all the time in the world, the world was still ours, there was no rot anywhere, the day was still fresh and new, we could do no wrong. We would grow, just not now.

Nominated by The Idaho Review

MAN AT THE MOMA

by LAURE-ANNE BOSSELAAR

from SNAKE NATION REVIEW

Whose name will be on his lips when he
dies? Whose body (weight, skin, fervors of it)

will he remember? Who was his first
ugliness? What his first treason?

He won't stop walking, doesn't look at
anything, wanders from room to escalator,

hall to other space—for an hour now—
carrying that plastic bag, a thick hardcover

askew in it. Why do I follow him? What
is it that makes me do that, so often, in streets or

subways even, getting off before my stop
to follow a man, woman, couple?

Yesterday, on a park bench—they spoke
a language I didn't understand—I listened

long to the plucked, hushed vowels of two
women, their voices so drained I felt

hatred for something I couldn't name—and
still can't. It isn't *life* or *fate* or—

But this man today, with his knitted
scarf and polished shoes in this insufferably

civilized place—it's Larry I see, Larry
Levis: his casual gestures, that staring-beyond

schism in his gaze, the head always tilted back or
away too much. I would have stalked

him too from subway to street, bench to bus,
wanting answers then turning away.

What else can I do but turn away as I did
from my first ugliness, hiding my face in my arm to

stop seeing Hannah's gaze—we were only six
and I was already evil. I can't forget her,

Hannah the hare-lip. How horror
stalks us—as desire does, or love. Or hunger.

What answers do I want from this man
lost in a Museum?

Whose name will be on my lips when I die?
Whose stalker am I but my own?

Nominated by Alan Michael Parker, Snake Nation Review

SWEETHEARTS
OF THE RODEO

fiction by LYDIA PEELLE

from THE SUN

LATELY I'VE BEEN THINKING about that summer. We barely ever got off those ponies' backs. We painted war paint across their foreheads and pinned wild-turkey feathers in our hair and whooped and raced across the back field, hanging on to their necks. Some days they were a pair of bucking broncos, or unicorns, or circus horses, or burros on a narrow mountain pass. Other days they were as delicate and regal as the rich ladies' horses, and we were two queens, veiled sultanas crossing the Sahara under a burning sky. We were the kidnapped maidens, or the masked heroes. We braided flowers in their matted tails, dandelions and oxeye daisies that got lost in the snarls, wilted, and turned brown. We tore across the back field, our heels digging into their sides. We pulled them up short and did somersaults off their backs, or handstands in the saddle. We turned on a dime. We jumped the coop, the wall, the ditch. We were fearless. It was the summer we smoked our first cigarettes, the summer you broke your arm. It was the last summer, the last one, before boys.

Our mothers drop us off every morning at seven. We grab two pitchforks and fly through our chores. For four dollars an hour we shovel loads of manure and wet shavings out of the stalls, scrub the water buckets, and fill the hay racks, the hay sticking to our wet T-shirts, falling into our shoes, our pockets, our hair. We race to see who can get done first. The sooner we finish, the sooner we can ride. Late in the morning Curt comes out to the barn and leans against the massive sliding door. He wears sandals and baggy shorts, and under his thick, dark lashes his eyes are rimmed with red. He tells us what other jobs there are to be done: picking stones out of the riding ring, or refilling the water troughs in the pasture with the long, heavy hose. We whine and stamp our feet. He is the caretaker, after all, and supposed to do these tasks himself. *We were just about to go riding,* we say.

Girls, he says, winking, *come on now.*

He looks over his shoulder and whistles for his dog. You stick your tongue out at his back. Some mornings he stays in his little house and doesn't come out until later, when the ladies' expensive cars start to pull into the long driveway. They get out and lean against their shiny hoods, smoking cigarettes and talking to Curt in low voices. Sometimes only one or two of them show up, and other times they all come, a half dozen of them in the identical beige breeches and high boots that we dream of one day wearing. They never once get a streak of manure across their foreheads or water sloshed across their shirts. We turn down the volume of the paint-splattered barn radio to try to hear what they're saying, but we can't make it out. In the afternoon we eat the sandwiches our mothers packed for us and throw our apple cores over the fence to the ponies, who chew them carefully and sigh in the hot midday sun. Their eyes close, and they let their pink-and-gray-mottled penises dangle. We go to them with soapy water and a sponge in a bucket and clean the built-up crust from their sheaths, reaching our arms far up inside. The ladies see us do this and pay us five dollars to do their geldings', then stand by and watch us, wrinkling their noses.

The ladies' horses all have brass plates on their stall doors, their names etched in fancy script, with their sires and dams in parentheses underneath. They are called "Curator," "Excelsior," "Hadrian." The ponies' names change daily, depending on our game. They don't even have stalls, but live out in the field, where they eat all day under a cloud of flies. Nobody even remembers who they belong to. For the summer, they are ours. They are round and close to the ground, wheezy and spoiled, with bad habits. One is brown and dulled by dust. The other is a pinto, bay with white splashes, one eye blue, the other brown. The blue eye is blind. We sneak up on this side when we go out to the pasture to catch them, a green halter hidden behind your back, a red one behind mine. The ponies let us get just close enough, then toss their heads and trot away. Peppermints and buckets of grain don't fool them. After a while we decide just to leave their halters on. The grass in the pasture is knee high, full of ticks and chiggers, mouse tunnels and quicksilver snakes that scare the ladies' horses into a frenzy. But not the ponies. They are unspookable. When we cinch up their girths, they twist their necks around to bite our arms, leaving bruises like sunset-colored moons. As the summer gets hotter, we stop bothering with saddles altogether and just clip two lead lines to their halters, grab a hank of mane, and vault on.

We trot them through the field and down the hill to the pine woods, making them scramble up steep ridges. The ponies are much faster coming home than going. We get as far away as we can and then let them race home through the woods, spruce limbs and vines whipping our faces. We know we are close when we can smell the manure pile. We come up the hill, and there it is, looming like a dark mountain beside the barn. You make a telescope with your thumb and forefinger, your fingernails black to the quick. *Land ho!* you say. Crows perch on the peak of the pile and send avalanches of dirty shavings down its sides. The ladies' little dogs jump gleefully out of the open windows of their cars and come running to us, tags jingling.

The ladies hardly ever ride. All day their horses stand out in the sun, their muscles like silk-covered stone. Sometimes they bring them into the barn and tie them up in the crossties, then wander into Curt's house and don't come out. The horses wait patiently for an hour or so, then begin to paw and weave their heads. They can't reach the flies settling between their shoulder blades, the itches on their faces they try to rub against their front legs. They dance and swivel in the aisle, and still the ladies won't come out. Finally we unhook them from the ties and turn them out into the pasture, where they spin and kick out a leg before galloping back to the herd. When the ladies reappear in the doorway of the little house, late in the afternoon, they squint in the light as if emerging from a cave and don't ever seem to notice that their horses are not where they left them.

We do everything we can think of to torture Curt. Before he goes out to work on the electric fence, he switches off the fuse in the big breaker box in the barn. We sneak around and flip it back on, then hide and wait to hear his curses when he touches the wire. You slap me five. He comes back into the barn and flicks a lunge whip at us, and we giggle and jump. When he turns away, we both whisper, *I hate him.* We use pitchforks to fling hard turds of manure in his direction, and he hooks his big arms around our waists and dumps us headfirst into the sawdust pile. We squeal and throw handfuls of wood shavings at him as he walks away. Oh, how we hate him! We pretend we've forgotten his name.

In the afternoon we ride our ponies close to the little house to spy on Curt. Their hooves make marks in the soft lawn like fingerprints in fresh bread. We ride as close as we dare and peer in and see things we don't see in our own houses: dirty laundry heaped in the hall, a cluster of dark bottles on top of the refrigerator, ashtrays and half-filled glasses crowding the kitchen table, which is just a piece of plywood on two sawhorses. Your pony eats roses from the bushes under the windows. He wears a halo of mosquitoes. From the bedroom we hear voices, a man's and a woman's. It is the only room in which the blinds have been pulled. We try to peer through the cracks, but the ponies yank at their bits and dance in the rosebushes, and we don't really want to see anyway. *Come on*, you say, and we head out to the back field to play circus acrobats, cops and robbers, cowboys and Indians.

The ponies bear witness to dozens of pacts and promises that we make in the grave light of late afternoon and have every intention of keeping. We cross our hearts and hope to die on the subjects of horses, husbands, and each other. We dare one another to do dangerous things: You dare me to jump from the top of the manure pile, and I do, and land on my feet with manure in my shoes. I double-dare you to take the brown pony over the triple-oxer jump, which is higher than his ears. You ride hellbent toward it, but the pony stops dead, throwing you over his head, and you sail through the air and land laughing. We are covered in scrapes and bruises, splinters buried so deep in our palms that we don't remember they are there. Our bodies forgive us our risks, and the ponies do, too. We have perfected the art of falling.

We know every corner of the barn, every loose board, every shadow, every knot in the wood. It is old and full of holes and home to many things: bats and lizards and voles; spiders that hang cobwebs in the corners like hammocks; house sparrows who build nests in the drainpipes with beakfuls of hay until one day a dead pink baby bird drops at the feet of one of the ladies, who screams and clutches her hair. You scoop it up and toss it on the manure pile, and Curt comes out with the long ladder and pours boiling water from a kettle down the pipe, and that is the end of the sparrows. Curt laughs at the lady and rolls his eyes behind her back and winks at us. We wink back. There is a fly strip in the corner that quivers with dying flies. When it is black with bodies and bits of wing, it is our job to replace it, and we hold our breaths when we take it down, praying it won't catch in our hair. And there are rats, so many rats that we rip from glue boards and smash with shovels, or pull from snap traps and fling into the woods, or find floating in water troughs where they've dragged themselves, bellies distended with poison and dying of thirst.

Along the edges of the manure pile we catch skinks and salamanders and yellow-striped millipedes that give off the scent of almonds when we rub them. We lock them up in mayonnaise jars, punching air holes in the rusty tops with Curt's hammer and screwdriver. We kneel in the filth and watch an army of ants dismantle a mouse carcass. We see a hawk drop a squirrel from a branch of the old white oak. The squirrel gets up, shakes itself, and runs right back up the trunk of the tree. We are in the hayloft the morning that the barn cat has kittens. Crouching beside her, we watch her contortions, her straining face, and we see the slick, blind kittens wriggle their way to the seam of teats. Afterward we watch in wonder, our faces inches from hers, as the cat eats the afterbirth with delicate bites, the hay around her dark with blood. In a few weeks, when the kittens have become fuzzy and playful, the ladies grow delighted with them, and we forget about them altogether.

In the basement is the workbench where Curt never works, rusty nails lined up in baby-food jars, their lids screwed to a low beam. The manure spreader is parked down there in the dark, like a massive, shamed beast. When we open the trapdoor in the floor above to dump loads from our wheelbarrows, a rectangle of light illuminates the mound of dirty shavings and manure, and mice scurry over it like currents of electricity. The ladies never go down to the basement. It is there that we sometimes sit to discuss them, comparing their hair, their mouths, the size of their breasts. Did you see that one throw up behind the barn on Friday afternoon? Did you see her diamond ring? Did you see that one slip something into Curt's shirt pocket and smile at him? What was it?

We hear them call their husbands' offices on the barn telephone and say they are calling from home. We watch two of them go into the little house at once, shutting the door behind them. We see Curt stagger from the house and fall over in the yard and stay where he falls, very still, until one of the ladies comes out and helps him up, laughing, and takes him back inside. The ladies hang around and watch the farrier, a friend of Curt's with blond hair and a cowboy hat, as he beats a horseshoe to the shape of a hoof with his hammer. He swears as he works, and we stand in the shadows by the grain room and listen carefully, cataloging each new word. When he leaves, one or two of the ladies drive off, following his truck, and return an hour or so later and go back to what they were doing, as if they'd never left. They lock themselves in the tack room and fill it with cigarette smoke. We sit in the hayloft and listen to their voices below us, high and excited, like small children's. The ladies wear lipstick, but it's gone by the afternoon. They wear their sunglasses on cloudy days. Some mornings the oil drum we use for empty grain bags is filled to the top with beer bottles. As we watch them, the rules that have been strung in our heads like thick cables fray and unravel in a dazzling array of sparks. Then we climb on the ponies' backs and ride away down the hill.

One afternoon Curt gives us each a cigarette and laughs as we try to inhale. *Look, girls,* he says, striking a match on the sole of his boot and lighting his own. *Like this.* We watch his face as he takes a drag, his jaw shadowed by a three-day beard. Later we steal two more from his pack and ride into the woods to practice, watching each other and saying, *No, like this!* We put Epsom salts in Curt's coffee and lock the tack-room door from the inside. We steal his baseball cap and manage to get it hooked on the weather vane. *Ha!* we say, and spit on the ground. *Take that!* He throws one of his flip-flops at us. He drags us shrieking to the courtyard and sprays us with the hose. He tells us we stink. We tell him we don't care.

There is one horse that was brought over on a plane, all the way from England. One afternoon we are sitting up in the hayloft, sucking peppermints and discussing all the horses we will own someday, when we hear a scream from below. The horse, left tied and standing in the aisle, has spooked and broken its halter and gashed its head open on a beam. Blood drips from its eyelashes and pools by its hooves, and it sways like a rope bridge. We grab saddle pads from the tack room, the ladies' expensive fleece ones, and press them to the wound. They grow hot and heavy with blood. It drips down our arms into our hair. The horse shakes its head and gnashes its teeth at us. We look over at the little house, all the blinds drawn tight. Who will knock on the door? We flip a coin. I don't remember whether you won or lost, but you are the one who cuts through the flower bed, stands on the step, and knocks and knocks, and after a long time Curt comes out in jeans and bare feet with no shirt. I hide in the bushes and watch. *What?* he says, frowning. You point at his crotch and say, *XYZ!* He zips his fly in one motion, without looking down, like flipping on a light switch. And then in the shadow of the doorway is the lady the horse belongs to, scowling, her blond hair half undone, looking at you as if she is having a hard time understanding why you're all covered in blood. After the vet comes and stitches up the wound, the lady eyes us suspiciously and whispers to Curt. Later he makes sure she is within earshot before scolding us. When the vet has left and they have gone back into the house, we knock down a paper-wasp nest and toss it through the open window of her car.

There is a pond in the back pasture where the horses go to drink, half hidden by willows and giant honeysuckle bushes that shade it from the noonday sun. On the hottest days we swim the ponies out to the middle, and when their hooves leave the silty bottom, it feels as if we are flying. The water is brown, and rafts of manure float past us as we swim, but we don't care. We pretend the ponies are Pegasus, and we grow quiet, both thinking about the same thing: Curt. His arms, the curve of his hat brim, the way he smells when he gets off the tractor in the afternoon. You trail your hand in the water and say, *What are you thinking about?* And I say, *Nothing.* When we come out of the water, the insides of our thighs are streaked with wet horsehair, as if we were turning into wild beasts ourselves. The ponies shake violently to dry off, and we jump down as they drop to their knees to roll in the dust. Other days it is too hot to swim, or even move at all. We lie on the ponies' necks as they graze in the pasture, our arms hanging straight down. The heat drapes across our shoulders and thighs. School is as unthinkable as snow.

Rodeo is our favorite game, because it is the fastest and most reckless, involving many feats of speed and bravery, and lots of quick turns and trick riding. One day in late July, out in the back field, we decide to elect a rodeo clown and a rodeo queen. The ponies stamp impatiently while we argue over who will be which. Finally the games begin. There is barrel racing and a bucking bronco and a rodeo parade. We discover that we can make the ponies rear by pushing them forward with our heels while holding the reins tight.

Yee haw! we say, throwing one arm up in the air. The ponies chew their bits nervously, and we do it over and over again. We must lean far forward on their necks, or we will slip off. Once, when the pinto pony goes up, you start to lose your balance. I am doubled over laughing until I see you grope for the reins as the pony goes higher, and you grab them with too much force and yank his head back too far. He hangs suspended for a moment before falling backward like a tree onto his spine. You disappear as he rolls to his side, then reappear when he scrambles to his feet, the reins dangling from the bit. I jump off my pony and run to you. Your arm is broken from the looks of it. *Oh, shit*, I say. You squint up at me through a veil of blood. *Doesn't hurt*, you say.

Curt was the one who rescued you. He drove his pickup through the tall grass of the back pasture, lifted you onto the bench seat, made you a pillow with his shirt. And when no one could get ahold of your parents, it was he who drove you to the emergency room. I rode in the truck bed and watched through the rear window as you stretched your legs across his lap, your bare feet on his thighs. I could see his arms, your face, his freckled hand as he brushed the hair, or maybe tears, from your eyes. I sat across from him at the hospital and waited while they stitched the gash on your forehead and put your left arm in a cast, and I came in with him to check on you. I hung back in the corner when he leaned over the table, and I heard you whisper to him in a high, helpless voice. I watched your hand grope out from under the blanket, reaching for his. And I saw him hold it. With both hands. Of course I was jealous. I still am. You must have a scar to remind you of that summer. I have nothing I can point to, nothing I can touch.

It was early August when the brown pony died. It happened overnight, and no one knew how: whether he colicked and twisted a gut, or had a heart attack, or caught a hind foot in his halter while tending an itch and broke his own neck. When we found the body, we didn't cry. I remember we weren't even very sad. We went to find Curt, who lit a cigarette and instructed us not to tell the ladies. Then we went back and looked at the pony's still body, his velvety muzzle, his open eye, his lips pulled back from his big domino teeth. We touched his side, already cold. Later we rode the pinto pony double out to the pond, your arms around my waist, your cast knocking against my hipbone. Behind us the tractor coughed as Curt pulled the pony's body to the manure pile with heavy chains. We slipped off the pinto, let him wander away, and sprawled out in the grass. You scratched inside your cast with a stick. Grasshoppers sprung around us. We lay there all afternoon and into the evening, your head on my stomach, our fingers in the clover, trying to think up games we could play with only one pony.

Weeks later we were alone in the barn. We were sweeping the long center aisle, shoving push brooms toward one another from opposite ends, the radio flickering on and off, like it always did. When it faded out completely, we heard the squabbling of dogs out back. We dropped our brooms and ran to see what they were fighting over. Through a cloud of dust we could make out Curt's dog, his back to us, bracing himself with his tail in the air and growling at one of the ladies' fierce little dogs, who was shaking his head violently, his eyes squeezed shut. Between them they had the brown pony's head. It took us a while to recognize it. It was mostly bone, yellow teeth, and gaping eye sockets, except for a few bits of brown hair that hung from the forehead, some cheek muscle and stringy tendon clinging to the left side. And then we saw it, both at the same time: the little scrap of green against the white. The pony still had its halter on. This was what the dogs had gotten their teeth around. Curt had never bothered to take it off. With a final shake of his jaws, the little dog managed to snatch the pony's head away, and he dragged it around the corner of the barn, Curt's dog bounding after.

We stood in the slanting September light and listened to the dogs' whines and rumblings, the scrape of the skull against the ground. Then we picked up our brooms, and when we were done sweeping, we went and got the pinto pony and rode double down the hill and didn't think much about it again. Death was familiar to us that summer: it was on the road, in the woods, under the floor of the barn; it was the raccoon rotting on the pavement and the crows that settled there to pick at it until they, too, were flattened by cars, and their bodies swelled and stank in the heat; it was the half-decayed doe we found in the woods with maggots stitching in and out of its flesh; it was the stillborn foal wrapped in a decomposing amniotic sac in the pasture where the vultures perched. We caught a whiff of it, sniffed it out, didn't flinch, touched it with our bare hands, ate lunch immediately afterward. We weren't frightened of it.

And a few summers later, spinning out of control on a loose gravel road in a car full of boys and beer, we weren't scared of death then, either. We laughed and said to the boy at the wheel, *Do it again.* We learned to fear it only later, much later, when we realized that it knew our names, and, worse, the names of everything we loved. At the height of that summer, in the dog days, I would have said that we loved the ponies, but I see now that we never did. They were only everything we asked them to be, and that was enough.

Nominated by Salvatore Scibona, The Sun

SHELLING THE PECANS

by LORNA DEE CERVANTES

from OCHO

I knew what a woman's hand could do:
shred the husk into threads, weave lips
together at the seam. Rock to hard body,
empire to thrust into knave—the native
touch tocando música up the spine
of the violin, some song of silk and gut.
I knew race was a matter of degree,
that inch in the face, that notice
of dismissal. How to work all day
at a posture, at a stance, at attention
paying attention to none but the awl.

I put my hole into you, this notch
between the breasts, this discovery
and treason. Hembra a macho. Fixed.
O defined in the still shell of history,
a destiny written in the charts and lost. Lost
in the unnoticed memories of you, a flicker
of change, some small scrimp
of light. Tu luz. Ahí allá—a la ala
and the scoop. Your aguila eyes sweeping
up the dawn's desire. This night. I remember

shelling the pecans. Nothing but a bucket.
No ride exceptional. Nothing but a dream

to entertain us. I dreamed this moment—
all the sweet meats in a risen weight going
higher to the rim. The price and the pricing.
I could eat what I missed or messed. Outside,
the birds bending to it on a summer day.
The great age of my grandmother's banded
hand weighing me down. The paper
of tutelage blasting me away

at that age. Now, I still remember
how to shuck, how to fetch it, how to
step it. Stepping up to you, I ask.
The point enters the ventricle without
shattering the meat. How a woman
on a good day can rip out the heart
whole.

Nominated by OCHO

CHILDREN OF CAIN

by JEFF P. JONES

from PASSAGES NORTH

In Madeline L'Engle's novel *A Wrinkle in Time*, ultimate evil resides in a disembodied brain called IT. Nothing could be less personal—a thing without gender, a brain without a body, an entity stripped of any relation to recognizable humanity.

I.

On good days, I imagine the parents are arrested or deemed unfit by Social Services, that my wife and I take a special interest in the child, adopt the baby girl, and she becomes our very own cooing body of flesh and slobber. On the worst days, when he rages above our ceiling, hurling things to the floor and calling his diminutive wife a "filthy bitch" and a "slut," I fantasize about crippling the father with a blow to the knee from a baseball bat, then working over his body, because I want to make this man—this man whom I choke even to label a man, this monster then—feel the helplessness of a victim. For once, I want him to be on the receiving end of rage.

Though they never become reality, I cannot stop these fantasies from arising each time I hear the shouts upstairs, where the couple and their baby live. The fantasies become like pornography or alcohol. I routinely inventory my apartment for weapons—broomstick, garden hose, shotgun, butcher knife, screwdriver—and each one generates a new daydream of destruction. I derive pleasure from them, but it is a pleasure that stains my mind with guilt.

———

The house we all occupied, in a posh Seattle neighborhood, was not originally designed as separate apartments. Built in 1929, it was a three-story Victorian with turreted windows and expansive views of Puget Sound's Elliott Bay. The landlords who bought it in 1962 divided the single family dwelling into four apartments. They hoped to make a profit off the predicted influx of people for the World's Fair that year, the same year the Space Needle was built. The front door led to a narrow staircase that climbed the heart of the house to the very top where the landlords carved out a tiny garret room with a low ceiling in the attic. For $400 per month, the couple with the baby girl named Sarah rented the attic apartment. We paid $600 for the considerably more spacious one-bedroom on the third floor. For the late 1990s in Seattle, both rents were bargains.

Two blocks away, the Show-Me-Seattle tour buses coursed Seventh West twice a day in the winter and almost hourly in the summer, showcasing some of the city's finest homes. The house where we lived, with its leaky pipes and four layers of carpet, its rickety wooden stairs along the backside of the building, wasn't on the tour route. It was a residual piece of old Seattle, a piece that should've been razed years before. Still, my wife and I liked it, because it had character, and the neighborhood was great. Sundays, we stopped for lattes at Tully's or Starbucks or the Rain Dog Café—we had our pick of coffee shops—before walking to church. While we maintained the basic Protestant beliefs with which we both had been raised, by our late twenties, my wife and I had grown wary of the fundamentalist tendencies of Baptist churches, so finding a progressive one just five blocks away, with a pastor who was both intellectual and compassionate, was refreshing.

The night the upstairs neighbors, Derrick and Sheila, moved in, they arrived in an old Buick. It was spring, and the raspberries loaded the bushes on the side of the house. We shook hands in the parking lot. They wore raingear and looked as if they had been camping for some time, perhaps out of necessity. Derrick had thin lips, a pale, stubbly face and a long blond ponytail. She was barely five feet tall, slight, and had thick red hair that flowed almost to her waist. Freckles dotted her cheeks.

Yell at us if our big feet stomping around ever gets too loud, she said. We've never lived above anyone before.

Don't worry about it, I said.

That night, from what had been an empty, silent space for more

98

than a month prior, my wife and I heard footfalls. We hoped the new couple's dog, a Doberman pinscher, would get along with our dog. It really was better, we told each other, to have someone in that space. After all, it couldn't stay empty forever.

Sound traveled easily through the walls and floors of that house. Mornings, I taught English-as-a-Second-Language and, afternoons, returned home to write. After they had been there several months, Derrick began lifting weights in his living room two or three times a week. He set them down with a thump, and the sound destroyed my concentration.

That spring, on afternoons when the weights thudded down, my life in Seattle closed around me. A heavy sky, the color of dirty goose feathers, often pressed low and menacing against our third-floor bay window as I watched mesmeric swells in Elliott Bay surge and subside. I had never felt further from my boyhood home, 1300 miles away in Denver, where my father still lived. For five years after high school, I lived at home with him and bused downtown to college. During those oppressive Seattle days, I longed for Colorado—its sunshine and wide open sky. I recalled days when I left college books at home and drove east of town, away from the Rockies, where the plains open up flat and dry. There, I tramped along narrow creekbeds, past groves of cottonwoods and stagnant pools of water. My favorite place was called Sand Creek, and my dog and I spent many afternoons along its banks. Ironically, it wasn't until I moved to Seattle that I seriously began to study my home state's history. I was surprised to find references to Sand Creek. It turned out that this was a different creek by the same name, and it is one that stains Colorado's history.

On the night of November 28, 1864, across the desiccated plains of what would become southeastern Colorado, a band of seven hundred cavalrymen rode through sagebrush and soapweed. This was a volunteer regiment, led by Colonel John Chivington, a former Methodist minister who had gone on the "warpath" against Indians in the Colorado Territory. He had given his men orders to "Kill all the Indians you come across . . . Nits make lice."

Before them, in the winter dawn, was a sleeping Cheyenne village of buffalo hide lodges. Orders passed quickly through the ranks, and the men goaded their horses into a gallop. Hundreds of hooves drummed the barren sand flats. A few people, some naked, appeared at the openings to the lodges. Some began to mill around; others clustered in groups. One old man whose teepee occupied a prominent spot in the village rushed out and swung a lodgepole overhead. At the end of the pole, visible in the dawn's early light, flew a white rag topped by an American flag. The soldiers did not know (and perhaps most would not have cared) that the flag had been presented by a US colonel to the old chief, Black Kettle, in a ceremony attended by Abraham Lincoln, with the assurance that his people would be safe under those colors. The galloping soldiers opened fire on the people. Several women and children fell in the first volley. People from all over the village crowded around the old chief, his face tanned from sun and wind, as he swung the American flag back and forth overhead.

In the summer, a couple of months after Derrick and Sheila moved in, she asked me if I would relieve their dog. She gave me a key.

Their living space was oppressive, with a double-sloped ceiling and small windows. It stank of sweat, mold, and spilled beer. Their dog Molly wagged her stubby tail wildly each afternoon when I opened the door. She jumped up on me, licked my hands, then turned circles. I had never seen such a sweet Doberman. We traipsed downstairs, and she romped in the yard.

One day, after releasing Molly back into their apartment, I looked around. Dirty clothes lay piled in their bedroom, and their living room was dark except for the tinfoil-covered aquariums housing ultraviolet lights and marijuana plants. Their kitchen sink brimmed with filthy dishes and, on their table, lay a pipe and some baggies. This explained his heavy coughing every morning and night.

A few weeks later, on a Friday night, my wife and I heard the first of what would become commonplace—shouting overhead. Locked out, Sheila pounded on their glass door and bawled. This was to become our toughest dilemma—when to dial 911. Do you reach for the phone when you first hear shouting? How about when you hear something heavy, like a bookcase or a dresser, crash to the floor? When you no longer hear her voice responding to his shouting? What about when you hear him yelling, Get up, get the fuck up, you aren't hurt? What about when he threatens to blow her brains out? And, when there's a sudden, chilling silence? That night, we did call the police. The next week, I returned the key to their apartment. The less I had to do with them, I reasoned, the better.

That fall, when we first noticed Sheila's swelling belly, we were sure she wouldn't keep it. Yet she did. As she came to term, we assured each other that a baby might be just what they needed, a settling presence in their chaotic lives. Four days after Sarah came home, the shouting started all over.

The next spring, when they had lived over us for nearly a year, Derrick resumed weightlifting. After enduring the thuds on my ceiling for a week, I reached into the closet for the broomstick. Three rapid thumps against the ceiling. The pounding from the weights subsided. Not many days later, though, the thumps started again. My temples throbbed with blood. My dog cowered at my feet, panting. I considered going for a walk, but that would mean I was being driven from my own apartment. I taught part-time and had carved out my afternoons to write. We were subsisting mostly on my wife's paycheck. What would I do two days later when it happened again? The challenge was being offered. This called for a confrontation.

Even that early on, I imagined reaching inside my closet for the twelve-gauge double-barreled shotgun, my grandfather's old home defense issue. I imagined ascending the staircase with the weapon in hand, shoving it in his face, saying through clenched teeth, Don't push me, motherfucker. This is what a real man would do, I told myself.

Instead, I climbed the steep, narrow staircase, my heartbeat drumming a ragged rhythm. I knocked on the door, and it opened.

Derrick, man, you've got to knock that off. I'm trying to work down here.

Yeah, yeah, he said and slammed the door shut.

Back in my apartment, the dumbbells thundered down. I felt each one hit, an explosion of hate aimed not at my ceiling, but at me. So this was Derrick's payback for all the times I had called the police.

How's that for trying to work! followed hard on the crashes. The floor was so thin I could hear every word. I had never been the target of such direct hate. I could only understand it in terms of demonic possession. It wasn't a man with problems hurling weights onto his floor. It was Satan riverdancing on my ceiling.

I don't remember what triggered me to make the anonymous call. It may have been just a routine fight or a weight-lifting session. It might have been the time my landlord hung up on me, weary of my com-

101

plaints, afraid of getting shot himself. It may have been getting laid off from my job at the end of that second summer living under them, with no prospect of saving up enough money to move out before winter. Or perhaps it was the time I saw Derrick and Sheila out walking in the neighborhood. She was pushing the baby carriage. I smiled; he flipped me off.

Whatever it was, I sat in the cramped coatroom of our church five blocks away. I didn't want the call to be traceable. To the woman who answered the non-emergency line, I reported that my neighbor was growing marijuana, definitely using, and perhaps dealing other drugs. By then, Derrick had purchased a brand new Suzuki motorcycle and often roared out of the parking lot in the middle of the night. I gave no name. A rock sat in my gut. Was I just a narc? I could care less whether he smoked pot in his apartment, but here I was, using his addiction as the pretense for calling the police, hoping the authorities would take care of my problem. If only I had called before Sarah was born. What kind of a person informs on a father, surreptitiously, anonymously, and with information more than a year old, meant only to eliminate him as a neighbor?

I justified my action by reasoning that it might curb the abuse. I walked the five blocks back to the house, wondering how long it would take for anything to happen. For more than a year, I had wanted to make that call, and it had always been my ace in the hole. Instead of relief, though, a new thought surfaced as I trudged home. What would happen when the cops did show up at his door? Wouldn't he know it was me?

Two weeks later, I flew home to Denver for a friend's wedding. I called my wife on the phone, and she told me they were fighting upstairs again.

I'm so glad you never talk to me like that, she said. I just can't imagine how horrible their relationship is. Fear colored her voice, and that was the first time I noticed the situation's effect on her. All along, I had been the one home during the day, the target of Derrick's animosity. All along, I had also been the one most intrigued and disturbed.

When I returned, my wife told me that she had asked Derrick to move his motorcycle from behind her car, and he had unleashed a torrent of slurs against her. She didn't go into detail about the specific words he used, but they were easy enough to imagine. They were the same words he used on his wife, I was sure.

The next night, with my wife working late, I go to the closet. I reach for the shotgun. Its polished stock is solid, its metal cool, its heft reassuring. From a drawer, I take two shells, slide them smoothly into the barrels, then snap the gun shut. I raise the gun to firing position and imagine the figure in the mirror is Derrick. I recognize the hatred in his eyes. My finger rests on the trigger, while my thumb brushes the safety.

II.

Accounts of the slaughter at Sand Creek are corroborated by scouts who had been forced to guide the soldiers. Chivington's men killed without discretion for seven hours. Then they mutilated the bodies. Lieutenant James Connor, who surveyed the killing grounds the following day, records this: "I did not see a body of man, woman, or child but was scalped, and in many instances their bodies were mutilated in the most horrible manner." Some men cut out the women's genitalia and stretched them over their saddle-bows, made tobacco pouches out of them, or wore them on their hats while in ranks. Not long after, the men paraded their trophies through the streets of Denver in celebration.

Who were these men who could kill unarmed, defenseless people and then parade their trophies along the same streets I had walked for five years in college? Were they pathological monsters? After reading about the attack, I began to wonder if all men aren't walking towers of ugly potential. After all, I can't deny my own obsession with violent fantasies while living in the Seattle apartment. It was an irresistible addiction, the only thing that soothed my anxiety, while also feeding it.

Reading a recent issue of *The Atlantic Monthly*, a quote from a major twentieth century figure caught my eye: "Mind and soul ultimately return to the collective being of the world. If there is a God, then he gives us not only life but also consciousness and awareness. If I live my life according to my God-given insights, then I cannot go wrong, and even if I do, I know I have acted in good faith." These words speak to me of my own search for meaning. I see in their concept of God a reflection of Leo Tolstoy's belief that a greater web of consciousness connects all life. I find in the final phrase a resonance of my own belief in listening to the still, small voice inside—what some call a conscience. Adolph Hitler spoke these words in December, 1941, at the time when the first crematoriums were being built to handle the "Final Solution," Germany's genocidal "answer" to the "problem" of European Jews.

Hitler is often held up as the twentieth century's greatest example of a person who embodied evil. We listen to the stories of his demented philosophy, of his twisted, grandiose psyche, of his pathological thinking. We listen for strains of the "other," the mad Nazi we know must lurk inside him; we listen for the mistral wind tugging him toward a place of darkness. To me, the words he spoke don't sound like those of a madman. They sound like thoughts I myself have had.

In one fantasy, I ascend the outside staircase to their deck. I knock on the door. Derrick answers and we begin to argue. He rushes for me. I dodge to the side and shove him through the dilapidated railing. He screams four stories down, and his life ends with the wet thud I heard once when I witnessed a man commit suicide from the fifth floor of a parking garage in downtown Denver. In another, we slug it out toe-to-toe in the parking lot. With bloody faces, we wrap garden hoses around each other's throats, bash each other's skulls with a fire extinguisher, fight to the death. Though I'm badly injured in some scenarios, I never lose. Perhaps I imagine myself injured to atone for the guilt I harbor for feeding Derrick's anger with my calls to the police, my thumps on the ceiling. Unstoppable, these daydreams recurred, stacking up on one another like clouds gathering at the horizon.

To counter the fantasies, I studied scripture. Also, on Thursday nights, in a small group from our church, I complained about Derrick. Though I didn't go into detail about my violent daydreams, I told them about my inner struggles, how I blamed this man, who filled my days with trepidation and hate, for my own ugly thoughts. His violence spilled into my mind, and I hated him for poisoning me. They reminded me that, as a believer, I should pray for my enemy.

One afternoon I overhead voices in the parking lot. It was Derrick cussing out our downstairs neighbor, a middle-aged single woman who was a close friend. That night, with my wife working late, I stifled my anger and climbed the rickety stairs to knock on his door. In preparation, I humbled myself, ready to meet him on whatever terms he offered. He answered with Sarah resting in one arm.

What the hell do you want?

I just want to clear the air between us, Derrick. I want to help. It's obvious you've got some problems.

He gazed at me. Sarah batted at the gold security chain hanging from the doorframe. I could tell Derrick was weighing the sincerity of my words, deciding his next move. His eyes narrowed. It seemed for an instant that he might invite me in, and I smiled at Sarah. When I looked back at his face, it was as if a veil had closed over it.

What the fuck do you know about my problems?

He was right. I didn't know about his problems. I felt stupid—of course, this was how it would work out. He swore at me, threatened to kick my ass. I edged away from the dilapidated railing around the deck. The hatred that had become so familiar surged through me. Yet he held that baby in his hands; in mine, I held a Bible. I walked away.

What was I thinking to climb those stairs carrying a Bible? I was no evangelist. I hated it when strangers tried to "witness" to me. I sympathized with people who, like Kurt Cobain, believed that Jesus didn't want them for sunbeams. At the time, when I was struggling to redefine my faith and find a new anchor in old beliefs, I felt compelled to reach out, if only once, in pure humility.

I remember clearly the rest of that night. This is how I'm able to pray for Derrick: I'm on my knees in our living room, the dog shivering in fear beside me from the crashes and thumps overhead that my visit incited. The curses flow down through the ceiling; the Psalms are open before me. I can't read the celebratory or the penitential ones. I go to the imprecatory Psalms, and this is what I pray, echoing David's own words:

Contend, oh Lord, with those who contend with me; fight against those who fight against me. May those who seek my life be disgraced and put to shame. May they be like chaff before the wind, with the angel of the Lord driving them away; may their path be dark and slippery, with the angel of the Lord pursuing them.

Here, even in my prayer, a new fantasy arises: I imagine Derrick on his motorcycle, roaring down a twisting, rain-slicked Seattle street late at night. Pursuing him, and from which he cannot escape, is an avenging wing, a spirit that sweeps the tires out from under him and sends him screaming headfirst into a wall. A motorcycle wreck is the best thing that could happen to his family. His wife and baby girl would finally get some peace. We would all get some peace.

My thoughts drift back to the danger he poses to my wife, my dog, myself. What feels natural is to reach into the closet and close my hands around the shotgun. To end it all with one flurry of violence seems like what a real man would do. I imagine the relief I would experience by succumbing to this gut-level response. After all, who could blame me if I acted purely on instinct? On a realm almost outside myself, I realize coldly that all my education, spiritual and secular, is supposed to counter this feeling, to illuminate its irrational, immoral nature. Yet, pent up inside me, quivering so that I can barely keep it lidded, is a masculine rage that aches for release.

When news of the Sand Creek Massacre spread, the public was duly horrified. The federal government opened three separate investigations, none of which found any of the soldiers guilty due to confusion over their status as either civilians or soldiers, since they belonged to a volunteer regiment. As Dee Brown observes in *Bury My Heart at Wounded Knee*, after the massacre, any claim by the Cheyenne and Arapaho to the Colorado Territory was abandoned, and all the Indians were eliminated from the area, which was the real motive behind the attack. When I read Brown's and other historians' accounts, I think of the other Sand Creek, the one near my boyhood home. It is wide and barren and flat, very similar to southeastern Colorado. It is also empty.

After we had lived two years under Derrick and Sheila, a friend loaned us $1200, and we moved out. Then, a year later, just before we moved again, this time several hundred miles away, my wife and I returned to the place of our former apartment. The house had been razed, and in its place were condominiums. How perfect, I thought—from the cheapest digs on Queen Anne to the most expensive.

We walked along the clean white sidewalks bordering beige stucco walls. I had hoped to experience a sense of reclamation, of justice finally served, but instead I felt displaced—the house was nothing like the home I had known. Condos sprawled over everything. Although there were no bay windows, the people on the south side still would have an expansive view of Puget Sound. I wondered if they knew it was the deep soundings of Elliott Bay that had originally drawn the Denny Party to found the city of Seattle. They arrived to find a native population recently decimated by disease, the area ripe for colonization. I wondered if any of the new tenants would lose themselves in the inscrutable patterns of light playing off the swells that roll unceasing over the depths of Puget Sound.

Now, in our new lives, in a small town on the other side of the Cascade Mountains, we rent a house at the edge of town on a hill that overlooks a wheat field. At sunset, my wife and I sit on our deck and watch the shadows formed by the hillocks across the field stretch and lengthen until they dissipate in the dusk. Our dog dozes nearby in the grass. The plum tree in the corner of our yard is heavy with fruit. The wheat field sits, always empty, and only the occasional car passes soundlessly along the highway in the distance. It is so peaceful I feel as if I could live here forever.

Today, the land around the bend in Sand Creek is an undistinguished field used for grazing. A single small monument atop a hill overlooks the supposed site of the massacre. The exact location has been forgotten. In less than 150 years, this place that provided the setting for what sociologist James Waller calls "extraordinary human evil" looks no different from the miles of flat, desiccated plains— farm and ranchland—that stretch away in all directions. It would be grossly unfair to suggest that the Sand Creek Massacre was singular in its horror. The genocide carried out in North America is unparalleled in history, and, because of this, it is becoming increasingly harder for me to escape the idea that the soil of the land itself is cursed, in the way God cursed the land where Cain slew his brother Abel. Fear of native inhabitants and an agricultural obsession have emptied and scarred the land. This genocide is something more than an arbitrary act of history. It required ordinary men, men no different from me, to take hold of a weapon, lift it against another, and unleash its power. An act that begins in the imagination.

This is the first spring in our new home, with its peaceful view. Recently, one day at dusk, a muted stillness lay over the field, as if the atmosphere itself was holding its breath. Birds darted rapidly past. In the west, dark clouds gathered.

As night came on, I retreated to my office. A groan rumbled through the open window. It was the farmer's tractor. He had been busy plowing the field behind our house for three days. I was sure he would quit at the loss of light. Instead, as dark settled, he switched on two lamps. One shone forward, and the other cast its light behind, glinting off the harrowing blades as they sliced through the soil. The tractor's silhouette finally faded, leaving the ghost lights to float across the blackness that had overtaken the field. A relentless breeze brushed and popped the loose screen against the window frame as the first drops of rain began to fall.

Nominated by Kim Barnes, Passages North

SLOAN-KETTERING

by LYNN SHAPIRO

from RATTLE

One thing they don't tell you about Sloan-Kettering
is how beautiful the workers are, shepherdesses, sirens,
brawny football players, ready to lift the heaviest bodies. One,
rosy as a mountain child moves like the most even glare of light,
never turns away till you have risen to follow her.
She holds your paper file near her breasts, but not too tight.
Walls are paved with photographs, scenes of mountains, forests
carved by light. The chemotherapy suite is a skylight, a bubble.
You pass posters for support groups presented on easels like paintings
in progress. There are private rooms for each patient with chairs
and blankets and a straight-backed chair for a companion if you have one,
and a little television with its snake arm, riveted into the wall.
In the center of all these private rooms are gatherings of high stalked
    flowers,
magenta, purple, amber, bursting higher than churches, in golden vases
everywhere, and the carpet is gold, too, so padded you can hear
no sound of walking. There are so many workers here,
and your surgeon, Alexandra, is the most beautiful worker of all.
Her office where you wait is the color of cool green and mountain cream.
A computer pulses out deep blue insignias, next to it
is a magazine, half the cover missing, torn, or half-eaten,
waiting for you to touch it in the same place as the person before you.
You don't and this decision, its stillness, its inability to reverse is profound
and stagnant. Outside, in the hallway other doctors stand leaning, writing
with the concentration of animals eating food, whose only purpose
is to become blind to everything but their own sustenance.

And she is the Sun. She is beautiful when she enters, says *How
are you?* You lean on her *are*. She opens your robe like the earth,
and you say, *I used to have beautiful breasts,* and she says, *You still
do,* and she cups your breasts. This is her special way. She cups
each one, then combs down, down with her fingers as if down
the side of a mountain she is scaling tenderly so as not to fall
once. She half-closes your garment and you close the rest.
You watch her fingers leave your robe how they arc in the air
to papers on her desk, and you realize that at various times
in the past five years you have thought of her fingers, their short
nails, and how she called you and said into the mouth of her phone,
really as an afterthought, that *in the site of the malignancy we found
a little milk. A little* she said, like the purr of a cat, and you could see
her fingers, her surgeons fingers holding her own children's milk bottles,
and then as you will always, you will want to be like her, to save lives
during the day, then go home, feed your children at night.
You remember the way out on the soundless carpet.
Your husband is with you, murmurs, your husband,
the lobby, just as you remember, in subtle shades, tones of green and gold.

Nominated by Rattle

LUCKY CHOW FUN

fiction by LAUREN GROFF

from PLOUGHSHARES

EVERY VILLAGE HAS ITS RHYTHM, and every year Templeton's was the same. Summer meant tourists to the baseball museum, the crawl of traffic down Main Street, even a drunken soprano flinging an aria into the night on her stagger back to the Opera. With fall, the tourists thinned out, and the families of Phillies Phanatics ceded the town to retired couples with binoculars, there to watch the hills run riot with color.

Come winter, Templeton hunkered into itself. We natives were so grateful for this quiet—when we could hear the sleigh bells at the Farmers' Museum all the way to the Susquehanna—that we almost didn't mind the shops closing up. It was in winter that we believed in our own virtue, when we lauded ourselves for being the kind of people to renounce the comforts of city life for a tight community and spectacular beauty. We packed on our winter fat and waited for spring, for the lake to melt, for the cherry blossoms, for the town to burst into its all-American charm, and the rapid crescendo of tourists.

This was our rhythm, at least, until the Lucky Chow Fun girls. That year, the snow didn't melt until mid-May, and the Templeton High School Boys' Swim Team won the State Championships. That year, we natives stopped looking one another in the eye.

I was seventeen that spring and filled with longing, which I tried to sate with the books of myth and folklore that I was devouring by the dozens. I couldn't read enough of the stories, tiny doors that opened

111

only to reveal a place I hadn't known I'd known; stories so old they felt ingrained into my genes. I loved Medea, Isolde, Allerleirauh. I imagined myself as a beautiful Cassandra, wandering vast and lonely halls, spilling prophesies that everyone laughed at, only to watch come tragically true in the end. This feeling of muteness, of injustice, was particularly strong in me, though I had no particular prophesies to tell, no clear-sighted warnings. On the nights I stuffed myself with myths, I dreamt of college, being pumped full of all the old knowledge until I knew everything there was to know, all the past cultures picked clean like delicious roasted chickens.

All March, I skidded home from school as fast as I could in my ratty Honda Civic to look for my college acceptance letters in the mailbox; all of my friends had gotten early acceptances, but because I was recruited for swimming, I had to wait for the regular acceptances. All March, there was nothing. By the time my little sister, Petra—Pot—trudged the mile home over the snowdrifts, I would be sitting at the kitchen table, having just eaten an entire box of cereal plus a bowl of ice cream, feeling sick.

"Oh, God, Lollie," she'd say, dumping her backpack. "Nothing?"

"Nope," I'd say. "Nothing."

And she'd sigh and sit across from me. Her days were also hard, as she was too weird for the other fourth graders, too plump, too spastic. She never once had a sleepover or even a best friend. But instead of complaining, Pot would try to cheer me up by mimicking the new birdsongs she'd learned that day. *"Drop-it, drop-it, cover-it-up, cover-it-up, pull-it-up, pull-it-up,"* she'd sing, then say, "Brown Thrasher," her dumpling face suddenly luminous. That year, Pot was on a strange ornithological kick, as if her entire pudgy being were stuffed with feathers. She fell asleep to tapes of tweets and whistles and had a growing collection of taxidermied birds scattered around her bedroom. I had no idea where she had gotten them, but was too moony with my own troubles to ask. I avoided her room as much as possible, because she had one particular gyrfalcon perched on her dresser that seemed malicious, if not downright evil, ready to scratch at your jugular if you were to saunter innocently by.

Those melancholy afternoons, Pot would chirp away until my mother came home from her own bad day at the high school in Van Hornesville, where she taught biology. No: my mother never came in, she blew in like the dust devil of a woman she was, stomping the snow off her boots, sending great clouds of it from her shoulders.

"Oh, God, Lollie, nothing?" she would say, releasing her springy gray hair from her cap.

"Nothing," Pot would trill, then leap up to rejoin her stiff little aviary upstairs.

My mother would look at the wreckage of my snack, frown, and hug me. "Elizabeth," she'd say, and I could hear the vibration of her words in her chest, feel the press of each individual bone of her rib cage. "Don't you worry. It will all work out in the end. You're no Podunk idiot like the kids I teach—"

"Spare me," I'd interrupt, and give her a kiss on the chin. Then I'd stand, late for swim practice, and leave my nervous little mother to peep out the window at me as I pulled away. That spring she was dating The Garbageman, and when I came home I may have seen her before going to bed, or I may not have seen her until morning, singing during her preparations for school.

There are hundreds of versions of the Cinderella story throughout the world: Serbian Pepelyouga, Norwegian Kari Trestakk, Chinese Yeh-hsien, German Aschenputtel, French Cendrillon. What most of the stories have in common is both an absent good mother and an evil present one. Fairy tales are not like real life in all its beautiful ambiguity. There are no semi-good semi-absent mothers. Or, for that matter, semi-present very good ones.

It was only in the pool that winter, feeling the thrust and slide of my body through the water, that I felt good. Only then could I escape the niggling terror of what would happen to my mother and sister when I left them, the image of their sad dinners, my sister talking only of birds, my mother talking only of the crap day she had at school, neither heard by the other, neither listening.

I was the captain and the only girl on the varsity boys' swim team that year, though not much of a leader. During the long bus rides, I only giggled nervously at the boys' boasts about boning chicks I knew they never touched. I wasn't chosen as a captain because I was a leader, but rather because of my teammates' small town gallantry and my minor celebrity as an oddity in the papers. I was the fastest butterflier around, and could beat everyone, boy or girl, in the region, save for one lightning-swift boy from Glens Falls. The papers all the way to Albany couldn't stop chortling over this fact. They ran photos of me every week, careful to only take my fairly pretty face and leave my—let's face it—overweight body on the cutting-room floor. I was very heavy. "Rubenesque," my mother called it, but the boys were clearly no aesthetes because they never looked directly at me, not even when I was on the block, waiting for the start. I was no pushover, though. If a boy made fun of the way I bulged in my bathing suit, calling me "Moby Dickless," for instance, that boy would find himself stunned on the pool bottom, having been swum over by my own impersonation of a great white whale.

One Friday night in March, after an exceptionally hard relay practice, Tim Summerton leaned over the gutter when I came trundling in from the last race. He was no looker, all wonky-eyed and stippled with pimples, but had a heart so kind he never went without a date to any school dance. He spat a stream of warm water into my face, which I ducked and spat back at him, laughing. Then he grinned.

"Hey," he said. "The divers and I are going to the Lucky Chow Fun. Want to come?"

I looked at the little clump of divers snapping each other with towels. Those three boys were the exhibitionists of the team, with, truly, a little more to look at in their picklesuits than the swimmers had. I would know: I saw underwater remarkably well. "Oooh, Fun, Fun," the divers were saying in a vaguely ethnic impression. "We have fun fun at Fun Fun." They were not the smartest boys, our divers, but I suppose anybody who tries to shave his neck with the end of a diving board must be a little lacking in brainpower.

"Yeah," I said. "Sure."

"Great. Meet you there," Tim said, tapping my head with the pull-buoy he had in his hand. I was overwhelmed with the desire to grab his hand, clutch it to me, cover it in kisses, laugh like a madwoman. Instead I smiled, then went back under the water, holding my breath until I could hold it no longer, then sent it up in a great silvery jellyfish-bubble of air. When I came up, Tim had gone.

That night, I showered with special care, washed the chlorine off my body, lotioned, powdered. And when I walked out into the cold night, all the gym's lights went out behind me, and the last employee locked the door behind my back. I left my hat off to let my hair freeze into the thin little snakes I liked to crunch in my fingers, and thought of moo goo gai pan.

It was a Friday night, but there was a basketball game at the high school, so the town was very still as I drove through it. Only the Ambassador's mansion gave a sign of life, every window burning gold.

114

The Ambassador was our local hero, former ambassador to France and Guyana, and once upon a time my father's great friend, and I always felt a wash of fondness for him when I passed his fine fieldstone mansion on the river. He was an erect, gray man of eighty years old with fine bluish fingers and canny eyes. He had, they said, a huge collection of rare goods from all over the world: a room entirely devoted to masks, one for crystal bowls, one for vases, even one for his miniature schnauzer, with paintings done by great artists of the snarly little beast. Nobody knew for sure, though, because when we were invited, we only saw the ground floor. In any case, my family hadn't been invited since we lost my father.

Now, on Main Street, only a few shop windows had left their lights on, casting an oily shine to the baseball bats in the souvenir shops, making the artificial flowers in the General Store glow. The Red Dragoon Saloon was open, and there were three Harleys in the sludge on Pioneer Street, but still I was able to park right in front of Lucky Chow Fun, behind Tim Summerton's Volvo.

The restaurant was newish, maybe two years old, and the town's first tentative step toward ethnic food, unless one counted Gino's Pizzeria and the Mennonite Bakery on Main Street. It was a cheap linoleum joint, with an ugly, hand-drawn sign flapping in the wind off the lake, lit from above with a red light. It served a lot of sticky Americanized Chinese food, like General Tso's Chicken and Fried Rice, and I loved it all, the fat and salt, the scandalous feeling of eating fast food in a hamlet that banned all fast food places, the miniature mythmaking of the fortune cookies.

That night, when I stepped out of the car and around to the sidewalk, I almost knocked into a small, shivering figure in an overlarge T-shirt, sweeping the new snow from the walk. "Sorry," I mumbled, and stepped away, not really looking at the girl I had nearly trampled, only gathering a vague impression of crooked teeth and a jagged haircut. She was just one of the girls who worked at the Lucky Chow Fun, one of the wives or daughters of the owners. Nobody in Templeton cared to figure out who the girls were, just as nobody figured out who the two men who ran the place were, only calling them Chen One and Chen Two, or Chen Glasses and Chen Fat. Only later did we realize that no part of their names remotely resembled Chen, nor did the girls resemble the men in any way, either.

I feel the necessity of explaining our hard-heartedness, but I cannot. Templeton has always had a callousness about outsiders, having seen so many come through town, wreak destruction on our lake, trash the ancient baseball stadium, Cartwright Field, litter our streets, and move off. This wariness extended even to those who lived with us; anyone who wasn't related to everyone else was suspect. Newcomers meant people who had only lived in town for fifteen years. The one black family who lived in Templeton during my childhood promptly pulled up roots and moved away after a year, and, to my knowledge, there were only three Jewish children in school. The only Asians were preternaturally cheery and popular, adopted kids from the wealthiest of the doctors' families in town. This was a town that clung ferociously to the shameful high school mascot of The Redskins, though if we were any skins, we should have been The Whiteskins. I was born and raised in this attitude. That night, without a second thought, I stepped around the girl and into the fatty brightness of the restaurant, past old Chen Glasses, snoozing over his Chinese newspaper at the door.

The restaurant was nearly empty, the long kitchen in the back sending out a fine oily sizzle, girls like ghosts in white uniforms chopping things, frying things, talking quietly to one another. The backlit photos above the register struck me so powerfully with their water chestnuts and lovingly fried bits of meat that I didn't at first see the divers, who were pretending to be walruses, chopsticks in their mouths like tusks. When they saw me, they took the chopsticks out so fast it was clear who they were imitating. I was not unused to this. In fourth grade, the Garrett twins had named their science project, a miniature zeppelin, *The Lollie*. That night, I did what I always did, stifled the pang, pretended to smile.

"Very funny, boys," I said. "Have you ordered?"

"Yeah," said Brad Huxley. He was in my grade and blessed with a set of eyelashes that made every girl in school envious. He gave me a dimpled smile, and said, "We ordered by ourselves. These two freaks don't like sharing," nodding at the other two. It was his sorrow in life that he was not endowed with hand-eye coordination; otherwise he would have been on the basketball court that evening with the cool kids. He overcompensated in the diving pool, and in a few weeks, at States, would come so close to the board on his reverse back pike that he had a strip of flayed skin from neck to mid-back, and a perfect score for that dive.

I was standing at the front, deciding what to order from solemn and scornful old Chen Fat, with his filthy apron, when Tim Summerton came from the back where the bathrooms were. His face was drawn and pale, and he looked half-excited, half-horrified. He didn't seem to see me, as he walked past me without a glance. He sat down at the table with the others and began to hiss at them something I couldn't quite make out.

Huxley sat back with a little smirk on his face. "Duh," he said just loud enough for me to hear. "Everybody knows." The other two divers looked pale, though, and smiles broke out over their faces.

I was about to ask what they were talking about, but Chen Fat said, "Hem hem," and I turned toward him. His pen was poised over the pad, and his eyelids were drawn down over his eyes. I couldn't quite tell if he was looking at me or not.

"General Tso's, please," I said. "And a Coke."

He grunted, and rang up the bill on the old register, and I forked over my hard-won babysitting money, two dollars an hour for the Bauer hellions. When I sat down, the boys were already digging into their food, and the girl who had served them was backing away, looking down, holding the round tray before her like a shield. This one was pretty, delicate, with pointed little ears and chapped lips, but the boys didn't seem to notice her at all. Tim Summerton, I noticed, was just pushing around his mu shu pork, looking sick.

"You okay?" I said to Tim. He looked up at me, and looked away.

"He's just a pussy," said Huxley, a grain of rice on his lips. "He's all nervous about Regionals tomorrow. Doesn't want to do the five-hundred free."

"Really?" I said. "But, Tim, you're the best we've got."

"Eh," said Tim, shrugging. "Well, I'm not too nervous about it." Then he blinked, and making an effort to change the subject, said, as my plate of crispy chicken was placed before me, "So, who are you taking to the Winter Dance?" None of the boys really wanted to talk about this, it was clear, but spat out names: Gretchen, Melissa, maybe Gina, maybe Steph. Tim looked at me. "Who you going with, Lollie?"

I shrugged. "I don't know," I said. "Maybe just my friends." Depressing thought: my friends were the girls I ate lunch with, all buddies from kindergarten who knew one another so well we weren't sure if we even liked one another anymore.

Huxley gave me his charming smile and said, "Because you're, like, a dyke, right? You like chicks? It's okay, you can tell us." He laughed, and the other divers laughed with him.

"No," I said, putting my chopsticks down, feeling my face grow hot. "What the hell? No, I'm not a whatever, I mean, I like guys, Jesus." My excitement, the invitation, soured a little in my gut. I looked hard at the curls of chicken on my plate.

"Relax, Lollie," said Tim, grinning at me, his wonky eye traveling over the window, where the world was lit pink by the light over the sign. "He's just teasing you. Brad's a dick."

And, charmingly, Huxley winked at me and showed me his mouthful of half-chewed food. "I know you're no dyke," he said. "But you could tell us if you were."

'Yeah," one of the other divers said. "That's totally hot." And when we all looked at him a little funny, he blushed and said, "Well. Maybe not you, Lollie. But lesbians in general." He gathered high-fives all around, hooting, until something in me burst, and I gave him a little high-five on his cheek, and he sat down again, abashed.

In the Chinese myth, the goddess Nü-gua created the first humans from yellow earth, carefully crafting them with her own hands. Though they pleased her, these handicraft humans took too much time, and so to speed the process along, she dipped a rope into the darker mud, and swung it around her head. In this way, she populated the earth with darker mudspatters who became the lowly commoners, while the handcrafted were the wealthy and higher-caste nobles.

Nü-gua, they say, had a woman's upper body but a dragon's tail. She invented the whistle, the art of irrigation, the institution of marriage. How terrible that this dragon-goddess was also the one who granted children to women; that this impatient snob of a goddess was the intermediary between men and women.

It was late when I came home because we sat around after we ate, as if waiting for something to happen. At last, Tim stood and said, "I'll escort you out, Lollie?" and I had the brief and thrilling fear that he was going to ask me to the Winter Dance. But Tim only opened my car door for me, then pulled off, his old Volvo spitting up smoke. I drove home over the black ice, and into the drive of our cottage on Eagle Street.

My mother's car was gone, and only one light was on in the kitchen when I came in. Pot was sitting in the half-shadow, looking at me with a tragic face.

118

"Potty?" I said. "What's wrong, honey?" Her little face broke down until, at last, her eyes filled, huge and liquid, with tears.

"I wanted your food to be warm," she said, "so I put up the heat. But then you didn't come home, and it burnt a little, and so I put it down. And then I got scared because you still weren't home, and so I put the heat up again, and now it's all ruined," and she poked the foil off the plate, and her lip began to tremble.

"Oh, I'm so, so sorry. We went out for Chinese," I said, looking at the charred remains of the chicken and couscous my mother had saved for me. I hugged my little sister until she began to laugh at herself. Then I said, "Petra Pot, where's Mom?"

She made a frowning face and said, sourly, "The Garbageman's." We called our mother's new boyfriend The Garbageman though he was actually a Ph.D. in garbage science, and owned a lucrative monopoly on trash removal in the five counties surrounding ours. He certainly didn't look like a garbage man, either, being fastidious to the point of compulsion, with his hair combed over a small bald spot on his head, his wrists doused in spicy cologne, with the beautiful shirts he had tailored for him in Manhattan. Though Pot hated him, I was ambivalently happy for my mother's sudden passion: since we lost my father, she hadn't seen anyone, and this, I privately assumed, had made her become as nervous and trembly as she had been in recent years.

When I say we lost my father, I don't mean he died: I mean that we lost him when we were on a sabbatical to England, in the bowels of Harrods department store. This was back when Pot was five and suffering acutely from both dyslexia and ADHD. Her inability to connect language in her head, combined with her short attention span, frequently made her so frustrated she didn't actually speak, but, rather, screamed. "Petra the Pepperpot," we called her, affectionately, which was shortened to "Pepperpot," then "P-pot," then "Pot," or "Potty." The day we lost my father was an exceptionally trying one, as, all morning, Pot had screamed and screamed and screamed. My dad, having coveted the Barbour oil jackets he'd seen around him all summer long, had taken us to Harrods to try to find one for himself. But for at least fifteen minutes, he was subjected to the snooty superciliousness of the clerk when he tried to describe the jacket.

"Bah-Bah," my father kept saying, as that's what he heard when he asked the Brits what kind of jacket they were wearing. "It's brown and oily. A Bah-Bah jacket."

"I'm sorry, sir," the clerk returned indolently. "I've never heard of a Bah-Bah."

Thus, my father was furious already when my little sister fell into an especially loud apoplectic fit, pounding her heels into the ground. At last, my father turned on us. His face was purple, his eyes bulged under his glasses, and this mild-mannered radiologist seemed about ready to throttle someone to death. "Wait here," he hissed, and stalked off.

We waited. We waited for hours. My mother rubbed her thin arms, frightened and angry, and I was sent to the vast deli in the basement for sandwiches. Cheddar and chutney, watercress and ham. We waited, and we had no way to contact him, and so, when the store was about to close, we caught a cab back to our rented flat. We found his things gone. He was in a hotel, he said later when he telephoned. He had arranged our tickets home. My mother shut the sliding doors in the tiny kitchen, and Pot and I tried to watch a bad costume drama on the telly, and when our mother came out, we knew without asking that it was all over. Nowadays, my father lives in an Oxford town-house with a woman named Rita, who is about to have their first child. "Lurvely Rita, Meeta-Maid," is what my mother so scornfully calls her, though Rita is a neurologist, and dry in the British manner to the point of unloveliness.

But the evening of the Lucky Chow Fun, my father wasn't the vil-lain. My mother was. Who leaves a troubled ten-year-old alone in a big old house in the middle of winter? There were still a few tourists in town, and anyone could have walked through our ever-unlocked front door. I was filled with a terrible fury, tempted to call her at The Garbageman's place with a sudden faux emergency, let her streak home naked through the snow. And then, after some reflection, I re-alized *I* was the villain: my mother had thought I'd be home by the time she went out, Pot had said.

Stricken with guilt, I allowed Pot to take me upstairs to her own creepy ornithological museum. In the dark, the birds' glass eyes glit-tered in light from the streetlamps, giving me the odd impression of being scrutinized. I shivered. But Pot turned on the light and led me from bird to bird, solemnly pronouncing each one's name, and giving a respectful little bow as she moved on. At last, she stopped before a new addition to her collection, a dun-colored bird with mischievous eyes.

Pot stroked its head, and said, "This is an Eastern Towhee. It goes: *hot dog, pickle, ickle, ickle.*"

"Neat," I said, feeling the gaze of the gyrfalcon on the tenderest parts of my neck.

"*Hurry, worry, blurry, flurry,*" Pot said. "Scarlet Tanager."

"Cool," I said. "I like it. Scarlet Tanager. Hey, you want to watch a movie?"

"*Quick-give-me-a-rain-check,*" giggled Pot. "White-eyed Vireo."

"Pots, listen up. Do you want to watch *Dirty Dancing*? I'll make popcorn."

"*If I sees you, I will seize you, and I'll squeeze you till you squirt,*" my baby sister said, grinning so hugely she almost split her chubby little cheeks.

I blinked, held my breath. "Uh," I said. "Where'd you get that one, Pot?"

"That's the call of a Warbling Vireo," she said with great satisfaction. "Let's watch *The Princess Bride.*"

My mother was up before we were in the morning, flipping omelets and singing a Led Zeppelin song. "Kashmir," I think. She beamed at me in the doorway, and when I went to her and bent to kiss her on the head, she still stank of The Garbageman's cologne.

"Ugh," I said. "You may want to shower before Pot gets up."

She looked at me, frowning. "I did," she said, pulling a strand of her springy peppered hair across her nose. "Twice."

I took a seat at the table. "That's the power of The Garbageman's scent, I guess," I said. "Indelible. He sprays you like a wildcat, and you belong to him."

"Elizabeth," my mother said, sprinkling cut chives atop the egg. "Can you just try to be happy for me?"

"I am," I said, but looked down at my hands. I wasn't sure what I was happy for, as I had never been on a date, let alone done anything remotely sexual, and it wasn't entirely because I was fat. The hard truth was that nobody really dated at Templeton High. Couples were together, or broken up, without really having dated. There was really nowhere to go, the nearest theater in Oneonta, thirty minutes away. And though I suspected there was some sexual activity happening, I was mystified as to how it was instigated.

My mother took my hand in a rapid little movement, kissed it, and

121

went to the stairs to shout up for Pot. My sister was always a furious sleeper, everything about her clenched in slumber—face, limbs, fists—and she never awoke until someone shook her. But that morning, she came downstairs whistling, her hair in a sloppy ponytail, dressed in all white, a pair of binoculars slung around her neck. We both stared at her.

"I am going bird-watching on the Nature Trail," she announced, taking a plate. "I'm wearing white to blend in with the snow. Yummy omelets, Mom."

"Oh. Okay, Honey-Pot. Sounds good," said my mother, sitting down with her own coffee and plate. She had decided when my father left to be a hands-off parent, and went from hovering nervously over everything I did to allowing my little sister the most astounding latitude.

"Wait. You're going alone, Pot?" I said. I glared at my mother, this terrible person who would let a ten-year-old wander in the woods alone. What would she do when I was in college, just let my little sister roam the streets at night? Let her have drunken parties in the backyard, let her squat in the abandoned Sugar Shack on Estli Ave., let her be a crack whore?

"Yup," Pot said. "All alone."

"Mom," I said, "she can't go alone. Anyone can be out there."

"Honey, Lollie, it's Templeton. For God's sakes, nothing happens here. And the Nature Trail is maybe five acres. At that."

"Five acres that could be filled with rapists, Mom."

"I think Pot will be fine," said my mother. She and Pot exchanged wry glances. And then she looked at the clock on the microwave, saying, "Don't you have to be at the gym in fifteen minutes?"

I stifled my protest, warned Pot to take the Mace my mom carried as protection against dogs on her country runs, and struggled into my anorak. Then I stuffed a piece of toast down my gullet, and roared off in my deathtrap Honda. When I passed the Ambassador's mansion, I saw him coming up the walk, back from the Purple Pickle coffee shop, steaming cup in hand, toy schnauzer on a lead in the other, and they both—man and beast—were dressed all in white, with matching white pomponned berets. *Curious*, I thought, but that was all: I was already focusing, concentrating on the undulations of my body through the water, envisioning the hundred butterfly, watching myself touching all the boys out by an entire body length.

In the Grimms' story of *Hansel and Gretel*, it isn't the witch in the gingerbread house who is the wickedest character, as the poor wandering siblings easily defeated her with their small cunning. Rather, the parents of the children were the ones who, in a time of famine, not once, but *twice*, concocted the plan to take their children into the dark forest and leave them there to starve. The first time, the children dropped stones and found their way back. The second time, the forest gobbled up their trail. The witch did what witches do. The parents were the unnatural ones. This speaks to a deep and ingrained fear: that parents could, in their self-interest, lose sight of their duties to their children. They could sell them to the dark and dank wilderness, send them to the forest, let them starve there. And each time, those two little children, starving for home, would come struggling so bravely back.

But nothing happened to Pot that day, and we won Regionals, as nobody could dent our team that year. It was late when we returned, and I was reading *Bullfinch's Mythologies* for the nth time, under the red exit light in the back of the bus. I was marveling over the tiny passage on Danae: *Daughter of King Acrisius of Argos who did not want her to marry and kept her imprisoned because he had been told that his daughter's son would kill him. Jupiter came to her in the disguise of a shower of gold, and she became the mother of Perseus. She and her child were set adrift in a chest and saved by a fisherman on the island of Seriphos.* There was something so haunting in the story, drama packed so tightly into the words that images burst in my head: a white-limbed girl in a dark room, a chink in the roof, the shower of gold pouring over her dazzled body; then the dark chest, the baby squirming on her stomach, the terrifying rasp of the scales of sea monsters against the wood. A story of light and dark. Purely beautiful, it seemed to me, then.

I was daydreaming so happily as we trundled over Main Street that I didn't at first notice what was happening until one of the freshman boys gave a shout. The bus driver slowed down to rubberneck as we went around the flagpole on Pioneer Street, and I saw it all: all eight of the town's squad cars up the hill to our left, all flashing red and blue in syncopated flashes, glaring on the ice and snow, and the ambulance with the stretcher being swallowed up inside it, the running police, the drawn guns, the Chens, both Fat and Glasses, up against the Lucky Chow Fun's vinyl siding, arms and legs spread. A huddled

123

ring of the Lucky Chow Fun girls on the steps. I could pick out the girl with the jagged haircut, her arm around a plump girl with hair to her waist.

"Ohhhhh. Shit," breathed Brad Huxley in the seat before mine. And then the bus passed the scene, and we rolled down Main Street toward the one stoplight in town. From there, the hamlet looked innocent and pristine, a flurry of windblown snow turning the streetlights into snow globes, icing the trees. Over the hills, the March moon was pinned, stoic and yellow, reflected in pieces on the half-glassy lake.

We were already halfway up Chestnut Street, silently looking out the windows, when someone said, "One too many cases of food poisoning?"

And though it wasn't funny, though we all had the flashing red and blue images lodged firmly in us, somewhere just under our hearts, we—all of us—laughed.

I slept late on Sunday, into the afternoon. I never sleep late, and I know what this means: the worst cowards are the ones who refuse to look at what they fear. When I went downstairs, my mother and sister were still in their pajamas. Though Pot was almost my tiny mother's size, and twice her width, she was cradled on my mother's lap, sucking her thumb, her hand up in her infant gesture to stroke my mother's ear. They were watching television, the sound off. I stood in the door, looking at the screen, until I realized that the snowy roads I was seeing on the television were roads I knew as intimately as my own limbs, that the averted faces of the men on the screen were men who knew me well, who followed my swimming in the paper, who thought nothing of giving me a kiss when they saw me. Hurrying down the snowy streets now, shame on their faces, shame in the set of their shoulders.

Then up came the faces of the Chens, stoic, inexpressive, and the scared faces of the Chinese girls, ducking into Mr. Livingston's limousine. He was my ninth-grade history teacher, his limo the only car in town large enough to hold all the girls and their lawyers at once. That car drove legends of baseball all summer from museum to hotel to airport. It drove brides and homecoming queens for the rest of the year. Now it was driving the Lucky Chow Fun girls wherever they were going. Somewhere, I hoped, far away.

I went to the television and turned it off. I stood for a minute, letting the swell die down in my gut, then sat beside my mother and said, "What happened?"

And my mother, who always made a point of being frank about sexual matters, describing biological functions in great detail so that her daughters would never be squeamish or falsely prudish, my mother turned scarlet. "Sit down," she said, and I did. She opened her mouth to speak, then closed it. She bit her lips.

Pot said, pulling her thumb from her mouth, "The Lucky Chow Fun's a whorehouse."

"Pot," said my mother, then sighed. She looked at me, her thin mouth twisting, patting my thigh. "She's right," she said.

"What?" I said. "Wait, what?"

"Last night," my mother said, slowly, as if trying to order the fragmented truths, "one of the girls at the Lucky died. She was locked in her room with her sister—seems they were being punished—and there was some kind of accidental gas leak. One of them died, and the other one almost did, too. And one of the other girls who knew a little English called the police and tried to leave a tip before the Chens found out. But there are not too many poor speakers of English in this town. The police figured it out. They arrested the Chens."

"Oh, God," I said. I thought of the little huddle of the Lucky Chow Fun girls the night before, flushed red and blue in the flashing lights, how quiet they were, how I never saw their eyes. I never looked. "Mom," I said. "Who were those girls?"

My mother brushed Pot's hair out of her eyes, and kissed her on the forehead. She seemed to hesitate, then she said, "They were bought in China and brought over here, it seems. They were poor. They worked in sweatshops. The Chens gave money to their parents, promised a better life. Apparently."

"Slaves," I said.

"On TV, they said that, yes," said Pot, stumbling over her words. "And some of them, they said on TV that some of them, they're younger than you, Lollie."

We sat there, in silence, thinking about this. My mother at one point stood and made us some cocoa, but for once, my tongue tasted like ash and I wanted to take absolutely nothing in. I was sick, could never again be hungry, I thought. At last, thinking of Chen Fat glaring at me over his notepad, the sticky smell of the food, Brad Huxley, the delicate girl with the chapped lips, I said, shuddering, "Do they know who visited? Do they have names?"

"Well," said my mother, who paused for a very long time, "that's almost the worst. The Chens wrote down the names of the men who visited the Lucky Chow Fun." It was hard to hear her, even in the preternatural stillness of the town on this day, even in our snow-muffled house. "They had a ledger. They made sure to write in English. The reporters said that they were going to blackmail the men who visited. Apparently, it's not just tourists. Apparently, a lot of men from the town went, too." She looked at us. "You should know. Some of the men you know, some you love, some of them may have gone."

And there was something so uncertain in my mother's face, something so fearful it struck a note in me. I looked at the clock over the mantle: it was already four o'clock: my mother hadn't left the house yet. Unusual: she was the only person I ever knew who could never sit still. Especially now, when she was dating The Garbageman, for whom she often cooked most meals and who, by this time on Sunday, had usually called our house to chat for hours, as if they were silly teenagers in love.

"Oh," I said. I looked at her face under her mop of curls, the weary circles around her eyes. "The Garbageman call today?"

My mother flushed again and stood to carry the mugs back to the kitchen. "Not yet." She tossed this over her shoulder, as if it meant nothing to her at all.

I looked at Pot, who was frowning solemnly on her perch on the living room couch. She looked beyond me at a bird that landed on the tree outside, and cried, "A Song Sparrow! *Hip, hip, hip hurrah, boys, spring is here!* That's what they say," she said, beaming. "The Song Sparrows. They say *Hip, hip, hip hurrah, boys, spring is here!*" She was tapping her feet in her excitement, blinking so rapidly and nervously that she reminded me of my mother.

"Pot," I said. "Have you taken your medication today?"

"Whoops," she said, grinning.

"Pot," I said. "How long has it been since you took your medication?"

She shrugged. "A week? Maybe a week. I stopped. I don't believe anymore in medicating children," she said.

I shuddered because I heard in her words the distinct voice of an adult, someone who never saw Pot as she was in her awful years. A teacher, perhaps, or some judgmental village crone. I went to the kitchen, slamming the door behind me. "Mom," I said. "Pot's not taking her medication. And by the way, don't you think she's too young to understand all this Lucky Chow Fun crap? She's only ten. She's just a baby. I don't think she can handle it."

My mother stopped washing the mug she was holding, and let the hot water run. The steam circled up around her, catching in her frizzy gray hair, spangling it when she turned around. "Lollie," she said. "I'll make sure she takes the Ritalin from now on. But nobody in town is going to be able to escape what happened. Not even the kids. It's better that we tell her the truth before someone else tells her something much worse."

"What's worse?" I said. "And I don't think people are made to take truths straight on, Mom. It's too hard. You need something to soften them. A metaphor or a story or something. You know."

"No," she said, "I don't." She turned off the water with a smack of her hand. "Why don't you teach me, since you seem to know everything."

"Well," I said, but at the moment when we most need these things, they don't always come to us. I couldn't remember a word. I opened my mouth, and it hung open there, useless. I closed it. I shrugged.

My mother nodded. "That's what I thought," she said, and turned away.

Years later, I would have had the presence of mind to offer the tale of Fitcher's Bird, from the Brothers Grimm, to offer up an allegorical explanation. I would have told my mother how a wizard dressed as a beggar would magically lure little girls into his basket. He'd cart them to his mansion, give them an egg and key, and tell them not to go into the room that the key opened. Then he'd leave, and the little girls would explore the magnificent house, finally falling prey to curiosity and opening the door of the forbidden chamber.

There, they'd find a huge basin filled with the bloody, dismembered remains of other girls. In their surprise, they'd drop the egg in the vat, and wouldn't be able to wipe the stain away. When the wizard would come home to find the stained egg, he would dismember the girls and toss their remains into the vat.

Eventually, he did this to the two eldest girls from one family, and came back for the third daughter. This girl, though, was uncommonly clever. She hid the egg in a safe place, and brazenly went into the room, only to find her dismembered sisters in the bloody vat. But instead of panicking, she pulled their severed limbs out and pieced them back together again, and when the parts were reassembled, the girls miraculously came back to life.

The clever girl hid her sisters in a room to await the wizard, and when he returned and saw she hadn't bloodied the egg, he decided to marry her. She agreed, but said first that she would send him home with a basketful of gold for her parents. She hid her two sisters in the basket, which he carted home, now a servant of his clever bride. In his absence, the little girl dressed a human skull in flowers and jewels and put it in the attic window. Then she rolled herself in honey and feathers to transform herself into a strange feathered creature, and ran out into the bright day.

On her way home, she encountered the wizard, who thought she was a wonderful bird and said, "Oh, Fitcher's feathered bird, where from, where from?"

To which she responded, "From feathered Fitze Fitcher's house I've come."

"And the young bride there, how does she fare?" he asked, imagining his marriage night, and the soft young body of his wife.

And she, smiling softly under her down and honey, said, "She's swept the house all the way through, and from the attic window, she's staring down at you."

When the wizard arrived home to find the skull in the window, he waved at it, thinking it was his bride. When he went inside, the brothers and father of the little stolen girls locked the door and set a fire and burnt the terrible murderer up.

In the story, of course, the community at last cleansed itself by fire, and in the aftermath came out righteous and whole. This did not happen to Templeton.

We were under siege. The media trucks were parked all along Main Street. Our town, though small, was famous for the baseball museum, for its beauty, an all-American village. Right-wing pundits on television, in the mega-corporation-owned newspapers, held our town as a symbol for the internal moral rot of America, a symbol of the trickle-down immorality stemming from our Democrat president who went around screwing everything that moved. People from Cherry Valley and Herkimer roared into town, pretending that they were natives, and the whole country saw us as drawling mulleted hicks in whole-body Carhartt, and hated us more. The handsome newscasters shivered in their furlined parkas, sat at our diner, trying to eavesdrop, but really only eavesdropping on other newscasters.

Our shell-shocked mayor appeared on television. He was the town know-it-all, a bearded hobbit of a man who gave bombastic walking tours to the tourists and wore shorts all year because of a skin condition. He had to pause to wipe his mouth with a handkerchief, choking up throughout his speech. At the end, he said, "Templeton will survive, as we have survived many other disasters in our illustrious history. Be brave, Templeton, and we will see each other through." But there was no applause at the end, as there were no Templetonians in the audience, composed as it was of disaster-gawkers and newscasters.

Our Ambassador appeared on CNN and 20/20 to defend our town. "We are not perfect," he said in his quivery old man's voice. "But we are a good town, full of good people." His cloudy eyes filled with fervor. It was very affecting.

We stayed inside. We went to the grocery store, if we needed to, to the school, and a few of us went to the gym. Our team practiced in virtual silence, the only sound the water sucking in the gutters, the splash of our muscled limbs. In school, the teachers came to classes with red-rimmed eyes, traces of internal anguish happening in the homes of people we never imagined had private lives. The drama kids pretended to weep at lunch on a recurrent basis. There was a hush over the town as if each of us was muted, swaddled in invisible quilts, so separate from one another as to not be able to touch, if we wanted to. Girls began walking in groups everywhere, as if for protection. The Templeton men did not dare to look at the Templeton women, furious as we were, righteous. And in this separation, in our own sorrow, we forgot about the girls, the Lucky Chow Fun girls, and when, after some time, we thought of them, they were the enemies. They had brought this shame into our town.

Two terrible weeks passed. My mother stopped talking about The Garbageman, *tout court*. He stopped calling. She stopped visiting him with plates of food. She grew drawn and pale, spent a lot of time in her flannel nightgown, watching *Casablanca*. She picked a new fight with the principal, and came home spitting. The Winter Dance was cancelled. I spent that evening dating a pizza and an apple crumble, watching Fred and Ginger glide across the floor, pure grace. Pot acquired two new taxidermied birds, one finch, one scarlet macaw, its head cocked intelligently even in death.

129

One day, I came home, skirting Main Street and its hordes of news cameras. I went to the mailbox, and found six envelopes from colleges all over the country, all addressed to me.

I went inside. I sat at the table with a cup of tea, the six letters splayed before me. One by one, I opened them. And what would have been a personal tragedy before the Lucky Chow Fun was now a slight relief. Of the six colleges, all of which had recruited me for swimming, though I had indifferent grades and mediocre SATs, I had only gotten into one.

Rather: I had gotten into one. One, glorious, one.

I tossed out the bad five, and waited for Pot. My tea cooled, and I made more, and it cooled again. I peered out the curtains for my little sister, but she didn't come. I made cookies, chocolate chip, her favorite. I had a half an hour before swim practice, and she still wasn't home when my mother came in, with her energetic stompings and mutterings. "My God, Lollie," she said, "you'll never guess what that ass-muncher of a princip—"

"Mom?" I interrupted. "Do you know where Potty is?"

"Isn't she here?" she said, massaging her neck, peeping in from the mudroom. "She was supposed to come straight home from school to go to the grocery store with me."

"Nope," I said. "And it's getting dark."

She came into the kitchen then, scowling. "Do you have any idea where she could be?" she said. We looked at each other, and her hand floated up to her hair.

I stood, nervous. "Oh, God," I said.

"Calm down," she said, though she had become flustered herself. "Think, Lollie. Does she have any friends?"

"Pot?" I said. I looked at her. "You're kidding, right?"

"Oh, God," she said.

"Let's think, let's think," I said. I paced to the window, then back. "Mom. Let's think. Where does Potsy get her birds? The stuffed ones. Do you know?"

My mother looked at me, then slowly lifted her hands to her cheeks. "You know," she said, "I never actually wondered. I guess I assumed your dad was sending them. Or she was buying them with her allowance. Or something. I never wondered."

"You haven't given us allowance in six months," I said. "So where are they from?"

"Is she stealing them?" said my mother. "Maybe from the Biological Field Station?"

"Pot?" I thought of this, wondering if Pot could have the gall to waltz into some place, open up the display cabinets, hide the birds under her shirt, and waltz on home. "I don't think so. It's not like her," I said, at last.

"Well," said my mother, her voice breaking. "Who'd have a collection like that?"

And my mother and I looked at one another. There was a long, shivery beat, a car driving by outside, its headlights washing over my mother's face, then beyond. And then we both ran out coatless into the snow, we ran into the blue twilight as hard as we could up the block, forgetting about our cars in our hurry, we ran past the grand old hospital, over the Susquehanna, we ran fleet and breathless to the Ambassador's house, and then we burst inside.

The house was extraordinarily hot, the chandelier in the hallway tinkling, and the ugly miniature schnauzer barked and nipped at us. Our shoes slid on the marble floor as we sped into the living room. Bookcases, Persian rugs, leather armchairs; no Pot. We flew through the door, into the library; no Pot. We ran through the hall and stopped short in the dining room.

There, my little sister was dressed in a feather boa and rhinestone starlet glasses, in her undershirt, crouching on an expensive cherry wood chair and looking at a book of birds that was at least as big as she was. She looked up at us, unsurprised, when we came in.

"Hey," she said, "Mom, Lollie, come here, look at this. This is a first edition Audubon. The Ambassador said I could have it when I'm eighteen."

"What the hell are you doing here?" my mother said, snapping from her surprise, and charging over to her. She ripped the glasses from Pot's face, and pushed her arms into her little cardigan. Pot looked up at her, her face open and wondering.

That's when the Ambassador appeared in the doorway and said, "Oh, dear. I told Miss Petra here she should have been home hours ago. But you know her and birds," and he gave a tinkly little laugh.

"You," I said, charging at him. "What in the fuck are you doing with my sister? Why is she in her undershirt?"

"Pot," my mother was saying at the same time. "Has he touched you? Has he hurt you? Has he done anything to you?"

131

The Ambassador blinked, his milky eyes canny. "Oh, my," he said mildly. "Oh, I'm afraid there's been a misunderstanding. Pot told me you knew she visited with me."

"We did *not*," I said. "Are you hurting her?"

Pot gave a little bark of surprise. "Oh, God," she said. "No. Jeez, you guys. I mean, like. I don't think he even. You know. Girls," she trailed off.

We looked at her.

She sighed. "No girls. He doesn't like them," she said.

My mother and I looked at the Ambassador, who flushed, ducked his head. "Well," he said. "Well, Petra. Oh, my. But yes, you are right. And no, I have never touched Petra. She comes here after school, and I give her one object of her choice every week. I have no heirs, you know," he said. "I have so many beautiful things. Petra is an original. She is a pleasure to talk to. She will one day be something great, I warrant."

"He lets me wear a boa," said Pot. "He lets me be a movie star. He knew Grace Kelly. And it's always hot in here so I have to take off my sweater. It's always one hundred degrees exactly. I *die* if I don't take off my sweater."

"Yes. I'm afraid I am anemic," the Ambassador said delicately. "I cannot bear cold." He looked at our shoes, dripping slush onto his fine floors. He said, "Could I make some tea for you before you three ladies return home?"

My mother and I stared at the Ambassador for a very long moment. And then, in shame, we gathered ourselves up. We apologized, we clutched our little Pot tightly to us. And he, ever the statesman, pretended we hadn't offended him. "These times," he sighed, escorting us to the door, where the wind had blown a great heap of powder onto the priceless rug. "In these dark days, there is so much distrust in this town. I understand absolutely. You never know quite what to think about people you believe you trust." Then he shivered, and Pot reached up and squeezed his hand. In the glance between the two there was such adoration that, on the long walk through the dark, I stole small looks at Pot to try to see what exactly he had seen in her, the budding wonder he saw. The one she would become, in time.

It took a lot of time. Templeton could not heal quickly. There was still much scandal, many divorces, many people leaving town to start over. The dentist I had been to all my life. The school custodian, the principal, the football coach. My postman; the town librarian; my best friend's brother; the owner of the boatyard; the manager of the Purple Pickle; the CFO of the baseball museum, all divorced. Brad Huxley sent to military school. The Garbageman moved to Manhattan, though his trucks still rumble by every Thursday morning. And there were many more.

But the newscasters trickled away when a professional football player killed his wife, and charged the country with a new angst. The tourists returned as if nothing had happened, and there were motorboats again on the lake, my tearful graduation, the Death-by-Chocolate binge the night before I drove off to school. The Chens were shipped back to China, and the girls were taken to San Francisco, where most of them decided to make a new life. To heal. I read of their trial in the *Templeton Journal*, from the safety of my dorm room my freshman year. In the end, time smoothed it all away.

But for those of us who return periodically, there is always a little *frisson* of darkness that falls over us when we see the candy shop where the Lucky Chow Fun once had been.

Only now, many years later, can I imagine what the real tragedy had been. It had not been the near-death of my town, though that was where all my sympathy was at the time. I mourned the community that almost buckled under the scandal, for the men in the town, for our women. How we were split. As was my training, I forgot about the poor Lucky Chow Fun girls. Only now, years later, do I dream of them.

Once upon a time there were seven girls. They were girls like any other girls, no cleverer, no more or less wealthy than others in their town. They were pretty as young girls are always pretty, blooming, rose-cheeked, lily-skinned. The factory they worked in was gray, the machines they worked on were gray, the nighttime streets they walked back to their crowded apartments, all gray. But they dreamt in colors, in blues, and greens, and golds.

One dark night, the girls' parents closed the doors. Conferred. When they came out, the girls were told: we are sending you to America. There should have been joy in this, but the parents' smiles were also taut with fear.

How much? the girls asked, trembling.

Enough, the parents responded, meaning: Enough money, enough of your questions.

And the seven girls were taken to the docks. They crawled into the boxes, they were sealed inside with the water and candy and pills. There, with the bones of their knees pressed to the bones of their ribs, hearing the roar of the tanker, they saw nothing in the darkness but more darkness.

They arrived, weak and trembling. They were unpacked. They were taken to the house where they were trained to be quiet, absent, to press themselves to the mattresses and not say a word. In that house, they slowly became ghosts.

The seven ghosts were put then into the van, driven to the cold town on the lake, where nobody knew who they were, nobody cared if they were living or dead, where they cooked silently, cleaned silently, lay on the mattresses, and did not say a word. Men went into their rooms, men left their rooms, other men came in.

One ghost stopped eating, and she died. In the middle of the night, the ghosts were forced to row her to the middle of the black lake. They tied her limbs to grease buckets filled with stones, and they dropped her in. She sank under the water and seemed to blink up at them as she went. The ghosts rowed back. Wordless, as always.

Then there were six ghosts. The two that were sisters were punished, locked into a room. The air was bad, and one died, the other almost did. And one of the remaining ghosts found the dead girl and her half-dead sister. She touched the blue cheeks of the dead girl, and she only felt cold. Something old rose in her, some small courage. She stole one moment with the phone, spoke words, clumsy, ugly, perhaps, but those words breathed life back into the girls, brought liberty in the form of flashing red and blue lights.

In the end, after the long trial, the men who'd imprisoned them were imprisoned themselves. The girls went to San Francisco, where they chose to stay, where, slowly, they went out into the streets. They saw the green of the water, the gold of the sky, and they learned what it meant to be girls again. I imagine them there, together, walking in some garden, their hair gleaming under the sun. I imagine them happy.

And it is a happy ending, perhaps, in the way that myths and fairy tales have happy endings; only if one forgets the bloody, dark middles, the fifty dismembered girls in the vat, the parents who sent their children into the woods with only a crust of bread. I like to think it's a happy ending, though it is the middle that haunts me.

Nominated by Ploughshares

GULF MUSIC

by ROBERT PINSKY

from POETRY

Mallah walla tella bella. Trah mah trah-la, la-la-la,
Mah la belle. Ippa Fano wanna bella, wella-wah.

The hurricane of September 8, 1900 devastated
Galveston, Texas. Some 8,000 people died.

The Pearl City almost obliterated. Still the one worst
Calamity in American history, Woh mallah-walla.

Eight years later Morris Eisenberg sailing from Lubeck
Entered the States through the still-wounded port of Galveston.

1908, eeloo hotesy, hotesy-ahnoo, hotesy ahnoo mi-Mizraim.
Or you could say "Morris" was his name. A Moshe.

Ippa Fano wanna bella woh. The New Orleans musician called
Professor Longhair was named Henry Roeland Byrd.

Not heroic not nostalgic not learnëd. Made-up names:
Hum a few bars and we'll homme-la-la. Woh ohma-dallah.

Longhair or Henry and his wife Alice joined the Civil Defense
Special Forces 714. Alice was a Colonel, he a Lieutenant.

Here they are in uniforms and caps, pistols in holsters.
Hotesy anno, Ippa Fano trah ma dollah, tra la la.

Morris took the name "Eisenberg" after the rich man from
His shtetl who in 1908 owned a town in Arkansas.

Most of this is made up, but the immigration papers did
Require him to renounce all loyalty to Czar Nicholas.

As he signed to that, he must have thought to himself
The Yiddish equivalent of *No Problem*, Mah la belle.

Hotesy hotesy-ahno. Wella-mallah widda dallah,
Mah fanna-well. A townful of people named Eisenberg.

The past is not decent or orderly, it is made-up and devious.
The man was correct when he said it's not even past.

Look up at the waters from the causeway where you stand:
Lime causeway made of grunts and halfway-forgettings

On a foundation of crushed oyster shells. Roadbed
Paved with abandonments, shored up by haunts.

Becky was a teenager married to an older man. After she
Met Morris, in 1910 or so, she swapped Eisenbergs.

They rode out of Arkansas on his motorcycle, well-ah-way.
Wed-away. "Mizraim" is Egypt, I remember that much.

The storm bulldozed Galveston with a great rake of debris,
In the September heat the smell of the dead was unbearable.

Hotesy hotesy ahnoo. "Professor" the New Orleans title
For any piano player. He had a Caribbean left hand,

A boogie-woogie right. Civil Defense Special Forces 714
Organized for disasters, mainly hurricanes. Floods.

New Orleans style borrowing this and that, ah wail-ah-way la-la,
They probably got "714" from Joe Friday's badge number

On *Dragnet*. Jack Webb chose the number in memory
Of Babe Ruth's 714 home runs, the old record.

As living memory of the great hurricanes of the thirties
And the fifties dissolved, Civil Defense Forces 714

Also dissolved, washed away for well or ill—yet nothing
Ever entirely abandoned though generations forget, and ah

Well the partial forgetting embellishes everything all the more:
Alla-mallah, mi-Mizraim, try my tra-la, hotesy-totesy.

Dollars, dolors. Callings and contrivances. King Zulu. Comus.
Sephardic ju-ju and verses. Voodoo mojo, Special Forces.

Henry formed a group named Professor Longhair and his
Shuffling Hungarians. After so much renunciation

And invention, is this the image of the promised end?
All music haunted by all the music of the dead forever.

Becky haunted forever by Pearl the daughter she abandoned
For love, O try my tra-la-la, ma la belle, mah walla-woe.

Nominated by Poetry

CONFESSION FOR RAYMOND GOOD BIRD

fiction by MELANIE RAE THON

from AGNI

Raymond, I remember everything about the day: the heat, the rain, the cold wind after. I remember Danny was sick, bloated up like a toad and moaning on the cot, so I took the call alone, which never happens on TV, but can happen twice a week out on Rocky Boy Reservation.

The situation didn't sound extreme: one forty-four-year-old man down on the floor in his sister's kitchen. Drunk, I thought. Heat and alcohol, a bad combination. I was simple that way, prejudiced against my own people.

I figured I'd cool you down with rags and ice, take you to the river for a reservation baptism. It was Fourth of July, almost. People had been celebrating or mourning three days now. If things were worse than I thought, we'd have a rough ride, the rocky roads of Rocky Boy to the hospital in Havre, where the medicine men use masks, but not the kind we know.

Doctors in town never appear as Owl or Coyote. They don't chant or smoke to heal your heart or sing the spirit back to your body. They carry drills and knives: they want to look inside; they need to open you. Doctors in green cut and cleave, suture and staple—they have miles of gauze to bind your wounds, respirators to help you breathe, electric paddles to jump you off the table.

If you swallow twenty-seven Darvocets with a pint of gin like Arla Blue Cloud, they pump your stomach dry, but they won't love you

139

back to life—that's not part of the treaty. No hospital doctor ever pressed his ear to the flesh of Arla's womb to hear the bones of her lost children shatter.

Three months later, Arla chopped a hole in the ice and went down naked. In a dream, I'm swimming after her, and I can't breathe, and I'm so cold I'm so cold forever, but I don't care because Arla Blue Cloud is quick as a pike and laughing like an otter; Arla is blue and green, beautiful as ice and water, and I think I can see—but I can't see—straight through her.

Nothing like that was going to happen to you and me, Ray. When I got the call from your sister Marilee, she didn't whisper, *No breath, no heartbeat.*

Danny Kite, my partner, my driver, tried to sit up, but his belly bulged with poison gas, something stuck deep in the bowel—roasted squirrel or kidney pie, blue cornbread and fried okra—something he ate two nights before, harmless once, and now gone rancid.

The woman on the phone, Marilee Dancy, older sister of Caleb and Raymond Good Bird, mother of Roshelle and grandmother of baby Jeanne, cousin of Thomas Kimmel, and granddaughter of Safiya Whirling Thunder, said, *Six of us here, seven, counting Raymond.*

I told Danny plenty of people to help me lift the man, carry him to the bed, the river, the white station wagon we called our ambulance.

Whatever seemed right.

Whatever proved necessary.

I don't know why I didn't feel you, Ray, sticky as the sticky heat, already here, already gone, already breathing down my lungs, already deep inside me. I told Danny: *Sit, lie down, stay,* and like the sick little dog he was, Danny Kite obeyed me.

We're not real EMTs, not even Woofers, WFRs, Wilderness First Responders, but we did get a crash course, five hours one day in Missoula, three pink-skinned dummies to rescue and resuscitate, 1982, nine summers ago, the year we started fighting fires.

We go every year we can—Arizona, Utah, Idaho, Wyoming. *Summer vacation,* Danny says. Stomping flames and plowing firebreaks is good work for a hungry Indian. We don't throw firecrackers in the grass. We don't torch timber. We're hungry, yes, but not that crazy. We've seen our own forests blaze—Mount Sentinel, Lost Canyon. We're Chippewa-Cree, some cloudy mix with French and Oglala. We've been wandering half our lives, dazed and unemployed for a century. When the smoke signals rise, when the fire is somewhere else, we give thanks for strange mercies.

Back home on Rocky Boy, we run the ambulance, our magically rebuilt Falcon Futura. We answer anybody's call, any day, any hour. We come when the dispatcher in Havre won't answer, when there's no money and no insurance to ferry the half-dead in a real ambulance with trained medical technicians and a pulsing siren.

Maybe Nadine Hard Heart slips us two dollars for gas. Maybe her husband Kip who almost choked on a bone asks us to sit down, share their dinner: two little ducks, canned peas, a heap of instant mashed potatoes. Mostly we don't get paid, and it doesn't matter. Five terrified, not-so-hard-hearted children breathe their silent praise, and we feel lucky. Seven months later, one of those skinny kids appears at the door with three pounds of elk steak to sustain us on our journeys. Luisa Hard Heart's offering means her father survived, lived to hunt again, met the elk face to face high on a ridge in the Bear Paw Mountains. Now there's food to spare: this flesh, his flesh, our flesh, a miracle.

Danny and I don't keep track. It isn't necessary. We do this for us, all of us, our people, because we learned one day with pale dummies how to breathe into another man's body, how to slow the blood from a severed artery, how to pump a child's heart with our hands, how to count and not stop and keep our faith, the old one. We don't have a choice: things you know but don't use eat you inside out, starved weasels biting hard, furious in your belly.

Saving you is saving me. It's not a good deed: it's my own body.

Looking at Danny rolling on the cot, I thought I'd have to resuscitate him before helping you. *Stay*, I said. *Trust me*, I said, like a fool.

We were boys together, Danny Kite and me, one mother and one father between us. We'd rescued each other plenty of times. I rolled him home in a wheelbarrow the day he flew off Wendy Wissler's roof and broke his ankle. Six-year-old Danny pulled my head out of a pail the morning I passed out proving how long I could stay under water. In a summer storm, we scrambled into the highest branches of a ponderosa pine to let the wind thrash us side to side; to spin, to heave, to be the storm, to think like wind and rain, to be that wild. Danny's father Earl had to climb the tree twice to save us.

One January night, my father drank six shots of tequila and walked out into the snow barefoot and naked. He wanted to prove that the

141

real world is beyond this one, that everything here is only a shadow, that fire could not scar and ice would not burn him. We found the man two days later, the blue shadow of him, and it was true: nothing before or after seemed real.

Danny's mother lived in Billings, in prison, sixteen years for forging a hundred-dollar check. Joella Kite wanted bourbon and cigarettes, a pink blouse embroidered with white daisies. She brought us banana cream pie and frozen Cool Whip, Orange Crush and spicy tortilla chips. I remember thinking nobody on Rocky Boy had ever been this happy.

Then Joella was gone, but between our houses, we had a whole family, and so it was: Danny Kite and I loved each other as brothers.

Trust me, I said when your sister Marilee called. Trust was all we had. Trust and luck and some kind of weird, hopeful vision.

My mother Pauline died of a toothache. *Abscess*, the doctor told us. *If she'd come to town in time, we could have taken the tooth, drained the hole, given her antibiotics.* I suppose he meant to comfort us with knowledge. In Pauline's little house on Rocky Boy, bacteria spilled into her blood and brain. My mother's feet and hands and ears turned black before Hector Slow Child found her. She said, *I don't think we'll make it. Please*, she said, *just lie down here beside me.*

Danny's father died of old age at forty-seven. Earl Kite drowned in his own bed, wheezing with emphysema, rattled by double pneumonia. *It's a good day*, he said. *I'm tired.* Joella Kite got out but went back and got out again and drove into a semi.

Now we were orphans.

Raymond, I see your face, a dark brown Chippewa face, pocked and pitted deep, like lava that bubbled up from the center of the earth to cool rough and ravaged on the surface. Raymond Good Bird, scarred by acne or disease, scorched like the earth itself, a face that revealed the suffering of a thousand homeless Indians or the aftermath of some spooky chemical explosion—like the trees of Vietnam, you'd erupted.

Yours was a face to love: without love, there was no way to look at you.

Marilee's kitchen steamed. Your sister had been simmering beans all day, frying bread and onions. She'd boiled up two sad, sorry, reservation chickens to shred the meat and make fajitas, a family feast to welcome you home, Raymond Good Bird, their soldier returned from the jungle war, then lost again, twenty-two years, working tug-

142

boats, hauling garbage, killing rats and roaches, grinding fat and flesh to stuff sausages, hosing hogs, plucking cherries, lying down drunk in the street and waking up half-frozen in jail—losing three toes, losing two fingers—Raymond found, Raymond recovered, Raymond come home at last only to lie down and die in the heat of your sister's kitchen.

You were skinny as a skinny chicken yourself, blistered from childhood and all the diseases of all our ancestors, wounded three times in the war, three times before, four times after it: firecracker, hand grenade, white boy's BB gun, brother's arrow—fishing knife, M-16, electric drill, broken bottle—shrapnel in the thigh, straight-edge razor across the belly.

Raymond Good Bird, cut up inside every hour of every day from the war you'd fought and the wars that killed you, sliced for forty-four years and sewed back together with invisible thread, invisible sinew of the last white buffalo.

You had no alcohol in your blood today, nothing to preserve you, only the homemade root beer you'd been drinking with your big sister Marilee and your blind, toothless grandmother Safiya. Your brother Caleb and cousin Thomas snuck nips out back and pretended nobody noticed, but you stayed straight to be with Marilee and your niece Roshelle. You stayed sober to hold Roshelle's baby Jeanne, eight months old and already speaking some secret language.

I see you eating chillies from a jar, ten green jalapeños and seven fiery orange habarneros. The buzz was quick, but the burn lingered. Thomas and Caleb swallowed their peppers whole, a wild Raymond-Good-Bird-welcome-home contest.

You cradled wide-eyed, wonderful baby Jeanne against your wounded chest, and Roshelle, too beautiful for whiteman's words, Marilee's I've-come-to-break-your-heart daughter, gazed at you as if you were the child's long-lost beloved father.

Roshelle was just a baby herself the last time you saw her, round baby Roshelle two years old when you dressed up as a soldier boy and said goodbye forever. She kissed you on the mouth this morning and swore she remembered. She kissed you on each pitted cheek. *Uncle Ray.* She held you tight—scrawny, pocked you—and you felt whole and young, pressed up that way against her just-turned-into-a-woman, just-became-a-mother body.

Lovely she was, your niece, long and lovely, smooth, as tall as you and much stronger, like Marilee before she swelled, soft and warm to touch like your mother Minnie before cancer curved her spine and turned her skin yellow.

In the light of Roshelle Dancy, in her body reflecting the morning light, *this* morning's light before the heat grew terrible, in the sweet golden light spilling through the worn-thin-as-gauze curtains, in the radiant love of Roshelle, your whole family came alive, the long-dead and unborn. All your wandering people filled the house and yard, and their voices surged, a song inside you.

That was morning, Ray, and now it was afternoon, getting on toward evening, and you rocked baby Jeanne to sleep, and you handed her back to her mother, and the silly boys came inside, not drunk, not quite, not really, and you swallowed jalapeños and habarneros, and the peppers made your head hum, and you said, *I need to sit down*, but you didn't make it.

You collapsed on the kitchen floor, and you stayed there till I found you. Now, in the thick glaze of afternoon, everything looked filthy. Bubbling beans and sizzling onions splattered; the smell of boiled chicken filled the house; orange cheese melted.

And it was hot, so hot, and I stood in the doorway, and I couldn't move: I didn't even try to help you. I've knelt over three dummies and twenty-seven real live human beings and thumped their chests to get their lungs heaving, but I saw you on the floor, and I saw something yellow above you in the terrible heat, a cloud of smoky yellow dust like the puff off a mushroom; I smelled something underneath the smell of boiled-to-smithereens chicken. Something a hundred times hotter than red chilli dust seared my nostrils; and a voice that sounded like God's if God had died with the Ghost Dancers, if God had been shoveled into a pit in the snow and buried, if God had lain dry in the dry earth for more than a century, *that* crackling voice said, *Too late, little brother*.

It could have been you, Ray, or the pinto pony at the window over the sink, or the little black dog with one white ear and one white paw that wouldn't stop yapping.

I think now it was the wind, the hot wind, the useless fan beating hot air into the hot kitchen. This voice from the whirlwind said, *Who are you?* And the voice inside my chest said, *You can't*. And the dry silence from your body said, *Don't bother*.

Maybe it's all an excuse, something I imagined after. I was scared, it's true. I don't know why you scared me.

I can still feel Roshelle's fist hammering my back, can still hear

Marilee whisper, *Do something*. The frenzied dog ripped the cloth of my pants and sank her sharp teeth into my ankle, and the little spotted horse put her whole head through the open window by the sink, and I looked at the faces of all your people—Caleb, Marilee, Roshelle, Thomas, Jeanne, Safiya—and I thought if they loved you so much, why couldn't they save you?

Once upon a time you tried to come home, but you couldn't live in peace among us. Every dark-eyed boy was one you'd killed, every child a gook, every woman your enemy. A thin teenage mother at the grocery store in Havre propped her plump baby on one hip and stared at you with unmitigated rage or benevolent wonder, her look as impenetrable as the gaze of the wounded Vietnamese mother bleeding out, five holes: chest, thigh, belly. She held her child in one arm on one hip—yes, like this—and with miraculous grace, the tiny Vietnamese woman slit her son's throat, clean and deep through the vein: so he wouldn't starve when she died, so he couldn't be spared, so you would not shoot him.

Your platoon lost thirteen men in nine days to booby traps and sniper fire. You burned the first village you found, unnamed on your lieutenant's map, just a cluster of huts at a slow bend of the Cua Viet River. You shot the people as they ran. You killed their pigs and dogs and chickens. Later, you found three women and two boys bleeding into the water. You knew these people, five slender Cheyenne cut breast to bowel and trampled at the banks of Washita, slaughtered to the joyful noise of bugles and gunfire. The ones whose thick blood swirled into the muddy Cua Viet were Pocatello's stunned Shoshone, five of the four hundred forty-three slain at Bear River. These five were Nez Perce in flight, awakened to die, skulls crushed by the boot heels and gun butts of drunken soldiers at the Big Hole.

If you opened their bodies, would you find your last word, a curse spat out and long forgotten? What did it matter? You fired. Their blood spilled. You witnessed. You'd murdered them all: brothers, sisters, ancestors, grandchildren.

You didn't want forgiveness. You wanted the wounded Vietnamese mother to take you in her arms as her own child—to comfort, and to kill you.

For twenty-two years you lived without faith, without love or the hope of it. *Bozeman, Coeur d' Alene, Walla Walla, Wenatchee*. You thought if you moved fast enough the dead might lose your scent and stop following.

You dangled sixty feet in the air, washing windows, downtown Boise. You met yourself face to face, the blue-skinned man hanging in dark glass, flesh pocked by soap and water. You hauled thirty-seven dead sheep down a hillside west of Helena. They'd died as one, skulls fractured by lightning, the head of each sheep resting tenderly on the rump of another. They were filthy now, their gray wool rain-soaked, their shocked bodies bloated. Flies swarmed you and them. Crows and hawks and kestrels circled. You lifted them by their broken legs, you and two Colombian men who called themselves Jesús and Eduardo, who jabbered as they worked, quick Spanish words muffled by bandannas. You tore your own rag from your mouth and nose to be with the dead, to know their smell, to breathe their bodies. The Colombian brothers laughed when they heard you choking. *Estúpido*. Even then you didn't hide your face. You heaved the pitiful animals into the bed of the rancher's truck. You saw that each face was distinct, with a certain space between the eyes, a soft curve of the mouth, a singular tilt of nose and forehead. Each one of them— and you, and Jesús, and Eduardo—secretly made, silently beloved. Why were you whole? Why were they shattered?

You left that night. *Issaquah, Butte, Aberdeen, Seattle.* You slept in the woods, in a cardboard box, in a barn with a whiteman's cow, in a bed of leaves under a freeway. You dove in dumpsters for bruised fruit, half-eaten buffalo wings, cold biscuits and gravy. You snatched three perfect blue eggs from the nest of a robin. The birds woke you for a hundred nights, beaks sharp as barbs in your lungs and liver. You stole corn from pigs and a gnawed bone from an old wolfhound. He rose on his crippled hips to tug his chain, too sick and slow to nip you. A goat gave you her milk, and for this offering you praised her.

North of Spokane, you walked up a dirt road to a weather-wracked farmhouse. You meant to ask for work mucking stalls in exchange for one meal. Nobody answered your knock, but you touched the doorknob and it turned. You breathed, and the door opened. The sweet smell of cherries sucked you inside, pulled you in a dream down a long passage to a sun-dazzled kitchen.

There it was, all for you, a cherry pie with a lattice crust, cooling on the table. In the freezer, a half-gallon tub of vanilla ice cream waited—untouched, perfectly white, unbelievably creamy.

You thought, *Just one piece or maybe a quarter.* The pie vanished. Who could blame you? You tried to stop, but you couldn't do it. In your swollen stomach, seven scoops of ice cream swirled.

Your head throbbed. You felt hot and cold at the same time, stunned by bliss and suddenly so tired. You staggered to the living room, but the couch was old, too short, too lumpy. Somehow you gathered the strength to climb the stairs. You opened three doors before you found the room you wanted, cool and dark with a wide bed and a down comforter.

You were afraid to sleep, but a voice that was your own voice gone mad and mocking said, *Why stop now? Why resist this last pleasure?* You knew you might die in this bed, victim of your own delight and a farmer's righteous fury. You woke to a woman's voice, insistent and gentle. *Mister, you best get up now, go down those stairs, and keep walking.* She was white-haired but not old—thin, but not frail. A farmer's wife, yes, without the farmer. The widow cradled an unraised rifle. She was kind: she wanted you to go, but she didn't want to scare you.

That night it rained and you slept in a child's treehouse. You crept out hours before dawn. If the boy came with his BB gun, he'd aim for your right eye and kill you.

Raymond Good Bird, twenty-two years gone. You walked close to death every hour, but somehow you survived, and then one day you came home to rest, and I let you die in your sister's kitchen.

Yesterday, Thomas said he wouldn't believe you were home till he touched you with his own hands. But he didn't touch: seeing was enough, too much in fact—Thomas wouldn't look you in the eye. *The light,* he said, *I can't do it.* Late last night, in the shelter of darkness, your delicate, almost pretty cousin Thomas picked you up, lifted you a foot off the ground and held you high to dance you in a circle dance. Your grandmother felt your face and skull, traced your chest and ribs to see you whole with her fingertips. Long after, when the others had fallen asleep on the couch and floor and single bed, your big brother pulled you close and breathed you in. Caleb, like a mother and a father now: wide shoulders, soft breasts. You were twenty-two years lost again. Rocking in his arms, you thought, *I'm him.*

Now you lay on the floor, and I heard you say, *Let the dead stay dead.*

Your brother and sister rolled you onto a wool blanket. These two, and blind Safiya, and doubting Thomas lifted you by four corners. You swung in their grip, a man in a hammock. Roshelle cradled baby Jeanne to follow behind you.

147

Marilee's turquoise Catalina sat on cement blocks in the yard, its rusted engine propped against a stump, its hood torn off, crumpled in some junkyard. Sunflowers and thistle grew high and wild in all its open spaces. Your people slid you, most beloved one, into the back of my white Falcon. Roshelle gave the baby to Thomas so that she could lie down with you, *Uncle Ray*, close, and hold you tight, *my love*, and keep you from rolling.

I resisted no one. Caleb took my keys and left me to walk seven miles. What did he care? Your people drove you to town, the dead man, the wounded-ten-times, the resurrected-and-returned-home and now dead-for-true Raymond Good Bird. They delivered you to the hospital in Havre, as if some man of faith might call you out of the cave of yourself, punch a hole in your vein or throat, split your chest, and work his miracle—as if some scrubbed nurse might forget her latex gloves, just this once, and lay her naked hands on your heart to close these last wounds, the wounds that saved, the wounds that healed you.

By then the rain had started, soft at first and still hot, more like dust than water falling, then hard and cold until the whole sky filled, a wailing, weeping rain of river.

I stood in your sister's yard, *estúpido*, cut by icy rain, jolted each time a drop hit me. At least you didn't die alone, foolish as our fathers, mine playing Crazy Horse in the snow, yours failing to jump a freight train east of Fargo. I didn't want to die today, another frozen Indian. I pictured my wife Delilah at our doorway, face blown open by the storm, long hair loose and dangerous, a tangled net whipping around her. I conjured Lulu, thin and dark, already too wise, strange and silent, old at seven. I heard tinkling Kristabelle, just three, our child of joy who burst into the world laughing.

That laughter fell from the sky, arrows of rain, sharp enough to pierce me. I dreamed myself home and safe, though I knew I didn't deserve it.

The wind spun, as if it wanted to speak, as if it were trying to become a person. I hoped to make it to Hector Slow Child's house, prayed that the man who loved my mother might let me sleep in his bed for a few hours, but I was barely a mile up the road, stung by rain, already staggering. I thought I'd fall, die here in a rut, drown in three inches of water.

God roared behind me. In a rush of breath, *his* breath, two angels thundered out of the storm, Luc Falling Bear and Leroy Enneas, my saviors, Luc driving Leroy's once-shiny-green-now-mostly-gray Torino. They didn't know yet what I'd failed to do, how I refused to kneel, refused even to try to help you. They didn't sense I was a ghost, gone like you, a dead man walking. They'd been drinking rum and Mountain Dew all day. To Luc and Leroy, I was still visible.

They were thoughtful drunks: I tried to slip in back, but they cried *no* in unison. They wanted me up front, soaked and shivering between them. They offered rum, straight from the bottle. I don't remember anything on earth for which I ever felt more grateful.

They ate corn chips with extra salt. *To stay thirsty*, Luc said. *You think drinking all day is easy?*

They were polite, the way Indians are polite. They didn't ask where I'd been or wonder aloud why I was walking. They didn't make jokes about my ambulance. They didn't mention my father.

They waited for me to speak or not speak. They lived on reservation time. They had forever.

I couldn't go home. Lulu and Kristabelle would grab my legs to pull me down on all fours and ride me like a pony. Delilah would say, *Let him go. Your father's cold and tired.* But somehow I'd find the strength to carry them, *my sweethearts, my darlings.* I'd buck and whinny. I'd be myself again, whole, Jimi Shay Don't Walk, father, husband, wet mustang. I wasn't ready for that much love. I thought the weight of it, of them, might crush me.

I must have said, *Drop me at Danny's*, because suddenly I was there, trembling in my brother's doorway. Without Luc and Leroy close, my skin hardly held my bones together. There he was, Danny the betrayed who didn't know it, Danny Boy curled up like a baby, smiling in his sleep, soothed by the sound of rain, back inside his mother's body.

Danny Kite was his thin self again, and I could smell the stink coming from the toilet, his bowels clean at last, the dam burst wide open. My Danny woke all sweet and groggy. He said, *Sorry, brother,* and, *How did it go?* And I said, *Fine, everything's fine.* I said, *Everything happened just the way it was supposed to happen.*

Let him sleep in peace, I thought. *Let the story find him.*

There are stories I like to tell, things I believe though I can't prove them. Sometimes I think Hector Slow Child is my real father, that he came to my mother as starlight falling through an open window, a constellation broken on her bed, the Great Bear, the White Buffalo.

My wife tells another story, how her mother died with Delilah

149

inside her. Nona Windy Boy skidded on ice, side-swiped Martin Cendesie's truck, and rolled fifty feet down a gully. *Brain dead*, the doctor told her husband Joseph. *Fractured ribs—fractured feet, femurs, pelvis. No hope*, he whispered. *Fractured skull, massive hemorrhage.*

Somehow Delilah lived. Delilah, unborn, rocked herself to sleep in a windy cradle. The doctor stood amazed, listening to her heart beat. Softly he said, *We should take the baby now while we can save her.*

Joseph saw tiny flecks of his wife's blood spattered on the young man's glasses. Joseph said, *Let the child stay inside as long as her mother wants her.*

Nona's mother and Auntie Bea chanted thirteen days and thirteen nights without ceasing. I tell you now: on the fourteenth day, Nona Windy Boy breathed again, no respirator. She lived thirty-four more days, and the child came in her own time of her own will, and the mother with her own breath released her.

Delilah says, *I'm my father's bitter miracle.*

Delilah says, *My mother turned herself into a trout and swam down into her own womb and swallowed me and kept me safe for seven weeks until I got too big to hold and then my mother writhed three times and spat me out to live in the world without her.*

Nona never opened one eye to see her child. Auntie Bea swore she laughed when the baby howled, but the nurse who witnessed said, *The poor woman was finally choking.*

Tonight, when I lie in Delilah's arms, when we lie entwined, her long arms and long legs wrapped around me, when I tell her our story in the dark, the story of Raymond Good Bird and Jimi Shay Don't Walk, my wife will say, *Not everybody wants to be saved. Not every body can bear it.*

Raymond, three months ago you took a real job, the first you wanted to keep, as a janitor, a custodian at Lewis & Clark Elementary School in Missoula. The urinals set to a child's height, the little desks, the low mirrors, the windows decorated with butterflies and birds broke your heart, and you let them. You wanted to hurt, and the hurt was love, and love roared back into you. You stole children's drawings from the walls and took them home to your motel, the River's Edge, a run-down dive where you paid by the week to live among prostitutes and addicts, where you shared bread and beans with bewildered half-bloods.

A little girl named Tania colored a family of bright angels—
mother, father, sister, brother—even the purple dog had a halo. Max
and Arturo drew a house on fire and a galaxy exploding. Coral
painted a child in a garden where red tulips grew taller than she was.
Darnell Lasiloo saw seventeen Appaloosas from the sky, as if he were
God, as if he were White Bird in flight over the Bear Paws. The spot-
ted horses lay on their sides, all sixty-eight legs splayed, all sixty-eight
legs visible. The ponies seemed to float along a trail of tears beside a
winding river. You taped the pictures to your walls and door and mir-
ror. So many children alive to love! The miracle was endless. The
dead whispered through the radiators. *Don't forget us.* They wished
you no harm. They were hungry, like the rest of us. You saved six dol-
lars the first week and nineteen the week after. You thought someday
soon you'd send all your extra money and a child's vision home to
Roshelle and your sister.

One night in a whiteman's bar, a half-Kootenai, half-Mexican
woman danced you across the room, and you thought this was the
end of hope, your last possibility. She asked you to come home with
her, to her trailer up a rutted road north of Evaro. She was twenty-
seven years older and fifty pounds heavier than you, but still, in your
eyes, beautiful. You refused. Refused even to kiss, though her mouth
looked soft as a girl's mouth. Her face was scarred, it's true, pocked as
yours, but her lips bloomed full and ready. *No, please.* You thought if
you kissed her once, you'd never stop kissing.

Fear made you unkind, and for this you were sorry.

The heads of elk curving out from the walls, the bighorn sheep,
the pronghorn antelopes all watched you drink your beer and crack
your nuts and keep your silence. The big Kootenai woman, Mag-
dalena Avalos, drifted away to dance alone, and then to spin with a
one-armed man by the jukebox. Three whitemen in the booth behind
you bragged about the ducks they'd slaughtered last autumn. The
creatures made a terrifying sound, mallards and pintails hissing and
chewing. The first three shots cleared a path: dozens lay strewn,
wounded and dying. The others rose, a jabbering cloud. The men
fired again, three more shots, then another three—that was all it
took—the sky opened. They stood stupid in a rain of ducks, stunned
by a storm of feathers. A hundred and eight birds dropped dead be-
tween them. They laughed now, remembering the crime, ninety-nine
ducks past the limit. The men spent all day gutting and plucking.

You tried to be Tonto, one of those two-syllable wooden Indians,

151

but your thoughts roared, and the men must have heard them. You looked into the eyes of the auburn bear whose head and skin hung from the ceiling, and you meant to whisper only to him, but your heart betrayed you.

Father, you cried, *Father, forgive them.*

Then you laughed a wild Indian laugh and you whooped one last wild whoop and the three white hunters lifted you high and danced you out into the alley, not in a tender way, not soft like Magdalena. They pushed you to your knees. They wanted you to be sorry.

You were sorry: for the ducks and the elk and the bear and the children, for the sheep on the hill and a black man in Florida, electrocuted twice because the first time the chair sparked and fizzled and he didn't die: only his hair and slippers caught fire. His picture in the paper last week looked so familiar, so much like you, you taped it on your mirror, beneath the bright angel family.

The men wanted you to pray, and you wanted this too, wanted to believe in a god that hears, and comes, and loves in mercy. Your pants were torn, your knees scraped, your palms full of grit and bloody. You felt the first kick and the second, and the blow to the back of your head, and you closed your eyes, and the god who answers in mysterious ways spared you all joy and pain, all desire, all language.

You woke in the moonlight, face down on the rocks by the Bitterroot River. They must have dumped you here, and you thought, *This is fine,* and you saw ponies swimming and a dog with a halo. When you woke again, Magdalena Avalos and her one-armed friend Gideon Daro were rolling you up in a tarp and carrying you to her Chevy. They were strong, these two, despite age and afflictions. Gideon had a story like yours, an arm of his own left back in the jungle.

In her trailer, in her bed, Magdalena splinted your broken fingers with sticks and bandaged your slashed belly with rags torn from a child's Superman pajamas. *Try not to move,* she said. *You're leaking.*

Twenty-two years you'd waited for this. You loved your own precious life. You couldn't help it. You wanted to stay alive—one more hour, one more day—to lie here like this while a woman who wasn't afraid touched you.

When you were strong enough to kiss, you kissed. When you could dance, you danced Magdalena Avalos out under the stars. She wore a heavy shawl, sewn with acorns and shells and juniper berries. It opened and closed, violet and green, one great wing whirling around you. It sang with its thousand bells, this shawl with a voice like no other. You fell in the tall grass. You thought you had fallen forever.

But Magdalena wouldn't let you stay. She said, *If you have a home, go home. If anybody wants to love you, let them.*

Twenty-two years, and then you were home, holding baby Jeanne in your sister's kitchen. Blessed was the God who hears, who had kept you alive and sustained you and delivered you whole to this moment. Blessed was Roshelle's kiss full and wet on your sweet mouth in the soft light of morning. Blessed was the child you held, the child reborn, the one come to save you.

Your people thought you'd stay for days and years to come.

The living, the left behind, the bereft think of all the days unlived—tomorrow and tomorrow. But you thought only of today, each holy moment. Blessed was this God who belonged to no one, who was the spark in all things, in everyone, everywhere. Blessed was this life, not held, not in you alone, not contained in one body: *this* life, *this* God, moving here as breath, as light, as love between you.

The wounded Vietnamese mother took you in her arms at last, Raymond Good Bird, her own, her most beloved child. Blessed was the mother of God. You and she knew only comfort.

Nominated by Michael Martone, Erin McGraw, Agni

WAVES

by GRACE SCHULMAN

from CIMARRON REVIEW

The burst, the lilt and rock, the wheel of spray,
the flash of waves exploding in hard rain.

Perhaps they are the dead, their watermark
the signatures of shipwrecked passengers,

or coded messages from men and women
desperate to tell what they have seen.

Speed, thunder, surprise. The jarring thump
of low bass drums, the dancer's leap and bow,

the gospel singer's growl, the pause, the shout,
dodging the beat, notes jammed with syllables,

the hums, mumbles, and cries, the choruses,
cymbals that gleam in sudden white-gold light.

Breakers roared when Caedmon sang Creation
in a new verse with the rhythmic pull of oars.

Rollers boom on a shore I cannot see
and tie me to flood-dead, quake-dead, war-dead,

disaster-dead, or dead ripped from the stars.
As I trudge in the shallows, sliding in wrack,

order snapped apart like a broken string,
each end still aloft, trembling in air,

the sea ahead, the roadways drowned behind,
a wave shimmers, taking its time to fall.

How all that matters is to stand fast
on the ridge that's left, and hear the music.

Nominated by Arthur Smith, Joan Murray, Marilyn Hacker, Philip Appleman

JUICE

by PAUL ALLEN

from THE SOUTHERN REVIEW

Behind me it is tomorrow. I'm on the outer edge of the troposphere, my body numbed by the vibration of some six million airplane parts holding together at 600 miles per hour. Somewhere between the Southern Cross over Zimbabwe and the last scene in *Spiderman*, I've entered the hemisphere I know. Toilets will flush counterclockwise again. The hot water spigot will be on the left, and light switches will go up for *on*, down for *off*. I'm told that dogs will circle the other way before lying down. Six weeks of trying to pay attention, and I never noticed how my host's Rhodesian Ridgeback gets ready for bed.

But I'll be able to understand the logic of the newspaper's classifieds again. In Harare, I found guitars—under *L*. Silly me, and I was looking under *M* for music, *G* for guitars, even *I* for instruments (musical). Why *L*? "Lead and Rhythm Guitars."

My little entertainment screen, which looks straight into the medulla oblongata of the snoozing Afrikaner in the seat before me, no longer shows the little airplane symbol indicating where we are—probably a good thing, since there's nothing below us but the Mid-Atlantic Ridge. I suspect British Airways will let us see ourselves again when a continent appears to be within swimming distance if we go down; it's good psychology. But we're so in the middle of nowhere that we've been given a movie—several of them—to keep us entertained (read, *distracted*). And we've been given juice, lots of it.

Why Zimbabwean poetry? I don't know, except that just shy of sixty, I'd been in a funk about poetry in general for a few years. I was

156

hoping for rejuvenation. Well, also my host invited me, and like other academics, I wanted to come up with a project in my field for a grant to go. The trip, I know now, was one of those trying-to-recapture experiences which those of us who've moved beyond middle age get. Some men my age collect younger women, twinks, or older cars. I suppose if I could get a grant for a '64 Mustang, I'd jump at it. When I was planning my trip—and a shoddy plan it was—I had little idea that Zimbabwe's poetry was anything but a few noted authors like Charles Mungoshi or Musaemura Zimunya. I had heard of Flora Veit-Wild, one of the top scholars on Zimbabwean poetry, but didn't have her *Patterns of Poetry in Zimbabwe* (1988) until I arrived.

I might have been looking for the poetry of my youth, or even of my in-full-career days. I first became passionate about poetry when I was in college. I knew nothing about it; not the history, the schools, the difference between an image and an abstraction. But I read Carl Sandburg until I was lost in the elegance of the teeming masses; reading him was a resurrection into some other world where people and beauty and cities and plains mattered. I wore out two copies of Lawrence Ferlinghetti's *A Coney Island of the Mind* (1958) in as many years. Percy B. Shelley made me cry; Walt Whitman's erotic lines gave me an erection. Ronnie and I would sit on top of a car in a field drinking beer, quoting Robert Burns until dawn. The "quality" of the poetry was all about the quality of the feeling I got. Naïve, of course. But I miss it.

I'm only just now realizing that I probably miss it because the passion was replaced, seamlessly, by a different enthusiasm. Intuitive love became calculated awe, "blown away" by idea became admiration of epizeuxis. With the schools, the degrees, the professional lecture replacing reading aloud to friends, my interest in myself turned into an interest in how a poem was made. The exchange slipped in on me.

I thought my students would enjoy poetry even more if they understood the technique of the poet, the craft, because I believed that was what had happened to me. Not so. I didn't enjoy the poem more, just in a different way, different poems.

No matter. I doubt that one can be enamored with Carl Sandburg's poems and wowed by Geoffrey Hill's poems at the same stage of his aesthetic development. That's probably OK. Fascination with craft lasted me a long time, a career, in fact. But by the time the fad of L=A=N=G=U=A=G=E poetry was hot, it was too late for me. I didn't have the mind or energy for Mikhail Bakhtin or Jacques Derrida, and

157

the poems just looked like typing tricks. There was not even enough in them for me to dislike. The slam poetry I encountered—change that: During the one slam event I subjected myself to, I kept wondering, "Why are these people yelling at me?" Three blocks away I still felt like I was hearing, "You just wait till your father gets home, young man!"

So looking for a kind of rejuvenation, I went to Zimbabwe. I thought I would meet contemporary poets and introduce myself to the poetry one can't get through American presses or stores. I thought I was looking for something that would make reading poetry pleasurable again.

The state of the country under President Mugabe makes finding poets a bit difficult. All but one interview I'd planned fell through. At present I know only a little more about Zimbabwean poetry, and that little is thanks to the Zimbabwe International Book Fair (ZIBF) and the Harare hub for writers, the Book Café. What I know, though, is what I knew about poetry of the United States and hadn't quite come to grips with: I'm not very interested in poetry at all anymore, as art anyway. I remember years ago John Frederick Nims's telling me, "I don't like poetry. There are just certain poems I like." I understand that better now.

Trying to locate authors in a phone book that seems to have been created as a test in chaos theory, with computer-generated numbers, is difficult. Three-fourths of the numbers I called were incorrect. And some of the poets must keep a low profile for political reasons. So I began at the ZIBF, an annual event hosted in the Harare Gardens, adjacent to the excellent National Gallery, the primary repository for Zimbabwean stone sculpture. (On technical grounds, some critics avoid the term Shona sculpture, since the sculpture is also Ndebele, a coexistent though minority culture in Zimbabwe). With Veit-Wild's book, I picked up several others. There were plenty available, poets and presses working hard. I bought a library. Books are cheaper there, and a collection that at Barnes & Noble might require my getting a second mortgage can be purchased with US $100–120. Coming from the southeastern United States, browsing on a bright, hot winter day, I was enchanted to encounter at ZIBF these words first: "In the heart of Appalachia,// parts of Africa and Asia too,/ prosperity is talked about,/known by its absence, like God or a lost tooth" ("Lament of the Third World Worker," in *Footprints about the Bantustan* by Tafataona Mahoso).

Back at my host's house, sitting down in my nest of books, I began my disenchantment. As I read, I remembered Veit-Wild's comment on the poetry of the sixties and seventies:

> I find the Zimbabwean poetry of those years, stylistically, rather shapeless, unstructured, discursive and non-lyrical. Poetry as a craft with its special means of rhythm, sounds, images, metaphors, etc. had not been explored enough or used in such a way as to open to the reader a different dimension of perception, feeling or spiritual experience. . . . Many of the Zimbabwean poems of that time to me appear crude, clumsy, heavy and undigested.

I was gathering the same conclusion about poetry of the eighties and nineties as well.

Most Zimbabwean poetry is like most American poetry—dull, cliché-ridden, and self-indulgent. Zimbabwe is a beautiful land populated by some of the most pleasant people in the world. No one can come out of Zimbabwe without a better attitude toward human beings. And there are wonderful resorts. I took a vacation from my reading to go on a week's safari. In the southern region, elegant safari camps are built into the hills. In the more central regions, one stays in comfortable tree houses, wakes to elan grazing below. These are built in national game preserves and parks, and with the handsome, friendly people, anyone with a couple thousand dollars who wants to take the family on the vacation of a lifetime ought to go. The mostly Dutch and French families I met around the fire when the Land Rovers came in agreed that the Western press gives Zimbabwe a bad rap. The resorts and lodges have few tourists, yet offer a rich world to experience.

But in the other world, the political world—where AIDS kills hundreds per day; where the people are beginning to starve; where drought has been around so long that it's a way of life; where the long queues are broken by an occasional scuffle for mealie-meal or sugar; where the largest segment of the workforce labor as maids, gardeners, and guards for European expats—one damned well has the right to be self-indulgent in her poems.

In *Chronicles* (2004) Bob Dylan recollects standing at a window, having recently arrived as a pup in New York City:

Across the way a guy in a leather jacket scooped frost off the windshield of a snow-packed black Mercury Montclair. Behind him, a priest in a purple cloak was slipping through the courtyard of the church through an opened gate on his way to perform some sacred duty. Nearby, a bareheaded woman in boots tried to manage a laundry bag up the street. There were a million stories, just everyday New York things if you wanted to focus on them. It was always right out in front of you, blended together, but you'd have to pull it apart to make any sense of it.

For most of my career, the poems that I read and wrote "pulled it apart" to make sense of individual moments. But the poetry of Zimbabwe, in my view, is panic poetry, uttering statements about issues and meaning, none of which is much different from others. It's as though each poem is saying, "I don't have time to be a neat little package—the world's collapsing." I guess that's what comes of poets living in a milieu of death, disease, and disappointed hope in a black leader, one of their own. The poetry tends to be an inarticulate scream out across the flatlands, the great expanses of fallow farms, rather than a collection of individual voices singing particular songs.

But what kind of poem would we in the United States write if, say, our house were on fire and we had to complete a poem before we escaped? I doubt that we would have the wherewithal to compose like William Carlos Williams:

> So much depends
> upon
>
> a red wheel
> barrow
>
> glazed with rain
> water
>
> beside the white
> chickens.

In Zimbabwean poetry, most often, I don't get to experience the moments. Speakers and characters seem mere stick figures, even in a love poem. I feel the broad strokes of its "big meaning" keep readers at a distance from the syllables and lines. It's as though while we're in a poem by a Zimbabwean either unknown or famous, we're listening to a communal, even generic voice. This is true even in works by a major poet like Charles Mungoshi. Here are lines from "Home" (1986):

> Home . . .
> Aftermath of an invisible war
> A heap of dust and rubble
> White immobile heat on the sweltering land
> Home . . . the sharp-nosed vulture
> already smells carrion—
> the ancient woman's skirts
> give off an odour of trapped time
> Home . . .
> Return science to its owners
> The witch demands a ransom for your soul
> Your roots claim their rightful pound of clay

Here's an example of a poem that plays with sound, a little heavy-handedly to my ear, only to abruptly terminate the play in the final stanza. It's "Beneath the Glare," from Musaemura Zimunya's *Country Dawns and City Lights* (1985):

> Beneath the glare of the lamp
> under the stare of the light
> he left some pus
> neon-watched knife-blood
> trickle and dry to a plastic crater.
>
> The dog that roamed and sniffed the city
> escaped a stone thrown
> trajected from the red-light district
> with a curse and laughter
>
> and ran stiffly.
>
> His gait resisted the anger of humans,
> defied disgust and authority.

Where is your morality?
Beneath the glare of the lamp
under the stare of the light
love and death made a deathly embrace.

The next example, "I Collapsed" by Titus Moetsabi, shows what I mean by a sense of panic beginning midpoint, a voice that lacks verisimilitude, a rush to get it all said at once. It begins at a measured pace, but at the beginning of stanza two, it seems he's discovered the house is on fire, and he hurries. Here is the whole poem:

Friends
When your death
Reached my ears
I was preparing dinner
In the kitchen
I collapsed

I have seen those robbed
Of relatives
Dead in the face
And hopeless
When it was a natural death
But
Assassins butchered you
Sadists dragged you
Dug many holes
Ripped your stomachs
Punctured your noses
Slit your throats
Slashed your ears
And fled

No good Samaritan was near
To rescue
Nor authority keen
To investigate

Friends
With others already gone.

This poem is typical of the problems I see in the greater part of Zimbabwean poetry, black Zimbabwean poetry anyway: awkward music, overreliance on abstraction, collapse of meaning or structural integrity in their later stanzas. I was not really interested in the poetry written by white Zimbabweans and am unable to understand the Shona or Ndebele, though I enjoy the music of that poetry more.

All of Zimbabwean poetry in English is informed by orality yet it doesn't demonstrate the rhythms of English speech. English is the nation's official language, but the people begin their speech and hearing in Shona or Ndebele. From their poetry in English, I get an impression similar to one made by our creative writing undergraduate students back home: Most of those have not decided whether to go for the sometimes dull, well-made MFA type of poem, or for the wilder, broader sweeps of performance poetry. So we get a kind of amalgam, often a prosy stew. Anyway, I don't know why Zimbabwean poets want to write in English. The sculptors seem to have found a more truthful voice than the poets; only a clod would call the sculpture "primitive." If I were a publisher, I'd have bilingual books with a CD of poets reading in Shona or Ndebele.

Hearing Shona or Ndebele songs and poems is a beautiful experience. Many citizens will sing them, though most are rather reluctant to give the appearance of showing off to strangers—a charming reticence. Safari guides are more used to performing, and several safari lodges have a staff chorus who will sing in the evening; many hotels and night spots have such entertainment as well. At the Book Café in Harare and at similar venues in Bulawayo there are mbira bands, with pickups for their amps attached with Duct tape, that create a magnificent mix of African language and English. Three or four mbira, or African thumb pianos, played well, draw one in like a spell. As with America's hip-hop, the music that accompanies the performance poetry redeems what would otherwise be uninteresting. The rhythms and sounds are haunting.

Of all the poets and poems I found, few match the beauty of the song delivered at Cecil Rhodes's funeral. This seriously funny farewell sung to the gods translates, "Forgive us, we are burying a white man (outsider)." Our guide sang it for us several times at my request while he and I stood at Rhodes's burial site and watched the sun go down on the red rocks from what Rhodes called "View of the World." Guides will take you to Rhodes's grave marker, a brass plate set in granite, and they will ask whether you want to hear their

163

canned spiel about Rhodes—the railroad and such—but they are also glad not to give it to you. Cecil Rhodes is not venerated among the indigenous peoples, although they are too charitable to speak his name through clenched teeth, as southerners do the name "Sherman" in my home state of South Carolina. Silence or unadorned facts deliver the message, though.

There is the Ndebele proverb that sounds something like "*Langa lapuma lindabe, lashona lindabe,*" which translates roughly to, "The sun rises with the stories of the night, takes with it the stories of the day." This from a tourist's ear and memory. We hear "Shona" in that saying, as metaphor, because to the Ndebele, the Shona are known for running away, for leaving the hard work. It's a holdover from when the Ndebele came into the southern region from South Africa and pushed the Shona farther north.

Who's to say? Maybe the spigots are correctly placed with cold on the left, and maybe *L* is the right place for listing *guitar*. In *Chronicles* Dylan says, "I never looked at songs as either 'good' or 'bad,' only different kinds of good ones." At twenty or forty, I would not have believed that, but it's sounding more right to me now. Maybe there's no such thing as a bad poem. There is only a kind of poem for a kind of audience. If one's poems are rejected by the academic big-name journals, the poet needs to decide whether he wants to work toward writing that kind of poem, or whether he wants to find another audience—Hallmark greetings, his mother, his friends with their black berets passing around a doobie. Publishing poetry is a matter of finding an audience. And if the poet is happy with the reception her poems receive, then good on her. The problem seems to come when we write black-beret poems and then get frustrated because *The Georgia Review* doesn't take them. If I'd wanted a new poetry from Zimbabwe, I'd have had to be a new person doing the reading. I don't know who that person would have to be.

As one rambling, swing-wild student poet told me back home, "I write this kind of poem 'cause it gets me laid." Reason enough, I say. Or because my mother puts them on her refrigerator. Or because Richard Howard selects them for *The Paris Review*, *Western Humanities Review*, or any of the dozens of contests he judges. My problem at twenty or forty was in confusing "kind" and "quality."

To be accepted into the MFA club doesn't mean simply that one's poems are better than others' poems; they aren't "better" because of their "quality," they are "better" because the audience he or she approves of accepts them. Gold has no value in Moore's *Utopia*, and it makes a poor plowshare. It only has value among those who say it does, like baseball cards. Judging one poem good and another bad is like saying a Willie Mays 1953 is worth $1,050 and the Steve Lyons is worth $1.49; we need to add, "among baseball card collectors." It's that way with anything, of course, and poetry is just another thing valued by those who value it, whatever its kind. There's no ultimate standard, no touchstone.

What does it mean, anyway, that my poems get into certain magazines or win a contest? It's a contest made up of entrants like me being judged by members of a club I've tried to join. My poems aren't good to many judges and editors who keep the door. They aren't good to the maintenance staff at my apartment building. They are good to some people whose work I admire and to some editors who have taken them. It's a small circle.

I've spent too many years reading dust jackets. Nowadays, the positive ones seem to come from a world of bumper-sticker blurbs, blurbs which could fit any poet of any kind of poetry. I guess for the essay that I'd intended to write about Zimbabwean poetry, I could have composed fifty such blurbs and simply stuck in poets and poems from Zimbabwe. Here's one from a publisher's Web site: One poem in the collection "stirs Eliotic grandeur with Stevensian absurdity for a cocktail of delirious observation." What?! Or these taken from book ads in *Poets & Writers*, March/April 2004:

- Through revelations, paradoxes, and the kind of startling connections we cherish in dreams, _____'s poetry gives us the secret lives of our surroundings, lovingly and beautifully rendered.

- Here, politics and aesthetics invade each others' circuses, and they admit—slyly, sheepishly, or sometimes with a sonic boom—that they were already each other anyway.

- Dazzling poems, wholly taken in by where the words are going.

Alternatively, we can make up our own, have them at the ready to apply to someone's work: "_____'s poems shock us into the expanse of

smallness, opening for us the larger world of our own kitchen table."
Or "_____'s dazzling lines and images paint our lives with the colors
of Miro as we walk through our own *film noir*."

Reviews—same thing. Worse are the mean-spirited reviews of
poetry (or fiction, for that matter) whose authors seem to delight
in composing slashing phrases for their mean-spirited sycophants.
Who can phrase a cut most memorably? It's a trick, a trick of lan-
guage that comes from our most evil natures. (Some may call it "up-
holding standards of Western civilization and culture," if they wish.
But at bottom it's just a trick). In college, I adopted that kind of mind
and polished that facility of phrasing in order to gossip about those
not in my clique and thus win acceptance from those in my clique. I
suppose I'll have to answer for it in the hereafter. Grown-ups ought
to know better, though. Commentators of this sort simply sound like
theater critics in the thirties and forties, or fops in the salon in eigh-
teenth-century Paris or London. Witness the new and, I would argue,
much diminished *Poetry*. For the most part, simply a blog in print.

I don't know. I'm just tired of it all. You want some blurbs for Zim-
babwean poets? Try the ones supplied above. Fill in Aaron Hodza,
Solomon Mahaka, Eddison J. Zvobgo, Barbara Makhalisa, Bianca
Mahlunge: Me, I've had enough of it.

In 1980, when the change from the colony of Rhodesia to the nation
of Zimbabwe took place and Robert Mugabe took office, there was
an optimistic, nationalist movement in art. Such high hopes. Poets
flourished, and their poetry—though not technically interesting to
me, tainted as I've been by the MFA aesthetic—was passionate in its
message promoting strong nationalist sentiment and reviling British
colonialism.

Nevertheless, when the voices roared *freedom*—like the diesel sa-
fari jeep in the cold morning, the elephant at dusk, the lion at mid-
night—there was no freedom. True freedom of speech requires that
poets be allowed to publish anti-Mugabe poems as well. They can't.
Nothing in art is more sad than a record of hope followed by a period
of silence.

Immediately after Mugabe took over, the poetry published was
that which had been hidden during British rule. Indeed, Colin Style
notes in his excellent introductory essay for his and O-lan Style's
Mambo Book of Zimbabwean Verse in English (1986):

The long period of colonial rule and its disruption of the
Ndebele and Shona past; the stranglehold of life under the
proto-apartheid system; the culmination in the long, guer-
rilla war; all meant that a common poetic tradition was es-
tablished, painfully and spasmodically.

But here's the sad part: When Mugabe leaves office, the same thing
will be said of the next poetry: "The long period of Mugabe rule and
its disruption of . . ." When Mudereri Kadhani and Musaemura
Zimunya called for poems for their anthology, *And Now the Poets
Speak* (1981), they considered it "a celebration of the People, for the
People of Zimbabwe . . . a communion of voices . . . once and for all
defying enslavement and imprisonment, death and destruction,
bombs and bullets; and castigating human indignity and the oppres-
sion of man by man." Both anthologies are important introductions
to contemporary Zimbabwean poetry. Both represent the idea that
during colonialism the real talent was suppressed, and with the new
government of Mugabe, now the poet can speak. More blatantly cel-
ebrating this optimism, *And Now the Poets Speak* proclaims that the
editors were unprepared for the "deluge" of submissions from Zim-
babweans and expatriate Zimbabweans of all stripes:

> Our belief was based on the simple observation that pro-
> gressive literature had been considered as anathema to
> the dead regime, so that, particularly in the mother
> tongue, only novels with cheap sentimental themes were
> supported and promoted. Consequently, there is many a
> tale of heart-broken authors who were compelled to com-
> promise their feelings and so to expunge vital messages
> from their works because they were found to have been
> "politically or religiously offensive."

Sadly, now twenty-five years since the first publication of that book,
the same is true, only substituting "Mugabe's government" for "the
dead regime." Thanks to POSA, the Public Order and Security Act,
there are as many unheard voices and expatriate voices as there ever
were in colonial times.

Colin Kajokoto was a young street poet in Harare three years ago.
His poetry is much like we in the United States expect from our

street poets. He gave readings when and where he could, accompanying himself on the mbira. People liked him, and he was starting to get a little press.

Then in 2002 Colin was first arrested for sedition. After his release he tried not performing for a while, but as he said, not to perform was worse than death. It meant slow starvation on the streets. Unlike in the United States, a beginning poet in Zimbabwe can eke out a living by passing the hat. He went back to performing. He knew the risks. He e-mailed me on the day of his first reading following his time in jail. The Book Café hosted him for their "African Night"—an irony, it turns out. Here is what he wrote to me when he decided to take the risk:

> I'm going to read again. To me writing is like blood—it flows within. It is like breathing. Now tell me who chooses between breathing and eating? If I stop writing it is the end. During the quietest hour of the night I ask myself, should I or should I not write—the answer is ALWAYS an emphatic "DO." If I stop writing to "save" my life this would be tantamount to cutting my throat to save my neck. If you are facing an unjust death you are not worried about your real demise but FREEDOM—freedom to express yourself to the outer world that you are dying, but innocently. You want to write the poetry that you were murdered, butchered, tortured, raped, hanged despite the fact that there was gross miscarriage of justice. And let me write this poetry the same way I demonstrated against Mugabe: so as not to be judged cruelly by the next generation.

So he performed. The audience loved him, and he was still running on pure adrenaline the next day. He could have done well were he not under Mugabe's close watch. But he was. Soon after the Book Café reading, Colin and three other poets were arrested. A weekend in Harare's jail is a year of hell. Shelter is crowded and personal space minimal at best. Your time is spent in a gray-dirt compound. No television, basketball courts, or free weights here, no date certain for release. If you are fed, it's because some friend or family member on the outside brought you food that day. I shall let an intermediary—Dr. Simmons, I'll call him—speak through his e-mail to me.

Dear Sir:

After some bribery and a lot of painstaking and relentless search I have finally got hold of the poet. I'm surprised he is in high mood. He said he hopes to be a free man again although he was in great pain after being tortured and severe interrogation. If he fails to appear in court tomorrow he has to spend the weekend in police custody until Monday. His clothes were all soaked in blood. I just hope he will survive to see another day. All I can guess is that they might charge him. I only can afford the bail amount of about ZIM $15,000 [worth about US $25] and the legal fees are just beyond my reach. Unfortunately there is little information.

Here is how the system works, in Dr. Simmons's words. This e-mail came to me in December 2002:

Sir Allen Paul: I have another brief with Colin. He is being denied food and water. He wishes to express his gratifications to you. Clearly he is not in the best mind unlike yesterday. I have however managed just to go a step further. The police are keen to have the buy out money. I was holding on to ZIM $15,000 as bail. This I have given to the investigation officer as surety that more money is coming from U.S. I have convinced them that the money is coming today although to be frank I do not know the story from your other end. The plan: If the money arrives the investigation officer will take Colin out to probe and investigate at Colin's place of residence. Instead they will then proceed to Western Union where Colin will collect the money [about US $300–$350]. Everything done, Colin shall be released tomorrow for lack of evidence to prosecute. This should be done before the police hand over the docket to the Attorney General otherwise it would be expensive to buy his freedom.

The story goes on to book-length proportions and complexities. After that buy-out came another jailing (as a British spy) in order to extort more money from me for the guards; more torture from the jailers when the money was not paid; Colin's mother's suicide with rat

169

poison, the preferred form of suicide there; his own attempted suicide with rat poison, which damaged his throat; his escape to Ireland, where he was put to work under indenture at a brothel and was finally deported back because, at my suggestion, he demanded that the brothel keeper either give him back his passport or provide a written accounting of how much she was making off of Colin's readings, indicating how much his debt was thereby being reduced.

Then the indenturer's henchman followed him to Zimbabwe and hired two goons to smash his hands so that he could not play the mbira. Two fingers had to be amputated. A year later, he tested positive for HIV, which he probably contracted during a transfusion in the hospital (a common occurrence), given he had been celibate since 1997. Then, though Colin didn't commit it, there was the murder of one of the goons. The police blamed him for the murder, though a dozen witnesses testified that he was not even at the scene. The actual murderer escaped to Zambia; Colin escaped again, this time to Denmark. Colin presumably left Denmark and tried to settle in Austria, since that is where he learned two months ago that he was to be extradited back to Zimbabwe, and where he jumped from a high-rise to his death.

You know, the familiar ups and downs of poets paying their dues.

Meanwhile in Matabeleland—the land of the Great Zimbabwe, the ancient stone fortress, and now wasted farmland—the people are faring worse than those in Harare, where President Mugabe resides. In the April 2005 elections, though Mugabe made it known that he would not step down even if voted out, Matabeleland supported the wrong candidate, so Mugabe punished them by holding back food and medicine and other international relief. Such deprivation is starting to show on the people. On the road from Masvingo that swings west and north toward Victoria Falls on the border with Zambia, they walk with less bounce in their step and do not stand as tall as the people of Harare. They are beginning to starve. Natural events, too, seem to conspire against Zimbabweans. The drought has been hardest in Matabeleland. There one crosses dry riverbeds of small rivers like the Khami, Umganim, Tegwani, which look like they would normally only run dry in the winter of August. But the older, more permanent rivers are dry as well, or nearly so. Women wash clothes in the middle of the Nyantue, in little pools sprung up within the bedrock of what was once a wide, deep river. The families of baboons in groups roadside seem to have more hope than the people: They talk amongst themselves loudly. The people whisper.

In looking at the poetry of Zimbabwe, I've come to the realization that I don't laugh at or turn up my nose to poems which in the United States I would have condemned. For much of my career, "bad" American poetry angered me, yet reading Zimbabwean poetry I feel no contempt at all.

So much Zimbabwean poetry is dull, uninspired, and technically sloppy. It's full of mixed or dull metaphor, or drips with self-indulgent political cliché. So what? That holds for much American poetry. But what seems like pure arrogance, megalomania, or the-emperor's-new-clothes in a prosperous country full of poets with advanced degrees, in Zimbabwe seems acceptable. The real poetry of Zimbabwe is not the poem on the page; it's the will to poetry, the commitment to it, the need for it.

In a country scraping to get by on all levels, and not actually getting by on any, the "bad" poetry has a kind of nobility to it. To my mind, lines that here read as blatant schlock, in a crash-and-burn country like Zimbabwe seem to add to the angst and affect of the poem. Writing it in such a world is all the art we need.

> Will these dreams come true, my friend?
> Will these dreams come true?
> We dream and dream
> In broad daylight or lamp lit rooms;
> We dream dreams of the unity of the seed of Pharaoh
> Scattered by time, region and tongue,
> And by the wily coos of the parasitic Vulture;
> Unmindful of the common roots,
> Unmindful of the common goal,
> Too blind to look back,
> Too blind to look forward—
> We dream dreams of glorious shadows, my friend.

These lines are by the noted scholar Emmanuel Ngara, from "Let Us Dream Our Dreams" (*Songs from the Temple*). Few of America's eminent literary journals or publishing houses would be interested in publishing these lines. Putting aside the "coos of the parasitic Vulture" (vultures being neither cooing nor parasitic), some nice lines

171

occur in Ngara's poems—surprises such as in "Elegy to the Memory of a Hero," a poem elegizing Josiah Magama Tongogara, who was a leader in the struggle for liberation: "[His] legs broke like china models/And the giant of a warrior slumped and shrank to the size of a coffin." But this interesting image, bringing a man who took on gigantic proportions to the size of a coffin, comes after these:

> I wondered at the glinting strides of the stilted giant
> Till that damned and fateful day
> After the blowing of the whistle of peace. . . .

"Stilted giant"? "Damned and fateful day"? "Whistle of peace"? How would you be inclined to read these phrases? I might have laughed or raged at one time, but I can't laugh at them now, not anymore.

I remember getting so angry over some description in David Ignatow's "Each Day"—". . . and me with kidneys straining to capacity/with piss I had no chance to release/all night . . ."—that I threw the book across the room where it slid into my give-it-to-a-student-who-wants-it corner. "Kidney" rather than "bladder"? One body part is as good as another if you're an important poet, a kingpin in the club, I thought.

For different reasons I cringed reading Ai's "Why Can't I Leave You?" which ends thus:

> I undress, then put on my white lace slip
> for you to take off, because you like that
> and when you come in, you pull down the straps
> and I unbutton your shirt.
> I know we can't give each other any more
> or any less than what we have.
> There is safety in that, so much
> that I can never get past the packing,
> the begging you to please, if I can't make you happy,
> come close between my thighs
> and let me laugh for you from my second mouth.

That laughing "second mouth" would send most men running for the door with their overalls around their ankles. I grumbled through the broken-lined prose, and when I hit that ridiculous last line, I laughed heartily. *Then* I threw the book toward the giveaway corner.

I'm seeing my problem then more clearly now with the help of Zimbabwe's poetry. It's me. So I sometimes found Ignatow silly and Ai ridiculous? So I felt like Lucille Clifton's poems were just notes for real poems yet to be written? So I felt in the middle of a John Ashbery poem that I should be doing something else—catching a bus, cleaning my rug—and I was glad for any interruption? So what? Whose standards was I upholding? Why do I not feel equally wronged by missteps I perceive in Zimbabwean poetry, or equally merciful toward those in American poetry? Surely Clifton, Ai, Ignatow, Ashbery write or wrote their best with a hunger in their souls, under the burden of personal struggle, aches and pains, crushing losses. They, too, are committed to their art. They—and their suffering devotees—have a need for poetry that goes beyond taste. Their success amounts to no more than their poems' acceptance by people who want or need them. As with my wild student who writes to get laid—reason enough.

When I returned from Zimbabwe wistful, it wasn't due to disappointment with the poetry, spoken and written, I had encountered. And it might not even have been a consequence of the poetic rejuvenation I sought having been thwarted. I think it was a byproduct of newfound self-acceptance that I don't belong to whatever club gathers around whatever particular poem. No more than that. No hard feelings. Every poem has its own fan base, its own standards for membership.

Here, toward the end of my career, when retirement or death is not long off, I see I was asking Zimbabwean poetry to do something it couldn't do. Were I twenty, I would have been taken by its message: the grand statements, the politics, and the pain. Were I forty, I'd have been derisive for its lack of interesting line breaks, its tin ear, its incompleteness and immaturity—though I would have been too politically correct to say so.

I know now that poems won't move me as they did when I was full of piss and vinegar, and they won't fascinate and excite me in the way they did when I knew stuff, or thought I did.

Often I've heard and said among my craft-loving professional poet friends, "I liked his early stuff." Any writer who lives long enough gets that said about him. Now I wonder whether I'm just learning what some poets knew all along. You see the end coming, and you decide, just decide, to let the bother and blather of standards go, drop it all as excess weight on a long flight. Intuitive or analytical, my devotions served me well for forty years. I'll let students worry about excellence of feeling; I'll let those in full career worry about excellence of craft. There will be "certain poems I like," but it will be for whatever reason or whim or moment I'm in. It won't be because they measure up to anything.

Postscript: My father is ninety-six, and dying: severe dementia for a few years. It looks like the end is in sight for him. I've gathered some poems to read to him, some I remember his quoting to me back when I was a boy battling all night with asthma. He learned most of them when he was a boy—"Home" by Edgar Guest, Joyce Kilmer's "Trees," Sidney Lanier's "The Marshes of Glynn," and the like.

I bend his straw, and he finishes his juice. Then I turn to "Trees," the poem I've used for years as an example of metaphor run riot. It's one of my showpieces; I can always make students laugh when I tell them there's a whole forest of such trees in North Carolina: the Joyce Kilmer National Forest.

"I think that I shall never see," I begin. Dad brightens like a boy, quotes the next line, "A poem as lovely as a tree." I congratulate him, pat his knee, read, "A tree whose hungry mouth is pressed." And he responds, "Against the earth's sweet, flowing breast." I'm amazed. Next couplet. Next. He nails each one with no hesitation. I do the penultimate line, and with voice cracking, tears starting, Dad recites the closing, "But only God can make a tree." As a kid, I was afraid of this man? As a youth, I was rebellious against this small person enjoying a poem now in ways I could never have imagined?

I wonder whether, when I'm in his shape, I'll be so filled with gratitude for the music of lines, with joy—pure joy in language—as someone reads to me "One Art" or "Prufrock" or any of the known and lesser known contemporary poems from among my favorites. Or for that matter, knowing as I do how tangled the synapses get, poems by Mungoshi or Zimunya. Who knows what's in there?

I'll continue to teach "Trees" in my classes as an example of ridiculously extended metaphor, but I don't think I'll have quite the arrogance and showmanship I've displayed before now. And I'll save some time in the period to discuss legitimacy and audience.

When I kiss Dad good-night, I tell him that in the morning we'll read "The Marshes of Glynn." He is looking forward to that. He asks me to come early.

Nominated by Michael Heffernan, The Southern Review

BON VOYAGE

by TONY HOAGLAND

from SMARTISH PACE

Here's a narrative for you:
my friend Charlie conducting his great experiment with adultery
with his pale young British mistress
in the hotel room next to mine,

exercising their right to be as sinful as possible
on the faux Victorian four poster bed
under a framed photograph of the Royal Family
launching a brand new battleship—
What does one say on such occasions? Bon Voyage? Happy sailing?

Wishing to be polite by not imagining
any explicit details of their fornication,
I interpret that vague thumping through the wall
as the sound of someone restless

moving the furniture around;
or maybe using the bed as a trampoline
to change the light bulb in the ceiling.

How thin is the wall between two lives!
between happy and unhappy;

between before and after.
It is thin as the page between chapters;
Thin as a pair of panties
            thrown on a blazing fire.

I remember that kind of heat
scorching my delirious face. I recall
trading one life for another.
What I feel now is mainly relief
that it's not me in there next door,
in the molten center of the drama.

Happy now to be simply reading my book,
and sailing. Sailing, out on the edge
of the solar system;
out on the silent periphery.
One of the cooler planets

orbiting the sun.

Nominated by Charles Harper Webb, Laura Kasischke, Smartish Pace

NOWHERE

fiction by JOYCE CAROL OATES

from CONJUNCTIONS

1.

*M*Y MOTHER, I WISH . . .

The first time no one heard. So softly Miriam spoke. In the din of raised voices, laughter. In the din of high-decibel rock music. She was into the beat, sweating with the percussion. Shaking her head from side to side and her eyes closed. Leaking tears but closed. *My mother, I wish someone would . . .* At the crowded table no one noticed. It was the Star Lake Inn, the deck above the lake. Music blared from speakers overhead. Had to be the Star Lake Inn though it didn't look familiar. The moon was rising in the night sky. She'd lost her sandals somewhere. Couldn't remember who'd brought her here six miles from home. Then she remembered: the boy from the marina driving the steel-colored Jeep. Not a local guy. He'd been flirting with her all week. Her heart skidded seeing him. Big-jawed boy with sun-bleached hair, had to be midtwenties, father owned one of the sleek white sailboats docked at the marina but Kevin wasn't into taking orders from the old man like a damn cabin boy, he said. Anger flared in his pale eyes. He was from downstate: Westchester County. Half the summer residents at Star Lake were from Westchester County. He'd thought Miriam was older than fifteen, maybe. Gripping her wrist not her hand helping her up into the Jeep. A stabbing sensation shot through her groin.

Had to be past 11 p.m. The moon continued to rise in the sky above Mt. Hammer. She'd gotten off work at the boathouse at 6 p.m. In the

Jeep she'd called home on her cell phone. Left a message for her mother she'd run into friends from school, wouldn't be home until late.

Please don't wait up for me, Mom. Makes me nervous, OK?

The boy in the Jeep didn't know Miriam's brothers, hadn't known Miriam's father. *Orlander* meant nothing to him. Maybe to his father who owned one of the new A-frames on East Shore Drive *Orlander* meant something. In the Adirondacks there were local residents and there were property owners from downstate. If you were a local male you worked for the downstate property owners: carpentry, roofing, plumbing, hauling away trash. You paved driveways, you exterminated vermin. You fenced off property to keep out deer hunters like yourself. The expensive new lakeside houses were always in need of upgrading: redwood decks, children's rooms, saunas, tennis courts. Les Orlander had been a roofer. His brother-in-law Harvey Schuller siphoned out waste from buried septic tanks and dug new septic fields. *Your shit smells sweet to me* was a joke bumper sticker Miriam's father had had printed up but Harvey kept it displayed in his office not on his truck. If you were a local female you might work inside the summer residents' houses: cooking, caring for children, cleaning. You served at their parties. You picked up after their drunken houseguests. Uncomplaining, you wore rubber gloves to retrieve from a stopped-up toilet a wadded Tampax or baby diaper someone had tried to flush away. You wore a nylon uniform. You smiled and hoped for a generous tip. You learned not to stack dirtied dishes from the dinner table but to remove each plate ceremoniously murmuring *Thank you!* as you took the plate away. *Thank you!* you murmured as you served dessert and poured wine into glasses. *Thank you!* mopping up spilled wine, on your hands and knees picking up shattered glass. Your employers called you by your first name and urged you to call them by their first names but you never did. Ethel laughed to show she thought it was funny, such bullshit. Not that she was a bitter woman for truly Ethel was not.

Beggars can't be choosers, right?

Miriam's mother thought this was an optimistic attitude.

Three years of his five-to-seven-year sentence for assault Miriam's father served at Ogdensburg Men's Facility and during those years of shame her mother worked for summer residents and for a Tupper Lake caterer. Often Ethel stayed overnight at Tupper Lake twenty miles away. It began to be said in Star Lake that she met men there, at the resort hotels. She took "gifts" from them. At this time Miriam

179

was in eighth grade and deeply mortified by both her parents. Her father she loved and missed so badly, it was like part of her heart was locked away in the prison. Her mother she'd used to love but was beginning now to hate. *Wish! Wish to God something would happen to her.* When Miriam's oldest brother, Gideon, confronted their mother one day, Ethel shouted at him that her life was her own not her damn children's. Her "money life" and her "sex life" she said were her own business not some damn loser inmate's who'd let his family down. Shocked then by the fury of the words roiling from her, Ethel had tried to laugh, saying it was a joke, some kind of joke, anyway isn't everything some kind of joke, the way life turns out?—but Gideon would never forgive her.

Quit roofing, moved to Watertown, and impregnated a woman he never married and a few months later enlisted in the U.S. Marines and got sent to Iraq.

Even when their father was paroled and returned to Star Lake to live, Gideon avoided the family. Every time Miriam came home she steeled herself for news of him: he'd been killed in that terrible place. Or for the sight of Ethel, disheveled, lying on her bed in the waning hours of the afternoon.

I wish. Why don't you. Why, when you're so unhappy!

"Looking lost, Miriam? Where's your rich boyfriend?"

Miriam was a girl to be teased. A hot blush rising into her face. Her eyes were warm glistening brown with something shrinking and mocking in the droop of the eyelids. Her hair was streaked blond-brown, the commonest color. Before meeting Kevin after work she'd hurriedly brushed out her hair, pursed her lips applying dark red lipstick to make her appear older, sexier. Now it was hours later and the lipstick was eaten off and her hair was in her face and so many guys looking at her, laughing at her, all she could do was shake her head, blushing and embarrassed.

Oz Newell, who'd been Gideon's closest high-school friend, was calling down the table: "What'd he do, the fucker, take a leak and fall in? Want me to break his head?"

Nervously Miriam laughed, shaking her head *no*. She was scared of something like this. Older guys relating to her like she was their kid sister, wanting to protect her and somebody getting hurt.

Her brothers had gotten into fights at places like the Star Lake Inn. Her father.

Star Lake Resident Pleads Guilty, Assault.

Reduced Charges Lead to 5-7 Years at Ogdensburg.

The kind of work men did here in the Adirondacks. A belligerent attitude was natural. Drunk Friday night was natural. It was sheer hell to take orders from foremen, bosses. Rich men from downstate like Kevin's father. "Manual laborer." By age forty-five you'd be limping. By age fifty your back is shot. Natural to want to break some fucker's head. Miriam thought, *I had fists like theirs, I'd feel the same way.*

Must've been Miriam had wandered past their table looking lost. Looking like a girl who's been dumped by her boyfriend, trying not to cry. Also she's underage. Also she's never had sex. Also she's been sick feeling, gagging in the restroom in one of the smelly toilet stalls but nothing came up. Whatever he'd given her, *Baby, you need loosening up.* In the Jeep, a joint they shared that made her cough, choke, giggle insanely. At the Star Lake, vodka and cranberry juice for Miriam. She was confused where Kevin had gone, exactly where they'd been sitting, couldn't find the table, someone else had taken the table, but maybe Kevin was inside at the bar, maybe Kevin was looking for her? Cigarette smoke made her eyes sting and blur, she couldn't see. Somebody grabbed at her arm, grinning faces lurched at her: "Miriam? Miriam Orlander? What're you doing *here*?"

So she was sitting with them. Practically on Brandon McGraw's lap. Like she was their little-girl mascot. Maybe because she wasn't *beautiful*. She was fleshy, warm skinned, but not beautiful. These were older guys in their twenties who'd gone to school with her brothers or who'd worked with them. One or two of them might've worked with Miriam's father. And one or two of them with Miriam's uncle Harvey Schuller. Where their girlfriends and wives were, Miriam wondered. When she asked, they told her it was boys' night out. She figured they'd come to the Star Lake Inn immediately after work to begin drinking. In summers you worked late, until 7 p.m. Miriam's father and brothers worked even later. The table was strewn with dirtied plates, empty bottles. The remains of hamburgers, deep-fried shrimp, pizza crusts. Onion rings, cole slaw, ketchup. A grease sheen on the Formica surface. The table was outdoors, above the lake; still the air was heavy with smoke from their cigarettes. They were drinking beer, ale, whiskey. They were drunk, high, stoned. Miriam saw the red-rimmed eyes she knew to associate with drugs: speed, crystal meth. These guys weren't into smoking dope like the kids she knew. Beyond wanting to feel mellowed out and restful like they could love mankind. She shivered to hear: raw male laughter like a braying of coyotes. Their young faces were reddened, coarse and prematurely lined from outdoor work. Their shoulders, necks, upper arms were thick with muscle. Their hair was buzz-cut short, or straggling past their collars. Martin had worn his straggly hair tied back in a kind of pigtail. The loggers and tree trimmers, who worked with chain saws, were likely to be scarred or missing fingers. If Miriam got drunker/sillier she'd count how many fingers were missing from the table. Sex energy lifted from the men's heated skins frank as sweat. Most girls would be uneasy in the company of so many men but not Miriam Orlander, who'd grown up in a household with three older brothers she'd adored.

Well, mostly. Mostly she'd adored them.

And her father, Les Orlander, she'd adored.

"Drown the fucker in the lake, who'd know? His rich daddy can drag the lake for his corpse."

This was Hay Brouwet. The subject seemed still to be whoever it was who'd brought Miriam to the Star Lake Inn, then abandoned her.

"What d'you say, Miriam? Pick out which one he is."

Quickly Miriam said, "He isn't here now. I don't see him."

Hay cupped his hand to his ear, not hearing. The rock music was so loud. The braying at the table so loud. Miriam caught her breath, seeing the smooth-shiny stub of Hay's right forefinger. Hay was a logger, must've had a chain-saw accident. Miriam felt faint imagining having to kiss that stub. Suck that stub, in her mouth. *If he asks me to, I will.*

In the Jeep, in the parking lot, Kevin made some joke about Miriam sucking him off, but Miriam pretended not to hear. In the tussle she'd lost her sandals. He hadn't meant to hurt her, she was sure. *Hey, baby, I'm sorry: just joking.*

Except Hay was married, wasn't he? One of the older guys at the table, had to be thirty. Seeing Miriam's eyes on him, winking.

"You see the asshole, let me know, OK?"

It was pretty clear Hay was high on something. That mean-happy red-eye-glittering look and he'd sweated through his shirt.

Crystal meth. Each of Miriam's brothers had instructed her individually never to try it. Not ever! Miriam was scared but intrigued. She knew that Stan, who was twenty-three, had had something to do with a methamphetamine lab—a cook-shop, it was called—but he'd never gotten caught and now he lived up in Keene. Ice was for older guys, not a fifteen-year-old girl whose hope was to go to nursing school at Plattsburgh State. An immediate high, wired straight to the brain. Her brother Martin was back in rehab at Watertown. *Fries your brain like nothing else. Makes you shiny and hard. Why's that bad? What's better you got to offer?*

Ethel had slapped him, he'd been yelling and laughing and stomping in the house so hard the windowpanes shook like an army bomber from Fort Drum was passing too low over the roof. Martin had hardly felt the blow, only brushed Ethel away like you'd brush away flies.

A few minutes later they heard him outside. A noise of breaking glass.

"Miriam, what the hell? You crying?"

It was the smoke. Making her eyes water. Her eyeballs burned in their sockets. She was annoyed, shaking her head *no*, why'd she be crying? She was having a great time.

Her left wrist where Kevin had grabbed and twisted was reddened in overlapping welts. Half consciously she was touching the skin, caressing.

"He do that? Your wrist?"

"No."

Brandon McGraw's blood yellow eyes were peering at Miriam's wrist. His bristly eyebrows nearly met over the bridge of his nose, which was large, red flushed, with deep, stretched-looking nostrils.

A look of shocked tenderness in Brandon's face so you'd almost want to laugh. Like the look she'd seen once on her father's face as he squatted in the driveway to stare at something small, wriggling, dying, a fledgling robin blown out of its nest.

"Like hell, Miriam. This looks like a guy's finger marks."

"Really, no. I'm just clumsy."

Miriam drew her arm away. Shrank both arms against her chest.

How she'd got there she didn't know. Six miles from home. Too far to walk in the dark. Missing her shoes. She was drunk, she'd been sweating so. *Miriam! I've been sick with worry.*

She hated Ethel. Couldn't bear to see Ethel.

Alone. The two of them. In the house on Salt Isle Road. Ethel, Miriam. Where there'd been six people, now reduced to two.

These guys felt sorry for her, Miriam knew. Seeing her they were thinking *Orlander: bad luck.*

183

"He didn't hurt me. I don't care about him. See, I'm having a great time. I want to dance."

Dance! Miriam wanted to dance! Stumbling and almost falling. The floor tilted beneath her like was the deck a boat? Were they on a cruise boat, on the lake? choppy waves?

Through the speakers blared heavy metal rock. Maybe you could dance to it. Was anybody dancing? Miriam wasn't the girl this was happening to. Miriam wasn't the type. How she'd got here to the Star Lake, which was a biker hangout on the marshy side of the lake, she didn't know. Underage but looking eighteen at least. No one asked her for ID. The kind of place the bartenders stayed inside and there were no waiters. You pushed your way in, got drinks from the bar, pushed your way back out onto the deck. Lights on tall poles. Insects swirling around the lights like demented thoughts. Miriam's brothers had come here. She'd been eating cold french fries from one of the greasy plates. Hadn't eaten since lunchtime. None of this was remotely like Miriam Orlander. At the boathouse she was the girl who blushed easily. The girl who didn't flirt with men. Had not wanted to waitress so she worked in the store where she was the youngest sales-clerk who got stuck with the hardest work like unpacking the merchandise, stocking the shelves. What embarrassed her was the female employee uniform she had to wear. Red T-shirt with white letters AU SABLE BOATHOUSE straining against her breasts. Worse yet the white cord miniskirt trimmed in red. The miniskirt rode up her thighs. Sitting, she had to keep her knees pressed tightly together. Walking, she had to tug at the skirt, uncomfortably aware of her thighs rubbing together. Men stared. Some smiled openly. Miriam was a healthy girl: five feet six, one hundred thirty pounds. Ethel had crinkled her face at the uniform. *Miriam! I don't think this is a good idea.* She'd wanted to come with Miriam to the boathouse to speak with Andy Mack, who'd hired Miriam and provided the uniform for his "girl" employees but Miriam had screamed at her and run out of the house.

Now Miriam was dancing. Wild and tossing her body like it's impaled on a hook she's got to wriggle, wriggle, wriggle to get free. Oz Newell was dancing with her and for a while Hay Brouwet. For such burly muscled guys, they got winded fast. Miriam laughed at them. Miriam loved how the music poured like something molten into her veins. The beat was so fast her heart raced to keep up. Maybe it was ice he'd given her, maybe this was the ice-rush and she loved it. Breathing through her mouth, panting. Bare feet, kind of pudgy-pale feet, toenails painted dark to match the sexy lipstick, she's picking up splinters in the tender soles of her feet from the raw floorboards but doesn't feel any pain. Not a glimmer of pain. No more pain! Maybe it doesn't matter if she isn't beautiful the way Oz Newell is looking at her. His eyes on her breasts in the tight red T-shirt, his eyes on her soft rounded belly, her hips and thighs in the tight white miniskirt trimmed in red. Rivulets of sweat trickle down Oz's sunburnt face. Oz does construction work for Herkimer County. Oz had some kind of disagreement with Gideon; they didn't part friends. Miriam is weak with sudden love for him. Laughs to think how surprised Oz would be, she slipped her bar arms around his neck and tongued his face, licked away the sweat droplets like tears. Oz is twenty-five or - six. Ten years older than Miriam. Gideon's age. Not a boy but a man. His hair is a blond buzz cut. Eyebrows and lashes so pale you almost can't see them. Gray eyes like pinwheels, spinning.

Hay Brouwet is back, and another guy, fattish and drunk-silly, grimy baseball cap on his head advertising WATERTOWN RACEWAY. The dancing, if you can call it dancing, is getting out of control. Hay is shaking his shiny stub-finger in Miriam's face, gyrating his hips like some stoned rock star, collides with an older man carrying beers, two beers in the stretched fingers of each hand, and the beers go flying, there's a comical scene like something on TV, Miriam is helpless, laughing, panting, and breathless and almost wets herself. There's a feeling like fire: wild fire. The guys' eyes on her, the heavy-metal vibrations thundering inside her head. Like, with a fire, the wind blows it in one direction and not another—it's the difference between somebody's property going up in walls of roaring flame and some- body else's only a few hundred feet away, untouched. There are con- trolled burns in the Adirondacks. You have to get permission from the country. And there are uncontrolled burns—lightning, campers' fires, arson.

Arson. There's times you are so angry, so bitten down, you need to start a fire. Toss a match, evergreens dead and dried from acid rain, it's like a fireball, exploding. Miriam remembers one of her brothers saying this. *Hey: just joking.*

Miriam's father had been a volunteer fireman for Au Sable town- ship. There'd been years of the excitement and dread of hearing the siren, a high-pitched wail from the firehouse a mile away, seeing Daddy roused to attention, hurriedly dressing if it was night, running out to his pickup. Often they'd smelled smoke, seen smoke rising above the tree line, heard sirens. Those years Miriam had taken for granted would go on forever. But after Ogdensburg, Les hadn't rejoined the volunteers. Maybe there was a law against ex-convicts being volunteer firemen, Miriam hadn't wanted to ask.

Abruptly the deafening rock music stopped. For a moment Miriam didn't know where she was. Her eyeballs were burning as if she'd been staring stupidly into a hot bright light. Inside her tight-fitting clothes she was slick with sweat like oil. Damn miniskirt had ridden up to practically her crotch. Like a child Miriam wiped her damp face on her T-shirt. Somebody's arms came down heavy on her shoulders, somebody stumbling against her, a big guy, soft-fleshy belly, a smell of whiskey and heat pouring off his skin. Quick as a cat Miriam disentangled herself and backed away. Ran barefoot to the edge of the deck where, overlooking lapping water just below, it was quieter, smelling of the lake. Miriam recalled as if through a haze that she was at Star Lake: six miles from home. The way the moon was slanted in the sky, now east of Mt. Hammer, it had to be late. *Worried sick about you. You're all I have.*

Star Lake was dark, glittering by moonlight. Said to be in the shape of a star but, up close, you couldn't see any shape to it only just glittering water and opaque wedges of shadow that were trees and, on the farther shore, the east side, lights from the new houses, not visible from the shore road. Miriam had never been in any of these houses, she had no friends who lived in them, mostly these were summer people who kept to themselves. Their houses were architect-designed A-frames, split-levels, replicas of old Adirondack log lodges. The last months of his life Miriam's father had worked for a roofing contractor on several of those houses. He'd been disbelieving, the prices people from downstate were paying. *Like another world,* he'd said. *It's another world now.* He had not seemed especially grieving, that day. Quiet and matter-of-fact informing his daughter as if it's something she should know.

"Hey, baby. Where you goin'?"

A hand came down on Miriam's shoulder. Fingers kneading the nape of her neck beneath her damp crimped hair. Miriam felt a stab of panic even after she saw it was Oz Newell. Now the music had stopped, she wasn't so sure of herself. *I don't want this. This is a mistake.* Miriam managed to twist away from Oz, but grabbed his hand, as a girl might do, to pull him back to the others, to the table. Oz slung his arms around her shoulders and nuzzled her hair, called her

186

baby as if he'd forgotten her name. Miriam felt weak with desire for the man, unless it was fear. "I miss Gideon. Damn, I miss your dad." Oz's voice sounded young, raw, clumsy. He had more to say but couldn't think of the words. Miriam murmured, "I do, too. Thanks."

Halfway back to the table Miriam saw the jut-jawed young man from the marina, weaving through the crowd. It was a shock to see him, she'd taken for granted he'd dumped her. Was Kevin his name? Was this Kevin? Miriam hadn't remembered him wearing a Yankees cap but she remembered the arrogant jut-jaw face, the streaked blond hair. He was walking unsteadily and hadn't seen her. Or, seeing her, had not recognized her. He was alone, appeared to be looking for someone. Miriam wondered if maybe he'd been in the men's room all this while, being sick to his stomach. His face looked freshly washed and not so arrogant as he'd seemed with just him and Miriam in the Jeep when he'd bragged of his father's sailboat and twisted Miriam's wrist. Miriam pointed him out to Oz: "That's him."

2.

Did it to himself.

This was a way of speaking. It was the way she knew they were speaking. It was a way of wonderment, and of accusation. It was a way of consolation. In Au Sable County and Star Lake and where Les Orlander had been known. A way of saying *Nobody else is to blame, no one of us. Nobody did it to him, he did it to himself.* Yet it was a way of admiration, too. It was a way of saying *He did it to himself, it was his free choice.* A way of acknowledging *He did it to himself, he had the guts for it and not everybody has.* In the Adirondacks, a man's guns are his friends. A man's guns are his companions. Les Orlander had not been a fanatic gun collector like some. Like some of his relatives and in-laws. Shotguns, rifles. Legal weapons. Les had owned only a shotgun and a rifle and these were of no special distinction. *Did it to himself, used his rifle* was a tribute to the man's efficiency. *Did it to himself, out alone in the woods.* A gun is a man's friend when friends can't help. A friend to protect him from shame, from hurt, from dragging through his life. A gun can make a wounded man whole. A gun can make a broken man stronger. No escape except a gun will provide escape. *Did it to himself* had to be the legacy he'd leave his family.

You know I love you, honey. That will never stop.

He'd said that. Before he went away. Miriam was staring out the school-bus window. Her breath steamed faintly on the window. Her eyes were glazed, seeing little of the landscape: trees, fields, roadside houses, mobile homes on concrete blocks at the end of rutted driveways.

. . . come see me, OK! Promise!

There came the tall, clumsy Ochs girl lurching toward her. As the school bus started up, lurching along the aisle staring and grinning at Miriam. She was at least two years older than Miriam: fourteen, one of the special education students at school. Her face was broad and coarse and blemished in dull red rashes and bumps. Her small cunning eyes had a peculiar glisten. Lana Ochs wasn't retarded but said to have "learning disabilities." Her older sister had been expelled for fighting in the school cafeteria. On the bus, no one wanted Lana to sit with them, she was so large boned, fidgety, and smelled like rancid milk. Miriam's backpack was in the seat beside her. She was saving a seat for her friend Iris. Miriam stared out the window as Lana approached, thinking, *Go away! Don't sit here.* But Lana was hunched over her, grinning. She asked, "This seat taken?" and Miriam said quickly, "Yes, it is." For Iris Petko, who was in Miriam's seventh-grade homeroom, would be getting on the bus in a few minutes, and Lana Ochs knew this. Still she hung over Miriam, swaying and lurching in the aisle, as if about to shove Miriam's backpack aside. In a whiny, insinuating voice she said, "No it isn't. It isn't taken, Miriam." Miriam was sitting halfway to the rear of the bus. There were several empty seats Lana might take. In another minute the bus driver would shout back at her to sit down; it was forbidden to stand in the aisle while the bus was in motion. Miriam said, "It's for Iris. You can sit somewhere else." Her eyes lifted to Lana Ochs's flushed face, helpless. Lana's hair was matted and frizzed. Her lips were fleshy, smeared with bright red lipstick. Older boys on the bus called Lana by an ugly name having to do with those lips. Lana leaned over Miriam, saying in a mock whisper, "Hey Miriam: your father and my father, they're in the same place." Miriam said, "No, they're not." Lana said, "Yes they are. That makes us like sisters." Miriam was staring out the window now, stony faced. She was a shy girl but could be stuck-up, snotty. In seventh grade she had that reputation. Her friends were popular girls. She received high grades in most subjects. She'd had three older brothers to look after her and there had been a certain glamor accruing to the Orlander boys who'd preceded their sister in the Star Lake public schools. Now the youngest, Martin, a sophomore at Star Lake High, no longer rode the school bus but got a ride into town with friends. Miriam was vulnerable now, not so protected. She could smell Lana Ochs leaning over her, saying in a loud, aggrieved voice for everyone to hear, "You got no right to be stuck-up, Miriam. Your father is no better than my father. You think you're hot shit but you're not." Miriam said, "Go away. Leave me alone. I hate you," and Lana said, "Fuck you!" swinging her heavy backpack against Miriam, striking her on the shoulder. Now the driver, who should have intervened before this, braked the bus and shouted back at them, "Girls! Both of you! Stop that or you'll get out and walk." Lana cursed Miriam and swung past the seat, sitting heavily behind her. Miriam could hear her panting and muttering to herself. Miriam fumbled to open her math book: algebra. Her heart was beating frantically. Her face burned with shame. Everyone on the bus had been watching, listening. Some she'd thought were her friends, but were not. Wanting to scream at them, *Go away! Leave me alone! I hate you.*

At this time, Les Orlander had been incarcerated at the Men's Maximum Security Prison at Ogdensburg for just six days.

4.

Ogdensburg. Almost as far north as you could drive in New York State. And there was the St. Lawrence River, which was the widest river Miriam had ever seen. And beyond, the province of Ontario, Canada.

Miriam asked Ethel could they drive across the bridge to the other side someday, after visiting Les, if it was a nice day and not windy and cold, and Ethel said, distracted, glancing in the rearview mirror, where a diesel truck was bearing close upon her, on Route 37, "Why?"

It added something to the prison, Miriam wanted to think, that it had once been a military fort. Built high on a hill above the river, to confound attack. From the access road the prison was too massive to be seen except as weatherworn dark gray stone like something in an illustrated fairy tale of desolation and punishment. Beside the front gate was a plaque informing visitors of the history of the prison: "Fort La Présentation was built in 1749 by French missionaries. It was captured by the British in 1760 and its name changed to Fort Oswegatchie. After the Revolution, it was the site of several bloody skirmishes in the War of 1812. In 1817, its name was changed to Ogdensburg and in 1911 it was converted into the first state prison for men in northern New York State. In 1956—" Ethel interrupted irritably," As if anybody gives a damn about history who'd be coming here." Miriam said, stung, "Not everybody is like you, Mom. Some people actually want to learn something." Miriam made it a point to read such plaques when she could. So much that was shifting and unreliable in her life; at least history was real.

It was a way, too, of telling Ethel: *You aren't so smart. You didn't graduate from high school. As I am going to do.*

Probably Ethel was right, though. Visitors to Ogdensburg had other things on their minds.

Everywhere were signs. PRISON PERSONNEL ONLY. RESTRICTED AREA. TRESPASSERS SUBJECT TO ARREST. VISITORS' PARKING. VISITING HOURS. PENALTIES FOR VIOLATION OF CONTRABAND RESTRICTIONS. A ten-foot stone wall topped with coils of razor wire surrounded the prison. Once you got through the checkpoint at the gate, you saw an inner electrified six-foot wire fence, angled sharply inward. Whenever she saw this fence, Miriam felt a clutch of panic picturing herself forced to climb it, like a frantic animal scrambling and clawing to twist over the top, cutting her hands to shreds on the glinting razor wire. Of course, she'd have been shocked unconscious by the electric voltage.

No one had escaped from Ogdensburg in a long time.

Ethel was saying with her bitter-bemused laugh, "Damn prisons are big business. Half the town is on the payroll here. Guards run in families."

Once you passed through the first checkpoint, you were outdoors again, waiting in line with other visitors. It was a windy November day, blowing gritty snow like sand. The line moved slowly. Most of the visitors were women. Many had children with them. Many were black, Hispanic. From downstate. A scattering of whites, looking straight ahead. *Like sisters*, Miriam thought. No one wanted to be recognized here. Miriam dreaded seeing someone from the Ochs family who would know Ethel. She hadn't told Ethel what Lana Ochs had said on the bus that everyone had heard. *Your father and my father. In the same place.*

Miriam didn't know why Lana's father was in prison. She supposed it had to do with theft, bad checks. Though it might have been assault.

It wasn't uncommon for men in the Star Lake area to get into trouble with the law and to serve time at Ogdensburg, but no one in the Orlander family had ever been sent to prison before. Miriam remembered her mother screaming at her father, *How could you do this, so ashamed, ruined our lives, took our happiness from us and threw it into the dirt and for what?*

Miriam had pressed her hands against her ears. Whatever her father had answered, if he'd shouted back or turned aside sick and defeated, Miriam hadn't known.

It was true: Les had taken their happiness from them. What they hadn't understood was their happiness because they'd taken it for granted, not knowing that even ordinary unhappiness is a kind of happiness when you have both your parents and your name isn't to be uttered in shame.

Les had been incarcerated now for nearly eighteen months. Gone from the house on Salt Isle Road as if he'd died. *Doing time.*

Miriam had constructed a homemade calendar. Because you could not buy a calendar for the next year and the next and the next, at least not in Star Lake. On the wall beside her bed she marked off the days in red. *Wishing-away time* was what it was. Miriam overheard her mother saying on the phone, *You wish away time, like wishing away your life. Goddamn if I'm going to do that.*

Miriam hadn't understood what Ethel meant. She'd understood the fury in her mother's voice, though.

Les Orlander's sentence was five to seven years. Which could mean seven years. Miriam would be nineteen when he was released and could not imagine herself so old.

"Move along. Coats off. Next."

They were shuffling through the second checkpoint, which was the most thorough: metal detector; pockets and handbags emptied onto a conveyor belt; coats, hats removed, boots. Ethel was flushed and indignant struggling to remove her tight-fitting boots. Each visit to Ogdensburg was stressful to her. She seemed never to accept the authority of others to peer at her, examine her belongings, query her.

She was an attractive woman of whom men took notice, if only to stare at her, then dismiss her: a face no longer young, a fleshy, sloping-down body. Breasts, hips. Since her husband's arrest and imprisonment she'd gained weight. Her skin seemed heated. Her dark hair was streaked with gray as if carelessly. In the parking lot she'd smeared dark lipstick onto her mouth, which was now downturned, sullen. The black female security guard was suspicious of her. "Ma'am? I'm asking you again, all the contents of that bag *out*." Ethel's hands were shaking as she fumbled to comply. Miriam was quick to help. Under duress, she immediately became Ethel's daughter. She would side with her mother against others, by instinct.

Orlander, Ethel and *Orlander, Miriam* were checked against a list. A guard directed them into another crowded waiting room. Hard not to believe you were being punished. Related to an inmate, a criminal, you deserved punishment, too.

Everywhere they looked was glaring surfaces. Rooms brightly lit by fluorescent tubing. Linoleum floors, pale green walls. Where a surface could be buffed to shine, it shone. Miriam had never smelled such harsh odors. Disinfectant, Ethel said. "One good thing, there's no germs in this damn place. They'd all be killed."

"I wouldn't be too sure, Mom. We'd be killed before that."

"God, I hate it here. This place."

"Think how Daddy feels."

"Daddy.' " Ethel's voice quavered with contempt.

Don't hate Daddy! Miriam wanted to beg. *We are all he has.*

The night before, Miriam hadn't been able to sleep. Misery through the night. She could feel her skin itching, burning. Her sensitive skin. Rehearsing what she would tell her father that would make him love her. That was all it was, trying to make Daddy love her. When she'd been a little girl, the baby of the family, it had been so easy, Daddy had loved her, and Mommy, and her big brothers, who'd adored her when they had time for her. Then something happened. Miriam had gotten older, Daddy wasn't so interested in her or in his family. Daddy was distracted, Daddy was in one of his moods. Drinking, Miriam knew. That was it. Part of it. He'd had disagreements with the roofing contractor for whom he worked. He'd tried working on his own but that brought problems, too. Ethel said, *Things change, people change. What's broke can't be whole again* but Miriam didn't want to believe this.

Driving to Ogdensburg that morning, Ethel had been unusually

192

quiet. That week she'd worked at Tupper Lake for two days, two nights and so she'd had that drive and now the drive to Ogdensburg and she was tired. She was tired, and she was resentful. Not one of Miriam's brothers was coming this time, which meant Ethel had to drive both ways. Miriam was only thirteen, too young for a driver's permit. Ethel had her own life now. In Tupper Lake. At home, the phone rang for her and she took the portable out of the room, speaking guardedly. Miriam would hear her laugh at a distance. Behind a shut door.

She's seeing men. Les better not know. Miriam's brothers were uneasy, suspicious. Gideon hadn't yet confronted Ethel. Miriam was frightened, preferring not to know.

Her skin! Her face. Broken out in hives and pellet-hard little pimples on her forehead; her fingernails wanted to scratch, and scratch.

"Miriam, don't."

Ethel caught Miriam's hand and gripped it tight. What had Miriam been doing, picking at her face? She was stricken with embarrassment. "Do I look really bad, Mom? Will Daddy notice?" Ethel said quickly, "Honey, no. You look very pretty. Let me fluff your bangs down." Miriam pushed her mother's hands away. She was thirteen, not three. "I can't help it, my face itches. I could claw my ugly face off." Miriam spoke with such vehemence, Ethel looked at her in alarm.

"Yes. I know how you feel. But don't."

At last they were led into the visitors' room, where Inmate Orlander was waiting. Ethel poked Miriam in the side. "Smile, now. Give it a try. Look at Momma, I'm smiling."

Miriam laughed, startled. Ethel laughed. Clutching at each other, suddenly excited and frightened.

"Go on, honey, Your daddy wants to see *you*."

Ethel urged Miriam in front of her, like a human shield. The gesture was meant to be playful but Miriam knew better. Ethel would hold back while Miriam talked with Les; she wasn't so enthusiastic about seeing him as Miriam was. They had private matters to discuss. Their transactions were likely to be terse, tinged with irony and regret.

Miriam smiled and waved at her father, who was standing stiffly behind the Plexiglas partition waiting for his visitors. Les Orlander in olive gray prison clothes, one inmate among many.

Here was the shock: the visitors' room that was so large, and so noisy. You wanted the visit to be personal but it was like TV with everyone looking on.

And the plastic partition between. You had to speak through a grill, as to a bank teller.

Les was frowning. Seeing Miriam, he smiled, and waved. Miriam didn't want to see how he glanced behind her, looking for Miriam's brothers and not seeing them.

Third visit in a row, not one of Les's sons.

"Sweetie, hi. Lookin' good."

He would look at her, smile at her. He wouldn't ask about the boys, in Miriam's hearing.

". . . got something for me there?"

They brought Les things he couldn't get for himself: magazines, a large paperback book of maps, *Civil War Sites*. These Miriam was allowed to give to her father, with a guard looking on. Harmless items, printed material. Les seemed genuinely interested in the Civil War book, leafing through it. "We'll go to Gettysburg. When I get out."

It was unusual for Les to allude to getting out to Miriam. There was a kind of fiction between them, in this place, of timelessness; so much energy was concentrated on the present, cramming as much as you could into a brief visit, there wasn't time to think of a future.

"So—what's new, honey? Tell me about school."

School! Miriam couldn't think of a thing.

For visiting Daddy she'd cultivated a childish personality not her own. Like auditioning for a play, reading lines with a phony forced enthusiasm, and smiling with just your mouth. Bad acting and everyone knew but it had to be done for you could not read in your own flat, raw voice. To sound sincere you had to be insincere. Miriam told her father about school. Not the truth but other things. Not that, this past year, her teachers seemed to feel sorry for her or that she hadn't many friends now, in eighth grade; she'd lost her closest girlfriends, like Iris Petko she'd known since first grade, guessed their mothers didn't want them to be friendly with Miriam Orlander, whose father was incarcerated in a maximum-security prison. Miriam supposed that Les didn't know what grade she was in or how old she was exactly, for he had other things on his mind of more importance. Still he seemed to want to hear her news, leaning forward cupping his hand to his ear. In prison he'd become partially deaf in his right ear, the eardrum had burst when someone (guard? inmate?) had struck

194

him on the side of the head shortly after he'd arrived at the prison. Les had not reported the injury as he hadn't reported other injuries and threats, saying if he did, next time it would be his head that was busted, like a melon.

Miriam's father was a stocky, compact man in his late forties. He'd had a hard-boned good-looking face now battered, uncertain. Scars in both his eyebrows like slivers of glass. His dark hair had been razor-cut military style, leaving his head exposed and vulnerable, the tendons in his neck prominent. He was prone to moods, unpredictable. His eyes were often suspicious, guarded and watchful. Miriam loved him but also feared him, as her brothers did. So much of her life had been waiting for Daddy to smile at her, to single her out from the others in his sudden, tender way; as if Daddy's feeling for Miriam overcame him, caught him by surprise.

Hey, sweetie: love ya!

He'd been wounded by life, Miriam knew. The hurt he'd done another man had rebounded to him, like shrapnel. Les had the look of a trapped creature. You never wanted to antagonize him; he had a way of striking out blindly.

At Ogdensburg, Les was assigned to the metal shop. Making license plates, dog tags. His pay was $1.75 an hour.

Again he was thanking Miriam for the Civil War book. The Civil War was one of Miriam's father's interests, or had been. Les had never been in the army but his father, Miriam's grandfather she'd never known, had been an army corporal who'd died in his second tour of Vietnam, long ago in 1969. Les's feeling for his father was a confusion of pride and anger.

"We'll go, baby. I promise. When I get out. I'll be up for parole in . . ." Les tried to calculate when: how many months.

It was time for Ethel to talk to Les. Ethel's hand on Miriam's shoulder, to release her.

Miriam waved good-bye to her father, smiling hard to keep from crying. Les mouthed *Love ya, baby!* as Miriam backed away.

In the visitors' lounge there were vending machines, a scattering of vinyl chairs. Everyone who visited an inmate at Ogdensburg seemed to be hungry. Cheese sticks, potato chips, candy bars, doughnuts, soft drinks. Mothers were feeding children from the machines. Children sat hunched and eating like starving cats. Miriam was faint with hunger but couldn't eat, here.

She never wanted to hear what her parents talked about. Never

195

wanted to hear that low quivering voice in which Ethel spoke of financial problems, mortgage payments, insurance, bills, work needing to be done on the house. *How can I do this without you. How could you leave us. Why!*

There was no answer to *why*. What Miriam's father had done, in a blind rage: use an ax (the blunt edge, not the sharp: he had not killed the other man, only beaten him unconscious) against a man, a home owner, who owed him money for a roof-repair job, and Les had been charged with attempted murder, which was dropped to aggravated assault, which was dropped to simple assault to which he'd pleaded guilty. If Les had been convicted of attempted murder he might have drawn a ten-to-fifteen-year sentence.

Everyone said, *Les is damn lucky, the bastard didn't die*.

"Hey: want some?"

A fattish boy of about seventeen surprised Miriam, thrusting out a bag of CheeseStix at her, which Miriam declined. Out of nowhere the boy seemed to have stepped. He had a blemished skin, a silver ring clamped in his left nostril. He wore a jungle fatigue jumpsuit with camouflage spots that looked painted on the fabric, crude as cartoon spots. He was a head taller than Miriam, looming close. "Hey: where're you from?" Miriam was too shy not to answer truthfully, "Star Lake." The boy whistled, as if Miriam had said something remarkable. "Star Lake? Oh man, where's it? Up by the moon? That's where I'm headed." Miriam laughed uneasily. She guessed this was meant to be funny. She hadn't ever quite known how girls her age met boys outside of school, what sorts of things they said. Miriam knew from overhearing her brothers how cruel, crude, jeering, and dismissive boys could be about girls to whom they weren't attracted or didn't respect and she wasn't able to gauge others' feelings for her." . . . your name?" the fattish boy asked, and Miriam pretended not to hear, turning away.

Wishing she'd asked Ethel for the car key so that she could wait for her outside. She needed to get out of this place, fast.

"We could go outside, have a smoke. I got plenty."

The fattish boy persisted, following Miriam. He seemed amused by her as if he could see through her pretense of shyness to an avid interest in him. Asking again if she wanted a smoke, tapping his thumb against a pack of cigarettes in his shirt pocket with a suggestive leer. Miriam shook her head no, she didn't smoke. She was aware of the boy's shiny eyes on her, a kind of exaggerated interest like

196

something on TV. Was he flirting with her? Was this what flirting was? Miriam was only thirteen but already her body was warmly fleshy like her mother's, her face roundly solid, not beautiful but attractive, sometimes. When her skin wasn't broken out in hives. The boy was saying, "I saw you in there, hon. Talking to, who's it, your old man?" Miriam backed away, smiling nervously. She was becoming confused, wondering if somehow the boy knew Les, or knew of him. He was saying, mysteriously, "There's something nobody ever asks in here, who's an inmate," and Miriam said quickly, "I have to go now, I have to meet my mother." Again the boy spoke mysteriously, "Not what you think, hon. What nobody ever asks." Miriam was trying to avoid the boy, making her way along the wall of vending machines where people were dropping in coins, punching buttons, but the boy followed her, eating from his bag of CheeseStix. "We're up from Yonkers visiting my brother, he's gonna max out at six years. Know what that is? 'Max out'? Six years. What's your old man in for? 'Involuntary manslaughter'—that's my brother." The boy laughed, sputtering saliva. "Like, my brother didn't 'intend' what happened, that's the deal, only know what, hon?—that's bullshit. Bullshit he didn't. You max out, you don't get no fucking parole officer breathing down your neck." Miriam was walking more quickly away, not looking back, trying not to be frightened. They were back at the entrance to the lounge where another corridor led to restrooms. The boy loomed over her, panting into her face. "Hey, hon: nobody's gonna hurt you. Why you walking away? Think somebody's gonna rape you? Any guy tries to talk to you, think he's gonna rape you? That is so sick, hon. What'd you think, Baby Tits? Your ass is so sweet, a guy is gonna jump you, the place crawling with guards?" The fattish boy spoke in a loud, mocking drawl. Miriam heard the anger beneath. She hadn't understood, something was wrong with this boy. Like the special ed. students at school, you tried to avoid because they could turn on you suddenly, like Lana Ochs. A female guard approached them. "Miss, is this guy bothering you?" Miriam said quickly, "No." She hurried to the women's restroom, to escape.

Igneous. Sedimentary. Metamorphic.

Miriam was underlining words in her earth science workbook. In green ink writing in the margin of the page. Beside her, driving, Ethel seemed upset. Wiping at her eyes, blowing her nose. Each time they visited Les at Ogdensburg, Ethel came away upset, dis-

197

tracted. But today seemed worse. Miriam pretended not to notice.

Miriam hadn't told Ethel about the fattish boy in the camouflage jumpsuit. She would recast the experience, in her imagination, as a kind of flirtation. He'd called her hon. He'd seemed to like her.

Ethel said suddenly, as if the thought had just surfaced, in the way of something submerged beneath the surface of the water that suddenly emerges, "I wanted to go to nursing school at Plattsburgh. You know this, I've told you. Except that didn't happen." Ethel spoke haltingly, with an embarrassed laugh. "Seems like my life just skidded past. I loved Les so much. And you, and the boys. Except I'm not *old*."

Miriam could make no sense of her mother's words. She dreaded hearing more.

They were headed south on Route 58, nearing Black Lake. A windy November day, gray sky spitting snow. Ethel drove the old Cutlass at wavering speeds.

Miriam especially dreaded to hear why Ethel had dropped out of high school at seventeen, to marry twenty-year-old Les Orlander.

"Miriam, I told him."

Now Miriam glanced up from her textbook. "Told him—what?"

"That I've been seeing someone, and I'm going to keep seeing him. I have a friend now. Who respects me. In Tupper Lake."

Ethel began to cry. A kind of crying-laughing, terrible to hear. She reached out to touch Miriam, groping for Miriam's arm as she drove, but Miriam shrank away as if a snake had darted at her.

Ethel said, "Oh God. I can't believe that I told him . . . and he knows now." Repeating, as if her own words astonished her, "He knows."

Miriam shrank into herself; she had nothing to say. She was stunned, disgusted, and frightened. Her brain was shutting off, she wasn't a party to this. Maybe she'd known. Known something. Her brothers knew. Everyone knew. Les Orlander, whose relatives visited him at Ogdensburg, had probably known.

". . . nothing to do with you, honey. Not with any of you. Only with him. Your father. What he did to us. 'I don't know what happened. What came over me.' My own life, I have to have my own life. I have to support us. I'm not going to lose the house. I'm not going down with him. I told him."

A heavy logging truck had pulled up behind the Cutlass and was swinging out now to pass, at sixty-five miles an hour on the two-lane country highway. Ethel's car began to shudder in the wake of the enormous truck. Miriam felt a sudden desire to grab the steering wheel, turn the car off the road.

I hate you. I love Daddy, and I hate you.

"Can't you say something, Miriam? Please."

"What's there to say, Mom? You've said it."

The rest of the drive to the house on Salt Isle Road passed in silence.

5.

. . . in silence for much of the drive to Gettysburg. And hiking in the hilly battlefield, and in the vast cemetery that was like no other cemetery Miriam had ever seen before. *All these dead,* Les marveled. *Makes you see what life is worth, don't it!* He hadn't seemed depressed or even angry, more bemused, shaking his head and smiling like it was a joke, the grassy earth at his feet was a joke, so many graves of long-ago soldiers in the Union Army, dead after three days of slaughter at Gettysburg: a "decisive" battle in the War Between the States.

They would question Miriam about that day. Afterward.

The long drive in the car with Les, what sorts of things he'd said to her. What was his mood, had he been drinking. Had he given any hint of how unhappy he was, of wanting to hurt himself . . . .

Wanting to hurt himself. The words they used. Investigating his death. *Hurt* not *kill.* Les's relatives, friends. Miriam's brothers could hardly speak of it, what he'd done to himself. At least not that Miriam heard. And Ethel could not, there were no words for her.

Les had been paroled five months, when they'd made the trip to Gettysburg they'd been planning so long. Five months out of Ogdensburg and back in Star Lake picking up jobs where he could. The roofing contractor he'd worked for, for years, wasn't so friendly to him now. There was a coolness between Les and his brother-in-law Harvey Schuller. Les had served three years, seven months of his sentence for assault. In Ogdensburg he'd been a "model" prisoner, paroled for "good behavior" and this was good news, this was happy news, the family was happy for Les, the relatives. If they were angry with him for what he'd done, bringing shame to the family, still they were happy he'd been paroled, now his drinking was under control, his short temper. Though Ethel had her own life now, that was clear.

Take it or leave it, she'd told Les, those are the terms he'd have to ac-
cept if he wanted to live with her and their daughter, I am not going
to lie to you, I don't lie to any man, ever again. By this time Ethel had
been disappointed with her man friend in Tupper Lake. More than
one man friend had disappointed her, she'd acquired a philosophical
attitude at age forty-seven: you're on your own, that's the bottom
line. No man is going to bail you out. Ethel had gained weight, her
fleshy body a kind of armor. Her face was a girl's face inside a fleshy
mask through which Ethel's eyes, flirty, insolent, yearning, still shone.
Miriam loved her, but was exasperated by her. Loved her, but didn't
want to be anything like her. Though Ethel had a steady income now,
comanaging a local catering service, no longer one of the uniformed
employees. Ethel didn't need a husband's income, didn't need a hus-
band. Yet she'd taken Les in, how could she not take Les in, the
property was half his, he'd built most of the house himself, they'd
been married almost thirty years, poor bastard, where's he going to
live? Nowhere for Les to take his shame, his wife had been unfaithful
to him and worse yet hadn't kept it a secret, his wife barely tolerated
him, felt pity for him, contempt. Maybe she loved him, maybe that
was so, Ethel wasn't sentimental any longer, all that was drained from
her when Les lifted the ax to bring the blunt edge down on another
man's skull, but what kind of love was it, the kind of love you feel for
a cripple, Ethel didn't mince words. Take it or leave it, she'd told
him, things are different in this house now. So far as the Ogdensburg
parole board knew, Les Orlander was living at home with his family.
P.O. Box 91, Salt Isle Road, Star Lake, NY. *Makes you see what life is
worth*, Les said. *Dying for a good cause.*

It was early June. A few days after Memorial Day. Everywhere in
Gettysburg Cemetery were small American flags, wind whipped.
Miriam had never seen so many graves. And such uniformity in the
grave markers, in the rows of graves. Row upon row of small identi-
cal grave markers, it made you dizzy to see. Miriam imagined a
marching army. Ghost army of the doomed. She felt a shudder of
physical revulsion. Why for so long had she and Les planned to come
here?

For an hour, an hour and a half, they walked in the Civil War
memorial. It was a cool bright windy day. Warmer in southern Penn-
sylvania than it would have been in Star Lake in the Adirondacks. Of
course there were other visitors to the memorial. There were fami-
lies, children. Les was offended by their loud voices. A four-year-old

boy clambering over graves, snatching at miniature flags. Les said something to the child's father that Miriam didn't hear, and the young father pulled at his son's hand, rebuked. Miriam held her breath but there was nothing more.

Stocky and muscled, in a hooded pullover, jaws unshaven, and a baseball cap pulled down low over his forehead, Les wasn't a man another man would wish to antagonize unless that man was very like Les himself. Was your father angry about anything, did he seem distracted, what was his mood that day, Miriam would be asked.

As if, after her father's death, Miriam would betray him!

She did tell Ethel what was true: on the drive down, Les had been quiet. He'd brought tapes and cassettes and a few CDs of music he wanted to hear or thought he wanted to hear, rock bands with names new to Miriam, music of a long-ago time when Les had been a kid, a young guy in his twenties just growing up. Miriam was disappointed; some of the songs Les listened to for only a few seconds, then became impatient, disgusted. Telling Miriam to try something else.

It was awkward, in Les's company. Just Les alone, not Ethel or one of Miriam's brothers. She had to suppose it was the first time they'd ever been alone together in the car like this though she could not have supposed it would be the last time. Somehow, the trip to Gettysburg had come to mean too much. They'd planned it so long. It seemed to have something to do, Miriam thought, with her father's memory of his own father. Not that Les said much about this. Only a few times, in the way of a man thinking out loud. If Miriam asked Les what he'd said, he didn't seem to hear. She was sitting beside his right ear, that was his bad ear. You didn't dare to raise your voice to Les, he took offense if you did that, even Ethel knew better than to provoke him, for sometimes he seemed to hear normally, and other times he didn't, you could not predict. And so sometimes he talked without hearing, without listening. In the cemetery at Gettysburg, the wind blew words away. Miriam saw how Les walked stiffly, like a man fearing pain. Maybe one of his knees. Maybe his back. His shoulders were set in a posture of labor; he'd done manual labor most of his adult life. Roofers are particularly prone to neck and spine strain. Miriam watched her father walk ahead of her, along the rows of grave markers, hands jammed into the deep pockets of his jersey pullover. He seemed to her a figure of mystery, still a good-looking man though his face was beginning to look ravaged, his skin sallow from prison. After he shot himself to death with his deer rifle

201

a few weeks later, in a desolate stretch of pine woods beyond the property on Salt Isle Road where he'd used to hunt white-tailed deer and wild turkey with Miriam's brothers, Miriam would be asked if he'd said much about the cemetery at Gettysburg, or about his father, or Gideon, who was stationed in Iraq, and Miriam said evasively she didn't remember.

Les hadn't said much about Gideon. He hadn't seen Gideon in nearly a year. He was bewildered and angry that Gideon had enlisted in the army without consulting him, Iraq was a dirty war, a sham war like they'd said of Vietnam. Like Gideon had wanted to put distance between himself and Star Lake, was that it? Between himself and his family.

Miriam was walking fast to keep pace with Les. She'd thought he was going to head back toward the parking lot but he seemed to be walking in the opposite direction, back into the cemetery. Overhead clouds were shifting in the sky, like soiled sailcloth. Miriam didn't want to think that the trip to the Gettysburg memorial had gone wrong somehow. Maybe it was too late. Les should have taken the family, all of them, years ago when Miriam's brothers were young, and Miriam was a little girl. Somehow, the trip had come to be too important to Les and Miriam, there was a strain to it like the strain of a balloon being blown bigger and bigger until it threatens to burst. And then it bursts.

There was a tall plaque beside the roadway. Miriam read aloud, in fragments: " '. . . Lincoln's Gettysburg Address, November 19, 1863, the greatest speech of the Civil War and one of the greatest speeches ever given by any American president. *Four score and seven years ago. All men are created equal. Brave men, living and dead, who struggled here. The world will little note, nor long remember, what we say here, but can never forget what they did here . . .'* " and Les interrupted, "Bullshit. Who remembers? Who's left? Just Lincoln, people remember."

It was the afternoon of June 3, 2004. Miriam's father would disappear from her life on June 28.

6.

Months after the funeral, after Labor Day, when Star Lake emptied out and the downstate homeowners were gone, they trashed one of the new houses on East Shore Drive. Stoned on crystal meth like lighter fluid inhaled through the nostrils and a match lit and whup! whup! whup! it was like a video game, wild. A replica of an old Adirondack lodge of the 1920s except the logs were weatherized and insulated; there were sliding glass doors overlooking the deck, and the lake. Maybe it was a house their father Les had worked on, the brothers weren't sure. Not Gideon (after the funeral he'd flown back to the Mideast, his duty had been extended) but Martin and Stan and some of their friends. Forced a back door and no security alarm went off that they could hear. Trashed the place looking for liquor and found instead above the fireplace mantel a mounted buck's head, six-teen-point antlers, shining their flashlights outraged to see a Mets cap dangling from one of the points, a small American flag on a wooden stick twined in the antlers, sunglasses over the glass eyes so they pulled down the buck's head to take away with them, stabbed and tore leather furniture with their fishing knives, smashed a wall-screen TV, smashed a CD player, tossed dishes in a frenzy of break-age, overturned the refrigerator, jammed forks into the garbage disposal, took time to open cans of dog food to throw against the walls, took time to stop up toilets (six toilets!) with wadded towels; in the bedrooms (five bedrooms!) took time to urinate on as many beds as their bladders allowed, it had something to do with Les Orlander though they could not have said what. Sure, they'd remembered to wear gloves, these guys watched TV crime shows. Martin wanted to torch the place but the others talked him out of it. A fire would draw too much attention.

Miriam wasn't a witness to the trashing, had not been with her brothers. Yet somehow, she knew.

7.

"My damn mother, I wish . . ."

This second time. The words came out sudden and furious. What-ever was in her bloodstream had got into her brain. And the music was hurting. It scared her, the way the blood arteries beat. ". . . wish somebody would put that woman out of her misery, she'd be better off." What was his name, he'd been Gideon's close friend in high school, Oz Newell was Miriam's friend here. Oz Newell was protect-ing her. Leaning his sweaty-haired head to Miriam, touching her forehead with his own in a gesture of clumsy intimacy asking what's she saying and Miriam says, "I want somebody to kill my mother, like

203

she killed my father." So it was said. For months it had needed saying, building up in Miriam like bile and now it was said and the guys stared at her but maybe hadn't heard her, even Oz laughing so certainly he hadn't heard. Hay Brouwet was trying to tell him something. Nobody could talk in a normal voice, you had to shout so your throat became raw. Hay was cupping his big-knuckled hands to his mouth, so Miriam could see that Hay was shouting but the music was so loud, must've been she was so stoned, she couldn't hear a thing.

Whatever is done. Whatever you cause to be done. It will have happened always. It can never be changed.

In that other time, before her father had killed himself. On the drive home from Gettysburg. If Miriam had said: what words? If Miriam had said *I love you, you are my father. Don't leave me.* Of course, she'd said nothing. Underlining passages in her earth science workbook as her father drove north on the thruway, home.

It was later, then. They were somewhere else, the air smelled different. There was less noise. The vibrations had ceased. When they'd left the Star Lake Inn, Miriam didn't know. Possibly she'd passed out. An inky mist had come over her. She remembered laying her head down on her crossed arms, on a table to which her skin was sticking. Though she knew better there was the fear that her brothers would see her, drunk, disheveled, sluttish in the company of older guys, some of them bikers, stoned, excited, looking for a way to discharge their excitement, a dog pack sniffing for blood. In this pack, Oz Newell was her friend. Oz Newell swaying on his feet and oozing sweat would protect Miriam, she knew. There was an understanding between them. Miriam believed this. For Oz carried her to his beatup Cherokee, lifting her in his arms, Miriam was limp, faint headed, her mouth slack and eyes half shut, she could feel his arm muscles straining, the tendons in his neck. Oz's face was a strong face like something hacked from stone. The skin was coarse, acne scarred. The jaws were unshaven. It was late, it was past 2 a.m. Miriam had to be carried, her feet were bare, very dirty, the soles scratched, bleeding. One of those dreams where you have lost your shoes, part of your clothing, strangers' eyes move onto you, jeering. The stained red T-shirt and cord skirt riding up her thighs, Miriam tried to tug the skirt down, her fingers clutched, clawed. She'd been running in the gravel parking lot. Hair in her face, panicked. "Don't! Don't hurt—" but no one was listening to her. Kevin had left the inn, the pack had followed him, Miriam clutching at Hay Brouwet's arm, he'd thrown her off as you'd flick away a fly. Miriam had not remembered that Kevin was wearing a Yankees cap but this had to be Kevin, big-jawed boy with sun-bleached hair straggling past his ears, Kevin with the rich father, Kevin complaining of the sleek white sailboat, he was headed for a Jeep, ignition key in hand he was headed for a steel-colored Jeep parked partway in weeds at the far end of the lot when Oz Newell and Hay Brouwet and Brandon McGraw and their friends advanced upon him cursing—"Fuckface! Where ya goin'!"—and Kevin turned to them with a look of utter astonishment so taken by surprise he hardly had time to lift his arms to protect his head, the men were whooping and rushing at him fierce as dogs in a pack. Kevin tried to run but they caught him, cursing him, slamming him against the Jeep, the Yankees cap went flying, Kevin's head was struck repeatedly, Kevin fell to the ground as the men circled around him punching and kicking with their steel-toe workboots. Miriam clutched at their arms, pulled at them, begged them to stop but they paid no attention to her, even Oz Newell shoved her from him, indifferent to her pleas. And a part of her was thinking, *Hurt him! So he will know.*

There was justice in it, such a beating. You felt this. Though you could not acknowledge it, not even to Oz Newell and his friends.

In the gravel, partway in the weeds at the end of the lot, the bleach-haired boy lay writhing and vomiting. His clothes were torn, his chest exposed. He had not been hurt. It hadn't been a serious beating. They laughed in derision watching him crawl toward the Jeep. Bleeding from a broken nose but a broken nose isn't serious. His front teeth were maybe loosened. The pretty-boy face had been roughed up, he'd had to be taught a lesson. Rich fucker. Rich guy's fucking son. Stay away from the Star Lake Inn, fucker. Stay away from our girls. Next time it's your head that'll be broke. Your brains you'll be puking. The guys were feeling good about this. They were grateful to Miriam, who was their friend Gideon's young sister, for needing them. For turning to them. The adrenaline high is the best high, the purest high. Laughing so tears stung their faces like acid. Except they had to get the hell out, fast. What if somebody inside the inn had called 911. Two or three of the guys had come on their motorcy-cles, some in pickups. Oz Newell had his beat-up Cherokee that smelled like he'd been living in it. There was a plan to meet at an-other place a few miles up the road at the Benson Mines, open till

4 a.m. But Oz Newell said he'd better get Miriam the hell home.

On Salt Isle Road the wind was moving in the tops of the trees like a living thing. There was the moon sliding in the sky, about to disappear behind clouds. And the clouds so thin and ragged, like torn cloth, blowing across the face of the moon. "Look!" Miriam pointed. "Makes you think there's some reason to it." Oz glanced sidelong at Miriam, sprawled in the seat beside him. He'd had to toss soiled shirts, Styrofoam wrappers, beer cans into the back to make room for her. ". . . like the moon makes a center in the sky. So the sky isn't just . . ." Miriam was losing the thread of what she was saying. It was an important thing she meant to say, might've said to her father, maybe it would have made a difference. The Cherokee was lurching along the narrow lakeside road. Whatever had gotten into Miriam's brain was making her feel like she wasn't inside her skull but floating a few feet away.

Oz Newell said, surprising her, his voice was so deliberate: "Back there, Miriam, what'd you say, about your mother? I didn't maybe hear."

So Oz had heard. Heard something. Miriam thought, *He will do it. For me.* It could be an accident. There were so many accidents with guns. All the men owned guns. Boys owned guns. Even off-season you heard gunfire in the woods. Les Orlander had not been one of those who'd owned many guns, just two. The shotgun, the rifle. The rifle taken into custody by the county sheriff's department, then released to the family, and Stan had appropriated it, and the shotgun, to take back to Keene with him. Oz could use a rifle. Oz could fire through Ethel's bedroom window. Oz could hide outside, in the bushes. Oz could fire through the windshield of the Cutlass. When Miriam was driving into town. It could be a robbery. A stranger. This time of year there were many strangers in the Star Lake area. There were many strangers in the Adirondacks. There were break-ins, burglaries, vandalism. There were unexplained beatings, killings. It would happen swiftly and then it would be over and Miriam could live with Martin in Watertown where he was out of rehab now and working as a roofer and he'd seemed lonely, and Ethel had said, honey, come home, live with your sister and me, and Martin pushed her off, saying he'd sooner be in hell.

In childish bitterness Miriam said, "My mother. What she did to my father. She should be punished," and Oz said as if perplexed,

"Punished how?" and Miriam said, wiping her mouth on the shoulder of her AU SABLE BOATHOUSE T-shirt, "Some way." Miriam's brain was becoming vague again. It was like clouds being blown across the face of the moon, you couldn't see what was behind the rapid flowing movement, if it was moving also. Oz, driving the Cherokee, braking at curves, said nothing. He was driving more deliberately now, as if he'd realized that he shouldn't be driving at all. Miriam could hear his panting breath. She said, "I'm not serious, Oz. I guess not."

Oz said, hunching his shoulders, "Shouldn't say a thing like that. About your mother. See, somebody might misunderstand."

Turning into Miriam's cinder driveway, Oz cut his headlights. Miriam saw with a pang of dread that the front rooms of the house were darkened but the outside light, at the carport, was on, and lights were burning at the rear of the house: kitchen, Ethel's bedroom. "Miriam, hey! Christ." Oz laughed, Miriam was clutching at him. She was kissing him, his stubbled jaws, the startled expression on his face. He pushed her away and she crossed a leg over his, jamming against the steering wheel. She was desperate, aroused. It felt like drowning, wanting so to be loved. Should be ashamed but it was happening so quickly. Her mouth against the man's was hot and hurtful, her hard, hungry teeth. She had no idea what a kiss is, the opening of mouths, tongues, the softness, groping. Oz laughed, uneasy. Pushing her away more forcibly. "Miriam, c'mon."

She was too young, Gideon's kid sister. She was a sister to him, or she was nothing. He was sure she'd never had sex with anyone and damned if he'd be the first.

"I love you. I want to be with *you*."

"Sure, baby. Some other time."

Miriam jumped from the Cherokee, made her way wincing barefoot into the house. So ashamed! Her face pounded with heat.

The kitchen was two rooms, one a former washroom. Les had knocked out the wall between. There was a long counter with a scarred white enamel sink. The beautiful cabinets of dark polished wood Les had built. On the linoleum floor were scattered rugs. Miriam saw that Ethel wasn't in the kitchen even as, in her bathrobe, a cigarette in hand, Ethel entered the kitchen, from the direction of her bedroom. Ethel's eyes brimming with emotion, fixed on Miriam in the way of one staring at a blazing light, blinding.

Miriam's heart gave a skid. She loved this woman so much, the two of them helpless together, like swimmers drowning in each other's arms.

Her voice was brattish, exasperated. "Why aren't you in bed, Mom? I told you not to wait up."

Now that Les was gone and would not be coming back, Ethel was in mourning. Her face was pale and puffy without makeup, raw. Yet strangely young looking, her mouth like a bruise, wounded. In the chenille robe her body was slack, ripe, beyond ripeness. The loose, heavy breasts were disgusting to Miriam, who wanted to rush at her mother and strike at her with childish, flailing fists. Miriam who was staggering with exhaustion, limping barefoot, hair in her face, and her ridiculous tight red T-shirt and white cord skirt stained with her own vomit. Wanting to hide her shamed face against Ethel's neck that was creased, smelling of talcum.

Somewhere distant, in the mountains beyond Star Lake, a melancholy cry, a sequence of cries. Loons, coyotes. Les had taken Miriam outside one summer night to listen to plaintive cries he identified as the cries of black bears.

Ethel smiled uncertainly. Knowing that, if she moved too suddenly, Miriam would push her away, run from the room. Barefoot, wincing in pain. The door to her room would be slammed shut, it would never open. "You look feverish, honey." Ethel must have smelled male sweat on Miriam. She smelled beer, vomit. Unmistakable, the smell of a daughter's vomit. But shrewdly deciding not to go there, in that direction. So grateful that the daughter is home. Coming to press a hand against the daughter's forehead. Miriam flinched, dreading this touch. For hours she'd been dreading it. Yet the hand was cool, consoling. Ethel said, her voice throaty, bemused, "Where've you been, are you going to tell me?"

For a moment Miriam couldn't remember. Where had she been? Her mouth was dry, parched as sand. As if she'd slept with her mouth open, helpless in sleep as a small child.

"Nowhere. Now I'm back."

Nominated by Conjunctions

NOTE TO A PINE RIDGE GIRL WHO CAN NO LONGER READ

by ADRIAN C. LOUIS

from NEW LETTERS

I keep dreaming these dreams
where I lose you, literally lose
you like misplaced car keys
and wake up sweating and
call and cuss, mutter for you
to reveal yourself, not in dream
but in my wide-awake frustration.
Thank God my closest neighbors
are simple Hmong who think all
Americans are crazed cannibals.
Ah, sweet mumbling darling,
I've been offered a great job
far from these mindless Plains
at a white castle of utmost
pay and supreme prestige.
Oh love, what are we to do?
A decade of intense meds
has made your face puffy.
I don't look any better, but
you cannot talk—little light

breaks in your eyes when I visit.
The *wasicu* staff tells me your
chanli will now be cut off
because you keep putting
the lit end in your mouth.
Pain and indignity floods
our being and our memory.
I can't tell you how many times
we've sat holding hands while
you've dirtied your diapers.
Two of your toes have curled
into claws—two of your fingers
did until they chopped them off.
God forgive me for okaying that.

When I catch your attention
and stand before you and do
the twist, you sometimes still
smile crazily, my little one.
That you smile at my dance
of tears is enough, my love.
Dearest woman, that is enough.
That is *all* I need. That's plenty.
Forgive me once and again
for thinking only of myself.
Everything is clear now and
I will not be crawling away to
some new life at this late date.
I'll keep playing the game
for the paycheck and
you, my love—
eternal

Nominated by New Letters

THE DINNER PARTY

by GALWAY KINNELL

from THE THREEPENNY REVIEW

1

In a dream, as in a dream,
they sit around a round
table, seven of them, friends
of each other and of me, too,
including two of my oldest
and closest. They look like
a bunch so loving they have
made it into paradise, as, in fact,
in life, they probably have—so far,
Aristotle would have us add.
Chunks of tiny sakras, bright
with the light drained from
the worldly sky, fulge from
the tips of the waxen stalagmites
like heads of salamanders
that have wiggled themselves
into existence. At the table
they talk a kind of talk
I know I don't know, sometimes
they smile it, sometimes chuckle
to each other their arrays
of oral finery. At these moments
their ears bunch up in the somewhat

bizarre natural screwiness
of ears at any sudden thrill.

2

In space as yet untracked
by feet of flies, still unpurged
by Pontic waters or by the Ajax
of the love of things earthly,
they look up, and smile.
"This empty chair. It's for you.
Come." O my dears. Yes, except
of course I'm only dreaming you,
the impossibility of you, of being
one of you. I can't. They take
the straitjacket off. So what?
The lunatic continues to hug himself.
Across the table I clink
eyeballs with several of you.
Space sings. My ears gaggle. Why?
I'm making you up, as I glidder
through the human dream.
Sometimes, rising from my desk
thick with discarded wretched
beginnings, the only way
I know I'm alive is
my toe- and fingernails grow.
O what I could have written! Maybe
will have written . . . Tonight
I will work late, then bed,
then up, then . . . then we'll see.
By then the busgirls and busboys
may have already come and lapsed
me into the lapping waters of ever
more swiftly elapsing time, and then
sat me down propped up on a chair
alone with knife, fork, and spoon
and bright empty glassfuls of desire.

Nominated by Henry Carlile, The Threepenny Review

THE BEST JEWELER

fiction by CLANCY MARTIN

from NOON

OLD JOHN WAS A FORMER HELICOPTER GUNNER who held the first bench in my jewelry store. We had a strict system: the best jeweler sat up front, where he could watch the teenage girls go in and out of Victoria's Secret through the front window. Larry, our second-best bench man, sat behind Old John, and behind Larry Tommy, et cetera, down to the back of the store where the polishing wheels were. I kept a list of best to worse. The one exception was my wax carver Christian Hilburn, who always held the last bench because he claimed you couldn't carve waxes with people watching. Unlike many jewelry stores we kept the jewelers out where the customers could observe them. I knew my customers would worry about their jewelry less, while it was being worked on, if they could keep an eye on it. We always kept exactly seven guys on the bench.

Although Old John used solder to fill in the gaps in his channel setting he was a patient jeweler, and was the only one who could reliably work with platinum without costing me money. He never broke diamonds, not even the corners on princess cuts. He worked late like me. But I came in early and we never asked Old John to come in before noon. Often, after the store was closed and everyone else had gone home, he would tell me about his time as a gunner in Vietnam, or his year in prison in Mexico, or the seven years he did at Leavenworth, in Kansas, where he learned to be a jeweler. It's a fact many people don't know, that most jewelers and watchmakers learn how to sit on the bench while in prison.

He dyed his hair jet black. He kept a jade-handled forty-five

213

chained to his bench. At Christmas he brought his boa in for the late nights and fed it mice in the store. He was five foot five. He drove a small, light, bruised Ford truck. His cheeks were as yellow and shiny as the belly of a lizard. His lunch and his dinner came to work with him in Tupperware, and he brought his own special coffee in a canteen. He did not drink or smoke, and unlike almost every other jeweler I have ever known, he didn't take speed or cocaine. I admired his asceticism. He kept the store square because he gave me a model to live by.

Good years Old John would make two hundred grand working for me, which is more than I ever paid myself. That didn't include the gold sweeps, colored stones and diamond melee that went home with all our jewelers at night in the pockets of their aprons. For years I had washed the aprons at night for the sweeps but two years ago I had stopped doing that, for personal reasons. Old John on the other hand was very good about that. He made a living and he did not want to cheat me. He never stole any sweeps or melee. He never did side work on company time, either.

Old John was the best jeweler in the Dallas-Fort Worth metroplex. I knew it and I was grateful for him. Everyone tried to steal him from me. But no one could. Those evening talks of ours made a difference, I believed. Normally I refused to make friends with employees but in Old John's case it was crucial. Then the woman came. Her name was Jane. You think, an ordinary name, but oh ho, look out. He did not tell me himself, of course, and you wouldn't have heard it around the shop because the other jewelers were afraid to tease him, but I finally got the word out of our shop manager Nathan. "John's got a girl," he said. We were sitting in my office talking about the new Plano store. It was losing twenty grand a month. I hoped to close it down. He was trying to convince me not to, and I worried why.

Old John lived with his mother and had never dated anyone as far as we knew, so this was alarming news. I had supposed on the way home he usually stopped at Rosie's Gentleman Tan. "What?" I said. "She's a new saleswoman over at Victoria's Secret. John's been watching her for weeks. Now he's started coming in before nine to watch her on her way in." I came in at seven, turned off the alarms and opened the safes, and then worked in my office until it was time to put out the cases, so I had not noticed. Nathan was grinning. He stroked his nose with his index finger. He had nice fingers and a long nose. "Has he spoken to her?" I asked him. I was not grinning. I un-

214

derstood Nathan was warning me. He often did that, perhaps without realizing it. "No," Nathan said. "But I'm going to go and give her a coupon for a free tighten and polish and invite her in. She wears a lot of jewelry." "Jewelry?" I was surprised. Some people should own jewelry and others should not. "No, cheap stuff," he said. "You know, titty-dancer jewelry." I said firmly, "Be certain to tell me when she comes in." I knew she would be in. I made Nathan shop manager not because he knew the business—he couldn't do much more than stretch rings and polish—but because he could sell and his look. I can tell you now, that is the secret to a successful shop: have a manager who can sell the job. That was our trouble up in Plano. Lisa couldn't sell. She knew jewelry. She was a GIA-certified gemologist. But she looked like hell. It frustrated and confused me that I had made her a manager.

Nathan went to work on Jane like he could when he wanted to and before you knew it Jane and Old John were going to lunch three times a week. Jane looked exactly like the young woman you picture when you picture the young woman who works at Victoria's Secret. She called him John, which we all did, but she could call him John to his face. That made me angry. She would ring on the phone in the afternoon and say, "May I speak to John, please?" True, she said please. Old John only received phone calls once or twice a month and then it was his mother. He took Jane's calls in the same place he took his mother's: in the back bathroom, with the door closed, and the phone cord stretched all the way under the door. The cord wasn't that long and you wondered if he had to lie on the bathroom floor to get the phone up against his ear. He was so clean I doubted it. His fingernails were like clear epoxy. You do not see that in jewelers. Down on the floor in the piss. We had our own bathroom on our side. But this was the jeweler's bathroom.

I could manage Old John's affair but then Jane decided to come to the regular showroom, our showroom, and befriend my salespeople. Normally the Victoria's Secret girls knew better than to come in our place. They were modest enough. There was no point coming in if you couldn't spend a thousand bucks. We didn't have anything for less than a grand, not even in the watchcases. We didn't waste time with porcelain figurines and crystal vases. We were a luxury jewelry store.

The problem was obvious. This woman Jane hung around in Martin's, flirted with Jim and Clancy, and then bounced over to waggle

215

her tits at Old John and the boys on the bench. It was worse than untidy. She was taking over. I admit it was my fault because initially I was too busy to consider her. We were in trouble at the bank with an old line of credit and one of our investors was unforeseeably closing out a buy line he had funded that I had expected to use to pay back the bank. But the saleswomen were in and out of my office all day complaining about her. Especially Janice, who was trying to steal Clancy away from his wife and did not appreciate Jane's interference.

"She doesn't buy anything," Janice said. "If she bought something it would be different. She's not even a customer." She was standing by the door of my office cleaning her left ear with a pair of thirty-two dollar titanium-tipped diamond tweezers. "You know you shouldn't stick those in your ears, Janice," I told her. She looked at the tweezers. "Sorry," she said. She wiped them clean with a diamond cloth an appointment had left on my desk. That's why you put things away, Baron, I thought. "That's disgusting. I'm sorry. I do it without even knowing I'm doing it." "No," I said. I had the same problem. There was something in the air of the store that made your ears itchy. I think it was particles of red and yellow rouge from the polishing wheels. "But you could lose an ear drum." I hoped she would go away. Please go away, Janice, I thought. Then I thought, Baron, what kind of a boss are you? Suddenly I had no control over my people or my environment. It was as though the walls of my office momentarily fell down around us and my chair turned upside down. I was sick to my stomach. But she went on. "She just stands around all the time. I can't sell with her standing around like that. She acts like she works here. She doesn't work here." I wanted to ask her: Janice, when was the last time you put a number up on the boards? Things settled back into place. But the goal was for Janice to leave. Then if necessary I could put away Jane. "I'll talk to Old John about it," I said. "Sure you will," Janice said and made that face of hers that kept anyone from honestly trusting her. That face is why you cannot even sell a lousy TAG Heuer, Janice, I wanted to say. But at least she walked and I could get back to work.

I figured these things never solve themselves. The sooner I interfered the better. Then again, she might get bored of the attention and go back to Victoria's Secret where she fit in well.

But I also acknowledged that my argument, though valid, was not sound, because one premise was false. Titty dancers do not grow bored of attention. Not that Jane was a titty dancer in the strict sense so far as I knew. Truly I'd never known a titty dancer. I don't even use the expression. But she was a kind of socioeconomic equivalent.

Many jewelers I have employed show an angry face at the bench. The metal is their enemy. That's one way of doing it. But Old John wore a precise, cunning smile while he worked. He was holding a secret. So when I saw Old John Friday afternoon setting my three-carat padparadscha sapphire with his lips folded together like a pair of scissors I knew I had a problem I could no longer afford to tolerate. On the one hand I wasn't worried about the sapphire, corundum is tough, it was an oval so no corners, and it was one of my new twenty-two carat designs, a Late-Byzantine Elizabeth Gage knock-off, so the metal was as soft as frozen butter. I knew Old John wouldn't let even Jane affect his work at the bench. On the other hand it makes me mad but most times you lose good people you lose them for personal reasons, so I called Nathan into my office.

"Nathan," I questioned him, "fine, you were right. You knew and I didn't. So now tell me what I need. What must I do about Jane?" Nathan squirmed. He played with something in his lap. I thought: No. No warning. Of course. Not Nathan. "I didn't mean to," Nathan said. His head wandered childishly. "She licked my neck," he apologized.

Thousands of people every year fall in love in jewelry stores. My employees were constantly fucking each other. Dating policies were useless. They even fell in love with customers. Customers! It is because of the diamonds and platinum, the rubies and gold. You should not mix them. That is why the great jewelry cultures—Thailand, India, Israel—are all grossly oversexed. Think about Canadians. They hate jewelry. But who has ever fucked a Canadian?

So now because of my slovenliness and Jane too it was Nathan or Old John. This was of course an inadmissible disjunction. The next day Jim was late for work and when he called in I already knew so, resigned, I told Julie to put him through to my office. I checked my Patek. It was nearly eleven-thirty. I noticed through the one-way glass that the Anteater, the Gypsy, was snooping around the antique case. I hoped all the cases were locked. Clancy was not on the floor. The Anteater waved at a piece and I watched Janice turn and run for the back. The soles of my feet were sweating and I kicked off my wingtips. I picked up the phone.

"You're not going to believe this, boss," Jim whispered over the line. He always called me boss because he thought it kept him on my good side. It was true from him I enjoyed it. "You're at Jane's," I said. "What? How did you know?" he said. I could tell he was smiling on the other end. That was why Jim was one hell of a salesman, my second-best, because he was joyful like a little boy. He was cute, too, he was the kind of guy you would sleep with and in the morning he would tell you he loved you and then he would be mystified and in-sulted when you laughed. He was sincere. Like a boy or an angel. No brains though.

"Take the day off," I told him. I saw my opportunity now. "Keep her out of the store. Keep her out of Arlington if you can. I have to figure this out." I thought I understood what to do. Then I wondered if I was merely panicking. I suffered a vision of Jane fucking Jim. She was on top. I called Nathan. He picked up the phone and asked me, "Have you heard from Old John?" Christian asked me. I could hear sloppy polishing in the background. The wheels were shrieking. Larry. Probably drunk. That kind of metalwork cost me ten cents a second. "What?" At this point I did not precisely want to shoot my-self but I wanted to shoot someone else. "He left early yesterday and he hasn't called." I thought, What about my two-carat bezel-set studs? Stan Bowler had an appointment at one. That was twenty-three grand I had to have in the bank at opening Monday morning or my checks to Davidoff, IDC, Simons, all of them would bounce. "I put Christian on the platinum studs," Nathan said. "He's hobnailing them now. I checked." Good Nathan, I thought. "But his pistol's gone too," Nathan said. "Okay," I said. "Remind Christian the studs are screw backs," I said and hung up the phone. Then I found Clancy, put him in charge, and drove to Old John's.

I knew to go to Old John's because once before, years ago when we were all at Fort Worth Gold together, Old John had taken a customer hostage in the mailroom. It was a confusion over a ring. The cus-tomer claimed that Old John had switched stones on him. He was wrong, of course, but that was not the point. The point was that Old John fell into a Vietnam regression or who knew what and took the customer hostage, tied him to a chair with copper alloy wire and kept him there in the mailroom with the barrel of this same missing jade-handled pistol stuck in the customer's mouth. No one knew what to do: it was Old John, after all. We weren't going to call the police. But Ronnie Popper, who was the owner of Fort Worth Gold and Silver Exchange, and who was a kind of uncanny salesman-avatar who could close a deal just by gesturing, like a magician, without even speaking

218

to the customer, intuited that we needed Old John's mother. I was seventeen years old and the head runner then. I did everything but the bank deposits, so I was sent to get her. She was calm and gentle. When we arrived at the store she walked into the mailroom without speaking to him or anyone else, took the gun away from Old John, put it in her red leather purse, and packed them both into the car. Old John and herself, I mean, the customer was still tied up. They sat there and waited for me to drive them home. I was eager to hear the conversation from the back seat but they sat silently together the whole way. She only spoke once, to ask me to pull into a McDonald's and get them Filet-O-Fish sandwiches. Later I heard Mr. Popper gave the customer a Rolex so he wouldn't press charges. Mr. Popper was that kind of a boss. When I sold my first Men's President, before I was even on the sales floor, he had hugged me and tucked a hundred dollar bill into my shirt pocket.

With Jane, Old John and Jim I held a similar situation in my hands. Hopefully it wouldn't be necessary to give away any Rolexes. We weren't making the kind of money Popper used to. But when I got to Old John's mom's place the cops were already there. Two prowlers were parked in the driveway with their lights spinning. I hung my jacket in the car, then thought twice and folded it in the passenger seat, and approached. The door was open. It was my job to go in. From upstairs in the house I could hear people laughing. This was disorienting. It should be encouraging, I thought. I was abruptly unsure whether or not I should involve myself so I wandered back to where I imagined the kitchen must be to wash my hands. And there at the kitchen table was Old John's mother with Jane, a policeman and another old woman I didn't know. They were drinking coffee and picking at a vegetable tray. Old John's mother stood carefully and I saw she was bent like a violin from osteoporosis but otherwise unchanged. She said, "Baron dear! See how you've grown!" I must have looked frightened because she said, "Don't worry." Then she asked me, "Do you know John's friend Jane?" "Hi Jane," I said. Jane winked at me. She was wearing a white tank top with a round pink bird on one breast. The cop introduced himself, he had a Coke in his hand, and I met Pearl, who was Old John's mom's sister. Unlike her sister, Pearl stood perfectly straight. "Where's Old John?" I asked. "Old John?" his mother asked. "He's upstairs with Jim," Jane said.

"Nathan's here too, Baron," Old John's mom said.

Without realizing what I was doing I sat down in Old John's mom's chair. The cop gave me a look and then rose and fetched a chair out of the dining room for Old John's mom. "I'm sorry," I said. Old John's mom said, "Never mind, honey," and sat back down. She passed me a cup. "Would you like some coffee, Baron?" I didn't know what to ask next. Jane abruptly laughed. I wanted to explain that I was only trying to help. Then I wanted to ask everyone to get back to work. "I think I need to get back to the store," I said. "We are in trouble at the bank." "Everything is going to be all right, Baron," Old John's mom said and took my hand in hers. Her palm was wet. I thought, these people are living lives I cannot conceive. I looked at the four of them and they smiled generously back at me. They tried to draw me out into a circle of their laughter. I realized I would never enjoy an explanation.

Nominated by Deb Olin Unferth, Noon

WINGED MERCURY
AND THE GOLDEN CALF

by REBECCA SOLNIT

from ORION

I

FOR A WHILE in the middle of the twentieth century, economists liked to model their subject as hydrology. They built elaborate systems of pipes, pumps, and reservoirs through which water traveled, allegedly modeling the movements of money, wealth, capital. They were funny devices, stuck halfway between literal-mindedness and metaphor, and they begged many questions about the nature of economies and the nature of water. Since that time, water contamination and scarcity have become global issues, and water privatization an especially heated one. But even if you left aside all the strange things we do to water, water was never exactly a good model for economies, since the implication was that the flow of capital is natural, that money moves like water.

Even water doesn't move like water in our systems. Our economies produce lots of strange uphill pumping (as Los Angeles does with the Colorado River's water, as the Bush tax cuts do with the nation's wealth), as well as hoarding, flooding, squandering, false droughts, and unnecessary thirsts unto death. What model explains the hundred-foot yachts and fifth homes U.S. captains of industry accumulate while hunger, homelessness, lack of access to medical care, and general precariousness overtake more and more of the population? Or Bechtel Corporation privatizing the water supply in a Boli-

221

vian town and jacking up prices to the point that the poor were expected to do without—what kind of economic model is that? Could we model as a flood the uprising that forced Bechtel out?

But there's another problem with the attempt to represent wealth as water, which is that wealth was for millennia embodied for monetary societies not by the two-hydrogen, one-oxygen molecule that makes life on Earth possible, but by a true element, a heavy metal, and a fairly useless one: gold. The real movement of wealth and poverty through an economy, or at least our economy, might better be modeled by the movement of gold out of the California ecosystem during the Gold Rush and by the release of deadly mercury into the same system during the same rush.

The gold was the point. The mercury was the secret. The former yielded a one-time profit and was thereafter mostly sequestered, made into coins or worn as ornaments, not even much of a speculative commodity during the century and more that the price of gold was fixed. The latter was dispersed in all the streams in which and near which gold was mined, mercury being useful in securing the gold with the old technologies of ore refinement. More than a century and a half later, the mercury continues to spread, pervading thousands of miles of stream and river, continually flowing with the rivers of the Gold Rush into the San Francisco Bay, and moving outward into the great ocean. Mercury travels from other mining operations into other water systems too, including the Salmon River in Idaho and the Amazon in Brazil. In stream, river, bay, and ocean, it enters the bodies of aquatic creatures, moves up the food chain into bigger fish, and then into other predators, including our own species, where it particularly affects the mental capacities and nervous systems of young children and unborn children, so you can say that at least indirectly gold dims the minds and drains the futures of the youngest among us. The gathering of gold then and now is the spread of mercury. The making of wealth along this extractive model is often also a far more widespread and long-lived generation of poverty.

In the popular version of the California Gold Rush, every man is free to seek his fortune, and flannel-shirted miners panning for gold in mountain streams strike it rich. This picturesque vision of the bearded prospector with his pick and pan is still re-enacted at places like Knott's Berry Farm amusement park near Disneyland in Orange County and celebrated in tourist-dependent towns up and down Route 49, which runs through the old Mother Lode, the gold-bearing belt in the Sierra Nevada. It's a vision of natural riches naturally distributed, a laissez-faire and free-market system in which all start out even, with the implication that all thereby have equal opportunity to benefit. It was almost nearly briefly true, if you ignore the racist laws and the violence that deprived Asians and Latinos of mining access and basic rights. Non-Europeans were subject to special taxes, denied the right to stake claims or work them independently, intimidated, lynched, driven off the richest sites, and barred from legal recourse, but their lot was far more pleasant than that of the native Californians. Bounties were paid for their scalps or ears, and they had no legal or treaty rights. (Though they owned the mother lode from which the gold came, most received nothing from the rush but ruin.) Disease, deracination, starvation, despair, and outright murder reduced the indigenous population by about four-fifths during those early years of the Gold Rush. So if you imagine a world in which everyone is a young white man, you can picture the gorges, ridgelines, and canyons in which the Gold Rush unfolded as the level playing field of which free-market enthusiasts sing.

Distinguished historians once endorsed this version of the Gold Rush as a paradise of opportunity: California historian and former *Nation* editor Carey McWilliams wrote in 1949, a century after the rush began, "Few could conquer with Pizarro or sail with Drake, but the California gold rush was the great adventure for the common man." McWillams went on to say, "Since there was no 'law of mines' in 1848, the California miners adopted their own rules and regulations in which they were careful to safeguard the equality of opportunity which had prevailed at the outset." But within a decade of James Marshall's January 1848 discovery of gold on the American River, mining in the Mother Lode shifted from simple pans and sluice boxes to complex mechanical systems. The mining organizations built larger washing devices to get the gold out of the streams, introduced hydraulic mining—the use of high-powered jets of water—to hose it out of the nearby landscape, and launched hard-rock mining operations, whose tunnels and shafts still riddle the Sierra landscape, in order to get underground ore that could then be crushed and processed in a stamp mill.

The technological changes were paralleled by a shift from individual endeavor to increasingly industrialized large-scale process requiring capitalization and eventually producing stockholders and distant profiteers, as well as bosses and employees. By that point, it took wealth to get wealth. Charles Nordhoff in his 1873 guidebook to California mentions a three-thousand-foot tunnel dug near the Yuba River at a cost of $250,000, completed before "a cent's worth of gold could be taken out of the claim"—not the kind of investment option available to everyone. Some of the earlier photographs are astonishing. Whole rivers were diverted so that men could pick more easily at the bed, and if the economy is imagined as flowing like water, these evicted rivers provide some interesting metaphors.

Many of the men who joined the scramble for gold spent much to get to California only to become destitute or die by malnutrition, disease, violence, suicide, accident, or other typical mining-camp misfortune. Many others became ordinary laborers working for ordinary wages, with no chance of striking it rich. It was a colorful world, with lurid newspapers published seemingly in every small town, touring singers, theaters, and even opera in San Francisco, writers like Joaquin Miller and Bret Harte, a tsunami of alcohol consumed in taverns with concomitant brawls, delirium tremens, brothels—ranging from courtesan palaces to child-rape mills—and a lot of vigilante injustice. Maybe it's all evident in the names of their mining camps. Murderer's Bar, Hangtown, Rough and Ready, and Sucker Flat all existed by 1849.

Of course the division of labor and inequality were there from the beginning. Walter Colton, a Protestant minister who had settled in Monterey when it was still part of Mexico, wrote on August 12, 1848, "Four citizens of Monterey are just in from the gold mines on Feather River, where they worked in company with three others. They employed about thirty wild Indians, who are attached to the rancho owned by one of the party. They worked precisely seven weeks and three days, and have divided $76,844—nearly $11,000 to each." That is, if you leave out the thirty who likely worked for trade goods and food. Or leave out that the Feather River ran through the territory of the Maidu, who had not sold or surrendered their land by treaty, so that all riches extracted and lands ravaged were done so illegally. Today's equivalent, the gold rush that would make Nevada, were it an independent nation, the world's third largest gold producer, is taking place on land never quite obtained from the Western Shoshone.

Perhaps the terrain of gold rushes should be described as a level playing field riddled with mineshafts and poisoned waters.

Just as one of those useful commentators from another culture or galaxy might perceive the purpose of drinking heavily to be achievement of a splitting headache and furry tongue in the morning, so she might perceive mining as a way of ravaging great swaths of the land, water, and air about as thoroughly as it is possible to do. For from an ecological point of view, mining produces large-scale, long-term poverty of many kinds while producing short-term wealth for a small minority. When it comes to iron, aluminum, copper, and other metals essential for industrial society, you can argue that the mining is necessary, but about 80 percent of the world's current gold production is made into jewelry destined for India and China. The soft yellow metal has had few practical uses throughout history. The U.S. government even now has 8,134 tons hidden away and recently recommitted itself not to sell, helping to buoy up the metal's current high price (after dropping to about $250 in the 1990s, it has recently soared to more than $700 an ounce).

Gold was itself money and money was gold throughout most of Near Eastern, European, and American history, right until August 15, 1971, when President Richard Nixon took the wartime U.S. off the gold standard for various then-expedient reasons, and most of the world followed. Until then the bills that circulated were essentially receipts for gold held in vaults, and the gold coins still in circulation into the twentieth century were literally worth their weight in gold. During the long era of the gold standard, the metal was the means by which all else was quantified, the measure of all other things. Its value when extracted and abstracted from the landscape was obvious. The difficulty of quantifying the true cost of extracting it is the basic environmental failure of accounting, or maybe of money.

Contemporary accounting does sometimes speak of "externalized costs," those borne by others than the profiteers, and by this measurement the Gold Rush was very expensive. Today's environmental and social justice advocates would like to see "true cost" accounting, in which the value or cost of an item takes into account its entire impact from creation to disposal or recycling. Moves to measure costs in this way are increasing as communities begin to recognize the ways that a corporation, industry, or enterprise may bring specific benefits to their region, but may also potentially wreak pervasive or long-term damage, social and ecological. Similar analyses could be performed on many enterprises previously framed as profitable simply by asking, For whom? And who pays? For how long? You can look at an individual automobile, for example, as conveying profit to the seller and usefulness to the buyer and noxious fumes and social ills to the larger community.

The California Gold Rush clawed out of the foothills of the Sierra Nevada considerable gold—93 tons or 2.7 million troy ounces in the peak year of 1853 alone, an estimated 973 tons or 28.4 million troy ounces by 1858, more than 3,643 tons or 106 million troy ounces to date. In the course of doing so, everything in the region and much downstream was ravaged. Wildlife was decimated. Trees were cut down to burn for domestic and industrial purposes and to build the huge mining infrastructure that was firmly in place by the 1870s. That infrastructure included huge log dams to make water available on demand—the photographer Carleton Watkins took some pictures of them, looking alarmingly precarious as they stoppered deep valleys full of water. According to environmental historian Michael Black, "Within its first five years of operation, California's hydraulic cavalry dismembered whole forests to construct five thousand miles of ditches and flumes. This figure was doubled by the close of the decade." The earth was dug into desolation and later hosed out so that some landscapes—notably the Malakoff Digging and San Juan Ridge near Nevada City—are still erosive badlands of mostly bare earth. But most of all, the streams and rivers were devastated. The myriad waterways of the Sierra Nevada were turned into so much plumbing, to be detoured, dammed, redirected into sluices high above the landscape, filled with debris and toxins. Water as an industrial agent was paramount, and water as a source of life for fish, riparian creatures, downstream drinkers, farmers, and future generations was ignored.

By 1853, the Sacramento River's once prodigious salmon run was in steep decline, and so were those of most of the rest of the streams and rivers that flow into the San Francisco Bay. Black continues, "Three years later, an exasperated commissioner reported that owing to mining, fish runs on the Feather, the Yuba, and the American rivers were dead." Also in 1853, an Indian agent wrote of the native peoples in the region.

They formerly subsisted on game, fish, acorns, etc. but it is now impossible for them to make a living by hunting or fishing, for nearly all the game has been driven from the mining region or has been killed by the thousands of our people who now occupy the once quiet home of these children of the forest. The rivers or tributaries of the Sacramento formerly were clear as crystal and abounded with the finest salmon and other fish. . . . But the miners have turned the streams from their beds and conveyed the water to the dry diggings and after being used until it is so thick with mud that it will scarcely run it returns to its natural channel and with it the soil from a thousand hills, which has driven almost every kind of fish to seek new places of resort where they can enjoy a purer and more natural element.

There was no new place of resort; the fish mostly just died off.

At the time, the costs of the Gold Rush were perfectly apparent to its witnesses; only later was it reconfigured as a frolic. As Nordhoff said in 1873,

At Smartsville, Timbuctoo, and Rose's Bar I suppose they wash away into the sluices half a dozen acres a day, from fifty to two hundred feet deep; and in the muddy torrent which rushes down at railroad speed through the channels prepared for it, you may see large rocks helplessly rolling along. . . . Of course the acres washed away must go somewhere, and they are filling up the Yuba River. This was once, I am told by old residents, a swift and clear mountain torrent; it is now a turbid and not rapid stream, whose bed has been raised by the washings of the miners not less than fifty feet above its level in 1849. It once contained trout, but I now imagine a catfish would die in it.

The volume of mercury-tainted soil washed into the Yuba was three times that excavated during construction of the Panama Canal, and the riverbed rose by as much as eighty feet in some places. So much of California was turned into slurry and sent downstream that major waterways filled their own beds and carved new routes in the elevated sludge again and again, rising higher and higher above the surrounding landscape and turning ordinary Central Valley farmlands and towns into something akin to modern-day New Orleans:

places below water level extremely vulnerable to flooding. Hydraulic mining washed downstream 1.5 billion cubic yards of rock and earth altogether. "Nature here reminds one of a princess fallen into the hands of robbers who cut off her fingers for the jewels she wears," said one onlooker at a hydraulic mine.

The Gold Rush was a huge giveaway of public or indigenous resources to private profiteers, a mass production of long-term poverty disguised as a carnival of riches. Which is to say that the profit the mining operations made was contingent on a very peculiar, if familiar, form of enterprise it might be a mistake to call free: one in which nature and the public domain could be squandered for private gain, in which the many were impoverished so that a few could be enriched, and no one was able to stop them in the name of the public, or almost no one.

Only one great battle was fought against the mining, by downstream farmers. They too were invaders transforming the landscape, but in that pre-pesticide era of farming with horse and plow, their impact was at least comparatively benign and they had, unlike any miners anywhere, an interest in the long-term well-being of the place, not to mention a useful product. The farmers took the hydraulic mining operations of the central Sierra to court for polluting the rivers, raising their beds, and rendering farms extremely vulnerable to flooding, and they won in 1884. Robert L. Kelley, in his 1959 history of the lawsuit, called it "one of the first successful attempts in modern American history to use the concept of general welfare to limit free capitalism."

III

Gold is heavy, and it sinks to the bottom of a pan, a rocker, a long tom, or whatever device you might have used to get the metal out of the stream in the early days of the California Gold Rush. Some of the gold always slipped away—unless you added mercury, also known as quicksilver, to the water and silt in your pan. The mercury amalgamated with the gold, making it easier to capture, but then some of the mercury inevitably washed downstream. With hydraulic mining, the same methods were used on far larger scales. You hosed out riverbanks, hillsides, mountainsides, breaking the very landscape down into slush and slurry that you then washed for the gold. Then you poured mercury, one flask—seventy-five pounds—at a time, into the washing device. This was one of the most extravagant uses of mercury during the Gold Rush, and much of it escaped into the environment. With hard-rock mining, as the 1858 *California Miner's Own Handbook* describes it, you put pulverized ore into "an 'amalgamating box' containing quicksilver, and into which a dash-board is inserted that all the water, gold, and tailings may pass through the quicksilver." Here too the mercury helped capture the gold. You dissolved the amalgamation by heating it until the mercury vaporized, leaving the gold behind, and then tried to capture the vapor in a hood for reuse. Inevitably some of it would be atmospherically dispersed, and breathing mercury fumes was one of the more deadly risks of the process.

During the California Gold Rush, an estimated 7,600 tons or 15,200,000 pounds of mercury were thus deposited into the watersheds of the Sierra Nevada. The U.S. Geological Survey estimates that placer, or stream-based, mining alone put ten million pounds of the neurotoxin into the environment, while hard-rock mining accounted for another three million pounds. Much of it is still there—a U.S. Fish and Wildlife biologist once told me that he and his peers sometimes find globules the size of a man's fist in pristine-looking Sierra Nevada streams—but the rest of it ended up lining the bottom of the San Francisco Bay. Some of it is still traveling: the *San Jose Mercury News* (named after the old mercury mines there) reports that one thousand pounds of the stuff comes out of gold-mining country and into the bay every year, and another two hundred pounds comes from a single mercury mine at the south end of the bay annually. Some of this mercury ends up in the fish, and as you move up the food chain, the mercury accumulates. According to the San Francisco Estuary Institute, "Fish at the top of the food web can harbor mercury concentrations in their tissues over one million times the mercury concentration in the water in which they swim." All around the edges of the bay, warning signs are posted, sometimes in Spanish, Tagalog, and Cantonese, as well as English, but people fish, particularly poor and immigrant people, and some eat their catch. They are paying for the Gold Rush too.

Overall, approximately ten times more mercury was put into the California ecosystem than gold was taken out of it. There is something fabulous about this, or at least fablelike. Gold and mercury are brothers and opposites, positioned next to each other, elements 79 and 80, in the Periodic Table of the Elements. And they also often coexist in the same underground deposits. Gold has been prized in part because it does not rust, change, or decay, while mercury is the only metal that is liquid at ordinary temperatures, and that liquid is, for those who remember breaking old thermometers to play with the globules, something strange, congealing into a trembling mass or breaking into tiny spheres that roll in all directions, ready to change, to amalgamate with other metals, to work its way into the bodies of living organisms. The miners called it quicksilver for its color and volatility. Half gold's goodness is its inertness; it keeps to itself. Mercury's problem is its protean promiscuity.

Gold was never more than a material and occasionally a curse in the old stories, but Mercury was the deity who shared with his namesake element the elusive fluctuant qualities still called mercurial, and it is as the god of commerce and thieves that he encounters the "precious" metal gold. Perhaps in tribute to the element's talent for engendering fetal abnormalities, Mercury is also the Roman counterpart to the Greek god Hermes, father of Hermaphrodite, though mercury-generated birth defects are never so picturesque.

At least from Roman times onward, mercury was critical for many of the processes used to isolate both gold and silver from ore. Thus mercury was a crucial commodity, not valued in itself, but necessary for obtaining the most valued metals. Sources of mercury were far rarer than those of gold, and so one of the great constraints on extracting wealth from the New World was the limited supply of mercury (in forested parts of the world, heat could be used in gold refining, but in the fuel-poor deserts, mercury was the only means). The Almaden Mine in Spain and then the Santa Barbara Mine in Huancavelica, Peru, were the two major mercury sources in the Western world from the sixteenth until the mid-nineteenth century, and when the Spanish colonies gained their independence, they (except for Peru, of course) lost easy access to this supply of mercury.

So dire was this lack that the Mexican government offered a reward—$100,000 by one account—to whoever could discover a copious supply. In the northwesternmost corner of old Mexico, in 1845, a staggeringly rich mercury lode was discovered by one Captain Don Andres Castillero. Located near San Jose at the southern end of the San Francisco Bay, the new Almaden Mine was well within the territory seized by the United States by the time it was developed. And only days before the February 2, 1848, treaty giving Mexico $15 million for its northern half was signed, gold was also discovered in California. Thus began the celebrated Gold Rush, which far fewer know was also a mercury rush, or that the two were deeply intertwined.

One anonymous 1857 visitor to the New Almaden Mine published his (or her?) observations in *Harper's Magazine* a few years later. "One of the most curious circumstances connected with the New Almaden Mine is the effect produced by the mercurial vapors upon the surrounding vegetation," said the report.

> *Despite the lofty chimneys, and the close attention that has been devoted to the secret of effectually condensing the volatile matter, its escape from the chimneys withers all green things around. Every tree on the mountain-side above the works is dead, and some of more sensitive natures farther removed exhibit the influence of the poison in their shrunken and blanched foliage. . . . Cattle feeding within half a mile of the hacienda sicken, and become salivated; and the use of waters of a spring rising near the works is guarded against. . . . The workmen at the furnaces are particularly subjected to the poisonous fumes. These men are only able to work one week out of four, when they are changed to some other employment, and others take their place for a week. Pale, cadaverous faces and leaden eyes are the consequences of even these short spells; and any length of time continued at this labor effectually shortens life and impregnates the system with mercury. . . . In such an atmosphere one would seem to inhale death with every respiration.*

Without the torrent of toxic mercury that poured forth from this and a few smaller mercury mines in the Coast Range, the California Gold Rush would probably have been dampened by foreign monopolies on mercury. Though the New Almaden mining operation closed more than thirty years ago, the mercury there is still leaching into the San Francisco Bay. A series of Gold Rush era mercury mines has gravely contaminated Clear Lake a hundred and twenty miles or so to the north, where the local Pomo people have seven times as much mercury in their systems as the regional normal. In many places, mercury contamination of water forces native North Americans, who have traditionally relied on marine animals and fish as primary food sources, to choose between tradition and health.

231

Gold is the paradise of which the bankers sang; mercury is the hell hidden in the fine print. The problem is not specific to the California Gold Rush, which only realized on a particularly epic scale in a particularly lush and pristine landscape the kinds of devastation gold and mercury can trigger. The current gold rush in northeastern Nevada, which produces gold on a monstrous scale—seven million ounces in 2004 alone—is also dispersing dangerous quantities of mercury. This time it's airborne. The forty-mile-long Carlin Trend on which the gigantic open-pit gold mines are situated is a region of "microscopic gold" dispersed in the soil and rock far underground, imperceptible to the human eye, unaffordable to mine with yesteryear's technology. To extract the gold, huge chunks of the landscape are excavated, pulverized, piled up, and plied with a cyanide solution that draws out the gold. The process, known as cyanide heap-leach mining, releases large amounts of mercury into the biosphere. Wind and water meet the materials at each stage and create windblown dust and seepage, and thus the mercury and other heavy metals begin to travel.

As the Ban Mercury Working Group reports, "Though cumulatively coal fired power plants are the predominant source of atmospheric mercury emissions, the three largest point sources for mercury emissions in the United States are the three largest gold mines there." The Great Salt Lake, when tested in 2004, turned out to have astonishingly high mercury levels, as did wild waterways in Idaho, and Nevada's gold mines seem to be the culprit. The *Reno Gazette-Journal* reported that year, "The scope of mercury pollution associated with Nevada's gold mining industry wasn't discovered until the EPA changed rules in 1998 to add mercury to the list of toxic discharges required to be reported. When the first numbers were released in 2000, Nevada mines reported the release of 13,576 pounds in 1998. Those numbers have since been revised upward to an estimated 21,098 pounds, or more than 10 tons, to make Nevada the nation's No. 1 source of mercury emissions at the time." Glen Miller, a professor of natural resources and environmental science at the University of Nevada, Reno, estimates that since 1985, the eighteen major gold mines in the state released between 70 and 200 tons of mercury into the environment.

Maybe some of this is already evident in the Greek myth of King Midas. Dionysus, the god of wine and revelry, gave Midas a single wish and regretted the mortal's foolish choice: the ability to turn anything he touched into gold. The rest is familiar. The king transformed all he touched so that what he tried to drink became gold when it touched his lips, and his thirst grew intolerable. Worse yet, he touched his daughter and his greed turned her to inanimate metal, and it was with this that he begged the god to take back his gift, resigned his crown and power, and became a rural devotee of the god Pan. In this ancient tale, gold is already associated with contaminated water and damaged children.

Midas is mythological, but true tales of gold-as-horror checker the history of the Americas. There is an extraordinary print from Girolamo Benzoni's 1565 *La Historia del Mondo Nuovo*, a report by an embittered witness to fifteen years of Spanish colonization. In the image, unclothed native men, tired of being savagely forced to produce gold, pour the molten metal down the throat of a captive Spaniard in pantaloons. Thus literal fulfillment of a hunger for wealth leads to death, and thus revenge for the brutality of the gold economy begins in the Americas. Another tale comes from the Death Valley Forty-Niners, seeking an easy and finding a hard route to the California gold fields. On their parched sojourn across the desert, one gold-seeker abandoned $2,500 in gold coins to lighten his load in the hopes that thus unburdened he might make it to water and life. Another of these desperados snapped at his companion that he had no interest in what looked like gold-bearing ore along the route through the dry lands: "I want water; gold will do me no good."

Gold is a curse in Exodus too, when the Israelites, having lost faith during their pilgrimage in the desert, come to worship the golden calf made out of melted-down jewelry. Moses comes down from the mountaintop, grinds the golden idol into powder, throws it into a stream, and forces them to drink it.

For us, perhaps the golden calf is the belief that the current economic system produces wealth rather than poverty. It's the focus on the gold to the exclusion of the mercury.

Nominated by Orion

WE STARTED HOME, MY SON AND I

by JAMES HARMS

from WEST BRANCH

after Jaan Kaplinski

We started home, my son and I.
Evening begining. The small stains
of streetlight spreading across the sidewalk,
thinning to darkness every few yards.
My son paused at the edge of each
then leapt, one hand in mine,
to the next. Ahead, his mother
touched the meat twice before
turning it, rinsed the lettuce, called out
for his sister to wash her hands.
He said each spot of light
was a great land, each span
of darkness the sea. And we
followed his map home
out past the edge of town where night
filled the long blocks between
streetlights with oceans.
We rowed when we could, swam
the last few miles. Until the moon
reared up like an old man
startled from his nap. And once

234

again the roads of the world rose
beneath us. Before long, my son
and I were home. I watched him climb
the brick stairs to the front door,
whose key I no longer owned.
His mother waved as he fell
into the house, the bright rooms
splashed with light. The ottoman
covered with horsehair; a damask
draped over the sofa: I couldn't see
these or any other emblems of my
previous life. I felt the waters rise
around my feet, heard in the distance
the loose rigging in the wind, a buoy bell.
So far from the sea, I rolled up
my trousers, wading in
for the walk back.

Nominated by William Werthe, B.J. Ward, Robert Cording, Edward Hirsch,
Ted Deppe, Joan Connor, Robert Wrigley, West Branch

DEPARTURE

fiction by ANDREW PORTER

from ONTARIO REVIEW

THAT SPRING WE WERE SIXTEEN Tanner and I started dating the Amish girls out on the rural highway—sometimes two or three at the same time, because it wasn't really dating. There was no way of getting serious.

This was in 1992, over ten years ago, and things had not yet begun to change in our part of Pennsylvania. I think of that year as a significant one now, a turning point in our country, the first year the town of Leola started growing and becoming a city and also the first year the Amish started leaving, selling their property and heading west toward Indiana and Iowa.

There had been several cases of runaways among the Amish that year—mostly young men, barely in their twenties, tempted by the shopping malls and bars popping up along the highways near their farms. Leola was expanding quickly then, it was becoming more common, and it worried the elders in the Amish community. And I think it explains why that spring some of the Amish teenagers were given permission to leave their farms for a few hours on Friday nights.

Out on the other side of town there was an intersection on the rural highway where they would go to hang out. It was a remote area. A strip mall with a K-Mart sat on one side of the intersection and across the road there was a twenty-four hour diner. You would sometimes see them on Friday evenings traveling in a long line like a funeral procession, their buggies hugging the shoulder of the road as tractor-trailers rubbered by. They would park out of sight behind the

K-Mart, tie their horses to lamp posts or the sides of dumpsters, and then the younger ones would go into the K-Mart to play video games and the older and more adventurous would cross the street to the diner.

The diner was a family-style place, frequented only by local farming families and truckers, and it was usually empty. Inside, the Amish kids would immediately disappear into the bathrooms and change into blue jeans and T-shirts that they had bought at K-Mart, clothes which never seemed to fit their bodies right. Then they would come out, their black wool clothes stuffed into paper bags, and order large platters of fried food and play country songs on the juke boxes, and try to pretend they weren't Amish.

That spring Tanner and I had begun stopping by just to see them. We never bothered them, just watched. And it never occurred to us that there might be something unnatural about what we were doing, or even wrong. We were simply curious. We wanted to know if the rumors we had heard in school were true: that there were spectacular deformities to be found among the Amish, that few of the children possessed the correct number of fingers, the results of extensive inbreeding.

We would sit in a booth at the far end of the diner and glance at them from behind our menus. We were amazed to hear them curse and see them smoke cigarettes. Some of them even held hands and kissed. Sometimes other people, people from town like us, would stop by, just to watch—and you could tell that it worried them. People were still scared of the Amish then, they were still a mystery and a threat because of their wealth and the tremendous amount of land they owned—and so naturally they were disliked, treated as outsiders and freaks.

At eleven o'clock, they'd change back into their clothes and very politely pay their checks. Then they'd cross the street in a big group, climb back into their buggies and leave. And Tanner and I would stand out in the diner parking lot and watch them, still not believing what we had seen, but also somehow sad to see them go.

Once the other kids at school found out about the diner, they started coming regularly in their jeeps and BMWs—not to watch like Tanner and I—but to mock and torment. It was cruel and it saddened us to see, though we never once tried to stop it. Instead we sat back in the corner and watched, angry, but also privately relieved that for once it was not us who were being teased or beat up. In the midst of targets so uncool and vulnerable as Amish teenagers, the popular kids seemed to have practically forgotten us.

There was one Amish kid who looked older than the rest. He could have been in his twenties. Tanner and I had noticed him the very first night because of his size and because of his face which always looked angry. He came every week with the rest of them, but always sat off by himself in a separate booth, smoking cigarettes and punching heavy-metal songs into the juke box at his table.

His anger scared us more than the others. That and his size. He had the body of a full grown man, a laborer—his shoulders broad, forearms solid and bulging out near his elbows.

When the fights started he was always involved. They usually happened out by the dumpsters in back of the diner. The odds were never even: always five or six against one. Having been raised strict pacifists, almost none of the Amish would fight. But he would. And despite his size he would, of course, always lose—though he'd last longer than anyone would believe, moving with the grace of a young boxer, gliding, ducking. His style was to stay low and bring his punches up from way down under. He was quick, had a powerful jab, and knew how to protect himself. But the beauty of his moves never lasted long. Inevitably he'd lose his focus, turn his back or look away for a second, and there would be a pile-on.

A few minutes later, his face cut up and swollen, he'd retreat across the street to K-Mart, followed by the rest of the Amish teenagers. And the next week, to everyone's surprise, he'd be back again—not even bitter about it, just sitting there at the edge of the booth, waiting.

It wasn't until late April that Tanner and I started dating the girls, but like I said, it wasn't really dating. They were all extremely shy and there wasn't a whole lot of common ground. Mostly we would ask them questions about their lives, and they would nod or shake their heads and giggle, and then we would sit and watch as they nervously stuffed their faces with cheeseburgers.

Later, we would walk them back across the street to K-Mart, and then sometimes, if no one else was around, they would kiss us in the shadows. And then—almost like it never happened—they'd be gone again and we'd have to wait a whole week. Sometimes they'd never come back, and we wouldn't know why. We couldn't exactly call them up. Usually we didn't even know their names. So if they didn't show the next week, we'd try to meet two new ones.

Back at our school, pretty girls wouldn't look at us. We were unexceptional—failures at sports and our fathers didn't manage banks or practice Orthopedic medicine. But out on the rural highway we dated the most beautiful of the Amish girls. They were attracted to our foreignness; and we, to theirs.

At school, there were jokes about us naturally. Mainly inbreeding jokes. Someone had heard that our girlfriends had two heads, three nostrils, tails coming out of their backbones. It was almost summer and so we tried to ignore it, ride it out, though it made us think about what we were doing.

And it was not right, what we were doing. We were aware of that. And in a way we were still scared of the Amish. Even the girls. There was something unnatural about them. It's hard to explain: they would only let you so close—and it was always in private where no one could see. Sometimes they would kiss you and then run away, or else you would be thinking about making a move, not even doing anything, and they would start to cry for no reason, like they knew.

I wonder now if it was not worse to let them leave the farms only once a week—if giving them only a small taste of freedom did not make the temptation stronger. Perhaps that's why so many never came back: it was simply too hard.

Tanner came from country people, though he had grown up in town like me. It didn't seem to make a difference. The wealthy kids still called him a hick and made fun of the way he talked and dressed. And you did not want to have the stigma of being from the country in our high school. Tanner and I both lived on the edge of the wealthy area, just across the street from it really. We were in the seventh grade when the school zone switched and the school district agreed to let us finish out our education at Ceder Crest High where all the beautiful and wealthy kids went, the only decent school in the country.

I had grown up with them, the wealthy kids, and even sometimes felt aligned with them when I'd see some of the dirty and disreputable country kids raising hell at our dances. But among them, sitting in class or walking in the hall, I was aware of our differences. Up until the ninth grade I had lied about my father's occupation, told people that he did a lot of work overseas, that his job was sort of secretive and I was not at liberty to discuss it. College wrestling coach didn't sound that great next to heart surgeon or judge. But I don't think anyone believed me anyway. They knew where I lived and knew that I was not a member of the country club, and that I was friends with Tanner. We were not one of them, Tanner and I, though we were not as low as country people either.

There was one girl I saw consistently that summer. Her name was Rachel. She wasn't shy or afraid of the outside world. And her hair smelled like tall field grass, a sweet smell. She was beautiful, too. She did not look like the other Amish girls; she lacked the full-bodied German figure, the solid thighs, the broad shoulders, the round doughy face. She was thin, small-framed and with different clothes could have easily passed for one of the popular girls at Cedar Crest.

She was curious, too. Some nights she would want to leave the diner and ride around in Tanner's truck. She would beg Tanner and me to take her into town. Or else she would want to drive out to the Leisure Lanes bowling alley to shoot pool and smoke cigarettes. She was always excited, anxious, wanting to do and see as much as possible in the few hours she had.

When we were alone, Rachel wanted to know everything about me. She wanted to know what my school was like, what my house was like, what it was like to go to Ocean City. She wanted it all described to her in detail, almost like she was saving it up, collecting it.

Only once when we were parked outside the diner did she tell me about her family. It was an enormous family, she said. More than twenty of them lived in one house. Her father was seventy years old, the patriarch of the entire household, and he had set up rules and standards based on the very first order of Amish, now three hundred years old. These were standards that she was expected to uphold and pass down to her children. She had an obligation, she said, being one of the chosen very, very few. But she seemed upset as she told me these things. I could tell it made her feel guilty to think about her family, especially when we were together. And after that one night we never talked about them again.

All summer the heat was getting worse. It had not rained for a record six weeks. Out in the deep country the crops were drying up and in town the grass on people's lawns, even in the wealthy areas, was turning into a yellow thatch. There was no escaping it. Even at night the air was thick with humidity and stuck to your skin like wet towels.

One thing Rachel liked to do was go down to the river valley where there was an old railroad track that had been out of service for more than fifty years. In all that time no one had ever thought to take down the tracks. They were rusted now, covered with weeds, and you could follow them for a mile or so to where they crossed over the river on an old wooden bridge, more than thirty feet high.

Rachel liked to have barefooted races across the planks of the bridge. The planks were evenly spaced, about two feet apart from each other. With a full moon it was easy, you could see where you were stepping, but other nights it would be pitch black and you would have to do it blind. It came down to faith. That and timing. If you slipped once, if your timing was just slightly off, your foot would slide into an empty space and you might snap a shin bone, or worse, if you were unfortunate and slipped through, you might fall thirty feet into the water. And of course we were young and confident and so we never once slipped, or fell, or even stumbled. The trick was always to get a rhythm in your head and to concentrate on it. But like I said, it mainly came down to faith, an almost blind trust that the wooden plank would be right there when you put your foot down. And it always was.

Tanner would sometimes come along with a girl he had met that night and we would all take a blanket and some iced tea down by the river and sit out underneath the stars. Some nights it was so hot Tanner and I would take all our clothes off and jump in the water, and the girls would watch us and giggle, never once thinking to join us; and we, of course, never asked. We knew the limits. We knew how far to push things and the truth was we never wanted to push, being inexperienced in those matters ourselves, and also not wanting to ruin what we had. We were young and somehow sex seemed intricately entwined with those other things—responsibility and growing up— and we were not interested in anything like that.

By then we had stopped hanging out at the diner altogether. It was no longer exciting to watch the fights and Rachel said it depressed her. More and more people had started coming out to watch and he was becoming somewhat of a local celebrity. Rachel told me one night that she knew him. She said his name was Isaac King and that she'd gone to school with him up until the third grade when his parents pulled him out to work. She said that that past winter he had watched his brother die in an ice-skating accident and that everyone thought he had gone a little crazy from it. He had stopped going to church, she said, and it was only a matter of time before he left the community altogether.

Some Fridays we'd just drive, the three of us, with Rachel sitting between Tanner and me. Tanner liked to take his father's truck onto the back country roads that were all dirt and race it with the head-lights off. It was terrifying and more fun than almost anything I've ever done—coming around those narrow curves at a high speed, not knowing what to expect, sometimes not knowing even if we were on the road or not, and then flying a little, catching some air when there was a bump or a small hill. Rachel loved it the most, I think. She'd close her eyes and laugh and sometimes even scream—she was not afraid to show her fear like Tanner and me—and finally, when she was on the verge of tears, she would beg Tanner to stop.

"No more!" she would scream. "Pull over!" And he would.

By July everything was changing quickly. Many of the Amish were already leaving, selling their farms to the contractors who had ha-rassed them for years. Rachel never talked about it much, though I know that it was on her mind. People she had known her whole life were being driven off their land. Corporations even wealthier than the Amish themselves had moved in, offered sums of money that seemed impossible to refuse, and then, when that didn't work, had threatened them.

Rachel was beginning to change too. I knew she had strong feel-ings about leaving the Amish community by then, vanishing like the others had, though she never came out and said it to me, only hinted at it. For the first time, she had begun to complain about the te-diousness of her life. Once she had even tried to leave, she said. She had packed up a bag with clothes and food but had stopped when she got to the highway near her farm, realizing she had no money and did not even know which direction led to town. With each Friday our time together seemed to go by quicker, and each time it got harder for her to go back home.

I think now that she wanted me to do something. It was not un-usual for Amish women to marry at fifteen or sixteen, and I know that she was under a lot of pressure that summer to get married. Some-times I tried to imagine what my parents would say if I brought her home with me, explained to them that she would be moving in. I imagined her coming to college with me and taking classes. I would get carried away sometimes, ignoring the absurdity of it, wanting to believe it could work.

It was a good summer for Tanner and me, our best, I think. Though we did very little until Friday nights. Days we stayed inside because of the heat and watched horror movies and drank iced tea by the gallon and nights we drove around by ourselves in Tanner's truck planning what we'd do the next Friday. We were wasting time, wasting our lives our parents said, and it felt good. That next year would be our last in high school and I think we were aware, even then, that we were nearing a pinnacle of sorts: the last summer we would still be young enough to collect allowance and get away without working jobs.

Our parents were never home that summer. There were cocktail parties and barbecues five or six times a week on our street and it seemed that almost every night the parents in the neighborhood got trashed, never stumbling home before one or two in the morning. Sometimes Tanner and I would show up at a party just to steal beer. We would stick ten or twelve cans into a duffle bag and then go back to my house and drink them on the back porch, and sometimes end up falling asleep in the backyard by accident.

In late July we started driving the truck out into the deep country during the days. The roads were all dirt out there and illegal to drive on. Occasionally we'd go out on a Saturday afternoon, hoping maybe to see Rachel or one of the girls Tanner had met the night before.

It was different out there. Aside from the humidity and the bugs, it was somehow depressing to watch all the young Amish kids working in the fields in such heat, fully dressed in their black wool suits, struggling with their ancient and inefficient tools, horse drawn plows, steel-wheeled wagons. It seemed cruel.

One Friday night I borrowed Tanner's truck and took Rachel to the other side of town to see my house. We parked outside, just looking at it, not even talking. That night my parents were having a party and inside we could hear people laughing and the record player going. I could imagine my father slumped in his big leather recliner, surrounded by a circle of drunk guests, telling stories, and my mother carrying around trays of pierced olives and glasses of cold gin. Later on I knew my father would step outside and begin wrestling people, and everyone would yell "Go coach! Pin 'em!" My father had been a wrestling star in college and whenever he drank, he'd start challenging his guests.

The thought of my father rolling around on the lawn with another grown man depressed me and I suddenly wanted to go back to the diner. But Rachel seemed happy listening to the music and laughter from inside.

After a few minutes she said, "Let's go inside."

I looked at her then and suddenly thought of what my father would do if I brought my Amish girlfriend into his house while he was throwing a party. My father, like most, did not like the Amish.

"Let's go," she said. "I want to try a beer."

I told her that it would be easier if I went inside and snuck the beer out to the truck myself.

A few minutes later I emerged with a couple of six packs and we drove down to the river and drank all twelve beers. Afterwards we lay down in a patch of grass near the water and acted silly. We felt loose and we were affectionate with each other. It was Rachel's first time being drunk and she was being funny about it, kissing me in strange places: my elbow, my eyelid, my pinky.

Then at one point—I can't remember exactly—I started to understand that she was trying to tell me something: that it was okay. We could. That is, she would, if I wanted to. She was gripping my body tightly then, and it surprised me. And it scared me, too—because it did not feel tender anymore, but angry almost—and I know now that whatever she was trying to do, whatever she wanted that night, did not have anything to do with me.

And even though we never did, she still cried for a long time that night, and I held her. And later, when I drove her back to the diner and we said good night, I was scared that I would never see her again.

In late August Tanner and I drove out into the deep country for the last time. Rachel had not showed up at the diner for two weeks and I had hopes of seeing her. I needed to talk to her. And Tanner, my best friend, drove me around all day.

We never did see her. Though we did see Isaac King as we were driving out toward the highway. It surprised us to see him and we stopped for a while and watched him working in the field. He was the equivalent of a foreman, in charge of the younger boys, probably his brothers and cousins. It was strange to watch him at work. He was a different person out in the fields, not quiet like he was at the diner, but loud, animated. He moved around the fields swiftly, like an animal, and the young boys listened to him and even seemed a little scared of him.

We parked up on a hill, out of sight. We were still scared of him ourselves, even from a distance. I can tell you now that I did not really hate him. But those nights I had watched him take on four or five kids at once, I believed that I hated him. I hated him for never acknowledging the futility of the situation, for not bowing his head like the others and going home. For not accepting his place like the rest of us—like my parents did, like Tanner did, and like I did.

He must have spotted us before, because he came up slowly from behind the truck and surprised us. He might have thought we were two of the kids from the diner who beat him up every week, looking for some more action. But if he did, he didn't say anything. It was illegal for us to be on that land, even illegal to be driving a car on those back roads, but he never asked us to leave. He just stared at us until he realized we were not there to fight him and then he turned around and went back to the field.

Rachel finally showed up at the diner the last Friday in August. She was shy with me and distant. She told me that a lot of families in the community, including hers, were moving to Indiana at the end of November, after the harvest. The town was growing quickly, she said. It was just a matter of time before they would be forced to leave. She looked at me very solemnly as she said this.

"So what does that mean?" I said. "You're leaving for good?"

She nodded. "I think so."

I took her hand. "That's terrible," I said.

"I know," she said. "I know."

I've sometimes wondered what would have happened had I asked her that night to leave her community—to marry me and come live with me and my family. I thought of asking her even then, that night, but it would have been a cruel thing to suggest. My parents would have never agreed. It was an absurd thought, when you got right down to it. I was a pretty good student, after all, college bound.

Rachel had been begging me to take her to a movie all summer.

She had never seen one before. So instead of spending our last night talking as we usually did, I took her to a rerun of an old Boris Karloff film playing at a place called the Skinny-Mini.

After the movie we drove around for a long time, just talking, though neither of us ever brought up that last night we had been together. I am certain now that she had been thinking about something else as we had watched the movie, and then later as we drove around. And somehow I could tell, even before she said the words, that she wasn't going to miss it.

We drove through town without talking. Rachel seemed disinterested, not even looking out the window. And the town seemed sad now, in the way every town looks sad right at the end of summer. It seemed cold already and empty, as if all the possibility Rachel had seen in it that summer had disappeared and now it contained only the same dismal potential it had every year.

It's strange, but I was not angry at her for leaving like this. I could tell she was not happy about it. And as we drove back to the diner I suddenly wanted to tell her how much I had enjoyed the time we had spent together, how much it had meant to me. I wanted to assure her that I would not forget her. But I never did.

When we got back to the diner, there was a crowd in the back lot, as usual. We walked over and saw Tanner watching. He was alone.

"Ten minutes," he said. "Fucking unbelievable."

Isaac King had been up for ten minutes. It was a record.

Kids were gathered around the circle, shouting, some of them jockeying for position. I moved in closer to the group and found a spot near the edge. I could see that Isaac King was still up on his feet, his arms flailing.

What I never understood was why he never gave up. It shows that he was not right. Because even if he had been able to do the impossible—defeat five at once—there would be five more waiting on the sidelines. And then five more after that. And so on.

But that night it was clear that something was different. He wasn't going to let himself go down. In fact, he lasted a record twenty minutes. In the end, it took six or seven guys to finally get him off his feet and even after he'd been pinned down on his back he was still trying to move his arms and legs. Someone finally used a two-by-four to knock him out. It was an unnecessarily hard blow and even today I do not know which of the kids delivered it. His head split open near the hair line. And when the blood started, everyone scattered.

I walked over to Tanner. "Hey," I said. "What the fuck just happened?"

"I don't know," he said. "I have no fucking idea."

It took a half hour to get him across the street and into a buggy. He was losing a lot of blood by then and had passed out. I suggested calling an ambulance, but Rachel said they never used the hospital. I tried to insist but she was stubborn about it.

"No," she said. "They wouldn't like it."

"Who's they?" I said.

But she turned away.

I never got a chance to say goodbye to her. When she left she was crying, though I knew it was not because she would never see me again.

Tanner and I went home after that and never went back to that part of town or talked about that night again. Instead we went into our senior year of high school and took the SATs, and then off to college like everyone else. I never saw Rachel again. But a few months later I found out from Tanner that Isaac King had died of a brain clot six weeks after that night. It was a small article in the paper and no allegations were made.

These days almost all of the Amish have left. Most have sold their land off cheap to real estate agencies and contractors and gone west to Indiana and Iowa. We have new malls and outlet stores where their farms were, and out where Rachel used to live actors dressed in Amish costumes and fake beards stand along the thruway, chewing on corn-cob pipes and beckoning carloads of tourists to have their picture taken with them.

I am twenty-nine years old now and not married. I am not yet old but some days I am aware of it closing in on me. Tanner lives in California now with a woman who will one day be his wife. But I can remember when he still lived in Leola, just a few blocks away. And when I think about Rachel now, I think mostly about those races we used to have out across the railroad bridge, thirty feet above the water, and I still shudder at our carelessness, our blind motions, not watching where we were stepping, not even considering what was below us.

Nominated by Ontario Review

SOUTINE: A SHOW OF STILL LIFES

by EDWARD HIRSCH

from PLOUGHSHARES

It started with herrings, which he ate
with warm black bread as a child,
and ended with two pigs, the forbidden.

It started with the strict dietary laws
of his father, a pious Jew, a mender,
and ended with ulcers, which he disobeyed.

He was snubbed by a bouquet
of colorful flowers on a balcony
and a pretty pink vase with flowers,

but red gladiolas from the countryside
in a flower shop next to a laundry
suddenly reached out to him.

He never expected so much water
in a dead ray fish, so much fire
in a turkey hanging from a fireplace.

He never expected to find his soul
hiding in a chicken splayed
open-winged on the blue ground.

Who needed a mirror against the wall?
He found an enormous carcass of beef
with all of its entrails exposed.

He loved the savagery of the match
and slashed his brush into the canvas
until the painting wobbled on its legs.

He was a boxer forcing his opponent
into a tight corner, taking him apart
with quick jabs and a right cross.

One punch for a shack in Smilovitchi,
two punches for a pair of older brothers
who attacked him in the kitchen.

One punch for the village thug
who thrashed him for drawing a rabbi,
two punches for the Second Commandment.

"Thou shalt not . . . " But Rembrandt painted
the portrait of a bearded Jew, a woman
bathing in a stream, the slaughtered ox.

Homage to the Jewish painters in Paris:
a scrawny hen for Kikoïne, a donkey
for Chagall, a pheasant for Modigliani.

He traveled back and forth to the Louvre.
He carried a giant slab of meat
on his back through the graveyard.

His lover said that his studio looked
like a slaughterhouse on Friday afternoon.
He no longer kept the Sabbath,

but he could scarcely endure the stench
and sprinkled blood on the carcass
to keep it fresh, like an open wound.

Some days his brush was a knife,
some days a scalpel. Some days
he worked like a surgeon

separating the ligaments of a patient
wounded on the table, calmly
cutting the flesh away from the bone.

He could not forget the village butcher
who shouted out with joy
when he sliced the neck of a bird

and drained the force out of it.
He could not abandon the boy
who had stifled his cry.

Let's leave a space for the paintings
that he lacerated and destroyed
with the radical fury of the creator.

Let's leave a space for his portraits
of the wind in the French countryside,
invisible presences, awe-filled nights.

It was a calm day. A void encircled
a solitary figure of flayed beef.
A void enclosed the painter.

I stood in the middle of a silent room
and surveyed the beauty of carnage,
the dangerous carnage of beauty.

So many brushstrokes in a painting,
and so much blood. So much art
in a still life, and so much death.

Nominated by Charles Harper Webb

18½

fiction by ROBERT OLEN BUTLER

from ZOETROPE: ALL STORY

Employing recent developments in nanomagnetic imaging techniques, the National Archives and Record Administration has reexamined the Watergate-Nixon tape number 342, which was created June 20, 1972, on a Sony TC-800B recorder, and has recovered the 18 ½-minute segment that was erased, allegedly on October 1, 1973, on a Uher 5000 reel-to-reel player. The erased portion occurred in a conversation between President Richard M. Nixon and his chief of staff, H. R. "Bob Haldeman, in the Oval Office three days after the Watergate break-in. The following is a transcript of the recovered segment, in which the only speaker is President Nixon.

Elvis was right, Bob. You won't find it in the memo Bud Krogh wrote, but I had him leave me alone with that boy for a few minutes, after all the picture-taking and formal talk. You remember when he came to visit a couple of years ago, just before Christmas, asking me to make him a federal drug agent at-large. You were hiding in your office. But Bob, if you looked beneath the velvet cape and the gold necklaces, you'd find that he and I have a lot in common.

You know, as a boy I plucked chickens. For a butcher in Prescott, Arizona, to make money for the family. For years, it feels like. Years and years, though in fact it was only for a summer. I was a sideshow barker too, out there, at the Slippery Gulch carnival. We were poor, Bob. My brother Harold was dying of tuberculosis in Prescott, and we'd eat chicken feather soup some nights. It was all we had. You know how to pluck a chicken, Bob? You have to dip it first in boiling

251

water. If you do it too quick, if you don't let the chicken scald sufficiently, every feather will fight you. But if you leave it in too long, the feathers will come out fast all right, but the skin will go brown and start to break up. You see what I mean? You dip the sons of bitches long enough, but not too long.

I barked the Wheel of Fortune. I could really put out the patter too. "Step up, step up. Step up to the Wheel of Fortune. That wheel spins for you every day of your life, only you don't know it. So if you've got to face your fortune anyway, why not put your own hand to the wheel and maybe walk away with wealth and power and victory over your enemies. Or at least a Kewpie doll."

It was all horsefeathers, Bob. The wheel was fixed. The Kewpie doll sat there untouched all that July. When the carnival was closing down I asked the man who ran the Wheel how long he'd had that doll, and he said four years. So I stole the son of a bitch and took it home and I gave it to Harold. He said to me, "Dick, you little prick, what makes you think I'd want a Kewpie doll?" Harold was nineteen at the time, and he was acting pretty goddamn cocky for a guy walking around with a sputum cup. So I said to him, "It's all I have to give, you son of a bitch. You rather have chicken feathers?" I should have just gone ahead and given the Kewpie doll to my saint of a mother to start with, but I was sorry about Harold dying. I should have at least given her the doll after Harold said what he did. But he needed to be shown what I was made of, my goddamn brother. I took a ball peen hammer to the doll, right in front of him, where he sat swaddled in his deck chair out in the sun. The doll was made of bisque and shattered into a million pieces and a patch of yellow hair. Bob, I was mostly an ignorant runt of a kid at the time, but I was learning how to protect myself.

I'd walk to school in Yorba Linda barefoot. You hear the Democrats sneering at me for wearing my wingtips when I walk on the beach at San Clemente, but they never had to walk to school barefoot. If you walk to school barefoot, Bob, you treasure your shoes. You've had enough dirt and grit and little flaky things between your toes to last a lifetime. And if you still get lint in there and grit that comes from God knows where and your skin flakes on its own account, well you just keep it to yourself. You're the president. When my saint of a mother sent me off to school barefoot she'd put extra starch in my white shirt to make up for it. Starch was cheaper than shoes, Bob. It turns a collar into a razor, but she knew what she was doing, my mother. She set me apart.

Elvis was a barefoot boy, too. At some point, when he was sitting in that very chair you're sitting in, Bob, I said to him, "Elvis, I bet you were a barefoot boy, walking to school in your bare feet."

And he said, "Well, sir, I did walk around barefoot some as a boy."

"It sets us apart, you know," I said.

"It was pretty common in east Tupelo," he said.

"Don't let your enemies hold it against you," I said.

"No, sir, I won't," he said.

I said, "I bet you wear those funny high-top pansy shoes you've got on right now even when you walk on the beach, don't you?"

Elvis just blinked, knowing that we were set apart together in this way.

"You just keep your shoes on no matter what they do to you," I said.

He's a good boy, Bob. You have to look under the surface. He despises Jane Fonda and the Smothers Brothers. He understands that they're traitors to America. He said as much. And he blames the Beatles for starting the country down the road of pot and protest. And we're all barefoot down that gravelly road, Bob. All of us.

He even said to me, "I can go out among the protesters. They accept me. I can be your eyes and ears."

"And my voice," I said.

"Yes, sir," he said.

"Our voices are very similar," I said.

He threw his arms up in the air and made the twin V-for-victory signs and he said, "Let me make this perfectly clear," and, Bob, he sounded just like me.

I said, "Love me tender. Love me true," and it was unquestionably Elvis's voice.

"That's very good, sir," he said.

"I've been meaning to say," I said, "don't call me 'sir.' Call me 'Mr. President.'"

"All right, Mr. President. And you can call me 'King.'" He said this with a laugh, Bob. Don't get him wrong.

"Mr. King," I said.

"Mr. President," he said.

"I remember a strange, drunken young man playing your music

during the campaign of '68," I said. "It was early one morning when I couldn't sleep."

"I have trouble sleeping too," Elvis said.

"You and I have a lot in common," I said.

"What do you use to help, Mr. President?" he said.

"I'm the president," I said.

"Yes, you are," he said. "You deserve to get some help if you need it."

"Seconal and single-malt scotch," I said.

"Both very good, Mr. President," he said. "But if you feel you need a little something more, I'd recommend Nembutal, Carbrital, Amytal, Demerol, Valmid, and Valium. Those'll give you the rest you need to kick some Communist butt, sir."

"I'll keep that in mind," I said. "But if you're using Valium, I'd recommend Dilantin to you instead. Jack Dreyfus, who's made more money than both of us put together, introduced me to it in Key Biscayne a few years ago. Two or three a day will keep you focused. He sends them to me in bottles of a thousand."

"I've heard about that," Elvis said. "But the FDA says it only works for seizures."

"Fuck the FDA," I said. "This is a drug for presidents and kings."

"I appreciate the advice," he said. "And I'm sorry for interrupting. What was it about this young man playing my music in the early morning?"

And I told him a little story then. You'll want to hear this too, Bob. I know I caused you some anxious times in Houston, when I left the hotel before dawn on my own, and it's true enough that I wanted to get in touch with the working men and working women of this great country. But there was a little more to it, Bob.

I couldn't sleep that night. The wallpaper was crawling around, so I got dressed and went out of the room and I made the Secret Service agents keep their distance. I walked out of the downtown district and there was nobody around and I kept going till I found an all-night diner. I told the agents to stay the hell outside, and they did.

Inside, there were just two people. One was a Mexican-looking woman in an apron behind the counter, who was mixing a mud-colored liquid in a glass from a bunch of jars. The whole diner was vibrating from the jukebox going full blast. It was Elvis singing "Jailhouse Rock." There was a young man in chinos and loafers leaning forward with the top of his head against the jukebox, and he was not moving at all, in spite of the music that he was playing. I was thinking of finding another place, but suddenly the young man turned his face to look at me without removing his head from the jukebox. I had the impression that he'd somehow glued himself there. But he smiled and waved and gathered his resolve and stood up straight and made his way toward me.

He had beady, deep-set eyes and heavy eyebrows and a goofy hayseed smile. "Welcome to the Elvis Pretzel concert," he said. It didn't sound right to him. "I meant to say, 'Pretzel,' " he said. "You look familiar."

"Yes," I said.

"Famous even," he said.

"I'm Bob Hope," I said. If this young man—who was slightly retarded or still drunk or both—didn't know who I was, I thought I'd seize the chance for an unvarnished conversation.

"I love your shows for the troops," he said.

"I feel it's my duty," I said.

"I hope you'll come to the Texas Air National Guard this year," he said.

"Are you a guardsman?" I said.

He nodded and began circling the floor of the diner with his arms outstretched. I could hear his jet engine imitation under Elvis singing, "You're the cutest jailbird I ever did see."

The young man landed on a counter stool in front of the Mexican waitress's concoction and patted the stool next to him. I sat down.

"That was an F-102," he said. "And this," he said, taking the glass in his hand, "is Maria's Magic Head-Fixer. Upper." And he drank down the contents in a long, single swallow, ending with a fit of coughing and throat clearing broken up by three *boy-that's-goods*, two *boy-that'll-fix-yous*, and, finally, one *boy-that'll-put-the-peck-back-in-your- pecker*. After this latter he took on a sober demeanor and said to the waitress, "Not you, Maria." Maria smiled faintly and turned away. "Mucho gracias, Maria," the young man cried at the top of his lungs, and then sang, "Let's rock, everybody," along with Elvis.

He spun once completely around on his stool and then returned his attention to me. "Bob, do you have any F-102 jokes, preferably dirty?" he said.

"I'm afraid not," I said.

"Then maybe some jokes about guys with receding hairlines. Or maybe an Italian joke," he said.

"I'm sorry," I said.

He said, "There's a couple of guys in my unit who like to give me knucklies and talk some foreign language around me, laughing all the while. But they misunderestimate what I can do. One's going bald and the other's Italian, see, is why I'm asking."

"You want to tell jokes about your enemies?" I said. For some reason I'd begun to feel sorry for this young man.

"A good zinger or two," he said.

"Listen," I said, "I'll give you some important advice. Don't zing your enemies, destroy them. When someone tries to harm you—or you even have reason to suspect they will—then you are free to do whatever you feel is necessary to thwart them."

"Wow," the young man said, "lighten up there, Bob." And before I could back away he reached out and palmed the top of my head and he tousled my hair.

He continued to tousle and I knew the Secret Service men would burst through that door in another moment. I turned my face to the door and pushed the palm of my hand at them, even as their faces appeared in the window. They stopped.

When I turned back to the young man, he was goggling out the door. Then he looked at me and realized he still had his hand on my head, and finally he took it off.

"I think I may still be drunk," he said.

The diner was suddenly silent as "Jailhouse Rock" ended and the jukebox whirred and clicked, searching for another song. The young man was blinking into his empty glass of Maria's hangover drink.

He said, "So, Bob, it looks like the life of a comedian can get to be a little intense."

Elvis began another song, and the words turned my head to the jukebox. "Are you lonesome tonight?" he sang.

I looked back at the young man, who'd picked up his glass and was licking inside the rim.

I knew it was time to go back to the hotel. But I was like Henry V, the king in disguise among his troops, trying to understand what they really thought of him, and I wanted one more thing from this young man.

I let him fortify himself from his licking for a little while, and then I said, "Can I ask you a question?"

He stopped licking the glass and looked at me. His previous mood seemed completely restored. "Shoot, pardner," he said.

"Are you hoping to fly in Vietnam?" I said.

He looked at me and his beady eyes widened. "Hell no, Bob. The furthest I'm hoping to fly is Waco."

"Do you think we should pull out?" I said.

"Negatory to that," he said. "Not till we've whipped those Viet Conks. From what I hear, they've got some other countries they're hiding in over there, right?"

"Cambodia and Laos," I said.

"Then we should go on in there. Send a bunch of our best in there and kick some Cambodite butt till they won't help our enemies anymore," he said.

I was interested in this common citizen's impulse, even when he seemed a little backward about how to deal with his own personal enemies. I said, "What if there are some who would say that an invasion of Cambodia or Laos exceeds the president's authority? They'd say that, under the present war powers approved by Congress, it would be illegal to send troops into those countries."

The young man squared around and looked me steadily in the eyes and said, "Heck. If the president does it, it can't be illegal, right, Bob?"

This seemed to me to be the voice of the American people. But even as I understood this, I found myself wondering if Maria would make me one of those drinks too.

And from the jukebox Elvis sang the refrain once again, "Are you lonesome tonight?"

So, Bob, I told Elvis this little story about his music when he came to visit, and I looked into his sympathetic eyes and I said, "You were right. You spoke to me there in the diner in Houston. I was lonesome that night."

"I understand, Mr. President," Elvis said.

And I knew he did. "Could you sing me a song right now?" I said.

"I'm afraid I don't have my guitar," he said.

"A cappella," I said.

"What song would you like?" he said.

" 'How Great Thou Art,' " I said.

So Elvis began to sing, and I swiveled in my chair and looked out onto the South Lawn. He sang about awesome wonder and making worlds with your own hands. Which is what presidents do, Bob. He sang of rolling thunder, and I was pissed that Johnson had already grabbed that phrase for his own bombing campaign in Vietnam.

Johnson was an enemy we crushed pretty well, but not enough. He's down on his ranch in Texas right now, happily growing his hair as long as a hippie's. I never have trusted Texans, Bob. Even the Republicans, I'm sorry to say. And when Congressman Bush sent his son to Washington to have a date with Tricia and it turned out to be that dimwit boy from the diner, I was only confirmed in that distrust. But Elvis soothed all that over. I just closed my eyes and let him sing to me, "How great thou art. How great thou art."

Nominated by Zoetrope: All Story

SKINNY-DIPPING
WITH PAT NIXON

by DAVID KIRBY

from THE GETTYSBURG REVIEW

"That blonde kissed me," says Barbara, and I say, "The minx!"
but don't add that she kissed me, too, then said she and her friend
    are going to pull their clothes off and jump
in the pool, and do I want to join them, and I say yeah, kind of,
    only Barbara's in the next room, just-kissed herself, or about to be,

and I'm in enough trouble already: we're at a party following
the National Book Festival, and while nobody told me
    not to speak out against the war in Iraq, it's hard to pretend
nothing is going on as surveillance helicopters whack-whack
    over the poetry tent, and some of the peace marchers have

even plopped down in front of me, so I promise them, if elected,
(1) to bring the troops home, (2) to rebuild the city of New Orleans
    exactly as it was before Hurricane Katrina, and (3) to prevent
or at least minimize helicopter flyovers during all future
    poetry readings, and now my host won't talk to me, and all because

I have put a single raisin of doubt on the government's snowy
white cake of confidence. At the opening ceremony
    the night before, four writers spoke, but they all said
the same thing, which is that, if you work at it and keep smiling,
    everything will be fine. And at the dinner afterward, I'm talking

to a publishing executive who wants to know how I liked what
the writers said, and I say I about half liked it, and he says
        what does that mean, and I say I like all that Abraham
Jefferson Jackson stuff about America the beautiful,
    the sunlit, the fluoride-coated, the vitamin-enriched,

    but where's bad America, America the weird, the one that says,
"No! in thunder," to use Melville's description of Hawthorne,
        although I suspect it was himself he was talking
about when he said that, and the publisher keeps saying what do
    you mean, I don't get it, and I say doesn't every play or opera

    or TV show you like have something dark in it, something
bug-eyed and scary, and he says why would I watch anything like
        that,
        and I say okay, doesn't every great artist walk
the line between the sublime and the horrible the way Johnny
        Cash
        heel-to-toes it along the narrow thread between right and wrong,

    between the love of a woman he's known it seems like forever
and some nameless dance-hall pussy, though I don't use
        the *p* word, and the executive says why would
anyone write that way, I don't get it, what are you talking about,
    what do you mean. And then this morning, at the White House

    itself, there were four more speakers, but these weren't even
writers, because if you have too many writers at a book festival,
        people get the wrong idea. So there were two TV
personalities and two basketball players, but they said the same
        thing
        the writers did the night before: life's good, people are good,

    God loves you. Yet every portrait in the White House
is of a failure: Warren Harding, with his gang of unscrupulous
        shysters;
        LBJ, who went overnight from world's greatest
president to world's worst; even poor Eleanor Roosevelt, with
    her unfaithful husband and ugly buck teeth. But the portrait

I come back to again and again is of Pat Nixon, so dignified,
so sad, her hands folded in her lap, her eyes pained,
     her narrow chin almost trembling. You weren't good
enough for me when I was younger, Pat; I thought you scrawny
     and neurotic, and you were married to that evil turd Richard.

But now I'm the age you are in the portrait, and I can see
how hard it was for you, how different it would have been
     if you'd had a good marriage, a good man.
I would get in that pool with you, Pat; as the guests swirl, unseeing,
     you'd turn your back to me and wriggle out of

     your old-fashioned white undies, dive in and surface
where I wait, then throw your arms around my neck.
     I brush your hair out of your eyes and glance down
at your breasts, though I'm too shy to touch them.
     The guests nibble gingered beef and crab-stuffed cherry tomatoes,

     and the host pours another drink, a stiff one this time.
The sky over Washington fills with chrysanthemums, their light
     dappling
     the water and our pale skin as they flash and boom like bombs
or fireworks, though we can't tell which. Kiss me, Pat:
     heal me, heal the world. You've never been more lovely.

Nominated by Ed Falco, Joyce Carol Oates, R.T. Smith

AUGUST/NO RAIN

by DEBORAH KEENAN

from KINGDOMS (Laurel Poetry Collective)

Still summer, and on the steps of the museum
Poseurs and the arrogant gather in honor of art.

Your head was on fire—they couldn't let you in—
Those flames too weird and meaningful

Might touch off a golden storm inside the Monet.
Or not. You never, never know about art and money.

You never know about money and fire,
Their curious marriage, their rapture.

Nobody was drunk, though. I think the heat
Just makes people pray for rain that doesn't

Arrive. Nobody's drinking, nobody's cooking.
Too many people are forgetting they hate winter.

I'm not, though. I hate winter. And today,
I'm so uneasy standing near the rich.

I know it is not their fault they live under
The money tree, I know how hard it is for them

When the poor refuse to love art, refuse to pose
On the steps of the museum. Today

In the brilliant heat I would burn their money
And dip my brush into the cinders for art's sake.

Nominated by Jim Moore, Laurel Poetry Collective

THE DEAD FISH MUSEUM

fiction by CHARLES D'AMBROSIO

from A PUBLIC SPACE

"THIS KEY ISN'T WORKING," Ramage said.

Behind a thick sheet of acrylic, the desk clerk's face rushed up at him; it spread and blurred, white and without features, but never seemed to reach the surface. Ramage leaned forward and looked through a circle in the slab of glass, cut like a hole in ice. On the counter was a dinner plate with chicken bones and a few grains of rice hardening in brown gravy and, next to the plate, the splayed and broken spine of a romance. The clerk had been working over the chicken, cracking the bones and sucking the marrow. Her hair was thin and her teeth were leaning gray ruins in her lipless mouth. Her blue eyes were milky and vague, the pupils tiny beads of black. Ramage could not imagine a youth for her—it was if she'd been born fully ruined. She licked her fingers and swiveled heavily on her stool, unhooking a new key from a pegboard on the wall.

"Off season," she said. She seemed suspicious of him.

"I'm here for a job," Ramage explained. "A movie."

"Oh." A hand flew up to the crimped little mouth. The eyelids batted.

"Who's in it? Anybody famous?"

"No one," Ramage said. "No one famous."

"A movie, really?" she said. "You an actor?"

"Yes," Ramage said, lagging, caught in the confusing overlap of questions—"No." He tapped his new key on the counter. "Hope this works," he said.

Ramage went back to #7 and this time the door unlocked. He set his canvas tool sack in one corner and draped his coat over a doorknob and instantly they seemed to have been there forever. He changed out of his shirt and splashed cold water in his face. Next door, he heard a man and a woman laughing, perhaps making love. He'd gained weight in the hospital—two sedentary months chain smoking in the day room, drugged and without true hunger, yet an emptiness had kept him eating constantly. The food was institutional, flavorless, all of it boiled and pale, except for a bounty of fruit that arrived on the ward in pretty wicker gift baskets that no one wanted. One day a month into his stay, the vibrancy of an apple had started him crying. He'd been alone in the dining room and it was quiet except for the rumbling of the dumbwaiter dropping down to the basement and the singsong of black scullions rising up the shaft from the kitchen. A red apple rested on the windowsill in a beam of white morning light. Waxed and glowing, it was painfully vivid. It was perfect, he remembered thinking, but too far away to eat.

Ramage put on his coat and lingered in the doorway, trying to decide if he should carry his tool sack with him. In it was everything, his tools, a change of underwear, a clean shirt, a pair of jeans. Buried at the bottom of the sack, wrapped in a purple shop rag, was the gun that he had believed, for the past year, would kill him. The gun was his constant adversary, like a drug, a deep secret that he kept from others, but it was also his passion, a theater where he poured out his lonely ardor, rehearsing scenarios, playing with possibilities. Over time the gun had become a talisman with the power and primitive comfort of a child's blanket. It would horrify him to lose it. Ramage hid the canvas sack beneath the bed. He locked the door and checked it. Halfway across the parking lot, stricken with doubt, he returned to his room and tested the handle once more, making sure.

Ramage immediately went and stole an apple and a brick of cheese at a convenience store. The woman behind the cash register sucked on a whip of red licorice and read through a beauty magazine while a tinny radio wept sentimental favorites. As he was leaving, the woman gave Ramage the eye. She knew what he'd done, he was sure, but her stake in the scheme of things didn't warrant hassling shoplifters. Had she confronted him, he would have handed over the apple and cheese as obediently as a schoolboy. He wouldn't have run away, he wouldn't have become violent, he wouldn't have elaborated a lie. He'd have felt deep shame. Maybe the cashier understood that, maybe she thought he was ridiculous.

Back in his room, Ramage took a hacksaw blade from his tool sack and sliced up his apple, fanning the pieces out on the nightstand. He cut the brick of cheese and paired up a dozen open-faced sandwiches. Next door, a baby cried, and then a man yelled, telling it to shut the fuck up. A woman shouted, "For christsake, it's just a baby. It might be hungry or something." Ramage turned on his TV and blotted out the noise. He felt evil around young children; he avoided them on buses, in waiting rooms, in city parks. The night of his release, he'd been seated in a restaurant next to a family with a baby, not six months old. The child was snugly dressed in blue footed pyjamas, gurgling and burping a white liquid all over itself. After a few minutes, Ramage moved his steak knife to the other side of his plate. Something wildly uncentered in his mind had told him he was going to stab the baby in the eye.

The memory made him shudder, and he stepped outside for fresh air. The tourists were gone, and everything in town—the souvenir vendors, the picture-postcard shops, the ice-cream parlors, and arcades—had been closed for the season. Bits of popcorn blew across the highway; paper cones that had once held wigs of blue and pink cotton candy lay dirty and trampled flat in the parking lot. Ramage drew a deep breath and smelled sage or basil—something cooking in the spice factory down the street. A single stranded palm tree and the motel's blue vacancy sign stood at the edge of the lot. Toilet paper fluttered from the fender of his neighbor's car, a few crushed tin cans were strung from the bumper, and a Burma-Shave heart, pierced by an arrow, dripped from the rear window.

"This is the back road to Hollywood," Greenfield said early the next morning.

A steady procession of people moved from the van to the warehouse: a woman with a face pierced with pins, a punk with a hackle of red hair, a man with the shaved blue skull of a prisoner. They hauled trunks, hoisted lights and cameras, carried canisters of film, slung coils of cable over their shoulders. Best boys, key grips, gaffers—titles Ramage knew from his old habit of sitting in theaters, after the end, watching the scroll of credits bubble up from the bottom of the screen like a movie's last breath.

"Who am I kidding?" Greenfield said. "This doesn't go anywhere near Hollywood."

"You got lots of company," Ramage said.

"Everybody wants a little stardust to fall on them."

"Success could be all over your face next week," Ramage said.

"Sure," Greenfield said. He took a deep breath. "This town stinks."

"There's a spice factory a few blocks over," Ramage explained.

A blonde woman lifted a travel bag from the van. Greenfield nodded at her.

"My star," he said.

To Ramage, she looked like a rough outline for someone's idea of a woman, the main points greatly exaggerated.

Greenfield fumbled in his pocket and drew out a box of colored Shermans, lighting a pink one. He'd already put the box away when Ramage asked if he could bum a smoke. A cigarette might cut the gnawing in his stomach. Greenfield took a deep drag, and said, "Finish this one."

Ramage smoked. "You still pay in cash?" he asked.

"*Bien sûr.*" Greenfield lovingly patted a black shoulder bag at his side.

"How about an advance?"

"I can't do that," Greenfield said. "I've had people run out on me."

"Would it matter if I said I was broke?"

"Not much," Greenfield said. "How broke are you?"

"We've known each other a long time," Ramage said.

"I heard you were in the bin."

Ramage nodded.

"What's the least you need?" Greenfield said.

It was clear that asking for the full thousand would only bring derision. Ramage said, "Half."

Greenfield reached in his bag and separated two crisp bills from a bound stack. "Here's two hundred," he said. He held the two bills toward Ramage, then drew them back. "This doesn't mean I trust you."

Greenfield was wearing his signature black shirt and black pants; his cowboy boots were made of green-snakeskin, buffed and shiny except where fine lines of dust had settled between the scales. Ramage had worked with him off and on for twelve years, beginning shortly after he'd moved to New York. Before his hospitalization, Ramage had been rehabbing the homes of the rich, but he was still loosely connected to an underground of carpenters and waitresses and bookstore clerks who, in successive waves, struggled to make films. Greenfield had been a rising star ten years ago; porn was only supposed to occupy the space of an anecdote, a moment of amusement as he looked back, a dark tint in an otherwise bright career. Ditto for Ramage: he'd scripted the movie that established Greenfield's promise a decade ago.

They walked into the building and rode the freight elevator upstairs. "First thing you do," Greenfield said, "is board up all the windows. This is a non-union job."

"A union for porn?" Ramage said.

"Erotica," Greenfield corrected him. "There's a street tax we're not paying."

"What's the plot of this one?" Ramage asked.

Greenfield lowered his glasses and looked at him over the rims as if he were stupid.

"Boy meets girl," he said.

Ramage ran the carpentry crew. They'd boarded shut the windows and now, with fumes of fresh paint filling the warehouse, Ramage felt woozy; as a precaution, he set his hammer down and stepped off the ladder and waited for the room to resolve back into focus. With a prybar he yanked the nails from a sheet of plywood over one of the windows; the board crashed to the floor and the air rushed in. He was slightly winded by the effort. He took off his shirt and squatted against the wall and drank from a quart of warm beer and lit his last cigarette. He crushed the empty pack, feeling weak and isolated and craven; already he was dreading the next wave of desire. There would be no one in the crew to borrow from. RB smoked snowballs that tasted medicinal and Rigo didn't smoke at all.

Rigo was in the next room rolling red paint over the walls. He was a short, stocky man with a broad, flat plate of a face whose perfect roundness was carried out thematically in his dark eyes and in the purple, fleshy pouches encircling them and then again in the two wide discs of his jutting ears. These redundant open circles gave Rigo's face a spacious, uncrowded look that people routinely mistook for simplemindedness.

RB, the other carpenter, had watched Ramage step down from the ladder, and saw this as a cue to take another break.

"What say, Spooky?" he said, sitting beside Ramage. He took a swig from the quart and swished the beer around in his mouth. "You see the ladies out there this morning?" he said. He held his hands out in front of him to suggest breasts. He shook his head in disbelief. He looked at his empty hands and said, "I saw that blonde do a midget once. She's famous."

Ramage nodded neutrally.

"This little itty-bitty midget," RB said. "But he had the pecker of a full-grown man. About as long as his arm. Hey Rigoberto, how about pecker? You know what a pecker is?"

Rigo paused and held his roller aloft and red paint dribbled like blood between his fingers and down his arm. He had been a lieutenant in the army in El Salvador and his bearing was military; one could still sense in him the faint trace of his training at the hands of U.S. advisors. He never fully relaxed and he held to odd protocols— after a day's work he cleaned and organized Ramage's tools and insisted on carrying the canvas sack for him, moving the bag to and from the job like a bellhop. Leftist rebels had raided his house on the outskirts of San Salvador and shot his brother, who'd been spending the night, and sleeping in Rigo's bed. The bullet had been meant for Rigo, who'd skipped the funeral and fled El Salvador with his family, deserting the army and leaving the civil war behind. Now a jackleg carpenter who spoke only a crude, cobbled English, he worked with indefatigable energy, compensating for RB's tendency to goldbrick. He lacked a green card and preferred the clarity of labor, no matter how arduous, to the vagaries of talking in a language where even the simplest notion plunged him into loss and confusion. He was still learning the names of the tools he was using.

"Pecker?" Rigo said.

"Like dong, dink, dick," RB said. He spread his legs and pointed at his crotch. "Penis."

Rigo allowed a thin smile of recognition.

"Little guy doesn't know where he's at," RB said. He fingered a scar that cut across the base of his throat; the original wound had been stitched together without much concern for cosmetics; against his oily black skin, the tissue was red and smooth and protuberant, like a worm. "We watched fuck-flicks all the time in reform school."

"You were in reform school?" Ramage asked.

"You don't believe me?"

"You've never mentioned it before. How'd you end up there?"

269

"I got crossed by a guy I sold some chainsaws to."

"Seems to me they wouldn't allow porn."

"Shit," RB said. "Everything was allowed."

"You finish taping?"

"No."

"I guess you got that disease again."

"What disease?"

"That-sit-around-on-your-ass disease."

"Oh, you're kidding. I get it."

"I'm not kidding, RB. You hardly did jack today."

"Ah, Spooky."

"Why are you calling me Spooky?"

RB looked at Ramage, then shrugged. "That cartoon," he said. He turned to Rigo and shouted, "Hey Rigoberto, take a break. Stop. No paint."

"He's not deaf," Ramage said.

"He sure don't understand." RB beat on the floor with his fist. "Rigoberto, here, sit. Sit. Sit down. Down, man."

Rigo grabbed a wrinkled brown lunch sack he'd stashed behind a stack of Sheetrock. The sack had been folded and saved and used repeatedly. His clothes showed the same habitual thrift. He wore neatly creased khakis and a crimson T-shirt, the HARVARD nearly washed away.

"You ever killed a man?" RB said.

Rigo scraped flecks of red paint from his arm and didn't answer.

"Me, I don't have the heart to kill a man. You got to have heart to kill somebody."

Using his thumb Rigo made an inconspicuous sign of the cross on his knee and silently said grace and then made the same small cross again before unwrapping the wax paper from his sandwich.

"That must be some good-ass sandwich," RB said. "I hope it is. I sure hope to fucking God it's not baloney again."

Rigo lifted a corner of the sandwich.

"More baloney!" RB screamed, grabbing Rigo's sack and sandwich. "Jesus Christ, I swear, you're just like all them refugees." Then, as if they were co-conspirators, he said to Ramage, "See how it works, they all get together and send a man over, and he gets his shit together, eatin' baloney every damn day and savin' up his money. Never go to a movie or buy ice cream or nothing. Just baloney and baloney and more baloney. Then he sends back money so the whole family

270

can book out of Pago Pago and come over and they all live together, nine of them to one room, everybody eatin' baloney every minute!" RB lobbed the lunch sack out the window and, his tone lowered and confidential, addressed Rigo again. "America's so wide open, see, with you people coming here, I call you refugees."

"America's so wide open," Ramage said, "it seems to have filled up with shitheads. Go get his sack."

"Spooky, man, you can't have a grown man praying for baloney. Not in America! It ain't right, I'm sorry. Now Harvard, quit praying for that shit."

"Go get it."

"Every job we do," RB said, "every week, he eats five days of straight baloney. Not even fried! Give the baloney a break, Harvard. You understand? FUCK. THE BALONEY."

Rigo was gazing into the inscrutable square of black sky, out the empty window where his baloney sandwich had flown.

RB clattered down the fire escape and came back a minute later.

"The baloney got a little dirty," he said. He reached for his billfold. "Buy yourself something good to eat, Harvard. My treat. Something special. Get yourself a cheeseburger."

Greenfield looked about the warehouse, making no mention of the work that had been completed; it was as if the merest kindness might collapse the hierarchy. He stared up at the ceiling, inspecting a large skylight.

"I like that," Greenfield said. "I might use that."

Greenfield moved directly under the skylight where a waning moon was visible like an amulet in the bottom of a black velvet box.

"I might quote *Citizen Kane*, he said. "What do you think? We'll crane up over the warehouse and drop down through the skylight." He lit a long red Sherman. It moved obscenely like the tongue of a lizard between his lips. "What do you think of that? Huh?" He was asking RB. "Quoting *Citizen Kane*? What's your opinion?"

RB shrugged. "Whatever gets you off."

Ramage said, "You don't have a crane."

"So?" Greenfield said.

"So you need a crane to quote *Citizen Kane*."

"I'll call the movie 'Citizen Cunt,' " Greenfield said. He pointed to Rigo and said, "You like that? Would you buy a movie with that ti-tle?"

"Certainly," he said.

"The title's important," Greenfield said. "The title's everything."

Ramage felt a tightening at his temples. Impatient, he asked, "You got any more work for us?"

"Finish painting," Greenfield said. "I want that black room glossy, like a mirror. Rub some polish on the paint after it dries. Buff it out so we can see our reflections."

RB spoke up. "Greenwad, how about putting me in the movie?"

"It's not as easy as it looks," Greenfield said.

"I can handle it," RB said. "I popped my first cherry when I was eleven, just a little spike."

"Bullshit," Ramage said.

"Ask my sister if you don't believe me."

Greenfield looked him over. "You endowed?"

"Shit," RB said, reaching for his belt buckle.

"Please," Greenfield said. He made his face into a face expressive of distaste. He looked at RB again and said, "Although, it might be a kick."

The carpentry job was straightforward: build three boxes, paint them in three colors: one red, one black, one white. With the paint still drying, Ramage had Rigo and RB help him arrange a few pieces of rented furniture, chairs, tables, lamps, and now, nearly finished, they all sat down in one of the rooms they'd built, on the bed. RB propped a pillow beneath his head and leaned back. Ramage felt RB's cool moist skin rub against his; he inched away from the contact.

Rigo opened a beer and lofted the bottle above his head; it shone like a torch, golden in the dim light, as bubbles streamed to the surface. The outside world might have vanished, the warehouse was so suddenly quiet.

"You might be part nigger," RB said to Rigo.

Rigo sipped his beer; his face was freckled with paint.

"Spooky, don't he look like a nigger?"

RB's initials stood for nothing. "Just RB," he'd explained, when Ramage asked about his name, "straight up southern."

"Drink your beer," Ramage said.

"Look at his nappy head," RB continued. "Nigger hair. Me and Rigo could be brothers."

"I am Salvadoran," Rigo said, a little cold, prideful.

"Used to be, but now you in the U.S. of A., Jack."

"Drink," Ramage said.

RB drank, then asked, "When they start shooting?"

"Call's for seven tomorrow morning," Ramage said.

"You're all invited to my debut," RB said. "Those ladies are fine. They know all sorts a special tricks, too. You get with one of them, you'll be spoiled for life. I had this one old girlfriend that used to call me the wonder-log."

"Referring to what?"

"Hell, Spooky—"

"Why do you keep calling me Spooky?"

RB shrugged. "Just do," he said. "It's from that cartoon."

"Let's get out of here," Ramage said.

The head full of paint fumes, the numbness in the arms, the reluctant knees, the rigid back—the body's memory: Ramage felt this, and no one else moved from the bed, as if the day's work had brought them to a poise. Outside, there was nothing but the separateness of feeling used and spent, of rundown bones and sore muscles and another day, and at the narrow end of it a tub of tepid water that would instantly turn tea-brown and drain away, leaving a ring of crud around the porcelain. His first day of work in two months had exhausted Ramage; he was spacey with fatigue; they all were; and for a moment Ramage wished that they might rest and sleep and dream together on this bed until morning.

Back at the motel, Ramage washed his hands and face at the sink, listening to the baby cry next door. He sponged his chest and armpits and put on his clean shirt.

Standing outside, he heard the baby, still crying, and knocked on the door. No one answered. He pushed the door open slowly and saw the baby alone in the room; a crib had been squeezed between the bed and the sliding doors of a closet. Clothes were scattered on the floor, over the nightstand, flung across the TV screen. An empty bottle of strawberry wine with its cap resealed lay in the wastebasket along with a condom wrapper and a plastic straw and a nest of black hair someone had cleaned from a comb. A calendar hung on the wall, but no one had bothered to turn the page since the end of summer.

The baby shrieked. Its tiny hands reached through the slatted cage of the crib, opening and then closing into tight fists. Ramage saw the pacifier that had fallen to the carpet. He picked it up and rinsed the hair and grit away under the faucet. He set the pacifier in the baby's hand and the baby pitched it back to the floor. Ramage cleaned it off again, and this time stuck the rubber nipple in the baby's mouth. The baby's eyes softened and it sucked contentedly. The baby was maybe a year old. It was naked. It wasn't even diapered. Ramage touched it; he pressed his thumb into the soft skin.

Outside, he saw Rigo working his way up from the beach, over the sand, past a lifeguard station that had been knocked down for the winter. He waited for him to cross the highway.

"Buy you a drink?" Ramage asked.

"Certainly," Rigo said.

Certainly: it was one of Rigo's words, a magniloquence in his otherwise lean vocabulary. Ramage ushered him into the bar. Sawdust had been strewn about the floor; oyster shells broke like bones underfoot. A few other people sat at the scattered tables. Ramage saw a man and a woman he thought might be his neighbors at the motel. They were bending into the yellow light of the jukebox, looking for a good song.

Ramage saluted Rigo with a nod of his bottle and they drank down their beers in unison.

"RB, he talk too much," Rigo said.

"That's just RB," Ramage said. "He's having fun, he's goofing."

"In Jersey City," Rigo said, "outside my apartment, there is a telephone. All night, the niggers out there. They play their music, they talk their talk. I call police—nothing."

Rigo finished his beer, ordered another round. Ramage insisted on paying; he considered it part of his position as foreman of the crew, a way of building esprit de corps.

"So I take care of business myself, as a man must," Rigo said. "I chase them with a baseball bat. I chase them every night. They always come back."

"You're going to get yourself killed," Ramage said.

"RB is nigger, not me."

"Don't call him that. Not to his face, anyway."

"He calls that to us, to our face."

"What were you doing on the beach?" Ramage asked, changing the subject, although he knew the answer: Rigo was sleeping down there, saving the expense of a motel room, pocketing the modest per diem. RB's riff on refugees had not been far off. Rigo wired a remittance every month to an uncle exiled in Honduras.

"I love the ocean, Ramage." Rigo looked at his dirty hands, a little embarrassed; then he said, "When I first come with my family to Jersey City, everyday I fish. Every morning I go with my bucket to the park where I have a view of the *Estatua—Estatua de la Libertad*. They are cleaning her, she is—all everywhere—they put—"

"Scaffolding?" Ramage guessed.

"Scaffolding," Rigo repeated, reciting the lesson. "I catch many fish. I bring fish home I do not know the name of." Rigo broke off. He seemed bewildered, recalling the beginning, before names. "My wife, she no say the word *refrigerator* so good. She just learning. She say it, the dead fish museum."

"I like that," Ramage said. "The dead fish museum."

"We can no eat all that I catch."

"I'm surprised you ate any of it," Ramage said.

The bar door opened, and the blonde star took up a stool near the register. Her drink came in a goblet and the bartender produced a faded paper parasol, cocked over the frosted rim of the glass. It was a summer garnish but in the dim slow bar the parasol failed to add much in the way of gaiety.

"In El Salvador," Rigo said, "you go to the beach with the children, Sunday, you stay all day. The sand is clean and white and the man, he comes with *las ostras* for you. Limón, tabasco, pepper: you go down like nothing."

"I can taste them now," Ramage said.

"Certainly," Rigo said. "Here, the beach is garbage. Everything wash up. Tonight, I find a door to the house. A door to the man's house, Ramish."

Rigo held his hands above the bar, staring into the empty space they created; he seemed to be picturing the thing his words had just described, trying to put his hands around the hallucination of it; they tensed with frustration; he could not hold the thing, and the picture in his mind floated away. Rigo grabbed his beer and finished it off. He ordered another.

"I no eat on the beach here," he said. "But the ocean, she is the ocean still."

They crossed the necks of their bottles together in a sloppy swashbuckling salute, and Ramage drank with the image of blue water, of open sea, before him. The soreness deep in his body had risen into a pleasant hum on the surface of his skin. He felt loose and shallow.

"I do not know what kind of movie this is," Rigo said.

"No," Ramage said. "I didn't tell you."

"Now I know," he said.

Rigo drank his whiskey and spun the empty shot glass like a top on a tilted axis. The glass wobbled violently; it stopped and he spun it again. He seemed torn between maintaining dignity and getting trashed. Each word was the end of a very long journey. Every sentence jeopardized his loyalties.

"I am surprise how things are," Rigo said.

Ramage said, "It's only three days."

"Salvador," Rigo said, raising his bottle.

"Salvador," Ramage said.

They toasted each other, the bar, the empty tables, the jukebox that had fallen silent.

"Salvador," Rigo said again.

Another drink, and another after that: Ramage couldn't keep pace.

"I no choice. I must go away or die. I die, my family die. I come here. I don't know to what. To what, Ramish—*to what?*"

"You going back someday?" Ramage asked.

"They rape the women with rats," Rigo said. "A man from my town has a nail"—he pounded the air—"in his head, his—" and with a balled fist he knocked on his forehead.

"His skull," Ramage said.

Rigo shook his head. *"Su cerebro."*

"His brain?"

"Yes, he can no speak with a nail in his brain."

Rigo fashioned a gun out of his right hand; the hammer of his thumb slammed down rapid fire as he squinted and swept his aim along the glimmering funhouse row of bottles behind the bar.

"They kill my brother," he said. "But I go home, Ramish. One day I go home."

He slapped the bar and rose; Ramage watched him weave toward the door; it looked as though he was only taking a rough guess about the way out.

At different junctures, Ramage tried to recall what he and the blonde woman were talking about, but he found the words were just falling out of the back of his head as they went along, and he was arriving in the present always empty. When last call was announced, she suggested they buy a bottle and stroll along the boardwalk and keep drinking.

"You're right," she was saying. "My name isn't Desiree Street, good God—but we can just leave it at that anyway. I prefer it. Let's make up a name for you instead."

"Call me Payne, Payne with a *y*," Ramage said, "Payne Whitney."

"Payne's okay, Payne's a good porn name. Payne-with-a-y Whitney. Okay Payne, where to?"

"You smell that?"

As they drifted up from the beach and further from the ocean the damp cloying odor of kelp and sea lettuce was replaced by the arid and spacious scent of oregano cooking in the spice factory. It was if they'd entered a new, fairer latitude. They walked through a back section of town where the sidewalks were cracked and slabs of concrete heaved up to make way for weeds and tree roots. A wooden boat listed in the dirt of a vacant lot; a cat with yellow eyes watched them from the glassless wheelhouse. A brick building dominated by a high square clock tower was just across the street. The clock had a white face and roman numerals and the black hands were stuck at the pleasant hour of seven o'clock, a time of beginnings, of a new day, a new night. They leaned their heads through a window, canted open with a pull-chain; blue smoke rose from the ovens and spread and was sucked away by a whirring exhaust fan. Ramage shushed drunkenly with a warning finger to his lips. "Look," he whispered, "natives." Two men and a woman stood in front of a large spinning machine; they were dressed in white smocks and paper hats and surgical masks; behind them glass bottles filled with spice and were shunted down a metal chute and conveyed up a rubber ramp into waiting boxes; the clinking bottles made a cool Latin-flavored jazz in the cavernous factory; particles of oregano rained down in a fine green dust that settled over the cement floor; a faint trail of footprints was visible, the tread of sneakers stamped into the green spice, and the men and the woman were coated in green dust too. Ramage leaned in and inhaled the warm fragrant air, and he started choking and hacking; the woman inside the factory, laughing at the conclusion of some joke or story, lightly touched the elbow of the man beside her. They stiffened and the laughter went out of them. They stared uncertainly at Ramage and Desiree in the window; they ventured a wave. Ramage waved back.

"Somebody got married," Desiree said, when they'd returned to the motel. She pointed to the neighbor's car.

"They're on their honeymoon. That's why they came to this paradise."

"You are wasted."

"I'll tell you what."

"What?"

Ramage put a finger to his lips. He led her to his neighbor's room and tested the knob and it turned. Inside, the man and the woman slept naked on top of a tangle of sheets, the baby nestled between them like a puzzle piece. Whatever it was inside of Ramage that understood that he was outrageously drunk stifled the urge to scream. He quietly shut the door.

He put the key in the lock to his own room and then flopped over the threshold and crawled on his knees across the carpet to his canvas tool sack. He unzipped the bag and fumbled through an omnium gatherum of plumb lines and box wrenches and pencil stubs and ratchers and tape measures until he found his gun. Further searching produced a plastic case of shells. "Look," he said. He lay on his back like a playing child, holding the gun in one hand, the shells in the other. He smashed the gun and the case against one another and shells rained down on his face.

"Hello gun," he pantomimed. "Hi bullet."

The black polymer barrel waggled as the gun asked, "Will you marry me?"

"Is this like a kink or something?" Desiree asked.

"Let's have a baby," the bullet said.

"Fill me with your seed," the gun said.

Ramage loaded a shell in the gun. The bullet made a satisfying click in the chamber like a key turning in a lock.

"I'm pregnant," the gun announced.

"I'm out of here," Desiree said.

"They got a baby. The newlyweds have a child."

Ramage jumped into bed and beckoned Desiree with the gun.

"Why don't you give me that gun?"

"I came here to kill myself."

"Why?"

"Why kill myself?"

"Why come here?"

She walked out, leaving the door open, and for a while Ramage lay on the bed, listening to the crashing of the ocean across the highway. His display had been grotesque. He had humiliated himself and now it disgusted him, he was mortified and filled with self-loathing and yet he watched the open door, hoping she might return. He had almost felt decent, standing with Desiree outside the spice factory, watching the quiet green dust spin through the cavernous room, but now he couldn't stop his black ruminations. His mind went round and round, churning pitifully, and finally he pictured himself crossing the highway and wading into the sea and pulling the trigger; if he lost nerve and flinched and only managed to blast off part of his head the ocean would drown him. It wasn't so unusual to consider these scruples; it was like a math problem one worked until there was no remainder. Regina, his friend from the hospital, had dressed ceremoniously in her grandfather's bathrobe and soaked the terry cloth in gasoline and then struck a match, immolating herself, and what she remembered was the noise, the horrid rushing sound, the wind howling inside the flames—that was what made her want to stop it. She had rolled herself in the garden, digging into the dirt and desperately spinning, smothering the flames not to save her life, not to end the pain, but to stop the noise. She was hideously disfigured, her mouth a dry withered hole, her eyes drooping from their melted sockets, her graphed skin puckered and glossy, red and raw, as if she'd been flayed and turned inside out, but all she ever wanted to talk about, two years after striking the match, was the noise.

Ramage gulped a yawn to clear his head; tendrils of chalky saliva hinged his mouth and alcoholic tears welled in his eyes. Breeze from an open door did little to refresh him. When Greenfield cleared the set, Ramage went out onto the fire escape and found RB sitting on a metal step, furtively turning the crank on a hand drill and boring a hole in the plywood that blocked the window. When the half-inch bit punched through, he tested the peephole, and then enlarged it, carving away at the wood with a pocketknife.

"Spooky," RB said. He stopped to pinch at a blood blister on his thumb. "You smell that smell?"

"Clove today," Ramage said.

"I been trying to figure it out."

"There's a spice factory," Ramage said.

"This town is ugly," RB said, "but it smells good."

"I'm all tore up," Ramage admitted. "I got drunk with Rigo last night."

"Harvard," RB said, with a laugh. "He don't like me kidding him, do he?"

"He might appreciate it if you laid off."

"Good. Then I'll keep on." RB finally popped the blister, wiping the spurt of blood away on his pant leg. "Guy doesn't know where he's at."

They could hear Greenfield calling for quiet as the filming was set to begin. RB peered through the hole he'd made in the plywood.

"This shit's tame," he said after a while. "I thought there'd be monkeys in it." He closed his pocketknife. "Still, there's boys and girls inside about to get their rocks off. And you out here sicker than a dog."

"I think I'll head home," Ramage said.

"Have a look."

Ramage pressed his eye to the peephole and saw Desiree naked on the bed; she was alone on the set and seemed not to know where to place her hands; she leaned forward, resting her elbows on her knees.

"You look bored," Greenfield was telling her. "You got a dick in your mouth but you got a face like a postal clerk."

"Scolding me doesn't put me in much of a mood," Desiree said.

"You're a professional," Greenfield said. "You get paid to be in the mood."

"No monkeys," Ramage said to RB. He looked out over the town. "I think I'll head home."

"You said that."

Ramage stood, steadying himself with the handrail. The gray overcast sky tumbled and spun and his stomach heaved. He buckled and was seated again, throwing up between his legs. He propped his arms on his knees and spat chunks through the grated metal landing. RB closed his hand over Ramage's, and Ramage slowly turned his palm up and clasped hold of RB, weaving their fingers together, holding on tighter as each new wave of nausea hit.

"Spooky?"

"Yeah?"

"I could give a rat's ass where you been. Crazy or whatever, locked up, I don't mind. It's nothing to me."

"Thanks."

"But you're different. You changed."

"Different?"

"You used to be somebody else."

He woke with a parched mouth and put his head under the faucet and desperately lapped at the water like a poisoned animal. He undressed and was asleep again when a knock on the door woke him. He wound a sheet over his shoulders and slipped the chain off and found Desiree standing under the walkway light. Night had fallen; he had to ask what time it was.

"Ten-thirty," she said.

"Man alive," Ramage said.

Desiree wore jeans and a white T-shirt. She'd let her hair loose from its usual hard lapidary style, and an archaeology of treatments showed, strata of blonde and silver, a bedrock of dark brown at the roots.

Ramage asked, "How was work?"

"Greenfield's got notions," she said.

"I heard him go off."

"There wasn't any call for him to humiliate me in front of everybody."

She slipped off her sandals and walked barefoot across the gold carpet. She poured rum into a plastic cup and sipped from her drink, then tipped out a little more rum and sat on the bed beside Ramage, her legs raised. Their knees touched. Ramage felt the faint pressure and in silence he ran his finger back and forth along her pants seam, tracing the outline of her leg as it rose and fell from her hip to her ankle. She primped the flat airless pillows beneath her head; she ran her tongue over her lips and her mouth settled into a pout as she stared at the ceiling. Ramage wished for ice but he was too tired to dress and search for some. Desiree balanced the plastic cup on her stomach, over her bellybutton. Ramage kissed her woodenly and touched her breasts; he faked the kiss a moment longer and slipped his hand under her shirt. Beneath her breasts, two faint surgical scars, like the twin curved lines of a cartoon bust, were clearly visible. He traced his finger along the pink welted tissue. The cakey foundation she had applied to cover the scars for the shoot came off on Ramage's finger in a kind of powdery dust the color of putty. He looked at his finger; he wiped it clean on the bedsheet. She reached for his crotch. His penis curled like a burnt match between his legs.

"I knew a guy killed himself," she said, sitting up. "I always wondered why."

"It's not that interesting."

"Come on, if we hung out tonight, and then you were dead tomorrow, you wouldn't want me to feel anything?"

"Nothing."

"Not even weird? You wouldn't want me to feel a little weird?"

"I don't know."

"That guy used to come to our shows. I had this rock band. I was sixteen. He was a fan. He shot himself in the parking lot. He had some kind of drama. I wrote a song about it but the song stank."

The light that had been leaking into the room was briefly eclipsed and someone knocked on the door. Ramage pulled the sheet around his shoulders and answered. Rigo held a six-pack in one hand and Ramage's tool sack in the other.

"You are not at the bar," he said. Without the past tense he could only protest pointlessly against the present; his eyes shifted, staring into the room. Nothing was happening but Ramage felt awkward and compelled to account for himself.

"I see," Rigo said. Red and black paint spotted his face and sand crystals flashed in his hair. He set Ramage's tools inside. "You forget, I bring." He opened one of the bottles from the sixpack and offered it to Desiree, who declined. Ramage turned down the offer too and Rigo drank the beer in one long hard swallow. When he was finished, he knocked the empty bottle against his knee, waiting. "I see," he said again.

There was nothing Ramage could do, and his guilt gave way to anger. "Thanks for the tools," he said. He abruptly said good-bye and shut the door. Turning back to face the room, he was conscious of the tableau from Rigo's vantage, the poisoned scene, tawdry and familiar: the twisted sheets, the tangle of clothes, the uncapped bottle of rum on the table.

"He gives me the creeps," Desiree said. "You know the way you can look at somebody just for a second, and that's one thing, but if you look longer, that's something else? That's him—he just keeps staring. He doesn't know when's enough."

She reached for Ramage again, but gave up quickly.

"I'm getting this feeling of familiarity around you," Desiree said. "I don't mean cozy. I mean like a past life, like we've been here before. Not way back in history or anything. We weren't Roman emperors together. I mean a past life like maybe a couple weeks ago."

After the second day of shooting, Greenfield told Ramage to stay late and dismantle the sets, all except the black room. The weather had turned cooler; a light rain tapped against the plywood windows. Space heaters had been spread around the warehouse after some of the actors complained of cold. Ramage sent Rigo to the store for beer; he waited with RB, the warm air blowing over them.

RB looked out from the set to the tangle of equipment.

"All these people watching," he said. "You forget there's all these people looking on."

"This is some job," Ramage said.

"We've had lots worse."

"That we have, my friend."

Knocking down what they had only recently built hollowed their desire and didn't make either man inclined to work. When Rigo returned with the beer they loafed on the bed and drank.

RB said, "What side were you on, Rigo?"

"Side?"

"A good guy? A bad guy?"

"He was in the military," Ramage said.

"No side," Rigo said.

"I seen you looking through my peephole," RB said. "I should charge admission. I'd make some money off you, boy. You like these bitches."

"I am married," Rigo said.

"You can look, Harvard," RB said. "It's okay. Looking don't hurt nobody."

Rigo flipped a bottlecap at RB, hitting him in the face.

"Lighten up," Ramage said.

"Spooky, he just threw a bottle cap at me."

"Wah wah, let's get back to work."

"Back to work, you niggers!" RB laughed, his dark lips rolling back, exposing a gate of white teeth. "That includes you, Rigoberto."

"Go get my claw hammer, RB."

"You know about black men, right, Rigo?" RB said, as he rose form the bed. He lifted a 2x4 off the floor and duckwalked the length of the warehouse with the stud crotched and angled up between his legs. "You're definitely some kind a nignog," he said. He stuffed the board in one of the galvanized cans they were using to haul refuse. He laughed to himself as he searched in Ramage's tool sack. He found the hammer and beneath it the gun. "Hey Spooky, man, what the hell?" He held the gun delicately like a small wounded bird in the palm of his hand.

"Put it back," Ramage said.

"Is it loaded?"

"No," Ramage said. "Are my smokes in there?"

The kerosene heaters burned orange and warmed the hue of Rigo's olive skin. His cheeks flared up and Ramage watched his wide black silent eyes track RB's movement across the room.

"You want a world where you have to choose sides?" RB said, "Go to prison, man."

He offered Ramage the handle end of the hammer.

"It's prison now, is it?" Ramage said.

"What?"

"First it was reform school, now it's prison. Which is it?"

"It's all the same," RB said. "You'd know that if you'd been where I've been."

"Let's strike these rooms."

Rigo walked over to the lockbox and grabbed a small sledge and began pounding away the supports that held the room together. Gypsum shook loose as the Sheetrock buckled and white dust sifted into the air. The back wall caved-in and the others folded over like shuffled cards. A stud broke free and whacked against RB's leg. Ramage turned and calmly waited for things to surface. RB closed his hand around Rigo's neck and shoved his face to the floor.

RB said, "You got to be very careful. People get fucked up on jobs."

RB let go and picked up a prybar and began to rip nails loose from the discarded studs. Each nail screeched like a gull. Rigo was still lying on the floor.

"Get up," Ramage said.

"Just act right," RB said. He slapped the prybar in his palm. "Act right, you know what that means?"

"Enough," Ramage said.

"Fuck enough," RB said. "Little half-nigger almost fucked me up just being stupid."

"He's sorry," Ramage said.

"I didn't hear him say so," RB said.

For the rest of the night, Ramage worked with Rigo close by his side. His silence got on Ramage's nerves. After they'd hauled the last load of broken drywall outside, Ramage offered Rigo a cigarette.

"Don't get all quiet inside yourself," Ramage said. "It's a pain in the ass to everyone else."

Rigo said, "I quit."

"It's stupid to quit now. Hang in there. Get paid." Rain swept through the blue light of a streetlamp. Ramage squeezed Rigo's shoulder, giving it a pat. "The job's done," he said. "Gather up my tools and let's get out of here."

No one had arrived at the warehouse for the last day of shooting, and Ramage, after making coffee, sat alone in the black room; it was the only box still standing. The walls shone with the rich luster of ebony and his reflection floated as if submerged in dark water. Other than a bed the room was empty of furniture. The floor was carpeted in orange shag and a pine box stood against one wall. Ramage opened the lid and found the day's drama: a braided bullwhip, handcuffs, black leather chokers studded with chrome spikes. He lifted the bullwhip and gave it a crack in the air.

When Greenfield showed up, he stood in the middle of the warehouse, silently taking in the scene. He scuffed his cowboy boots on the floor. A long blue cigarette hung from his lips.

"Don't put RB in the movie," Ramage said.

"Why not?" Greenfield said. He looked at Ramage, and then up at the skylight, washed with gray.

"I just prefer it."

"I was never going to anyway."

"He'll say you promised."

"I can't get caught up in all that," Greenfield said,. "You're the foreman, you're in charge of the cheap seats. You tell him." Greenfield looked up at the skylight. "I still haven't quoted *Citizen Kane*," he said. "You know Rosebud was Hearst's pet name for his mistress's clit? You know that? Orson Welles knew that. Rosebud, Rosebud. It was an inside joke. It drove Hearst crazy." He shaded his eyes against the gray light. "I'd like to get at least one shot of all this from above."

RB was in back of the warehouse, dressed in slacks and a rayon shirt. The smell of pomade hung in the air around him, and he stood alone, rocking back and forth on the heels of his workboots, apparently the only shoes he'd brought with him. Ramage stepped next to RB, and for a full minute went unacknowledged.

Finally, Ramage said, "I talked to Greenfield. There might not be time to get you in."

RB hesitated, then resumed his rocking.

"It's an orgy," he said. "Everybody climbing all over everybody else, can't tell one person from the next. I get in there, who cares? It's all equal."

"You can't just walk on."

"Won't nobody know the difference."

Four strands of rope were anchored to the corners of the room, and Desiree waited, shackled at the ankles and wrists, crouched quietly in the convergent center. Enough slack played in the rope for her to crawl a few feet in any direction. Her sunken reflection swam below the surface of the polished wall, surrounded by a vague wash of white faces. The wall did not reflect the crews' eyes or mouths; black hollows bloomed in their heads like the holes in a skull. An assistant took a powder puff and dabbed away the glare from Desiree's forehead. The chalky cloud caused her to sneeze.

The set was cleared, and Ramage left RB, who insisted on staying there on the sidelines until Greenfield called him in. Ramage went to sit on the fire escape. Rigo was planted in front of the peephole, peering through it as if it were a telescope, subdued and quiet, his open mouth pressed against the plywood. With RB out of the way, this was his chance, his opportunity. Then Ramage looked too. Through a tangle of cameras and booms, he watched Desiree tug at one of the ropes binding her ankle. A hooded man cracked the bullwhip and the tasseled tip snapped against the back of her thigh. The contact was accidental, outside the choreography, and she lurched forward, trying with her bound wrist to protect herself. She howled, and then someone in the crew moved, standing in Ramage's line of sight.

Ramage left Rigo and climbed the fire escape, making his way up a ladder that curled over the parapet and onto the roof. The skylight was made of green tinted glass and reinforced with chicken wire. Ramage shaded his eyes against the dull glare. Twenty feet below, the full cast was assembled, the orgy well underway, a swarm of white bodies that gradually came apart as men and women, pairing up, crawled across the orange carpet. They moved silently, dividing like cells and then joining again, their skin pale and colorless under the burning lights. The hooded man loomed over Desiree from behind, holding onto her hair like the reins of a horse. It was hard to imagine what exhaustion, what wasting away of power, would bring the orgy to an end. Everything was eternally available, everything equal. Ramage sat up and looked out over the town. Nothing moved, not a car, not a pedestrian. It felt as if some vast Sunday had devoured the day. The sea was flat and the waves rolled evenly along the shore.

After an hour, a raucous cheer rose from the set, and Ramage went downstairs, entering the warehouse ahead of Rigo. Greenfield bowed first toward the cast and then toward the crew, sweeping his hand along the floor. "Thank you one and all."

Women wiped themselves off with towels. A few naked men stood nonchalantly in a huddle, asking one another about their itineraries, where they'd go next. Desiree's skin had a stung, hectic appearance, and one of her ankles was still bound, the rope trailing after her as she moved about the set, saying her good-byes.

RB was partly undressed, standing foolishly in his stocking feet and boxers and rayon shirt. He said to Ramage, "Greenwad fucked me."

Ramage didn't say anything.

"You get a bone on?" RB said, looking at Rigo. "You know what a bone is, right?" With a fist he feinted in the direction of Rigo's crotch. "Huh, Harvard? A bone? A woody? Huh? You like seeing women tied up? That what you do in your country?"

Rigo reached for RB's mouth as if to stop the flow of words, smashing it shut. An instant passed and then RB smiled, the gate of white teeth washed pink with blood. His lip was torn. RB slammed the butt of his palm against Rigo's chin, shoving back on his jaw as though pounding open a door. It was a moment before anyone noticed, but then a circle gathered, and the onlookers, by their steady gazes, seemed to freeze the fight in tableau: Rigo fallen on the floor, RB smiling down on him. Rigo rose once more and rushed RB and again RB knocked him to the ground. This time, Ramage bent over Rigo and told him to stay down. RB's hand filled with blood. He showed it to Ramage as if the substance puzzled him. "Fucking Harvard," he said, and then he slowly wiped the blood off his hand, painting Rigo's face with it.

After Greenfield paid him off, Ramage walked down to the pier, looking for Rigo. His encampment was on the lee-side of a restroom; a picnic table tipped on its side formed a second wall of his shelter and he'd made a roof of the door he'd scrounged from the ocean. A small pit in the sand was filled with sticks of driftwood and wet ashes. Rigo was gone.

Desiree came by the motel later that evening, carrying her suitcase.

"Where to?" Ramage asked.

"Los Angeles," she said. "Another job. You?"

"RB's coming by," Ramage said. "I've got to pay him. Then it's over."

"I had a dream about me and you last night. Somebody was taking us somewhere, they wanted to show us something. We were riding in the back seat of a limousine. There was a baby in it, this dead baby."

Ramage waited. "And?"

"That's it," she said. "The baby was dead, but it wasn't ugly and rotten or anything. It was just still."

There was a hard rap on the door and Ramage answered.

"Oh boy, what do we have here?" RB said. He pointed to the bottle of rum. "Don't mind if I do."

Ramage found another plastic cup in the bathroom. He removed the safety-seal and poured out a small measure of the rum and then watered it down. RB sat in the chair beside Desiree.

"I've got your money," Ramage said.

"There's no rush," RB said.

RB fingered the arm of his chair, running a nail back and forth through the fretted grooves, blindly retracing a rosette. In a minute, Ramage decided, he would give RB his money. The bills were crispy folded into a small manila pay envelope Ramage had slipped into his shirt pocket.

RB finished his drink and tapped the plastic cup against the arm chair. He looked at Desiree. "I was wondering, how is it you get paid? You get your money by the hour, or you get a salary, or what?"

"By the scene," she said. She was looking at Ramage when she answered; her voice was barely audible.

"The scene? You mean what you do, how many times you do it, like that?"

"Will you call me a cab?" Desiree asked Ramage.

"Like two men—you do two men you get paid more?"

She nodded.

RB said, "I seen you in a movie with a midget. I figure a dwarf can do it, I can too. You remember that guy, that midget?"

"Sure," Desiree said.

"That was sick."

She got up and went to the bathroom. RB and Ramage sat silently. Through the thin door, they could hear her peeing.

"Shouldn't hang no hollow core doors in a small room like this," RB said. "No privacy."

Ramage handed RB the envelope. "Here's your money," he said. "There's a bonus."

RB set the envelope aside.

"You all laid-in, you taken care of. Desiree Street, huh?"

"Take your money, RB."

"Couldn't have no nigger in on that." RB counted his pay, tossing one of the bills to the floor. "I don't want your bonus."

Ramage dialed the phone and ordered a cab.

"Bitch taking a long-ass time in the bathroom," RB said.

"Don't make this a bad scene," Ramage said. He twirled his drink as though there were ice in it.

Desiree came out of the bathroom. She sat on the bed and worked the strap of her sandals, refastening the tiny brass buckles.

RB said, "Why don't we all make a movie?"

Desiree took a drink. Over the edge of her glass she said, "Where's your camera?"

"In my head," RB said.

"Oh, that's right," she said. "You all got cameras in your head."

"I'm not like all them."

"None of you are like all of them."

"In my movie," RB said, "I wouldn't tie you up and whip you or anything. I'd treat you right."

"Sure you would," Desiree said. "In your movie you'd send me flowers every day."

Ramage followed Desiree out the door and through the empty lot to a waiting cab. She settled in the back seat and he waited, expecting her to roll down the window and say good-bye, but she didn't. He went back to the room and gathered up his stuff, zipping his tool sack shut. RB had moved from the chair to the bed.

RB said, "I come here, I see you got your own little movie in progress. You didn't want me in on your thing. You cut me out."

"You're wrong," Ramage said. "There was no thing."

"Spooky, man, how dumb do you think I am?"

He put his sack down in the motel lobby. Behind the glass, through a beaded curtain, he could see the blue glow of a television, could hear the snappy rhythm of sitcom repartee and the spurts of canned laughter. On top of the television, between a potted cactus and a jar of pennies, was a photograph of a young man and woman, circa 1950, the woman laughing, her light hair blown by some long-ago breeze, the man with a cigarette in his mouth and a collar upturned against the same stiff wind. Ramage couldn't see where they were standing; the photo was overexposed and the background had bleached away. The desk clerk was asleep on the couch, her fat, heavy leg resting on a coffee table cluttered with magazines, a plastic bowl of popcorn, a can of diet soda, a spotless green ashtray. Ramage tapped the service bell.

"I'm checking out," he said.

The woman looked through her files; she shrugged, hopeless.

"I can't find your thing," she said. "How long've you been here?"

"Three days," Ramage said.

"Seems longer," she said. She started the itemized math on a receipt.

Ramage separated seventy-five dollars from his pay and set the money on the counter. Outside, the motel's blue vacancy sign was just beginning to glow in a halo of mist blowing up from the beach.

"Seventy-five," the woman announced.

Ramage slid the money forward. "Kind of dead this time of year," he said.

She gave him the receipt. "You know the others, that was next to you? They skipped out."

"You should make people pay in advance," Ramage said. They waited in an awkward frozen silence, staring at each other. Ramage rapped his knuckle on the counter, breaking the spell, and left.

He walked across the parking lot and dropped his tool sack at the foot of the palm tree. The brown fronds spread above him and the air smelled of cinnamon. Bruised and sore, he sat back against the trunk and unzipped his bag. He pulled out his clothes and groped along the bottom and then turned the sack over and emptied his tools into the sand. A car drove by, and in the wake of its passing everything was briefly quiet. The gun was gone. He considered the probable suspects and decided that RB had taken it. A moment later he was convinced that Rigo had stolen it. Then he wondered if it was Desiree.

When his cab came, he repacked his things and stood to go. Behind him in the empty lot a string of tin cans his neighbors had cut loose lay twisted on the asphalt—too much clatter, he supposed, as they made their getaway. The desk clerk sat at the counter behind the sheet of bulletproof glass. He'd disturbed her sleep and now she was awake. She'd turned on a lamp and was reading, the white waste of her face set to the romance.

Nominated by A Public Space

WHAT FOR

by GERALD STERN

from FIVE POINTS

1946 there was an overcoat
with rows of buttons fifteen dollars and two
American flags for some ungodly reason
and a slight rise in the distance as the street
went over the river I would have breathed the air
both in and out for, I was a bellows then
and one by one my lungs were ruined but I wouldn't
change my life, what for? You wouldn't know
unless you crossed the river yourself, unless you
climbed a hill and turned around twice
to stare at the street behind you either mud
or cobblestone and count the wooden steps
or look through the windows longingly the houses
piled up, the one below the next, the dirt
supreme your breathing heavy the base of a cliff
even further below, a river shining from
time to time, your mind half-empty, your teacher
a curbstone, the mountain really hill upon hill,
you knew the details the porches pulled you up
your face turned white at a certain point I'm sure
you walked through a cloud how slow you learned how absurd
the goats of arcady or the baskets of apples
in New Jerusalem compared to that.

Nominated by Ed Ochester, Grace Schulman, Christopher Buckley, Joan Murray, Five Points

A GENIUS FOR GRIEF: MEMORIES OF SAUL BELLOW

by HERBERT GOLD

from THE REPUBLIC OF LETTERS

Postwar Paris—ration cards, public baths if a person developed an interest in cleanliness, and a romance of ambition, the most reliable means of winter heating—took up its honored role once more for a hive of young American would-bees. Bruised and lovely, the paradise of misery was still the capital of hope.

Along with Richard Wright, the most esteemed American writer in residence during my years there, 1949–1951, was Saul Bellow, approximately ten years the senior of such as James Baldwin, Evan Connell, Terry Southern, Otto Friedrich, George Plimpton, Max Steele, and my callow self. Bellow had two published novels, *Dangling Man* and *The Victim*, appeared regularly in *Partisan Review*, collected a Guggenheim Fellowship. The rumor got around that he was destined to be America's new great novelist. His confident and graceful lounging, on view especially at the café Le Rouquet near Saint-Germain-des-Prés, seemed to confirm the rumor. He had a contract with Viking Press. He was writing, and sometimes reading aloud, what would become *The Adventures of Augie March*. He was legal; the rest of us were stowaways.

We would-bees on our G.I. Bill money, our Fulbright money, or selling our clothes, cigarettes, and dollars on the black market, saw him as an Old Master in his early thirties. He had climbed the heights while some of us were still peddling hashish to gullible Frenchmen under the chic American name "marijuana," or serving as gigolos to existentialist millionaires, or worst of all, cadging hand-outs from family grinds back home. A few magazines, *Points, Janus, Zero,* and *DEATH* (the answer to Time Inc's *LIFE*) were started by young men and women of dependent means. We wouldn't get rich writing for Sindbad Vail's *Points*. Orson Welles gave the editor of *DEATH* a few bucks for food which he shared with me in return for translating French restaurant menus; otherwise, he was reduced to ordering "Jumbo Omelet, goddammit! Omelet Jumbo!" which myste-riously always came with ham.

I watched Saul from across a terrace, at his ease, and tried to fit this boyish person to his book *The Victim*, about a New York summer hot as Bangkok and the mutual sufferings of a crazed anti-Semite and his prey, which I had read during my first summer back at school af-ter the Army and the War. The dark-eyed young man with a shock of black hair and large-lipped smile was what a writer should look like. Also he wrote, I thought, as a writer should write, with acute sense, and an astringent alertness to events. Naturally, I didn't dare ap-proach this formidable personage strolling under the plane trees or holding court in the cafés of the quarter.

I don't remember exactly how we met; perhaps he was amused by my lurking shy shadow. Without telling him, I sent the manuscript of my first novel, *Birth of a Hero*, to Viking Press and it was dug out of the slush pile by a young editor, Monroe Engel, who shepherded it to higher authorities, including Malcolm Cowley. Since my return ad-dress was Paris, some prudent soul thought to ask Saul for an opin-ion—had I really written the book? Would I be likely to repay investment by writing another book?—and he gave a favorable ver-dict. Thanks partly to his generosity, I became a published novelist, returning to Cleveland, the Paris of northeastern Ohio, after my Ful-bright-G.I. Bill years in exile. I planned to buy a three-cent stamp at the post office in the Public Square which would surely have my pic-ture on it. (The novel came out, but it was still Benjamin Franklin on the three-cent stamp and Herb looking for work in a ham-and-eggs factory—whatever—to support self, wife, child, another child on the way.)

In Paris, with the news of imminent publication, I was adopted by some of the older expatriates, in addition to the French students, artists, and layabouts who had already become my Rive Gauche friends. Rodin's Balzac strutted belly-forward on his pedestal at Vavin-Montparnasse; encouraged by Sartre and de Beauvoir, huddling nearby at the Café de Flore and the Deux Magots, Diderot on his own pedestal pointed an accusing finger across the boulevard at the ancient church of St.-Germain-des-Prés. Bellow was not a stony challenger; rather, an amiable deity for the fresh crop of American would-be's seeking out the Paris of Henry Miller. Saul's generosity was not the sum of his appeal. His complaints, particularly marital, and his neediness, which went back to childhood or perhaps to the origins of the human species, gave him the charm of a genius for grief. His lamentations, which I thought of as "The Book of Saul," a long-run drama, had some of the eloquence of Job and Jeremiah; sackcloth, ashes, a wife who didn't understand him, and sometimes even worse, a woman who did. In that last variation, "The Book of Saul" departed scripture in the direction of modern happy endings.

When his marriage boiled over, the spillage was uncontained by the boundaries of family. The shock of seeing this hero in a state of frantic self-pity bewildered my twenty-two year old wife and my twenty-four year old self. He was a mature person, above the age of Jesus when crucified, but we were kids. With his first two books, his handsome lounging, and his renown as The Designated New Voice, his fall into despair made us feel awe. It was as if the mountain crumbled as we watched; we heard the shrieks.

Usually these family quarrels, hot tongue and cold shoulder, had to do with boredom (his) and jealousy (his wife's). He cultivated the admiration of pretty young women; he received it. He liked to recall how, when his first story was published in a national magazine, *Harper's Bazaar*, along with a photo, he received a telephone call from MGM pictures. Did they want to make a movie of his story?

He beamed; high wattage. There was an ironic glint in the large dark eyes. His smile delighted. No, they wanted to offer him a screen-test.

When he glanced around the circle of admirers on the terrace of Le Rouquet at the corner of rue des Saints-Pères and the Boulevard Saint-Germain, we all responded with an echo of his own joyous amusement, just as if we were receiving the tale for the first time. Sometimes there was at least one person present for whom it was new.

At the end of a sleety Paris winter, my wife Edith and I thought of hitchhiking south for awhile to pick figs and swim in the Mediterranean. Saul had another dreadful long-run battle in progress with Anita, his wife, and needed to get away. He decided upon a strategic retreat to Spain by automobile, invited us to come along. We hoped to find cheap digs in one of the French Basque towns near the Spanish border. This is how young we were; felt we were making a necessary political gesture by stopping short of visiting Franco Spain.

The trip in Saul's Citroën was no joyride. He wailed and wept as we drove. He was also funny and full of curiosity about himself and knew the map. I still connect his total recall for directions, his sensitive nose, with the quality of his gift, an almost metabolic perspicacity. Through the narrow medieval streets of Avignon he found our way, sniffing out the correct road. Ah, here would be a bread smell. And there it was—a good bakery. There was also an unnerving claim for attention to his marital agonies. His need was exclusive, unflagging, draining. He required an audience as devoted as the audience he gave himself.

Occasionally he rested from discourse about his conjugal griefs by talking about his book in progress, reading aloud from *The Adventures of Augie March*. Although my approval was a foregone conclusion, he asked for fresh and renewed bursts of enthusiasm. Occasionally, for a little variety, I tried to speak of my own novel-in-progress. But this really wasn't the program.

In a park in Avignon, amid Roman ruins and blood-red meridional blooms, we saw a white-haired old man lovingly dandling a child. I said, "What a beautiful grandchild you have," and the man said: "My daughter." Perhaps I was fated not to satisfy my elders.

By the time we reached Banyuls, a few miles from the Spanish border, Edith and I were exhausted by the pleasure of Saul's company. Enough; we were stopping. The long afternoon on those narrow roads of the Côte de Vermeil, hearing of how only oblivion could offer Saul release from his sorrow along with how his book would change the face of American literature, had left us hyperventilating. It was hot, bugs were swarming, and there may have been a mistral, that wind which makes folks crazier than usual.

We worried about leaving him alone in the hotel. We sat under an umbrella, drinking lukewarm soda, waving away the flies. We dreaded the meal we were about to have with him before he drove on into Spain. How would we cope with his paroxysms of despair?

She nudged my arm. "Look."

He was bouncing towards us with a boyish grin, hair slicked down after his shower, eyes bright and skin fresh, chipper and restored. We were drained by the sufferings he seemed to shed. He was ready for a glass of wine and a good meal of the local fish stew and his nose was twitching as he approved of the girls on their high wooden clogs in the town square of Banyuls-sur-mer.

✻

A few months later, with the eagerness of the would-be, I handed Saul a new story, "The Heart of the Artichoke." He was traveling to Italy and said he would take it with him. A week or so later I received the letter every young writer wishes to receive from a maestro (it even came from Rome, like an Encyclical). In his clear and comely handwriting it gave me the clear and comely news I wanted. One odd phrase stood like a monument at the end of the paragraphs of perfect enthusiasm: "All barriers are down."

Through the inevitable discouragements to come, I remembered this grace note from on high and would mumble to myself, *All barriers are down . . . All barriers are down . . .* Surely all barriers must come down.

The zestful generosity of which the young Bellow was capable fills me with gratitude despite the narrower judgements of later years. It fits a time when birds sang sweetly in the courtyards of Paris and all our sleeves were stuffed with manuscripts.

In the early Fifties, Saul's urban wit and angst—Kafka-out-of-Chicago, Dostoyevsky-from-the-*yeshiva*, polymathical, polylinguistical, playful about it all—offered just the ticket for a G.I. Bill generation which was heading from college into graduate work, although its parents had often not finished high school. He made fun of suffering, he made the suffering into fun, he was fully implicated in his own life. Only connect? It connected especially with himself.

His personal grace relieved the solipsism. It wasn't that he didn't need others; he wooed those around him with an eloquent performance. He enacted his inner life for his public on the stage he carried everywhere. Women loved him; men found him demanding but ingratiating. He managed to enlist the world in the narrative of his disasters. Later, *Herzog*, drawn partly as an act of revenge after one of his marriage and friendship convulsions, would depict a beloved protagonist in a state of despair. Herzog ranted comically and proceeded from the melodramatic scenes with his wife to episodes with women eager to offer nursery solace. Such a scenario is unreal to experience—when mired in despair, most of us are not beloved—but Saul's star turn, dominating his own theater, helped to make it seem possible in his special case. Of course, talent and reputation contributed to what in the Kennedys came to be called charisma. He banged on his high chair with his spoon and asked to be served. He demanded respect and was in a position to get it. If he sometimes seemed like a child, he was a beautiful baby.

Saul's prose style married classical elegance to Mark Twain and the pungency of street speech; Yiddish played stickball with Henry James. As a young man, he rode the elements with terrific energy. He could spritz like a lower east side comedian and then lament like the prophets. His fate as a writer was to insist that words matter, his own most of all; suffering matters, his own absolutely; and he was able to enlist an audience in his struggle to survive, marked and measured by the works in progress which devoured his life.

He performed jazzy riffs on his good Hebrew school, University of Wisconsin, and University of Chicago Trotskyite education, making neediness the baseline. ("I want, I want, I want.") He never questioned the appropriateness of his stance at the center of the stage. Among contemporary novelists, he was surely the most serious about reading, studying, learning, and using it all, adding it all up. It was unified by that keening cry from the heart. Saul needed, needed, needed.

> Time . . .
> Worships language and forgives
> Everyone by whom it lives . . .

*

One morning in the late Fifties, I drove along with Ralph Ellison and his big black dog to Tivoli, New York, where Ralph and Saul were sharing the rambling old Hudson River house in which another of Saul's marriages ended. The dog grew agitated from the long trip confined to an automobile, and when Ralph stopped at an office at Bard College to pick his mail, the dog began furiously barking and leaping. There seemed to be a discipline contest in progress between Ralph and his dog. Ralph said, "Don't let him out," while stately he proceeded to collect his mail.

Piteously disillusioned at this desertion by his master, the dog let go a flood, a sheet, an avalanche of dog piss. I leapt out of the car and the dog followed. Now the dog was zestfully leaping about on the green. My flanks were dripping. Ralph reappeared, and commented with extreme irritation:

"I told you not to let him out."

Later, while I stood naked in the yard of the house, hanging my soaked clothes on a line to dry, Saul talked about the state of his career. "I want to be like Tolstoy," he said, "more philosopher than anything else."

"More than a great novelist?" I asked, shivering, watching the steam rise from the clothes I had dipped into a soapy bucket. "The later Tolstoy? 'The Kreutzer Sonata?' 'What is Art?' Where he denied Shakespeare and *Anna Karenina*? Why that?"

"One more book," he said, "and my position will be impregnable."

In the house in Tivoli he read aloud from the manuscript of *Henderson the Rain King* while I tried to stifle my impatience, sometimes asking, "Couldn't I just read it by myself?" But he needed to hear his own voice, test his rhythms, bounce them off others. Since I was there, I would do.

In this novel I missed the gritty blues of other books, his authentic monologuing plaint, and it seemed to me he was trying to put himself into a WASP aristocrat body which he did not in fact possess. I wondered if he was competing with the New England writers he reacted against, while creating a fable indebted to Kafka and Melville. Was this part of constructing that "impregnable position"? I thought he was doing what he said not to do: writing from the head, not the heart; idea-writing, although in the end his heart's cry interrupted the plan.

As to building his reputation, *Henderson the Rain King* seems not to have been a mistake, even if the book had less appeal for some of his admirers. There are those who like it best of all his work. As he said of another writer's novels, it became a favorite for university instruction in American Lit courses. Professors enjoyed teaching it because there was so much to explain.

Himself, he didn't like to explain his writing, but he loved to read it aloud. "I'm a bird," he said, "not an ornithologist."

Until I came to live in San Francisco, our friendship went through ups and downs, with periods of intense intimacy; that is, Saul confided his troubles, I listened and felt warm about being invited in. Occasionally he stayed with me in New York and gave me the difficult gratification of hinting that I stood between him and some desperate act at the high window. These threats didn't interfere with his intent sessions bent over the notebooks with their ruled lines upon which his fountain pen tracked his imagination and indignation. I learned that folks don't usually kill themselves in the middle of composing the suicide note.

I sought his approval for my own writing and sometimes got it. His words were used in advertising my books. I was still a young writer; he was a maestro; I was both grateful and privileged to share his life's disasters.

When I left the east coast, thereby becoming unavailable during crisis, the ups and downs of our friendship transformed themselves into a prolonged down. We exchanged letters for awhile, but he needed regular nursing care. Others filled the requirement. I was irritated that he didn't include "The Heart of the Artichoke," a story which he had praised so highly, in an anthology he edited. "I forgot," he said, shrugging. "Why take such a thing seriously? I just forgot."

He was right. It was merely my own writer's vanity that was aggrieved, but the advice not to take it seriously was hard to accept, coming from a writer whose spirit could be broken by a slighting review in the *Deseret News*.

In the early Sixties, as a member of the international jury meeting in various European locales to award the Formentor Prize, I argued for Saul Bellow to receive the award. One year the favored French candidate was Nathalie Sarraute, a leader of the fashionable *nouveau roman* grouplet. As a friend of her daughter, I had known her during my student days in Paris. (The daughter's husband *pro tem* was the journalist Stanley Karnow. He and I bought little Renault 4-cv automobiles at the same time, and our wives had in common resentment of our rude habit of running outdoors when it rained, sometimes raining on them in our leaky rooms, to make sure our cars were not melting. Stan and I were enjoying the simultaneous strains of first wives and first vehicle ownership).

The Formentor deliberations were supposed to be secret; they were, of course, not, especially since the French delegation did not get its way about the Nathalie Sarraute. Saul Bellow received the prize.

Later, when I saw Nathalie Sarraute in Paris, the grand old lady looked me keenly in the eye and greeted me with a mantra which she repeated fairly frequently that Paris season: *"Ah 'Airbair'! C'est vous le gangster."*

Barney Rosset of Grove Press, organizer of the American delegation, asked me to present the award at a ceremony in New York. I felt pleased to have made a case, pleased for Saul, although at that point in our long friendship, we were not close. We were not really friends anymore. But as always when I saw him the old warmth and gratitude welled up.

I handed him the check. Photographs were taken for the newspapers. We ate canapés, drank wine. A woman showed up who had been a lover of Saul's, then found employment as a character in one of his books, and she picked an argument with me. "The really great writer, the one who should have been given the prize"—the writer she was currently studying—"is Ionesco. He's international."

"I like his plays." I said. *"The Lesson, The Bald Soprano*, they've been running forever at the Théâtre le la Huchette. When I'm in Paris and I see the posters, I know nothing has changed around there, no matter that everything has changed."

"Rhinoceros!" she cried. "The metaphors, the mythos! Compared to Ionesco, Saul is only . . ." She wouldn't say it. She shook her curls with that ferocity which he captured in his fictional portrayal. "And take it from me, I know," she announced, mandibles compressed, teeth gritting.

I remembered his image of a woman hiding a dagger in her stocking.

"Saul was, let me tell you how that bozo treated me—compared to Ionesco—"

Maybe it was in her garter belt, that dagger.

*

Herzog turned out to be Saul's most popular book, his best selling novel after *The Adventures of Augie March*, which had first broken through for a large public. Comic and sad, spiced with rants in the form of letters, *Herzog* was drawn directly from his personal travails, cuckoldry, a turbulent divorce, treason by a protégé. He put the wife, the protégé, and friends into the book with hardly any disguise, as if the story was intended not so much to be about them as against them. The letters Herzog wrote to world figures were entertaining, garrulous, alternately wise, crazed, and self-mocking. He poured himself into the man-with-heart, Herzog, ranting, wronged, the seeker betrayed.

Self-justification gave an aspect of troubling ambiguity to the book. He intended to be the American Dostoyevsky, but funny; the American Tolstoy, but a close witness to the times. But neither of his Russian masters would have portrayed themselves as innocently aggrieved and yet fatally attractive to women. Most men know from experience that, when overwhelmed by jealousy, they are in a mood to grovel, whine, and smell bad—not very attractive to women. They may find nurses, but the sexy and delightful women tend to cross the road when they slump into view.

Herzog, despite his frenzies, remains the most charming man in the world; or so Saul seemed to hope; or so he wrote him. This made his revenge on life too perfect. The novel was flawed by its special pleading, its lyric of self-love.

Perhaps what made me uneasy appealed to both the public at large and the Nobel committee. Herzog's dire suffering didn't get in the way of fun. The letters to the great, alive and dead, were elegant paranoid monologues, marinated in Saul's learning and his mortal passion to change the world, or at least punish it. The challenges of disaster in love and friendship, divorce laws and night sweats, were given chipper colors and a style which reached for the lugubrious in a middle-aged scholar's yearning. Bathroom spying approached French farce mechanism, with no French farce mechanism cool. Yet the book allows readers to perch on the benches as spectators at a circus of pain. It didn't disturb too much. The trapeze whirled, and the clown fell safely into the sawdust. The elephants danced, dropped their elephant doo on the fallen clown, and he arose as a hero, covered with flowers, embraced by all. The book was an original and intelligent entertainment, a consolation.

A mutual friend of ours, call him Professor X, wrote to Saul to congratulate him on his Nobel Prize and also to give his response to *Herzog*. Professor X, a man with severe and incurable physical problems, in lifelong pain, wrote admiringly of the book and with delight about the acclaim from Sweden, but added a fateful sentence: "Of course, your novel doesn't solve my problems."

Saul cut off all connection. Professor X was bewildered and hurt. He was about to retire from his job; his body was rapidly giving way. I hoped to be an intermediary, described the troubles of our friend and asked Saul why he was so angry. "I can't be interested in what goes on with him," he said.

"What happened?"

"He wrote me a poison pen letter."

The author of *Herzog*, with a protagonist who poured his advice, suggestions, and complaints into the mails, had received a letter from an old friend which ended a long association. This seemed a bizarre twist on the novel. I believe the letter must have been ruder than Professor X had said. I asked to see a copy, and of course like a good academic, Professor X had made one. The letter was dense with praise and goodwill. But it did contain that offense: Your novel doesn't solve my problems . . .

All the honors available worldwide couldn't relieve Saul's touchiness. Receiving hundreds of clippings with rave notices, he was still the man who could be thrown into a raging flunk by that bad review in the *Deseret News* of Salt Lake City (it may have been the *Rocky Mountain News* of Denver, Colorado).

※

Among the later books, *Humboldt's Gift*—not a favorite of many critics—stood out for me as a comic and terrified riff on desperation and madness. It was intended partly as a tribute to Saul's friend and contemporary, the poet Delmore Schwartz, who in his paranoia turned against Saul as he turned against almost everyone. Saul tried to help him, contributed money for treatment, but could not escape the wrath of a man spinning out of control. Schwartz died miserable and alone in a seedy Manhattan hotel.

The book celebrated the charm of a manic talent; it also memorialized the friendship of Bellow and Schwartz, contemporaries and buddies. The engrossing persuasiveness of Schwartz, the ranting and pathos, were named; and the book expressed the helplessness of those around him. What Saul couldn't do was to evoke the great gifts of Delmore Schwartz, the brilliance of his best writing, the loopy wit and the elegiac mourning. He named the madman; he couldn't name the perverse genius.

This is a most daunting task for a novelist, to suggest genius in one of his characters. But it also seemed that Saul couldn't really allow the competition from his friend, and instead needed to hold him up for regard as a pathetic specimen, a loser.

Out of the quarrel with ourselves, Yeats said, we make poetry; and out of the quarrel with others we make war. In his novels Saul made both poetry and his own kind of war, which could have resulted in mere vengeful tale-telling. At his best, he managed to transmute his antagonists, wives, lovers, and failed friends into grand sports and aberrations. Early on, he preserved in this circus world the sense of himself as a tragic clown, dancing amid the wreckage. Later, he seemed to feel that this image was beneath his dignity, and as his books became more severe, they lost some of their grace. *Mr. Sammler's Planet*, tense and controlled, was a parable of withdrawal, rejection of a world which lets us down. Through the optic of the aging survivor, Sammler, he makes a case for depression as the proper response to the disaster of modern history.

Still later, the wintry authenticity of *The Dean's December* is a confession of hopeless yarning. Flashes of the old comedy raise ironic signposts as the writer charts a continuing devolution into disappointment.

❖

In the early Seventies I found myself in Chicago with the woman who had become my second wife. I loved her, I was proud of her—called her the "statistical miracle" because it seemed such extraordinary good luck to find her—and I wanted Saul to appreciate my good fortune, too. He invited us to lunch at the club where he played racquetball. It was elegant and sparkly, with a panoramic view of the city, Saul's city.

The three of us had a polite and affable meal; fish, a good wine. In my pride I waited impatiently for a word alone with him. At last she stood up to go to the bathroom and I watched him as he watched her. Then he turned to me with his wide smile and said, "She has a sense of humor. I like that in a woman."

304

I was chagrined. I wanted him to express enthusiasm for my statistical miracle; this smug and bland okay was surely not enough. But it was all he had to give me just then. My joy was no pleasure to him during another crisis in his life. I was no longer one of his intimates.

Melissa returned to the table and my heart leapt with love and pride, and Saul's opinion didn't matter.

I was no longer an acolyte or disciple. The ten-year difference in our ages was becoming irrelevant as the years rolled by. Saul mattered, but not enough to spoil my time with the woman I loved. And also not enough to make me read his novels without judgment. The supple prose was engrossing; how he danced with ideas! Sometimes I didn't like the vision behind the prose.

At various times he championed the work of younger writers like Edward Hoagland, William Kennedy, and Cormac McCarthy, and he was often moving and generous in praise of suffering contemporaries like Isaac Rosenfeld, Delmore Schwartz, John Berryman, and John Cheever, especially after they died. He acutely felt the loss of his contemporaries, those who fought to stay afloat and failed at it, as he had fought and succeeded.

When he turned against old friends, such as a lawyer in Chicago whom he lampooned in one book, he was merciless and they felt crushed. I know three people who wrote novels intended as revenge for what he had written about them (the books were not published; rage and frustration provided unreliable fuel for inspiration). When Saul wrote a book against, he had larger things in mind than self-justification and punishment of enemies. Freshets of soul and wit scampered through the prose, as if his essence were a glacier, the top warmed by the sun, chunks breaking off and sparkling streams pounding down the ice.

When asked at a lecture to explain something about one of his books, boyish irritation, that winsome flirtiness he could summon, arose in his voice as he grinned, seemed to search, rediscovered his mantra for a new audience: "I'm a bird, not an ornithologist." Once again he was saying it for the first time. He threw back his head in laughter, encouraged others to relax and laugh, and even the questioner joined in.

In the fall of 1988 or '89, I heard he was depressed about the breakup of another marriage, the death of a brother and a childhood friend, and telephoned him. We had a few meals together; I attended a lecture he gave at NYU. At first, as we caught up with his life, there was a warmth that recalled our old friendship. The morning he left Manhattan, he invited me to meet him for breakfast at One Fifth Avenue, so I was surprised to feel over the toast and eggs that I was imposing on him. He was withdrawn and chilly. Had I said the wrong thing about his lecture? Had I offended him again by mentioning Jack Ludwig?

The son who accompanied him seemed embarrassed by his father, and made a point of being cordial to me. When we said goodbye, Saul stood there, nattily dressed as usual these years, in a stylish coat and hat like an international businessman, waiting stiffly apart from us as his son and I chatted. Finally he said impatiently, "Come on, we're going," and that was goodbye.

I had written him no poison pen letters, but somehow I fell into the category of those who offended. I tried to imagine how this happened—by growing up, by insufficient discipleship, by not being available to listen to his troubles since I lived in California, by admiring other writers besides him (he was annoyed by my enthusiasm for Vladimir Nabokov), by no reason that was clear to me. Like so many former friends, I was out of the privileged circle.

Some of the friends he kept played variations on the theme of disciplehood. One woman liked to say she only lived in Chicago "so I can be there for Saul." As she murmured, "Saul used to read his new pages to me every day," or, "When Saul's upset, I always tell him . . ." or the ever-popular, "Sometimes when Saul can't sleep, I . . .", people formed the natural habit of asking if she was having an affair with him. It was a question urged upon them; rude not to ask. Primly she would fall silent, a silence that cried, Yes! Yes! But having been urged toward the question, folks felt general relief that she was discreet enough not to admit to the affair she very likely hadn't had.

Literary groupies are much like rock groupies, but more literary (that is, older) and speak of "being there for him" instead of plaster castings.

*　*　*

More than fifty years of friendship and non-friendship include too many harsh memories. They begin, after gratitude, with that ordinary puzzlement that a writer and man who inspired part of a generation, altered the tone of a literary period, wrote with such grace, nonetheless lived his life with flaws both large and petty, like other people. The flaws seemed to be magnified by the fineness of his achieve-

306

ment. Saul wrote in the rhythms of city speech, stylized, pursuing the sense of his troubled American life. His anxiety made him frantic. He reflected upon each moment, defending himself with wit and charm. Again and again, he almost, temporarily, mastered his experience. And then the victory passed. He draped his life's story in a prose which served to calm him—almost, temporarily—by displaying his nakedness fetchingly clothed. The narrative sometimes had the innocence of a boyish daydream, sometimes of a boy's nightmare. The discourse both quickened and heartened his readers.

And it wasn't just style, the playful surface, the watchfulness. He really wanted to discover What It All Meant (he would never put it that way). His gifts enabled him to edge abruptly into scenes of vivid desire and grief, as in the last paragraphs of the great story, *Seize the Day*. During his best moments he shared his sense of our lives in a way impossible for writers of mere self-justification and confession. The path of self-justification, he used to say, has been worn so deep that all you can see is the top of the heads of the writers who follow down it.

The images in *The Victim* of a pair of tormentors chained together one hot summer in New York, or Augie March wrestling with Chicago, or Humboldt raving in the grip of mania, and especially Tommy Wilhelm, the protagonist of *Seize the Day*, weeping for himself and mankind at the funeral of someone he doesn't know, will endure as the memories of Saul's personal faults fade. Tolstoy, Dostoyevsky, Melville, Kafka, D.H. Lawrence, and Unamuno were not saints in real life, either. Their work and Saul's teach something about generosity.

The effect of his presence was also generous for other writers. The example of his success invited to the feast those who followed after him in the priestly—rabbinic!—calling of story-teller, lyric poet, questing philosopher. For a later generation, his rich use of vernacular speech energized the American language as Rabelais and Verlaine did for French, as Shakespeare and Laurence Stern did in English, as Whitman and Mark Twain did. Of this doing and redoing, there needs to be no end. The stylistic playfulness, grace, and grasp of American urban yearning by a writer from a Yiddish-speaking family resonated especially for other Jews. We too could be Americans in the American language. I am old enough to have been informed by a friendly editor that I should spell my name "Gould" when a first story of mine appeared in her magazine. Later, a writer who had changed his name to something bland and generic informed me, with a grin both stern and smug, that he could be a real American writer, but I, alas, burdened by the name "Goald," could not. After Saul's success, writers who once believed they needed names like "Shaw," "Harris," or "Algren" no longer required these 'Made in America' labels. They could call themselves Ginsberg, Litwak, Leavitt, Canin, Gold, whatever names they came with, and this was liberating.

Saul's persistent heartfelt *I want, I want, I want*—his own cry and that of his protagonists—really means, *I need, I need, I need.* Insatiability derived both from his condition as an outsider and increasing recognition that being inside is no solution, either. Sometimes he glamorized his neediness by turning it into heroic appetite, as in *Henderson the Rain King*, elegantly, but with a querulous edge, in a bewildering rush of haughty self-pity. No story or novel could settle matters for him. He never stopped trying. He turned away congratulations for his many prizes (Nobel, Pulitzer, National Book Award) by confiding that they interfered with his real business.

He wanted to be like Tolstoy, both a teller of tales and an inspirer, a moral philosopher; and he wanted to solve his own problems. Late in life, when he was ill with a failing heart, a friend said to him, "I hope you're getting better," and he answered, "I've been getting better my whole life, but look where it's gotten me." He kept on trying, sustained by the devotion of Janis, his fifth wife. He became something like a shadow Tolstoy, running toward a devoted woman instead of away from her. An older Tolstoy wrote his passionate novella *Hadji Murad*, hot-eyed and rampaging over terrain he knew from his youth, after the great periods of *War and Peace, Anna Karenina*, and *The Death of Ivan Ilyich*. Then, overwhelmed, he turned to the autumnal achievements of "What is Art?", "The Kreutzer Sonata," and the fabular tracts with which he sought to teach moral lessons while his own family life fell into ruins. The spare precision of Bellow's first novels, *Dangling Man* and *The Victim*, opened into the rich language-busting of *The Life of Augie March*. Swaggering and full of delight at rafting down the wide river of American speech, he broke patterns as Twain and Whitman did, giving the street and the library equal place. And then, avidity still the habit he lived by, he became less hungry. He judged the century and found it lacking. The rebellious dangling man, the Trotskyite who had studied the violin and anthropology, became a defender of the established order, frightened by rock music and the Chicago he helped redefine. It made me fear my own old age to look into those great dark eyes and see the laughter in retreat.

*

Strolling with Saul down the rue de Verneuil during the early days of our friendship, around the rue du Bac, back up to the café Le Rouquet at the corner of the Boulevard Saint-Germain and the rue des Saints-Pères—across the street from the garden of the Russian church—talking and talking amid that peculiar Paris smell of Gauloise Bleu, redwine piss, and flowers, I happened to speak of Sinclair Lewis, who was still alive and writing his worn-out, alcoholic last novels. As a boy, when I first discovered grownup books, *Babbit*, *Main Street*, and *It Can't Happen Here* opened doors to the world outside Lakewood, Ohio. But by 1950 it seemed that Sinclair Lewis' fingers were merely punching the typewriter, his rage had devolved to hysteria, the satire was diminished into abuse of a world he no longer fathomed. Sinclair Lewis' erotic yearning—I was in my early twenties—seemed pathetic in an old man.

Saul interrupted, turning his warm and amused gaze on me, with a reproach which was just, aimed exactly right, naming the lack of generosity in a young man's sniping against his elders. "Don't count any writer out while he's still alive."

These words imposed a long silence. I had a vision of eternity like the one called forth by Oscar J. Campbell, one of my freshman professors, when our class read Lucretius on time and death and he spoke of his stroke and then stopped speaking, lowering his head in contemplation of the unknowable. I accepted the shame Saul's reminder brought down upon me.

*

Through difficult times in a long friendship, the early paradox remains, young Saul in crisis, that smiling person with rosy cheeks and hair freshly wetted by his shower, bouncing down mossy steps toward the café in Banyuls where we waited for him more than a half-century ago. Edith and I expected someone exhausted by griefs without end on the roads from Paris to the Côte de Vermeil. Instead,

309

what appeared for the bouillabaisse and wine was an avid young winner, sure of his powers. We had been exhausted by listening to his suffering. He was refreshed by the telling of it.

The irritable old person in gray and black who warily and impatiently pulled away from our encounter in New York still lived by the standard of that passionate and spendthrift wilfulness. Since he was an artist, still alive, still alive, he couldn't be counted out. Within his irritability still swelled the indomitable young writer with pains he adored, restlessly seeking how to say them better.

*

Among my brother Sid's papers after his death, I found a letter from Saul to me, written in the early Sixties, in response to a story of Sid's which I had sent to *The Noble Savage*, the journal Saul edited. Saul's letter was full of good counsels, generous encouragement, and I gave it to my brother in the hope that it would nudge him toward finishing the endless, never completed novel which he spent forty years writing.

I wrote Saul in a flood of remembrance and gratitude, and in sadness for our faded friendship. His reply was immediate and full of compassion about losses, his own and mine, of my brother, and regret that we had "neglected to attend to our friendship." Again I recalled his reproach when, aged twenty-four, I ridiculed Sinclair Lewis for his frantic and decrepit late novels. Don't count any writer out until he's gone.

We were back in touch, attending to friendship. He wrote tenderly about Janis, his last wife, his fifth wife, who kept him alive, he said, through caring, love, and the example of her youth. When he was eighty-four and she was pregnant, some women expressed anger at what they considered sexist behavior. There is no symmetry in the matter; a man of eighty-four can father a child. "I try to keep in practice," he said. Justice is hardly the point here.

On a balmy day in October, 1999, we had lunch outdoors at the Nob Hill Café in San Francisco, and then sat in the sun on a bench in Huntington Park, both of us—I'm not reading minds here—remembering our Paris days when we used to pass the time like this. But we weren't talking about Sartre, Merleau-Ponty, or the daily news of the trials of Nazi collaborators. He talked about his life in Boston and Vermont, about his regret for needing to fly with a helper now that his wife's pregnancy was too advanced for her to travel with him. She wanted their child. She knew what the conditions were. He spoke of his end of the deal with a certain wryness, with an energetic resignation, his head cocked as he laughed about oncoming inevitabilities. "I always prided myself on my sense of smell. I always prided myself on my memory. I'm losing them." When he laughed, throwing his head back, he was a boy again.

And then he said it was time for his nap. He took my arm as we walked back to the Huntington Hotel. That night he was having dinner with his eldest son, Gregory, whom I had known as a child in Paris. "He has gripes about me he doesn't want to give up," he said. "I don't blame him." But this father, grandfather, and father-to-be intended to mend his fences at a crucial time.

✿

For me, Saul is still fully present. There was a generous dreamer locked within his vanity, a young poet and lover in the body of the wary old party; and when he emitted his voice, sent out his courting signals to the world which he desperately asked to understand him— often in scenes filled with pleading and tears—he managed to bring something gallant into our lives. He helped to create a new permission not only for Jewish writers, but also for others previously exiled to an odd regionality without regions—Blacks, Latinos, second and third generation immigrants, founding sons of not founding fathers. Like all artists, his personality was stuffed with surprises, and not always delightful ones; like all human beings.

When the days and nights end for a writer, something keeps going on if he has shed his magic light and darkness upon the miracle of life. "The death of the poet is kept from the poems." And Saul Bellow struggled to leave us a record of days and nights which would not disappear after his troubled and fortunate time on earth.

Nominated by The Republic of Letters

DIACRITICAL REMARKS

(For and after Dean Young)

by G. C. WALDREP

from CUE

> *"Meaning is being in a charged environment and making a choice."*
> —Dean Young

MEANING IS BEING in a charged environment and making a choice. Meaning has in fact been held hostage there since the thaw of the last ice age. The ropes have begun to fray, a bit, but still they hold tightly, the way music holds a piano to its cardboard stage. Meaning keeps making a choice—many choices—but nothing comes of it: the hedgehogs keep slaloming down the Chiltern Hills, deforestization in Sarawak proceeds apace, and attendance at the night auction keeps growing. The question of whether Caspar really doubled as the invisible spice merchant goes unanswered. Some of us rebuilt London. Dili burned. Meanwhile, deep in its arctic cavern, Meaning is flexing its muscles. Meaning is working out the last decimals of Zeno's paradox. Meaning is planning a cruise. Dearest partisans of pulchritude, gnosis, & light, the *General Slocum* will not be docking. Meaning has all the time in the world and refuses to give us any. It's trickle-up economics. At the night auction Henri Bergson is serving up another faux Vermeer. This one, like nearly all the others, features a domestic scene. Meaning's long shadow falls across the canvas. It's impossible to know the details of the composition. It's impossible to know who cancels the stamps. Meaning at one point expressed a considerable interest in philately. Meaning premeditates. Meaning is on its way home.

Nominated by Cue

HIMMELEN

fiction by HEIDI SHAYLA

from THE GEORGIA REVIEW

I'T'S A LONG STORY how I came to be walking down the industrial stretch of Highway 99 on a Thursday morning, looking like a prostitute after a hard night. I'm trying to ignore the truckers who blow their air horns at me and make gestures that aren't worth repeating. The dust from their tires makes spinning storms in the gravel when they swerve onto the shoulder of the road, not watching where they're going as they crane their necks to ogle me in their rearview mirrors. I can't blame them; my skirt is so short I can't bend over or squat down either one without revealing everything I came into the world with, and my heels are high enough to break my neck if I fall off them—which I'm likely to do stumbling and twisting my ankles along the graveled edge of the highway, stepping over the McDonald's cups and cigarette butts that people have thrown out their car windows.

The early July sunshine is just breaking over the Coburg Hills, lighting up the green of the mountains to the west, illuminating the endless rise of peaks and a patchwork of fir forests and clear-cuts shimmering in the distance. I trip again and limp forward, swearing out loud. I'd take off the damn shoes, would have taken them off five miles ago when I first started walking north from Eugene, except there's broken beer bottles all along the highway, jagged shards of brown and green glass mixed into the gravel, ready to lacerate anything fleshlike that comes their way. So I'm stuck in these heels and wondering where the hell I left my common sense, because I certainly appear to have misplaced it.

That's where I come back to the part where I said it's a long story how I got here. Let's just say it has something to do with a guy named Peder Shlolakov, who I now know to be a lowlife waste of my time, but until last night I thought was a law student from Gdan'sk, Poland, with a soft accent and a way of pushing my name between his teeth so that it sounded as if it were a part of his breathing: *Sar* on the inhale, *eena* on the exhale, Sareena. I'd never had a man breathe my name before. I would have gone back to Poland with him just to spend the rest of my life beneath the dripping honey of his accent. But instead, here I am looking like something from the red light district, tripping past the wrecking yard where the morning sun glints off the rusting carcasses of old automobiles, and then past the live-stock auction barns, the reek of hogs washing over me. All because of a jerk whose real name is Pete Schlotszky and whose only accent is the one he made up in Roseburg while he worked as a mechanic in a garage owned by a cigar-smoking second-generation Polish American named Floyd.

I know all about Floyd. Pete went on and on about him and his garage last night when he was confessing his real identity along with his everlasting love for me. Pete had given up the Polish accent after two margaritas and was spilling his fourth drink onto my knees as he slurred and nearly fell off his barstool. Floyd was part of Pete's plan for our future; we'd move to Roseburg, where he would go back to the garage and I would apparently spend my days dressing in next to nothing with matching high heels because that's what turned Pete on. It sounded sexier when Pete Schlotszky was Peder Shlolakov and I was thinking about being a Polish attorney's wife whose home over-looked the Baltic Sea.

He didn't have to be from Poland. He could have been Spanish or Chinese. He could have come from Bali or Denmark or the Czech Republic. I would have been just as happy to have a house on the Seine as on the Baltic Sea. Hell, he could have lived in Tijuana, Mex-ico, or Vancouver, Canada, right over the border—just someplace out of the ordinary. I can trace the earth right here in the gravel for you, show you places on a map so far from western Oregon that if you could go there you'd be standing at the edge of the planet with the winds of a different world on your face. Trust me, Floyd's garage in Roseburg is not at the edge of the planet, and Pete Schlotszky is no more exotic than the rattletrap rusted bucket of a Ford pickup that's stopping ahead of me to see if I need a ride. Great, just what I don't

314

need is some logger trying to buy a piece of my time or more likely a piece of something else that I'm barely covering with this skirt. Damn these shoes.

The man who leans his head out the driver's side window is more hippie than logger, though in the Pacific Northwest the two aren't necessarily mutually exclusive. His long beard is the color of stone-ground mustard, and the sleeve of his T-shirt is bright tie-dye against his skin as he rests his elbow on the open window. He's got ten years' worth of Country Fair and Farmer's Market bumper stickers plastering the tailgate and back window of his pickup. It's possible they are the only things holding that old truck together. Otherwise, the Ford is splotches of primer gray over the top of some color that might have once been red but now reminds me of dried blood or brick dust. The bed of the Ford is full of lumber scraps—cedar, redwood, and fir—1 × 6s, 1 × 8s, and some smaller pieces of teak. When I was growing up, my parents owned a lumber supply store; I can identify wood the way some women can spot designer shoes. That little talent wouldn't have done me much good in Poland maybe, but in western Oregon it has its advantages.

"I'm heading to Junction City," the man yells. "You want a ride?"

A log truck roars past and I hang on to my skirt, striving to keep it down against the rising gust of wind the truck leaves in its wake. I ought to keep walking, use the six more miles to Junction City to work off a little more of the raging disappointment that Peder— Pete—left me with. But I am generally a sane and practical woman (although I know you can't tell it by looking at me now), and spending much more time out here alone, dressed like this, is neither sane nor practical. Either I'm going to fall in front of a car and become someone's hood ornament, or I'm going to have to fend off some pervert with nothing but the spike heels of my shoes. Still, climbing into a pickup with a strange man doesn't seem that much smarter.

I look at the back of the man's head in the rear window, at the line of his shoulders. He's got no right arm! It's missing from just below the shoulder, the tie-dyed T-shirt sleeve hanging empty below it. When the surprise of that registers fully in my mind, it occurs to me that a one-armed man cannot simultaneously grope me and drive. So I tell him, "I appreciate you stopping" and stumble to the passenger door. The pickup seat is ripped and scratches my bare thighs as I slide in.

The man in the driver's seat is lanky, his long legs folded up beneath the steering wheel, his one arm seeming like it might reach from his shoulder to his thin knees. He swivels his body and thrusts out his big left hand to shake mine. "Name's Silas," he says, his voice soft beneath the whooshing rush of traffic noise.

My hand disappears in his much larger one. "Sereena," I tell him.

He nods and takes the steering wheel in his hand, accelerating onto the highway. "Well, it looked like you were struggling out there, Sereena."

"Yeah, struggling is a good word for it." I lean to pull off one shoe and rub my aching foot, but I can't raise my knee too far without making the skirt hike up my thighs. I kick off the other shoe, all the while noticing the way Silas' knuckles stand out on his long hand as he grips the steering wheel, like a row of starlings sitting on a phone wire, rubbing up against each other to keep warm.

Silas changes lanes to pass a chip truck. "Must be a man involved," he says as he accelerates past the long silver trailer. He tips his head at me. "Dressed like that out here, got to be a man behind it."

I don't know whether it's a question or just a statement of the obvious. I look out the passenger window. The silver of the trailer whirls in my vision for a moment and then abruptly ends, replaced by the rising up of the truck itself, and then that is gone too and there is only the golden blur of hayfields whipping past. Silas pulls in front of the chip truck. The hayfields go on and on, broken occasionally by the sudden green of a rye grass field or the gray slash of a side road. A grain barn looms up and disappears in the next instant, the industrial edge of Eugene well behind us now. My feet are throbbing and my eyes ache. There is something about the shuddering of the pickup, or the distorted streaks of color, or Silas' solid hand on the steering wheel, or maybe it's his other empty shirt sleeve, that is shaking my emotions loose, vibrating my barely held composure apart. "What are you building?" I ask, craning my head to see the short boards in the bed of the pickup. They are clear vertical grain, nice lumber.

"Birdhouses," he says.

"Birdhouses?"

He taps his fingers on the steering wheel, seeming to consider. "Bird condominiums." But that must not be right either because then he says, "Bird villages. Bird cities."

I laugh, because it's preposterous, because I have images of New Bird City, and Las Birdelas, and Birdingham.

Silas' grin is lopsided, short on one side, like his arm. "Bird apartment complexes, community centers, retirement homes, fire halls, police stations, all of that."

"You're kidding."

He shakes his head. "Nope, serious as a heart attack."

"You build bird towns for a living?"

"No." Silas slows as we come to a stoplight at the edge of Junction City. The chip truck stops behind us. "I'm a janitor at the high school." The light changes to green and he accelerates. "I build birdhouses on the weekends for collectors, bird enthusiasts, gardeners, that sort."

"Bird cities," I correct him. "Not just birdhouses, bird cities!" We are rolling past car dealerships now and vast lots of motor homes and RVs for sale.

Silas smiles that crooked smile. "Right. Whole bird communities."

I stretch my legs in front of me, feeling the scratch of the ripped seat on the back of my thighs, imagining cities in miniature pinned to the sky, elaborate aeries perched on poles over gardens and suspended in trees. "Avian metropolises," I laugh. "You could do replicas of all the great cities. Paris, New York, Prague, Moscow, London, Venice. Venice could have little waterways and bird gondolas."

"I have parts of London and Paris done, and New York and San Francisco are almost finished." He doesn't look at me when he says this, staring at the highway in front of the pickup, gripping the steering wheel in his hand as if it might jerk free of his grasp.

"London and Paris?" I breathe.

He nods. "In my backyard." And then he squints through the windshield at Junction City. "Not much happening here so early in the morning."

It's true, everything is quiet. The shops and businesses that line the highway are still closed, their window displays lit by the early morning sun. Everywhere I look, Scandinavian flags flutter from buildings, and elaborate delicate tole paintings grace the corners of offices, columns on porches, window boxes full of flowers. Junction City was settled by Scandinavian immigrants, who, as far as I can tell, hammered their heritage and their history so firmly into this valley soil that it is still, generations later, sprouting pure Danes, Swedes, Finns, and Norwegians. The descendents of those first pioneers have never forgotten the old countries. Downtown, there is even one building wall painted in a huge mural depicting blond helmeted

Vikings storming across the brickwork to pillage and plunder. We pass a Mexican restaurant, a quilting shop, a pharmacy with dala horses and trolls in the windows, a business that makes furniture for motor homes. The few grass seed farmers and truck drivers who are up already are guzzling coffee from Styrofoam cups they bought at the Dari-Mart.

Silas flicks a finger at the supermarket ahead. "I've got to buy some groceries. You want off anywhere in particular?"

The supermarket is open, every light on and glaring through the spotless windows. "There." I point to a row of shops across the highway.

Silas squints at the low-lying building. "You live there?"

"No, I work there. At my aunt's beauty salon."

He pulls into the parking lot, parks the pickup, and tugs at his beard. "You cut hair, huh?"

I smile, open the door, and slide out of the pickup, fishing for my keys in my purse, the ridiculous high heels in my hand. "Thanks for the ride, Silas."

He nods, looking past me to the salon, his long fingers still in his beard. "What time do you open?"

"9:00," I tell him.

He nods again.

I turn away, angling across the parking lot in my bare feet, my keys jangling against the shoes. Silas waits for me to get to the door. Only when I've unlocked it and stepped safely inside does he wave good-bye. He puts the Ford in gear and pulls across the highway to the supermarket.

I can see the fuzzy-edged reflection of the grocery store, the parking lot, and the highway in the mirrors of the salon. Silas' pickup is a slowly rolling, blood-colored blob pulling into the almost empty lot. It sits in the corner of my vision even as I go to the back room to change into the comfortable clothes and shoes I keep in a plastic bin on the shelf above the surplus towels and aprons. My blouse smells of Pete Schlotszky as I pull it off over my head. His cologne, spilled margaritas, cigarettes. Peder Shlolakov used to smell like books, paper and glue, and coffee. And Silas smells of pitch and wood smoke and rain. The mix of them in my nose is like the array of shampoo bottles that line one wall of the salon—a whole world of scents and promises, some true and others doubtful.

318

I slip into a T-shirt and skirt, and shove the high heels and miniskirt into the bin, pushing it back onto the shelf out of my sight. Then I sit at one of the hair-washing stations, turn on the water, lay my head back over the sink, and let the warm water pour over my hair, washing away the lingering odors of Pete Schlotszky. When I sit up, wrapping my shampooed hair in a towel, that brick dust–colored pickup is still sitting in the parking lot across the highway. It distracts me, drawing my attention as I clean the salon. Everything is already spotless, but I have two hours to kill before we open, so I wipe down my own station and then my aunt's and, finally, the nail tech table that is my cousin's domain. When I finish mopping the floor, the pickup is finally gone.

On Thursdays we offer a senior citizen discount. I am up to my elbows in gray pin curls and am having my third conversation of the morning about the advantages of Metamucil and glucosamine while my aunt makes small talk about the upcoming barbecue at the Sons of Norway lodge. My cousin has just talked an ancient frail woman into trying a hand waxing, and all the woman's friends are gathered around her like cooing, rustling pigeons, murmuring over the elaborate process of slathering her hands in lotion, dipping them in the warm peach-scented wax, slipping them into plastic bags and then big terry cloth mitts to hold in the heat. She looks as if she is about to take a roast out of the oven as she sits on the waiting area couch and reports every detail of the cooling process to her friends. They all laugh when my cousin pulls off the mitts and the baggies and peels away the wax. "Still old," they tease, "still wrinkled."

"Yes, yes," the woman rubs her hands together, "but soft as a baby's butt."

So then they all must have hand waxings, and my cousin is suddenly overwhelmed by elderly women in oven mitts. It is at this very moment that the bell above the door jangles again. I'm expecting another carload of women, but instead it is Silas who walks through the door, an enormous backpack slung over one shoulder, his hand pausing on the knob as he surveys the room full of women in big white mitts as if they are burn victims. He looks at me, mystified. "I was wondering, Sareena," he says softly, "if you might have time this morning to trim my hair."

There is an instant of electrified silence in the salon as my aunt,

319

cousin, and every one of the Thursday senior discount clients look between Silas and me. And then they erupt into laughter and chatter, whisking Silas inside, closing the door firmly behind him. My aunt saunters over to the scheduling book. "Melva honey, you wouldn't mind waiting half an hour longer would you?"

Melva, whose perm I wash and brush out every Thursday, does not mind in the least.

Silas shoves his hand in his jeans pocket. "I wouldn't want to put you out or anything . . ."

But Melva pulls him down to sit on the folding chair next to her. "Aren't you the janitor down at the high school?" The other women gather around. My cousin flits among them, pulling off mitts and baggies and hand wax. The smell of peaches drifts across the room. Silas looks helplessly in my direction, but there is no saving him from Melva. She is a stirrer of pots, a Loki, a mischief maker in brown polyester slacks.

"How is your love life, Sareena?" she calls, patting Silas' thin knee. "Still dating that Polish boy?"

"Turns out he ain't Polish," my aunt yells over the noise of the women. On Thursdays, my aunt is Melva's accomplice, her apprentice in training. "He was an imposter. One of them Roseburg fellows," she declares, as if all men from Roseburg are imposters of one sort or another. And then she is hustling my client out of the chair, and Melva is herding Silas toward a hair-washing station, with loudly whispered advice that he should have me trim his beard while he's in the chair because no man as handsome as him should be walking around looking like a scraggly Jesus.

Which is how I find myself leaning over Silas' reclined body, working shampoo through his hair and massaging my fingertips along the curve of his skull. I trace the tight arc of a scar that trails from above his ear into the hollow of one temple and slide my thumbs over the rise of bone on the back of his head as if I am following the contours of a topographical map, learning a new landscape. Despite the scrutiny of Melva and my aunt, Silas is completely relaxed in the chair, his long legs sprawled in front of him, his eyes closed. There is a comforting rhythm to the steady rise and fall of his chest as his breathing slows beneath the warm water, and I wonder if he might drift to sleep with his head in my hands. But when I'm done, he murmurs, "Damn! That was . . ." He waves his hand without opening his eyes, like he's trying to catch the words from the air, and finally settles on, "That was art. Pure and unadulterated art, Sareena." He says my name all on the exhale, on a sigh of satisfaction.

Cutting Silas' hair is like trying to herd cats. It curls and slips out of my fingers and from between the scissors, beautiful and soft, independent and difficult. Once I have corralled it, strands escape, and while I'm trying to pull those back in, the rest springs free out the other side. Finally I discover that it is better to cajole it, to lure it piece by piece into the scissors. He watches this slow process in the mirror and suddenly asks me, "What do Polish imposters sound like?"

"Liars," I tell him, "frauds, charlatans."

But he says, "No, really."

So I try to mimic the dripping honey voice of Peder Shlolakov. I reach to catch the heavy vowels and the way the consonants sounded like the echo of rolling thunder across distant hills. I struggle to breathe in the middle of words, the way Peder did when he said my name, but that is hopeless. I laugh because I'm embarrassed, and I turn back to Silas' willful hair instead. But now Silas has captured the gist of Peder, and he watches his mouth in the mirror as he sounds out the accent. By the time I'm finally done with his hair and am trimming his beard, he sounds a little like Vladimir Putin.

When I take the plastic cape from around his neck, he still looks like an Aryan Jesus, but he's a clipped and combed version that meets the approval of the Thursday senior discount crowd. They rustle and cluck around him as I wade through to the register to get his change. And then they buoy him out the door, and he waves to them through the window. They all wave back.

I turn away to sweep up Silas' hair and discover he has left a tip at my station, a tip he must have had hidden in his huge backpack all along. He has tucked a five-dollar bill into the most amazing birdhouse I have ever seen. Hardly a birdhouse but a bird palace, painted to look like shimmering marble with spires and iridescent domes and perfect, elaborate, impossibly delicate scrollwork. The gateway is surrounded by floral arabesques with faux gemstones and black inscriptions. In the yawning arch beneath the central dome, there is space for a nest, and feeders are tucked into the four corner towers. It is the stuff of fantasy and enchantment. Across the base, Silas has painted,

I push through the women to the door, cradling the birdhouse in my hands, but Silas' old pickup has already turned onto the highway and is rolling out of sight.

At home that night, I hang the birdhouse on the tiny back porch of my apartment and look up the Taj Mahal on the Internet. It turns out the palace is actually a tomb built by a Mughal king to honor the wife he adored above all others. He apparently had a perverse sense of humor about architecture, though; his palace tomb is a puzzle of optical illusions and hallways that were built to confuse and mystify, all of which Silas has exactly replicated in miniature. To build a palace tomb with architects and hundreds of workers at your beck and call is one thing. But to build the Taj Mahal in perfect detail from bits of scrap wood in the hours left to a man once he's done polishing the gymnasium floor, scrubbing the high school toilets, and painting over the graffiti is something more wondrous still. I lie awake in bed that night, wondering how he could possibly manage it with only one hand.

When I finally fall asleep, I dream of cinnamon-throated barn swallows nesting in my father's lumber warehouse. I am stumbling around pallets of boards and plywood in the half light, trying to find my way out, but the big door that is wide and tall enough for a freight truck isn't where it used to be. The birds are calling to each other in a thousand languages as they swoop in and out of the girders and joists. It is just inane gossip and insights about the quality of the air, but in Portuguese, Romanian, Gaelic, Afrikaans, Basque, Greek, Hindi, Russian, French, a Tower of Babel cacophony, too many swallows to count, all vying to speak over the others, and all of it echoing and bouncing from the metal walls and the concrete floor of the warehouse.

When I wake up late in the morning, with the sun already shining full tilt in my windows, my head is pounding from trying to understand their chatter.

By noon I have lifted the Taj Mahal down a dozen times to finger the scrollwork and the intricate Arabic lettering over the door. I hang it back up and walk away, only to find myself staring at it again. Finally

I call Melva. "How do I get in touch with Silas?" I ask her. "I want to thank him for the birdhouse."

"I think he's got a place up at Alpine," she tells me. I can hear the speculation in her voice. "You give me fifteen minutes and I'll find the number for you."

Twenty minutes later she calls back. Without saying hello, she announces, "I just got off the phone with Silas' mother. You got a pencil?"

After I write down Silas' phone number, Melva launches into a spiel about his genealogy. "Did you know his people have been in the area since before the Civil War? Danes and Norwegians, every one of them. Solid, stable, no flighty notions." In Melva's way of thinking, this is the highest praise.

"I've got to go," I tell her before she can get a full wind in her sails.

"You've been saying that since you were little," she clucks, "always in a hurry to leave. If you got off your pity pot and spent half as much time making a life for yourself as you do pining for places you've never been, you could find some satisfaction in this world." And with that, she hangs up.

I am still staring at the receiver with "pity pot" echoing in my ears when the phone rings in my hand. "Hello?"

"Sareena." Silas laughs. "My mother just called. She's been talking to Melva and your aunt. The three of them think I should ask you out."

I look again at the Taj Mahal hanging from my back porch. It is perfect and glistening in the morning sun, dangling over pots of yellow and white daffodils. "They're right," I tell him. And I mean that; Silas should ask me out. Should I accept, though? That's a more difficult question. I don't trust my taste in men since the Polish imposter. But the Taj Mahal is as exotic a thing as I have ever owned, and it has occurred to me that that birdhouse could very well be testimony to its creator's mind, the way the original tomb was testament to the abiding love of a grief-stricken Mughal king. What kind of man builds a palace tomb, and speaks of the endurance of a distraught heart, and fills his backyard with an avian metropolis?

"Will you let me take you to dinner, Sareena?" Silas asks.

"I want to see your birdhouses," I tell him.

"All right, then, we'll have a barbecue at my place. You eat steak?"

"If it's rare and comes with beer."

"Is there any other way to eat steak?" he laughs. "Tonight?"

When I hesitate, he hedges, "I mean if you've got nothing else going on."

I take a slow breath. It's probably the height of foolishness to judge a man by his birdhouses, but, all things considered, it can't be any worse than chasing after a foreign accent. "Tonight's fine."

"Good. I'll pick you up at 5:00."

Silas picks me up in the blood-colored pickup with the primer patches. When I open my front door, he exclaims, *"Du ser flott ut!"*

"Excuse me?"

"It's Norwegian," he tells me. "It means you look beautiful." He scuffs his boots on my doormat.

"Say it again," I prompt, looking with some amusement at my barbecue clothes—faded jeans, tank top, Birkenstocks.

"Du ser flott ut," he repeats, sounding like he means it. He reaches for my hand. I give it to him and lace my fingers through his as if we have known each other longer; the Norwegian makes me a little giddy.

He leads me to the pickup and opens the passenger door for me. He's thrown a blanket over the ripped seat and waxed the dash and cleaned the windows. I smile at him and slide in to the middle. Our thighs brush against each other as the pickup storms noisily out of Junction City, heading further west on Highway 99 toward Monroe and finally into the green hills on a long road to Alpine.

The community of Alpine is a wide spot in the road. There used to be a general store, but it has gone out of business. The tavern is still open, though. Silas turns onto Bellfountain Road, and we rocket past rolling hayfields until we dip between a stand of fir trees where the pavement ends and the tires churn up the gravel. Finally he turns the pickup into a driveway and parks in front of a garage. Morning glories climb one wall almost to the shake roof, snaking along the gutters. He turns off the pickup, which sputters and protests but finally gives up, and opens his door to get out. And then he reaches back for me. Once I am on my feet next to him, he steps away, sketches a bow, and says, *"Jeg vil danse med deg.* I want to dance with you."

I curtsy as best one can in jeans and Birkenstocks. *"Jeg vil danse med deg,* too."

He begins to hum a jaunty broken tune, slips his arm around my waist, turns and turns again, and we two-step, clumsy and laughing, away from the pickup and around the garage to a side door. "This is my shop," he tells me, still turning, two-stepping into the lawn and back to the door and to the corner of the garage and back again. He slides his hand from my waist to turn the doorknob and flips on the light switch with a flourish.

His shop is like something from James Bond. There are mysterious devices and gadgets, metal vices, clamps and pincers, armatures, power tools adapted to work for a man who has lost a hand, a dozen different places for him to secure things so he can hammer and glue and paint. There is a built-in industrial vacuum system that dominates one wall; the shop is clean and shining. There should be scientists or engineers in here, in white lab coats, building devices to destroy or save the planet. But instead there are birdhouses in various stages of completion. I stand and stare. In this one small corner of the world, Silas is not a man with only one arm; he is a man with twenty arms, all silver or black metal, shining and efficient.

Silas steps close behind me, so that I can feel his clothing brushing against my backside. He puts his hand on my shoulder. "There by the band saw is the Statue of Liberty. More of New York City is in the yard. And over there by the lathe is the . . ."

". . . the Sistine Chapel," I interrupt, because I can't help myself. "And what's that going to be? Is it the Palace of Versailles?" I've read about these places, and here they are in midconstruction. I want to touch everything.

Silas laughs softly. I can feel his breath on my scalp. "Yes," he tells me, "it's going to be Versailles."

"This is . . ." I spread my arms, completely at a loss for words, amazed by the ingenuity in this room.

"*Himmelen*," Silas whispers into my ear.

"What?"

"*Himmelen*," he says again. "It means heaven. This is heaven."

I don't know if he's talking about the shop or the fact that our combined body heat, rising in the small space between us, is a heady and combustible thing. I have to step away to catch my breath.

As much as I want to see the backyard, I can't pull myself from the wood shop. Silas has already gone to fire up the briquettes, and I should follow him, but I have been waylaid by his Statue of Liberty birdhouse, which is nearly completed. The Mother of Exiles is standing on an elaborate nesting box with the chains of tyranny lying bro-

325

ken at her feet and her crown shining the light of liberty over the seven seas. Counting her torch, she is three feet and two inches of wood and thin copper sheeting, the perfect folds of her gown made in *repoussé*, a way of shaping sheet metal by hammering it into a mold; these are the things Silas told me before he went to light the grill. There are also 142 narrow steps in the staircase winding round and round up to Liberty's crown; I know this because he has not yet closed up the back of the Lady, and I have counted each one of those stairs in miniature.

As he did with the Taj Mahal, Silas has painted an inscription onto the star-shaped base of the Lady:

LIBERTY ENLIGHTENING THE WORLD
GIVE ME YOUR TIRED, YOUR POOR, YOUR HUDDLED MASSES
YEARNING TO BREATHE FREE

When my great-grandparents immigrated to America, they sailed into New York Harbor, past the Statue of Liberty, en route to Ellis Island. They and twelve million other people who left behind home and family to get on dank, filthy ships and sail across the ocean to a new world in hopes that their children would have a better future. How is it that, only three generations later, I am sitting, disgruntled, in the land of plenty? What right do I have? That, I suppose, is what Melva was trying to say all along.

Outside, Silas must have turned on a CD player; Ray Charles comes bouncing into the wood shop. The shop door opens and Silas pokes his head in. *"Jeg vil danse med deg,"* he says.

"Again?" I laugh. But I'm already turning my back on the Statue of Liberty and moving to clasp his outstretched hand. I want to dance too, round and round in the grass of his lawn, beneath cities raised to the sky and propped in tree limbs.

In the doorway, I see that the sun is just dropping behind the hills, casting off orange shards and pink clouds. The evening air is soft and warm. And everywhere I look, there are great metropolises. New York City is perched on poles, with the Empire State Building, Rockefeller Center, the Twin Towers, the Brooklyn Bridge, the Guggenheim Museum. London is clustered in the lowest branches of an ornamental cherry tree. Westminster Abbey, the Globe Theatre, the Houses of Parliament, and Saint Paul's Cathedral shimmer in the trailing hues of the setting sun. There is Paris around a black walnut tree, and the Great Wall of China near some tea roses. The Sydney Opera House sits on a platform by a rock pool. The Aztec city of the gods, Teotihuacán, is surrounded by a raised bed of strawberries. Gaudi's Casa Batllo soars above a cluster of huckleberry bushes; every carved porch contains a nest. There are Buddhist temples, mosques, great cathedrals, synagogues, ancient Egyptian pyramids, Greek and Roman ruins, Mecca, even Taihe Dian—the Forbidden City—with its Pavilion of Supreme Harmony, on which any number of birds might perch.

I am standing at the edge of the planet in miniature with the winds of a hundred lands, a thousand languages, myriad histories and faiths churning the grass, blowing through the trees, whispering down the mountain.

This is Himmelen.

Heaven.

I would just stare at it forever.

But Silas' arm is already encircling my waist. "Come on, Sareena," he says. "Dance with me and I'll show you the world."

I wrap my arms around his neck, and we two-step out onto the lawn, past Oslo, Prague, Moscow, and turn and turn again to see Venice, and then we're off to Istanbul.

Nominated by The Georgia Review

ON HEARING
A RECORDING OF
THE VOICE OF
WALT WHITMAN

by JOHN BRADLEY

from TERRESTRIAL MUSIC (Curbstone Press)

This voice can crack
        river rock
                or mend broken bone.
This voice can mend river rock
        or crack
                mended bone.
This voice poured Lincoln
        a glass
                of elderbery wine.
This voice poured Lincoln
        into the roots
                of elder trees.
I can hear stars
        being born, stars dying
                inside this voice.
I can hear lilacs
        laying claim

                              to the soil,
the soil
      laying claim to the lilacs
                        in this voice.
This voice churns
                  with the nebulae
                              churning inside
every voice.
            This voice carries
                        everyone
even those
            who do not believe
                        they are returning
back
      to the source
                  of every voice.

Nominated by Curbstone Press

SHEPHERDESS

fiction by DAN CHAON

from THE VIRGINIA QUARTERLY REVIEW

1

THIS GIRL I'VE BEEN SEEING falls out of a tree one June evening. She's a little drunk—I bought a couple of bottles of hopefully decent Chardonnay from Trader Joe's on my way over to her house—and now she's a little drunk and a little belligerent. There is something about me that she doesn't like, and we've been arguing obliquely all evening. It's only our fifth real date, and though we've slept together once—it was the week after my mother died, pity sex, so it doesn't exactly count—we don't know each other that well.

For example, I just found out that she has an ex-husband who lives in Japan, who technically isn't an ex-husband since they haven't officially divorced.

For example, I didn't know that she thought I was a bad kisser: "Your kisses are unpleasantly moist," she says. "Has anyone ever told you that?"

"Actually, no," I say. "I've always gotten compliments on my kisses."

"Well," she says. "Women very rarely tell the truth."

I smile at her. "You're lying," I say, cleverly. But she doesn't seem to catch the interesting paradox. She looks at me blankly and downs the last bit of wine in her glass. Then she turns her attention to the tree that rises up alongside the railing of her deck, follows the trunk upward where it branches out, and locates her cat, Mr. Niffler, about ten feet above us where he has fled to escape the terror that is me,

330

his claws fixed tightly into the bark, an expression of dyspeptic alarm on his face.

"Mr. Niffler," she calls. "Kitty, kitty, kitty. What are you doing up there?" And then she gets up and goes to the base of the tree. She hoists herself up on the two-by-six ledge of the railing and stands there, teetering for a moment.

"You know," I say. "That doesn't seem like such a good idea."

2

My mother appears in the doorway, silhouetted in the morning light. Her dark hair stands up stiff, like a shrub. Smoke from her cigarette curls up. I'm half-awake but I can see how bony she is, a skeleton in a nightie, barely ninety pounds. She's not much heavier than the two Brittany spaniels that hover behind her—Lady and Peaches, my mother's dogs, watching as she wakes me, alert and so quiveringly shy around men that they sometimes pee a little when I speak to them. I can feel their tension as I stir in my bed.

"Okay," I murmur. "I'm up, I'm up." But my mother and her dogs just stand there. My mother is a few weeks away from her sixtieth birthday and I am nearly forty, but for a moment, here in my old teenaged room, we replay our roles from the past. She knows that if she leaves, I will roll over and go back to sleep. Lazybones.

So after a moment, I sit up. I'm an adult, and I wipe my fingers across my face. "What time is it?" I say, though she can't hear me.

She's been deaf for almost five years now. A freak infection shut her ears down despite various attempts at intervention by various doctors—but the truth is that in half a decade she hasn't done much to help herself. She stopped going to her lipreading classes early on, and forget about sign language or anything like that. She refuses to hang out with deaf people.

Mostly, to be honest, I don't know how she occupies herself. I don't know who her friends are or where she goes or what she does with her soundless days. The dogs make little anxious noises as I pull the covers off, and I watch as my mother turns, as her bare, crooked feet slide across the carpet toward the kitchen, where she will make me coffee and breakfast. It's about six in the morning, time for me to drive from Nebraska back to Los Angeles, where my fairly successful grown-up life is waiting for me.

I am between my second and third date with Rain at this point, and I'm looking forward to seeing her, things are going well I think. "I've met a girl I really like," I tell my mother. At the time, I have no idea that she will fall out of a tree. I have no idea that she thinks I am a bad kisser.

3

In the emergency room, there is a Plexiglas barrier between me and the receptionist, whose name tag says VALENCIA.

"I'm here with Rain Welsh," I tell her, and she asks me how to spell it. I have the purse and the billfold and I put Rain's driver's license and insurance card through the little mouth-hole at the bottom of the glass wall.

"Are you the husband?" Valencia asks me, and I shift awkwardly, looking at the stack of neatly rowed credit cards in Rain's billfold.

"I'm the boyfriend," I say. "I don't really know that much about her. She fell out of a tree."

"Please take a seat in the waiting area," Valencia says. She gestures toward the couches just beyond. A series of five Mexican children— boys and girls, aged approximately two to nine—are sitting politely together, watching a sitcom on the television mounted on the wall.

"Do you know how long it's going to be?" I ask Valencia. But that's not the right question. "Is she going to be all right?" I say, and our eyes meet for a moment. I am usually pretty good at these kinds of encounters—I have the face of a nice person—but Valencia doesn't approve.

"Take a seat," Valencia says. "I'll let the doctor know that you're waiting."

4

I've been talking to myself a lot lately. I don't know what that's about, but my mother was the same way. She hated to make small talk with other people, but get her into a conversation with herself and she was quite the raconteur. She would tell herself a joke and clap her hands together as she let out a laugh; she would murmur to the plants as she watered them, and offer encouragement to the food as she cooked it. Sometimes I would walk into a room and surprise her as she was regaling herself with some delightful story, and I remember how the sound would dry up in her mouth. She stood there, frozen in the headlights of my teenage scorn.

Now, as I close in on my fortieth birthday, I find myself doing a lot of the same sorts of things. An ant crawls up my leg and I say, "Excuse me? May I help you?" before I slap and crush it. I get up in the morning and narrate my way through the rituals of awakening. "Okay, we're taking a shower now," I whisper, and I mumble shampoo into my hair and toothpaste into my mouth and stand mesmerized in front of the coffee machine. At times, the procedure seems heartbreakingly complicated—grinding the beans into dust, separating the filter from the packet (which requires the same kind of fine motor skills as threading a needle), bringing water from the sink to the reservoir of the automatic coffee maker. My God, it's like building a house every morning, just to get a cup of coffee! I stand there at the counter holding my mug, waiting as the water burbles through its cycle and trickles into the pot. "Okay," I encourage softly. "Okay, go—Go!" At times I get very urgent with my coffee, as if I am watching a horse race that I have a lot of money riding on.

Now, in the emergency room parking lot, I am having a very involved talk with the contents of my girlfriend's purse. "I cannot believe this is happening," I mutter to the handbag, confidentially. "This is ridiculous," I say, and then I find what I'm looking for. "Well, hello, beautiful," I say, to a crumpled pack of extra-long, extra-thin, feminine cigarettes: *Misty*, they are called.

5

My mother collapses on the floor of her bedroom. She is perhaps on her way to the bathroom or to let the dogs out. I am sleeping in a motel outside of Provo, headed back to L.A., and she lies there unconscious, her face pressed against the carpet. The dogs are anxious, pacing from the bedroom to the back door in delicate circles, nosing my mother with their muzzles, whimpering introspectively. They lower themselves beside her and rest their heads against her side as her breathing slows and she goes into a coma. They lick her salty skin.

She is still alive when her neighbor friend comes by the next morning. The dogs have relieved themselves in the kitchen, unable to control their bladders any longer, and they hide in shame under the bed as the neighbor friend calls my mother's name. "Mary Ann!

Mary Ann!" the friend, Mrs. Fowler, calls. Even though my mother has been deaf for as long as they've known each other, Mrs. Fowler nevertheless continues to speak at her—loudly, steadily determined, oblivious. When she sees my mother on the floor, she screams like a maid in a murder mystery.

When I get back to Los Angeles, there is a message waiting for me on my answering machine. "Charles," Mrs. Fowler will recite in her most declamatory voice. "This Is Mrs. Fowler. Your Mother's Friend. I Am Sorry To Have To Tell You That She Is In The Hospital, And Very Ill."

After I've listened to the message a few times, I get on the cell phone and call Rain. "Listen," I say. "It looks like I'm going to have to cancel our date again. You won't believe this but I have to fly back to Nebraska. My mom's in the hospital! It must have happened practically the minute I left!"

"Oh my God," she says. Her voice is soft with concern, actually very warm and—though we've only dated briefly—seemingly full of genuine tenderness. I imagine her touching my hand, stroking my forearm. She has beautiful dark brown eyes, the ineffable sadness of a girl who drinks too much. I'm drawn to that.

"Actually," I say, "I think my mom's going to die. I just have this feeling."

"Go," Rain says, firmly. "Just get on that plane and go to her," Rain says. "Call me when you get there."

6

I know that she is going to fall, but I'm not sure how to stop her. I stand there with my hands clasped awkwardly behind my back as she shimmies unsteadily up the tree toward her cat. "You know," I say, and clear my throat. "Rain, honey, that doesn't seem like such a good idea." She pauses for a moment, as if she's listening to reason; and then, abruptly, she loses her hold on the branch. I watch as her body plunges down like a piece of fruit, not flailing or screaming or even surprised, but simply an expressionless weight coursing to earth. She hits the edge of the deck's railing, knocking over a plant, and I say: "Oh my God!" And then she lands on her back. "Oh my God," I say again, and finally have the sense to move toward the flower bed where she has come to rest.

"Are you hurt?" I say, leaning over her, and for a moment she doesn't open her eyes. I take her hand and squeeze it and a tear expels itself from beneath her eyelid and runs down her face.

The wind has been knocked out of her, and at first her voice is hinged and creaky. "I'm so embarrassed," she whispers, wheezing. "I'm such an idiot."

"No, no," I say. "Don't worry about it."

But she begins to cry. "Ow," she says. "It really hurts!"

I bend down and kiss her on the mouth, comfortingly. "It's okay," I murmur, and run my hand over her hair. But she flinches, and her eyes widen.

"What are you doing?" she gasps. "I can't feel my legs." And then she begins to cry harder, her mouth contorting with a grimace of sorrow like a child's. "Don't touch me!" She cries. "I can't feel my legs! I can't feel my fucking legs!"

7

Another hour passes. The five children and I sit in the waiting area and watch television together, and I keep my eye on them. These children seem to know what they're doing, whereas I have never been in a hospital waiting room before. Rain's purse sits in my lap and the children laugh politely along with the prerecorded laughter on the soundtrack of a comedy show.

I am not really sure how I am supposed to behave in this situation. I can't help but think that I should be sitting at Rain's bedside, pressing her damp hand between my palms. I should be arguing vehemently with doctors, demanding results, I should be surrounded by people who are bleeding and screaming and shocking one another with defibrillators. I sit there for a while longer, imagining this romantic pandemonium, and then finally I go to stand in line at the reception booth again.

When I sit down in the chair opposite the bulletproof glass, Valencia stares at me grimly. "Yes?" she says, as if she has never seen me before.

"Hi," I say. "I was just checking on the status of Rain Welsh. I've been sitting here for a while and I hadn't heard anything so I thought . . ."

"And you are . . . ?" Valencia says.

"I'm the boyfriend. I'm the one that called the ambulance. I've been sitting right over there waiting because you said . . ."

But she is already looking away, staring at her computer screen, which faces away from me, typing a little burst of fingernail clicks onto her keyboard. Pausing, pursing her lips. Typing again. Pausing to consider. Typing again.

"She's in x-ray right now," Valencia tells me at last, after several minutes.

"Well," I say. "Do you have any idea how long it's going to be? I mean, do you have any idea what the situation is? I've been sitting here patiently for a long time now, and I'd just like to know . . ."

"That's all the information I have, sir," Valencia murmurs firmly, and gives me a look that says: *Are you going to give me trouble? Because I know how to handle troublemakers.*

"So I guess I'll just wait," I say. "I'll just wait right over here."

8

No smoking on hospital grounds, so I head out to the bus stop, on the sidewalk just beyond the parking lot, and stand there to smoke one of the nasty Mistys that I found in the purse. It has a perfumey, mentholated flavor, like a cough drop dissolved in Earl Grey tea.

I had no idea that Rain smoked, and in some ways this makes me like her more. The fact that she was shy about it, that she wanted to hide it from me. That's kind of sweet.

I've always liked the idea of smoking more than I liked the actual smoke. Watching someone in a movie smoke, for example, is a lot more pleasant than waking after a pack of cigarettes and coughing up a yellow-green slug of phlegm.

But nevertheless I have a predilection for it. My mother was a fiercely committed smoker, and, growing up, I probably ingested half-a-pack-a-day's worth of secondhand smoke. I've always found cigarettes comforting, a taste of childhood, the way some people feel about Kellogg's cereal or Jell-O or Vicks VapoRub.

I'm just about finished with my smoke when I look up and see three women coming toward me. The women are being led out of the emergency room in their gowns and slippers, pushing their wheeled IV stands down the sidewalk. The IV stands look like bare silver coatracks; a clear plastic bag full of clear liquid hangs from each one, and a tube runs from each bag to each woman's arm. They walk along, single file, followed by an orderly who is talking on a cell phone. When they get close to me, they all stop, take out packs of cigarettes, and light up.

It's pretty surreal, I guess. I didn't realize that such things were allowed, but apparently they are desperate enough for nicotine that someone (the orderly, smoking himself) has decided to take pity on them. Has sneaked them out the back door for a quick fix.

This isn't, after all, the fanciest neighborhood in the world, nor the nicest of emergency rooms. The women are all poor to working-class, grim-faced, clearly having a bad day, and I can't help but think of my mother—who wouldn't go anywhere unless she could smoke. Had, in fact, once left a hospital in outrage because they refused to give her a "smoking room."

I stand up, gentlemanly, and nod as the women approach.

"Hello, ladies," I say. "Beautiful evening."

Having grown up kind of poor-to-working-class myself, I can't help but feel a kind of kinship with them. "You really romanticize the white-trash period of your life," Rain once said to me, which I thought was a little hurtful but—perhaps true.

There is, for example, this blond woman who reminds me of my mother's side of the family—all sharp cheekbones and shoulder blades, sinewy muscle, a body built for hardscrabble living—and I smile companionably at her as she breathes smoke into the night air. She is gazing off toward some cheap apartment buildings in the distance, the vertical rows of identical balconies, and I stare out with her. Together we look up and see the moon.

9

As expected, she's dead by the time I get there. By the time my plane touches down she's being moved from the hospital to the funeral home, and her friend Mrs. Fowler calls me on my cell phone as I'm standing in line at the rental-car place.

"Charles," Mrs. Fowler says. "Would you go and sit down somewhere for me, honey? Sit down in a comfortable chair." And then her voice breaks. "I have some terrible news."

About two hours later, I pull into the driveway of my mother's house in my rented car and it still hasn't sunk in.

The death of a parent is one of those momentous occasions, one of the big events of your life, but what do you *do*, exactly? My father died when I was three, so I barely even remember it, and my ex-wife's mother passed away during the early, happiest years of our marriage, and I had to do hardly anything at all, I just stood by looking sympathetic and supportive and people would occasionally nod at me or pat me on the shoulder.

So: sinking in. I sit there in my car, idling in the driveway, and I try to remember exactly what went on at the funeral of my late ex-mother-in-law but my mind has gone completely blank. Here is the door of my mom's house, well-remembered childhood portal. Here is the yard, and a set of wires that runs from the house to a wooden pole, and some fat birds sitting together on the wires, five of them lined up like beads on an abacus.

I left home when I was eighteen—more than twenty years have passed!—and though I came back dutifully every year, the connections that held us together grew more threadbare as time went on.

I can remember being about five or six and running around and around that lilac bush in the front yard, chased by Mother. Laughing, joyous, etc.

I turn off the ignition in the rental car and after a minute I take out my cell phone and call Rain.

I don't know why. We seem to have connected; she seems like a very bright, sensitive, caring woman.

"This is Rain," she says. She is in the middle of directing a commercial, a public-service announcement about teen suicide, and her voice has an official snap to it.

"I need some advice," I say. "I'm not sure what to do."

"Charlie?" she says, and I love the way that she says my name, a matter-of-fact tenderness.

"My mom's dead," I tell her.

10

A little past midnight, the television has been shut off and the children in the waiting room are huddled together in a row on the chairs, leaned up against one another smallest to largest, sound asleep.

How long are people expected to wait in these places? No one seems to know the answer, though as time has passed I've tried to engage some of my fellow waiters in conversation on the subject.

"I've been waiting here for five hours," I disclose, and people regard me with varying degrees of commiseration. "Does that seem normal?" I ask them. I don't know why I do this: why, after all these years in Los Angeles, I still have the Nebraskan's urge to banter with strangers.

I seem vaguely familiar to people, which is frequently a kind of advantage, particularly in Los Angeles. They are always asking: *Do I know you from somewhere?* And I shrug modestly. Probably they have recognized my voice from television commercials, or—especially if they have children—from one of several popular animated series such as *Fuzzy Fieldmouse and Friends*. One of my specialties is the earnest, disarmingly boyish voice. "I don't know if I can do it," Fuzzy Fieldmouse often says. "But I know I can try!" Anyone who watches children's programming on public television has no doubt heard me utter this phrase.

Which is not to say that this gives me any particular leverage in a situation such as this one. It's not as if I can throw my weight around with Valencia: "Do you realize that I am the voice of Fuzzy Fieldmouse?"—doesn't exactly open many doors. Though I have to admit that I am used to being a little better liked than I have been tonight. Valencia has glanced over at me once, but when I gave her a little hopeful wave her face went still and her gaze swept past. When I finally managed to catch her eye she emanated a serene kind of inhospitality, like Antarctica or deep space.

And so another hour has passed when a man comes out of the Authorized Personnel area to wake the children.

"Little ones," the man whispers, and I watch as head by head they lift their sleepy faces. "Do you want to go back and see mommy?" the orderly says. "Your mommy wants to see you guys."

It's kind of heartbreaking how delighted the poor kids are, how excited they are to see the mommy. *Yes! Oh yes!* They beam, and the girl of about four actually does a little hopping bunny dance, and the orderly gives me an indulgent look. "Cute," he says.

It occurs to me at that moment that no one will stop me if I follow them. I can just walk right through along with them, just shadow them past the AUTHORIZED PERSONNEL sign, past the security guard who stands holding the door open for them, following along as if I might be some kind of guardian, an uncle, perhaps, a neighbor or family friend.

Amazingly, no one says a word. I just line up behind the tiniest child and march right through, the security guard even smiles respectfully at me as if to acknowledge that, hey, I'm a good guy, to be

339

watching over these children. I glance over my shoulder at Valencia, and she's chatting with someone on the phone; she isn't even looking.

11

Shortly before she falls out of the tree, I think Rain is getting ready to break up with me. We have been circling around that sort of conversation all evening long.

She has been telling me about her husband. "Your ex-husband?" I say, and she says no, actually, they are still married, it's just that he has been living in Japan for the past year and they're going through a period of questioning. Deciding what to do, letting things drift, and so forth. "You know what I mean," Rain says, and takes a long drink from her glass of Chardonnay.

"Um," I say, and consider. "Hmm," I say. Did I know what she meant? Up until the moment that she told me about the husband, I'd thought things were going pretty well between us—so perhaps not.

"I'm a little surprised," I tell her. "About the husband thing."

She sighs. "I know," she says. "I realize that I should have told you. But—you know. All this stuff with your mother and so on. You seemed like you were in a very fragile state."

"Fraj-*ile*," I say, pronouncing it the way that she does—as if it might be a popular tourist destination in the Pacific, beautiful Fraj Isle with its white sandy beaches and shark-filled coves.

It's the kind of conversation that reminds me of my own former marriage, which fell apart abruptly, perhaps similarly, with a series of emotional signals that I had completely failed to interpret.

"Surely you realized how unhappy I've been for the past few years," my ex-wife murmured, and I recall this as Rain tilts another few ounces of wine into her glass.

12

The rooms where the patients are being kept are not exactly the way they appear on television. Everything very subdued, people huddled individually in their little warrens with the flimsy curtains pulled partway closed.

I fall back as the children are led toward the cubicle where their mother is awaiting them—no one has stopped me or even seems to notice that I'm here, and it appears that actually once you make it past Valencia that's pretty much all there is. Still, I'm feeling a bit wary. I slow my pace, let the children pitter-patter away. I try to peer surreptitiously into the little curtained roomlets, looking for Rain.

I can't help but think of the pens in an animal shelter, the stricken, doomy look of the strays as you pass by, that sense that it's a bad idea to make eye contact or pause.

I drift past several dreadfully intimate tableaux, trying to avert my eyes. Behind one curtain is the melancholy glare of a bleeding, tattooed hip-hop guy, emasculated by cotton smock with periwinkle pattern; behind another is the skeletal old man (woman?) in an oxygen mask, whose gaze of biblical despair trails along beside me as I pass.

"Hello," I say, at last, to a woman with a clipboard—my heart is beating very fast, I'm feeling as if I'm having a kind of panic attack, wouldn't that be a laugh?—"Hello," I say, whispering exaggeratedly, as if the nurse is an usher at a matinee I'm interrupting. "I'm looking for a woman named Rain Welsh—"

And then—as if I have been led directly to her curtained doorstep—there she is, I see her only a few yards away. She is sitting propped in her bed, wearing a neck brace and a metal halo that encircles her forehead, frozen there into an alert, attentive posture the way statues of empresses sit in their thrones.

"Charlie?" she says, and she watches with a kind of dreamy abstraction as I come toward her. It's not clear if she's glad to see me, but I hold up her purse like a treat: Look what I brought for you!

"Hey, sweetheart," I say, still in my whispery voice. "How are you?"

"Eh," she says. It seems like it takes her a lot of effort to compose a sentence. "I don't know. They've got me on pain meds, so I can't really tell."

"But you're okay," I say, encouragingly. "You're not paralyzed or anything, right?" I say this and then I realize that it has been a fantasy hovering in the back of my mind: what if she's paralyzed? Would I be courageous enough to stick with a wheelchair girl? Would I be amazingly, fiercely loyal, would she love me for it, marry me, etc.? I can feel this scenario passing again briefly through my future and my smile stiffens.

"Charlie," she says. "What are you doing here? It's two o'clock in the morning."

"I don't know," I say. "I couldn't exactly leave you."

"Oh," she says—her voice a dreamy, medicated sigh. "Oh, Charlie. I told them to tell you. You should just go home."

"Well," I say. "I'm just trying to be, you know. A good guy."

"I appreciate that," she says, "but—" and her brain seems to drift along down the stream for a ways before she lifts her head. "But honestly, I've been thinking. This is," she says, "really not working out between us. I've been meaning to tell you for a while that . . ."

She closes her eyes for a moment, five seconds, ten seconds, and when she opens them again it seems that she has lost her train of thought. She smiles up at me fondly, as if I'm an old dear friend she hasn't seen in a long time. "Did I tell you, Charlie? My husband is flying back from Japan! I'm going to be in traction for a few weeks and he's flying home to be with me."

I consider this for a moment. "Wow," I say. "That's wonderful," I say.

"Oh, I'm so sorry," she says, and I watch as she closes her eyes, blissful as a sleepy child. "I wanted our last night together to be . . ."

I wait for her to finish her sentence, but now she appears to be completely asleep, and her expression slackens and sags. "Rain?" I say, and I adjust the blanket on her bed, straighten the wrinkles underneath her hand. For a moment, I imagine that I could just sit here and talk, the way Mrs. Fowler used to talk to my mother, my mother sitting there deafly, the two of them watching TV, Mrs. Fowler chatting away.

I have this concept going around in my head, I would love to try to get it off my chest, but when I start to talk she makes a little sad face in her sleep. She moans lightly.

At last, I set Rain's purse on the bed at her feet. Her cigarettes are still tucked in my pocket.

13

This is one of those things that you can never explain to anyone, that's what I want to explain—one of those free-association moments with connections that dissolve when you start to try to put them into words.

But I consider it for a moment, trying to map it out. Look: Here is a china knickknack on my mother's coffee table, right next to her favorite ashtray. A shepherdess, I guess—a figurine with blond sausage curls and a low-cut bodice and petticoats, holding a crook, a staff, in one hand and carrying a lamb under her arm—a more mature Bo Peep, I suppose, and when I am eleven years old I will notice for the first time the way her porcelain neckline dips down to reveal the full slopes of her porcelain breasts. Years later, when I am nearing forty, I will notice a woman in a hospital gown and slippers walking through the parking lot of an emergency room, holding her IV stand like the crook a shepherdess carries, and I will lean over my sleeping ex-girlfriend and try to explain how I found myself in a Möbius strip of memory, traveling in a figure eight out of the parking lot and cruising past the glimmering sexual fantasies of an eleven-year-old noticing the boobs on a porcelain figurine and then curving back again to find myself in my mother's house, a few days after her funeral, hesitating as I'm about to drop the shepherdess into a plastic trash bag full of my mother's other useless belongings.

Alone in my mother's house, I am ruthless with her possessions. I live in an apartment in Venice, California, and I don't have enough room for my own stuff. For example, what should be done with an old cigar box full of buttons and beads that she has inexplicably kept? The collection of whimsical salt and pepper shakers? The cards and letters, the dresses wrapped in plastic in the closet, unfinished needlework, clippings from newspapers, her high-school yearbooks, her grade-school report cards, a doll she loved when she was two, all the accumulation she stuffed into drawers and boxes and the corners of closets? What can I do but throw it away? Though at last I spare the little shepherdess, I stick it in my pocket and eventually I'll find a place for it on my own coffee table.

The dogs, Lady and Peaches, are not so lucky. They hide from me most of the time that I am cleaning out the house. They sleep under-neath my mother's bed, crouching there as I haul bag after bag of junk out into the daylight, as I dismantle furniture and leave bare rooms in my wake. At last, almost finished, I tempt them out of their lair with a trail of luncheon meat that leads to a dog cage, and when I close the metal door behind them, they gaze out through the bars at me with a dull, grief-stricken stare. They are older dogs, and it seems cruel to take them to the pound, to try to find some new home for them after all the years they spent with my mother. Still, I don't look them in the eyes again. I do not stick around as the veterinarian "puts them to sleep," as they say, one after the other, with an injec-tion of sodium pentobarbital. I drop the dogs off at the veterinarian's office and drive away, back toward California, and driving along the interstate I realize that this is something I will probably never tell anyone, ever.

Perhaps such things will accumulate more and more from now on, I think. More and more there will be things I can never explain to anyone. More and more I'll find myself lost in parking lots at four in the morning, stepping through the rows upon rows, the long sea of vehicles spreading out beneath a canopy of halogen streetlights, and me with no idea whatsoever where my car might be. I'll find myself pressing the teeny button on my car's automatic antitheft alarm system. "Where are you?" I will whisper to myself. "Where are you?" Until at last, in the distance, I will hear the car alarm begin to emit its melancholy, birdlike reply.

Nominated by Martha Collins

TO THE SEA AT CADIZ

by PHILIP LEVINE

from TIKKUN

Tonight the land wind,
the Terral, works into the face
of the waves, spilling them back
one after another until music—
a wordless humming—rises
toward a moon that barely is.
On the run from a war not his,
my father arrived in the autumn
of 1919 and found a moon
here, full and promising,
and the wind blasting the sea's
breath into his lungs. Did
he think he could redeem
the lost years, did he weigh
his chances only to find water
in one hand, salt in the other?
I know he never returned.
He swapped forged passports
with an American and began
a life flogging Kosher table goods
in the Tri-state territories, married,
fathered three sons and died
in his thirties. Now I'm here

to beg the air to calm down,
the waves to freeze, the moon
to settle into the black waters.
Why? So I can be heard
by someone? Thirty-five years ago
in the high Sierras I asked
the wind-filled mountain oaks
to hold their breath long enough
for my words to return to me
as answered prayers. Overhead
an indifferent winter sun went
on falling below the coastal peaks
while the earth turned toward
other obligations. I came
down slowly, in no way smarter
than before. If my father were
here now he'd laugh to learn
a son with twice his years and half
his wits retraced all the wrong
steps to this sea and this night.
A single gull—my totem tonight—
circles above, lost or impatient,
to tell me another morning's on
the way with its gaudy light shows,
its cool new winds from the west,
its dawn songs, rumbling dirges,
their lyrics in the old language
of water, salt, and battered breath.

Nominated by Len Roberts, Christopher Buckley, David St. John,

Charles Harper Webb, Tikkun

OVERWINTERING
IN FAIRBANKS

by ERICA KEIKO ISERI

from THE NORTH DAKOTA QUARTERLY

LAYER BY LAYER I put on my winter gear—expedition weight Capilene top and bottom, snowpants, down parka, double-layered modular gloves that come almost to my elbow. I wear my heavy black Sorels, the kind some call hundred-below boots, a bright blue hat. I don't have a facemask so I wrap my polar fleece scarf around my head. I live in the Goldstream Valley where cold settles, stretches out for winters. My thermometer goes to -40 and I haven't seen any mercury for days. I tell Lucky to stay inside—she looks disappointed but obeys, as she always does, and lies down on her pad beneath the table. She is 13 and grew up with me in LA and her face is swollen with cancer and her body is gradually giving up. The two huskies though, their undercoats thick, run out in front of me, chasing each other down the driveway.

I have been spending most of my time lately with my dogs, preferring their constant company over people. I have learned to distrust human loyalty.

I whistle for the dogs as I walk around the corner of the cabin. I pass the outhouse and arrive at a small clearing, close enough that lights from the cabin will be visible but far enough to be hidden from the road. The two dogs run past, their powerful hind legs propelling them through the deep snow. Sally, a three-year-old malamute, is the most recent addition to my household which also includes a black cat, Kuro, who spends her time sleeping on my plates in the cupboard. Sally had been on the short list for euthanasia at the local pound when I met her there, having stopped by to give them the kibble that Lucky no longer ate. The tips of both her ears are missing, perhaps from frostbite, maybe a dog fight. Her nipples hung down from her skinny belly; she was lactating, the shelter worker said. They had no idea where her pups were as she had been alone when they caught her. She had looked at me with yellow eyes, skittish, unsure. That was winter solstice and Sally came home with me the same day we began to regain sunlight at four minutes a pop.

Although Sally's admission to my family was unplanned, I had been vaguely looking for a new dog when I found Kobi. I hadn't wanted a puppy—who has time for a puppy?—but I needed help coping with Lucky's slow decline. Kobi, another shelter dog, was a seven-week-old butterball, all fur and puppy breath. She is part Mackenzie River husky, a small part wolf. The vet predicted she could easily be a seventy-pound dog—Mackenzie River huskies, though not a registered breed, are big freight dogs that traditionally pulled heavy sleds in the Yukon Territory. I named her Yorokobi, joy in Japanese. Her wing-like ears still haven't decided whether to stand erect or not and her round brown eyes are doe-like.

When I first brought Sally home, her fur was dingy and she crouched, belly to ground, whenever I was near. She wouldn't take food from my hand, and I had to lay it down before she would slink over and wolf it. I wondered what sort of life she had led up to now that she sometimes yelped in fear when I placed my hand on her back. If I made a sudden motion, she cowered as if I was going to hit her. I learned about what body language means to dogs—kneeling down, turning sideways, and averting my eyes are all ways of letting her know that I am her friend. I could tell from the warmth of her eyes that she wanted to trust me, but others in whom she had placed her eager trust had obviously let her down. I can understand this distrust.

A year ago I gathered all the pills I could find in my cabin. I didn't know what would be a lethal dose, though I thought that if I took everything I could, I might fall into a sleep deep enough that my heart would stop. I sat for several minutes in my bed, opening child-proof caps and foil packets, putting all the pills into a teacup. There were large green gelcaps, small blue and white pills, round white chalky ones. I don't remember what they were all for, cold, fever, headache, cramps.

I sat in bed and swallowed the pills two, three at a time, taking big swigs from a bottle of water. Then I lay down to sleep, tried to examine how I was feeling. It seemed that I could hear my blood flowing, the pills dissolving in my stomach.

I don't know how much later I woke up, just that I woke up feeling more sick than I had ever thought possible. I had a small bucket by my bed and I threw up into it prodigiously. I wasn't able to get up out of bed, just lean over and vomit into the bucket, over and over. There wasn't a lot of food in my stomach, but what there was came up in chunks that I could feel passing between my teeth. After a short while there was only spit and bile coming up, and it seemed I had those in healthy supply. I vomited like a magician pulling handkerchiefs from a pocket. I would lie back after a World Series round of retching and feel the sickness all over my body. I wanted to cry but didn't have enough energy. I wanted to die—anything would be better than the feeling of the medicine, the poison swirling in my stomach. It lasted for what seemed like hours. It wasn't like being sick from too much alcohol. Tequila vomit hits me like a semi, trampling me under extra large wheels and flinging me against a tree, leaving me lying in a ditch, broken but oblivious. This vomit was insipid. It was like ivy choking an old building over decades, twining around my spine, traveling up each vertebra, curling its spiny fingers around the base of my neck, slowly crushing its way toward my nervous system. It was like a subterranean river carving through limestone, seeping into the folds of my brain and prying individual cells apart. Caverns formed within my body, spelunkers danced within my fingers.

I was sick, and I remember having only one actual thought. "What a great big fucking joke this would be," I said to myself, perhaps out loud, "if I wake up tomorrow morning and I feel just fine."

And I did wake up, and although I didn't feel just fine, I felt okay. I woke up and the sun was shining through the windows, my neighbor was starting his car. I caught a whiff of the vomit and carried the bucket outside, not looking at it. I turned it over into the snow behind the cabin. Out of the corner of my eye I saw the snow grow an alarming green under the bucket, a shocking, bright, gelcap green.

It was after first snowfall two years ago that I noticed Lucky's urine was red. I took a sample to my vet and was told she had transitional cell carcinoma. I got off the phone with the vet and looked down at my dog leaning against me, her cataract-clouded eyes closed while I

349

scratched behind her ears. She had been a shelter pup, and I had been nine. For four years while I went to school in Fairbanks, she lived alone with my parents, bored in the backyard, slowly losing interest in life. Arthritis plagued her and her left hind leg shook constantly. I brought her to Alaska as soon as I was living in a place that allowed pets and let her be a dog, exploring in the woods, chasing squirrels, riding in my car with her tongue lolling out and drooling on the windows. And then she began to urinate blood, violent red on the new snow.

I sat with my arm around my dog and she leaned against me, her neck wrapped against mine, sighing contentedly. The vet put her on antibiotics and an arthritis med that was effective for her type of cancer. Her leg stopped shaking, and she was almost young again.

But then, in August, a tumor began to grow in her mouth that made her look like she was sucking on a piece of hard candy. I took her to the vet at least every couple of weeks, checking and rechecking her progress. The tumor grew slowly and several medications were added to her regimen. I threw down my credit card, asking for anything that would help her.

And then one day she didn't want to eat. I had been feeding her only canned food, and now I scooped mouthfuls for her with my hand, pleading with her to eat. I heated up the dog food, ransacked my cabinets for anything she would eat, went to the grocery store and bought meat for her—hot dogs, chicken breasts, cold cuts. Sometimes she ate, sometimes I had to coax her, holding the food in my hand under her nose, sometimes she simply refused. Her tumor was getting larger, extending along her snout, under her throat. I called the vet. We decided to try chemotherapy.

I dropped Lucky off in the morning and picked her up in the afternoon. She was a little weak, happy to see me. A patch of fur on her right foreleg had been shaved off to give her the injection of chemotherapy. A week later she had another injection and came home with a matching shaved patch on her left foreleg. She was losing weight.

The tumor began to necrose in her mouth and the stench of the dead tissue filled the cabin. Unable to control the saliva around the growth in her mouth, she drooled when she lay down, leaving wet, foul-smelling circles. I mopped at her mouth with cotton balls, removing grayish saliva hot with dead cancer cells. I washed the dog beds, my sheets, the carpets, the couch, over and over.

In a stand of alder brush, I find a branch that looks long enough and use the saw blade of a Swiss Army knife to cut it down, do the same for another six-foot branch. I plunge one of the branches vertically into the snow roughly in the middle of a clearing—it sinks almost six inches. We have had an unusual amount of snow this winter. I lay the other pole on the ground and walk a circle around the vertical one, twelve feet in diameter. I leave the pole as a radius line within the circle. It will be a guide when I begin to dig out the snow cave. Feeling like a child throwing a tantrum, I tamp down the snow within the circle, hopping around in my heavy boots.

My fingers and toes begin to hurt. In temperatures this cold, it doesn't matter how thick my socks, how insulated my gloves—I will either have to start exercising soon or go back inside. I don't own a shovel so I have brought out the scoop I use to pick up my cat's litter and a five-gallon utility bucket that the kitty litter came in and wonder vaguely what I would have used if I didn't own a cat. I begin throwing snow onto the circle I have packed down, piling it around the vertical pole. The progress is slow and several times I stop, drawing my face down into the scarf, ball my hands into the palms of the gloves, curl my toes under.

The snow is loose and dry and I am able to scoop and then throw it easily. I wonder how long I will be able to continue before my back begins to ache. My scarf is damp from the condensation of my breath, and I can see wisps of my hair frosted white. My eyelashes are frosted as well and I can feel the cold in the corners of my eyes. My nose runs from the exertion and I do not try to wipe it away; instead, it freezes around my nostrils and along my upper lip. My fingers and my toes begin to warm up and they don't hurt anymore. I work steadily for an hour piling snow, but the mound does not develop as quickly as I had thought it would. That's a lot of snow I'm moving, I think to myself. But it's not, really—avalanches and the city of Valdez move a lot of snow. But with my scoop and my bucket, a child making sand castles at the beach, the job takes on mammoth proportions.

I look around and don't see my dogs. I walk back to the cabin where I find them huddled by the door, excited to be let back in. What a bunch of wimps, I tell them. You're supposed to be snow dogs. I open the door and they run in, grateful for the warmth. Kobi's paws click on the ground like she is wearing hard-soled shoes and I take off my gloves to dig out the ice balls that have formed between her toes. Sally settles onto a dog bed in front of the heater and falls asleep.

Leaving the dogs inside, I continue to build the snow cave. This time, having used up all the snow within throwing range, I scoop snow onto a plastic sled, five bucketfuls at a time, drag the sled to the slowly-growing mound, and dump it on top. The hill grows more quickly. It is getting dark. Days still aren't that long.

It wasn't the pills that landed me so decisively in the hospital. Several days after the teacup was a night that was the kind of clear that comes from being cold. It is mostly only this clearness, though, that I can remember. On Noatak Drive, just before it turns into Sheep Creek Road, just past the Experimental Farm, I stood in the dark next to my car holding a box of ammunition I had bought at Fred Meyer the week before. The bullets seemed to glow in the darkness. There was a 30.06 rifle in the trunk.

In the car was a man, the man who had decided he did not love me anymore. This thought filled me with fear and desperation and self-loathing. My intentions, as much as I can pin them down, was to threaten to shoot myself and have him stop me. This would make him love me again and happily ever after. I am unclear about what happens next. I know that I never got the gun loaded, that he took the bullets out of my hand and threw them deep into the woods. The gun, too, he took from me, ran down the road with it. I may have left him there in the dark while I drove back to my cabin.

Once I got there, I pushed a heavy table against the door and fell into bed. Some time later, two state troopers came and knocked, and I didn't get up. They shone their flashlights into my windows, saw me huddled under the covers. They called to me, they asked me to please let them in. After a time, maybe when I realized that they wouldn't go away, I opened the door and they came inside. They seemed large and out of place in my cabin. Their boots were heavy on the plywood floor, their belts squeaked when they moved. They said they had to take me to the hospital.

Apologetically, one of the troopers, young, not yet thirty, placed handcuffs around my wrists and strapped me into the backseat of his squad car. Protocol, he said. I tried to make conversation with him, to joke with him. It was four or five in the morning.

"Hey, I think that this seat should be more uncomfortable. Could you maybe put in a req for that?" I asked him. The seats were made of molded plastic to make wiping things up easier, he told me. He had that restrained good humor typical of police officers trying to be nice. Cops hide behind phrases like "the parties," "she stated to me," "at the time," trying to sound professional, thinking they come off as sincere. But I suppose that's not too different from me hiding behind a door jammed closed by a table.

It took a long time to drive to the hospital, going the speed limit, checking out other cars in the radar. Any hint of joviality evaporated, though, as soon as we got to the parking lot. It was bright out, the air cold, and in it I could feel the crisp of the time between dawn and when the world wakes. He opened the door for me and undid the straps, a freakish mockery of all the amusement park rides I'd ever been on. I stepped out into the clear air, though, and felt once again afraid. Two of my students worked at the hospital—what if they saw me? I gritted my teeth, trying not to cry, drawing my head as far down into my shoulders as I could. I held my handcuffed wrists before me as if they could shield me. The trooper led me into the hospital and admitted me. Voluntary Title 47, he called me.

I spent a week in the hospital, refusing to speak to anyone I knew, especially my parents who kept calling. They gave me Prozac, I had sessions with several psychologists, but in the rotation of three or four doctors later, I didn't feel they were telling me anything I couldn't figure out myself. One day, during a session with a new doctor, I kept looking at her feet. She had on a pair of gray, new-looking Merrell hiking boots that looked ridiculously large on her. They were grotesque in their magnitude. I imagined her stomping around in these gargantuan hiking boots, carelessly exterminating biota. She could decimate Angel Rocks with one well-placed roundhouse kick. I couldn't suppress a giggle. She asked me what was funny, and I said her shoes and laughed out loud. I asked her if I could go home. She said that perhaps I should stay for another day or so.

Bored one day, I folded several origami cranes that I brought to the front counter of the mental health ward. I shuffled over in my hospital gown and slippers, fluttered the cranes onto the nurses' clipboards, and said that they had flown in through the windows. One of the nurses followed me back to the common room, looking around. She said, "The windows in here don't open." I said, "I know."

I spent that summer in California with my parents. I threw away

353

the Prozac. I told my mother I didn't want to see any doctors, even though the hospital in Fairbanks had recommended it. I left with almost a month to go in the spring semester, threw away all of my responsibilities, the ones that had seemed so daunting that I wanted to put a bullet through my brain rather than deal with them. Someone took over my teaching, a friend took in my dog and my cat. I took an incomplete in my classes. I spent three months in Southern California, longer than I had ever been back since I left to go to college when I was seventeen. I had no responsibilities all summer. I did what I felt like. I cooked, I cross-stitched, I watched a lot of late night TV. I spent time with my sister and her husband in San Diego. I helped her pick out a new kitten, walked her dog.

I add an arctic headlamp to my ensemble, its battery pack hanging under my jacket from a little pouch around my neck so my body heat will conserve its energy. Working steadily, I continue piling snow around the poles for a few hours, dumping sledfuls countless times. My back aches. Although the vertical pole is not yet covered, the hill is almost six feet tall and I decide that it is enough.

I am to let the snow pile sit for several hours. I leave it though for the night, too tired to start digging, and the next day, I take the kitty litter scoop and begin to dig out the cave. This part goes quickly, the snow easily worked loose and hauled away. Eventually I am able to sit inside the cave and carve away at the walls and ceiling. As I scrape away layers of snow, I am reminded of my mother. According to her, one's soul, one's heart, is like a block of soap and life is the carver of that soap. Every day, with every stress or problem, a sliver comes off; tragedy gouges at the soap. The goal, she says, is to keep the scraped-off pieces small and in control. I think most people don't know what shape their soap is in—I had no idea mine had gotten so little.

I sit inside the hut, careful to keep the walls at least two feet thick in order to support the weight of the snow. The inside should be smooth so that any melted snow will run down the walls instead of dripping into the hut. I replace the headlamp with a small glass and metal lantern that holds a votive candle, giving off plenty of light in the small cave.

On my first morning in the hospital, while I lay in bed, a breakfast tray growing cold next to me, exhausted yet unable to sleep, unable to believe that I was actually in a mental health ward, a nurse asked me if I would like to speak to the chaplain. I thought I told her no, but the next day, he came to see me, a cross on his nametag and a bible in hand.

He told me he enjoyed fishing and that he had put some full-spectrum lights into his house because the darkness sometimes got to him. He had a round, pink, freshly-scrubbed face. His hair was a bright white, as was his mustache. He was very handsome.

He talked to me the way the doctors, even the nurses, didn't. He didn't talk to me like it was part of his job. Instead, he actually talked to me. And we didn't talk about God, he didn't tell me he would pray for me. Instead I told him about my mother's soap theory. Before I went in hospital, I felt as if I was constantly washing with my soap, lathered and losing shape, getting washed down the drain. I told him that I knew I wasn't revolutionary—I wasn't going to change the world. But the soap was all I had, and I desperately needed for it to stop getting smaller.

Of all the strangers I encountered that week, he was the only one who I felt comfortable with. I appreciated what everyone else was doing for me, but the chaplain was the only one who actually helped.

When it was time for him to go, he stood up, put a hand on my shoulder, and smiled kindly at me. "Maybe you are revolutionary," he said.

The snow cave stands completed behind my cabin. I had intended on sleeping out there at least one night, but I put it off, unwilling to sub-ject Lucky to a night out in the cold yet unable to spend even one night away from her. Recently she had debulking surgery and parts of the necrosed tumor had been sliced off. Her face is still swelled but she looks much more comfortable. There is significantly less odor.

One night I come home after class and Lucky is not on the couch. I hurry to the bedroom and find her struggling to get off the bed, am in time to see her legs fold under her. I kneel beside her as she tries to rise several times, but she sways and can't get her legs under-neath her. She has thrown up her dinner all over my bed. Panicked, we drive hurriedly to the after-hours vet who tells me that the tumor has probably grown into her middle ear, affecting her balance, and if it hasn't yet, soon will start pushing against her brain. She gives my dog fluids, some vitamins, recommends Dramamine for the dizzi-ness.

The next day, I take her to her regular vet who takes an X-ray and I see the mess that half my dog's face has become. Her jawbone is broken from the tumor pushing against it, and the growth is encroaching on her skull. A couple of weeks at most, the vet tells me.

I take my dog home. For the next several weeks on my drives back to my cabin, I steel myself to find her not moving on the couch. But every time I walk through the door, she lifts her wobbly head, gazing at me with eyes that do not focus. She keeps her small meals down with the Dramamine, and I take her for short walks outside as soon as she relearns how to balance. The sun becomes brighter, warmer as it heaves itself higher into the sky. Partway through the walk, Lucky gets tired and I pick her up, her bootied feet dangling, her head leaning against my chest.

And then one day I walk through the door and she is on the floor, lying in her own mess. She can't lift her head but I see her chest moving slightly. I pick her up carefully, clean her off, make her comfortable on the couch.

She will die tonight, slipping away by degrees as I stroke her fur. I will lift her stiffening body into a box and have her cremated. I consider scattering her ashes somewhere, perhaps in the Chena River, maybe somewhere up on Murphy Dome. But I do not like the idea of her blowing randomly about Fairbanks—I don't think she would like this either. Instead, I will put her ashes in a jar and keep them with me. I will keep her close to me, where she is happiest, to remind me of her always, to keep in mind her deep brown eyes, her unquestioning love.

I do not know what pain Lucky endured, anything of what she went through. All of her life, all she has wanted was to be with me, to please me in her doggy way. And that is what she did. She didn't let herself go until she knew that I was ready for her to. Her very last act, even when she was incapable of controlling anything anymore, was for me. She was a good dog.

The walls are blue, the filtered sunlight reflected in the thinning hard-packed snow. The temperature is near freezing and the warmth of each day's sunlight has begun melting away layers of the packed-snow roof. I am sitting on the cold floor, wrapped in long underwear, a sleeping bag, a blue tarp. One of the dogs runs over the snow cave, stripping away more layers of snow, and I am half-afraid that one of their paws will punch through. The walls, though, remain stable—there are several more weeks of cold left.

Sitting in my cave, I realize that the advantage of snow is its malleability. I am the sculptor of the snow around me: I can reinforce the sides of this cave, can add a room, a whole other wing. All I have to do is find more snow, drag it here in my sled, pack it down.

Kobi runs into the snow hut and lies down on the sleeping bag. We are both grateful for the coming of spring and of the warmth, and we stretch out for a nap. I half-anticipate when the sun will negate the need for this shelter, will compromise the sides of the snow hut enough that it will fall into itself, creating first just another pile of old snow, then a dirty puddle, and then finally becoming indistinguishable from the forest floor.

I think about how skittish Sally was when I first met her. She is sometimes nervous about entering the house. But she is getting better, stronger, as I spend time with her every day working on her confidence. Her face lights up when she realizes that I am praising her, and she smiles as I pet her.

I think about how I had allowed myself to get so entangled in the fact that one person did not love me that other things ceased to matter. I hadn't really wanted to kill myself. I think I knew it then, I certainly know it now; after all, I had sabotaged my own suicide attempt. I came back to Fairbanks in August, made arrangements to pick my life back up. I went to the animal shelter, I moved to a new cabin.

I see that man around every once in a while. We say hello, smile, and part. We are, if not friendly, at least civil with each other, and no one watching us would be able to guess that I put him through that awful night. Perhaps he has forgiven me, perhaps he has decided to forget it ever happened.

I have decided not to forget, but I have forgiven myself. I still deal with the things that led me to that point—I cry in my car as I drive, sobbing from somewhere behind my sternum. I often feel a great emptiness there. But these moments no longer overwhelm me. I have learned ways to keep them from consuming me—I ski, I run, I watch my dogs play in the snow. For now, it is the dogs that give my life meaning, the lessons taught to me by a 40-pound-and-losing shepherd mix who has been dead over a year. I am the center of these dogs' lives, and though they are in the end just dogs, I need them in the center of my life too. Although the outside world is hostile, the love that exists within my cabin is palpable and safe, and I know that slowly I will be able to expand that safety into broader and broader circles, to include human beings whose love is not constant and unquestioning as my dogs' love is. For now, though, I cling to the small circle I have and am grateful for it. It is the candle lantern in my snow cave.

Nominated by The North Dakota Quarterly

MODELS OF PASSION AND PAIN

by ELEANOR LERMAN

from WATER-STONE

In the morning, blue clouds ink the sky
like stained thumbs, pressing down
and the buildings lean down like giants
in steel kimonos, with cut-throat eyes.
This is the headache world, the other world
that no one believed in. But I get the message:
  Hello traveler. It is now

Who knew? That time, too, leans down
imposing pressure that has no mind behind it.
No god, aslant, asleep upon a plinth is
dreaming this. Who knew? That we
would have to make up a reason why;
in fact, we wanted a little more time.
  So do it now. Quickly. Run

Or not. My new plan is to make a
parable of the old days when we went
with Mama to the roof: when someone's
shirt might break free and fly off into the
good tomorrow. Someone's shirt might be
  a white sail, waving good-bye.

And still there would be men in the subways,
men in the factories, men as the models of
passion and pain. Now I remember that
I meant to marry someone. Slip into
        someone's heart. Stay safe.

But out here on the edge, I suppose I can
claim anything: *I didn't hear the phone ring.*
There was a fire. Or tell the truth: until recently,
I was an idiot. I thought the sky meant nothing
and that if you walked lightly upon the ground,
        no one heard.

Nominated by Water-Stone

BLACK OLIVES

by MICHAEL WATERS

from DARLING VULGARITY (BOA Editions)

In those days while my then-wife
taught English to a mustached young nurse who hoped to join
her uncle's practice in Queens,
I'd sip gin on our balcony and listen to her
read aloud from the phrasebook,
then hear the student mimic, slowly, *Where does it hurt?*
then my wife repeat those words
so the woman might enunciate each syllable,
until I could no longer
bear it, so I'd prowl the Ambelokipi district
attempting to decipher
titles emblazoned on marquees—*My Life As A Dog,
Runaway Train, Raging Bull—*
then stroll past dark shops that still sold only one item—
kerosene, soap, cheese, notebooks—
to step down into the shop that sold olives, only
olives in barrels riddling
a labyrinth of dank aisles and buttressing brick walls.
I'd sidle among squat drums,
fingering the fruit, thumbing their inky shine, their rucked
skins like blistered fingertips,
their plump flesh, the rough salts needling them, judging their cowled
heft, biding my time. Always
I'd select a half-kilo of the most misshapen,
wrinkled and blackest olives

sprung from the sacred rubble below Mt. Athos, then
had to shout "Fuck Kissinger!"
three times before the proprietor would allow me
to make my purchase, then step
back out into the smut-stirred Athens night to begin
the slow stroll home, bearing now
my little sack of woe, oil seeping through brown paper,
each olive brought toward my mouth
mirroring lights flung from marquees and speeding taxis,
each olive burning its coal-
flame of bitterness and history into my tongue.

Nominated by BOA Editions

THE BRIDGE

fiction by TIPHANIE YANIQUE

from THE SONORA REVIEW

1

The Parable of the Miniature Bridge Maker:
as told by an Island that is between things

THE PEOPLE WORE LITTLE BRIDGES around their necks. And when couples married they hopped over a little bridge. Everything was good.

There was a bridge maker. He made bridges that people put in their earlobes and around their fingers. Tiny little bridges. Ornamented and beautiful and perfect. He decided that when he died he would request a thin bridge fixed to his casket helping to connect him to his dead family under the ground.

His living family insisted that he leave a real legacy. He was famous for small things. They wanted him to be known for big things. So he built a real bridge. Paid for by the Yankees—not to honor his memory, but really for their own convenience. Like everything new. Huge and stretching from Guyana—the place in the world most South, to Miami—the place in the world most north. Before allowing the public to walk on the bridge he gathered all his family onto it for a picture. But the bridge was built like his others, the only way he knew how, delicate and pretty but not able to bear weight.

When the picture flashed—a big, beautiful, blinding light—the bridge fell apart. And not only in that spot but in places all over the Caribbean, so that the many families who had gathered to take pictures (without express permission) also went into the ocean. And though they were surrounded by the sea no one in any of the communities had bothered to learn to swim. The water never seemed as important as the land.

2

The Story of the Burka and the Habit:
as told by a Church Lady in a big hat

Margo was a kind of ghost. A living ghost. Don't say that because you're Catholic you don't believe in those things! She'd been living in St. Thomas for years but she had just up and sailed back to Dominica years ago. Not because she was young, but because she was old. She couldn't continue to suffer the lack of dignity she faced here in St. Thomas. Oh, yes. Right here. Everyone in their community knew what was happening to her and her splintering family. Her husband, Rashaad, living in St. Thomas like a proper Muslim man. Working even now that their children were grown. Their grandchildren almost grown. Great grands already on the way.

Back in Dominica their house was small and old and rolling down the hill inch by inch every year. No plumbing, she pissed in a pot. She did her business in a hole. Cooked her own food and withered away. This was okay. This was living. Going to Mosque every Friday—walking all the five miles on her own. Her legs sturdy and smooth. She walked fast—she felt she could live forever. In St. Thomas she'd felt she would die. In the small mosque in Dominica there was no separate place for men and women. And women could speak. Ask the Imam questions in Patois during the middle of his speeches. Margo asked the same question every Friday.

"Does a woman sin by not living with her husband?"

"Family comes first. You should do nothing that hurts your family, always doing what is best for them is best for you."

She was never satisfied. I wouldn't be either. Seems like imams and priests aren't so different.

What was best was for her to stay in Dominica. Her family had moved on. Her son was Rasta and had three wives—two of them were Ethiopian Orthodox and the other was a teen-age devotee of an Egyptian faith long dead in Egypt. Her daughter had converted to Christianity. Her husband had remained devoted to Islam. Becoming more devout as his children were swept away. Margo left for other reasons. But now she was returning. She'd heard about the bridge.

364

Who hadn't? All of the Caribbean was talking about it. An easy simple convenient way to connect, to unify the cultures. The next stretch was planned for the British Virgin Islands, though the ferry men complained and complained that they would go out of business. Proposals were in motion for the Bahamas and the ABC islands. A bridge soon to be under construction between Trinidad and Tobago. Next St. Kitts and Nevis. Bridges connecting the whole region.

She would see the bridge. Then she would go back to her husband. They had had happy years together. She was ready for the indignity. Urinating in a pot and moving one's bowels in a hole was not indignity. Indignity was her husband's house that was so ornate when there were so many poor in St. Thomas. Indignity was the black curtains he'd laid over all the windows to hide his shame at having children gone astray. Indignity was the burka he suggested she wear even in the hot Caribbean sun.

Their house in St. Thomas was at the very top of the island, at the tip of the highest peak. They'd bought it from the government. How, she'd never know. They'd left their nuptial house in Dominica, left it to slide down the little hill. That was where her son had been born. They moved to the US Virgin Islands when Rashaad was given a job by a cousin who was doing well. They'd returned only once to Dominica before her son left the Faith. Long before her daughter's betrayal. They'd been a family of tourists then. Ooohing and ahhing at the rivers and the water falls. Speaking Patois to their fellow natives and English to their fellow foreigners. Then her son had left and finally her daughter. And then she too, gone back home (home-home) for eight years. By now Rashaad would have another woman.

Margo walked to the corner store—four miles down the small Dominican hill, leaving her door unlocked so that anyone could get in if needed. She begged someone for money to buy a calling card. No indignity in being a beggar—Muslims were required to give alms.

"Rashaad?"

"Margo."

"I am coming home."

"Good. I have been waiting."

"Are the curtains still black?"

"They are more of a dark blue."

"Is there another woman?"

"Never."

"I'm coming soon, then."

"Come soon, then. Come soon."

What kept her away all these years? Was it really his fanaticism—something he used to steady himself as his children converted? Islam so in vogue now, every kid in St. Thomas wearing a "Go Aya-tolla!" t-shirt. Was it her son with his eleven children? Had that been the straw that sent her across the sea?

She'd left for Dominica on a whim. Just walking by the cargo ship of bananas in her burka. She'd been a shadow as she climbed aboard. Eating the sweet bananas grown on her mother island as the vessel island-hopped, dumping its fruit cargo, filling up with parcels of books and clothes from Aunties in Tortola to favorite nieces in Grenada. With the new bridge of course, these water ways would be obsolete.

What really made her get on the ferryboat is the question to ask. For mothers it's always the daughters. Living shadows haunting each other. Ayana was engaged to be married when the Catholics got her. Yes, we Catholics are always where the blame falls. She was engaged to a good Muslim boy whose parents were from Atlanta. Ayana said she was visiting him after school. But that was a lie. Margo knew that now. Ayana was actually staying after school in Catholic classes. All was revealed one Saturday evening:

"Mommy, come with me."

But what does that mean, really? Come with me down the street? Come with me so I can show you something? Come with me into the bosom of Jesus?

Oh, hush, dear. It was a trick either way. Unfair, really. Margo had to sit in the back row as her daughter let go of her hand and walked down the aisle. And the priest placed a white square on her waiting tongue. "I'm happy, Mommy. Be happy for me." And then Ayana kneeled right beside her mother and prayed. The indecency of that child. Didn't even think of her mother. Children nowadays!

Poor Margo had breathed in deeply, that horrible incense filling her nose, and kneeled beside her daughter. "Darling. Jesus never said he was God. You mustn't pray to him." Ayana didn't even nod at her mother. She seemed to have turned to stone. Margo left her daughter kneeling in the church. No energy to drag her out. Ayana was an adult in the eyes of God now anyway. Margo spat on the steps of the Cathedral. And cursed out loud the day that she'd sent her daughter to the parochial school. They'd lost her now. They'd failed.

"She'll find her way," said her son. "She's just exploring." But what did he know? He was lost too. His dreads all down his back. Dozens of illegitimate children swinging on his legs.

Her husband had taken her head to his chest. "Trust in Allah." But Ayana did not come home. Rashaad put his trust in Allah and darkened the windows; buying the burka Margo refused to wear, praying five times a day. Attending mosque every Friday, at least. And they heard nothing from Ayana. Nothing. Until she arrived one day. No longer stone—now habited. Nunned. In the full nun regalia, a brown rope hanging from her side. Oh, darling. Even I don't trust those costumed types. Who wants a nun in the family? Not me. Well, Margo slapped her at the door. Ayana turned the other cheek. Margo slammed the door. She wore her burka after that. Always ready. Ready to face her daughter on even terms if she ever came back. But she didn't. And then Margo, burkad, had slipped onto a boat headed for Dominica.

Now she was flying back to St. Thomas. Rashaad had insisted on flying and not hitching on a barge again. He'd even sent her the money. But she hadn't told him when she was coming. "Soon," she said. The plane was small but it took a long route, circling the north side of the island so the passengers could see the bridge. Steel and cords and everything known to man seemed to have gone into it. It could hold elephants, a whole tropical jungle. It looked so strong. Like the hand of God stretching over the sea and saying "come, come." Margo began to weep.

At the airport she had to wait a long while for her one bag which couldn't be found at first. When it was finally unearthed it was clear that it had been opened. The wood carving of a rounded thinking man with his head in his lap had been stolen. She had brought it as a gift for her husband. Now she was going home with nothing but herself. She took the burka out of her luggage and put it on right there in the baggage claim area. This would make Rashaad happy. She was being watched in such a way that putting on this extra cloth felt oddly as if she was stripping naked.

It was quite late and the airport was almost deserted, but as she walked to the taxi stand the remaining drivers looked uneasy on their bench. She was a woman, but she was also a ghost gliding towards them. She announced her destination in her French island accented English. The two older men slapped the younger one on the back and pushed him forward. He looked barely in his twenties.

367

The house was out Northside and they drove in silence through town where there were lights on and bars still open. There are no lights in the country. No lights at all in Northside. Just the occasional high beams of another car. When they reached the hills the young driver began to talk.

"So you hear 'bout the bridge?"

"Yes."

"They opening it tomorrow. Well, today, seeing as it done past mid-night."

"Yes, I have heard."

"Tomorrow is Emancipation Day here. You know? The day the slaves get free when Buddoe blow his conch shell."

"Yes, of course."

She didn't want to talk to this boy. She wanted to get home and talk to her husband. Wanted to make amends. Start a new life before they died.

"The bridge is that way." The driver turned away from the direction he pointed and made his way up a steep hill. The car revved angrily, jerked and obeyed. They made their way slowly. She hadn't seen the house for eight years. But is was still too large. Still too ridiculously ornate. Three stories on an island were two stories was already an excess. There were lights coming from the ground, lighting the driveway as they made their way. The columns at the entrance were emblazoned with light, making them look even more stretched than they were. There was darkness from the windows.

Margo opened the passenger door. The young driver carried her one bag to the steps of the grand house. Together they waited as she knocked. As she rang the door bell. As she screamed out her husband's name, causing wings to flap and a distant dog to respond.

"Maam. I have to head back to the airport. My dispatcher is calling." And perhaps he was. Perhaps that sputtering from the car was the boss. Perhaps it was a lover or his mother. Or perhaps it was just static.

"Young man, you can go. This is my house. My husband will come home soon. He's expecting me."

"Yes, but I need to get paid."

She couldn't pay him. She'd counted on her husband being home. There was no money. Rashaad had Western Unioned only what was needed. Now there was nothing.

"Well money or no money, I can't just leave you here at night. You like my grandmother or something."

Margo stared at him through the opening in her veil. He could see the wrinkles around her eyes. "I'll find you tomorrow and pay you. Now go." She watched the young man walk backwards, get in his car and then drive slowly down the hill. She wasn't afraid of the dark. She'd lived without electricity for eight years. She wasn't afraid of loneliness. She'd lived alone on a little hill for eight years. She was afraid that her husband was not coming home. She walked down the big hill. Still hearing the very end of the taxi's growl in the night's silence. It was a very bright night. The half moon was out, and the house was so high up that the only thing above her was the stars. She would see the bridge up close. She would walk on it. Perhaps she would walk all the way to St. Croix. Live there. Where the land was flat and there were no hills to walk up or down. Where people had to face each other on level ground.

Gravity helped her along, pulling her down the hill towards the magnet of the bridge. She had once felt unsafe in a burka. No peripheral vision. No easy way to get hands out in defense. But in the days that she'd worn it, ready to face down her daughter, she'd found a safety. A safety to be hidden. In the dark now, rushing towards the sea, she felt unseen. The walk was a long one and she kept expecting the sky to get lighter into the morning but it didn't. She thought about her children when they were little. How smart they'd looked in their Catholic school uniforms with dark blue socks pulled up to their knees. She thought about her husband when they first married and he'd built that house in Dominica with his own bare hands. He had promised her he would install plumbing and electricity. But then their son had been born and moving seemed easier. She thought of her own mother, who didn't trust Rashaad because he wasn't Pentecostal. How she had told her father that she loved Rashaad, even though she'd only brushed hands with him in the Juan Diego burial grounds where they'd both gone to mourn their different forgotten family member.

How could Margo have known then that she would leave behind her own faith and become Muslim to marry him. She'd only been seventeen. How could she have known anything.

By the time Margo reached the bridge she realized that she had seen her whole life in her mind. She was grateful. Now the bridge

369

was towering above her, dwarfing the house on the hill that she had hated for so long. She stepped onto the bridge, there were sidewalks for pedestrians and she ambled along these for some time. Aware that she was high above many things. She paused to lean over a railing and then consider the distance she had walked. She could still see where she was coming from, but where she was going was lost in the darkness. Far below her was a little boat with two figures lying languidly beside each other. One figure was quite larger than the other.

She knew what it was. Margo leaned deeper over the railing to get a better view of her husband and his other woman. They did not see her. She placed her feet on the railing, one after another until she stood there and screamed, her arms flying about. The young girl much further along on the bridge watched the woman tip. Heard her screaming: "You said you were waiting!" The couple in the little fishing boat saw Margo as a sparrow in flight. The bridge began to shake. Margo had the flighting feeling that she had been a little wrong, but as she soared she could not remember what she was wrong about. The water rose to meet her life like a wall.

3

The Fisherman's Tale:
as told by someone's grandfather in
a corner rumshop

Pour me a greenie. I like my Heineken in a glass, damn it. I'm a gentleman. And I tell you here and now that Tony Magrass wasn't no cheapster. He never weigh down the scale by leaning on it like some does do. His fish always fair and always fresh. He love the water. I mean is love he love the water. Spear fishing and all of that. The little wife is a waitress for a tourist food shop. She old now, but still good looking. Not wrinkle up at all. You seen her? She the type that too pretty for she own good. She been horning with the manager of the restaurant where she work for years. Years! Salli, that's she name, wasn't even sure that she and Tony son was really Tony son. The manager wasn't good looking, now. Just rich. Just keeping she in she job. Just helping she send Pete to Catholic school.

Pete make alright grades but he fish with his father more than he study books. Giving his teachers fish for free on Sundays. Going to mass out Northside like all the Northside Frenchies. But no one had been fishing on the north side for two years. You know, because of building the bridge and all. Less fish for the locals. Less fish for the tourists. Less fish at Salli restaurant. Tony had taken to fishing in town with the Frenchtown boys. They tease him but they pity all the Northside Frenchies. Their piece of the ocean take away by the bridge that supposed to help everybody—connect all the islands. St. Thomas to St. Croix goin be just a car drive away. Set up a toll in a year when it get popular and needed. Bring in money for the government. Money for the islands. Right? Well. On July 3rd the bridge would be opened. On July 3rd people would be able to walk even to their sister islands. But to Tony July 3rd don't mean bridge open, don't even mean Emancipation Day, don't mean the day before US independence. It just mean he could fish again. But now it was March still.

He wife calling him. "Tony. Tony, baby. I leaving."

He come home to the house half empty. The mahogany short leg table, for coffee she'd told him, gone. The rusted beveled mirror that her father self had brought during their first year of marriage, so they could hug up and stare at each other as she belly grow, gone. The art books that she buy second hand, hinting and hoping for the easel and paints he never buy she (settling for the pad and pencils Pete bring home from school), gone. In the kitchen there was food in plastic containers that they didn't own before. Meals done cook and freezing in the freezer. She'd gone shopping. She'd cooked. But the coal pots and iron pans that her mother had hand down, gone too. In the bathroom her little soaps. Her sweet smelly shampoo. The towel with Mini Mouse from their trip to Orlando back when money was good—gone. Only the Mickey Mouse one hanging alone.

Salli was in the bedroom. The linen bedspread that he parents had given them arrange neat over the bed. She lying on top of it. Fully clothed. Heels and stockings. Calf length skirt. White blouse. A nice purse at she side. Clothes he ain never seen before. That's a woman for you. She turn her head just so when he enter and watch him in the face.

"I goin with Mr. Kenny. I can't live off a fisher man's salary no more."

"And Pete?" Tony look at he wife, too pretty and laying out on their bed. He wanted to walk to her and unbutton her shirt slow. But he smell of fish. He know she hate that. She watch him hard.

"Pete's a grown man. Going to college in the States soon. He'll stay with you or us. No matter."

Tony leave the room before she did. If I were he I woulda swallow some cold Heineken. But Tony just walk out to the dining room where dinner for he and Pete sitting in plates covered in aluminum foil. He sit down at the tail of the table and begin to eat. He hear her heels clink behind him on she way out.

Pete didn't come home that night. The next day was school but he turn up at eight in the morning to his father's house. He find Tony in bed, wrap up in the linen bedspread, bloat up and sick from all the food he eat. Not just the dinner Salli leave but enough food for at least three days. Pete stand over his old man.

"Ma say you not my real father, Dad."

Tony roll around in his linen cocoon. See the man! Flinging heself onto the floor, onto the tile he had lay he ownself. The tile she had picked out. He fighting now, tearing the linen and old lace until he get free. He son watching from the doorway.

"Dad. Let me know what's true."

Tony reach a hand to he son and together they get Tony onto the bed. Pete sit down beside him. Tony look into he son eyes.

"Your mother is the Devil."

"Don't say that, man."

"She's a lying devil."

"Chill, Pops. Chill out."

Tony thought they should go fishing. At times like these that is what a proper Frenchy father and son should do. But Tony can't take Pete to Frenchtown—it already crowded down there. So they decide to wait until July 3rd. So long aways. And Pete leaving two days after that. He had gotten into a nice-up school in the States but they require him to do some summer classes cause he ain so good at maths.

So the father and son wait all that time. And at four in the morning of July 3rd they roll up their pants. They have their spear gun and dagger just in case, but really they only want to do some leisure fishing. Maybe bring something home for dinner so they don't have to eat the cooking Salli keep bringing in plastic tins. They push out their boat, and the bridge there gleaming. They see it stretching out across the ocean. They have nets and poles and flashlight and a bag of small live bait.

At the docks there weren't no other men. The other Northside Frenchies thinking to wait, thinking that the fish wouldn't come back so soon. Thought maybe the fish would never come back. Some had already moved from Northside permanently. You seeing them in town. Haunting the place looking for sea jobs, land jobs—anything. But those didn't have a son going away. They didn't have a wife who leave them for a better man.

The boat engine make a soft noise and though they just heading out to sea it seem like they heading toward the bridge. They wasn't. Not really. It only seem so 'cause the bridge feel like it everywhere. Like it a haunted rainbow, hunting you round the city. I have felt the feeling. The moon was out and shape funny, like a smile almost. They even see one or two people on the bridge.

"Yeah, Dad. I think we goin catch something, man. I think the fish must be curious to see a boat like ours after all this time."

"We counting on it." But the father didn't really think so. Not really at all. He only want to be with he son like this. Pete been living with his mother and Mr. Kenny all this time because Mr. Kenny could drop him to school while his father went fishing first thing in the morning. But Pete was still his son and Tony love-love he son. More than fishing even. More than life.

"Jesus. Pops, look." Pete was staring past he father shoulder. "Pops, she's frigging jumping." And sure nough. A woman was standing on the railing of the bridge with her arms spread wide.

She tip forward and Pete scream—like his mother's own son. A high pitch thing. And the woman above them spread her black wings and began to fly like a crow diving to the ocean. But Tony ain even see she cause he busy going blind from a light bright like a saint. It was just then that the bridge begin to collapse. And the water around their little boat begin to swell. And their boat itself begin to shake. And boulders of the bridge crash into the sea causing waves that lift highhigh. And then the sound like hell opening its dirty doors—loud like it coming from inside the chest somehow. The boat rip apart before it could capsize. Son holding on to the one half and spinning off into a whirlwind. Father grabbing on the next half rushing towards ragged land.

Tony Magrass knock on Mr. Kenny door that very morning. The easel hard and heavy under he one arm. The palate of paints dainty in he other. Salli open the door and look at her husband of seventeen years. The father of she dead son. She don' know for sure yet that she son gone, but she know this man ain come cause he hungry. Mr. Kenny not home as yet, so she watch the art ting hard. She look again at she husband and they lock eyes even harder. Despite their distance, there had never been a thing but love between them. "Set it up in the corner, Tony."

4

Lament of the Queen:
as told by a seventeen year old school
girl in patent leather shoes

Guadeloupe did it for love. Obviously. As they say in all the movies, nothing else is enough. Of course she wanted to kill herself. Attempted suicide is like, so in vogue now. Though she did more than die, of course. Juan Diego was a real man who knew not to ask about her past. About how she really won (well, almost won) all those teen pageants. He knew not to question anything that had happened before him, not even to question what was happening while she was with him. If it did not stop her from loving him, if it did not wrack her with guilt, if it did not make her different, than how could it matter to him? Yes, girl. Guadeloupe was a little whore.

When she said she was a virgin, he agreed. He accepted her with the illusions she presented. Loved her and didn't care about the lies. You know the type. He was a real college guy, mature about that kind of stuff. Dark skin and tall. Those sweet ones are hard to find, and then the wrongest girls are the one that find them, yes.

Anyway, she wasn't like him. She wasn't mature 'bout those things. Still in high school and one of those stupid girlie girls. I would have known better. Anyhow, she found a love note, dated like three years before she'd even met him. And she just crumbled from the thought that he'd loved someone besides her. Stupid, hey? Crumbled from the realization that he too had a past, that maybe she was not his greatest love in the whole wide world—I mean he had saved the note for three years and she would have been like a freshman in high school then. And like all girls who don't know how to forgive themselves—she could not forgive him. So she decided to win the crown, a tiara really, without the usual aids of her body and obeah-magic.

But it would be hard. Because she was Puerto Rican and light skinned and straight haired, though at least her hair was brown. Ms. Emancipation, the biggest title in St. Croix, was supposed to be a woman who celebrated the freedom of slaves. Guadeloupe decided to win the crown for the few slave-descended ancestors she had. To show Juan Diego that she could be whatever he wanted. Because when she found the note, she realized that he didn't think her pure, did not think he had her virginity, did not think her a girl who'd first runnered-up pageant after pageant by her own merit. But that he'd known all along that she was a fraud. And he'd loved her a fraud, when she'd thought she'd had him loving her pure. Thinking that his love made her pure, because he said he loved her as if she was like the Virgin Mary herself. Anyway.

Well, you saw it. She won. She'd sang for the talent competition something about God, and our people love that. And for the historical segment she'd been the Bridge, the thing to connect us; friends to family. While the other girls wore masks of famed teachers and religious leaders on all sides of their heads or boxes of the legislature building around their waists, the judges and the audience thought Guadeloupe was so innovative to bring the present into such significance by making it history. In the question and answer portion she talked about connectivity, diversity in unity. Despite her light skin, despite the obviousness that more of her ancestors had owned slaves than had been them, how could she lose? We're open like that. We like to know that people love us, we don't care how they look.

She'd competed without aid in pageants before. First with Carlos McEntire, when they'd been Carnival Prince and Princess. You remember that? Then in middle school she'd been Miss Junior May Fair Queen. Who could forget that one. She mimed for her talent. She was good, too. But then winning became serious, the prizes became substantial. She'd done what was needed to place first runner up in Miss Talented Teen, Queen of the Band, Miss Parks and Recreation, Lady Alpha. Incantations, meditations, all kinds of 'tations to win, to not lose. She competed in things she didn't even qualify for, like Mistress of Housing, though she didn't even live in the projects. And now she'd won Miss Emancipation. It wasn't as if she hadn't prepared like her whole life. All the singing lessons, and the walking lessons: until she figured out that learning to walk and learning to sing were the same. (Both required breathing and a straight back and hands clasped before the torso. Like this. She could tell a singer by the sway in the hips, though if you ask me you can tell a slut by the same thing.) Finally, she'd won all by herself.

They sat the skimpy little tiara on her head and her first walk as Miss Emancipation was announced. Her blue gown was covered in sequin stars and she really looked good, as if she was a piece of the sky. Her arms shimmered with the glitter her chaperone had applied carefully before releasing her to the formal gown segment. Strutting down the cat walk she was only aware of herself. The spot light does that. It blinds you, you know. So bright she couldn't see the audience, not even Juan Diego, in the front besides her mother. Both of them looking at her so proudly. She could only clutch the red roses tight in her hands, letting the few thorns prick her fingers but not the delicate dress. She felt her chest swell with heat while the darkened faces below smiled—well, they seemed to smile.

Backstage, the other girls congratulated her stiffly, their lips not touching her face at all. And somehow winning without seducing a judge or casting obeah on the other contestants still felt fraudulent. Maybe, like being a fraud might be her true-self? She got kinda crazy thinking about that then. She took off her heels in the changing room and put on her sneakers, still in the panty hose and sequined dress. And she ran. No joke. The people parted as she ran by because no one recognized her without her tiara on. She ran to the last place she should have. The Bridge. She had no food and no water but wanted to make it to the other side. She didn't know how long it would take. She didn't know why she chose this as a symbol. She didn't know that when one doesn't eat or drink for a whole day that one forgets to be hungry. That hunger doesn't matter. Only thirst. It rained the morning of the second day; this is the Caribbean after all. She titled her head back and kept walking. The worn make-up streaking down her face, then off her face completely. She realized, once the rain had stopped, that her face hadn't been so clean since she was seven years old.

A full day on the bridge. Not on the land, not in the sky, not in the water. She saw the sun set and then rise on this limbo life. Between the night of the second day and the morning of the third she could see the other side of the bridge. The land of the other island just there past the length of her tongue. The thirst for it like, I don't know, like mother love. Scratching at the back of her throat. There was a black sack figure crossing the bridge too. There were two figures in a boat just below. It was late, dark. The moon was high and crescented. She wanted to be on top of that moon. She wanted it at her feet—like a boat to get her across anything. She was such a frigging drama queen. She couldn't know what she had in common with these three figures. But she felt she had to choose one set or the other. The weight of her absent crown solid on her head. She knew that if Juan Diego was with her he would hold her up with his two hands like the angel he was until she became something holy, something to make these lands pure and able. His Guadeloupe.

Anyway, she walked towards the figure on the bridge, but the black-sack woman actually seemed to move further away, climbing the railing away from her. Perhaps Guadeloupe looked a little off, mad you know, a beauty queen in sneakers, hair looking like crap because of the rain and the ragged days of walking. Guadeloupe looked down where the woman was looking and saw the moon below, at her feet. Saw the little brown boy in the boat stand up to hold her. She felt the tingle of the glow. The halo covered her entire body. Not like a tiara; not even like a crown they gave the boys who won for Mister this or King that. The halo coming from her very bones and protecting her. She was pure. She could save lands. She was the most pure and the most good. A human bridge.

The other woman on the bridge looked now like a huge black crane steadying itself for flight. Guadeloupe, this mixed up girl who was just getting to know herself, watched on in her new state of grace, and the lovely crane leapt into the air, with its wings wide and open to the wind. Guadeloupe pressed her hands together so gently that her pinkies crossed and missed each other—she felt something glorious come from her and go out into the world. And, I kid you not, that was when the miracle of miracles happened. The bridge began to crumble. She was not afraid as the air opened and took her in.

Nominated by The Sonora Review

THE METHOD

by MARVIN BELL

from CRAZY HORSE

Of the knees we might say they beseech,
seen together on the floor, the head bowed,
wherefrom one senses penitence and dread.
From a future of the numerous, a single sword
is held aloft. It takes two hands. From the sound
of no-sound the soon-to-be-beheaded is aware
the steel blade is beginning to descend. At once
the stricken neck flowers, a thousand rosettes,
and the head, picked up by its hair, dripping,
is thrown thoughtless in the trash. For an instant,
if one could be measured, the mind must resist,
while in reality time stops. Something about it.
A kind of gumshoe diplomacy kicks into action,
asking for clear pictures it dare not show.

Nominated by Mark Irwin

FINE DISTINCTIONS

by BARBARA HURD

from FOURTH GENRE

Though the merman has nothing to do with my original reason for visiting Orford Ness, his story has complicated my musings about stones and shingle beaches. Local fishermen claimed they had caught him in their nets, a slithery creature, man from the waist up, fish from the waist down. They grabbed him under his arms and dragged him across the shingle beach, his tail flopping and flailing over the pebbles, which must have rolled and shifted a bit in his wake, darkened by seawater shaken from his scales. The villagers feared him. They took him to the bottom of the castle keep, bound him up in the dark and beat him, and finally, in a last resort to get him to speak, they hung him by his tail over a fire. "Burn," they tried to get him to say. "Scare."

The English warden who'd dropped me at the edge of the Orford Ness Nature Reserve on the southwest coast of Suffolk wanted to know what my interest was, why I'd searched out this place now closed to tourists. I didn't say anything about the merman, whom I'd first heard of just last night at a local art gallery when a woman who knew of my planned trip to the Ness had approached me, her eyes glittering. Nor did I say I'd been intrigued by the various descriptions of the Ness that I'd run across in my reading: "aura of mystique," "wild and hostile," "potentially dangerous." Debris, I told the warden, especially debris that's washed up by the sea—kelp, bottles, driftwood, stone. And shore regions formed by debris—coastal moraines and shingle beaches. He'd been understandably reluctant at first, but finally agreed to take me by boat and then by jeep out to this barren spit that juts into the North Sea. His only caution: stay off the shingle above the high-water mark. "If you're not back at the landing jetty in a few hours," he said as he turned the jeep around, "I'll come back out and look for you."

Last night in my hotel room after the gallery opening, I unwrapped a package the woman had delivered to me—a musty book published in 1700—and turned the yellowed pages carefully to the marked passage about the Merman of Orford. There the historian recounts the tale told by a monkish chronicler about a creature caught in the fishing nets off of what became, centuries later, the shingle beach at Orford. Half man, half fish, bearded and scaly, the story says, a wild man who fought the nets that tangled him and the men who locked him up in the dungeon of a nearby castle. The woman from the art gallery evidently believed in a literal merman. I think she wanted me to also.

On the beach this drizzly November morning, the castle keep and its dungeon behind me, I picture the fishermen on the sea, eyeing the wind, hauling nets, calculating the odds of a good catch just a few miles farther out, where survival depends on knowing what the water holds. They catch sight of something they can't identify, something that lures, as the strange often does, a vision or a fear that requires an explanation. A sea turtle with tendrils? A squid with expression? What to think of a creature who resembles you but lives in a way that you cannot? Did they fear the merman, finally, because he was too much like them or not enough? They did what we humans too often do: imagined what might scare them and then created that very thing so they could drag it ashore, tie it up in a castle, make it feel what they didn't want to: *burn, scare.*

The warden has driven off. To both sides and in front of me, a desert of pebbles extends almost as far as I can see, a vast mosaic of flindered ochre and gray. No honking horns, cell phones, the sound of anything human. Out here on the Ness, no trees provide shelter, no butte or peak breaks up the terrain. Just acres of tiny stones underfoot and a silence that's almost eerie. Even the sea is quiet. Unfolding old and current maps, I try to figure out exactly where they'd hauled the merman ashore and realize the beach I'm standing on wasn't even here a thousand years ago. On a 1601 map, the earliest one I have, the Ness, which means nose, is north of the town of Orford and extends farther up and out into the water, as if sniffing the North Sea a little snootily. Five hundred years earlier, when the merman came ashore, it would have been even farther north, somewhere up near my hotel in Aldeburgh.

So, I asked the woman last night in the gallery, was he fish or human? Both, she insisted. But how? How did he get that way? Human sex with a fish is preposterous, as is the notion of either of them giving birth to the result. No, she said, not like that. He just came into being. Appeared. This is the stuff I'm drawn to, these stories of transformation: Kwakiutl lore about salmon turning into twins, Inuit stories of bears into men, quick-change artists like Spiderman, Superman, Wonder Woman.

I like to imagine a slow-motion camera recording the change— scales thinning into skin, fur dropping out, fingers growing webby— and wonder whether we're ever aware of the drifts and shifts of our own lives, the moments when we find ourselves, through tragedy or good fortune, a slightly altered being, sprouting new strengths, new skills or vices, becoming more or less than we were. Is there ever a morning when we look in the mirror and suspect we're seeing a different face?

No, she insisted, it just appeared.

Today the Ness is about ten miles long, a shifting pile of the debris of ancient landforms. It's made up, almost exclusively, of pebbles, the round, polished, and transported bits of more northerly lands. Technically, "shingle" refers to sediment smaller than boulders but larger than sand or, more specifically, stones with a diameter between 2 and 200 mm. Somewhere up the coast of England there must have been, millions of years ago, ledges and mountains of granite and flint, maybe chert and quartzite that got hammered and battered by rain and the sea. Small chunks would have been broken off by waves that tumbled them for centuries, lifting and rolling, scouring and polishing, moving them southward in the direction of prevailing storms, piling them up along the coast in low ridges. Where the shoreline tucks a little inland, as it does just south of Orford, the storms decrease and the effect is even more dramatic: winds die down, the wave action slows, and the water, unable to keep moving its load of pebbles, drops it. The nose-like beach accumulates another layer there, grows a little deeper and longer. Today there's not a jagged stone in sight, no hooks or pocks or anything rough. Just globes and oblongs, glassy ovals and orbs, smooth-sided, sometimes perfect Os. Tiny petrified eggs.

Most shingle beaches are barren. Rain splashes against the pebbles and drops immediately into tiny interstices, millions of rivulets vanishing into the spaces between stones. There's nothing to slow the water, no tiny pit whose bottom doesn't lead to passageways farther below. Whenever it rains, these millions of pebbles are merely rinsed, never drenched. And it isn't just the lack of moisture that discourages plant life. These same glassy-smooth stones that shrug off water also refuse the dirt. This beach is the cleanest expanse of stones I've ever seen.

And, it seems, the most raked. Even from the ground where I'm standing, I can see the pattern of ridges and valleys running mostly parallel to the shoreline. The larger pebbles congregate in the valleys and the lighter ones, called "fines," pile up in mostly parallel ridges just a few feet away. The valleys are a hue darker; the ridges are lighter, more sand-colored, and delicate. The result is a subtle striping that changes slightly if I look across rather than lengthwise along at the ridges. It changes again when the fog lightens and clouds thin, as if this were a beach of wide-wale corduroy and someone's fingers were alternately smoothing and roughing up the nap.

That's an illusion, of course, the kind I enjoy anyway. It provides a moment's pleasure without the risk of hardening into dogma about the hand of any god or which way one should stand if the sun is shining or not. In actuality, stone-sorting here is the result of the waves' depositing the stones in a series of ridges and swales sculpted only by certain laws of physics—wave action and lift, pebble weight and deposition.

Most of us humans, on the other hand, sort with a certain degree of consciousness. It seems to be one of our traits to like things assigned to specific categories. Classifying is one of the first tasks of discrimination a young child learns: all the red objects belong in this pile, blue in another. Squares over here and circles over there.

When I was 12 or 13 and spending summer days on the beaches of the Atlantic Ocean, I used to try to classify seashells. With my bare foot, I'd draw around me four or five large circles in the sand, and then I'd stand with my bucket of shells like a kid at the start of a hopscotch game, tossing the fan-shaped shells into one circle, horns into another, turkey wings there, cones into the circle beside me. I didn't know the language of bivalves or gastropods, and function didn't matter. Shape did. When I found a shell that didn't fit any of my categories—too twisted or barnacled, too odd to be typed—I heaved it back into the water. Only a few merited their own miscellaneous category—ones with deep purplish color or an inside curve so lus-trous I'd keep my thumb in it half the afternoon. Beauty, I see now, could break the rules, but the grotesque could not. I don't remember making up stories about the shells, the way I did with stones in the backyard. Looking back, it seemed to be merely an exercise in the pleasure of sorting, perhaps a human tendency to group: golf balls in one pile, baseballs in another, scholars in one place, athletes in an-other. Large stones in the valleys, smaller ones on the ridges, humans in one category, fish in another.

For us, there's safety and efficiency to such clear categories, and often laziness. For the English sea pea, however, there's an impera-tive. Size-sorted stone is crucial, in fact, if the shingle is to support any plant life at all. Here's why: a larger stone has more rounded sur-face area than a small one and therefore can't nestle as closely next to surrounding, also rounded, stones. As a result there are larger spaces between the larger rocks, which means more space for rain and dirt to slip through. Picture pouring dirt through a clutch of ping-ping balls. The interstices gape, so that that which might support plant life slips through the holes and disappears.

Or, the holes in the mind-sieve widen too far, so that inhibi-tions drop away. Rationality can find no foothold. Nor can a tolerance for ambiguity or thoughtfulness about fantasies. And that which might ordinarily be repressed slips out too soon, appears only half-transformed: a merman, a centaur. Is this what can happen out at sea or wherever fear combines with lack of bearings? Subtleties vanish; the world becomes starker and the mind more coarse.

But on the ridges here, the pebbles are smaller and can therefore nestle together more closely, like lima beans or even lentils. The spaces between them are tighter, which is what the sea pea needs. Though it has a long taproot to snake and curl through the shingle, the rare plant depends on the bits of organic debris and the drop or two of moisture that only a congregation of smaller stones can trap. Records indicate that the sea pea was once abundant on the shingle in the mid-1500s, a few hundred years after the merman, when it was harvested by villagers in Aldeburgh during a famine. It isn't plentiful now. In fact, that it grows here at all makes the beach a designated Site of Special Scientific Interest. The story of its near extinction in this area is a story about secret radar and war and the triggering de-vices on atomic bombs.

Bouncing over the shingle in his jeep, the warden had told me part of the story. In the late 1960s, he said, when the American armed forces were hunting for a site on which to build the world's largest, most sophisticated, most powerful radar of its kind, they chose the shingle beach of Orford Ness. Isolated, quiet, uninhabited, the Ness provided the secrecy the military needed, a spot where, they calculated, reception would be unimpeded and the project could operate under a cloak of mystery. Cobra Mist consisted of a giant, fan-shaped array of aerials arranged in a 119-degree arc and, with its large aluminum ground net, covering over 80 acres. The aerials themselves ranged from 40 to almost 200 feet high. Costing more than a hundred million dollars, the project never worked. Its ability to receive signals was, from the start, hampered by the presence of a mysterious noise. "Clutter-related noise," they called it. "Severe background noise," "excessive noise of undetermined origin." Months of testing failed to find the source of the problem.

UFOs again, a local contingent muttered. Though the warden hadn't mentioned this, I learned from others that Orford Ness has long been a hotbed of spaceship stories, accounts of fireballs and strange lights, hovering, cigar-shaped aircraft. Perhaps, some hypothesized, UFO residue interfered with the radar's function. Maybe there were even UFO's still using the Ness as a landing site. More tests, more theories. In the end, the armed forces admitted they couldn't explain the interference and dismantled the huge array. But the damage to Orford Ness had been done—roads built, wells dug, and barracks erected, all of which meant boots, tires, and shovels in the shingle. Intent on cupping a huge ear to the sky, they shuffled the pebbles until the fines were mixed into the coarser, the distinction disappeared, dirt and rain slipped through the cracks, and most of the sea pea died.

In 2000, the National Trust tried reconstructing the shingle, using sieves and screens to re-sort the pebbles, move the small ones back to the ridges, the larger ones to the valleys. They measured the height and width of nearby undamaged ridges and swales and constructed the newly re-sorted mounds accordingly. On some of the new ridges, they experimented with adding extremely fine pebbles and on others, seeds, sometimes both. Using fixed-point photography, they monitored any plant growth. But months later, it all seemed futile. The rate of plant colonization did not increase, and the labor-intensive nature of the work made the whole experiment too costly.

The Trust concluded that no amount of human effort can replicate what the tides and the waves do naturally.

Restoring the shingle beach wasn't at all what Derek Jarman had in mind. Thirty-seven miles south of Orford on the shingle beach at Dungeness, the artist, dying of AIDS, moved rocks and pebbles, built basins with plastic liners, hauled in manure, fashioned a garden on the barren shingle. He raked the gravel into furrows and circles, up-ended larger stones, piled up pebbles of blue-gray that he ringed with flat flint, and collected debris from the beach. Around his cottage, sculptures of twisted iron scraps rise out of mounds of gorse and elder. Everywhere there's a sense of the deliberate—stones balanced on upright driftwood, a scavenged orange glove holding a yellow pebble in its palm. Poppies bloom and viper's bugloss, pink valerian and giant sea kale. "Paradise," he decided not long before he died.

Unlike the villagers inclined to torment fish-tailed men or the waves governed only by the laws of physics, Jarman did his work consciously and slowly. For eight years he walked and collected, dug and raked, planted and rearranged, stood back and reconsidered. That's the difference between a myth like the merman or the inattentiveness of the army and the work of an artist. Jarman took forms and rearranged them. He had an aesthetic in mind. What emerged in his garden wasn't by sudden metamorphosis—the shingle blooming overnight into lushness—but by the long slow business of beauty: worry, watering, the slow coaxing of an oasis of color and shape.

I turn and head north. Walking, even meditative walking, isn't easy. "Arduous," in fact, the warden had warned me. The pebbles can roll, give way underfoot, leave your ankle turned sideways. You can't predict if they'll stay still enough to give the ball of your foot something firm to push off of or if you'll stumble forward, lurch a little, leave a small stone-slide in your wake. With my foot, I could rake them—clean and rounded—into small ridges, much like Japanese monks have done with gravel and sand for centuries. Their gardens are serene and silent, just the conditions for opening the mind. I bend down and pick up a handful, let them dribble into mounds at my knees, small collapsing piles of pebbles—copper colored, adobe, gray speckled and plum, small nuggets with streaks of black. The pile builds until it can't keep itself together. Pebbles roll down its side, a pyramid of slowly avalanching, giant grains of sand.

I've done this hundreds of times on the beaches of my childhood, mounding the damp and silent sand with my feet, dropping to my knees to pat it into grainy sculptures. But shingle pebbles aren't silent; they ping and clatter and clunk. They do not cling to one another, hold any shape at all. Castles and forts are as impossible, finally, as the fantasy of a miniature me in a colossal garden of Zen. No monk raked the small stones, no hooded contemplative strolls silently by or sits cross-legged, trying to empty the mind. No tool is old or large enough to be the vast rake that the North Sea is, heaping and sorting the shingle for centuries. And no Zen garden I've ever heard of posts signs like the one to my left: "Danger. Unexploded Ordnance. Please Keep to Visitor Route."

To the south I can barely make out the outline of two Japanese-looking pagodas. The rooflines—gracefully curved—are consistent with the Zen-like feel of the place. Built 50 years ago, they were designed to shelter, not monks, but the triggers for atomic bombs. Below the roof was a pit into which the trigger mechanism of a bomb could be gently lowered. After it had been carefully placed and vibration sensors attached, the pit was sealed and the tests begun. They subjected the triggering device to various vibrations, temperature shocks, and a hydraulic ram that could produce g-forces. If the thing detonated, the roof, a light aluminum, would be blown off harmlessly.

I try to imagine the tests—the device buried in the well, the beach pebbled and still all around it, and then the vibrations and ramming, the temperature shocks, the shingle pounded, the small stones rattling, the trigger down in its well absorbing one blast after another after another until finally it's too much and the bomb explodes, blows off the aluminum roof. Surely the mind does likewise. Surely there's a point where what's been under the surface can absorb no more and erupts in passion or fear, fantasies and hallucinations. With no time or consciousness to shape what spews out, the mind must try then to make sense of whatever emerges: dreams, projections, hybrids, mutated beings.

In Gabriel García Márquez's story "A Very Old Man with Enormous Wings," heavy rains wash a creature ashore and into the courtyard of a young couple. He's a drenched and pitiful man who huddles in a corner, trying to get comfortable in spite of the enormous wings that sprout from his back. Is he an angel or a castaway? When the couple questions him, his answers are incomprehensible. When the villagers appear, they want to know what he is; his muttered, indifferent responses lead them to torment him, pull out his feathers, burn him with a branding iron. He backs away in his chicken coop, befuddled and withdrawn.

Though the villagers want to know what to call him, what category to put him in, nobody needs to ask how he got there. Oddities, after all, wash up from the sea all the time. Neither does anybody need to ask how he happened to have wings, whether he sprouted them slowly, if it took years of rubbing his back against a barn wall until the nubs appeared. Márquez and the villagers understand that most mythological transformations don't require the passage of time. They also understand, as do the merman's captors, that instant metamorphosis carries with it the possibility of magical wisdom. Winged and fish-tailed men wash ashore, UFOs descend to Orford Ness, and even though we're afraid, we long to know what they know. Speak to us, we plead. *Say something.* I know those fantasies, that wish for some benevolent mandate to revolutionize me, cause me to wake up in the morning kinder, smarter, more willing to fight for justice. If only we could do it that way—hear a magical cure, sprout wings, slit open the necessary gills, grow a new face, eat a little kryptonite, whatever it takes to suddenly become more than merely human.

And this, I finally see, is how the merman's story instructs. They're out there at sea; the deck is salt-sprayed and slippery. Home is elsewhere, and up onto the stern of the boat they haul a figure that has slipped through the censoring nets of their own minds and silenced their chatter. They stand around and stare at the chance to change their lives and they refuse it. Back on shore, the villagers refuse it. In the Márquez story, they refuse it. They become worse than they were: they burn and scare.

No wonder the force of mythology and art and the Rilke line in which he declares that in the face of Apollo's headless torso, "You must change your life." What frightens us might also have the power to transform us—aliens from underwater, outer space, some other sky—though we'd be wise to never count on those. Beauty can do it too, serve as a kind of merman for the soul. Whether we find it on our deck, on the page, in the garden, or on a gallery wall, we can be moved by it, stunned by how it disallows any wallowing or delay. Now? you want to ask. You mean I must change my life *right now*? Rilke's answer seems clear—*right now*.

Could I do it? Would I even recognize a merman at my feet? The men testing the trigger device might have been able to call out a number, a shock rating, a temperature drop, a specific point at which the trigger fired, but most likely for most of us there is no single igniting spark. If ever I've been able to measure any real catalyst in my life, it's been in retrospect: months later, years even, understanding the significance of a certain encounter with someone or a night of looking up at the stars. And even if I'd felt the trigger point approach, I'm not sure I'd be brave enough to allow the explosion to occur. Mythological transformations, after all, occur in an instant. There's no time for second thoughts, a careful reconsideration, no chance to sculpt the chimera that bursts forth, no guarantees at all. You get whatever hodgepodge emerges—fins, wings, a tail.

I blur my eyes and the shingle stretches out before me, acres of stonenubby carpet unrolled for miles beside a gray sea that reminds me I love myths of transformation because in reality human change is often so difficult. Incremental, tedious, the result of years and years of a dailiness that abrades and polishes, slowly changes our shapes. Dreams get fragmented, washed away, new foundations deposited. Not one of us wakes up one morning as a literal bug, as Kafka's character did, or an angel or a merman. Instead, we shift a little here, a little there. Perhaps the most we can hope for is the transformative power of beauty or love. Meanwhile, we mostly go on, accumulating and discarding what we can. Debris piles up. We ignore it or, given luck, patience, and a trace of consciousness, we sculpt it into something useful, know ourselves to be a bit buggy one day, a little fishy the next.

I unblur my eyes and look down. Underfoot is a bean-sized, putty-colored pebble with deep mauve blotches that look exactly like fish. And next to it, a stone inlaid with something resembling bone, and then a small potato stained with a topographical map of Asia. Here on this stretch of the literal shingle, gravel-bits aren't separated from stones, and so the sea pea won't survive. But if this were a shingle in some myth, we humans might. Maybe if we're willing to see—but not segregate—the coarse from the fine, we might even do more than survive. Maybe if every distinction we make between freak and human were tempered by uncertainty, then we might begin to change our lives. Faced with the winged and fishy, the buggy and scaled inside us all, we might find a way to be less monstrous.

The merman never spoke. Neither did the very old man with enormous wings, nor, as far as we know, did anything from outer space.

Whatever the Cobra Mist radar was trying to hear remained out of earshot, obstructed by some mysterious noise. No blazing message, no commandment to alter our ways, no explosion that means we must revise our lives. The sky is lighter now, the drizzle stopped. I'm aware if I don't head back to the landing jetty soon, the warden will be out in his jeep looking for me. I don't want that, don't want the jeep with its fumes and him with his concern, nor do I wish yet to leave this shingle, which seems even larger now than a giant's Zen garden and looks, in fact, stable, as if it's been here, like this, forever. But I know that's an illusion, that even as I walk here, it's graveling its slow way down the coast, inching southward with its litter of iron scraps, blocks of wood, and remnants of war, its lore of merman and UFOs, top secret radar projects and trigger testing. By my left foot, the tiny white tendril of a sea pea twines down between the finer stones in search of a smidgen of nutrition. In the 500 years since that early map, the nose that is Orford Ness has moved south a couple of miles, its tip now pointed a little more downward. If it were possible to film this drifting debris over hundreds of years and speed the action up, we'd see a nose held high begin to lower, as if the head it's attached to has grown sleepy, begun to nod off.

Nominated by Fourth Genre

SEVEN MARYS

by LI-YOUNG LEE

from WORLD LITERATURE TODAY

Father John,
I have seven Marys.
What am I to do?

Ancient when I was born,
each sings to me in three colors: Blue,
wishing, and following the river.

Growing younger while I die faster
every year, they speak to me
in four languages; Thinking, dreaming,
drowning, and guitar.

And one never knows what to do with her hair.
And one rocks me in and out of moonlight.
One cauterizes broken wing joints with black honey.
And one lifts my heart
onto the weighing pan opposite hunger.

Seven Marys, Father, and one
sets me on her lap and opens a book
and moves her finger from word to word

while I sound out evening's encrypted sentences.

And one is the book itself. A book,
yet not a book,
but a house called *Day*.

Seven, Father John, Marys, Father John,
the fulcrum, the eye, the heart enthroned, the dove
without person, homing.

And I can't tell the one who's always looking ahead
from the one who's always looking behind,

the one who's late for everything
from the one who's quick to remind me:

Be ever beginning.
At time's brim, abreast
of that dream
whose wake is each flown act, word,
wish, the stars, their dust,
who stays too long at childhood's window
leaves earth's shadow unsung.

Seven Marys, Father John, seven laughing Sarahs.

One to kiss my mouth and one to tie my hands.
One to build the pyre and one to assure me:

Don't be afraid. Find yourself
inside good-bye, one with life,
one with death.

Seven mothers, their backs turned,
walk ahead of me forever.

Sisters dancing, they're the hub
of all that wheels,
all that joins or comes asunder.

Rachels underneath my bed, they decide
the fate of my sleep.

Bells tolling my solitude,
they're seven zeroes
trumping every count.

Lure, slaughter, feast,
blood in the throat,

fire at the whispered gate, the song
that keeps leaving, they're seven wings
stalking my voice,

they're seven dragons marrying seven sheep
with their heads bent down
by seven enormous crowns.

Marys, Father, Rachels and Sarahs,
and I can't tell one from the other.

Is it Rachel who sings to remember the flood?
Is it Sarah who sings to forget it?
Is it Mary making my bed?
Which one can tell me
the shape of my destiny?

Nominated by World Literature Today

UNASSIGNED TERRITORY

fiction by STEPHANIE POWELL WATTS

from THE OXFORD AMERICAN

LESLIE PAWLOWSKI PARKS HER BLUE HORIZON on the shoulder of
the dirt road—the best shade we can find. July is always a killer in
North Carolina. It's always hot as blazes, hot enough to fry eggs, and
on and on. We are in the thick of it, midmorning, our dresses clinging
to our backs, way far in the middle of nowhere, preaching door to
door, working in our congregation's "unassigned territory." This is the
kind of dirt road, *Hee Haw*, overalls, straw-in-the-teeth place even
we Southerners make fun of. Did you hear the one about the country
girl who went to a town doctor? The doctor says to her mother,
"Ma'am, has this girl had intercourse?" and the mother, wringing her
hands, says, "I don't rightly know, Doctor, but if she needs it, you
make sure you give it to her."

The passenger-side window sticks in the middle of going up or
down. Piece of junk car. And on the way to every house, we shed bits
of polyfoam from the car's cracked upholstery. But Leslie has a great
attitude about her poverty: "Halcyon, salad days," she will say with a
withering chuckle when her future kids complain of their own first
cars.

We've visited too many houses without updating our field-service
records so we stop before we forget the details. We need to keep
records. Records for ourselves, for the congregation file on the terri-
tory, and for the official log at the Kingdom Hall.

"What was that woman's name at the blue trailer, Steph?"

I shuffle through my notebook knowing I won't find any useful
information. You are supposed to write things like: *Ruth Boaz,*

393

123 Main Street, blue trailer, lived in town all her life, no husband in the house, four kids—one still at home. Took the July 1989 brochure, Making the Most of Your Youth. *Expressed an interest in tarot. Bring brochure* Why Godly People Shun Spiritism.

My records are, to say the least, incomplete. I wrote: *Trailer is a nightmare. Looks like the time my brother and I played drug czar with an old suitcase and Monopoly money. Ryan threw my clothes and shoes out of the dresser and closet screaming, "Where's the real stash! Where's the real stash!"*

I'm praying that Leslie won't ask to see what I've written. I've been at this long enough that I don't need any guidance from my field-service partner. Sometimes Leslie will say things like, "You're writing a book over there, aren't you?" but she never pries.

"Shoot. I hate to leave her name off. She was nice, too," Leslie sighs.

"Nice" to Leslie means that she didn't cuss us, that she didn't shoo us away or hide behind her curtains, her hand over the mouth of her child like a kidnapper. "But Mama," the kid would manage through her fingers, "there's some girls on the porch."

"Shh," I imagine her saying, "Do you want to be saved? Is that what you want?"

This lady had stood sullen and quiet on her rickety porch, her eyes never leaving my brown face. Leslie, even with her Minnesota accent, was apparently okay. Brown woman on the porch trumps Yankee invader any day. To be fair, they don't get too many black Jehovah's Witnesses out here. There are only two black Jehovah's Witness families in town, for a total of six people. And though our congregation gets to every door in the city limit at least three times a year, the unassigned territory, this deliverance of woods, creeks, and black snakes, gets worked only once a year if we are lucky. More likely, these people won't see any of us for eighteen to twenty-four months. Imagine the odds of seeing a black Jehovah's Witness in the territory. That's Lotto odds.

Besides the absence of black people there are four things to remember about the unassigned territory:

1) You are as remote as you can get in this new world—way out in the boonies, mostly white Southerners who've been holed up here for generations, living on winding dirt roads that lead to more

winding dirt roads, with houses, the occasional mansion, trailers, and shacks out of sight from each other. They like it that way.

2) Everybody and his dog has a dog—at least one loose, ugly mutt with cockleburs in his unloved fur and filled with the kind of hatred that only comes from at last finding a body more miserable than yourself.

3) Apparently, the trauma of a visit from Jehovah's Witnesses is so great that just the glimpse of your *Watchtower* will act as a Proustian mnemonic causing the householder to wax nostalgic about your last visit. Never mind that someone from your or any congregation left a tract in the door two years ago. You will hear over and over, "Some of y'all was just here."

4) There is nothing good about the unassigned territory.

Leslie explained the "Offer of the Month," trying to regain the householder's attention. "This is our new booklet, *Enjoy Life Forever on a Paradise Earth*." Leslie dangled the bright red cover at the woman. Even the color pictures of laughing children and fluffy sheep nuzzling up to male lions (dubiously, I thought) didn't move the woman's eyes. She only had eyes for me.

Does the missus want I should jig, a little tap dance fuh yo pleasure? I wanted to ask, but instead put on my best yes-I'm-black-but-dog-gonit-not-*that*-black face.

"You got that same Bible?" the woman said to me.

"Yes, ma'am," I held out my paperback *New World Translation* for her to see. When I got baptized, I'd get a leather one.

"That's plenty," she said, folding her arms across her chest. "I know the Bible when I see it."

Leslie gave the woman an older *Watchtower* magazine because she wouldn't have to request a donation for it. Good move, Leslie. She can get the literature into the house and not risk rejection. Who knows? This woman might even read it. She might change her life and be side-by-side with us in this very territory next year. You never know. That's why Leslie is a pro. She thinks about these kinds of things. I've seen her talk to grief-stricken and depressed people, whip out the Bible she seems to know by heart, and without a blink tell them that God is a fortress, a rock, a high place, a God of comfort, love, and forgiveness. And for a few seconds, I think she really lightens those people. It is no small thing to give a person even a moment of hope. Of course, when we go back the next week to follow up, those same people, looking like they could kill us, order us away—"Don't you tell me God loves me. Don't you dare"—and slam their doors.

Leslie is grooming me, though she doesn't think that I know. I have a big decision to make next year. To serve Jehovah during my youth (which *Making the Most of Your Youth* recommends) or to go to college. I know that my congregation elders have urged Leslie to help me do the right thing.

On the way past the car, past the tired, old dog, through the patchy yard, I can't be sure, but I think I heard the woman say "wetback." I don't know, it could have been the heat or bigoted cicadas, but I think she called me that. I wanted to put my finger in her crumpled face, her skin like the film from Krazy Glue, and say something wise and cutting like, "Get your racial epithets right, Ms. Einstein." But fighting in the field service is looked down upon. Truth be told, at ninety-seven degrees and counting, Unnamed Householder had the virtue of being accurate in a literal sense. Not nice, but accurate. Apparently, the Mexicans who are coming into the county taking all the glory jobs (like picking apples for fourteen hours a day at less than minimum wage) and preaching door to door in glamorous locales like Millers Creek will make anybody sick with envy. I wanted to tell Leslie, but she was the sort of white person who refused to acknowledge racism. Just deny it and it won't exist. She'd say, "Well, I'm sure she didn't mean anything. Maybe she was concerned about the heat."

"What about the man on the tractor? Where did he say he lived?" Leslie asks. "I knew we should have stopped right then."

"Oh yeah," shuffle, shuffle. I want to ask Martin Luther King: Is this the dream you meant? Me and this sweet girl from Minnesota in a steaming car? Dr. King, I am hot today, but I'm trying to remember you at 1400 High Rock Road.

"1400 High Rock Road," I say.

"Okay, you are good for something," Leslie grins, acting like a mother. She's only six years older than I am, but preaching is her career. Her family moved to North Carolina only three years ago to serve "where the need was greater," but Leslie is easily one of the most popular people in town. She's a good girl, with a sweet disposition, and she has committed herself to the fieldwork. Leslie is a pioneer—out in service at least sixty hours a month every month. Sixty hours of door-slammings; "I have my own religions"; "I was just on my way outs"; and lonely old women who will even talk about Jehovah to hear another voice in the room.

"Okay," Leslie says, handing me a Shasta from her cooler; she always gets the cheap sodas. "Let's do two more houses. One if it's too far, okay?"

Thank God, thank God. Thank you. Thank you, Dr. King, thank you. "Are you sure? I'm up for another hour or so," I say, willing the bouncing thing of hope in my chest to stay still for a few minutes; she might change her mind. "I mean, if you need the time. I'm up for it," I manage to say.

"I'll just have to make it up next week," Leslie says breezily. But I know that this month will be especially hard for her. She has all those hours to complete in these backwoods. Think about it. You can't just come any old time. You have to arrive at decent hours, after nine in the morning and before eight at night but not during the dinner hour. You can only count the time you actually preach. That means the forty-five minute drive out there—gratis. The ride in between these houses in the territory—if it is more than ten minutes, you eat it. The fifteen-minute lunch break is on your time, sister-friend. Jehovah's Witnesses need a union.

Leslie dribbles soda all over the bodice of her dress. No loss, as far as I'm concerned. Leslie shops at Granny's Rejects or Let's Repel Men or some store like that. I can't believe the kinds of things this young woman puts on her body: shifts (really!), baggy sweaters, long full skirts, gaudy prints. A style my Daddy dubbed, "To' up from the flo' up."

Leslie has mostly given up on men. I know that the secret wish of her heart is that Bruce Springsteen comes to the Truth, but she was only hoping in her heart, not in her head. Lately, I've noticed her saying strange things like, "when I was young," or "if I were your age," or "that's for the kids." She is twenty-four. To be honest, she *is* getting a bit too old to be a Jehovah's Witness bride. The faithful marry young rather than burn with desire (according to 1 Corinthians 7:9), and they marry fast to get the pick of the litter of endangered young male believers. The congregation has already picked out my husband for me. A nice-looking white boy with a flounce of blond hair, unswiveling hips, and clunky, clod-buster shoes. Bobby Ratliff. I like Bobby, don't misunderstand me, but only twelve-year-old virgins look at a dopey sixteen-year-old and think, "What great marriage material!" Lord knows that by rejecting Bobby I am dooming myself to Lesliedom. There is precious little else to choose, few kids my age to even compare and contrast.

Jim, another teenager in the congregation, is a possibility, but he and his sister, Lisa, are bad—really bad. Once they brought a dirty magazine on the school bus, passed it around like candy to the other kids. I noticed when it came to Bobby's seat, he wouldn't even look at the filthy cover, wouldn't even touch it. The worst, the absolute limit, was when Jim and Lisa brought a Prince song for us to listen to. When Prince said "controversy" (and he said it often), Jim and Lisa led the bus in a rollicking, racy mispronunciation at the tops of their heathen lungs. Bobby and I didn't tell on Jim and Lisa, though we were tempted. We did explain to the other kids (at every opportunity) that though Jim and Lisa attend the Kingdom Hall, they aren't really of our sort. We insist that we are the real Jehovah's Witnesses. Sure, Jim and Lisa are clever and cool and fun, but salvation? I don't think so.

Lingering in a parked car in someone's driveway is a definite no-no, an unwritten rule; you can't look like you're casing the joint. But we are in slow-motion today, staring ahead at the gravel road, the high weeds and bushes covered with a thick layer of red dust. It hasn't rained for days. We can't see the house that the record indicates is directly in front of us. Somehow this seems important to me. If I had the words, I would say to Leslie, Isn't it funny that we can't see the next house? Doesn't that mean something? I want to tell her that, to take her deeper into my head. I want her to understand me. Leslie wouldn't get it. She would coax me to pray for guidance and direction and she'd be right. I know she'd be right. What is the alternative, really? The house record warns us of one place at the edge of the territory to avoid: "NOT INTERESTED. GUN." I can't help but think that the gun fact should come first. We'll have to come back when we're sure that Jim Caudle—gunman—has moved or is dead. Today we won't even check.

"Your door," Leslie says. "You can have the last door of the day."

The house is small, with a red tin roof. Someone must love the sound of the rain. Hippies probably. This gravel driveway looks fairly new and, sure enough, there is no record of the house in our files.

Another rule: Wait for the dog. Some come on strong, yelping and moaning like they've been stranded on Jupiter with a host of unheralded moons. Others give a quick impotent yap when you least expect it, their only surprise attack.

But this time: nothing. Just the pleasant walkway of paving stones, dotted without any discernable pattern, with terra-cotta pots full of red geraniums. I like this place. I like the porch and bentwood furniture, the chunky table in the center with a photo of a toddler on the potty. An instance when pervs and parents have the same taste in art. But nothing is pervy about this place. Just solid and permanent.

"Hello," I say to the outline of the woman's face behind the screen door.

"Yes?" she asks. Her accent is Yankee.

"Good morning," I say. "We are sharing a word from the Bible with our neighbors this morning."

"Your neighbors?" the woman moves onto the porch.

"Yes, ma'am." I smile. Stupid. Stupid. Leslie would never have used a canned line like that.

"You've got a generous idea of neighbors," the woman grins.

"We've been going for a few hours now," I say, not sure of what I'm getting at.

"You must be hot, then. Let me get you some drinks." The woman starts back into her house. When my mother was a teenager she ironed clothes for Mrs. Rowe, an old white woman in town. When the black man who tended the yard needed a drink of water, Mrs. Rowe would grab the glass from under the sink, bring the water or tea out to him herself. When he was done, she'd rinse the glass out with Clorox water; store it back in its place. Something told me that this woman will not scurry to her kitchen for the Colored glass. Something tells me she is for real.

"Oh no, ma'am," I begin. "We are ready to go home. You are actually our last stop today." Why did I say that?

"You are Jehovah's Witnesses, then?"

She got the name right. The number of people who just can't manage the name is astounding. We are the Jehovahs or simply Jehovah or, worse, the jokes: Are you a Jehovah's Witness? they ask. No kidding, well, where's the accident?

"I knew some Witnesses a few years back. I worked with one. Nice people. I admire the work you do."

"Thank you," I say.

"I've studied a number of faiths—as a lay person, I mean. The spiritual life is important."

I was right. She is a hippie.

"Well, we want everyone to hear the good news," Leslie chimes in. I'm blowing this call. She is saving me. "We are always happy to find people of faith in these times. You know that the perilous conditions we live in have been predicted in Scripture," Leslie pulls out her Bible. Some householders recoil, as if you've just pulled out a gun. Okay, okay, put the Bible down. You don't want to do anything crazy.

"Well, I'm not much for organized religion, but I do try to keep an open mind. I'm glad that God is available to everyone. Are you sure you don't want a drink? It's brutal out there."

"No," I say too vehemently. "But I'm Stephanie. Nice to meet you."

"Well, take this then." The woman pulls out a couple of bills from her jeans pocket. "I'm Phyllis. I'd like to give you a donation for your work."

"Thank you." Leslie hands the woman some new magazines, taking only one of the dollars from her open hand.

"Okay, so that was Phyllis, new magazines," Leslie says, writing in her record. "I'm giving you credit for placing those. We'll come back to see her next week." Leslie pretends she doesn't know quite what to write, but, of course, she is pondering the best way to make this last call a teaching moment. "Listen, Steph, don't worry if you forget your sermon. I've done it. We all have. As hot as it is, I can hardly remember my name. Anyways, you got a magazine placement. That's the important thing. I don't see much working out with Phyllis." Leslie screws her face into a conclusion. "She's fine, nice really, but we're not going anywhere with her." Leslie pauses, trying to find the most encouraging angle. "Of course, Jehovah is the judge, but she seemed to me too comfortable. I don't think we're going anywhere. If you don't stand for something, you'll fall for anything, right?"

But I am hardly listening. All I can think about is that I am in love with Phyllis. It is too easy to point to her middle-class manners, the slick magazines with no celebrities on the covers, the coasters on the willow furniture, her kindness at the end of a long, hot day. I want her. Wouldn't it be great to walk up to someone's house and just say, I am here and I want to be your friend? Kids do it all the time. No misunderstandings. None of that rooting around for larger meaning. Like with God. He has the key, right? He holds the keys to happiness and to life. Why can't we just show up at the door, just ask for them? I'd open a door, any door, and He'd be on the other side with a whole host of Phyllises saying, "Here you go. Enjoy."

Before being a Jehovah's Witness, I'd been a member of my grandmother's African Methodist Episcopal church. Another world of dogged believers. Mama Ruby preached on lonely dirt roads, black neighborhoods, none of this white man's religion. Black places like Warrior, Freedman, and Dulatown. "Do you need to make water?" she'd admonish before the services, because once we commenced, there was no stopping. Remember: no hair-fooling, no gum, no candy, no giggling, no turning to look at the opening door, no smiling, no eye-darting, no talking, no tapping of feet or fingers— clapping at up-tempo songs only, but not too vigorously, like I've had no home-training, no syncopation with the claps (leave that to the elders). No staring at anyone, even the spirit-filled or pitiable. And these are the easy rules, the ones for the very young. No problem. No problem, I say with nods. And if you are very good, do it all to your utmost like Noah, so you too will be rewarded with belief. Oh Phyllis, to believe anyway. What are you made of? I start my house-to-house record:

> To poet Philip Larkin: I have felt your breath on my heart today. Phyllis said she likes to keep an open mind and I fear this is the beginning. I will not go down the long slide with you, but stay safe, a dirtroader myself. It is safe here. The copse of pines, poplars, and weeds choking everything but light. Don't you see that? If you can't, I can't love you. Doesn't Scripture say to stay away from bad associates? Friends who will see you dead, all in the name of opening your mind? What about knowing every single thing for sure? What about that?

"A good day. A realy good day," Leslie says. "How did you like your first visit to the territory? Different, huh?"

I nod.

Leslie starts the engine. "You seem preoccupied. Are you thinking about a certain young man?" She grins at my surprise, which she takes as proof of her suspicion. My body cringes at the thought. I'll see Bobby at the Kingdom Hall when Leslie drops me off. I'll see him tomorrow morning at the Sunday service and the day after that on the bus. But the thought of his thick fingers any place on my body, his short-sleeved dress shirts with the sweaty armpit stains that never seem to come out completely, the idea of spending one day of life forever with him makes me angry. Though I love him in God's way, I want to stomp him. I will say none of it to Leslie. I don't even want to.

"Maybe," I say.

"I knew it." Leslie wags her finger at me. "Don't wait," she says, "don't wait."

Nominated by The Oxford American

FLICKERS OF LIGHT BECOME THE MOVEMENT OF THOUSANDS

by GRETA WROLSTAD

from THE CANARY

As when Orson Welles ran for governor, and the cinematographer
filmed a crowd drawn in ink, pricked pin-sized holes and waved
a candle behind the paper. The hand moving, withheld
from sight. Across the room, a blackened window doubles
the distance to my image, and last century there were mediums
who brought forth an unraveling white shapelessness from their
   bodies—
cloth, cobwebs, proof of duration. In photographs
their faces are pained, their hands gripping the dark curtains
as an ectoplasm gauze falls from their open mouths. Some nights
I find myself in an old mill town, sitting beside the train trestle,
watching rustling water flint the light. Across the river
a man weaves along the ties, his mouth gathered as if whistling.
It would be enough for his voice to reach me.

Nominated by The Canary

FATHEAD'S
HARD TIMES

by W. S. DI PIERO

from THE THREEPENNY REVIEW

WHEN I'M STANDING AT THE OPERA—at ten dollars a ticket it's the best cheap show in San Francisco—I look along the balustrade and think on the kinds and degrees of backache people will tolerate in exchange for a certain order of beauty. Regulars have to think things through in advance. The difference between the one-act *Salome*, a quick hundred minutes of sexed-up hysterics, and the nearly five-hour evening of the bitterly sweet *Così Fan Tutte*, may entail significant medication. About opera I am the complete amateur, musically untrained, patchily familiar with the repertoire, but a concentrated listener and, like so many other hounds attracted by ripe scents, a helpless softie. Mostly I roll in it. Nothing else in my life induces the dark elation I feel at a performance of *Don Giovanni* or *Così*. Passages in *Rigoletto*, *Peter Grimes*, and *Jenufa* melt me down; and while I'm losing my mind during *Butterfly* I give no thought to Pound's crack in the *Cantos*: "Spewcini the all too human / beloved in the eyetalian peninsula / for quite explicable reasons."

I didn't grow up in the eyetalian peninsula, I grew up (in the 1950s and 1960s) in South Philadelphia, an operatic culture that gave no thought to opera. My neighborhood was working class, Italian-Americans mostly, small congested squared-off red-brick row houses with shared stoops and walls, here and there a heroic sycamore, big voices aroused night and day, women's voices usually, shrieking at their misarranged ungrateful kids or at husbands coming home from miserable jobs. In the late 1950s through the 1960s, music of other sorts washed over every street and corner. They were the days of Berry Gordy's Motown Records and the sassy, big-finned-car vocals of Martha and the Vandellas, whose "Heat Wave" was an anthem to gluey city summers and sex. Phil Spector was crafting his "wall of sound" dynamics for The Ronettes, one of the early tough-girl groups, all beehive hairdos and goth eye shadow. ("Be My Baby" still kills.) One of Spector's groups, The Teddy Bears, performed their hit "To Know Him Is To Love Him" on the TV dance show, *American Bandstand*, broadcast from Philadelphia, which soon had its own city sound in The Delfonics (featured in Quentin Tarantino's *Jackie Brown*), two of whose singers were born the same year I was, 1945.

I listened with sunny transport to doo-wap groups. The Delfonics and The Deftones. The Clovers and The Cadillacs. The names alone would entice any daydreaming misfit to become some sort of writer. Transistors fizzed their portable sounds around the clock, indoors and out. On August nights men slept in deck chairs on the sidewalk, radios tuned to top ten programs ("We're livin' in a heat wave / a pain in your heart"), which in those days still featured vocals by Tony Bennett, Della Reese, and Sinatra. On summer weekends certain guys (bad guys taking a break from badness) did pretty much what you see in movies, cluster and croon on corners, leaning into the central harmonies they made. I sang a little myself, a passable falsetto, though I didn't go off with them later to make trouble at the local dance. Our *basso profondo* occasionally brought along a shot-putter's shot, which he once laid against the head of a black kid, a dark-complexioned, kinky-haired boy who danced with a white girl but who, the shot-putter later learned, was actually Sicilian.

My experience of music took a hard-angled and inauspicious turn when as a young boy I entered Pat's parlor, with its deeply folded odors of tomato sauce, cabbage, and garlic, down the block from the house I grew up in. Pat played mandolin and violin, it was said, though nobody had actually ever heard him play. My parents, who didn't care much about music of any kind, didn't know what to do with me. A multi-disc set of Sigmund Romberg's operetta *The Student Prince* had mysteriously turned up in our house. My father, who as staff handyman at a hospital had occasional access to useless pilfered goods like test tubes and fat rolls of butcherpaper, might have acquired it after hearing me howl in the shower whatever stuck in my head from AM radio. (For weeks it was Jerry Lewis's nasal "Rockabye My Baby.") Or it may have been the remnant of opera sets some unknown immigrant uncle two generations back had owned. His collection, on acetate 78s, which in those days ran to twelve or more disks and weighed at least as much as a meat-slicer, had all been given to the Salvation Army when he died, or moved away, or disappeared. (Nobody could tell me what became of him.) "For Chrissake," my mother would say years later. "If I knew you'd end up liking that stuff, I'd've kept them." For weeks I played *The Student Prince*, sang along with Mario Lanza (Alfredo Arnold Cocozza adopted his mother's name, Maria Lanza), a South Philly boy from Mercy Street, where he and my uncle Mike played stickball, lustily shredding my voice just as he was shredding his. Shredding, too, the already threadbare fabric of family peace. And so I was sent to Pat, as some parents send their children to Boy Scout camp or matinees.

I didn't expect so much silence. Pat spoke little English and taught me by the Italian method that had formed him. His parlor was like others in the neighborhood, an overcast weather with low clouds due to a high pressure system—thickly upholstered, hard-spring furniture, statuettes of the Sacred Heart and Infant of Prague, and leaky table lamps. I was terrified. I didn't know what to expect but vaguely thought I'd soon hold an instrument. Instead, to learn tempo, I clapped, for weeks. Clapped then waved my hand, side to side, as if in benediction of a privileged moment which never arrived, because along with the clapping Pat tried to teach me to read music. He wrote down and told me to copy notes and phrases that to me meant nothing, because they weren't voiced or sounded. Each week he *showed* me music, then sent me home to study it, clapping. I lived in a constant state of anxious boredom, stupefied by abstraction, and as unwilling to master unvoiced notes on the stave as I was to memorize the Latin that would have cleared me to become an altar boy. I felt so alive when my puny voice swelled alongside Mario's light tenor. But music, while I was learning it, became not just dephysicalized—it's made of nothing, after all—but abstract, virtual, a metronomic code embodied only by that robotic clapping and waving.

Weeks passed and I still hadn't seen an instrument. The idea was to start with mandolin then work up to violin. What did I know? One day Pat drifted off like a poltergeist and returned with a mandolin, which he played a bit and let me touch but not hold. Next week, out

406

came the violin. Same routine. He held out the instrument so that I could stroke it with my hand as if it was his pet, but infinitely remote, an actuality (it seemed an extension of his body) sealed off in a medium of mere possibility. I was Tantalus in the Parlor. Tantalized all the more when he tickled the mandolin into sound, then coddled and stroked long sonorous lines from the fiddle. Why wasn't I ecstatic? What I had known as a physically enthralling medium that came straight onto my nerves in mysterious, scary ways was becoming Idea. Luckily, that part of my musical education didn't last long. When I was eighteen and finally experienced live performance other than the snare drums and wheezing clarinets of wedding combos, it was at the Academy of Music during Eugene Ormandy's long stewardship of the Philadelphia Orchestra. Ormandy's predecessor Leopold Stokowski had created the plush, deep sonorities that came to be known as the "Philadelphia sound," as specific and laudatory a designation in the classical world as the Delfonics' sound was in theirs. I couldn't get enough. In the mid-1960s the orchestra performed a lot of Bartók and Mahler—I remember feeling that I was listening to "Concerto for Orchestra" with my *stomach*—and I started paying attention to whatever was available on radio and the occasional LP I could afford. But my musical intake was what it still is, eclectic, a polite term for an indiscriminate mess that took in Sunday morning gospel broadcast live from local Baptist churches, early Beatles and Stones, and (critically, it turned out) jazz of any kind. In the end, probably because I always had rock and roll, *Bandstand*, and Mario singing "Golden Days" to fall back on, my interlude with Pat, instead of putting me off music or decisively cooling it into abstraction, jacked up music's nervous immediacy and made it even more systemic, brute, and ardent.

That physicality intensified when I was twenty years old and got sick, when music fused to physical pain. I've been in bondage, more or less, ever since, but it's a bondage—or bonding, a cellular hybridizing—I can't imagine living without. And it's formed by music of all sorts, especially, in my later life, by voice—Dawn Upshaw singing Marc Blitzstein, any good tenor's "Un aura amorosa" from *Così*, Sarah Vaughn accompanied by Clifford Brown, Dion's "The Wanderer," or Sting's a cappella "Roxanne" (which a dog I once knew, a Shih-Tzu, sang along to with sonorous conviction). Physical pain is like personality: it's involuntarily expressive and idiosyncratic, but ex-

407

pressive only to the person experiencing it, and so idiosyncratic that any verbal representation of it is sickly inadequate and, to listeners especially, tedious, though talking about pain is boring first and most of all to its owner. It's an idiolect, a language specific to one brain and comprehensible only to the nervous system that activates and networks messages from that brain. It's grotesquely companionable to the person experiencing it but unfriendly toward others. It islands and isolates. When Philoctetes, dragging around his evil-smelling wounded foot, describes his island to the visiting Neoptolemus, he's also describing the exile pain causes:

> There's no anchorage here, nowhere anyone
> can land or trade or have a good time.
> No sensible person sails this way,
> though now and then sailors come by,
> and when they do, they pity me,
> at least they say they do, and in their pity
> give me scraps of food and cast-off clothes.

Pain becomes you, becomes so capillary that even though it's local it colonizes the entire body and is coextensive with it. It saturates perceptions and your sense of consequence. While it's active, just as we say certain pieces of music irrationally change our lives, it can permanently alter your sense of sense.

Ankylosing spondylitis is a severe inflammation that breaks down ligaments and cartilage and fuses them to bone. If in the vertebrae, you end up with "bamboo spine." If the lower back, the sacroiliac joints become an inelastic bony mass. In 1965 the syndrome was unknown, so the pain that put me in the hospital for three months, then plateaued for ten years (a steep plateau, it was), and has faithfully stood by me in varying degrees—depending sometimes on the length of the opera—ever since, had no evident cause. The physical pain was fraught with the spiritual dread unknowingness creates. I was tested for slipped disc, neurological damage, and psychosomatic dysfunction (i.e., derangement). Because the pain wasn't identifiable, my body felt invaded and occupied by hostile unreason. A person my age whose A.S. went untreated now usually looks like a broken matchstick or twig, someone who, as a chiropractor friend of mine says, walks around looking at his shoes. (Imagine Groucho's scampish glide turned herky-jerky, Mr. Hydeish.) I've often seen old men in

Chinatown shaped like grasshoppers, bent over a cane, looking up through inverted bifocals. Now I know why they look like that. My A.S. wasn't diagnosed until 2000, when a rheumatologist I consulted for a different ailment took an interest in my medical history and solved the mystery. He was rather surprised to see me standing upright. I *don't* walk around looking at my shoes, and for this I'm grateful to, among others, David "Fathead" Newman.

While in the hospital and for a long time thereafter, at night I kept by my ear a transistor radio like those the men who slept on sidewalks listened to. So whenever pain spiked me awake—*it* seemed deranged, because it migrated: now in my lower back, now knees, now upper legs—I had sounds running into my ear that instead of being a balm or distraction layered me more deeply into the pain, its rhythms and registers. The pain and its music, as one entity, took on the sort of casual familiarity Nietzsche describes in *The Gay Science*: "I have given a name to my pain and call it 'dog.' It is just as faithful, just as obtrusive and shameless, just as entertaining, just as clever as any other dog—and I can scold it and vent my bad mood on it."

My night music was jazz, spun by Joel Dorn at Philadelphia's FM station, WHAT, which programmed around the clock. Early Nina Simone, Oliver Nelson's *The Blues and the Abstract Truth*, Miles Davis playing Gil Evans's arrangements, Oscar Peterson's sweet and melancholy *Canadian Suite*, and the celestial Charles Lloyd. Dorn, who went on to become an astute, adventurous record producer, hosted an evening show to which he brought some interesting backstory. In 1958, as a teenager already possessed by blues and jazz, he went to a small joint outside Philadelphia called The Ambler Sporting Club, where Ray Charles and his group were performing. Charles was mostly a rhythm and blues instrumentalist starting to break ground as a pop vocalist and jazz artist. The sax player in Charles's ensemble was a young and handsome fellow named David "Fathead" Newman. (When he flubbed an arpeggio in his high school band, the leader called him a fathead, and the moniker stuck.) Dorn cornered him during a break between sets and promised him that someday, when he became a D.J., he would use a number he heard that night, "Hard Times," as his theme song.

And so he did, every night at ten P.M. All day every day I felt the urge to take to my bed and settle into whatever occult infirmity waited there for me. I didn't know, of course, that if I did so, my body would shape itself to its illness and once I put on my shoes I would spend a long time looking at them. We now know that certain rheumatic disorders require the body to stay in motion lest it stiffen for good. Some impulse, maybe fear of inertia—I became terrified, still am, by enforced immobility—or mule-headedness, made me want to stay in motion. With the help of stout canes given me by my Mario-Lanza Uncle Mike, who lost a leg in the war, I rode the bus into center city, went up and down subway stairs and the stairs in our small dim house (occasionally harangued by my impossible mother about how much suffering I was causing her), and walked endless circles—ovals, actually—around the dining room table, to train my legs again, to walk the dog. Keep moving, I told myself, like jazz, which is most alive in its changes.

By late evening the pain was running high; I'd be exhausted and had to rest. "Hard Times," Charles on piano opening with a brief, tripping statement of theme, was always waiting for me. Fathead's sax line, a climbing plea resisting the drag of melancholy, became a resting place for (not from) pain, became pain's reliable nocturnal climate and substance. I loved the number all the more, with the kind of exasperated love that doesn't fade but gets more acute in memory, even after the pain dampened. I never owned the album, though, until a few months ago, when I ran down a remastered CD of the original 1958 LP, *Fathead: Ray Charles Presents David Newman.* "Hard Times" is the opening track, and when I played it, not having heard it for over thirty years, I wept like a child for the past, and then I whistled along.

In the hospital, I had nothing but time on my hands and pain in my brain. I spent time practicing apotropaic mind games I hoped would help with the pain. What they now call "pain management" is really a way of establishing terms of ownership. One tactic is to contrive likenesses. Pain is a language, a story, a journey, it's a busted gearbox's teeth, a bed of nails, a heat gun. Another, and one I practiced for years, is to imagine the means of eliminating it. Extirpating it. I imagined marking its boundaries, as one traces the frontiers of a small country on a map, then surgically knifing it out, carving it clear of its surrounding mass of nerve and flesh, as Filippino hoo-doo men magically insert their hands into a sick person and extract the ailing part. I could, I thought, use a trowel or ice-cream scoop or child's sandshovel and remove it cleanly. I wouldn't want to see it or dedicate it to science. I wanted an old high school pal, a racketeer trainee, to take it away and feed the gorgeously veined, placental mass to the rats and feral cats at the dump.

My reading kept pain company. I read Thomas Mann's *Doktor Faustus*, his "Nietzsche book" about the inseparability of sublimity and pain. Adrian Leverkühn, a prodigious young composer and inventor of tone-row music, in order to break through ("like a butterfly emerging from its chrysalis") to an original musical language for feeling, to something really new—it turns out to be plainsong—sells his soul to the devil by contracting the syphilis that kills him and bargaining away love. Immobilized, often in hip-harness traction ("counter-indicated," they would now say), I moved laboriously through Mann's high-toned, immobile prose. What else was there to do? Except in movies and TV, hospitals are generally uneventful places, the sick waiting to learn more about sickness, lose it, or succumb. So I was cheered by the occasional visits of an African-American orderly who would stop by on his rounds to chat with the poor young bastard in bed. Actually, I was cheered before he walked in. I knew he was approaching because he'd be whistling, pitch-perfect, some jazz standard, and so in addition to the emotional boost he brought, he reminded me of a character in *Doktor Faustus*, the violinist Rudolph Schwerdtfeger, who "whistled with such artistry that one laughed for sheer pleasure, whistled more like a violin than a flute, the phrasing masterly, the little notes, staccato or legato, coming out with delirious precision."

The eeriest jazz stylist then (featured, of course, on WHAT) was Morgana King. After cutting a few albums and drawing a small but devoted following, she shunted into an acting career, so that most people now know her only as Don Corleone's stolid wife in the *Godfather* movies. Her repertoire was jazz classics and pop ballads like "A Taste of Honey," the title of her first LP. Some singers emulate the solidified sound of string instruments. King's voice went the opposite way. Her delivery was wound tight, breathy, flute-ish, air tremulously whisked into resonance, closer to moody, throaty whistling than to song. Her singing reminded me of the orderly's whistling. That was a time when you still heard people whistling everywhere, in hospital corridors and buses, in work places and on the street. I once read a lament by some poet about the passing of those sounds from public and private life. But they haven't entirely passed. The day I was reading the lament I could hear my adolescent daughter about the house whistling some Chopin she was working up

411

on piano; that reedy vitality gave me a rush of affection and hope, for her and for all breath in life, but rattled me, too, because it made me think of breath passing, my own, hers. And a childhood South Philly friend was visiting at the time, who in the many years I've known him whistles phrases the way people whoop at ball games and concerts, violent gusts and surging wingbeats of sound, but always only a phrase or two, which seems to exhaust him, because he never completes a melodic line. It's true enough that outdoors—I have no car so spend a lot of time waiting for and riding public transit—I hardly ever hear anybody whistling, and I don't have to catch myself if I start doing so because heads immediately turn my way, as if I'd burst into song. But who can say that's a bad thing? There's not much whistling going on because so many people are listening to music, ears muffed or buttoned up by headsets.

I tried another tactic while I was laid up, whistling through (or along with) the pain while the music was playing. Pain breathes forth its rhythms and tonalities through its instrument, the body. If I breathed too deeply, cleared my throat or, God help me, coughed, the pain spiked. Once I sneezed and nearly passed out. ("Give that boy more Darvon and muscle relaxers.") When people around me whistle, I listen up, thinking I'll hear some essence revealed. I sat vigil with my mother until she stopped breathing. Before he died my father's breath thinned to a hesitant narcotized hum. An old neighborhood friend of mine recently died in his sleep. Our lunch dates every couple of months were a ritual, the sort of little social celebration that refreshes and sustains affection: we ate at the same time in the same neighborhood place, even ate the same dishes—I did, anyway; he flopped between two favorites. Inside the restaurant, when I sat or stood, the standard but by now dampened pain flicked its blowtorch, as it likes to do. (My darling remembers me.) But I was happy when we settled down to catch up, gossip, talk books and movies and mutual friends, then say goodbye with a peck on the cheek, until next time. He loved to eat and drink and get lost. One night after dinner at my apartment, I was playing Dion and the Belmonts, and when he stood to leave he starting juking and pumping his fists to "The Wanderer"—"I'm a wanderer / Yes, a wanderer / I go around around around around"—right there in my kitchen. Whenever I phoned to make a lunch date, while fumbling for his book he whistled in a way that bespoke his personality, a bit diffident, unobtrusive, more air than tone, and no tune really, just a happy-go-lucky breathy jaunt. Now I wait for a streetcar on our neighborhood corner where I sometimes ran into him, hearing no whistling at all, and feel as if he disappeared into his own breath, the small music he made, and took all that beautiful rough vitality with him.

Nominated by The Threepenny Review

BICAMERAL

by LINDA GREGERSON

from THE KENYON REVIEW

1.

Choose any angle you like, she said,
the world is split in two. On one side, health

and dumb good luck (or money, which can pass
for both), and elsewhere . . . well,

they're eight days from the nearest town,
the parents are frightened, they think it's their fault,

the child isn't able to suck. A thing
so easily mended, provided

you have the means. I've always thought it was
odd, this part (my nursing school

embryology), this cleft in the world
that has to happen and has to heal. At first

the first division, then the flood of them, then
the migratory plates that make a palate when

they meet (and meeting, divide
the chambers, food

from air). The suture through which (the upper
lip) we face the world. It falls

a little short sometimes, as courage does.
Bolivia once, in May (I'd volunteer

on my vacations), and the boy was nine.
I know the world has harsher

things, there wasn't a war, there wasn't
malice, I know, but this one

broke me down. They brought him in
with a bag on his head. It was

burlap, I think, or sisal. Jute.
They hadn't so much as cut eyeholes.

2.

(Magdalena Abakanowicz)

Because the outer layer (mostly copper
with a bit of zinc) is good for speed

but does too little damage (what
is cleaner in the muzzle—you've begun

to understand—is also cleaner in
the flesh), the British at Dum Dum (Calcutta) devised

an "open nose," through which
the leaden core, on impact, greatly

expands (the lead being softer). Hence
the name. And common enough in Warsaw

decades later (it was 1943), despite
some efforts in The Hague. I don't

remember all of it, he wasn't even German,
but my mother's arm—

that capable arm—was severed at
the shoulder, made (a single

shot) a strange thing altogether.
Meat. I haven't been able since

to think the other way is normal, all
these arms and legs.

This living-in-the-body-but-not-of-it.

3.

Sisal, lambswool, horsehair, hemp.
The weaver and her coat-of-many-

harrowings. If fiber found *in situ*, in
agave, say, the living cells that drink

and turn the sun to exoskeleton,
is taken from the body that

in part it constitutes (the
succulent or mammal and its ex-

quisite osmotics), is
then carded, cut, dissevered

in one fashion or another from
the family-of-origin, and

gathered on a loom,
the body it becomes will ever

bind it to the human and a trail
of woe. Or so

the garment argues. These
were hung as in an abattoir.

Immense (twelve feet and more from upper
cables to the lowest hem). And vascular,

slit, with labial
protrusions, skeins of fabric like

intestines on the gallery floor.
And beautiful, you understand.

As though a tribe of intimates (the
coronary plexus, said the weaver) had

been summoned (even such
a thing the surgeon sometimes has

to stitch) to tell us, not unkindly, See,
the world you have to live in is

the world that you have made.

Nominated by David Baker, Rosanna Warren, Sherod Santos, Susan Hahn

LOTTO

fiction by ANNA SOLOMON

from THE GEORGIA REVIEW

THOSE DAYS AND MONTHS I spent with Alma, I was new to Providence. I'd left New York after Ben left me, and I was living in a valley inside, pale and uncluttered and mute. I knew no one. I spent my days wandering the Portuguese neighborhood where I lived, avoiding the storefronts crammed with sweetbreads, the corner grocer with his nuts and fruits. I survived on saltines and peanut butter. I walked on across bridges, past schools that looked like industrial wastelands, along brick-cobbled streets where professors strolled with antisocial dogs. I was working nights at a call center answering pleas from people who'd maxed out their credit cards.

I found Alma on a flier in a coffee shop, where I was staring at ads for roommates and futons and Cuisinarts. I didn't need these things, but it was a great relief to see other people's lives coming apart. I wondered who they were, what sorts of hopes they allowed themselves, whether they'd created their own pandects of self-denial. One flier stood out: EXTRA HOURS? VOLUNTEER TO SPEND TIME WITH AN ELDER. I had hours, and I had a lonely guilt—or guilt at my self-pity for being lonely—so I went for an interview and left with Alma's address on an index card that read *African-American, 98 years old. Department of Social Services visits daily to medicate for Crohn's disease.*

Her social worker was Prairie, a dyed blond who wore push-up bras and a wide smear of fuchsia lipstick outside the line of her lips. The first day I came, Prairie was on the verge of tears trying to get

Alma to take a plateful of pills. Alma shook her head, the skinny shreds of her braids whipping, her mouth clamped shut, her left leg hooked over the ragged arm of her chair.

Prairie shouted, "She won't be reasonable about anything!"

The place was overheated and smelled sour. I stood in the doorway, still in my coat, thinking I might slip back into the hall. Then I saw Alma's eyes. Despite their zombie-ish swing, they were certain and clear, the whites as bright as hard-boiled eggs.

Prairie rattled open the refrigerator and shoved a jar of applesauce at Alma. "This," she said, "is the only way she'll take them."

"Not today I won't."

Prairie turned to me. "Leslie?"

"Leah," I said.

"Lee. This woman is a pain in the ass. You get in the elevator, she pushes the button for every floor down. You bring her flowers, she tapes them to the wall. She won't go to the doctor unless you bring her chocolate, and she's not supposed to eat chocolate."

I looked at Alma's bare walls. I imagined her standing, one foot on each arm of her chair, reaching for the wall with a rose.

"I can understand that," I said.

"I bring cards? She plays solitaire."

I said, "My favorite. Especially in poor company."

Alma looked at me then. Her mouth twitched.

I committed myself to getting rid of Prairie. I made sure to be there every time she showed up. I moved her purse when she wasn't looking, and to further confuse her I convinced Alma to take her medicine greedily to show how she'd reformed. "Oh thank you, Lotto." This is what Alma called me; she said it made her think of luck. "Please could I have more water, Lotto?" Alma made me out to be the savior, and all the effort felt worthy, almost revolutionary, as if together we were disturbing some larger order. I brought boxes of saltines and stayed all day.

When we were alone, I let Alma do what she wanted. I bought her coffee, though she wasn't supposed to drink it. I turned up Nina Simone louder than the vacuum. I watched her play a game with her pills in which she lifted each one grandly toward her mouth until, at the last instant, with a flourish of her arm, she stuffed it under the cushion of her chair.

One afternoon, as I was leaving, she said, "Pick me up some dirty magazines."

"Are you serious?" The only reading material I'd ever seen in Alma's apartment was a pamphlet next to the toilet titled *This Book of Divine* HELP. I'd assumed it belonged to Prairie.

Alma leaned forward. "I like girls." She raised her eyebrows, mocking my surprise. "You 'spect old people not to be as many ways as everybody else?"

"Of course not."

"Liar. Then don't ask me if I'm serious."

Alma had a way of making me feel my cowardice all raised up like hives. It stung, but like peroxide, as though it would make me cleaner, better.

"Do you want anything special, then?" I asked. "Girls who like girls? Butch? Asian? There's something for everybody."

Alma squinted. I couldn't tell if she mistrusted these magazines or the fact that I knew what I was talking about.

"My boyfriend and I used to look at all of it," I said. Though, actually, I was talking about a few run-of-the-mill *Hustlers*, and I'd been alone when I discovered them stuffed into the back of our file cabinet. I was disturbed, flipping through, to find myself turned on. I felt smashed up all over again, as if he would still be there next to me if he'd known I was the sort of woman he didn't have to hide porn from. Or that I could have been. This line of reasoning was ridiculous, of course. Ben had not run off in search of sex. He'd run off to an orthodox yeshiva in Israel.

Alma said, "I don't care what girls or what types of people it's done for."

Her neighborhood was a dead zone, all tenements and parking lots. When the sky was gray, which seemed like most of the time, it felt apocalyptic. I had to buy the magazines across town, at the minimart near work. I felt no desire looking at them now. I'd tried masturbating once since Ben left, but it felt desperate and false, and I didn't make it anywhere. And there was Alma, at ninety-eight, still wanting to get it on. I pictured her leaning back in her chair—was it the same at that age, the same fickle, predatory process?

I settled on *Playboy*, *Penthouse*, and one called *Busty Beauties*. On my way to the register, I spied a co-worker—or rather, I spied the frosted bangs I spent my nights watching over a putty-colored divide. I started to shove the magazines under my shirt, then realized I didn't care enough to bother. I didn't know her name, and there was no one for her to tell. The call center was a solitary place. We were almost all women, just vessels for voices; the only closeness I felt to anyone was based on what I heard in the bathroom: some talked on cellphones as they peed, others vomited without shame, some sniffled and coughed. One, who wore only socks, punched the stall doors. It was a stricken scene but alive, and sometimes it got me close to crying. You could feel men crawling all over the walls, like roots and fires under all that pain. Ben was there, too, just before he left, when his arms seemed harder, as if dowels had been planted in them.

Alma and I worked out a spot under the rug where she could hide the magazines from Prairie.

"She just be jealous," she said.

"Did I do okay?" I asked.

"You did good."

"You haven't even looked at them."

"Later I will. Don't be so worried. I trust your way of thinking."

"Why?" I needed to hear something good about myself.

"You don't make me do what I don't want to do. You let me die in peace."

"You're not dying."

Alma laughed. "Everything's got to end someplace. Your little man again, to take an instance. You were together and then you weren't, see?"

Salt rose in my throat. All I'd told her was that I had an ex-boyfriend. "That's not dying," I said.

"Sure it isn't."

I shoved the magazines under the rug.

"This man went off why?" asked Alma.

"He didn't go anywhere. I left."

"What for?" Alma's mouth hung open. I saw how chapped her bottom lip was, the pink-brown flesh lined with gray cracks.

"It's complicated," I said.

Sometimes I pretended Ben had in fact died. Then the damage was simpler, my mourning less pathetic. There was a shape in my mind that held death. But how to say this to Alma's eyes with all their detached cool? She was rock-like, and I envied her this.

I was saved by Prairie flinging open the door, shaking her umbrella like a pompom. Her blond hair was frizzed with mist; it looked silvery and aged, and for a moment I felt sorry for her.

That was the day she sat me down and showed me the schedule of Alma's appointments. She turned to the pills and whispered: this one for blood pressure, that for constipation, another for diarrhea, another for Alma's bones. She walked me through the possible side effects and mistakes. It seemed, for instance, that combining the diarrhea and constipation pills could result in some mental confusion. I said that made sense.

Prairie scowled. "These pills are what keep her alive." Her eyes widened. Even under all the makeup, I could see her cheeks flush. She didn't think she was leaving Alma in my care alone. She was leaving Alma with the pills. She believed in them the way Ben now believed in religion and restraint.

When he'd told me where he was going, he said it wasn't about spirituality or politics, but discipline: this, he said, was the only thing he'd never tried. We'd just finished dinner, and his elbows were up on the table, his left sleeve clinging to his wrist with dishwater. There were nights when I'd leaned forward to lick his wet skin, to push him back against his chair. Now his eyes were small, backing away.

"We're taught," he said, "to follow our true selves, as if we'll end up where we need to be—but really we're just trying on everyone else. Take you. You want to act, but you spend most of your time waitressing, and when you're not doing that you're all conflicted about how to be a woman—how much to cook or clean, whether to have babies. Too many choices. Too much freedom. But if you commit to something and believe in it, then somewhere it will intersect with *you*. What it is may not even matter. What matters is, you're in it. You've surrendered." His eyes met mine, shy and wet, and I almost thought he might still be himself—then he pounded the table with his fist.

"Who told you this?" I asked, but he never answered.

After showing me the pills, Prairie left. It had taken us almost a month, and she was barely out the door when Alma said, "Hallelujah. Now I want to go for a walk."

"Let's wait," I said. According to Prairie's directives, walking was too strenuous. "She could run back here, saying she made a mistake."

"Bullshit. I'll be dead before that buttercup gets back."

"Alma," I scolded. Her eyes glittered with irreverence, and I was hit by the cracked-up-ness of what I was helping her do. But if I changed my mind, I knew she would kick me out. She would die faster and alone. I forced a grin. "Tomorrow. I'm sorry. Tomorrow. I promise."

My shift at the call center was 8 P.M. to 4 A.M. The later people called, the more desperate they were.

"This is my life you're screwing with."

"Who the hell are you to judge?"

I found it perversely satisfying to hear people's anger come so fully and predictably out of their mouths. They seemed wholly unashamed, as if the gorging pace at which they shopped was a discipline in its own right. I would have liked to help them.

"I'm sorry," I said to a single woman with three kids who spent a thousand dollars a month at Sears and a few hundred at Victoria's Secret, "but you've generated debt exceeding the allowable expected burden for a consumer in your circumstances."

"My what? Fuck you."

At four, a company van drove us home. Providence looked fake in the blackness. Nothing moved but leaves and plastic bags. The tight cluster of downtown scratched the sky like a dimly lit apology. My apartment was just as dark and silent, a steeply angled attic with windows at knee level. But I didn't mind the emptiness, or being awake on the backside of most people's days. It was easier this way; since Ben had left with his absolute faith, I'd felt my own fall away completely. Not my religious faith—I barely considered myself a Jew anymore—but the miniscule particles of faith it takes to get through a day. The sort of faith I didn't realize I had until I lost it. Some people call it optimism, but I came to see it as a willingness to let yourself be persuaded. You must be persuaded that the sun will come up again, persuaded that the homeless are not your fault, persuaded that your friends are not sick of your complaints, persuaded that a child who steals change from your hand is not beyond help. You don't realize all the work this takes until you are no longer persuaded.

The floors in my apartment were painted green, and on the spot where I stood to do my few dishes someone had painted, in gold, the delicate head of a woman sniffing a bouquet of flowers. The night after Prairie left, I looked at my floor and thought, That's no woman, that's a lady—but from what world, what century? I couldn't think of a single lady I knew, and I wondered, if I'd been one, whether I would have followed Ben and been rewarded in some way I couldn't now fathom.

When I arrived the next day, Alma was ready in her coat, a giant, brown, sack-like thing that made her head look like a vegetable growing out of the top of a compost heap.

"What you smiling at?" she said, pushing up from her chair.

"Did you eat?" I asked.

"Nope." She walked into the hall and started bouncing on her toes. "Grab my coffee, please, Lotto?"

In the elevator, she looked at me sideways. "Did *you* eat?"

She knew I hadn't—that I didn't, anymore, not until I absolutely had to.

We walked a few blocks to a vacant lot, where Alma sat on an old cable spool, picked up a newspaper someone had left, and pushed it into my chest. "Sit," she said. "Tell me who died."

I found the obits. "June Matthews. Michael Brown. Ruth Ritchie—"

"I knew Ruth."

"I'm sorry."

"Fah." Alma took a long swallow from her mug. Something creaked in her stomach. "She was a hoarder. Kept grocery lists. Melon seeds. Fingernails. Hung onto that shit like it would hold onto her. Cried like a baby. Just because she never married."

"What about you?" I said. "Were you always alone?" That I didn't know struck me suddenly as wrong, a symptom of my general disconnection. A breeze tossed a red straw behind a tree and I had to resist an urge to follow it.

Alma looked at me with a face I hadn't yet seen, her eyes dry and blank.

"No," she said. She grabbed the paper and stood. "Let's go back now."

The next day a fresh paper was on the spool. A man named John Johnson was dead, someone Alma knew vaguely through a cousin. She tossed her hand dismissively, but when I started to read on she interrupted me.

"Twenty-three years old, and there's Alma," she said. "Along comes this fine young chick-a, Grace Grace Grace, comes in dresses so tight Alma wants to pinch her just looking." Alma sucked her teeth.

"And?" I asked.

She rolled her eyes skyward.

"So you—dated?"

"You could call it that. Wasn't public. Grace wouldn't have it. Grace was still a princess, prim as Betty Crocker." She looked at me and smiled demurely. "Didn't matter that she'd never be white."

Each morning Alma knew someone in the obits, and each morning she told me a little more. One day, after a Minnie Jackson had suffered a stroke, Alma said, "Grace left when she turned thirty. Couldn't take it anymore. Married her a real man."

"Oh, Alma," I said.

I waited for something more—some sort of fury or hurt—but Alma went on in the same breezy voice, "A real man, yes, and had babies and grandbabies." She pulled a photograph from her pocket and kissed it. "Alma had some others, of course. Lieutenant Richards. He's the one Alma said she was waiting for. Waiting, but he never came back from the Orient."

The lieutenant was handsome, his skin darker than Alma's, smiling stiffly in army green. "How did you meet him?"

"Found him under the cushion of a train seat. Fine looking, no?"

"So you lied," I said.

Alma grabbed the photograph and stood. "I don't think it like that. But if that's how you do, Lotto baby . . ."

I felt a sudden desire to tell Alma everything, to take back my distortions about Ben, to tell her how the world looked to me lately, crumbling and dreamless. Then anger, that she'd never pressed me, never made me defend myself and my lies. This was, I knew, part of our agreement, just as I'd agreed not to make her take her pills, and up until now I'd liked it: she didn't bother me about the fact that I was sickly pale and didn't have any friends, or that my eyes were often purple underneath as if I'd just finished crying, though I hadn't. And I knew that if she did ask me to explain, I wouldn't. I would be too afraid of the quakes and groans my voice might make. Alma would shrug and pshaw and look into her mug, and there I'd be next to her unable to breathe, let alone tell my story. Not the way she told hers. As if it had happened to somebody else.

We'd been going to the spool for a few weeks when Alma bent over in the elevator one morning and threw up a flood of liquid, all coffee brown except for a few reddish chunks from a pomegranate she'd asked me to buy.

I went to the basement to leave a note for the super. When I got back, she was standing outside. Her whole body shook. Her lips were tinged blue.

"Let's go."

"You need to eat something," I said.

"I don't."

I took a pack of saltines from my bag. "These are good for an upset stomach."

"It's past upset. It's done being upset."

"I'm not going with you," I told her.

"I'll go alone."

"You can't go alone—if you could go alone, why wait for me? Why should I come every day?"

She wouldn't look at me.

"Do you want me to leave? Is that what you want?" I grabbed her arm and pulled her inside and held on until the elevator opened. Then I felt how tightly I was gripping, how tiny and soft she was beneath the layers of coat and dress, like she might not break but just disintegrate. "I'm sorry," I said, letting go, and we rode up with the stink of her vomit.

After that, we stayed inside. Alma's face was always damp. Her lips cracked and flaked as if molting. She barely ate or drank, even coffee. I'd continued picking up her refills, but I'd lost the med schedule and the doctors' names. I looked up Crohn's disease, but the treatments were drastic—steroids, enemas, nothing I could do without Alma knowing. I bought the paper and opened to the obits, but she didn't want to listen. Mostly she slept, and eventually I forced myself to go to the call center. I never showed her my terror. I practiced accepting her death. Ben would have called it surrender—he would have said it was a test of my strength—but I could already see how he'd gotten it wrong, how allowing yourself to be led was in fact the easier way, the way to avoid the darkness, the forks. It was as easy and as pitiful as being sold a lawn mower at Sears.

One afternoon I was on Alma's floor, responding to a wedding invitation from one of Ben's friends. The font was rhapsodic, the envelope lined in pink. *Ben's gone to the Homeland to make babies*, I wrote.

Alma woke in her chair with a rapid, sucking breath.

"What's wrong?" I asked.

"Bring the old soap box from the back my hanging clothes."

I went to her bedroom and knelt in the closet. I pushed through skirts and coats and mothball fumes until I found the box. Across the side in an arc, it read, FRESH, SWEET, AND FEMININE, and underneath the words, staring at me slyly, was a woman who looked eerily like the gold lady on my floor.

I carried it out to Alma. Inside was an album with a bent, blue, fauxleather cover, but when I lifted it toward Alma, she shoved it away with her mug. Her lips were nearly blue. "You look."

On the first page there was only one photograph: a young black woman in a frilly yellow dress. She wore white gloves and tipped a white-feathered hat at the camera.

"This is Grace?" I asked.

Alma wouldn't look. I turned the page. There was Grace in her wedding dress, the arm of her groom around her waist. Just an arm. No body, no face.

"You were there?" I asked. Alma wagged a finger. Turn it over. On the back, in wide, cursive letters: *Alma. You said you didn't want to see, but I can't have that. You're stubborn, but I'm smarter, and I know you.*

I put the picture back and turned the page. There was Grace and a baby. Grace and a toddler and a baby. Alma was humming now, a broken seesaw of a tune. Her eyes were closed, her face somewhere between smirk and collapse. Grace's husband's hand shook their grown son's hand. Grace held out a cake at her daughter's birthday party. *Happy 21st, Darling Alma.*

"Darling?" I said. "I bet you never let her call you that."

Alma fought off a smile. Her lips trembled.

The final shot was Grace under a tree, wrinkled and holding spectacles in one hand, her mouth tight with concentration.

"What happened?" I asked, but when I looked up, Alma's shoulders were shaking. She'd let her mug fall to the floor. She was holding her ears and rocking, her face spilling tears. I pulled myself up next to her and stared. I had to lift her slightly in the chair so I could slide in. Then I let Alma down onto my lap and felt the first weight I'd known in months.

I'll never know what made Alma want to see those pictures. Maybe it was the end of our obits routine; maybe she had used them like a wall of death, had leaned Grace up against them, tried to cover her with their moss and mold. It could have been a dream from her nap, or a voice she'd heard, or simply how close she was to her own death.

Even then I understood that memory and desire are not reasonable. I knew the stiller you are, the harder they claim you. This was why I walked all over that city, why I never ate enough to feel satisfied, to grow lazy. Sometimes, when I felt beaten, when I couldn't help but lie down, my exhaustion tasted as sweet and dangerous as my Friday memories of Ben, after work, when it was already getting dark, and we would stumble home from the loud streets of that loud city and want nothing but each other and sleep—unable to tell the difference.

The next morning I found Alma sitting in the bathtub with the shower running. Her nightgown was bunched around her waist. On the floor her underwear was smeared with shit and blood. I turned off the water and lifted her by the armpits, but she doubled over, grunting, in my arms. I'd barely set her on the toilet when something gushed into the bowl, and then there was a violent noise as if her stomach were trying to expel itself from her body.

"I'm calling the doctor," I said.

"No." Alma struggled against my grip.

I tried to catch her eyes. I said, "Why do you want to be in pain?"

"I don't want. I am."

I walked her back to the shower. She looked made of the gauzy paper that colors stage lights, the skin hanging off her bones out of habit. Her face was growing more horse than woman, gray and long and heavy. I sponged her with warm water. I tried to touch her as if she wasn't a person, but a plant or a chair.

I said, "There are places where they'd let you die. They would make you comfortable."

"I don't want strangers near me."

"I'm a stranger."

Alma looked at me. "You're harmless."

I stopped sponging. I felt a pressure in the air like a note going higher. I became aware that whole parts of me were gone.

"I'm not," I said. "Look at what I've done." I meant my body, I meant her dying—but Alma was wincing and didn't seem to hear. Carrying her to bed, I smelled her skin for the first time, not her perfume or her old woman breath but something like how I remembered myself smelling—the simple odor of skin touching skin in the junctions and crevices where air can't reach.

Alma said, "Forget about the exact right temperature."

Her eyes were yielding and terrifying. I left the bedroom door open as I went, digging her pills out from under the cushion, putting her prescriptions in order. I found the number Prairie had left in case of an emergency. I picked up the phone and put it down, then I went to the basement and put Alma's underwear and towels in the wash. I threw her coffee down the trash chute, along with my saltines.

When I returned, she said, "You can't go 'round, baby girl, you go through."

I told her, "I'm going to take a shower now." I spoke in the voice I'd avoided, the voice people use with infants. "I'll leave the door open. Call if you need me."

"Go on now, Lotto. Go."

Alma shifted under the blankets. I expected, wanted, to see her throw them off, but soon the only motion I detected was a silent rise-fall—more like the infinitesimal settling of a sidewalk than a breath. I called work and said I was sick.

In the bathroom I undressed and stood in front of the mirror. I couldn't remember the last time I'd looked at myself. My hip bones stabbed the air, my shoulders looked like rocks, my breasts were shrunken and loose. I touched one nipple and wagged a finger over it, holding my breath until it came forward, pink and standing. I placed two fingers in the cave between my ribs. The bones on either side felt soft. I turned on the shower as hot as it would go. My whole body reddened and stung, and as I dried myself and dressed, I remembered Alma's porn stash. I knew one day those magazines would be in the basement of my house, and some child or lover would discover them and wonder how well he really knew me.

Under the rug, I found the glossy covers unbent. I hadn't considered whether Alma was strong enough to bend over and reach the floor. I hadn't thought to ask if she needed help. She had seemed too proud.

She was trying to sit up in bed.

"Brush my hair," she said.

"But your braids—"

"Take them out."

I got in behind her. I lifted her to sitting, held her ribs with my knees, and started to take apart her braids. As her hair puffed free, I leaned around and saw her face grow gentler. I combed until I felt oil reach the ends. Alma was asleep, her narrow chest rising and falling, still persuading itself to go on. I fell asleep thinking about Lotto—whether maybe it didn't mean luck, but chance.

I woke at four, when my shift would have been ending. The room was hot and stale. Alma breathed. I slipped out from under her and went down to the street. I needed air before the sun rose, before offices opened, before I called DSS.

A bus slid by. I heard every one of its grunts and clicks and sighs. Someone hollered, "Hey!" from a window above, and another voice answered across the street. The voices trailed and echoed against the bricks, and I thought of Ben in his desert, of whatever he might shout with nowhere to land. *You can't go 'round.* I'd assumed this was Alma's head unraveling, synapses firing years, or decades, too late. But she'd seemed lucid after that. She would hate my doubting her. *Don't ask me if I'm serious. Go on now.*

A box truck pulled out of a warehouse down the street. It drove past carrying the thick scent of bread, then kept on heading west, where the sky was still the darkest purple. *Yes,* Alma said. So I breathed it in, too, even though it was everything I wanted.

Nominated by Kevin Moffett, The Georgia Review

REAR VIEW MIRROR

by JOAN MURRAY

from AMERICAN POETRY REVIEW

If you'd seen her there, trying to rise, you'd understand
why I didn't make a sound. If you'd seen how many times
her spindly forelegs dug themselves forward, trying to
lift the stone cart of herself off her yearling flanks—
if you'd watched her head toss left and right,
searching for instructions from any corner—
if you'd seen how she finally broke through
the cowl of her pain and pulled
herself upright, you'd know
why I sat there paralyzed.

Then you'd have seen how she was denied the heady
moment given to any flimsy fawn who makes it to its feet—
how she couldn't pause a second to feel gravity
pull away from her hooves and slink back in the earth.
And you'd have stayed there with her too,
hanging onto the wheel like an exhausted god
till she tossed her death on the heap of her shadow
and hauled herself to the woods,
one leg scratching jaggedly behind her
like a lie on a lie-detector test
until she disappeared.

Only then would you have pulled apart your harness
and stepped out and seen the smashed side mirror

pressed flush against the window where your shoulder
had just been. Only then would you have
touched the caved-in door that held the
sudden wave-like thud of her wriggling spine.
Only then, Demeter-like, would you have
brushed the tufts of fur, still stuck in the
rear window gasket—and probed
a finger through the wet grassy smear
that her flailing hoof had left there.

Only then would you have figured out the strength
to go after her into the dark place where she'd gone—
to search for her and keep searching—
just the way you'd have done if you'd come to
in a dark room after labor, and found no one there,
not a cry, not a sound—like that time—
when I slid down on a sheet below a mirror—
so I couldn't see my daughter come or go.
But this time, with the cars rushing by,
I watched in the mirror. I watched.
And I saw where she'd gone.
And I followed her in.

Nominated by Colette Inez

THE BOOK
OF WILSON

by ANDREW RICE

from THE PARIS REVIEW

His FATHER CALLED HIM SUNDAY, for the day he was born. But he hated the name, thought it churchy and effeminate, and as soon as he was old enough, he became someone else. That was his way. At the time when we were friends, before distance and hardship and repulsion intervened, he called himself Wilson Obote. He had spent most of the first half of his life in combat, as a fighter of shifting allegiances—sometimes a government soldier, sometimes a government soldier, sometimes a rebel—in his country's civil wars. "I grew up knowing that fighting, torturing, and killing is what proves the might of a man," he said. In his view, the world was divided between people with guns and people who did their bidding, and he was proud to say he'd lived his life accordingly. Wilson intrigued me as someone who seemed to personify Uganda's legacy of violence, and also the country's potential to reclaim itself from the abyss. In civilian life, he had become a schoolteacher and a performing artist: a musician, a dancer, and above all, an actor. It was on the stage and the screen—through his talent for impersonation and self-dramatization—that he'd come as close as he thought possible to finding peace and satisfaction. Then, in October of 2002, teenage fighters from the Lord's Resistance Army, a cultish rebel force that terrorizes northern Uganda, kidnapped Wilson's two oldest sons. "Things were getting out of hand," Wilson said, "so I decided to handle the gun again."

When we met, at a hotel bar in Kampala, Wilson introduced himself as an army lieutenant. This rank was a bit of make-believe—an embellishment, like the garish suit he wore, a tie-dyed topcoat and matching trousers that, he announced proudly, he had designed himself. In fact, Wilson had joined a government intelligence agency, the Internal Security Organization, and was working as a reconnaissance scout in the badlands of the north, leaving written messages for his sons wherever he went—at wells, in mango groves, anywhere he thought they might stop for a moment's rest. Wilson cut a striking figure: tall and sinewy, with his oblong head shaven, a look that drew attention to his protruding ears and cheekbones. His arms were thick and powerful, his eyes narrow and mistrustful. "I think I must have done something to make God angry," he said. "Bad things have been happening to me ever since I was young." He handed me a computer disk on which he told me I would find his autobiography, and he asked if I knew any Hollywood directors.

Wilson's book, "Born in the Barracks," ran to eighty-three digression-filled, syntactically twisted single-spaced pages, and it was unfinished. As a self-portrait, it is as self-deceiving as it is revealing, and yet it offers an extraordinary account of a childhood in wartime Uganda: he commits his first killing at five (braining a playmate with the metal wheel of a wheelbarrow), runs off to live with a band of cattle thieves, becomes a street hustler, burns down his mother's house, is thrown in a prison cell with a decaying corpse, flees to the big city, enlists in the army at fourteen, butchers civilians, takes a child bride, runs for his life when the government is overthrown, joins a rebellion, deflowers a nun, becomes a vagabond, and is imprisoned again.

At times, as he recounts his exploits, Wilson seems to glory in his faults, carrying his confessional tone to operatic extremes. Early on, for instance, he adopts his mother's voice to describe his own birth: "So my son, I labored all this time for this kind of reward? If I knew you would be this kind of brute, I would have squeezed your bloody head between my thighs and suffocated you to death during your birth." Although Wilson swore to me that every word he wrote was true, it was obvious that there was plenty of exaggeration, and even much outright fiction. But so much of his story checked out that it was impossible to take comfort in one's disbelief.

Uganda is cut roughly in two by the Nile, and the divide is as much political as it is geographical. Antagonism between the north and south, which was fostered under British colonial rule, turned bloody after the country gained independence in 1962, when northern tribes seized control of the state. For the next twenty-five years, Uganda was dominated by a succession of dictators from the north. Wilson was born in 1966, the year that army tanks attacked the palace of Uganda's first president, a southerner, consolidating power in the hands of the prime minister, Milton Obote. Obote was a member of Wilson's tribe, the Langi, and five years later, when General Idi Amin ousted him, Wilson's father was one of many Langi military officers who were publicly executed. Wilson says that he was in the audience, and in his book he describes in minute detail how his father and several other officers were tied, naked and hooded, to poles in the yard of their barracks and then shot by a firing squad:

> Within very few minutes, I saw pa drop his head on his chest. . . . I did not know how many bullets struck him. But when he was roughly untied and left to fall down, one would not wish to see the holes the bullets created. It was just like smashed beef mixed with shit.
>
> No one was allowed to cry, women, men swallowed their tears in their heads. Within no minutes the bodies were piled in a standby lorry, and off to the destination none of pa's relatives, including me, knows. Moroto barracks is situated just adjacent to Matheniko Game Reserve, from which at night stray hyenas and even lions came into the barracks from the northern side.
>
> So the last night we spent in the barracks had no roaring of the lion. Neither did the hyenas complain. This therefore gave a clear testimony that the beast had a fair fill of their tummies from pa's fatty flesh, and his friends'.

After that, Wilson writes, "Human life became chicken life to me. . . . I would do whatever it means with my gun to the satisfaction of my vengeance." He became "a brute who loved to swim in human blood," and he claims to have killed at least ten people.

In 1986, when Yoweri Museveni, a guerilla leader from the south, led his army into Kampala and installed himself as president, Wilson fled back across the Nile and became a rebel, marauding around the northern countryside, until he was captured by government troops and sent to a political reeducation camp. Wilson emerged a changed man, determined to create a civilian life for himself. He married, started a family, moved to Kampala, and drifted into artistic circles. He joined a theater and dance troupe, where he sang tenor, played a traditional harp, and performed the intricate knee-pumping steps of the northern tribes. The troupe's director cast Wilson as an army commander in one of his plays, and his performance was so convincing that the director sponsored Wilson's enrollment in a teacher's college. On one occasion, when he was at school, Wilson suffered a nervous breakdown. He chased off his roommate and marched military-style around the campus compound with a stick, until an uncle, a real army officer, came and had him tied up and taken away. There were many smaller outbursts, but they gradually subsided. Wilson landed a job as a primary-school instructor, began writing his memoirs, and was cast in leading roles in several Uganda plays and movies.

Wilson's progress was very much in keeping with the country's. Museveni was an autocrat, but a saner, more benevolent one than Uganda had ever known, and under his eloquent, often enlightened rule, the country steadily recovered from its self-destruction. By 2002, when I arrived, Uganda's economy was thriving and Kampala was a boomtown, as a new generation came of age without any direct experience of political violence. I had come to see this rare phenomenon: an African success story. But it didn't take long to notice that the peace and prosperity stopped at the southern bank of the Nile. In the north—a swath of the country the size of Belgium—the war had never ended.

Wilson loved Kampala and his life there, but in Uganda a man doesn't count for much until he has some property of his own, a piece of land that he can cultivate and use as a retreat, and which, one day, can serve as his burial ground. So Wilson built himself a house in his ancestral village of Amugo, a collection of tumbledown shops and mud-wattle huts along a derelict railway line in the north. Wilson's wife Josephine and four of their children were staying there, visiting his mother, when the rebels attacked. They crept in early on an October morning in 2002, about a dozen youths in ragtag clothes, carrying axes, machetes, and machine guns. A neighbor who spotted the beams of their flashlights screamed and scrambled for the hut where Josephine and the children were sleeping. "We are all dead," she shouted hysterically, and the shooting began.

A rebel appeared in the hut's doorway. He wore gumboots, a trench coat, and a baseball cap. He was a boy, really, no older than fifteen. "Where are yours?" he barked at Josephine. She wailed and the boy called for a rope. He and a comrade then tied her eldest sons together at the waist—Jimmy, who was fourteen, and Oscar, a year younger—and marched them into the bush.

Wilson was asleep in Kampala, and he didn't hear of the attack until later that morning when he was at school, teaching. He left immediately and headed north. Wilson was no family man. He talked to me unabashedly about his many women—hardly remarkable in polygamous Uganda—and he boasted of fathering fifteen children, counting the illegitimate ones that he knew of. But Josephine was his "official" wife, and he loved the big messy family they'd made together. He took enormous pride in Jimmy and Oscar, who were promising, well-educated boys, and as he left Kampala he told his friends that he was going to find his boys. It seemed a febrile plan, but he could not be dissuaded. "We could see the violence in him," one friend recalled. "There was a change in him," said another. "He was heartbroken. . . . He had that self-blame." Any father might have such feelings at the loss of his children. Wilson had something else, too, when he thought of his sons' ordeal: he had been there himself.

During his last years as a bush fighter, in the late eighties, Wilson had fallen in for a time with the Holy Spirit Mobile Forces, a rebel army that sprung up in the north during the first years of Museveni's rule, led by a young, Bible-quoting soothsayer named Alice Auma, who preached both rebellion and religious revival. Auma claimed to be channeling a local warrior spirit named Lakwena—the word means "messenger of God"—and to be in communion with animals, mountains, and waterfalls. The north's malady, she said, was spiritual, and if only northern fighters were cleansed of sin they could easily defeat Museveni. Auma's message drew thousands of recruits, whom she commanded from a thatch-roofed temple. She enforced a strict code of conduct—no drinking, no fornication—and instructed her soldiers to anoint themselves with a holy oil that, she promised, would make them invulnerable to enemy fire. Wilson, who was not disposed to blind belief, quickly soured on Auma's crusade. To declare your forces bulletproof, he felt, was pure suicide. Sure enough, the Holy Spirit army was soon defeated and Auma fled into exile, but a young cousin of hers, Joseph Kony, claimed that Lakwena's powers had passed into him, and he started his own rebellion, which he called the Lord's Resistance Army.

Kony had been born around the same time as Wilson, in nearly the same place, and as a young man he had found power in cultivating a reputation as a sorcerer. He was a lanky, dreadlocked former altar boy who wore white robes and purported to be inhabited by warrior spirits and imbued with gifts of prophecy and healing. He had a mesmerizing voice and messianic pretensions, and when he began the LRA in the late eighties, he drew support from some of the renegade forces of the old dictatorships who regarded Museveni as a usurper. But most northerners declined to follow him, and Kony, enraged, turned harshly against his own people. He declared that if fathers would not rise up with him he would take their sons, and kidnapping became the LRA's primary means of recruiting. It was a fiendishly effective tactic. Children made malleable, disposable troops, well-suited for the campaigns of murder and mutilation by which Kony gained an international reputation in the nineties. Eighty percent of his army of abductees were believed to be between seven and seventeen years old—and for the most part he sent them to attack not an enemy army, but their own brothers and sisters.

A Ugandan clergyman who served as a government intermediary during a short-lived attempt at peace talks with the LRA once described to me a summit meeting with Kony in a remote northern meadow. The rebel arrived wearing military fatigues and aviator sunglasses, escorted by a cadre of children who poured holy water from calabashes before his feet. He raised a Kalashnikov above his head and told the peace negotiators: "Look at the gun. I have fought with this gun for seven years, and the government has also fought with the gun—and yet they have not defeated us."

In fact, defying defeat was Kony's signal accomplishment. Nobody could say for sure what else the LRA stood for. Kony claimed his orders came directly from God and that he planned to rule Uganda according to the Ten Commandments. But the religion on which the LRA based its holy war was entirely invented—a muddle of animist superstition, Biblical fundamentalism, and shamanism—and its politics were even less coherent. Because Kony's victims are overwhelmingly from the north, his war has been called an auto-genocide. Still, many northerners blame Museveni equally for their continued suffering. They are convinced he could squelch the LRA anytime he likes, but that he prefers to let the fighting continue in order to keep the north crippled. "I don't believe in turning the other cheek," Museveni has said, explaining why he refuses to engage in serious peace talks with Kony's rebels. "We are killing them."

When Wilson reached Amugo the day after the attack he found his house burned to the ground. Josephine was gone; she'd fled to her mother's village, which was some distance away. Wilson kept going north, following the path the rebels had taken out of town. At first he hired bicycle taxis. But the bicyclists were only willing to go so far. LRA troops often kill the riders they encounter, or hack off their legs, because the rebels believe them to be government spies. So Wilson walked.

He walked for days, passing through the flatlands around Amugo and the malarial swamps where the rebels collected water, then crossed the Moroto River and traveled on to rockier terrain. This land was barren, depopulated. When Wilson did encounter people, they fled in terror at the sight of him. In this area, any stranger was assumed to be a threat. He also encountered some children who'd escaped the LRA, and they gave him bits of intelligence.

Following one such tip, Wilson left the road and headed west. He came to a clearing where he found the remains of an encampment. Several makeshift crosses stood planted in the ground amid small plots of soybeans and sorghum. Wilson found four children's bodies there. They had been bludgeoned to death. The children appeared to Wilson to have been eleven or twelve years old. He knew that the LRA often executed abductees who were slow or injured or who simply cried for their parents. These killings served as a lesson to those who were allowed to live.

The rebels had abandoned the encampment a few days before, and the bodies had already begun to decompose in the tropical heat. Wilson was drawn to one of the children, who lay facedown, his head atop a log, as if he had been forced to the ground and clubbed from behind. The dead boy wore blue, just as his son Oscar had been wearing when he was taken. Then Wilson noticed the belt. It was white and bore a crocodile insignia, just like Oscar's. He tried to study the features of the corpse. "They had beaten him with a lot of canes so the body was swollen," Wilson told me later. "The whole face had already been eaten by maggots. Even though he was my son, I couldn't recognize him." But Wilson was certain: Oscar was dead.

———

439

Shortly before I began seeing a lot of Wilson, in January of 2004, President Museveni had announced in his yearly holiday address: "The Kony terror in the northeast has been defeated decisively." But it was just his usual bluster. Out on the street corners, hawkers flogged newspapers that told a different story. The front pages were covered in gruesome photos and alarming headlines. At times, the daily toll of nameless battles and repetitive atrocities—"LRA KILL 3 ON XMAS EVE"; "KONY AIDE SHOT DEAD"—could lend this bizarre war a lulling sense of normalcy, and in the cosmopolitan remove of comfortable Kampala the news from the north seemed to come from a foreign country.

So, on a Sunday morning at the end of February, when the radio reported an attack on a refugee camp up north, I didn't pay much attention. Squeezed from their homes by the LRA and the Ugandan army, more than a million northerners were living, more or less permanently, in wretched camps, and Kony's raiders attacked them all the time. In one incident just a few weeks before, the rebels had killed roughly fifty civilians, and no one outside Uganda had noticed. But this attack, in a place called Barlonyo, proved to be different. Over the course of the day, the death toll rose, ticking past one hundred and continuing steadily until it passed two hundred. Somewhere along the way, the Barlonyo massacre crossed the nebulous threshold that separates a routine African horror from an international news event. CNN aired video footage of the smoldering ruins of the camp. Many of the victims had been hacked to death or burned alive inside their huts. The Nairobi-based foreign press corps hastened to Lira, the nearest town.

I left before dawn the next morning, driving north in my jeep on a two-lane highway. I wound through hills outside the city as sunrise swirled the sky purple and orange. The mists clung briefly to the rolling terrain, then dissipated, revealing an expanse of grassy pastures and green banana groves. Uganda flattened as the road neared the Nile. Greenery gave way to savannas, empty except for the occasional anthill or thorny acacia or giant cactuslike euphorbia, standing alone against the voided landscape. The last town before the bridge, a dusty stretch of beer shacks and trucker motels, had the air of a border post. I passed through a military checkpoint and crossed the bridge over Karuma Falls that links the south to the north.

On the other side, the road was overgrown and deserted save for a family of baboons. I pressed hard on the accelerator. The sky turned overcast and it started to rain. A signpost said that Lira was thirty kilometers away. I noticed a pickup truck ahead. It was in my lane, and it was slowing down. It had no brake lights. I stomped hard on my brakes and skidded on the wet road. The crash came with a low, hollow crunch. The hood of my jeep crumpled before my eyes. My glasses flew off as the seat belt jerked me back. I twisted the wheel, trying to stay on the road. Finally, after a long split second, the car came to rest, teetering at a thirty degree angle on the edge of a steep ravine.

I touched my face, wiggled my fingers and toes. Everything moved. I climbed out of the car, grateful to be alive. Then, with a rush, the fear came. I was outside and alone in the north. A passing soldier stopped to tell me there wasn't much danger from the rebels; they hadn't been through in some time. The mob of villagers that had rushed to the accident scene was another matter. The pickup, which had come to rest in a clearing across the way, belonged to the pastor of the local Catholic church. He'd been rushed to the hospital, and there were angry murmurs that I'd killed him. The soldier suggested I stay close—he had a gun.

Hours later, I was still there, sitting crouched on my haunches in the midday sun. It turned out the priest was fine, but I wasn't so sure about myself. A group of young villagers I'd hired to hoist my jeep back onto the road were arguing wildly about how to do it. The village madman was dancing around the wreckage. A potbellied cop stopped by. He told me not to worry, which seemed like a bad sign. I was trying hard to keep my eyes off the papyrus-choked marsh that surrounded us. I knew the rebels lurked in swamps.

Then a bus bound for Lira screeched to a halt beside me. Its door opened, and out stepped Wilson. I had never been so glad to see anyone. He wore military fatigues, and his olive beret was twisted at a jaunty angle. He seemed pleased to play the savior, and pleased by my surprise. He marched over and ran his hand along my car's twisted front end. "Sorry," he said. He told me he'd been rushing to Lira—the government was mounting a counteroffensive following the camp massacre—and when he recognized my car from the bus, he ordered the driver to stop. He said I was lucky. He said we were safe. He could protect me. Wilson's position with the Internal Security Organization allowed him to wear army clothes when he traveled. The uniform made him more feared than admired, but he was happy to accept the respect—and, on this day, out on the road, I was happy to be his friend.

As the sun fell toward the horizon, a truck towed us into Lira. The sprawling town, officially home to ninety thousand people, was bursting with thousands more war refugees who were crowded into tent villages and dismal shanties on its outskirts. The massacre had only underscored what everyone already knew: the army couldn't protect the countryside. At night, the slightest rumor of rebel movements or rustle in the bush would bring those who still lived in the surrounding villages rushing into the city center—men and women of all ages, children laden with book bags and sleeping mats. They came with their cattle, with their belongings heaped on bicycles, and set up camp beneath hand-painted business signs that seemed to speak for them: GOOD HOPE STORE, GOD PROVIDES LOUNGE, JOBLESS BARBER SALON.

The Lira Hotel, which offered cheap, cramped rooms around a courtyard bar that served warm beer and plates of beans and goat, was crowded with foreign correspondents. Earlier that day they'd visited a refugee camp with President Museveni's military convoy. The locals had given the president a chilly greeting of slow claps and perfunctory ululation.

The people were furious, and not just with Museveni. In Lira, which is a city dominated by the Langi tribe, the radio waves were crackling with anger directed against Kony and his tribe, the Acholi. The two peoples lived side by side, spoke the same language, and shared the same grievances against the south. But they also harbored considerable hatred for each other, as neighbors often do. Some said the feud went back to ancient times. Others said it dated from the 1980s, when an Acholi dictator overthrew a Langi dictator. But Kony's war had driven the tension to a violent extreme. In Lira, the LRA was seen as an Acholi army, and this latest offensive, which had cut a destructive path through Langi lands, was considered an attack on their people.

That night, seeking to calm tempers, some local politicians went on the radio to announce that in the morning Lira would rally for peace at the town soccer pitch, an open field of patchy grass situated next to the police station. I went there after breakfast. Thousands of people were carrying leafy branches, a traditional symbol of mourning, and there were signs that read: STOP KILLING LANGI and THE UN MUST INTERVENE. I'd attended a similar event in Lira a year before, where priests offered prayers for peace and everyone joined in a rendition of "We Shall Overcome." But this time Lira didn't want prayers. It wanted revenge.

As the rally began, I saw a group of about a hundred young men streaming away from the larger crowd, chasing a solitary, terrified boy. He barely escaped his pursuers, jumping a wall into the safety of the police station's grounds. I asked someone what was happening.

"They are beating Acholis," he replied.

Suddenly, another scrum developed. Beneath a banner reading PEACE, the mob massed around a wraithlike figure and beat it with fists, sticks, and shoes. Somehow, the victim—a man—managed to break free. He ran for his life, through a stand of trees and down a dirt road to a primary school, dashing through an open metal gate. By the time I got there, men were hoisting each other over a high brick wall onto the school's grounds.

Inside, against the wall, the mob had cornered its quarry. Dozens surrounded him in an impenetrable semicircle. All I could hear was a sickening rhythm of dull thuds. A man in an orange shirt turned to me and gave a gleeful cackle. "He is killed now," he said.

I walked back outside, dazed, wondering whom to alert. A thin, neatly-dressed man called out to me: "The killing is not intentional, Mr. Journalist. We have been suffering for so long." He introduced himself as Geoffrey Obello, a twenty-seven-year-old schoolteacher from Ogur subcounty, near where the Barlonyo massacre had taken place. He told me that the crowd had recognized the boy as an outsider by his accent. "These Acholis," Obello fumed, "have been killing us, stealing our property, burning our houses."

"We must kill them all!" a passerby shouted.

Behind us, people were filing through the school's gates. I went back inside and saw onlookers competing to get close to the corpse. Boys stood balanced on bicycles to see; women pushed their children to the center of the crowd. Every so often someone gave the body a kick or ceremonial thwack with a mourning branch. A man saw me and yelled something, and the knot of people loosened enough to allow me to view the broken, splayed body of a young man. The mob wanted me to see. It was proud of what it had done.

Nearby, at the police station, a few dozen officers were sitting in the shade of leafy mango trees, armed and in riot gear, waiting for orders to deploy. "If we try to control them now," the police chief said, "it will be a bloodbath."

I returned to the hotel, but the mob's cheers followed me—growing louder, full of adrenaline, heading toward the military barracks. Not long afterward the shooting began, and it continued for several hours as the army restored control. That evening, after the tear gas cleared, Wilson came to see me. The hotel bar's television was switched to the BBC, which was airing footage of Acholi huts set on fire by the mob. Five people were reported dead, including the lynching victim. He turned out to have been a Langi after all.

Wilson was clad head to toe in a flowing outfit of green *kitenge*, a kind of brightly patterned Congolese cloth. The Langi were his people but he was annoyed at them. The rioters had smashed his car's side mirrors and windshield. "It was a little childish," he later reflected. "I don't see any reason why this tribe could point an accusing finger to any other. Not only Acholis are in the LRA."

The next day, a Ugandan photojournalist told me more of the story. He'd happened upon the mob as it surrounded a government office building and attacked a dented Toyota. A strange tall man in green *kitenge* had emerged from the building. "I've lost children," the man yelled, "and I am not reacting the way you are reacting." The rioters paid no attention. So the man walked back into the building. He reemerged brandishing a Kalashnikov. At the sight of the gun, the mob moved on.

"This thing has disorganized my family seriously," Wilson told me one afternoon as he welcomed me into his apartment, a dim and dingy cold-water flat located in a far-flung Kampala suburb. Josephine and the children were in the living room, sitting solemnly, as if for a formal occasion, on tatty foam-cushioned furniture. Josephine was barefoot in a bright orange dress, her hair swept back high. She held the baby, Ruth, who was wearing pink chiffon. Wilson was relaxed in a tight white T-shirt, surrounded by his other children. And sitting on a wooden box in the far corner, wearing a khaki school uniform and a look of sad detachment, was Wilson's son Oscar.

The rebels hadn't killed Oscar. They'd made him into a soldier. It was another boy whose bludgeoned body Wilson had discovered in the bush. Nine months after he'd given Oscar up for dead, Wilson had received a phone call: his son had reappeared in Amugo. Oscar

444

had escaped from the LRA by playing dead during a battle. He'd walked sixty miles back, dodging the rebels and surviving on raw mangoes. Wilson had rushed back to the village, where he embraced Oscar and started to cry. "It wasn't joy," he told me. Jimmy was still missing, and Oscar's return only made the older boy's peril seem that much more profound.

Oscar was trying to readjust to home, but it wasn't easy. "His temperament has changed so much," Wilson told me. Once cheerful, Oscar had become dour and argumentative. When he was angry, he talked harshly, like a rough adult. Oscar attended the school next door, where Wilson had once taught English, but the other kids teased him, called him a "rebel," and he often got into fights. The headmaster was losing patience with his aggressive behavior.

Wilson had pulled Oscar out of class to talk to me. When his father introduced us, the boy shook my hand with limp deference. He was slight, with big almond-shaped eyes, and he looked younger than his fourteen years. He seated himself on the couch and curled up, crossing his arms tight across his chest and rubbing his elbows. When the conversation turned to the war, Josephine stood up without a word and padded off into the kitchen. Pots and pans clanked in agitated rhythms. "I think you can see it is hurting her," Wilson said. "Whenever I am talking about this, she doesn't feel right."

Oscar could understand English, but he preferred speaking in Luo, his tribal language. So I asked questions and Wilson translated the boy's answers. In a high singsong voice, Oscar recounted the morning of his abduction. Several other village children had been lashed together with him and Jimmy and pulled by their ropes down the road. One of them was a fourteen-year-old girl, whom an LRA officer soon took as a concubine. On the way out of the village, the rebels had looted some nearby shops and forced their unwilling porters to carry away crates of soda, boxes of biscuits, and bags of beans and sesame.

After a long march, a camouflage-clad rebel commander addressed the abductees. He had a reputation as a fearsome killer, and he spoke harshly. The commander told the children that they were to address him as *apwony*—"teacher." He promised that they would be fighting men, and they would "have freedom." But if they tried to escape, he warned—if they so much as cried or complained—they were dead.

The captives walked for two days without much food or water. Finally, they reached a rebel camp—the same place Wilson discovered, abandoned, a few days later. A number of raiding parties converged there with a great many abductees, perhaps several hundred. Jimmy and Oscar were assigned to different battalions. Then there were prayers. All the abductees were anointed with sheanut oil, which the officers smeared in the shape of a cross on their foreheads. The ritual, they were told, bound them to Joseph Kony forever.

Oscar never met Kony, who was said to be hiding out in Sudan. But he was still terrified of him: LRA abductees believed their army's leader was omniscient, capable of tracking them anywhere if they ran. The boys in Oscar's unit carried crosses made of grass or wore rosaries, which they were told would offer miraculous protection during battle. Oscar marched long distances every day and learned how to shoot in the evenings.

LRA commanders often force fresh recruits to murder other children, frequently their friends or relatives, because such killing binds the abductees to the LRA. Having done the unthinkable, the new recruits feel that they can never go home. Through violence, they are reborn as rebels.

Oscar said he killed eight people in his nine months with the LRA. When I asked him how he did it, he answered in a precise monotone, and Wilson translated: "The first time he contributed to killing was when a boy tried to escape." This was soon after Oscar's capture. He and a group of recent abductees were ordered to gather around the condemned boy and were handed sticks. "They just clubbed him to death," Wilson said.

I didn't say anything, and after a moment, Oscar thought of something else to tell. "He got used to the killing," Wilson translated. "It wouldn't get him scared."

"Do you think about it now?" I asked.

Oscar shook his head resolutely, no. He stretched and yawned. Class had let out at the school next door, and the sound of children's voices lilted into the living room.

"He liked the work," Wilson said. "He was enjoying it." Oscar said he had participated in the abduction of fifty children for the LRA, and when I asked if he felt bad for them, Wilson told me, "No. He was happy, because he was also revenging what happened to him." I didn't understand, so Wilson elaborated. "The way he was abducted, he didn't feel good. But now that he was abducting the rest, he knew

446

he was also doing the same thing that happened to him. So that's why he was happy."

"He may be a liar," a friend of Wilson's once told me, "but sometimes he will tell you the truth." The problem was you never knew. Wilson told me, for instance, that he'd once acted in a film by a famous American director named Robert Altman. I'd ignored him, but the boast turned out to be true, or at least sort of true. The film, *War Child*, was a television drama by a director named Bob Altman, of Darien, Connecticut. He was not the creator of *Nashville*. But this Altman did have a contract to make a miniseries about the Lord's Resistance Army, and in early 2001 he'd come to Uganda to shoot on location. He worked with a local crew, and he initially hired Wilson as a military consultant, to train his young cast to act like child soldiers. But Wilson had a way of cultivating patrons. He managed to talk Altman into giving him a starring role: Joseph Kony. "He understood it on a gut level," Altman said. "It was clear to me that it was a role that he had really lived and breathed."

Three years later, on a pleasant Easter weekend, *War Child* had its Kampala premiere. It was rare for Ugandans to see their country on film, and the opening night, held at an outdoor amphitheater, attracted a large and curious crowd—mostly families with children. The movie, projected against a white bed sheet, rolled when the sun went down. Wilson had prepared for his performance by studying rare archival footage of Kony, and he played the warlord with a bug-eyed snarl. He first appeared midway through the film, shirtless, whirling a wig of beaded cornrows, shouting, "Hallelujah!" He waved a Bible and, wagging his finger, preached to a group of abducted children, telling them that God had anointed him to do his will. "Go now," he bellowed, "and kill!" A gasp hissed through the audience.

Wilson stole the show, and he should have been savoring it. But he sulked through the premiere. It was as if every joyful moment mocked him. One morning that weekend, I met him at one of his favorite bars. His voice was sluggish, his eyes were deadened, and he complained of a cold. "I have lost a lot of weight," he said. "I think it is because of the worries I have." Wilson looked like he'd been up all night drinking or arguing—probably both. He and his wife were quarreling constantly. "We started blaming each other," Wilson said.

His infrequent visits home from the north inevitably turned into excruciating interrogations. Josephine would demand news of Jimmy. Wilson would say he had none. Then the recriminations would start. Sometimes the fights got physical. Jimmy was the darling of the family. He was bookish, mature, a scholarship student. Josephine was so devastated by his loss that she had become a born-again Christian. She spent much of her time at a ramshackle church, praying for a miracle. Wilson coped by talking of Jimmy constantly, as grieving parents do, calling him "a pillar in my house."

"Among all the children I had," Wilson said, "he was the person I would least expect to belong to an army. He's a very sentimental person. And I believe that these people have played with his psychology. They have played with his ego. And they have confused him. In fact, when I have this discussion it makes me a bit . . ." His eyes filled with tears. "I don't always like to discuss it." After all, Wilson was spending a lot of time at the front, and he said, "We know we are fighting our own children."

Wilson tried not to dwell on the possibility that he might actually meet—or even kill—Jimmy in battle. He clung to a distinction in his mind between the forces he called "the enemy" and the innocent children he wanted to save. But, in reality, the LRA's killers were also its victims: there was no distinction. This was the war's defining perversity. It was also why most Ugandans were in favor of ending the war through negotiation, even if that meant Kony would escape punishment. You didn't have to be an LRA sympathizer to question the moral implications of the government hunting children with attack helicopters. ("Innocent," an army spokesman told me, "is a relative term.") Each week, the army released figures of "enemies" killed and "abductees" rescued, but everyone knew that the only real difference between the two categories was that one group had been captured alive, while the others were dead. They were all just children.

The day after Easter, as Wilson was preparing to head north again, I met him at an outdoor café next to the amphitheater where *War Child* was shown. He was wearing another tie-dyed outfit, with a T-shirt emblazoned with the image of a spear and a machine gun and the baffling message WAR STORIES ABDUCTION SHIELD. In Wilson's more puffed-up moments, he liked to call himself a "freelance child activist." He was always determinedly vague about what he did with the army up north, but he claimed to have participated in the rescues of hundreds of abductees. He never mentioned casualties.

"To be sincere, what I am fighting for now is not my son," he told me. "My son is nothing—I mean, he is my prior objective. My objective now is to rescue these children and to have a peaceful country. If my son happens to be among those people, if he dies in the crossfire and the situation is calm, I will have been happy to sacrifice his life for the betterment of the nation."

Every once in a while, Wilson caught some wisp of a rumor: Jimmy wanted to come home; Jimmy was dead. Sometimes he would hear that his son had been sighted passing through some remote village, and he would make a desperate pilgrimage. But Jimmy was never there, and Wilson said he'd stopped counting Jimmy when he was asked how many children he had. "He is still my child, but the life is now . . ." He paused. "I entrust the life to God."

Even if he were to find Jimmy alive, Wilson doubted he would be the son he once knew. Oscar had told him that he had sometimes encountered his brother in the bush, and that Jimmy was no longer a gentle boy. He had become the aide-de-camp of a feared rebel commander. He carried himself like an officer. He barked orders. He didn't act like someone who wanted to come home.

Wilson understood that. The LRA didn't need psychology or witchcraft to brainwash children. It was much simpler than that. "For someone who has never handled a gun," he said, "when he's given a gun he will find that when he orders someone to sit down, he sits down. He will really be very pleased. He will love the situation. He will not want to get out of that."

Two nights later, my mobile phone rang, and Wilson said, "I've got my son." The joy in his voice exploded over the line. "I'm with Jimmy."

He was calling from the road, but he'd be home in Kampala the next morning, and he asked me to come over. I arrived to find the place overrun by friends and family.

"God is great!" Josephine shouted. The prodigal son was sitting on a three-legged stool in a corner of the living room. Oscar sat beside him, and their other siblings were on the floor at his feet, clinging close. Jimmy was now fifteen, as tall as his father, and skinny, with a child's soft face and an adolescent's awkward bearing. He wore a monstrously baggy blue denim suit. When he'd escaped, Jimmy had been dressed in rags, and even before seeing him again, Wilson had rushed to a clothing store. "I didn't have any idea what size to buy him," he later said. As always, he'd erred on the side of exaggeration.

Jimmy had rolled up the legs of his new trousers, revealing his bare feet, which were toughened and covered with terrible blisters from marching in poorly sized boots.

"Life is really very funny," Wilson said, beaming at his sons. "I could not imagine these people coming back."

Everyone clamored for Jimmy's attention. Overwhelmed, the boy sat with his eyes cast down and fidgeted with his hands in his lap. Then one of the well-wishers who'd stopped by, a girl named Sarah, shared a story about how her own brother had been kidnapped by the rebels and taken into the bush. "He stayed there for one and a half weeks," she said.

"Only one and a half weeks?" Jimmy said. He smiled and cocked his head. "Then he wasn't there."

He began talking with a confidence I'd rarely heard from a teenager in Uganda, a rigidly hierarchical society in which elders demand deference. His voice hadn't yet broken, but in the LRA he'd been a man of authority. Jimmy had some education, which set him apart. He said he'd quickly won promotion to second lieutenant. He told us that for a time he'd commanded a unit of a hundred and seventy rebels. He had only escaped, after a year and a half in the bush, when a fellow officer suggested it. "I'm tired of killing," his friend had said. So they'd stolen away, following a road south to a refugee camp, where they surrendered. The next morning, Wilson received a telephone call. "*Baba*," said the voice on the other end of the line. "It's Jimmy."

Wilson had traveled north to collect the boy that same day. He found him at a rehabilitation center, a vast tented camp filled with wounded and traumatized children. Ignoring the objections of administrators who said Jimmy needed intense counseling, Wilson checked him out and took him home. "I told them, if it means taking him by force, I am taking him," Wilson said. "I got him across Karuma Falls immediately. I wanted him on the side where I was feeling safe."

But Wilson knew that Jimmy and Oscar hadn't entirely escaped. Medical studies have found that ninety-seven percent of former LRA abductees experience symptoms of trauma. Jimmy spoke of "demons" that torture kids like him, and he meant it literally: the LRA's commanders warned their young soldiers that if they ran away, the spirits of those they had killed would pursue them forever. "I just try to forget whatever happened in the bush," Jimmy said. "Otherwise it could be very dangerous for me." Oscar couldn't shake his demons so easily. He had terrible nightmares, and sometimes, suddenly, he smelled human blood.

Wilson thought psychology was Western mumbo jumbo. He couldn't see any good in making his boys relive their darkest moments. Instead, he fell back on the traditions of the northern tribes, which have their own ways of cleansing souls and consciences. So, not long after Jimmy's return, Wilson decided to hold a special homecoming ceremony for his sons in his mother's village. My jeep was back from the shop, and one morning in April we loaded the family's battered plaid-patterned suitcases into the back of the jeep and went north.

With Jimmy home, Wilson's family had regained the appearance of normalcy. On the ride up, Wilson, who was wearing his army uniform and shiny sunglasses, pointed out landmarks to little Ruth, who was sitting on his lap. Josephine, who hadn't once returned north since the attack, looked excited and relieved and about a decade younger. In the back, Jimmy and Oscar were locked in animated conversation, as they had been incessantly since being reunited. And that night, at the hotel bar, Wilson was as contented as I'd ever seen him. He told anyone who'd listen about Jimmy's miraculous good fortune. When our waiter responded with a Christian blessing, Wilson smiled widely. "I am not a man of God," he said. "But for the last two days we have been friends." He talked of his son the rebel—the second lieutenant!—as if he were a tennis prodigy. Wilson said he was just trying to free his boy from his feeling of shame. But he couldn't hide it: he was genuinely proud. Over giddy retellings, he promoted Jimmy to lieutenant, then colonel.

The next morning, a Sunday, we left Lira on a rutted dirt road, driving several miles until we reached a mud-brick church. Behind it stood several round thatch-roofed huts arrayed in a rough circle around a bare patch of dirt and attended by a few scrawny chickens and goats. It was a makeshift village, occupied by refugees from Amugo who had fled to the Lira area when the war had intensified. But for the purposes of a homecoming, the place would have to do.

Jimmy and Oscar were treated like returning warriors. In keeping with Langi rituals, the women of the village, in worn floral-print dresses, laid three forked branches on the path leading to their grandmother's hut, symbolic arrows pointing the way home. Beyond the sticks they placed an egg. The boys stepped over the branches,

451

and then Jimmy, who was first in line, crushed the egg with a stomp. The women shook leaves dipped in water over the boys' heads, commanding the rebel spirits to leave the children. To the sound of ululating voices, the elders of Amugo performed a shuffling thanksgiving dance.

As lunch was prepared, Oscar sat alone in front of his grandmother's hut, toying quietly with a pink stuffed animal, while Jimmy took a seat on a wicker chair. The village children gathered around, and Jimmy regaled them with war stories. It hadn't been so miserable, he said. He and his comrades are well, lived off the land, stole anything they needed. They were no longer children once they carried a gun. They were different people entirely. Most of the LRA kids, Jimmy said, took a nom de guerre. His was "Jimmy Olwol."

Jimmy Olwol did terrible things. Josephine watched him with a fretful look as Jimmy spoke with tough-guy assurance about the atrocities he'd committed. He demonstrated how the rebels tied their captives' arms behind their backs. He said he'd killed many people. With a giggle, he added that LRA commanders sometimes ordered him and his comrades to desecrate the bodies of those they had killed and to ceremonially drink their blood. His appalled audience laughed uncomfortably. A few women clicked their tongues—whether with pity or disapproval, I couldn't tell.

In a small, stuffy brick house, the home of the village's richest man, we sang "A Mighty Fortress Is Our God," Martin Luther's martial hymn. Wilson addressed us, praising his sons for their bravery and loyalty to each other. Then a reverend said some soothing words: God had protected the boys; he had preserved them for his own invisible purposes. There was a reading from Isaiah. And then Jimmy and Oscar knelt on a woven papyrus mat. As Wilson looked on, the minister laid his hands on the boys' heads and said a blessing. They were forgiven.

Months passed. I returned to New York, and Wilson occasionally e-mailed. He asked about my presidential election and told me about his war. But the warmth had gone out of our connection. Wilson had always imagined that I would write about him and he would become rich and famous, and when I'd told him, before leaving Uganda, that it might be some time before I wrote his story, he'd acted betrayed, as if I'd borrowed something valuable and wasn't giving it back. Now, in his brief messages, he was always asking for something from me.

He wanted me to bring Jimmy to America; he wanted money for his story. I told him, guiltily, that I couldn't be that kind of friend. Our e-mail exchanges became less frequent, until eventually they stopped. Then, one afternoon, I got a phone message from a friend in Uganda telling me that a few days earlier Wilson had shot a woman dead with an AK-47 and then turned the gun on himself. Wilson was alive, though badly injured. He was in prison now, facing a murder charge. That was all my friend knew.

I returned to Uganda a few months later, and as soon as I got there, I called one of Wilson's closest friends, a man named Richard Nixon Okello. He was a thoughtful man with a kindly manner, and he'd known Wilson for nearly twenty years. But Okello hadn't seen Wilson for a while, even though his friend was in Lira prison, not far from where he lived. "I got annoyed with him because he was not repentant," he said. "He was behaving like a hero after killing a woman in cold blood."

Wilson had always cursed his deprived upbringing, but in the story Okello told me, it was good fortune that ended up destroying him. In May of 2004 a highly fanciful account of Wilson's search for Jimmy had appeared in a Ugandan newspaper. The article was read by some Austrian philanthropists, who invited Wilson to Vienna to speak about the war in northern Uganda. "They wanted to hear the story of how he fought the monster," Okello said. Wilson obliged, with his usual flair for embellishment. He presented himself to his audiences as an army batallion commander and talked of leading his troops on a mission to rescue his sons. He said that he planned to start a radio station to coax LRA fighters to lay down their arms, and the Europeans were greatly moved. They sent Wilson back to Uganda with ten thousand euros and a desktop computer.

Wilson used much of his new wealth to buy a home at one of Lira's best addresses: a brick house, wired for electricity, with a columned porch and a sheet-metal roof. He became a big man in town. His position in the Internal Security Organization made life's routine problems—a dispute with the phone company, say, or an expired car permit—magically disappear. He had money, especially after he used his imaginary radio expertise to score a consulting contract with an American AIDS charity. He was popular; late at night, he could be found buying rounds at a bar favored by white people and visitors from Kampala. And, in keeping with his heightened status and with Ugandan custom, he took a new, younger wife—a longtime girlfriend

453

named Grace, with whom he already had two children. Josephine, back in Kampala, had little choice but grudgingly to accept the situation.

Wilson finally had the life he'd always wanted, and yet, when the fleeting feeling of satisfaction passed, he was as vexed as ever. When he drank, he fought, mostly with Grace. She was pretty, but as an educated woman, willful and temperamental, she was a bad match for a man like him. Grace accused Wilson of sleeping around. (He was, of course.) She refused to have anything to do with his troubled sons. Wilson hated Grace's mother, who thought he was a good-for-nothing. When the relationship went bad, Wilson's mother-in-law told him she didn't believe his Austrian patrons even existed. She was sure he'd stolen the money.

Grace moved out, moved back in, fled again, forgave him. Finally she asked for a divorce. One morning, a cousin went to visit Wilson at his new house. He was drinking gin and talking murder, and he had his AK-47 out. Wilson's cousin tried to calm him down and took the gun's clip with him when he left. But Wilson had more bullets. Later that day, he got into his battered Toyota and drove to his mother-in-law's, where Grace was staying. He made a scene there, brandishing the gun. Wilson yelled that his wife was coming home one way or another. Grace came outside to talk. What happened next is disputed: Okello said Wilson claimed he meant to fire as a warning: a witness later told me, "He just shot her." In any case, Wilson emptied the gun's clip. Grace was hit four times. With the last bullet, Wilson shot himself. "But I think he was a coward. He did not do it properly," Okello said. "When he realized he wasn't dead, he got up, drove his car to the police, and told them, 'I have killed many people. Put me in.'"

Following Wilson's imprisonment, Josephine could no longer afford the apartment in Kampala, and she was afraid to take the family back to Lira, in case Grace's relatives tried to take revenge on Wilson's sons. So she had retreated to her mother's village, where the boys were attending a local school for which Josephine could no longer afford the fees. The north was calmer now; the LRA, reduced to remnants by a government offensive, was hiding out in a Congolese jungle, cut off from its weapon suppliers in Sudan. The International Criminal Court had issued an arrest warrant for Joseph Kony. The refugees were returning to their land. Still, when I found Josephine and the boys, in a village so remote that it could only be

454

reached by a footpath, the boys told me they used false names at school in case the LRA ever came back. "If they abduct me a second time, they will kill me," Jimmy said. "That's their motto." There wasn't much to eat in the village—just beans and cassava—and the boys missed Kampala. But what they really missed was the security of having a father.

Wilson's legal situation was bleak. The penalty for murder in Uganda was death by hanging, and the justice system was so overburdened that Wilson would probably spend years in jail before seeing a judge. But Wilson had managed to secure the services of a defense attorney. I found the lawyer at his Lira office, a file-strewn storefront lit by a naked bulb. He informed me that if Wilson could come up with seven head of cattle, he could pay "blood compensation" to Grace's mother. Then he could pay off a judge—it would cost a few thousand dollars—and the murder charge would evaporate. "In these circumstances—I mean, the fact that it's his wife—he can get away with it," the lawyer said happily.

The prison, a compact and grimy building, was on the other side of town. Okello went there with me, bringing Wilson some provisions: a pound of sugar, a few bars of soap, a one-liter bottle of Coke. Wilson, attended by a red-bereted prison guard, met us in the lobby. He shook my hand and said, "You've gotten fat." This was both a compliment and an accusation. In Uganda, a man who is prospering is said to be "eating," and girth is considered synonymous with wealth. Wilson, by contrast, had been winnowed by seven months in the lockup. He was barefoot and stuffed into a too-small prison uniform, a stiff canary yellow shirt and shorts. His face was gaunt and scarred from his suicide attempt. There was a little furrow where the tip of his nose used to be.

The guard led us across to a dingy visiting room that was lit by a small barred window and crowded with families bringing bags of rice and bowls of stew to their jailed relatives. The room had rules: visitors were to sit on the hard wooden benches that lined the walls, while prisoners squatted on the concrete floor. But Wilson refused to kneel. He sat beside me on a bench. A beefy matron rapped a baton against the doorjamb in reproach. Wilson stood up and gestured to his shoulders as if they bore epaulets. "I am a lieutenant in the army," he yelled. "You wait until I get out!"

Wilson sat back on the bench and smiled. His mouth was a mess: three of his incisors were missing, and a fourth was just a sharp stump. "I put the barrel here," he explained, sticking his index finger below his lower lip. "Then the bullet passed here"—he rubbed what remained of his top row of teeth—"and it blew off my nose."

I asked Wilson what had happened. "How could I kill the mother of my two children?" he asked. "I would have to be insane." His eyes met mine. "To be sincere," he said, "it was an accident."

The room emptied; visiting hours were over. Through the window, the sound of voices in harmony, a prison choir, floated into the room. Wilson told us that lately he'd been getting right with God. "You know that I am a very good preacher," he said. Okello and I rose to leave. A guard held open the prison's heavy front door, and we walked out into the bright afternoon. I looked over my shoulder to catch a last glimpse of Wilson, standing at the prison's entrance, costumed in his coarse yellow uniform. He shouted goodbye with a wide, jagged smile. He'd made me promise to come see him again. I told him I would, though I knew that I wouldn't.

Nominated by The Paris Review

THE BUNNY GIVES US
A LESSON IN ETERNITY

by MARY RUEFLE

from POETRY

We are a sad people, without hats.
The history of our nation is tragically benign.
We like to watch the rabbits screwing in the graveyard.
We are fond of the little bunny with the bent ear
who stands alone in the moonlight
reading what little text there is on the graves.
He looks quite desirable like that.
He looks like the center of the universe.
Look how his mouth moves mouthing the words
while the others are busy making more of him.
Soon the more will ask of him to write their love
letters and he will oblige, using the language
of our ancestors, those poor clouds in the ground,
beloved by us who have been standing here for hours,
a proud people after all.

Nominated by Ralph Angel, David Wojahn, William Olsen, Michael Dennis Browne,
David Riverd, Molly Bendall, Poetry

MULATTO

by ROXANE BETH JOHNSON

from JUBILEE (Anhinga Press)

GRANDMA IS WASHING ME WHITE. I am the color of hot sand in the bleached sea light. I am a stain on the porcelain, persistent as tea. Stay in the shade. Don't say she was the only one. Cousins opposite say: you too white. I am a night-blooming flower being pried open in the morning. My skin a curtain for a cage of bones, a blackbird coop. My heart is crusty bread, hardening. Hardening. This way, I feed my own fluttering. Under shade, the day looks like evening and I cannot bear the darkness. Don't say, I can't stand to be touched. Say, I stare into the sun to burn off the soiled hands that print my body with bloody ink. Don't say, *Mulatto*. Say, I am the horse in Oz turning different colors, each prance brightening flesh. A curiosity. Don't say, Bathwater spiraled down into the pipes. Say, I never did fade. Say, Skin holds the perseverance of my days. Folding, folding, the water continuously gathers, making wrinkles in a map.

Nominated by Anhinga Press

PAMPKIN'S LAMENT

fiction by PETER ORNER

from MCSWEENEY'S

Two-TERM GOVERNOR Cheeky Al Thorstenson was so popular that year that his Democratic challenger could have been, my father said, Ricardo Montalban in his prime and it wouldn't have made a five-percent difference. Even so, somebody had to run, somebody always has to run, and so Mike Pampkin put his sacrificial head into the race, and my father, equally for no good reason other than somebody must always prepare the lamb for the slaughter, got himself hired campaign manager. Nobody understood it all better than Pampkin himself. He wore his defeat right there on his body, like one of his unflattering V-neck sweaters that made his breasts mound outward like a couple of sad little hills. When he forced himself to smile for photographers, Pampkin always looked constipated. And he was so endearingly down-homely honest about his chances that people loved him. Of course not enough to vote for him. Still, for such an ungraceful man he had long, elegant hands, Jackie O hands, my father said, only Pampkin's weren't gloved. Mike Pampkin's hands were unsheathed, out in the open for the world to see. He was the loneliest-seeming man ever to run for statewide office in Illinois.

It was 1980. I was a mostly ignored thirteen-year-old and I had already developed great disdain for politics. It bored me to hatred. But if I could have voted, I must say I would have voted for Cheeky Al also. His commercials were very good and I liked his belt buckles. Everybody liked Cheeky Al's belt buckles.

Probably what is most remembered, if anything, about Mike

Pampkin during that campaign was an incident that happened in Waukegan during the Fourth of July parade. Pampkin got run over by a fez-wearing Shriner on a motorized flying carpet. The Shriner swore it was an accident, but this didn't stop the *Waukegan News Sun* from running the headline: PAMPKIN SWEPT UNDER RUG.

My memory of that time is of less public humiliation.

One night, it must have been a few weeks before Election Day, there was a knock on our back door. It was after two in the morning. The knock was mousy but insistent. I first heard it in my restless dreams, like someone was tapping on my skull with a pencil. Eventually, my father answered the door. I got out of bed and went downstairs. I found them facing each other at the kitchen table. If either Pampkin or my father noticed me, they didn't let on. I crouched on the floor and leaned against the cold stove. My father was going on as only my father could go on. To him, at this late stage, the election had become, if not an actual race, not a total farce either. The flying-carpet incident had caused a small sympathy bump in the polls, and the bump had held.

Yet it was more than this. Politics drugged my father. He loved nothing more than to hear his own voice holding forth, and he'd work himself up into a hallucinatory frenzy of absolute certainty when it came to anything electoral. My mother left him during the '72 presidential primaries. My father had ordained that Scoop Jackson was the party's savior, the only one who could save the Democrats from satanic George Wallace. My mother, treasonably, was for Edmund Muskie, that pantywaist. The marriage couldn't last, and it didn't. After the New Hampshire primary, my mother moved to Santa Barbara.

My father in the kitchen in October of 1980, rattling off to Pampkin what my father called, "issue conflagrations," by which he meant those issues that divided city voters from downstaters. To my father, anybody who didn't live in Chicago or the suburbs was a downstater, even if they lived upstate, across state, or on an island in the Kankakee River. He told Pampkin that his position on the Zion nuclear power plant was too wishy-washy, that the anti-nuke loons were getting ready to fry him in vegetable oil.

"Listen, Mike, it doesn't matter that Cheeky Al's all for plutonium in our cheeseburgers. The only meat those cannibals eat is their own kind."

Pampkin wasn't listening. He was staring out the kitchen window, at his own face in the glass. He didn't seem tired or weary or anything like that. If anything, he was too awake. In fact, his eyes were so huge they looked torn open. Of course he knew everything my father was saying. Pampkin wasn't a neophyte. He'd grown up in the bosom of the machine, in the 24th Ward. Izzy Horowitz and Jake Arvey were his mentors. He'd worked his way up, made a life in politics, nothing flashy, steady. Daley himself was a personal friend. And when the Mayor asks you to take a fall to Cheeky Al, you take a fall to Cheeky Al. That Daley was dead and buried now didn't make a difference. A promise to the Mayor is a promise to the Mayor and there is only one Mayor. Pampkin didn't need my father's issue conflagrations. He was a man who filled a suit. Didn't a man have to fill something? At the time he ran, I think Pampkin was state comptroller, whatever that means.

So the candidate sat mute as my father began to soar, his pen conducting the air.

"So we go strong against nuclear power in the city on local TV here. But when you're down in Rantoul on Thursday make like you didn't hear the question. Stick your finger in your ear. Kiss a baby, anything—"

"Raymond."

Pampkin seemed almost shocked by his own voice. He was calm, but I noticed his cheeks loosen as if he'd been holding my father's name in his mouth. Then he said, "My wife's leaving me. It's not official. She says she won't make it official until after the election. She's in love, she says."

My father dropped his pen. It rolled off the table and onto the floor, where it came to rest against my bare toes. I didn't pick it up. On the table between the two men were precinct maps, charts, phone lists, mailing labels, buttons, and those olive Pampkin bumper stickers so much more common around our house than on cars.

"Can I get you a cup of coffee, Mike?"

I watched my father. He was gazing at Pampkin with an expression I'd never seen before. Drained of his talk, he looked suddenly kinder. Here is a man across this table, a fellow sojourner. What I am trying to say is that it was a strange time—1980. A terrible time in many ways, and yet my father became at that moment infused with a little grace. Maybe the possibility of being trounced not only by Cheeky Al but also by the big feet of Reagan himself had opened my father's eyes to the existence of other people. Here was a man in pain.

461

They sat and drank coffee, and didn't talk about Mrs. Pampkin. At least not with their mouths. With their eyes they talked about her, with their fingers gripping their mugs they talked about her.

Mrs. Pampkin?

My inclination before that night would have been to say that she was as forgettable as her husband. More so. Though I had seen her many times, I couldn't conjure up her face. I remembered she wore earth tones. I remembered she once smelled like bland soap. She wasn't pudgy; she wasn't lanky. She wasn't stiff, nor was she jiggly. Early on in the campaign, my father had suggested to Pampkin that maybe his wife could wear a flower in her hair at garden events, or at the very least lipstick for television. Nothing came of these suggestions, and as far as I knew the issue of Pampkin's wife hadn't come up again until that night in the kitchen, when, for me, she went from drab to blazing. She'd done something unexpected. If Mrs. Pampkin was capable of it, what did this mean for the rest of us? I remembered—then—that I had watched her after Mike got hit by the carpet. She hadn't become hysterical. She'd merely walked over to him lying there on the pavement (the Shriner apologizing over and over) and the expression in her eyes was of such motionless calm that Mike and everybody else around knew it was going to be all right, that this was only another humiliation in the long line that life hands us, nothing more, nothing less. She'd knelt to him.

Pampkin's hand crept across the table toward my father's. Gently he clutched my father's wrist.

"Do you know what she said? She said, 'You have no idea how this feels.' I said, 'Maureen, I thought I did.' "

"More coffee, Mike?"

"Please."

But he didn't let go of my father's wrist, and my father didn't try to pull it away. Pampkin kept talking.

"You get to a point you think you can't be surprised. I remember a lady once, a blind lady. Lived on Archer. Every day she went to the same store up the block. Every day for thirty-five years. She knows this stretch of block as if she laid the cement for the sidewalk herself. It's her universe. One day they're doing some sewage work and some clown forgets to replace the manhole cover and vamoose. She drops. Crazy that she lived. Broke both legs. It cost the city four hundred thousand on the tort claim to settle it. I'm talking about this kind of out-of-nowhere."

My father sat there and watched him.

"Or let's say you're on Delta. Sipping a Bloody Mary. Seatbelt sign's off. There's a jolt. Unanticipated turbulence, they call it. It happened to a cousin of Vito Marzullo. All he was trying to do was go to Philadelphia. Broke his neck on the overhead bin."

When I woke up on the kitchen floor, the room looked different, darker, smaller, in the feeble light of the sun just peeping over the bottom edge of the kitchen window, Pampkin was still sitting there, gripping his mug of cold coffee and talking across the table to my father's shaggy head, which was facedown and drooling on the bumper stickers. My father was young then. He's always looked young; even to this day, his gray sideburns seem more like an affectation than a sign of age, but that morning he really was young, and Pampkin was still telling my father's head what it was like to be surprised. And he didn't look any more rumpled than usual. Now when I remember all this, I think of Fidel Castro, giving those eighteen-hour speeches to the party faithful. There on the table, my father's loyal head.

I was thirteen years old and I woke up on the floor with a hard-on over Mrs. Pampkin. One long night on the linoleum had proved that lust, if not love, had a smell and that smell was of bland soap. I thought of ditching school and following her to some apartment or a Red Roof Inn. I wanted to watch them. I wanted to see something that wasn't lonely. Tossed-around sheets, a belt lying on the floor. I wanted to know what they said, how they left each other, who watched the retreating back of the other. How do you part? Why would you ever? Even for an hour? Even when you know that the next day, at some appointed hour, you will have it again?

Got to go. My husband's running for governor.

Pampkin droned on. He had his shoes off and was sitting there in his mismatched socks, his toes quietly wrestling each other.

"Or put it this way. An old tree. Its roots are dried up. But you can't know this. You're not a botanist, a tree surgeon, or Smokey the Bear. One day, a whiff of breeze comes and topples it. Why that whiff?"

I couldn't hold back a loud yawn, and Pampkin looked down at me on the floor. He wasn't startled by the rise in my shorts. He wasn't startled by anything anymore.

He asked me directly, "You. Little fella. You're as old as Methuselah and still you don't know squat?"

463

I shrugged.

Pampkin took a gulp of old coffee. "Exactly," he said. "Exactly."

Either I stopped listening, or he stopped talking, because after a while his voice got faint and the morning rose for good.

Pampkin died twelve years later, in the winter of '92. The subheadline in the *Chicago Sun-Times* ran: AMIABLE POLITICIAN LOST GOVERNOR'S RACE BY RECORD MARGIN.

I went with my father to the funeral. The Pampkins had never divorced. We met Mrs. Pampkin on the steps of the funeral home in Skokie. All it took was the way they looked at each other. I won't try to describe it, except to say that it lasted too long and had nothing to do with anybody dead. They didn't touch. They didn't need to. They watched each other's smoky breath in the chill air. Facing her in her grief and her wide-brimmed black hat, my father looked haggard and puny. It only ended when more people came up to her to offer condolences. I don't know how long it went on between them. I'm not even sure it matters. I now know it's easier to walk away from what you thought you couldn't live without than I once imagined.

She was taller than I remembered, and her face was red with sadness and January.

"Don't look so pale, Ray," she whispered to my father before she moved on to the other mourners, her hand hovering for a moment near his ear. "Mike always thought you were a good egg."

Nominated by Joseph Hurka, Elizabeth McKenzie

GROWING WINGS

by ROBERT BLY

from THE SUN

It's all right if Cézanne goes on painting the same picture.
It's all right if juice tastes bitter in our mouths.
It's all right if the old man drags one useless foot.

The apple on the Tree of Paradise hangs there for months.
We wait for years and years on the lip of the falls;
The blue-gray mountain keeps rising behind the black trees.

It's all right if I feel this same pain until I die.
A pain that we have earned gives more nourishment
Than the joy we won at the lottery last night.

It's all right if the partridge's nest fills with snow.
Why should the hunter complain if his bag is empty
At dusk? It only means the bird will live another night.

It's all right if we turn in all our keys tonight.
It's all right if we give up our longing for the spiral.
It's all right if the boat I love never reaches shore.

If we're already so close to death, why should we complain?
Robert, you've climbed so many trees to reach the nests.
It's all right if you grow your wings on the way down.

Nominated by Wesley McNair

MERCY

fiction by PINCKNEY BENEDICT

from ONTARIO REVIEW

THE LIVESTOCK HAULER'S RAMP banged onto the ground, and out of the darkness they came, the miniature horses, fine-boned and fragile as china. They trit-trotted down the incline like the vanguard of a circus parade, tails up, manes fluttering. They were mostly a bunch of tiny pintos, the biggest not even three feet tall at the withers. I was ten years old, and their little bodies made me feel like a giant. The horses kept coming out of the trailer, more and more of them every moment. The teamsters that were unloading them just stood back and smiled.

My old man and I were leaning on the top wire of the southern fence-line of our place, watching the neighbor farm become home to these exotics. Ponies, he kept saying, ponies ponies ponies, like if he said it enough times, he might be able to make them go away. Or make himself believe they were real, one or the other.

I think they're miniature horses, I told him. Not ponies. I kept my voice low, not sure I wanted him to hear me.

One faultless dog-sized sorrel mare looked right at me, tossed its head, and sauntered out into the thick clover of the field, nostrils flaring. I decided I liked that one the best. To myself, I named it Cinnamon. If I were to try and ride it, I thought, my heels would drag the ground.

Horses, ponies, my old man said. He had heard. He swept out a dismissive hand. Can't work them, can't ride them, can't eat them. Useless.

Useless was the worst insult in his vocabulary.

We were angus farmers. Magnificent deep-fleshed black angus. In the field behind us, a dozen of our market steers roamed past my old man and me in a lopsided wedge, cropping the sweet grass. They ate constantly, putting on a pound, two pounds a day. All together like that, they made a sound like a steam locomotive at rest in the station, a deep resonant sighing. Their rough hides gleamed obsidian in the afternoon sun, and their hooves might have been fashioned out of pig iron.

The biggest of them, the point of the wedge, raised his head, working to suss out this new smell, the source of this nickering and whinnying, that had invaded his neighborhood. His name was Rug, because his hide was perfect, and my old man planned to have it tanned after we sent him off to the lockers in the fall. None of the other steers had names, just the numbers in the yellow tags that dangled from their ears. Rug peered near-sightedly through the woven-wire fence that marked the border between his field and the miniature horses', and his face was impassive, as it always was.

The teamsters slammed the trailer's ramp back into place and climbed into the rig's cab, cranked up the big diesel engine, oily smoke pluming from the dual stacks. The offloaded horses began to play together, nipping at one another with their long yellow teeth, dashing around the periphery of the field, finding the limits of the place. Cinnamon trailed after the others, less playful than the rest. Rug lowered his head and moved on, and the wedge of heavy-shouldered angus moved with him.

Another livestock van pulled into the field, the drivers of the two trucks exchanging casual nods as they passed each other. I was happy enough to see more of them come, funny little beggars, but I had a moment of wondering to myself how many horses, even miniature ones, the pasture could sustain.

More of the midgets, my old man said. What in hell's next? he asked. He wasn't speaking to me exactly. He very seldom addressed a question directly to me. It seemed like he might be asking God Himself. What? Giraffes? Crocodiles?

This valley was a beef valley from long before I was born. A broad river valley with good grass, set like a diamond in the center of a wide plateau at twenty-four hundred feet of altitude. For generations it was Herefords all around our place, mostly, and Charolais, but our angus were the sovereigns over them all. My grandfather was

467

president of the cattlemen's association, and he raised some trouble when the Beefmasters and Swiss Simmentals came in, because the breeds were unfamiliar to him; and my old man did the same when the place to our east went with the weird-looking hump-backed lop-eared Brahmas. But they got used to the new breeds. They were, after all, beefers, and beef fed the nation; and we were still royalty.

Then the bottom fell out of beef prices. We hung on. Around us, the Charolais and Simmentals went first, the herds dispersed and the land sold over the course of a few years, and then the rest of them all in a rush, and we were alone. Worse than alone. Now it was swine to the east, and the smell of them when the wind was wrong was enough to gag a strong-stomached man. The smell of angus manure is thick and honest and bland, like the angus himself; but pig manure is acid and briny and bitter and brings a tear to the eye. And the shrieking of the pigs clustered in their long barns at night, as it drifted across the fields into our windows, was like the cries of the damned.

Pigs to the east, with a big poultry operation beyond that, and sheep to the north (with llamas to protect them from packs of feral dogs), and even rumors of a man up in Pocahontas County who wanted to start an ostrich ranch, because ostrich meat was said to be low in fat and cholesterol, and ostrich plumes made wonderful feather dusters that never wore out.

The place to our west wasn't even a farm anymore. A rich surgeon named Slaughter from the country seat had bought the acreage when Warren Kennebaker, the Charolais breeder, went bust. Slaughter had designed it like a fortress, and it looked down on our frame house from a hill where the dignified long-bodied Charolais had grazed: a great gabled many-chimneyed mansion that went up in a matter of months; acres of slate roof, and a decorative entrance flanked by stone pillars and spear-pointed pickets that ran for three or four rods out to each side of the driveway and ended there; and gates with rampant lions picked out in gold. That entrance with its partial fence made my old man angrier than anything else. What good's a fence that doesn't go all the way around? he asked me. Keeps nothing out, keeps nothing in.

Useless, I said.

As tits on a bull, he said. Then: Doctor Slaughter, Doctor Slaughter! he shouted up at the blank windows of the house. He thought her name was the funniest thing he had ever heard. Why don't you just get together and form a practice with Doctor Payne and Doctor Butcher?

There was no Doctor Payne or Doctor Butcher; that was just his joke.

Payne, Slaughter, and Butcher! he shouted. That would be rich.

The horses started testing the fence almost from the first. They were smart, I could tell that from watching them, from the way they played tag together, darting off to the far parts of the pasture to hide, flirting, concealing their compact bodies in folds of the earth and leaping up to race off again when they were discovered, their hooves drumming against the hard-packed ground. They galloped until they reached one end of the long field, then swung around in a broad curve and came hell-for-leather back the way they had gone, their coats shaggy with the approach of winter and slick with sweat. I watched them whenever I had a few moments free from ferrying feed for the steers.

I would walk down to the south fence and climb up on the sagging wire and sit and take them in as they leaped and nipped and pawed at one another with their sharp, narrow hooves. I felt like they wanted to put on a show for me when I was there, wanted to entertain me. During the first snow, which was early that year, at the end of October, they stood stock still, the whole crew of them, and gaped around at the gently falling flakes. They twitched their hides and shook their manes and shoulders as though flies were lighting all over them. They snorted and bared their teeth and sneezed. After a while, they grew bored with the snow and went back to their games.

After a few weeks, though, when the weather got colder and the grass was thin and trampled down, the horses became less like kids and more like the convicts in some prison picture: heads down, shoulders hunched, they sidled along the fence line, casting furtive glances at me and at the comparatively lush pasturage on our side of the barrier.

The fence was a shame and an eyesore. It had been a dry summer when it went in, five years before when the last of the dwindling Herefords had occupied the field, and the dirt that season was dry as desert sand, and the posts weren't sunk as deep as they should have been. They were loose like bad teeth, and a few of them were nearly rotted through. I was the only one who knew what bad shape it was getting to be in. My old man seldom came down to this boundary after the day the horses arrived, and nobody from the miniature horse farm walked their border the way we walked ours. We didn't know any of them, people from outside the county, hardly ever glimpsed them at all.

It wasn't our problem to solve. By long tradition, that stretch was the responsibility of the landowner to the south, and I figured my old man would die before he would take up labor and expense that properly belonged with the owners of the miniature horses.

Cinnamon, the sorrel, came over to me one afternoon when I was taking a break, pushed her soft nose through the fence toward me, and I promised myself that the next time I came I would bring the stump of a carrot or a lump of sugar with me. I petted her velvet nose and she nibbled gently at my fingers and the open palm of my hand. Her whiskers tickled and her breath was warm and damp against my skin.

Then she took her nose from me and clamped her front teeth on the thin steel wire of the fence and pulled it toward her, pushed it back. I laughed. Get away from there, I told her, and smacked her gently on the muzzle. She looked at me reproachfully and tugged at the wire again. Her mouth made grating sounds against the metal that set my own teeth on edge. She had braced her front legs and was really pulling, and the fence flexed and twanged like a bow string. A staple popped loose from the nearest post.

You've got to stop it, I said. You don't want to come over here, even if the grass looks good. My old man will shoot you if you do.

He surprised me watching the horses. I was in my usual place on the fence, the top wire biting into my rear end, and he must have caught sight of me as he was setting out one of the great round hay bales for the angus to feed from. Generally I was better at keeping track of him, at knowing where he was, but that day I had brought treats with me and was engrossed, and I didn't hear the approaching rumble of his tractor as it brought the fodder over the hill. When he shut down the engine, I knew that I was caught.

What are you doing? he called. The angus that were following the tractor and the hay, eager to be fed, ranged themselves in a stolid rank behind him. I kicked at Cinnamon to get her away from me, struggled to get the slightly crushed cubes of sugar back into my

470

pocket. Crystals of it clung to my fingers. He strode down to me, and I swung my legs back over to our side of the fence and hopped down. It was a cold day and his breath rolled white from his mouth.

You've got plenty of leisure, I guess, he said. His gaze flicked over my shoulder. A number of the miniature horses, Cinnamon at their head, had peeled off from the main herd and were dashing across the open space. What makes them run like that? he asked. I hesitated a moment, not sure whether he wanted to know or if it was one of those questions that didn't require an answer.

They're just playing, I told him. They spend a lot of time playing.

Playing. Is that right, he said. You'd like to have one, I bet. Wouldn't you, boy? he asked me.

I pictured myself with my legs draped around the barrel of Cinnamon's ribs, my fingers wrapped in the coarse hair of her mane. Even as I pictured it, I knew a person couldn't ride a miniature horse. I recalled what it felt like when she had thrust her muzzle against my hand, her breath as she went after the sugar I had begun bringing her. Her teeth against the wire. I pictured myself holding out a fresh carrot for her to lip into her mouth. I pictured her on our side of the fence, her small form threading its way among the stern gigantic bodies of the angus steers. I knew I would be a fool to tell him I wanted a miniature horse.

Yes sir, I said.

He swept his eyes along the fence. Wire's in pretty bad shape, he said. Bastards aren't doing their job. Looks like we'll have to do it for them.

He shucked off the pair of heavy leather White Mule work gloves he was wearing and tossed them to me. I caught one in the air, and the other fell to the cold ground. You keep the fence in shape then, he said. The staples and wire and stretcher and all were in the machine shed, I knew.

Remember, my old man said as he went back to his tractor. First one that comes on my property, I kill.

On the next Saturday, before dawn, I sat in the cab of our beef hauler while he loaded steers. There were not many of them; it would only take us one trip. I couldn't get in among them because I didn't yet own a pair of steel-toed boots, and the angus got skittish when they were headed to the stockyard. I would have helped, I wanted to help, but he was afraid I would get stepped on by the anxious beeves and lose a toe. He was missing toes on both feet. So he was back there by himself at the tailgate of the truck, running the angus up into it, shouting at them.

Rug was the first, and my old man called the name into his twitching ear—Ho, Rug! Ho!—and took his cap off, slapped him on the rump with it. Get up there! he shouted. I watched him in the rearview mirror, and it was hard to make out what was happening, exactly, because the mirror was cracked down its length, the left half crazed into a patchwork of glass slivers. The other angus were growing restive, I could tell that much, while Rug balked.

My old man never would use an electric prod. He twisted Rug's tail up into a tight, painful coil, shoving with his shoulder, and the big steer gave in and waddled reluctantly into the van. The truck shifted with his weight, which was better than a ton. The rest followed, the hauler sinking lower and lower over the rear axle as they clambered inside. My old man silently mouthed their numbers, every one, as they trundled on board, and he never looked at their ear tags once. He knew them.

When they were all embarked, when for the moment his work was done, his face fell slack and dull, and his shoulders slumped. And for a brief instant he stood still, motionless as I had never seen him. It was as though a breaker somewhere inside him had popped, and he had been shut off.

I made my daily round of the southern fence, patching up the holes the horses had made, shoveling loose dirt into the cavities they carved into the earth, as though they would tunnel under the fence if I wouldn't let them break through it. They were relentless and I had become relentless too, braiding the ends of the bitten wire back together, hammering bent staples back into the rotting posts. The sharp end of a loose wire snaked its way through the cowhide palm of the glove on my right hand and bit deep into me. I cursed and balled the hand briefly into a fist to stanch the blood, and then I went back to work again.

The field the horses occupied was completely skinned now, dotted with mounds of horse dung. Because the trees were bare of leaves, I could see through the windbreak to the principal barn of the place, surrounded by dead machinery. I couldn't tell if anyone was caring for them at all. I don't believe a single animal had been sold. Their coats were long and matted, their hooves long untrimmed, curling and ugly. A man—I suppose it was a man, because at this distance I couldn't tell, just saw a dark figure in a long coat—emerged from the open double doors of the barn, apparently intent on some errand.

Hey! I shouted to him. My voice was loud in the cold and silence. The figure paused and glanced around. I stood up and waved my arms over my head to get his attention. This is your fence!

He lifted a hand, pale so that I could only imagine that it was ungloved, and waved uncertainly back at me.

This is your fence to fix! I called. I pounded my hand against the loose top wire. These here are your horses!

The hand dropped, and the figure without making any further acknowledgment of me or what I had said turned its back and strolled at a casual pace back into the dark maw of the barn.

Most days I hated them. I cursed them as they leaned their slight weight against the fence, their ribs showing. I poked them with a sharp stick to get them to move so that I could fix the fence. They would shift their bodies momentarily, then press them even harder into the wire. The posts groaned and popped. I twisted wire and sucked at the cuts on my fingers to take the sting away. I filched old bald tires from the machine shed and rolled them through the field and laid them against the holes in the fence. The tires smelled of dust and spider webs. This was not the way we mended fence on our place—our posts were always true, our wire stretched taut and uncorroded, our staples solidly planted—but it was all I could think of to keep them out. The horses rolled their eyes at me.

And I tossed them old dry corn cobs that I retrieved from the crib, the one that we hadn't used in years. The horses fell on the dry husks, shoving each other away with their heads, lashing out with their hooves, biting each other now not in play but hard enough to draw blood. I pitched over shriveled windfallen apples from the stunted trees in the old orchard behind the house. I tried to get the apples near the sorrel, near Cinnamon; but as often as not the pintos shunted her aside before she could snatch a mouthful.

You know why we can't feed them, don't you? my old man asked me. We were breaking up more of the great round bales, which were warm and moist at their center, like fresh-baked rolls. The angus, led

473

not by Rug now but by another, shifted their muscular shoulders and waited patiently to be fed. I could sense the miniature horses lining the fence, but I didn't look at them.

They'd eat us out of house and home, he said. Like locusts.

Behind me, the hooves of the horses clacked against the frozen ground.

One morning, the fence didn't need mending. It had begun to snow in earnest the night before, and it was still snowing when I went out to repair the wire. The television was promising snow for days to come. Most of the horses were at the fence, pressing hard against it but not otherwise moving. Some were lying down in the field beyond. I looked for the sorrel, to see if she was among the standing ones. All of them were covered in thick blankets of snow, and it was impossible to tell one diminutive shape from the next. Each fence post was topped with a sparkling white dome.

I walked the fence, making sure there was no new damage. I took up the stick I had used to poke them and ran its end along the fence wire, hoping its clattering sound would stir them. It didn't. Most of them had clustered at a single point, to exchange body heat, I suppose. I rapped my stick against the post where they were gathered, and its cap of snow fell to the ground with a soft thump. Nothing. The wire was stretched tight with the weight of them.

I knelt down, and the snow soaked immediately through the knees of my coveralls. I put my hand in my pocket, even though I knew there was nothing there for them. The dry cobs were all gone, the apples had been eaten. The eyes of the horse nearest me were closed, and there was snow caught in its long delicate lashes. The eyes of all the horses were closed. This one, I thought, was the sorrel, was Cinnamon. Must be. I put my hand to its muzzle but could feel nothing. I stripped off the White Mule glove, and the cold bit immediately into my fingers, into the half-healed cuts there from the weeks of mending fence. I reached out again.

And the horse groaned. I believed it was the horse. I brushed snow from its forehead, and its eyes blinked open, and the groaning continued, a weird guttural creaking and crying, and I thought that such a sound couldn't be coming from just the one horse, all of the horses must be making it together somehow, they were crying out with a single voice. Then I thought as the sound grew louder that it must be the hogs to the east, they were slaughtering the hogs and that was the source of it, but it was not time for slaughtering, so that couldn't be right either. I thought these things in a moment, as the sound rang out over the frozen fields and echoed off the surrounding hills.

At last I understood that it was the fencepost, the wood of the fencepost and the raveling wire and the straining staples, right at the point where the horses were gathered. And I leaped backward just as the post gave way. It heeled over hard and snapped off at ground level, and the horses tumbled with it, coming alive as they fell, the snow flying from their coats in a wild spray as they scrambled to get out from under one another.

The woven-wire fence, so many times mended, parted like tissue paper under their combined weight. With a report like a gunshot, the next post went over as well, and the post beyond that. Two or three rods of fence just lay down flat on the ground, and the horses rolled right over it, they came pouring onto our place. The horses out in the field roused themselves at the sound, shivered off their mantles of snow, and came bounding like great dogs through the gap in the fence as well. And I huddled against the ground, my hands up to ward off their flying hooves as they went past me, over me. I knew that there was nothing I could do to stop them. Their hooves would brain me, they would lay my scalp open to the bone.

I was not touched.

The last of the horses bolted by me, and they set to on the remains of the broken round bale, giving little cries of pleasure as they buried their muzzles in the hay's roughness. The few angus that stood nearby looked on bemused at the arrivals. I knew that I had to go tell my father, I had to go get him right away. The fence—the fence that I had maintained day after day, the fence I had hated and that had blistered and slashed my hands—was down. But because it was snowing and all around was quiet, the scene had the feel of a holiday, and I let them eat.

When they had satisfied themselves, for the moment at least, the horses began to play. I searched among them until finally I found the sorrel. She was racing across our field, her hooves kicking up light clouds of ice crystals. She was moving more quickly than I had ever seen her go, but she wasn't chasing another horse, and she wasn't being chased. She was teasing the impassive angus steers, roaring up to them, stopping just short of their great bulk; turning on a dime and dashing away again. They stood in a semicircle, hind ends together, lowered heads outermost, and they towered over her like the walls of a medieval city. She yearned to charm them. She was almost dancing in the snow.

As I watched her, she passed my old man without paying him the least attention. He wore his long cold-weather coat. The hood was up, and it eclipsed his face. He must have been standing there quite a while. Snow had collected on the ridge of his shoulders, and a rime of frost clung to the edges of his hood. In his hand he held a hunting rifle, his Remington .30-06. The lines of his face seemed odd and unfamiliar beneath the coat's cowl, and his shoulders were trembling in a peculiar way as he observed the interlopers on his land. I blinked. I knew what was coming. The thin sunlight, refracted as it was by the snow, dazzled my eyes, and the shadows that hid him from me were deep.

At last, the sorrel took notice of him, and she turned away from the imperturbable angus and trotted over to him. He watched her come. She lowered her delicate head and nipped at him, caught the hem of his coat between her teeth and began to tug. His feet slipped in the snow. Encouraged by her success, she dragged him forward. I waited for him to kill her. She continued to drag him, a foot, a yard, and at last he fell down. He fell right on his ass in the snow, my old man, the Remington held high above his head. The sorrel stood over him, the other horses clustered around her, and she seemed to gloat.

The Remington dropped to the ground, the bolt open, the breech empty. Half a dozen bright brass cartridges left my old man's hand to skip and scatter across the snow. The hood of his coat fell away from his face, and I saw that my old man was laughing.

Nominated by Andrew Hudgins, Fred Leebron, Laura Kasischke,
Bonnie Jo Campbell, Ontario Review

STICK FIGURE

by GARY SHORT

from RUNES

There was light in the trees. An autumn brightness.
And light in the nothing beyond the leaves.
The weight of it, my father,
dull cinders and grit poured from the plastic bag.
I saw the round pile of ash
accumulating at my feet. And stopped.

When I began again, I reached
into the bag, let the fistfuls of ashes
sift through my hand
and tried to give him human shape.
Using the ash circle as a head,
I made an ideogram—

a simple stick-figure of a man,
legs an upside down V, arms spread, the way
I would have drawn him as a kid
with a big-lead pencil
on grainy first-grade paper.
And when I was done pouring him out,

I gave him a heart. A fallen red leaf.

Nominated by Susan Terris, Runes

THE SUBCULTURE OF THE WRONGFULLY ACCUSED

by THYLIAS MOSS

from POETRY

Ultimately improved by it: slant light
hitting his prison obliquely

near the state bird's pointed head   accentuated
crest, the black-ringed bill

from which *wheat-wheat-wheat-wheat*
from which *whoit cheer, whoit cheer;*   *cheer-*
cheer-cheer

inspired Ronald Cotton to listen
as in his head, the solitary cardinal   indulged in snails

which seemed like polished fossils
of trophy hog tails   (after prize   butchery)

that Ronald was able to recall,
his hair a mess of replicas of them

as industrious as the state
whose success was poultry & eggs   tobacco & soybeans

as well as convictions:

None as tightly knit as Jennifer's   (not even the state flag)
that she could identify Cotton

that cotton's taking on appearances   other than burst white
of a dense localized haze from which   to weave memory, following
pink-petaled start, rather a satellite   dish of a flower, pollen/
                                              sensor-
studded antenna protruding from   the center

undeniably; the jury couldn't acquit   Cotton
of its role in documenting and altering   Jennifer's history,
many lives changed

as result of consequences, sensors   that boast duality
of receptor and transmitter: witness: insects give and take, taint
what is put out, taken in; mix

it up so that interrelatedness   spreads
and the understandable error of   metaphor
becomes less erroneous over time:
eleven years in prison, innocence   locked up, protected

although in prison, it resembled   something else.
If Cotton strained, he could see   the top

of a Ferris wheel on the horizon   just a possible
segment of a rainbow the length   of a chain

of cardinal feathers

even though it wasn't that at all.   The eye witnesses all the
                                         time,
even the unseeing eye is turned   toward a focus
on black, saturation dense as   conviction; the eye

processes, pulls in whole vista to a   retinal speck
of convergence

which is to say there is some Cotton   in Poole,
some connection, independent   shared participation in cold
beer, occasional cards turkey-spread
in the right hand without knowing   the other
sank into the seat at the cinema   the same way

and sampled Funnel cake at the   state fair
within a week of each other

and more than that in common:both being men
and convicted for what men really can and really do, do.

Including sometimes confessions   and apologies; cash
                           reparations
after the innocence is free to extend its parameters
to unlocked doors, be an oversized   over-zealous white bird
floating down the aisle, its cottony   haze lifted
in order to kiss and marry Ronald's   calm delight in being able
to take his time

leave his longshoreman's mark on   ships
that take some of him to any port in the world: durable goods

such as the DNA whose precision   detects human exactitude,
and could build as many Ronalds as time would permit

something Jennifer now desperately wants to do, restoring
what was lost because it was like   something else,

because the fact of similarity   is compelling, convincing;
if connections could not be made,   there'd be no havens, no
                           fugitive
status lost to fusion, no links   to God, no human

murmurings whose   constant echoes
are also the gentle silvery hum   of fans praying

over computer motors to cool them and also mimic
motion of small wings amplified to make sound

in the distance much like the electric razor
preparing a head on death row clean as a light bulb.

Ronald was prepared to be believed;
he saw the quiet manner of his long days in court
as evidence of his rationality and contemplativeness

such as befits clergy; a potential propensity for order,
mercy, the steadiness required to dispense blessings
mostly on the undeserving without emotion or judgment
selfishness or preference

while he was being judged guilty for lack of emotion,
for Jennifer's incontrovertible emotional insistence
on Cotton's being the one—she had to finger him
to be comfortable within her survival. No way to mistake
to ever forget details documented in memory,
the event relived to the point that it resculpted her brain
into a Cottony bust (he was there to be the perfect model)

whose reality floated away in a Poole,
as only the reflection of Cotton

identified as source. A situation also called (must-have)
moonlight.

Here's the new & improved Cotton: eleven years in the making;
enough

time served to anger to ruin it; at that same room's temperature
it became doubt of clemency, pardon: peculiar butter that
erupted
as gratefulness for the miracle of absolute exoneration
when his impossibility as rapist was proven.

Even Cotton conceded that   the composite sketch
bore a just resemblance to Cotton, displayed a metaphor for
              men

like Cotton, the seeds of capability in the structure of the face,
the human repertoire that includes Cotton
who softly consents to meet Jennifer when she asks him to
funnel her regret and apologies deep into himself, accepting that
she meant no malice toward him   but toward
the perpetrator whom many men   resemble, all
brothers, family

of man resemblance; Cotton's   own daughter, Cotton's
                  own wife

could be in a similar position; no   offense
taken, captivated by the beauty of Jennifer; her superior logic

refusing to let the crime against her
silence her; as sure, as certain, as dazzling
about speaking up about mistaking Cotton for Poole
as she was in identifying   in the lineup
the closest thing there to Poole   the best
available, the incredible   likeness
that memory seized, filling gaps in the recollected Poole
with Cotton's particulars.   She felt better in her cotton-
                touched skin.

Metaphor is a form of forgiveness; a short rope of it knots-up
those that can't come together any other way into being defined
by the other. Strange

and estranged pairings give rise to mutable truth
that can yield to both dawn and twilight
demands that things be seen differently.

Jennifer in moonlight instead of being illuminated moon whose face
was also in Emmett Till's way, but this generation of Jennifer has
  another side
home late after a day of good faith in which she and Cotton
              team up

at a church to speak up about doubt   as less a shadow than
                                           certainty.

Memory is as accurate as metaphor, an overlay
that always fits something, that like the purest
most sparkling water is too naïve   not to submit
to any vessel into which it's poured.   Just to be guzzled.

Perhaps the vessel in which cotton   becomes a pool
in which North Carolina is shaped   like an embryo:

Humanity still on the brink   of infancy.

Nominated by Poetry

THE DOME

fiction by STEVEN MILLHAUSER

from THE AMERICAN SCHOLAR

THE FIRST DOMES, the precursors, appeared here and there in affluent neighborhoods, on out-of-the-way roads, where they attracted a certain attention before growing familiar and nearly invisible. The few outsiders who actually witnessed them tended to dismiss them as follies of the rich, comparable to underground heating pipes for winter gardens or basement bowling alleys with automatic pinsetters. Even the early newspaper reports did not quite know what tone to take, shifting uneasily from technical description to ironic commentary, with moments of guarded praise. And that was hardly surprising, since the domes, while having features that were judged to be admirable, displayed themselves in a way that could readily strike an unsympathetic observer as pretentious or irritating.

Each of the early models, made of transparent Plastiglas, was designed to fit directly over a house and its property. Now, emerging from the front or back door in summer, the owner of a dome could step comfortably into a world of air-conditioned lawns and gardens, thanks to a highly efficient system of filters and evaporator coils built into the Plastiglas. There were other advantages. Recessed fluorescent lighting with dimmer switches permitted the property to be illuminated at night, so that you could read a book or newspaper in the cool outdoors on the hottest, muggiest evenings. Owners were encouraged to practice their golf swings, play badminton after dark, and enjoy a bit of night gardening, in the always perfect weather under the dome. In fact it was a boast of the manufacturer, much quoted at the time, that "Inside our dome, rain never falls." As if that wasn't enough, the manufacturer promised future models that would heat the enclosures in winter, though a number of difficulties still needed to be ironed out. It was above all as technological achievements that the early domes impressed most observers, who nevertheless remained skeptical. Questions were raised about the extent to which such excesses were likely to be shared by the average American household, since the domes at that time cost nearly as much as the estates they encapsulated. Nor could a number of journalists resist reflecting on the metaphorical implications of those glistening, crystalline structures, which enclosed the rich in little princedoms that insulated them even further from the everyday world.

There were, moreover, serious flaws in the early domes, which became apparent soon enough. Grackles, jays, and sparrows settled in great numbers on the dome-tops, where they blocked the sky and left broad smears of yellowish-white excrement. To make matters worse, many birds, deceived by the transparent Plastiglas, flew directly into the thick walls and fell dead or injured to the ground below. Now the manufacturer had to send out daily cleaning crews, who washed the outsides of the domes, gathered up the dead and injured birds, and installed small boxes that made a grinding noise intended to discourage wasps, bees, birds, and Japanese beetles from settling anywhere on the shiny surfaces. Other problems began to reveal themselves. Rainwater as it evaporated left dusty streaks, which had to be removed; air-borne particles gradually formed a layer of grime. Trouble developed even on the insides of the domes, where mist from sprinkler systems collected on the inner surfaces, increasing the humidity and obscuring the view. The manufacturer devoted itself assiduously to every complaint, while pointing out in its own defense that many of the little annoyances were due strictly to summer and might be expected to vanish with the season. The owners waited; and as the weather turned cold, frost formed colossal and oppressive patterns on the transparent surfaces, which were further darkened by the falling of the first snow.

One might have been forgiven, at this point, for predicting the death of the domes. In many instances the owners did in fact have them removed, a costly business requiring a small army of workmen and fleets of flatbed trucks. Others remained steadfast through the winter, during which a number of benefits became evident. No snow fell on the walks and driveways; bushes and hedges were protected from harmful layers of ice; the air inside the domes, though still un-heated, grew pleasantly warm on cold but sunny afternoons. Such discoveries were offset by a burst of new drawbacks. Accumulations of thick-crusted snow froze to the tops of the domes, while spears of ice clung to the sides, and sweeps of high-drifted snow pressed up against the Plastiglas doors. By the end of the first winter, it was clear to most customer that the domes were more trouble than they were worth.

The change came in early spring. Three separate events took place within one crucial 10-day period: the manufacturer discovered a cheaper and stronger substance, Celudon, that reduced the cost of the domes by half; a pollution alert lasting an entire week drew new attention to the domes as pure environments; and a rash of kidnap-pings in small towns in Connecticut, Massachusetts, and Vermont led to a sudden interest in the domes as protective shells. Now the domes began to appear in less-exclusive neighborhoods, where crowds gathered to watch enormous strips of Celudon being lowered into place by towering cranes. Newspapers and weekly magazines paid close attention to the new middle-class phenomenon, which some journalists attributed to the influence of the mall, with its habit of combining disparate elements under a single roof. Others saw in the trend still another instance of a disturbing tendency in the Amer-ican suburb: the longing for withdrawal, for self-enclosure, for ex-pensive isolation.

As the domes began to spread slowly, rival manufacturers pro-duced less-costly varieties, composed of improved materials and marketed under an array of names (Thermolux, Vivinox, Crysto-phane), often with new and attractive features. One dome was equipped with a heating system for winter, another had retractable panels for controlling frost and mist, and one well-advertised version, promoted by educators, came with an artificial night sky that dis-played constellations, planets, and other heavenly bodies, scientifi-cally adjusted to latitude and longitude, which moved slowly across the inner surface and were far more vivid and convincing than those in the actual sky.

Yet this activity too might have run its course, leaving behind a scattering of domed properties in towns that had gone on to new di-versions, had it not been for an event that took many observers by surprise. Just when it seemed that the market for domed houses had reached its limit, a developer decided to enclose several blocks of newly constructed homes on fourteen acres of land beneath a single dome. The vast span of Celudon rose not only over individual properties but over a small park with swings, a communal swimming pool, a stretch of oak and beech woods, and nine freshly paved streets. Two weeks later, in a nearby town, a gated community voted to endome itself; and as the fashion for doming continued to spread, citizens at town meetings and city halls began to debate the question of enclosing commercial districts and public lands, while keeping them accessible to area residents.

It was during this phase of enlarged domings that the first town voted to enclose itself in a massive dome that was reputed to be one of the great engineering feats of the new millennium. The immensity of the structure, the sheer drama and bravado of it all, caused a sharp increase of interest, for the new magnitude represented a decision that could no longer be dismissed as a passing trend. Critics attacked the hostile apartness of the town, which in its hemisphere of Permatherm was said to resemble a walled medieval city, as if the advance in technology served only to conceal a secret atavism. Admirers, as might be expected, hailed the brilliance of the engineering, the grandeur of technological accomplishment, which placed the new dome in the noble line of the skyscraper, the suspension bridge, the hydroelectric dam, and the ancient pyramid. Others praised the domed town for its clean air—a system of escape vents permitted the expulsion of factory pollutants and gasoline fumes—while several took a more esthetic approach, finding in the space enclosed by the dome a spirit of gaiety, of pleasurable artifice, reminiscent of the old European plaza with its fountain and shade trees or the American mall with its food court and Santa's workshop, for under the roof of the dome the inhabitants of the town were said to feel a bond of community, a sense of uninterrupted gathering in a special place set aside for their common pleasure.

To the surprise of almost everyone, the new dome did not immediately spawn another. It was as if people felt that the doming process was moving ahead a little too rapidly and required a pause, during which the consequences of the new technology might be studied more carefully. It was recognized, to begin with, that the sheer cost of a dome this size far exceeded the annual budget of all but the wealthiest towns. At the same time, a broad range of practical problems had yet to be solved, such as the efficient flow of traffic into and out of the dome, the pattern and duration of nocturnal illumination, and the seasonal migration of birds living within the structure. People began to wonder whether they would be safer under a dome, or whether a permanent enclosure might prove harmful. But even as the issue hung in the balance, decisions were being made in remote rooms, behind closed doors, that would soon change everything.

We live in the aftermath of those decisions. To say that the Dome is the single largest achievement in the history of architecture is inadequate and misleading. It is a leap beyond, into some new domain without a name. The story of its building is well known: the drama of starting on both coasts, the erection of the great pillars, the early collapse of the northwestern foundation, the construction of the offshore airports, the closing of the final gap. Many of us can scarcely remember a time when we did not live beneath a soaring roof of transparent Celestite.

And yet the achievement is not without its detractors, even today. Critics argue that the Dome represents the complete triumph of the consumer society, of which it is the extravagant and unapologetic symbol. For the Dome, they say, has transformed the entire country into a gigantic mall, whose sole purpose is to encourage feverish consumption. The sensation of being under a common roof, of living continually under artificial lights, is said to stimulate in the average citizen a relentless desire to buy. And it remains true that the completion of the Dome has been accompanied by a sharp increase in consumer spending, as if everything beneath the Celestite roof—houses, lakes, clouds—were being displayed to advantage and offered ceaselessly for sale. Some have even claimed that our Dome is the final flowering of the 19th-century department store, of which the American mall was only a transitional, horizontal form. According to this view, the great empty spaces of the Dome will gradually be put to commercial use; there are predictions of transparent floors in the sky, level upon level, connected by hollow Celestite tubes containing motorized passenger platforms.

But those who dislike the Dome do not simply accuse it of serving the interests of late capitalism. They attack the name itself, arguing that the Celestite enclosure follows the irregular shape of the continental United States and is therefore no true dome. Defenders, while not denying that the base of the enclosure is irregular, are quick to remind their opponents that at the height of 400 feet the soaring walls of Celestite slope inward to provide the base for a classic dome that rises over most of the nation. Indeed, the forging of a true dome above a vast, irregular perimeter is one of the engineering triumphs of the entire project. But defenders are not confined to such quibbles. They point proudly to a host of benefits: the national regulation of climate, the protection of our coasts against hurricanes, the creation of 24-hour illumination and the consequent elimination of time zones, the Celestite shield against ultraviolet radiation.

Without choosing sides in the debate, we may note a number of subtler changes. Because everything lies beneath a single dome, because everything is, in a very real sense, indoors, our feelings about Nature are no longer the same. The Dome, in a single stroke, has abolished Nature. The hills, the streams, the woods, the fields, all have become elements in a new décor, an artfully designed landscape—designed by the mere fact of existing under the Dome. This experience of landscape as *style* has been called the New Interiority. In former days, a distinction was made between inside and outside: people emerged from their homes or apartments and arrived "outside." Today, one leaves one's dwelling place and steps into another, larger room. The change is dramatic. The world, perceived as an interior, shimmers with artifice. A tree growing in a park is indistinguishable from a lifelike tree in the corner of a restaurant. A lake in the country is a more artful version of a tiled pool in a mall.

This perceptual change has led in turn to another, which has been called the New Miniaturism. Things in the world now appear smaller, more toylike. An object that once towered above us—a tall pine, a steep hill, a snow-capped mountain—is itself dwarfed by the Dome, which by the ever-present fact of its vastness miniaturizes what it encloses. The Mississippi is nothing but a trickle of water in a child's terrarium, the Rockies are only a row of stones in a third-grade diorama. Events themselves, under such conditions, have receded in importance, have become estheticized. Experience is beginning to feel like a collection of ingeniously constructed arcade games. Is it because, living beneath the Dome, people are reminded of playful worlds in enclosed and festive spaces, such as movie theaters, bowling alleys, laser-tag arenas, video arcades, the old fun houses and circuses? Indeed one might argue that under the regime of the Dome, the country has become not a mall but an immense hall of entertainment, in which every citizen is a player. Certain unpleasant facts of life—rundown neighborhoods, traffic accidents, robberies, drive-by shootings—are in this view taken less seriously, since

489

they are felt to be part of the artificial displays under the Dome. Death itself is losing its terror, has come to seem little more than a brilliantly contrived effect.

There are rumors of grander plans; at a conference in Oslo, architects and engineers have proposed a transparent globe, supported by massive Lumenite pillars, which would surround the entire earth. That such a vision shall be fulfilled in our lifetime is unlikely; that it should have been dreamed at all is perhaps inevitable. For under the visible fact of the Dome, it is difficult not to imagine still vaster encompassings. Already, at certain moments, in certain moods, the famous Dome has come to seem a little diminished, a little disappointing. No doubt we shall never rest content until the great All is enclosed in a globe of transparent Celestite. Then solar systems, galaxies, supernovas, infinite space itself will become elements of a final masterwork—a never-ending festival, a celestial amusement park, in which every exploding star and spinning electron is part of the empyrean choreography. Meanwhile we walk beneath the Celestite sky, dreaming of new heavens, of impossible architectures. For a change is in the air. You can feel it coming.

Nominated by The American Scholar

BACK TO COUNTRY WITH PULITZER

by LIAM RECTOR

from THE EXECUTIVE DIRECTOR OF THE FALLEN WORLD (University of Chicago Press), AMERICAN POETRY REVIEW.

I left here at eight
And returned at 75.
In between

I largely wasted America.
I married, had children,
Distinguished myself in a profession

Full of fools, becoming one myself,
As is the way
Of this (or, I suppose, of any other) world.

I missed
The Nobel but I did bring down
The Pulitzer. The weather,

The politics, the stars,
And my own small contribution
All lined up, and I got one.

So "Pulitzer" became my middle name
Before I came here, where no one cares
A whit about such things.

I failed at love.
That's where I truly fucked up.
I couldn't.

The women in this town
Are mostly severe, resentful
—The men bitter, disappointed:

A perfect place for my purposes.
I stay in a room
In the house of an old woman

Who doesn't want to have sex any more
And neither do I
So we do not

Trouble each other on that front,
Which is good.
I do like to drink.

I used to love to eat
But then I don't much
Give a shit

About any of that now.
The old woman sometimes says wistfully
God will soon be calling both of us

Back home, but as an agnostic
I don't believe that.
As an American,

I don't buy that.
I came here to retire from love,
To face my failure to love

As I attempted to face everything
Else before, and that
Is exactly what I am doing and doing

With the exactness I used to put into
My work, for which I received the Pulitzer.
I hate a coward.

My son
Came here the other day and asked
Exactly when I might

Be coming back
And I sent him off without an answer.
The answer

Seems to be staying here,
Staying honestly here and coming to terms
With my greatest single failure.

My wife is dead. To me,
It seems I am left over
To eat a shit sandwich.

"Eat me," the world says,
Now that I have lost my appetite.
We used to say "Eat me"

To each other in high school,
Another thing from which no one
Ever recovers. America likes to think

Every one can recover from every thing,
But about this,
Especially, America is wrong.

Nominated by Ed Ochester, David Rivard, David St. John, Alice Mattison,
University of Chicago Press

BEAR STORY

fiction by SAGE MARSTERS

from THE NEW ENGLAND REVIEW

WE ARE WALKING SIDE BY SIDE and talking about what a real cowboy is when the car passes us, slowing, two heads inside leaning in our direction, eyeing the sight of us, I think, hiking girls from the East with all the gear, two girls together, two girls alone. Anyone we've met out here—the waitress, the hotel clerk, a honeymooning couple, a curious ranger—has had something to say about it right away.

The car pulls to the side of the road a ways up ahead, tires grating over the gravel; somehow you can hear the silence of this place in noises like that. Abby and I keep walking, thumbs hooked in our shoulder straps, feet slapping the road, blinking and squinting up at the snowcapped peaks and the sky, that high, flashing blue, like razor blades. And Abby keeps prattling, explaining how a cowboy is a skinny kid with a darting Adam's apple and soft cheeks and pinkish, wet looking acne rising across his forehead from wearing a sweaty hat all the time.

The car is older, black, a fierce pointed look to it, like a stinging insect. It reminds me of other cars: cars from high school owned by angular boys; the car with a broken windshield, bits of glass like pale teeth scattered across the dusty seat, that sat for years abandoned in the field behind my grandparents' house. Abby says her real cowboy's got a dead mother. It was stomach cancer, she tells me, that's why the cowboy can't stand flowers or medicine. And he has an abusive father and a couple of curly-haired twin sisters he's always looked out for, and a piece of land. Her voice is loud; she sounds brave and pleased.

The passenger door swings open and a woman wearing a dress steps out. She shuts the door behind her and waits for us, standing next to the car with her head propped to the side and her hands on her hips. I remember from an intro psychology class, a leaning head means interest. It's an innocent-looking dress, like a prairie woman who sweeps the floor all day, and I'm thinking maybe she'll ask us what we're up to, how far from home we are, and then we'll be walking again, and I'll ask Abby what's this cowboy's name and how long has the mother been dead, and feel my legs moving, hitting a rhythm, as she tells me.

"A ride," Abby says. "It's a ride, Kate." She hops in place.

"We're hitchhiking?" I ask.

"Why not?" Abby says. "My feet hurt." And something shivers up my calves, excitement and fear and pleasure, because Abby is the kind of girl I have always wanted to be friends with, my whole life, and here we are, and I will do whatever she wants. At times, I've imagined her being cruel to me on a playground, if we had known each other as children, and I feel like I've tricked her into something and I have to go on tricking her, making her believe somehow that I am pretty and lucky like her. This morning, sitting at a picnic table, our hair wet from quick, cold showers, she looked at me and said, "You don't look like you. You look like you have a brother named Sven."

"Early, isn't it?" the woman shouts, even though she's walked a little ways from the car to meet us and now we stand close to her, close enough to see that she's no prairie woman, not the kind with a clean-swept cabin. Her face is broad and blunt, colorless, the skin pitted, her hair pulled back in a greasy ponytail. The dress she's wearing is faded green corduroy, and it fits her strangely, her stomach rising in a tight, lopsided lump against the cloth, the hem crooked at her knees. There are gray hairs stuck in clumps here and there across the dress, cat fur maybe.

"Early for what?" Abby says. She crinkles up her nose in a curious bunny rabbit way she can do, and she shows her front teeth just a little; it's the look she's greeted people with all across the country, on the train on the way out, men in starched Wrangler jeans, and old couples with their own homemade chicken sandwiches in coolers waiting at their feet, and the obese man behind the desk at the motel we found on the first night. It gets people talking, it gets people thinking they know her, maybe, or she's someone they've known, or wanted to know, or missed. It's got something to do with those front teeth, I think, their slight overlap, and the mole on her neck, and her brown hair in a braid, sleek like a field hockey player, like a well-cared-for horse. I move just off to the side, the way I do, waiting, watching, chewing at the insides of my cheeks until I get a few shreds of skin I can twirl with my tongue.

"We're hiking the park," Abby says.

"Two girls hiking Glacier National Park alone?" the woman asks. She starts laughing loudly with her mouth hanging slippery and loose. "Didn't you ever watch *America's Most Wanted*?" She picks a clump of fur off her chest, flicks it into the dirt. "Did you ever notice, at the end, whenever they find those guys, those rapers and killers and lunatics, they always find them in Montana?"

I glance around, catching at once the pines, dense, endless, and the snow-streaked mountains, and the woman's pale forehead, and the sun glinting off the roof of the car, and the empty ribbon of road almost glittering in this kind of white light I can't get used to; it's a kind of clear you can't look away from but that also makes it harder to see.

A man with thick, blue-black hair leans his head out the window. "Offer them a ride," he says. Until now, I'd thought it was a woman, the long hair, and I'd thought, two women, you can get in a car with two women. He's wearing giant, mirrored sunglasses, gold rims, from another decade, like the car.

"What exactly is it you think I'm doing?" the woman shouts, turning to the car, her voice going guttural.

Abby looks at me, chin tucked over her shoulder, and I shrug and take a small step back, and Abby sticks her tongue out at me.

The woman looks down at her feet, chuckling, a wet sound. She's wearing black hightop Reeboks without socks and something about the dress and her bare legs popping out and the big shoes makes her look like a puppet. She points her sneakered toe and makes a careful half-circle in the dirt, and then she looks up at us, an inquiring smile slanting across her face.

"Girls, girls, girls," she says. "You do know about the grizzlies? Some awful things I could tell you. You know if you have your period those bears'll sniff you right out? Bears crave blood, you know. Intoxication. Addicts for it. You know there was a girl out here last year died that way? Poor thing died screaming, 'My muff! My muff!' "

Her voice goes high and hysterical. She raises her arms and flaps her hands at the sides of her face. "My muff," she says again.

Abby giggles, her hand cupped to her mouth, and I laugh with her, and the woman laughs; the three of us are laughing in the cold sun on the side of the road while the man sits in the car with his sunglasses on, until the woman takes a breath and says, "Sure. Sure. But bears are no joke. No joke. Four, five-inch claws. Rip your chest clean open."

"Everybody keeps telling us about the bears," Abby says. Before we left, Abby's Uncle Ray sent her an envelope with nothing in it but a yellow Post-it that said "Grrr," and pictures cut out of *National Geographic*: grizzlies on their hind legs sniffing the wind, muzzles bristling; flipping silvery trout out of a river; on boulders pawing at pink flesh. And men on the train enjoyed giving us advice over Heinekens in the bar car, leaning in close, flashing saliva and fillings. Make noise while you walk—talk, blow a whistle, shake a Coke can full of pebbles. Avoid mama bears. Bears have a method of flaying the victim and storing the body under a rock or an old log for a snack later. Wear cayenne pepper spray in a holster on your hip, bear spray, but never spray into the wind. And a gun will do you no good against the already slow-beating heart of a bear. Even if you get a good shot the bastard'll still have time to maul you, then wander off to die. As a last resort, drop into the fetal position. And never go to sleep wearing fruity perfume or lip-gloss or with chocolate on your face.

Yesterday we hiked three miles into bear territory, the path dim and quiet with pine, shouting back and forth the entire time, singing when we ran out of talking, and at night we put all our food in the steel box they have at every site, and we cleaned our faces with just cold water in the restroom, rubbing our fingers hard across our lips, and we changed out of the clothes that smelled of smoke from the beans we had cooked, and put those in the steel box too, and then we both lay in the tent listening for rustling, for the snap of branches, for sniffing, for the growl that is supposed to sound like a hog snorting.

The woman gazes off down the road, her mouth slack, thick, white spittle hanging at the corners of her lips. Then, quietly, calmly, she says, "I know it. Nobody shuts up about the bears. But save your feet, you know?" She jerks her head at the car. "Lester and I can give you a ride. Get in the car and take a ride."

"We can take a ride down the road," Abby says, her voice a bright chirping, only agreement, and without looking at me she swings her pack off her back and then she is climbing into the car, folding herself in, and I follow her, groping forward, awkward, suddenly hot in my chest and in my cheeks, entering that small, dark space. With the click of the door I think of the half-circle the woman's toe drew in the dirt like something I'm supposed to remember, a signal, a marker, and I sniff and Abby smiles at me and gives my shoulder a shove.

The man peels out onto the road, empty except for us. All the guidebooks say early June is when no one is here. This is when it is cold and pristine and there are no crowds and you can see the place how it's meant to be seen. The car has a pressing, stale smell to it, like old, burnt things, shoes and mattress springs and tires. We sit with our packs wedged between our legs. My neck starts to ache. There's junk everywhere: a quilt, a place mat, a gun, a fork with the prongs crusted in pale brown food, a bundle of T-shirts, an umbrella, a flip-flop, a hot pink plastic daisy. Like clues. Like one of those brain games in high school, make an invention from the following items. You are stuck on an island with only the following objects. I nudge Abby, make a motion at these things, but she only smiles at them. I study the gun. It's the first time I've seen an actual gun, I realize. It's the hunting kind, a triangle of wood to prop to the shoulder, an old black trigger, the pioneer kind, not the kind people get killed with, the small, cold, black or silver ones that get put in people's mouths. I press my thigh to Abby's.

"We've been on the road for a while," the woman says. "When you're on the road you carry everything you own with you. And add to that everything you pick up along the way. Right, Lester? We're collectors. We collect things."

The man nods his head thoughtfully, chin up and down in the light through the windshield, neck long, sinewy. White V-neck shirt, jeans. Thin hips. I try to piece together their lives. Cans of food, a cheap hotel room now and again. The T-shirts are his, she washes them when she can, rubbing at them, her hands in a river, knuckles red under the water, once in a while they hit a Laundromat, the quilt, everything they own in for a wash, a cigarette outside, waiting, maybe a restaurant, lemon meringue pie for a treat, he drives, mostly they skirt the towns, hunt and fish.

"Where are you guys from?" Abby says, like we're meeting over drinks somewhere. That smile again, an eager milk drinker.

The woman turns in her seat to look at us, her face bobbing between the two headrests. She stares for a minute, wide-set gray eyes, and it occurs to me that she isn't looking at us, she's looking at the road behind us, looking at no one following us. I think of movies, memorized license plate numbers, signs held to windows, Help Us, fingers scuttling for door handles, bodies tumbling to the road. Slowly, the woman says, "From here. From there. Neither of us is from the same place. I had a trailer once in Ohio. And kids, had those once too." She laughs her damp laugh. "Remember Ohio, Lester? Lester found me in Ohio."

"We're from New Hampshire," Abby says. "Abby and Kate. It's so beautiful out here." She makes a motion, sweeping her arm around the back seat.

"Hi," I say, and I move my hand like I'm waving at a baby.

"Call me Sandy," the woman says. "As in Sandra or Alexandra or Cassandra. Or Andrew for that matter. Take your pick of the litter. Which one can't be confirmed without ID. Me and Lester here both lost our IDs back in Canada, which is not far away. Whole other country, but not far away."

"Canada is empty," Lester announces, his head shooting forward as though he is addressing the windshield. Then he moves a hand off the steering wheel, and lifting his hips, he draws a joint from his pocket, fits it to his lips, and hits the cigarette lighter all in one fluid motion. His fingers are long and clean, soft looking, like they've been soaking in something.

"Abby," I mutter. She gives my shoulder three pats.

"That's two things to know about Lester," Sandy says. "One is he's quiet. Preserves his words. Understands that there are modes of communication other than talking. Two is he likes to smoke. Frees his inhibitions. I'm sure you girls have seen the stuff before. Everybody knows what college girls are up to nowadays. Drugs and sex on campus."

"That's totally cool," Abby says.

"Right, totally cool," Sandy says, slow and smooth and mocking. "Totally."

Lester lifts his graceful chin as he inhales. He gives that hair of his a shake. Lustrous, I'd actually call it, good enough for a shampoo commercial. I think he might be an Indian and I feel guilty about it. The air turns thick-sweet with smoke.

"We believe in a lot of things not everybody believes in," Sandy says. "Destiny routes, the powers beyond, star guidance."

Abby keeps nodding slowly. "I'm into that stuff," she says.

Sandy bobs her head, her lips pursed. "Of course you are."

She turns away and opens the glove compartment, roots through some papers and plastic bags and then takes out a square-shaped piece of purple metal, the size of a drugstore novel. "See this?" she says, holding it up for us. "I got it from a magazine. A healing plate. Doubt whatever you want, but it works. Pulls the healing energy of the universe into you."

"Wow," Abby says. "It's kind of pretty."

Sandy turns the plate in her hands and it glints in the light, sparkly. It reminds me of roller skates with fancy wheels, banana seats on bikes.

"Right now I have a toothache. Nothing like a toothache to put you on the edge," Sandy announces like an infomercial. "But this'll suck the pain right out."

She nestles down into her seat with the purple plate pressed to her cheek. I look over at Abby, but she just sits back, roams her eyes lazily over the car like she's looking around for some other fun tidbit to discuss with Sandy: tarot cards, cooking on the road. Sunlight filters in through the smoke, thick and drifting, golden and filled with slow dust motes. I watch the park slide away, the trees, and the alpine flowers that bloom in snow, the towering rocks, wet with runoff, the curves where the land drops suddenly away from the road, the places I meant to spend hours seeing, gone instantly. We drive past a glacial lake with one speck of an island rising in the middle, on the island one pine. I recognize it, I've seen it in a picture before, it's a famous island. The guidebooks are always talking about the glacial lakes, their depth and cold, the ancient movements that formed them, the turquoise color, something about sediment sifting down, the perfect reflection of the land in the still water.

"Look," I say to Abby. I hold my finger to the window.

"Nice," Abby says.

"See something you like?" Sandy says. "Pretty as a picture."

Sandy puts her hand on Lester's thigh, rubs up and down. The sound of her skin against his jeans is menacing, a scurrying sound, like a small animal in the bushes. It makes my stomach turn and I

burp up a bit of breakfast, Snickers bars and Tang and instant oat-
meal, joking about eating bear bait, swishing afterward with a mini-
bottle of Scope, spitting onto the charred logs from our fire. I press
my face to the window, hard to the cold glass, press to feel the ridge
of my cheekbone, press and look to see more, to see the distance
here, to see everything.

After a while there is an open stretch of meadow and Lester flicks
his wrist and the car leaves the road and we are hurtling across the
grass toward more forest, more mountains, and I think we are going
to be dead girls with our mouths hanging open in the grass, and then
I wish I knew Abby was imagining this too, could see herself with her
throat slit. It is embarrassing to be girls killed hitchhiking. I see a
perky anchorwoman standing out here later, new hiking gear on, her
foot propped up on log, telling the story of us, interviewing the clerk
at the hotel we stayed at that first night, he'll move his pudgy hands
across his desk as he remembers us, vaguely, vacantly, and I think
about my father, how he has always liked girls having adventures,
how I knew he was impressed by Abby, by her being my friend, with
her long legs and the color in her cheeks that makes her seem on the
verge of something, always. My father took us out for pastrami sand-
wiches the day we left; the three of us sat at a big wooden table,
chewing and smiling at each other.

"This isn't going anywhere," Abby says.

"Coyotes," the woman says. "Lester here is going after a coyote
now. Lester likes to skin things."

Lester speeds up, leaning forward. The grass thwaps against the
wheels. When the road is out of sight he slows and drives the car in
three wide circles, and then comes to a stop.

"Okey-dokey," Sandy says. "We drop you here." She opens her
door, steps out, and pushes her seat down for us. We stumble into the
grass, back into the day, dragging our packs with us.

"Anything to show your appreciation?" she says. "A thank you for
the ride? Let's have a look inside your packs here. Come bearing
gifts?"

"What gifts?" Abby says.

While Lester waits in the car Sandy opens our packs and riffles
through our clothes, unfolding them and holding them up against
herself, smoothing them to her body. She comments that we're all
three about the same size, even though we aren't. Abby and I stand
in the brilliant light, smelling exhaust. She will take our things, she

will tease us, I think, and then Lester will climb out of the car and reach his long arm into the back seat and grab the gun.

"What are you doing?" Abby says.

"Shopping," Sandy says. "Shop till you drop."

"You're taking it?" Abby says. She sounds annoyed. She is talking to Sandy the way she sometimes talks to me and I wonder if she still can't understand that something terrible is happening to her.

"Maybe she won't take all of it," I mumble, and Abby snorts, a thread of snot flecking out of one of her nostrils.

Sandy makes a pile of our best things, our sweaters and fleece jackets and turtlenecks and hats, our clean T-shirts, six pairs of wool socks, Abby's purple, lightweight shorts. I've had the sweater she takes for years, a gray pullover, the elbows and the neck sag, I like to sleep in it. She holds up a pair of my long underwear and gives them a shake. They dance in the air and look absurdly small. She tosses aside the guidebook.

When she finds Abby's make-up bag she makes a sound like purring and sits down in the grass with the bag in her lap, unzipping it and pawing through it, her pale fingers and wrists flashing in the sun as she grabs at soap and a tube of toothpaste and nail clippers and floss and deodorant. She goes over her mouth with Abby's Chap-Stick, smiling, leaving her lips thickened and pasty, a girl playing dress-up. She takes out a bottle of Neutrogena sunscreen, inspects the label, frowning, and then squirts a white squiggle into her palm and wipes it along her cheekbones and down her nose and across her forehead, holding her face up to the sky, rubbing with her fingertips, leaving a shine over her skin.

She takes the food, peanut butter, beef jerky, cans of beans and boxes of macaroni and cheese and graham crackers and Snickers bars and cans of beer from the dusty shelves in the store in St. Mary's. After inspection she decides to take our sleeping bags and the collapsible pans, and a pair of tin cups, speckled blue and white—all my father's things, he went up into the crawl space above the kitchen to find them for me and Abby—and I remember it all from years ago, camping with him in the Smoky Mountains, the hush of rain against the green walls of the tent, my father in a flannel shirt cooking eggs, the snail shells we found scattered across the trails as we hiked. Sandy takes our wallets of course, but out of obligation, or maybe out of habit, it seems, more than interest. They are stored in side-pockets, and she doesn't miss a pocket, unzipping and untying. My pack is old, red canvas, new leather strings strung through the eyelets. I remember packing it all, squatting on the floor, rolling the sleeping bags tight, counting out underwear.

She makes a few trips between us and the car before she's got all the stuff she wants, moving leisurely through the long grass, bending and picking up a few things at a time, carrying them held to her chest, tossing them onto the back seat. When she's done she gets in the car and swings the door shut. She says something to Lester and they laugh, a tired, intimate laugh, the laugh of shared labor, and then Sandy rolls the window down and leans her head out. "Well," she says, "thank you and pleased to meet you and God bless America."

Lester revs the engine and Sandy settles back in her seat, and then they begin to circle us, Lester's two huge, clean hands on the wheel like limp fish. Abby and I stand close together. The car will turn and run us down, maybe, I will hear the thump of our bodies, chests, thighs, against the hood of the car, a dull sound, and our hair and blood will fill our mouths. I hold my hands clasped in front of me, politely waiting. Mostly, I'm tired, my legs hurt behind my knees and I want to sit down. But there are rules I'm following: to stand, to be still, to be quiet. What I can do is follow the rules. No running, no back talking. Lester circles us, each circle just a little faster, and closer, I think, closer each time. My saliva tastes unfamiliar, like fingernails and glass, and the wheels plow the grass down around us in a ring. He makes his circles and I watch in pieces, sun, hair, wheel, metal, until light and sound shift, and as though distracted the car lurches, but not at us, away, and Abby makes a weird, short squeal, and the car is spinning away from us, and they are leaving, and we are watching the small, black car careen away across the meadow.

The car becomes a hum, the meadow returns to its own clicks and whirs. It is hard to breathe. I don't want to look at Abby yet. I imagine Sandy moving on with our things. Maybe a ways down the road they'll pull into a campground and Lester will wait outside the restroom with the car running while Sandy washes herself with Abby's soap and then brushes her hair with my hairbrush in the dim mirror. I see her, chin pressed to chest, holding up the hem of her dress, lathering up her crotch. I see her bare feet, her bluish toes on the cement floor. I think of her smelling like Abby, her wind-rough skin softening over time with face cream.

Abby sits down in the grass, her legs splayed out in front of her.

"God," she says. Her breath comes short and terse. "God," she says again.

"See?" I say. My chest feels tight and hard and small.

"See what?" Abby says.

I go around picking up our leftover things, grabbing like I'm picking up somebody's room, stuffing useless odds and ends back into our packs. Abby lies back, stretches out, her arms flung above her head. The wind pushes the grass in silvery waves, and I remember a show I watched, a PBS thing about the wagon trains, how the pioneers would get seasick, watching the grass move all day, lurching through it. In the distance a wall of rock rises against the sky, and you can see movement in it, dark lines like scars, where, I imagine, something, ice, earth, ancient trees, once heaved against it, wrenching and pulling. I think again how big it is out here, how wide, and my eyes don't know where or how to look.

Nominated by The New England Review

POWER POINT (I)

by KHALED MATTAWA

from THE CANARY

What is disclosed lies smoldering
in stackings one beside the other.
Never connect, remain in a state beyond privilege
for that is why the swimmer can pursue
such unlikely heroism, and when tragedy strikes
some things scoot over. A realignment
in the foodchain of sympathy, all laid out,
a horizon no further than bullet range.
That's what the swimmer sees
in 32 degree water, chunks of ice bump into
her head, the crew worried gesticulating.
Penguins zooming below her like torpedoes.

A change of clothes now—the warmth of the engine
room, even in Arctic weather,
an awakening, the flesh revealing its layers—the cold
a message sent out, victory's radiance absorbed.

A change of clothes again. Daylight
exterior shot, merchants selling tomatoes,
equatorial sun, old colonial building. Flash to dream
image of something monstrous, a jellyfish/dragon
pink hued green, bone breaker, blood sucker, leaves
corpses behind like mummies . . . Kampala, Nov. 13, 2:11 p.m.,
the Ugandan scientist heads out for lunch and nap.

As to the new vaccine—"Issues of equity in clinical research
preoccupy ethicists and public health officials."
But need for human subjects persists:
Email a team of programmers in Bangalore:
reams of actuarial spreadsheets
cost assessment charts, patent infringement,
distribution of affected populations, national origin
divided by the square root of race.

Flash to Black woman dancing with her German shepherd in post-
    industrial living room.
        Cut to
                a house with an American flag at half mast.
                            Tragedy in Palestine,
        Texas.

Flash to Arabic text of Yasser Arafat's letter of condolence to White
    House.

The German shepherd is blasé about the whole ordeal.

        Flashback to 19th century church in Norwich
the minister delivering the sermon, January, steam
rises from minister's mouth.
Front row dignitaries are seated with their dogs on their feet as foot
    warmers.
Minister shouts out the story of Ezekiel, and at the mention of the
    wheel
the dogs bolt out.

There's of course a case to be made for war:
But the empire is circumspect.
It does not like to do things for one purpose:

DESIRE	PROS	CONS
Fire	Practicality	Greed
Danger	Protectiveness	Delusiveness
Interlocutor	Acumen	Mischief

Solution:

Move to next point,

when that shows fizzle-effect, move on, repeat.

Return to first point.

Keep adding additional nuances.

Do not engage in dialogue.

Let them think you're practical, greedy, protective of citizens,
    trigger-happy, sissy,

Yes, the need for lyric persists, to love one person

you must (or will eventually) love the whole world.

There are loves that are demarcations of boundaries,

fears we wish to be contained within: a man who cooks

or does laundry, a woman at home keeping house,

a policeman on patrol, a field being tilled, a horizon.

Herein lies the lyric moment. A particularity that fences us.

And herein the obsession with death,

childhood, illness (of a certain kind),

something to expend one's life into and/or toward.

And so how can you talk to a man whose wife died of cancer

about anything when all the pain he's capable of has been already
    allotted and spent?

In the house where the Black woman is dancing with her dog, the
    dog is showing slight

discipline problems.

She consults guidebook:

The paw on the knee, the staring down, the leaning,

all these are gestures designed to convey higher status in clan or
    household.

Dog owner, if such behavior is demonstrated, must force dog to
    submission.

Never give dog anything for free.

Before you feed dog, make it sit,

before you pet it, make it sit,

before dog gets to go out, make it sit.

Sometimes with an undisciplined dog you will have to topple it over
    and prevent it from

getting up, even if that requires sitting on it for a minimum of five
    minutes, twice a day. If

dog fails to respond to a command, owner must roll dog onto its
    side and stare it in the
eye for fifteen seconds.

Pan shot across the street:
two men in their sixties, one blind
talking about a shade of color, having a moderately expensive wine,
engaged in the airy metaphysics that strikes citizens
of a certain achievement confirmed
by a certain unintrusive sociopolitical confidence.
There's an underwriting notice airing
from the classical radio station to which they're not listening.
This hour was brought to you by
                134 colonial adventures
                slavery
                depletion of fresh water, lumber, oil, and coal.

Everything meanwhile is coated with a substance as fine as Anthrax.
Even the swimmer who's grown her hair long so
that she'd pile it on her head like a turban for better insulation,
her face too is speckled with the dandruff of conquest.

Time now to ask the Nobel prize winner, "If the swimmer died,
    would she be a martyr?" A martyr dies unwillingly, he says.
    Someone has an important follow-up question, something about
    the fighters who died defending the Warsaw ghetto, and other
    possible places like it, but the questioner does not ask his
    question, because there are no places like it.

On her second try the swimmer went farther because she could not
    feel pain. Yesterday's swim killed some of her nerve endings.
    During hypothermia the cold blood from the extremities disrupts
    the heart's normal processes. There are potential applications for
    this concept in real world, but why take the dark turn, why
    mistake the swimmer's head-gear for that of the one-eyed mullah
    of Kandahar?

Why do so when there's a tide pulling at the mind's bearings?
It rises and at its peak nerve endings stand like nettles,

the soul's wheels spinning like a grinding mechanism,
the eyes are coated by previous visions that become the future.

Where are you off to my love/
on this cold rainy day/
The birds you hear singing/
are not on this land/
The rays that warm your arms/
on this cold rainy day
The dry firm earth you walk/
is no earth at all/

Hence, no way to shut down the sapphic pipeline. Traces of it were
    found near Baku by
Caltex geologists and in the blue eyes of late mujahideen leader
    Massoud Shah.

The film had commercials for The Gap, Kawasaki, Citibank, etc.,
    embedded in it. The film's main dilemma is whether the hero
    should kill or not kill.

Nothing is likely to happen in the present when we've grown to
    think that the moment lived is already in a chain of action,
    already slipped out of will's grasp, or is in unrecoverable past, a
    past through which events have been framed. Otherwise it's the
    future we must look forward to. Needless to say, it's horrifying, it's
    moving at a G force beyond our familiar disappointments. That is
    why the hero will need to acquire magical forces or the latest
    technology. That is the place where the hero resides, where he
    must choose between killing or not killing.

The dog owner opens a magazine and reads about the swimmer's
    accomplishment
which is to have become for a short while the cogwheel driving the
    second-arm ticking
within civilization's time,

because to say Empire is to say: the Tet offensive and one step for
    man,

and going out to the movies and making sure the dog does not maul
   the new sofa,
wherein the blind man's accomplishment, via an eye bank in
   Bombay, is another toddle unto revelation,
so many magic powers or advanced technology incorporated within,
the march of progress becomes loops and loops of human matter
   strung around the cineplex,
the human soul as a conglomerate, a spark plug winking in the
   universe's internal combustion,
triumphs like motes of pollen from a new epoch stinging the
   cyclops' eye,
so much dithering, a catharsis that leads us screaming unto the
   street, our faces coated with history.

Nominated by David Baker, Marilyn Hacker, The Canary

BLESSING THE NEW MOON

by A. P. MILLER

from AGNI

> On a little street in Singapore,
> We'd meet beside a lotus-covered door,
> A veil of moonlight on her lonely face,
> How pale the hands that held me in embrace.
> My sails tonight are filled with perfume of Shalimar,
> And temple bells will guide me to the shore.
> And then I'll hold her in my arms, and love the way I loved before,
> On a little street in Singapore.
>
> —On a Little Street in Singapore; lyrics by Billy
> Hill; music by Peter De Rose with Harry James
> and his Orchestra; Columbia Records, 1939.

1.

GLENN GOULD recorded Bach's *Goldberg Variations* twice: once at the beginning of his career, in 1955, at the age of twenty-two, then again in 1981, at the age of forty-eight. To coincide with what would have been his seventieth birthday (Gould died at age fifty), both versions have been reissued together—the "alpha and omega" as the critic Tim Page dubs them. In the liner notes to the CD package, one learns that the recording engineers for the 1981 version did not trust the digital technique, which was "in its infancy" at the time. So they simultaneously recorded in analog, a technology at its peak. The new release features the heretofore unheard analog recording for 1981, which, like the 1955 rendition, is digitally remastered. The sound is supposed to be better.

I put on the 1981 recording that I purchased sixteen years ago while in college. Darkly, Gould plays the opening aria, each note placed according to the laws of nature, each note round and full, planetary. But it is not just the piano that sings. A ghostly hum, or at times a low groan, adds to the ether. The last cadence slows gracefully, the gravity of the moment foreshadowing the true end of the piece when the aria returns, thirty variations later. Just before silence envelops the final note of the aria's first appearance, a beer stein crashes on a table and Variation 1 thumps in: a raucous dance.

2.

Wassily Kandinsky, in his introduction to *On the Spiritual in Art*, writes that human souls "are only now beginning to awaken after the long reign of materialism." That nightmare, he adds, "turned the life of the universe into an evil, purposeless game." Our souls are "only a weak light . . . a tiny point in an enormous circle of blackness." "[W]hen one succeeds in touching them [they] give out a hollow ring, like a beautiful vase discovered cracked in the depths of the earth." Kandinsky published *On the Spiritual in Art* in 1911. That same year, he began to exchange letters with Arnold Schoenberg. Exactly ten years later Schoenberg would be the first to use rows of twelve tones as a method of composition.

3.

Gould imbues Variation 15 with sorrow—not the sorrow of regret or nostalgia, but the sorrow of resignation. He reaches, sonically, for something that can no longer be touched. Gould is Orpheus reaching for Eurydice as she is swept back to the land of the dead. Tones repeat. A slow walk, exhausted, shoulders hunched. Tones rise, step by step.

4.

In twelve-tone composition, the composer creates what is called a tone row: a series of notes that functions as a kind of musical DNA. The tone row is the original sequence of the piece, which undergoes an almost mathematical reconfiguration and repetition. At the composer's disposal is a range of techniques, including *inversion* and *ret-*

rogade. The former flips the musical idea upside down. If a note from the tone row reached heavenward *x* steps from the last, it now takes *x* steps down. The latter technique reverses the musical idea, retracing the row's steps from last to first. Schoenberg claims, "[T]he method of composing with twelve tones grew out of a necessity."

5.

On my desk at school, I have an M. C. Escher calendar, the type with pages that tear off each day. The artist's name is printed on each upper lefthand corner, followed by the sign for a registered trademark: M. C. Escher™. The weekend in my pocket quotes him:

> Hearing [Bach's] music influences my feelings, yet despite or perhaps because of this, the flow of his sounds has an inspiring effect, evoking particular images or flashes of inspiration, and also, more generally, stimulating an unquenchable desire for expression. . . . In my periods of weakness and spiritual emptiness and lethargy, I reach out to Bach's music to revive and fire my desire for creativity.

According to the calendar, there will be a new moon on Saturday, the seventh of September, 2002.

6.

My grandparents used to live in New London, Connecticut, in an old, three-story house on Ocean Avenue. It was white with green shutters, and a long porch ran along the side of the house that faced the lawn. Just a quick climb over a rusty barbed-wire fence was Dr. Ellison's house, with its pool: a seamless blue into which we would explode in cannonballs.

Each morning my brother and I would wake up in the pink-furnished guest room to the smell of Shalimar perfume cut with nail polish remover. A gentle breeze from the Sound would swell the curtains in toward the beds, into which we had been shoehorned the night before. A vengeance of tucking: if a bomb had dropped on the house in the middle of the night, we would have been mummified, stiff sheets unmoved beneath our chins. When we woke, our clothes from the day before lay washed and folded on the pink chair.

After our breakfast and her handful of pills, my grandmother would take us to a private beach, where we dug holes and watched them fill with tide, or high-stepped around the sideways scuttle of hermit crabs, or flipped a lone horseshoe crab to watch its writhing legs. On occasion, beyond the sparkling microcosm at our feet, a submarine would pierce the surface on its way back to Groton Naval Base.

After an ecstatic visit to the rides and arcade at Ocean Beach Park (my grandfather breaking the speed limit there and back, gunning his red Triumph), we would huddle in the small room at the far corner of the house, watching TV. Knuckles swollen with arthritis, nails freshly painted, my grandmother would peel grapes and drop them into our cupped hands. They were slippery and sweet.

Later, my brother and I would sneak up behind my grandfather as he sat half-dozing, solving a crossword puzzle, and muss his perfect hair. This angered him to no end. Our grandfather prided himself on his impeccable grooming. He was *dapper*. Eventually, he'd fall asleep, head cradled in the L of his thumb and forefinger. A snore. A grunt.

Sometimes he would rise and walk to his podium, on which rested the behemoth *Webster's New International Dictionary Unabridged, 1956*. Just inside the cover was Noah Webster, expressionless, done up like a founding father. Webster revised his dictionary in 1841, just before his death, noting that it was meant to "illuminate and explain to the American people both their language and their culture."

The dictionary and its podium sit next to me now as I write. I read the definition of "new moon":

> **a** The crescent moon before reaching first quarter; also the phase when in conjunction with the sun. See 1st Moon.
> **b** Day when the new moon is first seen. Among the Hebrews the period of the new moon was anciently regarded as a religious festival, in postexilic times celebrated chiefly by the women, but still marked by the ceremony of "Blessing the New Moon." The periodical reappearance of the moon is taken as a symbol of the Messianic redemption or renewal of Israel.

Compare that to *Webster's New Universal Unabridged Dictionary, 1996*:

1. the moon either when in conjunction with the sun or soon after, being either invisible or visible only as a slender crescent. **2.** the phase of the moon at this time.

Near the end of his life, my grandfather lost the ability to speak, and then his motor coordination. The last time I saw him, he was propped up in a hospital bed, strapped in. A gown was tied around his neck. I kissed his cheek. It was rough. It smelled sour. My grandmother was spoon-feeding him vanilla ice cream.

It was not long after his death that my grandmother felt her heart fail and decided not to call anyone. Night after night she had prayed for death. She saw no reason to live without him, she'd said. So she lay there and waited. I suppose she must have been annoyed when she woke up in a hospital room. The family came to visit. Then, late at night, everyone gone home, she sat up. She stared (the nurse told me the next day) as though seeing someone. Then fell back onto the pillow, dead.

At my grandfather's grave in a Jewish cemetery on the outskirts of New London, the rabbi spoke Hebrew, words vaguely familiar from the bar mitzvahs of childhood friends. My grandmother was angry that day, because the rabbi had insisted on a ceremonial bathing of my grandfather's body.

For herself, she insisted on cremation. No ceremony. No words.

7.

A former student of mine went on to study psychobiology in college. One experiment, she told me, examined the brain chemistry of people's reactions to different types of faces. Flash a black man's face at a white woman. Flash an Asian woman's face at a white man.

My student knew I liked Kandinsky, so she gave me a small book of fine-art stickers that feature his work. I keep them on file in the study. The back of the booklet announces that the stickers are "an eye-catching way to enhance stationary and other flat surfaces." One sticker has been removed from the booklet: an empty rectangle. The remaining stickers are labeled "Subdued Glow," "Painting within a Painting," "Untitled."

8.

I had yet to buy the reissue of Gould's *Goldbergs*. Like Kandinsky's art as stickers, it would be a repackaging, a sending of the original through a machine.

I used to wear a tie that replicated Van Gogh's *Starry Night*. Another was a Miro. But is it possible to be any further from the smell of oil paint?

The repackaging of Gould's musical epiphanies would, inevitably, include new information about Gould, and about Bach's music. I had read a few things over the years. Bach had composed the variations to help Count Hermann Karl von Keyserling make it through neuralgia-induced insomniac nights in 1742. The music was played by the count's harpischordist, Johann Gottlieb Goldberg. The commission came while Bach was visiting Goldberg, his student, in Dresden. Keyserling, in return for the music, sent Bach a goblet filled with *louis d'or*. Glenn Gould liked to soak his arms in scalding water for twenty minutes before he played. He found it relaxing. His arms would be the color of a cooked lobster. And he liked to take pills: pills for his nerves, pills to stop sweating, pills to control his blood circulation. The building where he recorded the 1955 release had originally been a church. Sweaters. Muffler. An electric heater.

9.

On the radio this morning, Tim Page was interviewed about his knowledge of Glenn Gould, a brief segment to announce the release of the new three-CD package.

Page only knew him for two years. It was a telephone relationship: late-night conversations of an hour or more, two to three times a week. He finally met Gould in Canada, where the two recorded an "interview" at three in the morning. Gould had scripted the conversation, which was something like a short radio play. But Page's remarks were based on things he had said to Gould about his work on the *Goldberg* over the phone. So, as Page was at pains to make clear, he was not literally Gould's "mouthpiece" during the interview.

The third CD in the set includes the interview, as well as outtakes from the original 1955 recording session. You hear Gould creating, stopping, and restarting musical phrases. Gould's voice during the

Page interview is higher pitched: quick, incisive, clipped—like his playing.

Page says that Gould suffered from high blood pressure and, possibly, Asperger's syndrome, which may have accounted for his heightened sensitivity to the climate.

Gould chose Variation 25 for the sound score to the bombing of Dresden in the film version of Vonnegut's *Slaughterhouse-Five*.

Page characterizes the 1981 version of the *Goldberg* as "autumnal." Gould was a sick man at the time, though most people didn't realize it. He would die of a stroke two months after the release.

About the humming or the singing, Page says that Gould wanted to stop it but couldn't. When you were in the room with him, he says, it seemed much louder.

10.

A snow day: the twenty-fifth variation. Months ago I bought a DVD version of *Slaughterhouse-Five*. Books on Schoenberg, Kandinsky, and Gould line my shelf.

11.

It was just a few days ago that the second MRI came back. The nurse told my wife over the phone that a small part of our six-year-old son's brain appears to be swollen. Recently, there has been a change in his tics. Instead of shrugging, or snapping his head forward and back, he crosses his eyes, or they fly to one side as though he is peering around a corner. He says it doesn't bother him. Each night when he practices piano, the tics increase in frequency. Rarely, though, do they get in the way of the music.

Aidan's birth was not easy. After hours of labor, the umbilical cord got caught around his neck, and his heartbeat began to drop. The doctor attached a monitor to the top of his head. They prepared for an emergency C-section. Bach played in the background. When he was born, Aidan smiled, and the nurses rushed him, naked and slippery, to his mother's arms.

I want Aidan to know what I know about music, even what I can't articulate in words. When I was his age, I discovered a recording in my parents' collection of Arthur Grumiaux playing *Bach's Sonatas and Partitas for Violin Alone*. It was a two-record set. The liner notes said that Grumiaux had played a Stradivarius, which accounted for the singular sound. Time and time again, I returned the needle to one particular groove: the fugue from the C major Sonata.

When I became good enough to study the first sonata in G minor, my teacher told me that the tension building toward the final cadence of the first movement was like "the cruelty of humanity." He said that his own teacher had told him the same thing.

Bach's *Sonatas and Partitas for Violin Alone* are a violinist's Bible. According to my teacher, they trace the stages of life, from the murky beginning in G minor (the lowest string of the violin is G), though life's climax (the profound Chaconne: the tonalities of the middle strings, D and A), to life's close, the bright E major dances of old age. An optimistic view of the end.

12.

"I am enchanted," writes Kurt Vonnegut,

> by the Sermon on the Mount. Being merciful, it seems to me, is the only good idea we have received so far. Perhaps we will get another idea that good by and by—and then we will have two good ideas. What might that second idea be? I don't know. How could I know? I will make a wild guess that it will come from music somehow. I have often wondered what music is and why we love it so. It may be that music is that second good idea's being born.

Vonnegut writes elsewhere that trying to stop war is like trying to stop a glacier. In today's paper, a student protests the war in Iraq by taping her mouth shut. On High Street, people light candles and carry signs. A former student, now a marine, emails from the desert.

13.

June 25, 2003. I've played both new versions of Gould's *Goldbergs*. The blue CD (1955) is in the player downstairs, the red one (1981), in the player upstairs. Imagine that they play simultaneously, and that the two flights of stairs are drafted by Escher. Up and down we go: a dragon to a fish to a bird. Black and white modulations; you become me as I become you.

I am at Capital University with Aidan for a week-long music camp. I read through the selected writings of Schoenberg and Kandinsky while he sits on the floor with the other kids, playing games with the musical alphabet. A parent stalks around with a video camera.

In a letter dated April 24, 1923, Kandinsky writes that he rejects Schoenberg as a Jew. A rift opens between them. For twelve years, they had been deeply supportive and understanding of each other. It was almost as though a soul of artistic genius had found its twin in the lonely space atop Kandinsky's ever-ascending triangle—"a coworker upon the spiritual pyramid that will one day reach to heaven." But Kandinsky wants Schoenberg to recognize himself as a human being, not a Jew. "We should strive to be 'supermen.' That is the duty of the few." Schoenberg responds angrily: "[W]hen I walk along the street and each person looks at me to see whether I'm a Jew or a Christian, I can't very well tell each of them that I'm the one that Kandinsky and some others make an exception of, although of course that man Hitler is not of their opinion." Later, in the same letter:

> I am no pacifist; being against war is as pointless as being against death. Both are inevitable, both depend only to the very slightest degree on ourselves, and are among the human race's methods of regeneration that have been invented not by us, but by higher powers. In the same way the shift in the social structure that is now going on isn't to be lodged to the guilty account of any individual. It is written in the stars and is an inevitable process. . . . But what is anti-Semitism to lead to if not to acts of violence?

Near the end, "I shall not understand you; I cannot understand you."

14.

August 19, 1912. Schoenberg to Kandinsky:

> We must become conscious that there are puzzles around us. And we must find the courage to look these puzzles in the eye without timidly asking about "the solution." It is

important that our creation of such puzzles mirror the puzzles with which we are surrounded, so that our soul may endeavor—not to solve them—but to decipher them. What we gain thereby should not be the solution, but a new method of coding or decoding. The material, worthless in itself, serves in the creation of new puzzles. For the puzzles are an image of the ungraspable. And imperfect, that is, a human image. But if we can only learn from them to consider the ungraspable as possible, we get nearer God, because we no longer demand to understand him. Because we can no longer measure him with our intelligence, criticize him, deny him, because we cannot reduce him to that human inadequacy which is our clarity.

The letter ends with warmest regards.

15.

In the 1970s, back when my childhood friend D. B. was preparing for his bar mitzvah (it was to be an orthodox one), I was not allowed to see him. I was cut off. Why? Was it because my mother had converted to Christianity when she married, and I, therefore, had grown up going to a church and celebrating Christmas? Or was it because my mother had said to him that Jews felt guilty about everything and he had stormed out of our house? Maybe we were separated because his intensive training required it. He was going to become a man.

D. B. studied cello, and he and I, after school, would go to his house and play duets and listen to the stereo (he introduced me to his passion, Mahler). Or we would burn incense in his bedroom, or talk about girls, or get into his father's collection of pornography.

When his mother died, D. B. quit playing cello. He moved away. At first, we exchanged notes. Then silence.

16.

Somewhere between the third and sixth centuries, the *Sefer Yetzirah (Book of Creation)* surfaced, a short essay that contributes to the tradition of Jewish mysticism. The essay suggests that Creation occured along thirty-two paths. The author (whose identity is unknown) arrives at the number thirty-two by adding the twenty-two letters of the Hebrew alphabet and the ten *sefirot*—vessels, depicted as circles on the Tree of Life—through which the energy of God flowed in the process of Creation.

For Jewish mystics, each Hebrew letter manifests an internal force, and each letter is assigned a number. *Bet*, the first letter in the Bible, is given the value two. The last letter, *lamed*, has a value of thirty. Again, thirty-two. The interaction of God and the Hebrew language generates Creation.

17.

A tiny white pill, one at night before bed, has stopped Aidan's tics. No more jerking around, no more disturbances crossing his face. When I look into his eyes, which are light blue, I see flecks of gold.

18.

I listen to Schoenberg's *String Quartet No. 1 in D minor* for the third time, trying to connect with its frenzied meaning. Even though it was written well before Schoenberg's break from the traditions of tonality, the music's complexity offers few clues for ears trained on other centuries. Even Mahler, when presented with the score, said, "I have written complicated music myself in scores up to thirty staves and more; yet here is a score of not more than four staves, and I am unable to read them." Schoenberg's first string quartet was played at a music festival in Dresden in 1906. It caused a scandal.

19.

For six years I taught in a public high school in Bridgeport, Connecticut. I drag the cursor over the names of my four students who died, over words describing the violent circumstances of their deaths. The son who was left without a father, the mother who was left without a son. Dreams, images of faces. Now the letters that form their names are gone. Snow gently falls. A

of moonlight buried in the clouds above.

20

For Kabbalists, the number 4 corresponds to Hesed, one of the *sefirot* on the Tree of Life. Hesed represents lovingkindness. We are in a Hesed consciousness when we nurture a child. Hesed must be close to a teacher's heart.

From Hesed, you can travel paths to other *sefirot*: Tiferet (Beauty) 6; Gevurah (Strength) 5; Netzach (Victory) 7. Follow the vertically ascending path from Hesed to the top of the Tree and you enter the realm of Hochma (Wisdom) 2, which forms a triangle with Binah (Understanding) 3 and Keter (Crown) 1. Sometimes the top of the Tree is cloaked behind a veil. It is the hidden part of Creation.

21.

Thirty-Two Short Films About Glenn Gould starts with an image of Arctic whiteness. Eddies of wind sweep snow off ice. In the distance, a figure in black (a tiny point at first) walks slowly toward the camera. As the figure comes into focus, Gould plays the aria from the *Goldberg*.

Slaughterhouse-Five begins with a similar image of whiteness. The camera follows Billy Pilgrim as he trudges through high snow, lost behind German lines during the Battle of the Bulge. Gould plays the ethereal Largo from Bach's *Concerto for Keyboard and Orchestra No. 5 in F minor.*

The former film conjures Gould's need for isolation, his love of the north, his one-ness. Gould comes from a distant white planet and stands, finally, like a solitary black key, a human monolith, an enigma.

The latter shows Pilgrim swaddling himself with a snow-crusted blanket as he wanders in a state of near oblivion. He does not know that he will survive the fire-bombing of Dresden by taking shelter in a slaughterhouse. Nor is he aware that he will be abducted, put on display, and mated with the "blue-movie star" Montana Wildhack on Tralfamadore. Gould plays Bach's Largo again when the Tralfamadorians first appear to Billy as a wobbling ball of light descending from the star-filled sky. The ball hovers for a moment, then quickly ascends into the night.

22.

My father tried to write about his experiences in World War II, but he couldn't. Last summer he told me his story:

The impact of it [the bombing of Pearl Harbor] *didn't strike me immediately until I went to the movies . . . I saw some newsreels—actually, they were probably propaganda films presented as newsreels—of the Japanese throwing up Chinese babies and catching them on bayonets. And immediately I wanted to go take care of that. And I tried to join—I was not yet eighteen. But the moment I turned eighteen I enlisted in the Marine Corps. Which was . . . I don't know if it was catastrophic or remarkably good for me.*

23.

The Greeks had a word for a relationship between two men that was extraordinarily close but not sexual in any way . . . and I can't think of what it is, but that's what we had. I had never, to this day never met anyone with whom I felt the same as I did with Max. But, anyway, well, he was killed on Iwo Jima anyway, so. [Lights cigarette.]

On the ship going over [to Hawaii], *we were standing together at the rail of the ship one night, and we were talking. And he said he liked to sing, and I said I liked to sing. We started singing together. And we found a couple of other guys that liked to sing and we formed a quartet on the boat and continued it when we got to camp.*

His favorite song was "On a Little Street in Singapore." And to this day, I can hear somebody singing that and get tears in my eyes. Our affection for each other, at least mine for him, was that strong—I have no way of knowing how he felt, because he was killed on the first day at Iwo . . . We took over this house and we mixed up everything we could think of: gin and rum and bourbon and Scotch and Coke and we threw aspirin in—we'd heard if you mixed Coke and aspirin that was supposed to make you drunk in a hurry—that was one of those things you knew in high school. It was untrue, but you knew that. But we spent Christmas Eve [1944] *and well into Christmas morning singing Christmas carols and various other things we'd gotten to harmonizing with, and had just a frightful hangover the next day.*

But it was there that I learned of the efficacy of—oh, what the hell

523

do they call it now, pep pills—dexedrine. We couldn't get dexedrine in any form except inhalers. In those days, I think it was Vicks made an inhaler that was an accordian fold of thin cardboard that had been supersaturated with dexedrine and stuck in there with some kind of flavoring. And this is what you sniffed up your nose. Well, also if you put it in coffee or ate it and drank it with coffee you could get really energized. And I remember one day there was a little guy in our company called Hotoechin. Hotoechin was probably just an inch or two below the minimum size for getting into the Marine Corps, but he'd gotten in somehow or other. He was a miserable little shit, but he was small and we had this "problem," meaning a maneuver. We had to climb a hill, and I said to the sergeant, whoever, that I could beat him up the hill. He said, "You lazy sonofabitch, you don't want to go up the hill." And I said, "No, I don't." And he said, "Well, you can't make it anyhow." And I said, "Sergeant, tell you what I'll do. I'll make you a bet—I'll put Hotoechin on my back and make it to the top of the hill before you do." I don't know what we bet. I've forgotten. I think I didn't have to do anything but light duty for a week after that if I won. And so I ate two full inhalers of dexedrine. And I was really strung out. I was kicky and ready to go. I put Hotoechin on my back and ran up that hill and I beat him by twenty yards. When you come down off that stuff, it's really terrible. But I didn't have to do anything the next day.

24.

About New Year's, we were hot oil, we knew we were going, we were going to ship out . . . And so we were putting our equipment together and making sure our knives were sharpened, our bayonets were sharpened, and our equipment was ready to go and some bags packed up for shipment wherever. And just all in all getting ready to go out and kill people . . . And then they got us all together and told us we were going to a place called Iwo Jima. We knew nothing about it. We had topographical maps. And we had heard it was going to be a three-or-four-day affair, and we were going to have I think ten or twelve days of bombardment from three or four battleships and two carriers. And they were going to bomb the hell out of the place and nobody would be alive when we got there. Instead of ten days of bombardment, we had three. And the Navy left. The Air Corps continued to drop bombs on the place and strafe it.

We needed the airfields—there were three of them. We were told we'd land on, what was it, Red Beach? Our job was to land and go over the foot of Airfield One and do a blocking move and get this thing over in a hurry.

It didn't quite work out that way . . . They didn't know that the whole island had been honeycombed with caves, and that they were all dug in, so if we'd had ten, twelve, fifteen days of bombardment it wouldn't have made any difference. Fortunately, we didn't know that.

Early one morning [we had] a great meal, the only good meal we had on these ships, steak and eggs, as much as you could eat. Pie. Candy, dessert, everything. So in the bowels of this ship it had these amtracks, so called, we hadn't even seen them, tractor propelled. So we circled around for what seemed hours. And at first light, we started in . . . You never thought of yourself as being one of those who got shot. It was going to happen to somebody else. The only thing I worried about was losing an arm, so, I had just learned to smoke cigarettes and I practiced with paper books of matches, practiced lighting matches with only one hand, both left and right, in case I lost one arm or hand, so I could light my cigarettes regardless of whatever happened.

When we went in, we went under one of the guns of these battleships. It was the call of doom. These were sixteen-inchers. We were so close we got some of that powder stuff that landed on us that they fired, unburned powder, whatever they used to pack the things . . . About thirty of us went off the end right into the water, and the treads started going. Some were not properly constructed or something and just sank . . . [and if you went in] you went down because you were carrying probably 100 pounds of stuff with you. You had both frag and concussion grenades, you had your ammunition, you had a rifle, your entrenching tool, your pack, your gas mask. Straight to the bottom . . . I didn't see it happening but heard subsequent rumors around the island, and we had talked to guys who had seen it happen.

As it turned out, we were fortunate in being the first wave, because they waited for more people to come on the beach . . . until I think about the third wave landed and it was really crowded. Then they opened up with everything. But most of us were not off the beach, because the angle was probably about forty-five degrees and the sand— this is volcanic sand—was in several steps, layers, and you'd climb *two steps and slip back three and of course you were scared, and didn't know what was going to happen. Guys lying there, and guys shot, and you'd see dead people and wounded people, and you could hear the cries for MEDIC MEDIC I'M HIT, you know, this sort of thing. And the only thing I knew was I had to get off the beach, because that was where they were shooting at us. And we had been told, "Don't freeze on the beach, because you're going to get yourself shot." So we worked our way up the sand and worked our way up the foot of the first airfield . . . I had at this time lost contact with my whole company. Most people were that way . . . Later, I met up with my company. We had been fairly well shot up . . . A few days later we were down to about 110, and then, when I got hit on the seventeenth day of combat, we were down to fourteen. And most of us were taken out by the white phosphorous mortar shell that blew me off the cliff and got most of the other guys in the company who were left at the same time.*

25.

On the day that they raised the flag on Iwo Jima we were on what's called corps reserve. We were taken off the line and told to clean up our rifles, sharpen the bayonets and knives and all the crap, and relax. And the first night we were there, almost everyone is dug in—I for whatever reason had not dug in. We found a little kind of a pit . . . but we thought we were in corps reserve and nobody was going to give us any trouble, so we didn't . . . That was the night they hit the ammunition dump with something and it blew up, so we dug in that night, an hour and a half to dig in—big, deep foxholes. And the second night we were in corps reserve, the Japanese came out of the caves—they had no water, they were dying of thirst. And they would sneak down by ones or by twos, I don't know how many came, and they would try to find somebody they could kill and get their water. And that's when this guy came into my foxhole with me. He wanted my water. That was all. But he came at me with a knife. That's this [points to scar on forearm].

So he struck at me and I blocked it. I was awake, I had just come off my watch. I was lying down. The other guy was looking the other way. I guess he was probably asleep—in corps reserve you don't stand strict watches. But he landed on me, so he stabbed me in the arm. And fortunately the knife stuck there, went between bone. So I

did him in. And, actually, first I put out both his eyes, then I stran-
gled him to death.

And it didn't bother me for a while. But within an hour it all hit
me. My tongue was quivering, my hands were quivering. I was shak-
ing all over like a dog shitting peach stones. It was only less than a
minute, I'm sure. It takes less than a minute to strangle somebody.
And I had—my thumbs were all the way through his flesh into his
trachea, and so it didn't take probably thirty seconds. And he was
screaming, because he was blinded.

26.

Rabbi Moshe de Leon of Guadalajara, Spain, claims he did not
write the *Sefer Ha Zohar (Book of Splendor)*, which was written
around 1280. No, he says it was the book's main character, Rabbi Shi-
mon bar Yochai, who wrote what the Prophet Elijah had revealed to
him in a cave in which he had hidden with his son for thirteen years
after escaping from the Romans. The narrative, as described in *Sim-
ple Kabbalah*, "has no linear structure but instead jumps back and
forth, delivering information about such topics as the Creation of
man, the nature of good and evil, and how our actions affect the des-
tiny of our soul, all couched in stories, expositions, allegories, and lit-
tle Zenlike koans."

In one of the stories, one rabbi complains to another that he was
annoyed by an "old and simpleton donkey driver" who posed him ex-
asperating riddles, such as, "What commences in union and ends up
in separation?" or "What are they who descend when they ascend,
and ascend when they descend?" or "Who is the beautiful virgin who
has no eyes?" Later, the donkey driver reveals himself to be a learned
man. Great insight is to be found in the riddles. The rabbis, on learn-
ing this, fall to the ground weeping.

27.

On Saturday, July 19, 2003, at 10:30 a.m., just above a tree line, I
see the moon—just the upper part of a white powder circle in a blue
sky, almost transparent.

A few weeks ago it was gibbous. Then, one night: full and bright in
a black sky.

Now it performs its slow-motion vanishing act.

28

Disc 3, from the three-CD package, is colored gold and contains two tracks: "Glenn Gould Discusses His Performances of The Goldberg Variations with Tim Page, August 22, 1982, Toronto, Canada (50'47")" and "Studio Outtakes from the 1955 Goldberg Variations Recording Session (12'32")."

On the first track, Page asks Gould what he thinks of his 1955 recording. In an animated voice, Gould responds, "I could not recognize or identify with the spirit of the person who made that recording—it really seemed like some other spirit had been involved."

About this interview, Page writes:

> Glenn was dressed in his usual summer wear—two sweaters, a woolen shirt, scarf, gloves, a long black coat and a slouch hat. Moreover, he looked decidedly unwell: his face a mask of bleached parchment, his hair coming out in clumps. Gone was the extraordinary-looking youngster—ethereally beautiful rather than traditionally handsome . . . . In his place was a wise, gentle, stooped man who seemed much older than his 49 years, with the air of a delicate visitor ready to cast off his wasted body and metamorphosize as pure spirit.

Later on, Gould says rapidly, "The music that really interests me is inevitably music with an explosion of simultaneous ideas—which counterpoint, you know, when it's at its best, is."

On the second track, a click of a control switch sounds into a room with high ceilings, the former church. The recording engineer says, "Goldberg Variation, Aria, Take 1." A 22-year-old Gould plays the complete opening aria. After a rapid Variation 1, Take 1, Gould announces, "I think that's it, but we might try another one." Later, struggling with a variation, he sings it into shape as he plays.

"Okay," Gould says. "I think we should've got something between all of those."

Finally, an exchange punctuated by the sound of the control switch. Gould explains to the engineer that Variation 30 is a quodlibet, a combination of popular songs from Bach's time. The German family, he says, would sit in the living room and harmonize popular tunes together within the same harmonic framework. The tunes for Bach's quodlibet, Gould adds, are "very dirty songs."

29.

I have brought four CDs along with me: the red and blue ones from the three-CD package, the disc I bought back in college of Gould's 1981 performance, and the 1955 performance on CD that CBS Records released as part of its *Great Performances* series.

Headphones on, I place the college-bought version in a player, press play, and listen to the aria. Quickly I replace that version with the red CD and listen to the aria. Then I rotate in the blue disc and hear the young Gould's aria followed by the earlier release of the same recording.

Headphones, of course, are not $50,000 speakers. Nor did I use a state-of-the-art CD player. Worse yet, I'm in a restaurant where the sound competes with a country-music vocal, coughing, and conversation. At one table people play cards. A player drums his fingers. At another, a young mother burps her baby. Outside, a woman tilts her head back and blows a vector of smoke toward the yellow canopy.

30.

"Did you hit your brother? Huh? Do you want to see what it's like to be picked on by someone bigger than you?" A jolt of pure fear rushes through my body, and before I can react he grabs me hard and picks me up into the air.

At 6'1" and 210 pounds, my father was a physically powerful man. He knew how to leverage strength—I had seen him break a block of concrete with his bare hand. He had taught self-defense classes off and on, and worked the night shift as a security guard. Once, he knocked a man unconscious on the commuter train home from New York. Another time, he gouged the eye of a man who came at him in a parking garage. My father kept an axe handle next to the emergency brake of our car.

He was the one who taught me how to make a fist, how to wrap the thumb tight around the outside of the fingers to avoid a break. And when I was older, how to hit a man with the heel of the palm to drive the bone of his nose into his brain.

In the mornings, on weekends, I'd snuggle up to him, right in the crook of his left arm, an island rising from the expanse of his body.

He throws me across the bedroom, onto the bed. Somehow I get around him. I run down the hall to my room and lock the door.

I hear the doorknob turn. Then it stops.

The door explodes as though a bomb has gone off, shards of wood flying into my room. My father leans against the shattered doorframe and says, "Don't you *ever* lock your door on me again."

31.

As though on cue, the long line of a funeral procession—hearse, limousines, cars—takes a left onto High Street past the parked motorcycle cop, his lights flashing. Each vehicle flies its tiny purple flag with a white cross. The cop's vest says ESCORT.

I had planned for this section, the thirty-first, to be about Gould's death: about the two strokes; about how, while unconscious, his hand rose and he appeared to conduct; about the first notes of the *Goldberg*'s aria mortised in granite. Both his biography, *Glenn Gould: Life and Variations*, and *Thirty-Two Short Films* use the Voyager spacecraft missions (a recording of Gould playing the C major prelude and fugue from Bach's *Well-Tempered Clavier* is aboard) as a concluding metaphor. Gould's message transcends death as it travels beyond each planet, past the reach of solar winds.

In preparation, I reread the last chapter of the biography. I read about Voyager 1 and its twin, Voyager 2—the first spaceships from Earth sent to explore the distant universe and deliver information about human life. In addition to Gould's Bach and other music, greetings and sounds from Earth were recorded on a twelve-inch gold-plated copper disk. Scientists also sent visual data such as black-and-white images of a circle, a man, a woman with a baby in her uterus, and a twisting double helix of DNA.

In *Slaughterhouse-Five*, the Tralfamadorians live 446,120,000,000, 000,000 miles from Earth. Vonnegut's creatures ("two feet high, and green, and shaped like plumber's friends," each with "a little hand with a green eye in its palm" for a head) would have been good recipients of the Voyager's message. They would have known what the scientists forgot to include: images of a fire-bombed Dresden, the sound of one man killing another on the island of Iwo Jima.

Billy Pilgrim says that Tralfamadorians think "that when a person dies he only *appears* to die. He is still very much alive in the past, so it is very silly for people to cry at his funeral. . . . [W]hen a Tralfamadorian sees a corpse, all he thinks is that the dead person is in bad condition in that particular moment, but that the same person is just fine in plenty of other moments."

This morning, rather than dwell on those particular moments when Gould's condition was bad, I focus on a moment in 1981 when Gould, sitting in the chair that his father made for him, sings with his piano the "dirty songs" of Track 31, the quodlibet. Within Bach's harmonic framework, he transforms the two strands of song into a processional hymn of man's desire.

32.

The sky was blue today. Perfect blue, like Dr. Ellison's pool before we would dive in. But now it is dark. Stars dot the sky. The moon set a couple of hours ago. You couldn't see it all day, its lonely face veiled by the absence of reflected light. It is July 29, 2003, and all day the new moon has been and has not been in the clear blue skies.

In ancient times among the Hebrews, preparation for a religious festival would begin with the ceremony of "blessing the new moon." When the slim crescent appeared, it promised Messianic redemption. The sky would swirl and vibrate with starlight and the crescent moon. To celebrate, there was feasting and dancing.

"What?" I can hear the disgust in my grandmother's voice as I consider, momentarily, an ancient Jewish tradition. Once I asked her if she ever went to temple. "I send them a check. That's it. They get my money, not me."

It is late. I pick up the phone and push numbers. A few seconds later, the phone rings in your house. You don't want to get out of bed. You are exhausted. But maybe it's an emergency. You hobble around, manage not to stub your toe, grab the phone.

"Hello?"

"It's me. Hold on a second. I want to play something for you. You've got to hear this right now. Don't hang up. Hold on."

I walk over to the CD player I bought in college, and put in the red CD. I push the track button thirty-two times, press play, and hold up the phone.

As you stand in the dark, pale hand holding the phone to your ear, I know you'll be patient. I play the entire track, the aria da capo. It

531

lasts exactly 3'45"—a full 1'35" longer than on the 1955 recording. As Gould plays, I become concerned about the noise in the background: the laptop, the crickets, a car backfiring, a propeller plane, a distant train whistle, sirens. Even the highway on the other side of the river seems loud.

When all that quiets down, finally, Gould's vocalizing. It is as if he were in the room. Some people don't like that. But you keep listening until the end, even though you haven't heard a word from me in years. You listen until that last note is enveloped by the sound of a distant shore.

Nominated by Agni

THE WAY PILOTS WALK

by PATRICIA SMITH

from JAVA MONKEY SPEAKS (Poetry Atlanta Press)

Like their cocks and haunches are heavy with it.
Arrogant past Starbucks and baggage claim, past
flinching monitors and the C gates, pilots stride
navy and crease, chiseled heads swiveling in bare
tolerance of we, the ground-bound. Their faces are
chapped by a higher sun, their pompadours glossy
and blade cut. They live a huger life awfully close
to heaven, where blessings begin. How smug are
those little hats, dripping with mysterious medals,
shaped like a salute to the men beneath them?
We bear bowed, pissed witness to their dismissive
sniffs, the oh-so-holier-than-thou in their hips.
There's no bound script for that sexy moment when
the wide sky inhales their laughable machines and
folds their hurtling heartbeats into blue. Go on,
join the club. Envy their asses. And pray towards
them. Every flyboy is your fate wearing a crisp little
uniform. A quirk of pulse, a sleepless night, a flick
of his wrist could kill you, a hundred other yous.
And maddening as it may be, there's just no answer
to that strut. It says, *Fuck you. I've got the air.*

Nominated by Poetry Atlanta Press

BREAKER

fiction by RANDY F. NELSON

from THE IMAGINARY LIVES OF MECHANICAL MEN
(University of Georgia Press)

So MANY TIMES IT SEEMS ETERNAL. She whines. I lie. It's our fate. We'll be bound to each other in hell by tangled telephone lines, except this time she reaches me through the air, across an entire ocean, inside an airport terminal. It's like a wasp buzzing in my briefcase, and I extract it with the tips of my fingers, holding the sound as close to my face as I can bear. When I hear her voice, I realize that she can reach me anywhere.

She says, without greeting, "Charles, I need a favor."

"You'll have to speak up," I tell her. "I don't think we have a good connection."

"Charles, don't start. I need you to take Eric this weekend."

"Narissa? Is that you?"

"Anthony and I are doing a wedding upstate. I need you to take Eric. Camping or something, you're always promising to take him camping."

"Gee, Nariss, I'd love to help you, but I'm sort of tied up at the moment."

"Where are you?"

"Where am I?"

"Yes, Charles. Where. Are. You."

"You mean right now? Right this minute?"

"Charles, for God's sake!"

"Oh. Yeah, well, right now I'm in Marseilles. Might not be back for a while."

"You're in Marseilles?"

"Yeah. I do international maritime law, Narissa. You know, boats and water. This is a very logical place. You and Anthony ought to try it sometime."

"You're lying."

"You dialed the number."

I have a talent for finding the argument-stopper. It's a gift—knowing that she had got the maid to call my office and then dial this number before touching the phone herself. And also knowing she would never admit it.

The truth is that I was in Marseilles yesterday, where they sell cold medication at the airport shops. Today I am here, with a sinus infection, at another airport on an island whose name I have forgotten, just off the coast of Liberia. Barely able to breathe. Right now I am waiting for a man named Robert N'mburo, who is a local chieftain, or whatever they call them over here, hoping that he will be able to write his own name. He isn't really required to write his own name, but it would make this whole charade easier. So I pinch my nose. Take sips of air through my mouth. Then finally, at some point, look down and see that I really am fondling a cigarette.

Waiting, after I get rid of the phone call, the way you do in this section of Africa.

And what a dump.

I can say that because my employer—International Filth, Human Misery, and Contamination, Incorporated—owns everything in sight. Really. We own the airstrip, the island itself, approximately two hundred ships in various stages of disassembly, the trucks, the cables, the acetylene torches, the infirmary such as it is, the dead fish, the twenty-four miles of shoreline, and mineral rights. It's all in my briefcase, printed on 8½ x 14 legal sheets. We own the dump and most of the human beings who live here. On the island at the end of the earth, whose name I cannot at present remember. And we own the terminal building in which I am sitting. And of course we own me, down to the pinstripes and New Orleans accent—slightly adulterated by the necessity of living in Manhattan for the past fourteen years and representing said ironies in federal district court from time to time.

So I'll say it again because these little moments don't last. And because I like saying it. We own this part of the world. We *are* the government. We are the parent, the tribal elder, the proprietor, and savior of this island. We are God, and this is our Earth. It is our lump

535

of dirt until it outlasts its usefulness, a moment which, unfortunately, arrived about six weeks into our last business quarter. Paradise is still profitable, but when your legal liabilities—not to say the closing arguments of several lawsuits—begin to creep into the accounting. . . . Well, that's why I'm here. To shut it all down.

This particular building reminds me of a subway station, except that it has an oily teakwood floor and a few windows the size of portholes. Nevertheless, the air is subway air. I know it when I see it. And there's rust blossoming on the walls, like the mineral gardens in caves. I've never seen anything quite like it—great cankerous rust flowers, as crenellated as carnations, growing on the walls of a building. It's unnatural. Someone should pass an ordinance. The place smells like a fish market and echoes like a cathedral. I keep expecting someone to walk by and use the word *aeroplane*. That's the sort of thing that pops into my mind when I'm not thinking about the fact that I am seven hundred miles from the nearest aspirin. And the fact that no one in this room has ever heard of Robert N'mburo. And the further fact that my wristwatch is missing.

Someone should have shut this place down years ago.

Did I say International Filth, Misery, Etc.? I believe I meant to say International Recovery Systems, Inc., a Fortune 500 company of sterling reputation whose major concern at the moment is that I make those two hundred ship carcasses disappear. Before, of course, they generate further unfortunate publicity and a verdict or two.

The really interesting thing is that I can do it.

At least, I can make them disappear from my client's side of the table. As I said, I do not require Mr. Robert N'mburo's signature. I simply require evidence that my masters have made a good-faith effort to eliminate the atrocious conditions in which Mr. N'mburo's people labor, those impoverished shipbreaking members of his tribe who, as luck would have it, are also members of what might be the most dangerous profession on earth. Thank God they haven't yet discovered lawyers.

In any event, my name is Charles Metairie Allemand.

And it is my sincere belief that the only truly happy people in the world at this instant are the two little boys, as black as bear cubs, who have been roly-polying, climbing, and chasing each other through the one big room since we got off the plane together. Their mother is a dignified young woman who watches them, and me, with equal calm. And I watch them because they have just found the one oddity about this place that even sarcasm cannot explain. It is a large marine compass, of the kind they used to have on sailing vessels, which has been bolted to the floor near one of the windows. Twice as large as a fire hydrant and as shiny as a medallion. And here is the human hope for all of us. It is the universal and ineluctable fact that no two boys anywhere in the world will ask *why* there is a marine compass in an airport. They will simply run to it and climb like monkeys. They will strain to lift it from the floor. They will try to make the needle move. They will fiddle and finagle and go belly-polishing over every inch of brass until one of them has clambered to the top and thrown his arms up like a champion. That's what I like about this pair. They're not lawyers.

I wonder which of them has my watch.

You see, I understand that there is a terrible logic holding this island to the surface of the earth. Different rules and regulations. And I know that the next few hours, or the next few days, will pass like a dream and that it will be useless to pretend otherwise. Sooner or later someone will sign the documents in my briefcase, perhaps even someone named Robert N'mburo, after which I will deliver one set to the Interior Ministry in Monrovia and then board the next flight to any major city in North Africa. Whence I will fly to Paris. Pick up an aspirin or twelve. Then from Paris to New York, where I will be paid an absurd amount of money by my employer, International Recovery Systems, Incorporated, for making this place disappear.

It's amazing how we can manipulate reality. Ten minutes ago, when the phone rang in my briefcase, every person in this building stopped to listen. Every one of them heard me lie to a woman who was not my wife, for a reason that I cannot, even at this moment, explain.

"Where are you?" she said. Just a disembodied voice from very far away, like a conscience.

"Where am I?" I said. "Do you mean right now? Where am I right this minute?"

And the voice said, "Charles, for God's sake. We need . . ."

And I said Marseilles. "I'm in Marseilles."

While no one even blinked.

My greatest fear is of dying at sea. Of being swallowed by the ocean itself or by one of its creatures. I dream about it after watching the History Channel, those World War II sagas where they show subma-

rine footage and the old fellows talk about what it's like to be torpe-
doed. I have nightmares of being trapped in the bowels of a sinking
ship as the first foam rushes across the deck and steel doors go slam-
ming and then I realize that outside my ever-constricting bubble
there will be no one left aboard to hear the hammering of my fists. I
think of that from time to time and how easily the sea erases any hint
of our passage. All the old fellows who didn't make it onto television.
And I think how, in the midst of the gray Atlantic, five hundred miles
from the continental shelf, the largest vessels go down without a rip-
ple, slowly spinning through the first hundred feet of filtered light as
schools of halibut scatter and strings of kelp become tattered stream-
ers on the coffin as it drops into that darker deep, beyond anything
even remotely human. Down, down to the places where sea dragons
and skeletal, armor-plated worms wear their own luminescence and
stare with mindless curiosity at our own white orbs, while—still de-
scending—we drift far past the point where every breathing thing
has already imploded and the bones have turned to jelly. Until at last
we settle, the two of us, ship and self, into the sedimentary muck,
which oozes like cold syrup through the one open hatch and down
the vacant stair. Somewhere on the abyssal plain.

Or I think at times of drowning within sight of shore, drifting into
some sharp crevice between brown rocks or floating facedown in a
tidal pool like a tourist diver who's lost his mask and fins. Dying there
and being inflated by my own pompous gasses, only to be punctured
by an inquisitive crab so that I might become a holiday for the mil-
lions who feed from the bottom up, a bounteous plantation of
limpets and filter feeders, a pink crust of coralline algae outlining my
form like chalk marks at the scene of a crime. While the urchins re-
joice. I, bobbing like a buoy until all my fat has been suctioned away
and the blue-tentacled anemones have lost their sting. So that I sink
into a kind of immortality among a constellation of starfish, my ribs
pointing toward the sun like the fingers of the first astronomer. At
the bottom of a deep, deep sky.

And just before the jellied tentacles, when our marriage was
breaking up and Narissa and I thought we could cure everything with
a flight to that other paradise, I saw the battleship *Arizona*. Spectac-
ularly visible from the air, resting in less than twenty feet of water be-
neath a pane of wavy green glass. Turrets perfectly aligned, the
familiar white memorial like a crown on a hoary head. From my tiny

538

window I could detect a peculiar undersea motion that made the ship's outline indistinct—an unresisting ebb and flow of marine plants that carpeted *Arizona* as if to assert how thoroughly, even in this remote and shallow puddle, the ocean would reclaim its own. Think of it, a battleship consumed by plants, and you will understand why as we prepared to land I told Narissa that we would not be among the tourists dropping their wreaths. Because I had already sensed that within inches of the surface were the outstretched arms of 1,177 sailors, a thought that terrified me even at a distance of several miles. As she leaned across to gape.

And now all these images flood my mind as I contemplate the young man standing in front of me. I'm trying to comprehend his words. He speaks perfect English, which is, after all, the official language of Liberia, but simple comprehension is not the problem. Rather, it sounds as though he is saying, "I have come to take you to the ship." A message that complicates things, since I am sure he means one of the skeletal ships being consumed along the shore.

"Mr. N'mburo sent you, yes?" I say.

"Yes, yes. Robert. I will bring you directly to him. Everything is arranged. I hope you had a decent and comfortable flight."

He is stick thin and just under six feet, a boy really, whose face is less than twelve years old and whose white shirt is buttoned to the collar. Perhaps one of the Bassa people come down from the hinterland with his parents to make money in the shipbreaking trade. I do not care to explain to him the horrors I associate with ships, but neither do I intend to meet Robert N'mburo onboard one of the floating corpses at the edge of this island. "There has been a mistake," I say to him. "I am supposed to meet Mr. N'mburo here, at this place, now."

"A mistake with many apologies, Mr. Allemand, which most assuredly is being met with correction, as everything is now in order. I have transportation immediately outside."

"What is your name?"

"Call me Sammy, that is the easy way. I will drive you immediately to your arrangement."

The absurdity of being driven anywhere by a twelve-year-old does not occur to me; it's the other absurdity that tingles along my spine. "Sammy, there is no need for anyone to be on a ship. In fact, I'm here to close down the shipyard. As a protection, for the workers. It's already decided. This meeting with your representative is just a formality really. A signature is all that's required. There won't be any more ships."

"Yes, I will take you. It is immediately arranged. I am an utmost excellent driver with apologies for this slight change, although I must believe that there will be more ships."

For a moment a flicker of fear crosses Sammy's face, and I want to say to him of course there will be more ships. There will always be rotting horror and putrefaction. But what I say instead is "I need for Mr. N'mburo to be here."

"Here? At this ship?"

Now he has confused me, and I have to stand and start over. Several people have come to stand with me and to offer help in several dialects. "No," I say. "Not a ship. I need you to bring Robert N'mburo here. To sign papers only."

"Here?" Sammy says.

The people nod, and I nod. "Yes. Here."

"To *this* ship?"

Everyone looks at me.

I look at the rust on the walls. The oily teakwood floor. Then Sammy takes my hand and leads me outside, several dozen yards out onto the airstrip itself where we turn and look and see the whole of it—a silhouette that still reminds me of a terminal building at some small airport upon some New England coast. Although now of course the details bring out the truth. There is the horizontal stripe, faded but still visible, just beneath a terraced array of windows, some with wipers still attached. Stanchions like a row of unthreaded needles picketing the open deck. Boom and funnels at the aft. The twin flags of America and Liberia fluttering from the radio mast. It is the superstructure of a cargo vessel, cut at her traverses, and dragged by some Egyptian strength across the beach and to this level stretch of sand. The type of thing I have seen in this part of Africa before, a solution so practical in its conception and yet so insane in its execution that you had sooner believe that a ship had fallen from the sky, burying herself, like the *Arizona*, in a shallow grave.

The boy looks at the terminal building and then looks at me, smiling at the colossal joke. "I am thinking that you are finding this very hard to believe, the way things are done."

I feel like a man who's been lifted out of the grave, and for a moment I share his humor. "I don't find anything hard to believe,

Sammy. For the right money . . . , I'll believe anything you say."

This is something he understands and that unleashes a flood of enthusiasm. "Gbambhala is a most logical place. We are not part of Liberia at all, Mr. Allemand, I am hoping you understand. The entire island has been purchased by the United States, and we are working for America."

I don't contradict him. "Gbambhala? Has it always been called that?"

"Yes, always I believe. And now you are still wishing to meet here?"

I stare toward the harbor, but all I can make out are wild sea oats and a scattering of palms and *bilinga*. The sun is low enough to make the beach road look like a strip of silver. "No. No, I just need a minute to, ah, get oriented here, Sammy. I just need to . . . get this over with and then . . . When did you say was the last flight, to the mainland?"

"There is a flight to Marrakech very late. Usually eleven o'clock or perhaps midnight. And a ferry boat to Abidjan across the water, in that direction perhaps a mile. Sometimes it arrives in the evening." He has a future, this kid who can remember more details than your average litigator.

"That's fine. Let's try to get me on that plane. But first let's make the call on Mr. N'mburo, wherever he happens to be."

There are only three places in the world where shipbreaking occurs on a large scale: Alang in India; Chittagong in Bangladesh; and the six-mile stretch of beach at Gbambhala—a wholly owned subsidiary of International Recovery Systems, Inc. There are no large shipbreaking operations anywhere in the Western Hemisphere. Only desperately poor people can afford this work, and only a government ruled by a lunatic would sell an island to a private shipbreaking firm. Still, it is one of the most profitable enterprises on earth. The turbines alone from a twenty-five-year-old tanker will fetch nearly a million dollars. The unburned fuel and oil, electrical equipment and wiring, wood furniture and decking will bring in another half million. Then you are down to the precious metals—brass, copper, and steel—so much steel that Chittagong supplies the entire steel output for Bangladesh. There is not another steel mill in the entire country.

What is left after a ship has been broken is too small to be counted unless you count lives. The residue occurs in two forms—liquid and powder. The liquid will always be several hundred gallons of diesel fuel, refinery oil, insecticide, complex polymers, dyes, and fishery waste. It's the sludge you see along the coast. The powders will be invisible, occurring only as a haze hanging over the yard: it's made up of asbestos, silicon, steel filings, wood ash, and PCBs. Mixed together they form a gray paste or a gray-white dust that reminds you of Seattle mornings. When it settles on the water, it shines like a mirror for days, killing all marine life for one to two miles out to sea. The workers clean the shore by shoveling contaminated sand into levees and connecting them into one long road that parallels every shipbreaking operation in the world and separates the shore from the shantytown. Such roads can run for miles at six or eight feet above the gradient. Some of them require tunnels to cross from one side to the other. I once drove the shore road at Alang, drunk, late at night when it was most spectacular, speeding from one end to the other, just to watch the places where the sand was on fire, like the road into hell.

But the road at Gbambhala is no more than eight inches above grade. It gives an unobstructed view of the beach. On our left is the town, separated from us by a flooded ditch with numerous plank bridges. A mob of children chases our jeep past hanging clothes, cook fires, and the tangle of ropes that seem to hold the encampment together. Sammy looks like an adult as he drives, sounding the horn with an air of grave responsibility and waving casually at the youngsters who chase us like tattered ghosts. On the right are the ships, twenty medium-sized cargo vessels already grounded and another sixty trawlers and smaller craft being picked apart. Among the sharp-angled shadows of late afternoon we can see figures swarming over each corpse like an army of ants. That's the first thing that comes to mind; but they do not look like beached whales, these ships. They look like toppled buildings. Or like train wrecks at the edge of the ocean. And at first you cannot grasp what has happened because it does not seem logical that human beings would deliberately create this kind of destruction.

Sammy tells me that Robert N'mburo is supervising the lifting of the propeller shaft from the engine room of one of the freighters. We drive to the high tide line and begin to walk the rest of the way. They've made a path of palm fronds in honor of my visit. Everything has been arranged.

Farther out to sea are the silhouettes of another hundred vessels, all waiting for a vacant slot on the beach, some anchored, one already building up cruising speed. We stop and listen to the radioman fifty yards below us. He's directing the captain and engineer on a tanker that seems to be headed away from shore. "*Sendai Maru*, what is your heading?"

A barely recognizable English squawk comes back to him, "Heading two nine zero."

"Very well. Your distance from the port ship?"

"Eight cables. Closing to seven cables. Seven point oh."

"Very well, *Sendai*. Come to course zero-four-zero. Ahead one half."

"Zero-four-zero. Ahead one half."

The radioman drives a blinking red beacon into the sand as the huge ship begins its turn and gathers speed. Someone calls off course changes in degrees. A few men in *lungis* and turbans wander down to our section of beach to watch. After ten minutes the radioman gives a new set of instructions. "*Sendai*, come to one-one-zero. Ahead two-thirds. Please confirm, you are ballasting, yes?"

"Course one-one-zero. Ahead two-thirds. We are continuing to ballast, and we have your light."

"Very well, call out your course."

The ship seems to grow shorter as its bow swings to face us; then, for a long time, it seems not to be moving at all. There is another exchange of numbers over the radio and an acknowledgment from the captain that he is giving full power. The ship itself appears to be no closer to shore than it was twenty minutes before, though its shape has changed to a dark and bulging V atop a churning foam. Soon the bow wake resembles a cat's paw flicking at the water ahead. Then it becomes more of a sound pushing the men back from the wavelets. They plod upslope in twos and threes, as if to prove that they do not yet need to run. The rushing torrent of my imagination gradually becomes a jetlike roar competing with the engine's deep thum-thum-thum, both sounds merging at last into a concussion that seems to have swept in from some World War II battlefield, a sound that is not so much sound as it is a physical pressure in the lungs, a rhythm in the stomach. It is the moment that language becomes useless. As the V expands into a mountainous slope of metal, the wake itself reaches us first as a fine mist that we inhale and then wipe from our faces. When the keel strikes bottom, there is not the shriek that I expect but rather a totally unexpected slippage to one side as if the *Sendai Maru* had suddenly decided to avoid an unpleasant puddle. As the stern fishtails, the bow continues its slow progress, another indication of the vast power that has been put in play.

Some of the sand spills to either side like a huge furrow being cut into the face of the earth, but most of it simply disappears under the broadening shadow of the hull, now rising impossibly high above us. A shallow depression forms for thirty yards on both sides of the prow, which the tide and the ship's own bilges immediately fill. It is as though a giant has suddenly stepped away from the shore and nature now rushes to seal the vacuum. Long after the propeller loses its purchase, the *Sendai Maru* continues her course inland, her plates groaning under an earthly weight that they were never designed to bear and revealing a crusty underside that no one is meant to see.

I have heard that, from time to time, a man will break away from the crowd and rush down the shore as one of these ships emerges from the water under full power and is no longer controllable by the hand of any pilot. Whether from an excess of bravado or out of a desire to commit suicide, it is impossible to say. He stares out to sea as if indifferent to the danger or hypnotized by the prospect of something better and far away. Then, when the ship makes that final sideways lurch, he is either spared by blind chance or else simply annihilated, ground into the sand by abrasions above and below. In either case, he is rarely seen again.

I know of course that the *Sendai Maru* has never been animated by anything other than her engines, but in the sudden silence I am struck by the paradox that something has indeed just died. For a moment no one moves. It's like the awkward hush at graveside after the last prayer and the benediction. And I know that in the morning's low tide tiny creatures will swarm over this ship and begin to dismantle the body. But for one shared moment we keep quiet, each one of us with his private thoughts. Even I, counting what has been lost.

It is one of the sad and fundamental principles of maritime law that a ship out of water is no longer a ship, but a heap of metal. Like a marriage out of love.

Sammy steers me toward another ship farther down the beach.

We reach Robert N'mburo's wreck by walking over a plank pathway thrown across deep ruts in the sand and then after a few moments by wading to a rough scaffolding. Sammy takes off his sandals and throws them on the beach. I roll my trousers and tie my shoes to the briefcase because I remember reading that most deaths in the ship-breaking industry actually occur from tetanus and bacterial infections that began in simple cuts. I will return to my shoes as soon as I reach deck and then will watch my step thereafter. From that one thought arises a mild concern that grows, as we ascend the scaffolding, into an unreasoning fear that literally no one in the world knows where I am. I could slip and fall into the sea at any moment; I could be electrocuted by any one of the land lines snaking from arc lamps on deck down into the water and across the beach to a sputtering generator; or I could step onto a metal gangway that collapses like a fire escape tearing loose from rotting bricks and mortar. No one would know, because I've lied to Narissa and put myself into the hands of a child named Sammy. I could die like one of the workers. And for the first time I realize that I could be replaced just as easily.

I go over the railing and onto the deck with slow and careful movements, clutching the briefcase as if it were an infant.

Below us a man climbs the anchor chain with no more effort than someone climbing a flight of stairs. He disappears into the hawsehole, and after a moment comes the crackle of an acetylene torch and the haunting glow of blue-white light, as if he had been a ghost opening the door of another world. Already the ship has been relieved of her wood, glass, plastic, rubber, porcelain, canvas, hemp, copper, brass, and silver. What is left is a world of iron and a world of iron sounds. We have to shout now to hear each other because most of the "cutting" at this stage is done with sledgehammers. Acetylene torches are rare and precious in this part of the world, and they are dangerous, slicing into pockets of every vaporized chemical that can be hauled by ship and not infrequently exploding. This ship, like most, is simply being beaten apart and hauled away by hand, a process that takes up to a year for the supertankers that are the prized treasure-ships of men like Robert N'mburo, and the principal killers of his men. As we stand on the half-deck and peer into the canyon beneath us, it is like looking into a village that had been bombed from the air.

We step through a maze of cables and descend the first stair to a point perhaps twelve feet below the scuppers, a place that's shadowed by the uppermost hull plates and where we pause to adjust our eyes like men stepping into a darkened theater. In this dim twilight we have to be careful to step over buckets of bolts, coiled electrical wires, and one-inch steel plates stacked like rusty playing cards. Below us are more landings and more metal stairs, all taking odd turns and occasionally hanging like catwalks where former walls have been stripped away. The infrequent shafts of light coming from portholes resemble spotlights focused on the backstage machinery of an experimental drama, and I feel like an actor descending to some unseen production by M. C. Escher. The hammering, which should have echoed like gunshots, becomes no more than a faint tinkling, perhaps muffled by the insane geometry of the demolition or perhaps simply swallowed by the immensity of the ship. It is like walking into a skyscraper that someone has left lying on its side. I go with one hand on a railing and one, where possible, flat against the inner hull. Down and down, past cabins and storage holds, at each level getting a glimpse of the antmen at work, some banging with sledges, some hauling out miles of intestines, some carrying away iron slabs like leaf-cutters deep in the Amazon.

At last we reach a narrow passage leading through two iron hatches to the orlop, a half-deck just above the bilges where waste spills into the open ocean twenty feet below. The entire stern of our ship has already been cut away, and the unguarded view of the outer harbor, in less dangerous circumstances, might have looked like early evening from one of the antiseptic balconies of a cruise ship. There are the murmuring breakers below us, the quaint commercial vessels at a distance, and a reddening sun that must be setting Brazil ablaze. High above the artificial horizon is our evening star, a sparkling hole in the hull where a torch has just cut through. The sparks fall for thirty feet and then skid down the inner hull like marbles of molten glass.

Someone behind us says, "It looks like an amphitheater, doesn't it?"

The unexpected accent startles me more than actual violence would have done, and the man's demeanor seems almost as alien as my own. Taller than Sammy, and far more substantial in body, he resembles in my imagination a professional athlete or an American diplomat who has dressed in the local costume for an afternoon of celebrity touring.

"Whenever I look up from this point," he continues, "I always think of one of those paintings of nineteenth-century surgeries, you know, the ones with the medical students peering down into the pit, the one light playing off the surgeon in his bloody apron and cravat—

and of course the very pale lady on the table." He chuckles at some private amusement and extends a hand.

"Charles Allemand," I say. "You must be Mr. N'mburo."

"Yeah. For about a year now. Before that I was a white guy like you." The man I had come four thousand miles to meet waits to see if I will laugh. He studies me with an intensity that would have been considered rude, even insulting, in most African cultures. "You look a little wet," he says. "Why don't you chuck that overboard," he nods at my briefcase, "and let's sit and talk for a while. I've got a feeling you're going to miss your flight."

His words are both casual and sinister, like those of a soldier who's grown indifferent to death and to high-sounding causes. When he comes closer, I see that fate has in fact touched him. There is a bandage hanging loose at one palm like a boxer's hand wrapping. A gray scar over his left eye. And as he walks it becomes apparent that he favors one leg and that he is gradually being bent under whatever weight he has chosen to bear. Still, there's nothing wounded about his voice, and he speaks like a man who expects his words to have an effect. He lowers himself to his haunches and rests his elbows on his knees the way I had seen the Bassa people doing in pictures.

I say to him, "Maybe you'll forgive me for suggesting that you're not exactly what I expected."

"No shit?"

"You're American?"

"Used to be. Used to be a lot more than that."

"I see."

"I doubt that, chief. I doubt you have any idea what you're seeing."

"Look, Mr. N'mburo, or Mr. . . . ."

"Rosello. Can you believe that? Somewhere along the line my family must have been owned by the only slaveholders in Brooklyn. You think that might have been it? Now, I myself find the name Robert Rosello far stranger than anything I'm about to tell you."

"I appreciate that. But I want you to understand that I'm not here to do anything other than . . ."

"I know why you're here. I even have an idea of how much you're getting paid to cradle your little briefcase. I could tell old Sammy there, but he wouldn't believe that there's that much money in the world. This is a strange place, Chuck. A very strange place indeed. I want you to think about that. Then toss your goodies out into the surf there. And then listen carefully."

547

"I'm afraid I can't do that."

"Let me ask you something. Have things been going well for you since you got here?"

"How do you mean?"

"Me, I had a headache for weeks. Sinus, diarrhea, heat exhaustion. It takes a while to adapt, let me tell you. Then, after you adapt, it's a pretty good sign that you're going to end up like everybody else around here. Seen anything yet that makes you want to stay?"

"If I could just get you to sign these papers . . ."

"Chuck, listen to me. I'm the guy they sent out here before you."

"I'm sorry, I don't . . ."

"Listen to what I'm saying. I want you to toss the papers. Tell them nobody's signing anything. Tell them the breaking yard is staying open."

"For God's sake why? This place is a disaster. It's killing every man who works here and the environment too."

"You're right. And, besides that, you own it—or at least your clients own it. And they can shut it down, make a few bucks by selling off the scrap, and win the corporate clean-up award all in one afternoon. Is that still the plan?"

"It doesn't make any difference whether you sign or not. If you're the guy they sent out here before me, then you already know that."

"It can delay things, and that's all we want."

"It won't make any difference in the end."

"Nothing makes any difference in the end, Chuck. It's the middle that counts. And, whatever else happens, it's better than starving to death. Right? Every man out there understands that, except here's what he understands that you don't understand. When he starves, his family starves, and not just his immediate family either. Ever watch anybody starve to death? It's like cancer without the tumors. But for every man who dies in the breaking yard there are ten trying to take his place. Why? Because where they come from it's worse."

"You're preaching."

"Damn right I am."

"You're preaching to the wrong person."

"No, I'm preaching to the right person. You're a scumbag, Charles. I want you to do what scumbags always do."

"Which is?"

"Look out for yourself. Switch sides. I want you to drop a monkey wrench into the corporate makeover. I want you to lose your luggage. Whatever would cause a delay, that's what I want you to do."

"Wouldn't that be a slight conflict of interest?"

"Not if you came over to our side."

"Simple as that, eh?"

"Simple as that."

"And what I would gain for myself out of all this would be precisely what?"

"If we can get a long enough delay, we can form a corporation under Liberian law, a genuine co-op where the workers would own principal interest. Then we could begin modernizing, cleaning up, and paying a guy like you."

"Sorry."

"It could work."

"Maybe in the Land of Oz. Not here. You've got real problems out there, Robert. And I've got a plane to catch. So maybe next time. We'll do the whole world peace thing together. Nice meeting you. But don't get up; I can show myself out."

"That's what we thought you'd say."

I feel a sudden chill. A door bangs shut. And it occurs to me once again that no one knows where I am. I look up from the pit of his amphitheater and see faces looking back. My head aches, and I understand that if I sit down with this man I will be negotiating for my life.

I stand very still, looking at Robert N'mburo for a long time, trying to imagine him organizing documents at a conference table. I try to imagine him in the finest suits and sitting in leather chairs. Summoning his morning coffee with the push of a button, like me. It is a leap my mind cannot make. Robert is too scarred and warped, too taken by the life he's chosen, and probably, I realize, quite simply insane from the suffering he has seen. So I take a slow breath and consider my options. I do not sit. I do not make sudden motions. I do not look down at the churning sea.

I negotiate.

We begin with little things, the warp and woof of life among the lowly. I promise him oranges, dates, and cheese. Soy milk and wheat. Torches and winches and trucks. Within minutes we are outside of all reality, my own words sounding as hollow as those of any politician. Only the gathering darkness suggests that there can be any end to

549

this babbling, to my judicious monotone. And although the man across from me seems mesmerized, I do not doubt the truth—that he's following these words the way a cobra follows the flute.

I promise him medicine, tools, and fuel. Then books and building materials. Fresh water. Maybe a school. Whatever, in a word, might sound reasonable to a man who has lost his reason. But it is not enough. His darkened face grows darker, and I see the sadness that precedes some violent act. When he starts to stand, I know we've reached the end. I've tried and found no argument-stopping words. Now it's the shuffling mob or the foam beneath the stern.

And one last chance. Robert looks at my briefcase, raises his eyebrows in silent question, and seems unsurprised that I find the courage to shake my head. But it's all I've got. We both know the gesture won't help. And he starts to walk away.

From some deep well I hear a voice, quite clearly, proclaim, "Give me Sammy then."

It stops him and turns his head.

And suddenly I'm saying, "There's a midnight plane to Marrakech. Passports if you have the dollars. And if I can get him into France . . ."

He looks at Sammy and then looks at me, the muscles knotting at his jaw.

"I can do it. You know I can."

"Not just to France. All the way to America?" He's bargaining again. I can hear the hope in his voice and something else, a hint of something else in my own.

"All the way."

"You swear?"

"On the life of my son."

"And until he's grown?"

"Yes."

"You swear this?"

"Robert—listen to me. I can save him. You know I can."

Nominated by University of Iowa Press

SPECIAL MENTION

(The editors also wish to mention the following important works published by small presses last year. Listings are in no particular order.)

FICTION

Steps Through Sand, Through Fire—David H. Lynn (TriQuarterly)

Feeling It, Wanting—Jessica Handler (The Healing Muse)

The Understory—Tim Horvath (Carve)

Fletcher Knowles—Lee Siegel (Raritan)

The Storeroom of Playboy Males—Robin Hemley (Columbia)

The Abandoned Elders of The Peach Street Hospital—Shawna Ryan (ZYZZYVA)

Hollyhocks—Cary Holladay (Five Points)

Screen Door—Sarah Strickley (Quarter After Eight)

Kids Make Their Own Houses—Geoff Wyss (Image)

OBO—Antonya Nelson (Tin House)

California—Erin McGraw (Kenyon Review)

Morag—D.R. MacDonald (Epoch)

That Winter—H.E. Francis (turnrow)

A Season Of Regret—James Lee Burke (Shenandoah)

The Arch—Andy Mozina (Massachusetts Review)

Driving Picasso—Peter Selgin (Boulevard)

Collateral—Gayle Brandeis (Amazon Shorts)

Our Lady of Paris—Daniyal Mueenuddin (Zoetrope)

Dead-End MF—Greg Baxter (Cincinnati Review)

Like Dylan At Newport—Chris Bachelder (Cincinnati Review)

Speak to Me of Love—Edith Pearlman (Lake Effect)

The Absolute Space of Wisdom—E.R. Brown (Event)

Piebald—Jason Ockert (Mid American Review)

How To Be A Real Ballerina—Jane Berentson (Redivider)
Think Straight—Malinda McCollum (StoryQuarterly)
Travelougue—Sheila Kohler (Boulevard)
The Dulcimer Maker—Robert Morgan (Shenandoah)
The Bris—Eileen Pollack (Subtropics)
Dead Man's Nail—Dennis Fulgoni (Colorado Review)
Old Grimes—Dennis McFadden (South Carolina Review)
Favor—Shimon Tanaka (Missouri Review)
Stop Saying My Names—Rebecca Tuch (Briar Cliff Review)
Parting Gifts—Mike Ingram (Baltimore Review)
Baracuda—Dylan Landis (New Orleans Review)
River's Edge—Thomas M. Atkinson (Indiana Review)
Torchy's—Aaron Michael Morales (Another Chicago Magazine)
The Scratchboard Project—John Michael Cummings (Iowa Review)
The Adjuster—Alexi Zentner (Southwest Review)
Falling In Love With The Unconquered Real—Ezekiel N. Finkel-
    stein [sic]
Happy For You—Gregory Spatz (New England Review)
The Caterpillar—Lydia Davis (Noon)
One Little Cigarette—Cynthia Struloeff (ZYZZYVA)
The Book of Signs—Molly McNett (Crazyhorse)
Trichotillomania—Susan Hahn (Michigan Quarterly Review)
Morning, Noon, Night—Matthew Batt (Western Humanities Review)
Someone Like Sue—Rebecca Curtis (Noon)
Foreign Correspondence—S.L. Wisenberg (Transformation)
Uncle Lazarus—Gladys Swan (Sewanee Review)
The End of Narrative (1–29; or 29–1)—Peter LaSalle (Southern Review)
Celebrations—Gary Gildner (New Letters)
An Upright Man—Holly Goddard Jones (Epoch)
What Is The Cure for Meanness?—Brock Clarke (One Story)
Rodney Valen's Second Life—Kent Meyers (Georgia Review)
Mijo—Carolyn Alessio (TriQuarterly)
Muddy Water, Turn To Wine—Michael Parker (Epoch)
A Man—Pia Z. Ehrhardt (Spork)
A Fence Between Our Homes—Robin Black (Southern Review)
The Edge of The Pot—Liesl Jobson (Per Contra)
Jonathan and Lillian—Richard Burgin (TriQuarterly)
Sea Dogs—Lee Martin (Glimmer Train)
After The Parade—Jack Herlihy (Shenandoah)

Dubai—Anis Shivani (The Pinch)

How I Left Onandaga County—Jane Ciabattari (*Best Underground Fiction*, Stolen Time Press)

Conservation—Debra Spark (Massachusetts Review)

The Source of My Troubles—Jeff P. Jones (Sycamore Review)

Reel to Reel—J.D. Chapman (Faultline)

Reva—Jenny Dunning (CutBank)

1899—Erin McGraw (Southern Review)

NONFICTION

My Tears See More Than My Eyes—Alan Shapiro (Virginia Quarterly)

Essay On Where It's From—John D'Agata (Conjunctions)

An Act of Kindness—Alyce Miller (Divide)

The Life of the Letter—Judith Kitchen (Georgia Review)

How Good To Hear You Singing—Mary Kinzie (Poetry)

Spectacular Mistakes—Wendy Rawlings (Agni)

How I Lost My Religion—Valerie Martin (Conjunctions)

Deceptions of the Thrush—Franklin Burroughs (Sewanee Review)

Writing In Two Tongues—Wang Ping (Manoa)

Comfort Food—Ann Hood (Alimentum)

Simple Past—Elena Gorokhova (Southern Review)

Runes and Incantations—Brenda Miller (Missouri Review)

What Jesus Did—Garry Wills (American Scholar)

Empty Streets, Missing Children—J. Malcolm Garcia (Fourth Genre)

Jealousy, or The Autobiography of an Italian Woman—Gina Barreca (Creative Nonfiction)

Literature Unnatured—Joy Williams (American Short Fiction)

Reading Into Old Age—Jane Miller (Raritan)

My Mother's Body—Mary Gordon (American Scholar)

Practicing The Arts of Peace—John Crowley (Conjunctions)

Katrina Five Ways—Randy Fertel (Kenyon Review)

"King August": August Wilson In His Time—Philip D. Beidler (Michigan Quarterly Review)

The Birdmen—Bonnie J. Rough (Iowa Review)

The Beautiful City of Tirzah—Harrison Fletcher (New Letters)

The Piano Teacher—Rana Dasgupta (Missouri Review)

32nd Running of the Tempus Stakes—Moe Folk (New Letters)

Serving The Sentence—Sven Birkerts (Raritan)

Afternoon of the Sex Children—Mark Greif (N+1)

My Mother, The Ingénue—Seth Lerer (Southwest Review)

An Orgy of Power—George Gessert (Northwest Review)

Galveston Island Breakdown: Some Directions—Sue William Silverman (Water-Stone Review)

My Affair With Jesus—Rebecca McClanahan (Arts & Letters)

The Angel of Diversity—Martha Bayles (The Antioch Review)

Tell Me Again Who Are You?—Heather Sellers (Alaska Quarterly Review)

This Is Heyen Speaking—Philip Brady (Provincetown Arts)

The Boy With Blue Hair—Cheryl Strayed (The Sun)

Primary Next of Kin—Christopher F. Arnold (Northwest Review)

100 Percent—Lesley Quinn (Gettysburg Review)

The Art of War—Sarah Aswell (Gettysburg Review)

Language, Loss, and Metaphor—Ellen Hawley (Threepenny Review)

The Ghost Light—ArLynn Leiber Presser (TriQuarterly)

What Feels Like Destiny—Jamy Bond (The Sun)

Chores—Debra Marquart (Orion)

Russell and Mary—Michael Donohue (Georgia Review)

This Is Who I Am When No One Is Looking—Pico Iyer (Portland Magazine)

Confessions of A Telemarketer—Brandon R. Schrand (Colorado Review)

West Greene and River Bend: Gun and Bait—Melissa Delbridge (Antioch Review)

Your Anonymous Correspondent: Ezra Pound and The Hudson Review—Mark Jarman (Hudson Review)

In A Glance—Joanna Scott (Conjunctions)

Setting Forth In Their Footprints—Elizabeth Dodd (Southern Review)

Streetcar—William Jay Smith (Antioch Review)

The Scribe In the Woods—Elizabeth Dodd (Fourth Genre)

Playing for Grace: William Matthews—Dave Smith (Georgia Review)

Century Walker: The Tsunami Notebook—Margo Berdeshevsky (New Letters)

The Blood of Children—Allen Learst (Water-Stone)

Red Politics and Blue In Wyoming—David Romtvedt (The Sun)

Auguries of Decadence—David Bosworth (Salmagundi)

All Apologies—Eula Biss (Ninth Letter)

Comfortless—Amy Leach (Iowa Review)

Documentary—Paul Nicholas Jones (Make)

Work—Kim Barnes (Iron Horse Literary Review)

The Finest Writers In the World Today—Tom Williams (Connecticut Review)

Passion Flowers In Winter—Molly Peacock (PMS)

A Year At the Lake—Jenny Fiore (Brain, Child)

The Disease, Then, But A Constellation—Daniel Gutstein (Bellevue Literary Review)

Jambon Dreams—Floyd Skloot (Boulevard)

Six Degrees of Separation from Japan—Terry Caesar (Palo Alto Review)

POETRY

Code—Daniel Gutstein (Phoebe)

The Shaw Brothers—Afaa Michael Weaver (5AM)

The Body—Marianne Boruch (Poetry)

The Magdalen With the Nightlight by Georges de La Tour—Madeline DeFrees (Image)

Snake Key—Carol Frost (TriQuarterly)

From Afar—Ted Lardner (Rhino)

Bilbao, Spain—Eugene Gloria (Bat City Review)

Windows—Mark Irwin (Eleventh Muse)

Report From The Empty Room—Christopher Howell (Southern Review)

Receiving the Host—Frannie Lindsay (*Lamb*, Perugia Press)

Departures And Arrivals—Arthur Sze (Natural Bridge)

Yellow Morning—Robin Behn (PMS)

Just The Habaneros—Nin Andrews (Sentence)

Killdeer—Lisa Akus (Lake Effect)

"Request . . ." Brenda Hillman (Poetry Flash)

Cloud Country—Carl Phillips (American Scholar)

The Origin of The Specious—Richard Kenney (New England Review)

Singe—Bob Hicok (New England Review)

1400—Albert Goldbarth (Poetry)

The True Apology Takes Years—Dean Young (Tin House)

Pyro—Dana Levin (Poetry)

The Last Days of Elvis—D. James Smith (Epoch)

PRESSES FEATURED IN THE PUSHCART PRIZE EDITIONS SINCE 1976

Acts

Agni

Ahsahta Press

Ailanthus Press

Alaska Quarterly Review

Alcheringa/Ethnopoetics

Alice James Books

Ambergris

Amelia

American Letters and Commentary

American Literature

American PEN

American Poetry Review

American Scholar

American Short Fiction

The American Voice

Amicus Journal

Amnesty International

Anaesthesia Review

Anhinga Press

Another Chicago Magazine

Antaeus

Antietam Review

Antioch Review

Apalachee Quarterly

Aphra

Aralia Press

The Ark

Art and Understanding

Arts and Letters

Artword Quarterly

Ascensius Press

Ascent

Aspen Leaves

Aspen Poetry Anthology

Assembling

Atlanta Review

Autonomedia

Avocet Press

The Baffler

Bakunin

Bamboo Ridge

Barlenmir House

Barnwood Press

Barrow Street

Bellevue Literary Review

The Bellingham Review

Bellowing Ark

Beloit Poetry Journal

Bennington Review

Bilingual Review

Black American Literature Forum

Blackbird

Black Rooster

Black Scholar
Black Sparrow
Black Warrior Review
Blackwells Press
Bloom
Bloomsbury Review
Blue Cloud Quarterly
Blue Unicorn
Blue Wind Press
Bluefish
BOA Editions
Bomb
Bookslinger Editions
Boston Review
Boulevard
Boxspring
Bridge
Bridges
Brown Journal of Arts
Burning Deck Press
Caliban
California Quarterly
Callaloo
Calliope
Calliopea Press
Calyx
The Canary
Canto
Capra Press
Caribbean Writer
Carolina Quarterly
Cedar Rock
Center
Chariton Review
Charnel House
Chattahoochee Review
Chautauqua Literary Journal
Chelsea
Chicago Review
Chouteau Review
Chowder Review
Cimarron Review
Cincinnati Poetry Review

City Lights Books
Cleveland State Univ. Poetry Ctr.
Clown War
CoEvolution Quarterly
Cold Mountain Press
Colorado Review
Columbia: A Magazine of Poetry and
    Prose
Confluence Press
Confrontation
Conjunctions
Connecticut Review
Copper Canyon Press
Cosmic Information Agency
Countermeasures
Counterpoint
Crawl Out Your Window
Crazyhorse
Crescent Review
Cross Cultural Communications
Cross Currents
Crosstown Books
Crowd
Cue
Cumberland Poetry Review
Curbstone Press
Cutbank
Dacotah Territory
Daedalus
Dalkey Archive Press
Decatur House
December
Denver Quarterly
Desperation Press
Dogwood
Domestic Crude
Doubletake
Dragon Gate Inc.
Dreamworks
Dryad Press
Duck Down Press
Durak
East River Anthology

Eastern Washington University Press

Ellis Press

Empty Bowl

Epoch

Ergo!

Evansville Review

Exquisite Corpse

Faultline

Fence

Fiction

Fiction Collective

Fiction International

Field

Fine Madness

Firebrand Books

Firelands Art Review

First Intensity

Five Fingers Review

Five Points Press

Five Trees Press

The Formalist

Fourth Genre

Frontiers: A Journal of Women Studies

Fugue

Gallimaufry

Genre

The Georgia Review

Gettysburg Review

Ghost Dance

Gibbs-Smith

Glimmer Train

Goddard Journal

David Godine, Publisher

Graham House Press

Grand Street

Granta

Graywolf Press

Great River Review

Green Mountains Review

Greenfield Review

Greensboro Review

Guardian Press

Gulf Coast

Hanging Loose

Hard Pressed

Harvard Review

Hayden's Ferry Review

Hermitage Press

Heyday

Hills

Hollyridge Press

Holmgangers Press

Holy Cow!

Home Planet News

Hudson Review

Hungry Mind Review

Icarus

Icon

Idaho Review

Iguana Press

Image

Indiana Review

Indiana Writes

Intermedia

Intro

Invisible City

Inwood Press

Iowa Review

Ironwood

Jam To-day

The Journal

Jubilat

The Kanchenjuga Press

Kansas Quarterly

Kayak

Kelsey Street Press

Kenyon Review

Kestrel

Latitudes Press

Laughing Waters Press

Laurel Poetry Collective

Laurel Review

L'Epervier Press

Liberation

Linquis

Literal Latté

Literary Imagination
The Literary Review
The Little Magazine
Living Hand Press
Living Poets Press
Logbridge-Rhodes
Louisville Review
Lowlands Review
Lucille
Lynx House Press
Lyric
The MacGuffin
Magic Circle Press
Malahat Review
Mānoa
Manroot
Many Mountains Moving
Marlboro Review
Massachusetts Review
McSweeney's
Meridian
Mho & Mho Works
Micah Publications
Michigan Quarterly
Mid-American Review
Milkweed Editions
Milkweed Quarterly
The Minnesota Review
Mississippi Review
Mississippi Valley Review
Missouri Review
Montana Gothic
Montana Review
Montemora
Moon Pony Press
Mount Voices
Mr. Cogito Press
MSS
Mudfish
Mulch Press
Nada Press
National Poetry Review
Nebraska Review

New America
New American Review
New American Writing
The New Criterion
New Delta Review
New Directions
New England Review
New England Review and Bread Loaf
    Quarterly
New Issues
New Letters
New Orleans Review
New Virginia Review
New York Quarterly
New York University Press
Nimrod
9 × 9 Industries
Ninth Letter
Noon
North American Review
North Atlantic Books
North Dakota Quarterly
North Point Press
Northeastern University Press
Northern Lights
Northwest Review
Notre Dame Review
O. ARS
O. Blēk
Obsidian
Obsidian II
Ocho
Oconee Review
October
Ohio Review
Old Crow Review
Ontario Review
Open City
Open Places
Orca Press
Orchises Press
Oregon Humanities
Orion

Other Voices
Oxford American
Oxford Press
Oyez Press
Oyster Boy Review
Painted Bride Quarterly
Painted Hills Review
Palo Alto Review
Paris Press
Paris Review
Parkett
Parnassus: Poetry in Review
Partisan Review
Passages North
Pebble Lake Review
Penca Books
Pentagram
Penumbra Press
Pequod
Persea: An International Review
Perugià Press
Pipedream Press
Pitcairn Press
Pitt Magazine
Pleiades
Ploughshares
Poet and Critic
Poet Lore
Poetry
Poetry Atlanta Press
Poetry East
Poetry Ireland Review
Poetry Northwest
Poetry Now
Post Road
Prairie Schooner
Prescott Street Press
Press
Promise of Learnings
Provincetown Arts
A Public Space
Puerto Del Sol
Quaderni Di Yip

Quarry West
The Quarterly
Quarterly West
Raccoon
Rainbow Press
Raritan: A Quarterly Review
Rattle
Red Cedar Review
Red Clay Books
Red Dust Press
Red Earth Press
Red Hen Press
Release Press
Republic of Letters
Review of Contemporary Fiction
Revista Chicano-Riquena
Rhetoric Review
Rivendell
River Styx
River Teeth
Rowan Tree Press
Runes
Russian *Samizdat*
Salmagundi
San Marcos Press
Sarabande Books
Sea Pen Press and Paper Mill
Seal Press
Seamark Press
Seattle Review
Second Coming Press
Semiotext(e)
Seneca Review
Seven Days
The Seventies Press
Sewanee Review
Shankpainter
Shantih
Shearsman
Sheep Meadow Press
Shenandoah
A Shout In the Street
Sibyl-Child Press

Side Show
Small Moon
Smartish Pace
The Smith
Snake Nation Review
Solo
Solo 2
Some
The Sonora Review
Southern Poetry Review
Southern Review
Southwest Review
Speakeasy
Spectrum
Spillway
The Spirit That Moves Us
St. Andrews Press
Story
Story Quarterly
Streetfare Journal
Stuart Wright, Publisher
Sulfur
The Sun
Sun & Moon Press
Sun Press
Sunstone
Sycamore Review
Tamagwa
Tar River Poetry
Teal Press
Telephone Books
Telescope
Temblor
The Temple
Tendril
Texas Slough
Third Coast
13th Moon
THIS
Thorp Springs Press
Three Rivers Press
Threepenny Review
Thunder City Press

Thunder's Mouth Press
Tia Chucha Press
Tikkun
Tin House
Tombouctou Books
Toothpaste Press
Transatlantic Review
Triplopia
TriQuarterly
Truck Press
Tupelo Press
Turnrow
Undine
Unicorn Press
University of Chicago Press
University of Georgia Press
University of Illinois Press
University of Iowa Press
University of Massachusetts Press
University of North Texas Press
University of Pittsburgh Press
University of Wisconsin Press
University Press of New England
Unmuzzled Ox
Unspeakable Visions of the Individual
Vagabond
Verse
Vignette
Virginia Quarterly Review
Volt
Wampeter Press
Washington Writers Workshop
Water-Stone
Water Table
West Branch
Western Humanities Review
Westigan Review
White Pine Press
Wickwire Press
Willow Springs
Wilmore City
Witness
Word Beat Press

Word-Smith

World Literature Today

Wormwood Review

Writers Forum

Xanadu

Yale Review

Yardbird Reader

Yarrow

Y'Bird

Zeitgeist Press

Zoetrope: All-Story

ZYZZYVA

CONTRIBUTING SMALL PRESSES FOR PUSHCART PRIZE XXXII

A

Abyss & Apex, 7635 Jefferson Hwy., Baton Rouge, LA 70809
The Adirondack Review, 305 Keyes Ave., Watertown, NY 13601
Agni, Boston Univ., 236 Bay State Rd., Boston, MA 02215
Akashic Books, P.O. Box 1456, New York, NY 10009
Alaska Quarterly Review, Univ. of Alaska, 3211 Providence Dr., Anchorage, AK 99508
Alice James Books, 238 Main St., Farmington, ME 04938
All Nations Press, P.O. Box 601, White Marsh, VA 23183
The American Journal of Poetry, P.O. Box 250, Chesterfield, MO 63006
American Letters & Commentary, 850 Park Ave., Ste. 5B, New York, NY 10021
American Poetry Journal, P.O. Box 4041, Felton, CA 95108
American Poetry Review, 117 S. 17th St. Ste 910, Philadelphia, PA 19103
The American Scholar, 1606 New Hampshire Ave., NW, Washington, DC 20009
Ancient Paths, P.O. Box 7505, Fairfax Station, VA 22039
Anhinga Press, P.O. Box 10595, Tallahassee, FL 32302
Another Chicago Magazine, 3709 N. Kenmore, Chicago, IL 60613
Antietam Review, 14 W. Washington St., Hagerstown, MD 21740
Antioch Review, P.O. Box 148, Yellow Springs, OH 45387
Antrim House, 21 Goodrich Rd., Simsbury, CT 06070
Apex Publications, 4629 Riverman Way, Lexington, KY 40515
Apogee Press, P.O. Box 8177, Berkeley, CA 94707
Arctos Press, P.O. Box 401, Sausalito, CA 94966
Arizona Literary Magazine, P.O. Box 89857, Phoenix, AZ 85080
Arkansas Literary Forum, Henderson State Univ., Box 7601, Arkadelphia, AR 71999
Arkansas Review, P.O. Box 1890, Arkansas State Univ., State University, AR 72467
Arriviste Press, Inc., 2193 Commonwealth Ave., Boston, MA 02135
Arsenic Lobster, 1608 S. Paulina St., Chicago, IL 60608
Artemesia Publishing, P.O. Box 6508, Rocky Mount, NC 27802
Artful Dodge, English Dept., College of Wooster, Wooster, OH 44691
Arts & Letters, Georgia College & State Univ., Campus Box 89, Milledgeville, GA 31061
Asian American Writers' Workshop, 16 West 32nd St., Ste. 10A, New York, NY 10001

The Aurorean, P.O. Box 187, Farmington, ME 04938

Autumn House Press, 87 1/2 Westwood St., Pittsburgh, PA 15211

B

Backwards City Review, P.O. Box 41317, Greensboro, NC 27404

Backwater Press, 3502 N. 52nd St., Omaha, NE 68104

Ballyhoo Stories, 18 Willoughby Ave., #3. Brooklyn, NY 11205

The Baltimore Review, P.O. Box 36418, Towson, MD 21286

Barbaric Yawp, 3700 County Route 24, Russell, NY 13684

Barrelhouse, 3500 Woodridge Ave., Wheaton, MD 20902

Barrow Street, P.O. Box 1831. New York, NY 10156

Bayeux Arts, 4712 Bayard St., Pittsburgh, PA 15213

Bellevue Literary Review, Dept. of Medicine, NYU School of Medicine, 550 First Ave., OBV-612, NY, NY 10016

Bellowing Ark Press, P.O. Box 55564, Shoreline, WA 98155

Beloit Poetry Journal, P.O. Box 151, Farmington, ME 04938

Birch Book Press, P.O. Box 81, Delhi, NY 13753

BkMk Press, Univ. of Missouri, 5101 Rockhill Rd., Kansas City, MO 64110

Black Clock Magazine, 24700 McBean Pkwy, Valencia, CA 91355

Black Warrior Review, Box 870170, Tuscaloosa, AL 35487

Blackbird, Virginia Commonwealth Univ., Eng. Dept., Richmond, VA 23284

Blue Fifth Review, 267 Lark Meadow Ct., Bluff City, TN 37618

Blue Light Press, 600 Lyon St., San Francisco, CA 94123

Blue Mesa Review, 1108 Calle del Solne, Albuquerque, NM 87106

Blue Tiger Press, 2016 Hwy 67, Dousman, WI 53118

BOA Editions, Ltd., 260 East Ave., Rochester, NY 14604

Boston Review, Bldg. E53. Rm. 407, MIT, Cambridge, MA 02139

Boulevard, 7545 Cromwell Dr., Apt. 2N, St. Louis, MO 63105

Box Turtle Press, 184 Franklin St., New York, NY 10013

Brain, Child, P.O. Box 714, Lexington, VA 24450

Branches, P.O. Box 85394, Seattle, WA 98145

The Briar Cliff Review, P.O. Box 2100, Sioux City, IA 51104

Bridge, 119 N. Peoria, #3d, Chicago, IL 60607

Brilliant Corners, Lycoming College, Williamsport, PA 17701

Bullfight Review, P.O. Box 362, Walnut Creek, CA 94597

The Bunny and the Crocodile Press, 1821 Glade Ct., Annapolis, MD 21403

Byline, P.O. Box 5240, Edmond, OK 73083

C

Caduceus, P.O. Box 9805, New Haven, CT 06536

Cake Train, 174 Carriage Dr., North Huntingdon, PA 15642

Callaloo, Texas A&M Univ., 249 Blocker Bldg., College Station, TX 77843

Calyx, P.O. Box B, 216 SW Madison, Corvallis, OR 97339

The Canary, 512 Clear Lake Rd., Kemah, TX 77565

The Caribbean Writer, Univ. of the Virgin Islands, RR2-10000 Kingshill, St. Croix, U.S. Virgin Islands, 00850

Carve Magazine, P.O. Box 1573, Tallahassee, FL. 32302

Cellar Roots, EMU, Goddard Hall, Ypsilanti, MI 48197

Centennial Press, P.O. Box 170322, Milwaukee, WI 53217

Center, 107 Tate Hall, Columbia, MO 65211

Central Avenue Press, 2132A Central St., #144, Albuquerque, NM 87106

Cezanne's Carrot, P.O. Box 6037, Santa Fe, NM 87502

Chaffin Journal, Eastern Kentucky Univ., 521 Lancaster Ave., Richmond, KY 40475

The Chattahoochee Review, Georgia Perimeter College, 2101 Womack Rd. Dunwoody, GA 30338

Chautauqua Literary Journal, P.O. Box 2039, York Beach, ME 03910

Chelsea, Box 773, Cooper Sta., New York, NY 10276

Chick Flicks, 3108-B Westbury Lake Dr., Charlotte, NC 28269

Chicory Blue Press, Inc., 795 East St., North, Goshen, CT 06756

Cider Press Review, 777 Braddock Lane, Halifax, PA 17032

Cimarron Review, 205 Morrill Hall, Eng. Dept., Oklahoma State Univ., Stillwater, OK 74078

Cincinnati Review, English Dept., Univ. of Cincinnati, P.O. Box 210069, Cincinnati, OH 45221

City Lights Books, 261 Columbus Ave., San Francisco, CA 94133

Cleveland State University Poetry Center, 2121 Euclid Ave., Cleveland, OH 44115

Cloverfield Press, 429 N. Ogden Dr., #1, Los Angeles, CA 90036

Coal City Review. Univ. of Kansas, Lawrence, KS 66045

Coconut Poetry, 2331 Eastway Rd., Decatur, GA 30033

Colorado Review, English Dept., Colorado State Univ., Fort Collins, CO 80523

Concrete Wolf, P.O. Box 730, Amherst, NH 03031

Conjunctions, Bard College, Annandale-on-Hudson, NY 12504

Connecticut Review, English Dept., WCSU, Danbury, CT 06810

Cottonwood, Univ. of Kansas, Rm. 400, Kansas Union, Lawrence, KS 66045

Crab Creek Review, P.O. Box 840, Vashon Island, WA 98070

Crackpot Press, 10915 Bluffside Dr., #132, Studio City, CA 91604

Cranky Literary Journal, 322 10th Ave. E, #C-5, Seattle, WA 98102

Crazyhorse, English Dept., Univ. of Charleston, 66 George St., Charleston, SC 29424

Cream City Review, English Dept., Univ. of Milwaukee, Milwaukee, WI 53201

Crowd, 341 42nd St., #4, Oakland, CA 94609

Crumpled Press, 477 West 142nd St., #5, New York, NY 10031

Cue, P.O. Box 200, 2509 N. Campbell Ave., Tucson, AZ 85719

The Culture Star Reader, 45 Hudson Ave., #743, Albany, NY 12207

Curbstone Press, 321 Jackson St., Willimantic, CT 06226

Cynic Press, P.O. Box 40691, Philadelphia, PA 19107

D

Dana Literary Society, P.O. Box 3362, Dana Point, CA 92629

DC Books, Box 662, 950 Decarie, Montreal, Que., *CANADA* H4L 4V9

Diner, Box 60676, Greendale Sta., Worcester, MA 01606

The DMQ Review, 16393 Bonnie Lane, Los Gatos, CA 95032

Dogwood, English Dept., Fairfield Univ., Fairfield, CT 06824

Donatello Press, 2508 Stoner Ave., Los Angeles, CA 90025

Dragonfire, 3210 Cherry St., 2nd fl., Philadelphia, PA 19104

The Duck & Herring Co., 279 Josephine St., Atlanta, GA 30307

Dunhill Publishing, 18340 Sonoma Highway, Sonoma, CA 95476

E

Ecotone, 622 Waynich Blvd., #102, Wrightsville Beach, NC 28480

Edgar Magazine, RD Box 5776, San Leon, TX 77539

Edge Publications, P.O. Box 799, Ocean Park, WA 98640

elimae, 1420 R.V., El Paso, TX 79928

Elkhound, Box 1453, Gracie Sta., New York, NY 10028

Emergency Press, 531 West 25th St., New York, NY 10001

Epiphany, 244 East 3rd, New York, NY 10009

Epoch, 251 Goldwin Smith Hall, Cornell Univ., Ithaca, NY 14853

Esopus, 532 LaGuardia Pl., #485, New York, NY 10012

Eureka Literary Magazine, 300 E. College Ave., Eureka, IL 61530

The Evansville Review, 1800 Lincoln Ave., Evansville, IN 47722

Event, Douglas College, P.O. Box 2503, New Westminster, B.C. *CANADA* V3L 5B2

F

F Magazine, Columbia College, 600 S. Michigan Ave., Chicago, IL 60605

Facets: A Literary Magazine, P.O. Box 380915, Cambridge, MA 02238

Failbetter, 40 Montgomery Pl., #2, Brooklyn, NY 11215

Fairy Tale Review, English Dept., Univ. of Alabama, Tuscaloosa, AL 35487

Fiction International, San Diego State Univ., San Diego, CA 92182

Field, Oberlin College, 50 N. Professor St., Oberlin, OH 44074

Finishing Line Press, P.O. Box 1626, Georgetown, KY 40324

Firewheel Editions, 181 White St., Danbury, CT 06810

The First Line, P.O. Box 250382, Plano, TX 75025

Fithian Press, P.O. Box 2790, McKinleyville, CA 95519

5 AM, Box 205, Spring Church, PA 15686

Five Fingers Review, PO Box 4, San Leandro, CA 94577

Five Points, Georgia State Univ., P.O. Box 3999, Atlanta, GA 30302

flashquake, P.O. Box 2154, Albany, NY 12220

Floating Bridge Press, P.O. Box 18814, Seattle, WA 98118

Florida Review, UCF, P.O. Box 161400, Orlando, FL 32816

Flume Press, English Dept., California State Univ., Chico, CA 95929

Focus, English Dept., Spelman College, 350 Spelman La., SW, Atlanta, GA 30314

Fourteen Hills, San Francisco State Univ., 1600 Holloway Ave., San Francisco, CA 94132

Fourth Genre, 285 Bessey Hall, Michigan State Univ., East Lansing, MI 48825

Free Lunch, P.O. Box 717, Glenview, IL 60025

Free Verse, M233 Marsh Rd., Marshfield, WI 54449

Fresh Boiled Peanuts, P.O. Box 43194, Cincinnati, OH 45243

Frigg, 9036 Evanston Ave., N, Seattle, WA 98103

Frith Press, P.O. Box 161236, Sacramento, CA 95816

Frostproof Review, 3190 NW Blvd., Columbus, OH 43221

G

Gargoyle, 3819 13th St., W, Arlington, VA 22201

Garrett County Press, 614 S. 8th St., #373, Philadelphia, PA 19147

A Gathering of the Tribes, P.O. Box 20693, New York, NY 10009

Georgia Review, Gilbert Hall, Univ. of Georgia, Athens, GA 30602

The Gettysburg Review, Gettysburg College, Gettysburg, PA 17325

Ghost Road Press, 5303 E. Evans Ave., #309, Denver, CO 80222

Gin Bender, P.O. Box 150932, Lufkin, TX 75915

Givall Press, LLC, P.O. Box 3812, Arlington, VA 22203

Gloucester Spoken Art, 2066 Kings Grove Crescent, Gloucester, Ont., *CANADA* K1J 6G1

Gobshite Quarterly, P.O. Box 11346, Portland, OR 97211

Grayson Books, P.O. Box 270549, West Hartford, CT 06127

The Great American Poetry Show, P.O. Box 69506, West Hollywood, CA 90069

Great River Review, Anderson Center, P.O. Box 406, Red Wing, MN 55066

Green Hills Literary Lantern, 100 E. Normal, Truman State Univ., Kirksville, MO 63501

Green Mountains Review, Johnson State College, Johnson, VT 05656

The Greensboro Review, UNCG, P.O. Box 26170, Greensboro, NC 27402

The Grove Review, 1631 NE Broadway, PMB#137, Portland, OR 97232
Gulf Coast, English Dept., Univ. of Houston, Houston, TX 77204

H

Hanging Loose Press, 231 Wyckoff St., Brooklyn, NY 11217
Harp-String Poetry Journal, Box 640387, Beverly Hills, FL 14464
Harper's Ferry Review, Arizona State Univ., P.O. Box 87502, Tempe, AZ 85287
Harpur Palate, English Dept., Binghamton Univ., Binghamton, NY 13902
Harvard Review, Lamont Library, Level 5, Harvard Univ., Cambridge, MA 02138
Haunted Rowboat Press, 162 Longley Rd., Madison, ME 04950
The Healing Muse, Upstate Medical Univ., 750 E. Adams St., Syracuse, NY 13210
Heliotrope, P.O. Box 456, Shady, NY 12409
Historical Society of Ocean Grove, P.O. Box 446, Ocean Grove, NJ 07756
H-NGM-N Press, Northwestern State Univ., Natchitoches, LA 71497
Hobart: A Literary Journal, P.O. Box 1658, Ann Arbor, MI 48103
Hollins Critic, Hollins Univ., Roanoke, VA 24020
Hollyride Press, PO Box 2872, Venice, CA 90294
Home Planet News, P.O. Box 455, High Falls, NY 12440
Hopewell Publications, LLC, P.O. Box 11, Titusville, NJ 08560
Hotel Amerika, Ohio Univ., 360 Ellis Hall, Athens, OH 45701
The Hudson Review, 684 Park Ave., New York, NY 10021
Hunger Mountain, Vermont College, 36 College St., Montpelier, VT 05602

I

Ibbetson Street, 25 School St., Somerville, MA 02143
The Iconoclast, 165 Amazon Rd., Mohegan Lake, NY 10547
Idaho Review, English Dept., Boise State Univ., Boise, ID 83725
Illuminations, English Dept., College of Charleston, 66 George St., Charleston, SC 29424
Illya's Honey, P.O. Box 700865, Dallas, TX 75370
Image, 3307 Third Ave., W, Seattle, WA 98119
Indiana Review, 1020 E. Kirkwood Ave., Bloomington, IN 47405
Inkwell, Manhattanville College, 2900 Purchase St., Purchase, NY 10577
Invisible Insurrection, 925 NW Hoyt St., #231, Portland, OR 97209
The Iowa Review, Univ. of Iowa, Iowa City, IA 52242

J

Jabberwock Review, English Dept., Drawer E, Mississippi State, MS 39763
Jewish Women's Literary Annual, 820 2nd Ave., New York, NY 10017
The Journal, English Dept., Ohio State Univ., Columbus, OH 43210
Journal of New Jersey Poets, CO. College of Morris, 214 Center Grove Rd., Randplph, NJ 07869
Jubilat, English Dept., Univ. of Massachusetts, Amherst, MA 01003

K

Karamu, English Dept., Eastern Illinois Univ., 600 Lincoln Ave., Charleston, IL 61920
Kelsey Review, P.O. Box B, Trenton, NJ 08690

The Kenyon Review, 104 College Dr., Gambier, OH 43022
Killing the Buddha, 1986 McAfee Rd., Decatur, GA 30032
The King's English, 3114 NE 47th Ave., Portland, OR 97213
Kitchen Sink Magazine, 5245 College Ave, #301, Oakland, CA 94618
Knock, Antioch Univ., 2326 Sixth Ave., Seattle, WA 98121
Kyoto Journal, Minamigoshomachi, Okazaki-Ku, Kyoto 606-8334, *JAPAN*

L

Lake Effect, 5091 Station Rd., Erie, PA 16563
Land-Grant College Review, P.O. Box 1164, New York, NY 10159
Laurel Poetry Collective, 1168 Laurel Ave., St. Paul, MN 55104
Licking River Review, Nunn Dr., Highland Heights, KY 41099
Like Water Burning Press, 109 Mira Mar Ave., #301, Long Beach, CA 90803
Lillies and Cannonballs Review, P.O. Box 702, Bowling Green Sta., New York, NY 10274
Lily Literary Review, P.O. Box 76, Nucla, CO 81424
LIT Magazine, 66 West 12th St., Rm. 514, New York, NY 10011
Lorraine & James, 3727 W. Magnolia Blvd., Box 406, Burbank, CA 91505
Louisiana State University Press, P.O. Box 25053, Baton Rouge, LA 70894
The Louisville Review, Spalding Univ., 851 S. Fourth St., Louisville, KY 40203
Lyric Poetry Review, P.O. Box 2494, Bloomington, IN 47402

M

Mad Hatter's Review, 105 West 13th St., New York, NY 10011
The Malahat Review, Univ. of Victoria, P.O. Box 1700, Sta. CSC, Victoria BC V8W 2Y2 *CANADA*
Mandorla, Illinois State Univ., Campus Box 4241, Normal, IL 61790
The Manhattan Review, 440 Riverside Dr., #38, New York, NY 10027
Manic D Press, 250 Banks St., San Francisco, CA 94110
Manoa, English Dept., Univ. of Hawaii, Honolulu, HI 96822
Margin, 321 High School Rd., NE, PMB #204, Bainbridge Island, WA 98110
Marsh Hawk Press, P.O. Box 206, East Rockaway, NY 11518
Marsh River Editions, M233 Marsh Rd., Marshfield, WI 54449
The Massachusetts Review, Univ. of Massachusetts, South College, A103770, Amherst, MA 01003
McSweeney's, 826 Valencia St., San Francisco, CA 94110
The Means, P.O. Box 183246, Shelby Township, MI 48318
Memorious. Org, 60 Winslow Ave., Somerville, MA 02144
Mercer University Press, 1400 Coleman Ave., Macon, GA 31207
Me Three Literary Journal, 101 Lafayette Ave., Brooklyn, NY 11217
Micah Publications, Inc., 255 Humphrey St., Marblehead, MA 01945
Michigan Quarterly Review, 915 E. Washington St., Ann Arbor, MI 48109
Michigan State University Press, 1405 S. Harrison Rd., Ste. 25, East Lansing, MI 48823
Mid-American Review, English Dept., Bowling Green State Univ., Bowling Green, OH 43403
Mindfire Renewed, 2518 Fruitland Dr., Bremerton, WA 98310
Mind Prints, 800 S. College Dr., Santa Maria, CA 93454
The Minnesota Review, English Dept., Carnegie Mellon Univ., Pittsburgh, PA 15213
MiPOesias Magazine, 4601 SW 94 Ct., Miami, FL 33165
Mississippi Review, Univ. of So. Mississippi, Box 5144, Hattiesburg, MS 39406
Missouri Review, Univ. of Missouri, 1507 Hillcrest Hall, Columbia, MO 65211
The Modern Review, RPO P.O. Box 32659, Richmond Hill, Ont. L4C OA2 *CANADA*
Moon in Blue Water, 430 M St., SW-N600, Washington, DC 20024
Moondance, P.O. Box 92-3713, Sylmar, CA 91342
Multicultural Books, 6311 Gilbert Rd., Richmond, BC V7C 3V7 *CANADA*

N

N + 1, PO Box 20688, Park West Station, NY 10025

Nassau Review, Nassau Community College, 2 Education Dr., Garden City, NY 11596

The National Poetry Review, P.O. Box 4041, Felton, CA 95018

Natural Bridge, English Dept., Univ. of Missouri, St. Louis, MO 63121

New England Review, Middlebury College, Middlebury, VT 05753

The New Hampshire Review, P.O. Box 322, Nashua, NH 03061

New Issues Poetry & Prose, WMU, 1903 W. Michigan Ave., Kalamazoo, MI 49008

New Letters, see BkMk Press

New Orleans Review, Box 195, Loyola Univ., New Orleans, LA 70118

New Orphic Review, 706 Mill St., Nelson, B.C., V1L 4S5, *CANADA*

The New Renaissance, 26 Heath Rd., #11, Arlington, MA 02474

New York Stories, 218 Gale Hill Rd., East Chatham, NY 12060

Night Train, 212 Bellingham Ave., #2, Revere, MA 02151

Ninth Letter, English Dept., Univ. of Illinois, 608 S. Wright St., Urbana, IL 61801

Noon, 1324 Lexington Ave., PMB 298, New York, NY 10128

North American Review, Univ. of Northern Iowa, Cedar Falls, IA 50614

North Dakota Quarterly, P.O. Box 7209, Univ. of North Dakota, Grand Forks, ND 58202

Northwest Review, 369 PLC, Univ. of Oregon, Eugene, OR 97403

No Tell Motel, 11436 Fairway Dr., Reston, VA 20150

Not One of Us, 12 Curtis Rd., Natick, MA 01760

Notre Dame Review, English Dept., Univ. of Notre Dame, Notre Dame, IN 46556

O

Ocho, 604 Vale St., Bloomington, IL 61701

OFF the Coast, P.O. Box 205, Bristol, ME 04539

Old Mountain Press, 2542 S. Edgewater Dr., Fayetteville, NC 28303

Onearth, 40 West 20th St., New York, NY 10011

One Story, 425 3rd St., Apt. 2, Brooklyn, NY 11215

One Trick Pony, P.O. Box 11186, Philadelphia, PA 19136

Ontario Review, 9 Honey Brook Dr., Princeton, NJ 08540

Open Minds Quarterly, 630 Kirkwood Dr., Bldg. 1, Sudbury, Ont. P3E 1X3 *CANADA*

Open Spaces Publications, Inc., PMB 134, 6327-C SW Capitol Hwy., Portland, OR 97239

Opium Magazine, 40 East Third St., Ste. #8, New York, NY 10003

Orbis, 17 Greenlaw Ave., West Kirby, UK

Order and Decorum, P.O. Box 1051, Carlisle, PA 17013

Orion, 187 Main St., Great Barrington, MA 01230

Osiris, P.O. Box 297, Deerfield, MA 01342

Other, 584 Castro St., #674, San Francisco, CA 94114

Other Voices, English Dept., Univ. of Illinois, 601 S. Morgan St., Chicago, IL 60607

Oxford American, 201 Donaghen Ave., Conway, AR 72035

Owen Wister Review, 302 Carthell Rd., Laramie, WY 82070

Oyez Review, Roosevelt Univ., 430 S. Michigan Ave., Chicago, IL 60605

P

Pacific Review, California State Univ., San Bernardino, CA 92407

Palo Alto Review, Palo Alto College, 1400 W. Villaret Blvd., San Antonio, TX 78224

The Paper Journey, P.O. Box 1575, Wake Forest, NC 27588

Paper Street Press, P.O. Box 14786, Pittsburgh, PA 15234

Paradox, P.O. Box 22897, Brooklyn, NY 11202

Parakeet, 115 Roosevelt Ave, Syracuse, NY 13210

The Paris Review, 62 White St., New York, NY 10013

Parlor Press, 816 Robinson St., West Lafayette, IN 47906

Parnassus: Poetry in Review, 205 W. 89th St, #8F, New York, NY 10024

Passages North, N. Michigan Univ., Marquette, MI, 49855

Pathwise Press, P.O. Box 178, Erie, PA 16512

P.A.W. Magazine, 2720 St. Paul St., 2F, Baltimore, MD 21218

Pearl, 3030 E. Second St., Long Beach, CA 90803

Pebble Lake Review, 15318 Pebble Lake Dr., Houston, TX 77095

Penumbra, P.O. Box 15995, Tallahassee, FL 32317

Perugia Press, P.O. Box 60364, Florence, MA 01063

Phantasmagoria, 3300 Century Ave. North, White Bear Lake, MN 55110

Phoebe, George Mason Univ., 4400 Univ. Dr., Fairfax, VA 22030

Plan B Press, 3412 Terrace Dr., #1731, Alexandria, VA 22302

Pleiades, English Dept., Central Missouri State Univ., Warrensburg, MO 64093

Ploughshares, Emerson College, 120 Boylston St., Boston, MA 02116

PMS, 1530 3rd Ave. S, Birmingham, AL 35294

Poems and Plays, English Dept., Middle Tennessee State Univ., Murfreesboro, TN 37132

poetic diversity, 6028 Comey Ave., Los Angeles, CA 90034

Poetry, 444 N. Michigan Ave., Chicago, IL 60611

Poetry Midwest, Johnson Co. Community College, 12345 College Blvd., Overland Park, KS 66210

Poetry Miscellany, English Dept., Univ. of Tennessee, Chattanooga, TN 37403

Poetry Project, St. Mark's Church in-the-Bowery, 131 E. 10th St., New York, NY 10003

Poetry West, P.O. Box 2413, Colorado Springs, CO 80901

Pool, P.O. Box 49738, Los Angeles, CA 98849

Post Road, P.O. Box 400951, Cambridge, MA 02140

Prairie Schooner, Univ. of Nebraska, P.O. Box 880334, Lincoln, NE 68588

Press 53, P.O. Box 30314, Winston Salem, NC 27180

Pretty Things Press, P.O. Box 55, Point Reyes, CA 94956

Prism International, Univ. of British Columbia, 1866 Main Mall, Vancouver, B.C., *CANADA* V6T 1Z1

Provincetown Arts, 650 Commercial St., Provincetown, MA 02657

A Public Space, 323 Dean St., Brooklyn, NY 11217

Puckerbrush Press, 76 Main St., Orono, ME 04473

Puerto del Sol, English Dept., New Mexico State Univ., Las Cruces, NM 88003

Q

Quarterly West, 255 S. Central Campus Dr., Salt Lake City, UT 84112

R

Raritan, 31 Mine St., New Brunswick, NJ 08903

Rattle, 12411 Ventura Blvd., Studio City, CA 91604

Red Hen Press, P.O. Box 3537, Granada Hills, CA 91394

Redactions: Poetry & Poetics, 24 College St., Apt. 1, Brooklyn, NY 14420

Redivider, Emerson College, 120 Boylston St., Boston, MA 02116

Releasing Times, 6077 Far Hills Ave., Centerville, OH 45459

Republic of Letters, 120 Cushing Ave., Boston, MA 02125

Rhapsoidia, 6570 Jewel St., Riverside, CA 92509

Rhino, P.O. Box 591, Evanston, IL 60204

Rio Nuevo Publishers, 451 N. Bonita Ave. Tucson, AZ 85745

River City, English Dept., Univ. of Memphis, Memphis, TN 38152

River City Publishing, 1719 Mulberry St., Montgomery, AL 36106
River Teeth, English Dept., Ashland Univ., Ashland, OH 44805
Rogue Scholars Press, 228 East 25th St., New York, NY 10010
The Rose & Thorn, 3 Diamond Ct., Montebello, NY 10901
Runes, PO Box 401, Sausalito, CA 94966

S

Salamander, English Dept., Suffolk Univ., 41 Temple St., Boston, MA 02215
Salmagundi, Skidmore College, Saratoga Springs, NY 12866
Salt Flats Annual, P.O. Box 2381, Layton, UT 84041
Salt Hill, English Dept., Syracuse Univ., Syracuse, NY 13244
Santa Monica Review, Santa Monica College, 1900 Pico Blvd., Santa Monica, CA 90405
Sarabande Books, Inc., 2234 Dundee Rd., Ste. 200, Louisville, KY 40205
Saranac Review, 101 Broad St., Plattsburgh, NY 12901
Schuylkill Valley Journal, 240 Golf Hills Rd., Havertown, PA 19083
Scissor Press, P.O. Box 382, Ludlow, VT 05149
Seems, Lakeland College, P.O. Box 359, Sheboygan, WI 53082
Sensations Magazine, P.O. Box 90, Glen Ridge, NJ 07028
Shenandoah, Mattingly House, Washington & Lee Univ., Lexington, VA 24450
Silk Label Books, P.O. Box 700, Unionville, NY 10988
Skidrow Penthouse, 44 Corners Rd., Blairstown, NJ 07825
Slipstream, P.O. Box 2071, Niagara Falls, NY 14301
Smartish Pace, PO Box 22161, Baltimore, MD 21203
Small Beer Press, 176 Prospect Ave., Northampton, MA 01060
Small Spiral Notebook, 172 5th Ave., #104, Brooklyn, NY 11217
Smokelong Quarterly, 239 Corby Pl., Castle Rock, CO 80108
Snake Nation Review, 110 #2 West Force, Valdosta, GA 31601
Somerset Hall Press, 416 Commonwealth Ave., Ste. 117, Boston, MA 02215
Sonora Review, English Dept., Univ. of Arizona, Tucson, AZ 85721
So To Speak, George Mason Univ., 4400 Univ. Dr., MSN 206, Fairfax, VA 22030
Soundings East, English Dept., Salem State College, Salem, MA 01970
The Southeast Review, English Dept., Florida State Univ., Tallahassee, FL 32306
Southern Arts Journal, P.O. Box 13739, Greensboro, NC 27415
Southern Poetry Review, 11935 Abercorn St., Savannah, GA 31419
The Southern Review, Louisiana State Univ., Baton Rouge, LA 70803
Southwest Review, Southern Methodist Univ., P.O. Box 750374, Dallas, TX 75275
Speakeasy, 1011 Washington Ave. S, Ste. 200, Minneapolis, MN 55415
Spoon River Poetry Review, Illinois State Univ., Campus Box 4241, Normal, IL 61790
Spuytenduyvil, 42 St. John's Place, Brooklyn, NY 11217
Starcherone Books, P.O. Box 303, Buffalo, NY 14201
Stirring, 501 S. Elm St., #1, Champaign, IL 61820
Story Circle Journal, 5802 Wynona Ave., Austin, TX 78756
Story Quarterly, 431 Sheridan Rd., Kenilworth, IL 60043
Story South, 898 Chelsea Ave., Bexley OH 43209
The Storyteller Magazine, 2441 Washington Rd., Maynard, AR 72444
The Strange Fruit, 300 Lenora St., #250, Seattle, WA 98121
Streetlight, P.O. Box 259, Charlottesville, VA 22902
The Summerset Review, 25 Summerset Dr., Smithtown, NY 11787
The Sun, 107 N. Roberson St., Chapel Hill, NC 27516
Sun Rising Books, 724 Felix St., St. Joseph, MO 64501
Swan Scythe Press, 2052 Calaveras Ave., Davis, CA 95616
Sweet Annie Press, 7750 Hwy F-24W, Baxter, IA 50028
Swivel Magazine, P.O. Box 17958, Seattle, WA 98107

T

Tampa Review, 401 Kennedy Blvd., Tampa, FL 33606

Texas Poetry Journal, P.O. Box 90635, Austin, TX 78709

Third Coast, English Dept., WMU, Kalamazoo, MI 49008

32 Poems, P.O. Box 5824, Hyattsville, MD 20782

three candles, 5470 132nd Ln, Savage, MN 55378

Threepenny Review, P.O. Box 9131, Berkeley, CA 94709

Tikkun, 2342 Shattuck Ave., #1200, Berkeley, CA 94704

Timber Creek Review, 8969 UNCG Sta., Greensboro, NC 27413

Tin House, 2601 NW Thurman St., Portland, OR 97210

Toadlily Press, Box 2, Chappaqua, NY 10514

Traprock Books, 1330 E. 25th Ave., Eugene, OR 97403

Travelers' Tales, 350 Stonegate Lane, Front Royal, VA 22630

Triple Tree Publishing, P.O. Box 5684, Eugene, OR 97405

Triplopia, 6816 Mt. Vernon Ave., Salisbury, MD 21804

TriQuarterly, Northwestern Univ. Press, 629 Noyes St., Evanston, IL 60208

Tryst Poetry, 3521 Longfellow Ave., Minneapolis, MN 55407

Tupelo Press, P.O. Box 539, Dorset, VT 05251

Turnrow, English Dept., Univ. of Louisiana, Monroe, LA 71209

U

Underground Voices Magazine, P.O. Box 931671, Los Angeles, CA 90093

University of Chicago Press, 1427 E. 60th St., Chicago, IL 60437

University of Georgia Press, 330 Research Dr., Athens, GA 30602

University of Nevada Press, Reno, NV 89557

University of New Mexico Press, 1601 Randolph Rd, SE, Ste. 2005, Albuquerque, NM 87106

U.S.1 Poets' Cooperative, P.O. Box 127, Kingston, NJ 08528

V

Valley Contemporary Poets, P.O. Box 661614, Los Angeles, CA 90066

Vallum Magazine, P.O. Box 48003, Montreal, Que., H2V 4S8, CANADA

Val Verde Press, 30163 Lexington Dr., Val Verde, CA 91384

Velvet Mafia/Outsider Ink, 201 W. 11th St, Ste. 6E, New York, NY 10014

Verse Libre Quarterly, Box 185, Falls Church, VA 22040

Verse Press, 221 Pine St., #258, Florence, MA 01062

Vestal Review, 2609 Dartmouth Dr., Vestal, NY 13850

Virginia Quarterly Review, One West Range, University of Virginia, Charlotterville, VA 22904

The Vocabula Review, 5A Holbrook Ct., Rockport, MA 01966

The Voice, 8906 Aubrey L. Pkwy, Nine Mile Falls, WA 99026

Vox, P.O. Box 4936, University, MS 38677

W

Water-Stone Review, Hamline Univ., 1536 Hewitt Ave., St. Paul, MN 55104

Wayne State University Press, 4809 Woodward Ave., Detroit, MI 48201

We Press, P.O. Box 436, Allamuchy, NJ 07820

West Branch, Bucknell Univ., Lewisburg, PA 17837

West Wind Review, 1250 Siskiyou Blvd., Ashland, OR 97520

Western Humanities Review, English Dept., Univ. of Utah, Salt Lake City, UT 84112

Whispering Prairie Press, P.O. Box 8342, Prairie Village, KS 66208

Whistling Shade, P.O. Box 7084, St. Paul, MN 55107

White Pelican Review, P.O. Box 7833, Lakeland, FL 33813

White Whiskers Books, 726 Portola Terrace, Los Angeles, CA 90042

Wild Embers Press, 155 Seventh St., Portland, OR 97520

Wildside Press, LLC, 9710 Traville Gateway Dr., #234, Rockville, MD 20850

Willow Review, College of Lake Co., 19351 W. Washington St., Grayslake, IL 60030

Willow Springs, 705 W. First Ave., Spokane, WA 99201

Winged Victory Press, P.O. Box 16730, Chicago, IL 60616

Wings Press, 627 E. Guenther, San Antonio, TX 78210

Witness, Oakland Community College, 27055 Orchard Lake Rd., Farmington Hills, MI 48334

Wolverine Farm Publishing, P.O. Box 814, Fort Collins, CO 80522

Women in the Arts, P.O. Box 2907, Decatur, IL 62524

The Worcester Review, 1 Elkman St., Worcester, MA 01607

World Literature Today, Univ. of Oklahoma, Norman, OK 73019

The Word Works, Inc., P.O. Box 42164, Washington, DC 20015

Words of Wisdom, P.O. Box 16542, Greensboro, NC 27416

Words on Walls, 18348 Coral Chase Dr., Boca Raton, FL 33498

Writer's Chronicle, George Mason Univ., Fairfax, VA 22030

X

Xantippe, P.O. Box 20997, Oakland, CA 94620

Y

Yalobusha Review, Bondurant Hall, Box 1848, University, MS 38677

Yale Review, Yale University, PO Box 208243, New Haven, CT 06520

Z

Zahir Publishing, 315 S. Coast Hwy. 101, Ste. U8, Encinitas, CA 92024

Zoetrope, 916 Kearny St., San Francisco, CA 94133

ZYZZYVA, P.O. Box 590069, San Francisco, CA 94159

THE PUSHCART PRIZE FELLOWSHIPS

The Pushcart Prize Fellowships Inc., a 501 (c) (3) nonprofit corporation, is the endowment for The Pushcart Prize. We also make grants to promising new writers. "Members" donated up to $249 each, "Sponsors" gave between $250 and $999. "Benefactors" donated from $1000 to $4,999. "Patrons" donated $5,000 and more. We are very grateful for these donations. Gifts of any amount are welcome. For information write to the Fellowships at PO Box 380, Wainscott, NY 11975.

Janklow & Nesbit Asso.
Edmund Keeley
Thomas E. Kennedy
Wally Lamb
Gerald Locklin
Thomas Lux
Markowitz, Fenelon and Bank
Elizabeth McKenzie
McSweeney's
Joan Murray
Barbara and Warren Phillips
Hilda Raz
Mary Carlton Swope
Julia Wendell
Eleanor Wilner
Richard Wyatt & Irene Eilers
Anonymous (3)
Betty Adcock
Agni
Carolyn Alessio
Dick Allen
Henry H. Allen
Lisa Alvarez
Jan Lee Ande
Ralph Angel
Antietam Review
Ruth Appelhof
Philip Appleman
Linda Aschbrenner
Renee Ashley
Ausable Press
David Baker
Jim Barnes
Catherine Barnett
Dorothy Barresi
Barrow Street Press
Jill Bart
Ellen Bass
Judith Baumel
Ann Beattie
Madison Smartt Bell
Beloit Poetry Journal
Pinckney Benedict
Andre Bernard
Christopher Bernard
Wendell Berry
Linda Bierds
Stacy Bierlein
Bitter Oleander Press
Mark Blaeuer
Blue Lights Press
Carol Bly
BOA Editions
Deborah Bogen
Susan Bono

Anthony Brandt
James Breeden
Rosellen Brown
Jane Brox
Andrea Hollander Budy
E. S. Bumas
Richard Burgin
Skylar H. Burris
David Caliguiuri
Kathy Callaway
Janine Canan
Henry Carlile
Fran Castan
Chelsea Associates
Marianne Cherry
Phillis M. Choyke
Suzanne Cleary
Joan Connor
John Copenhaven
Dan Corrie
Tricia Currans-Sheehan
Jim Daniels
Thadious Davis
Maija Devine
Sharon Dilworth
Edward J. DiMaio
Kent Dixon
John Duncklee
Elaine Edelman
Renee Edison & Don Kaplan
Nancy Edwards
M.D. Elevitch
Failbetter.com
Irvin Faust
Tom Filer
Susan Firer
Nick Flynn
Stakey Flythe Jr.
Peter Fogo
Linda N. Foster
Fugue
Alice Fulton
Eugene K. Garber
Frank X. Gaspar
A Gathering of the Tribes
Reginald Gibbons
Emily Fox Gordon
Philip Graham
Eamon Grennan
Lee Meitzen Grue
Habit of Rainy Nights
Rachel Hadas
Susan Hahn
Meredith Hall
Harp Strings

Jeffrey Harrison
Lois Marie Harrod
Healing Muse
Lily Henderson
Daniel Henry
Neva Herington
Lou Hertz
William Heyen
Bob Hicok
R. C. Hildebrandt
Kathleen Hill
Edward Hoagland
Daniel Hoffman
Doug Holder
Richard Holinger
Rochelle L. Holt
Richard M. Huber
Brigid Hughes
Lynne Hugo
Illya's Honey
Susan Indigo
Mark Irwin
Beverly A. Jackson
Richard Jackson
David Jauss
Marilyn Johnston
Alice Jones
Journal of New Jersey Poets
Robert Kalich
Julia Kasdorf
Miriam Poli Katsikis
Meg Kearney
Celine Keating
Brigit Kelly
John Kistner
Judith Kitchen
Stephen Kopel
David Kresh
Maxine Kumin
Valerie Laken
Babs Lakey
Maxine Landis
Lane Larson
Dorianne Laux & Joseph Millar
Sydney Lea
Donald Lev
Dana Levin
Gerald Locklin
Rachel Lodin
Radomir Luza, Jr.
Annette Lynch
Elzabeth MacKierman
Elizabeth Macklin
Leah Maines
Mark Manalang
Norma Marder
Jack Marshall

Michael Martone
Tara L. Masih
Dan Masterson
Peter Matthiessen
Alice Mattison
Tracy Mayor
Robert McBrearty
Jane McCafferty
Bob McCrane
Jo McDougall
Sandy McIntosh
James McKean
Roberta Mendel
Didi Menendez
Barbara Milton
Alexander Mindt
Mississippi Review
Martin Mitchell
Roger Mitchell
Jewell Mogan
Patricia Monaghan
Jim Moore
James Morse
William Mulvihill
Carol Muske-Dukes
Edward Mycue
W. Dale Nelson
Daniel Orozco
Other Voices
Pamela Painter
Paris Review
Alan Michael Parker
Ellen Parker
Veronica Patterson
David Pearce
Robert Phillips
Donald Platt
Valerie Polichar
Pool
Jeffrey & Priscilla Potter
Marcia Preston
Eric Puchner
Barbara Quinn
Belle Randall
Martha Rhodes
Nancy Richard
Stacey Richter
Katrina Roberts
Judith R. Robinson
Jessica Roeder
Martin Rosner
Kay Ryan
Sy Safransky
Brian Salchert
James Salter
Sherod Santos
R.A. Sasaki

Valerie Sayers
Alice Schell
Dennis & Loretta Schmitz
Helen Schulman
Philip Schultz
Shenandoah
Peggy Shinner
Vivian Shipley
Joan Silver
John E. Smelcer
Raymond J. Smith
Philip St. Clair
Lorraine Standish
Michael Steinberg
Barbara Stone
Storyteller Magazine
Bill & Pat Strachan
Julie Suk
Sweet Annie Press
Katherine Taylor
Pamela Taylor
Marcelle Thiébaux
Robert Thomas
Andrew Tonkovich
Juanita Torrence-Thompson
William Trowbridge
Martin Tucker

Victoria Valentine
Tino Villanueva
William & Jeanne Wagner
BJ Ward
Susan Oard Warner
Rosanna Warren
Margareta Waterman
Michael Waters
Sandi Weinberg
Andrew Weinstein
Jason Wesco
West Meadow Press
Susan Wheeler
Dara Wier
Ellen Wilbur
Galen Williams
Marie Sheppard Williams
Irene K. Wilson
Steven Wingate
Wings Press
Robert W. Witt
Margo Wizansky
Matt Yurdana
Christina Zawadiwsky
Sander Zulauf
ZYZZYVA

SUSTAINING MEMBERS

Agni
Carolyn Alessio
Dick Allen
Henry Alley
Anonymous
Renee Ashley
Jacob M. Appel
Philip Appleman
Marjorie Appleman
Renee Ashley
Linda Aschbrenner
Ausable Press
David Baker
Jim Barnes
Catherine Barnett
Dorothy Barresi
Ellen Bass
Judith Baumel
Charles Baxter
Ann Beattie
Madison Smartt Bell
Joe David Bellamy
Beloit Poetry Journal
André Bernard
Pinckney Benedict
Linda Bierds
Carol Bly

BOA Editions
Bridgeworks Press
Ethan Burmas
David Caldwell
Steve Cannon
Fran Castan
Siv Cedering
Dan Chaon
Chelsea Editions
Suzanne Cleary
Martha Collins
Joan Connor
Bernard Conners
Tricia Currans-Sheehan
Ben Davidson
Kent Dixon
Dan Dolgin
Elaine Edelman
Clive Edgarton
Nancy Edwards
Dallas Ernst
Finishing Line Press
Sharon & Ben Fountain
Gina Frangello
Alan Furst
Eugene Garber
Loraine Gardner

CONTRIBUTORS' NOTES

PAUL ALLEN teaches at the College of Charleston in South Carolina. In 2005 FootHills published his chapbook *His Longing: The Small Penis Oratorio.*

RICK BASS is the author of many books of fiction and non-fiction, most recently the story collection *The Lives of Rocks* (Houghton-Mifflin, 2006). He lives in Montana's Yaak Valley.

MARVIN BELL is now retired from the Iowa Writers Workshop and teaches at Pacific University. His poem selected here is from *Mars Being Red*, just published by Copper Canyon Press.

PINCKNEY BENEDICT grew up on his family's dairy farm in southern West Virginia. His third story collection and second novel are forthcoming from Nan A. Talese/Doubleday.

ROBERT BLY has published many books of poetry, most recently from Eastern Washington University Press and HarperCollins. He lives in Minneapolis.

LAURE-ANNE BOSSELAAR won the Isabella Gardner Prize for Poetry in 2001. Her third collection, *A New Hunger*, was recently published by Ausable Press.

JOHN BRADLEY is the author of *Terrestrial Music* (Curbstone Press). He teaches at Northern Illinois University.

ROBERT OLEN BUTLER won the Pulitzer Prize for Fiction. His next volume of short-short stories, *Intercourse*, is due out soon.

LORNA DEE CERVANTES is the recipient of two NEA Fellowships for poetry, a Lila Wallace/Readers Digest grant and a Pushcart Prize, among many awards and honors. She teaches at the University of Colorado in Boulder.

DAN CHAON's short story collection, *Among the Missing*, was a finalist for the National Book Award. He is the recipient of the 2006 Academy Award For Literature from the American Academy of Arts and Letters.

CHARLES D'AMBROSIO is the author of *The Point and Other Stories*, *Orphans*, a collection of essays and *The Dead Fish Museum*, which was a finalist for the PEN/Faulkner Award.

W. S. DI PIERO's most recent book is *Chinese Apples: New and Selected Poems* (Knopf). He lives in San Francisco.

HERBERT GOLD's many books include the novels *Fathers* and *A Girl of Forty*, the non-fiction books *Haiti* and *Bohemia*, and a collection of short stories, *Lovers and Cohorts*. He is currently playing the role of an 80-year-old rock drummer in his son Ari's feature film.

LINDA GREGERSON is the author of four books of poetry and two collections of criticism. She teaches at the University of Ann Arbor.

LAUREN GROFF's stories have appeared in the *Atlantic Monthly*, *Five Points*, *The Beloit Fiction Journal* and elsewhere. Her first novel is forthcoming from Hyperion soon.

JAMES HARMS is the author of five books of poetry including *After West* from Carnegie Mellon University Press. He teaches at West Virginia University.

EDWARD HIRSCH, a MacArthur Fellow, has published six books of poems and three prose books. He is the President of the Guggenheim Memorial Foundation.

TONY HOAGLAND's third collection of poetry, *What Narcissism Mean To Me* (Graywolf, 2003) was a finalist for the National Book Critics Circle Award. His book of prose about poetry, *Real Sofistikashun* (Graywolf) appeared in 2006.

BARBARA HURD is the author of the forthcoming book, *Walking the Wrack Line*. She is the winner of the LA *Times* Best Book Award (2001), the Sierra Club's National Nature Writing Award, and a Pushcart Prize.

ERICA KEIKO ISERI teaches high school in Tsushima, Japan. She will soon make an 88-temple pilgrimage around the island of Shikoku, which will be the subject of her first book.

ROXANA BETH JOHNSON's poems have appeared in ZYZZYVA, *Chelsea*, *Sentence* and elsewhere. She won the AWP Intro Award In Poetry.

JEFF P. JONES was an editor at *Fugue* and he studied at the University of Idaho. His essays and short fiction have been published in the *Chattahoochcie Review*, *Mississippi Review* and elsewhere.

DEBORAH KEENAN helped found Laurel Poetry Collective. She is the author of eight collections of poetry including her newest, *Willow Room, Green Door: New and Selected Poems* (Milkweed Editions).

GALWAY KINNELL has published ten volumes of poetry. His work has won the Pulitzer Prize, the National Book Award in Poetry and a MacArthur Fellowship.

DAVID KIRBY teaches at Florida State University. His most recent book is *The House On Boulevard Street: New and Selected Poems*.

NAM LE was born in Vietnam and raised in Australia. He has received fellowships from the University of Iowa Writers Workshop, the MacDowell Colony, Yaddo and elsewhere. His debut collection, *The Boat*, will soon be published by Knopf.

LI-YOUNG LEE has appeared in our pages five times. He lives in Chicago.

ELEANOR LERMAN lives and works in New York. Her most recent books of poetry are *Our Post Soviet History Unfolds*, winner of the 2006 Lenore Marshall Award, and the *Mystery of Meteors*.

PHILIP LEVINE has been represented in these pages in eight different volumes starting with *PPII*. His most recent book is *Breath* (Knopf, 2004). He lives in New York and California.

ADRIAN C. LOUIS' most recent of eleven books is *Logorrhea* (2006, Northwest University Press). He has won numerous prizes and fellowships and currently lives in Marshall, Minnesota.

SAGE MARSTERS recently received an MFA from Emerson College. She teaches at Emerson and works in an independent bookstore.

CLANCY MARTIN in a former jeweler and an Assistant Professor of Philosophy at the University of Missouri. He lives in Kansas City.

KHALED MATTAWA is the author of two books of poems, the translator of five volumes of Arabic poetry and the co-editor of two anthologies of Arab-American literature. He teaches at the University of Michigan.

A. P. MILLER is a pen name. The author lives in the mid-West.

STEVEN MILLHAUSER has previously appeared in *PPXIX*. He lives in Saratoga Springs, New York.

THYLIAS MOSS teaches at the University of Michigan where she is a professor of English and also a professor of Art & Design. Some of her video and sonic poems may be experienced in Limited Fork podcasts at iTunes and on the Forkergirl Channel at Youtube.

JOAN MURRAY is a past poetry co-editor of this series and the general editor of *The Pushcart Book of Poetry* (Pushcart Press 2007), and the author of many titles from Norton and Beacon Press. She lives in upstate New York.

RANDY NELSON teaches at Davidson College. He is the winner of the Flannery O'Connor Award for Short Fiction, the Carson McCullers Award and the Frank O'Connor Prize.

JOYCE CAROL OATES is the author most recently of *The Gravedigger's Daughter* and other books from Ecco Press. She teaches at Princeton.

PETER ORNER is the author most recently of a novel and short story collection. His fiction has appeared in the *Atlantic*, *Paris Review* and elsewhere.

MEGHAN O'ROURKE is author of *Halflife*, a collection of poems. She is also a literary editor of Slate and a poetry editor at the *Paris Review*.

LYDIA PEELLE lives in Nashville. She was a recent Fellow at the fine arts Center in Provincetown and is currently at work on a collection of short stories.

ROBERT PINSKY's new collection of poems, *Gulf Music*, is just out from Farrar, Straus & Giroux. He lives in Cambridge, Massachusetts.

ANDREW PORTER teaches at Trinity University in San Antonio. His fiction has appeared in *One Story*, *Epoch*, *Ontario Review* and elsewhere.

LIAM RECTOR was founder and director of the Bennington College graduate writing seminars. His latest book is just out from The University of Chicago Press. He died in August, 2007.

ANDREW RICE's first book, *The Teeth May Smile But the Heart Does Not Forget*, will be published by Metropolitan books soon. He lives in Brooklyn, New York.

MARY RUEFLE is the author of ten books of poetry. This is her second Pushcart Prize appearance.,

GRACE SCHULMAN's sixth collection, *The Broken String*, is just published. The winner of several prizes, she is a Distinguished Professor of English at Baruch College.

LYNN SHAPIRO is currently working on a memoir. She was awarded fellowships from the Guggenheim Foundation, the Jerome Foundation and the New York Foundation For the Arts for her choreography.

HEIDI SHAYLA's fiction has appeared in *Prairie Schooner, Mississippi Review, Iron Horse Literary Review* and elsewhere. She lives in Eugene, Oregon.

GARY SHORT's most recent collection is *10 Moons and 13 Horses*. He teaches at the University of California at Davis.

CHARLES SIMIC has published twenty collections of poetry, five books of essays, a memoir and several books of translations. He has received the Pulitzer Prize, a MacArthur Fellowship and many other awards. He was just named the 15th poet laureate of the United States.

PATRICIA SMITH is a four time individual champion of the National Poetry Slam. She is the author of four books of poetry and the critically acclaimed history *Africans In America*. She was recently inducted into the National Literary Hall of Fame for Writers of African Descent.

REBECCA SOLNIT lives in San Francisco where she writes about politics, activism, ecology and the arts. Her most recent book is *Storming the Gates of Paradise: Landscapes for Politics*.

ANNA SOLOMON is a graduate of Iowa Writers Workshop and teaches at Sackett Writers Workshop in Brooklyn, New York.

GERALD STERN is a winner of the National Book Award for Poetry. His most recent title, *Everything Is Burning*, was published in 2005 by Norton.

MELANIE RAE THON's most recent book is the novel *Sweet Hearts*. She was born in Montana and now teaches at the University of Utah.

G. C. WALDREP teaches at Bucknell University and is author of the poetry collection *Goldbeaters Skin and Disclaimor* (BOA 2007) among other works.

MICHAEL WATERS has won three previous Pushcart Prizes. This year's selection is from his book just out from BOA Editions.

STEPHANIE POWELL WATTS teaches at Lehigh University. Her work has recently appeared in *African-American Review, Tampa Review* and the *Oxford American*.

GRETA WROLSTAD died in the summer of 2005 from injuries suffered in a car accident. She was a poet and vital presence at the MFA Program at the University of Montana where she served as poetry editor of *CutBank*.

TIPHANIE YANIQUE is originally from the Virgin Islands. She has been awarded a Fulbright scholarship in creative writing, the Academy of American Poets prize, and the Tufts University Africana prize. She teaches at Drew University.

PAUL ZIMMER is the author of thirteen books of poems and two books of essays. He is a former director of the university presses at Pittsburgh, Georgia and Iowa. He divides his time between a farm in southwestern Wisconsin and a small house in the south of France.

INDEX

The following is a listing in alphabetical order by author's last name of works reprinted in the *Pushcart Prize* editions since 1976.

589

594

597

607

609

611

613

614

618